THE ZOMBIE UPRISING SERIES

M.A. ROBBINS

COTTAGE STREET

THE AWAKENING

BOOK ONE IN THE ZOMBIE UPRISING
SERIES

CONTENTS

For George Romero, the Father of the Modern Zombie Film. Without his contributions, this book wouldn't have been written.

1

The day the sun is blotted from the sky, and the winds of hell are upon us, is the day death takes possession of our land.

His late grandmother's words burst unbidden into Leo Nageak's mind as he opened the ATV's throttle and sped along the coastal tundra to Wainwright. Scorching wind buffeted his face, sending his shoulder-length hair whipping behind him. It was the fiercest heat he'd ever felt in his eighteen years on the tundra.

But it would have been worse if the sun were out. Overcast as hell, with roiling black and gray clouds, the weather had forced him to turn on his headlights. *Death takes possession of our land.*

Thirty minutes after he left Point Wallace, the headlights revealed a gaping hole in the earth and he pulled the ATV to a shuddering stop. The damn crater was big enough to swallow him and his four-wheeler whole. He hopped to the ground and removed his rifle from the ATV's gun scabbard. Peering around in the dim light, he scanned the horizon for any movement. An elder had encountered an aggressive young grizzly in the area a few days before, so Leo wasn't taking any chances.

Satisfied no danger lurked nearby, he walked to the edge of the hole and sighed. There were more appearing every day. The damn heat had been so bad, he wondered if the coast wouldn't melt into the sea. Even the elders said they'd never seen weather like it. According to his uncle's ther-mometer, it had hit ninety-five degrees the day before. Had to be a record.

Gazing out over the whitecaps in the Chukchi Sea, he considered his options. He didn't want to turn around, but what other choice did he have?

Maybe the ground isn't so bad inland.

He turned toward the shadow of Iqsigi Mountain in the east. He could ride up to its base, cut south, and still make it to Wainwright in decent time.

They called it a mountain, but it was nothing more than a big hill. He peered at it just as a small break appeared in the clouds. Iqsigi Mountain. His Inupiaq wasn't so good, but that's one word everyone knew. Of course, no one mentioned it if they didn't need to. If they did, they called it by its English name. Fear Mountain.

He wiped the sweat from his brow and hopped onto his four-wheeler. The elders had long taught that spirits lived in the mountain and would carry any intruders inside, never to be seen again.

"Bullshit."

Leo smiled that he'd said that out loud. As much as he might deny it, the damn stories still got to him. But a little tough talk would help keep his childhood fears at bay.

"Screw it."

He eased the throttle open and guided the ATV toward the mountain. The clouds closed in, plunging the area into a dusk-like darkness. Fat rain-drops fell. Leo kept the speed low as the ATV bounced and bucked over the uneven ground, but the more inland he traveled, the smoother it became. He increased his speed.

The mountain grew larger, a big hulking shadow. He smacked his lips. His mouth had gone dry and he found it hard to swallow.

He'd swing by just in front of the mountain and be past it in twenty minutes. He increased speed again.

A flash of lightning shot across the sky, and thunder boomed, echoing through his bones. He gunned the throttle, and the ATV leapt. Rain poured down, and a lightning bolt spidered from the clouds, stabbing the mountain halfway up its slope.

Let me get through this. Let me get through this. Visions of spirits snatching him off his four-wheeler and dragging him into the mountain came unbidden.

Leo kept his attention on the glow from the headlights spread out in front of him. Tundra zipped by, with the occasional small bump shaking the lamp. Halfway past the mountain, the edge of a crater appeared out of nowhere. Leo released the throttle and jerked on the brakes. The ATV rattled and skidded. Hitting something solid, it stopped, but Leo kept going.

He flew through the air, weightless, then gravity kicked in and slammed him on his back to the ground, the impact knocking the wind from his lungs.

As he lay there, rain peppered his eyes and filled his open mouth, causing him to choke and struggle for breath. Then came the first jolt of pain. His back ached and his left calf burned, as if a hot poker were jammed in it. He coughed and cleared the water from his mouth. Taking a deep breath, he gagged at the thick smell of decay that assailed his nostrils. He turned his head and puked.

When he regained his breath, he looked around. Other than misty rain in the ATV lights shining above him, everything was blackness.

He moved his outstretched arms in the dark, and one hand landed on something cold and soft, almost like a fish's underbelly. He squeezed, and it made a disgusting squishy noise.

What the hell?

When he attempted to sit up, his left leg flared into agony. He fell back and panted.

No one knows I'm here. Gotta get up or I'll die.

He reached into his pants pocket and pulled his lighter out. The one his uncle had recently given him. He rubbed his thumb across the Marine Corps symbol on the outside, then flipped it open and rolled the wheel. Sparks flew and the wick lit, producing an orange-and-blue flame. Leo raised the lighter and his breath hitched.

He lay in a pit of frozen bodies, their mouths open in silent screams, arms outstretched, and legs in mid-stride. It was as if they'd been flash-frozen.

Or buried alive in the permafrost.

Leo cried out and sat up, the searing pain making him light-headed. He gritted his teeth and held the lighter over his left leg, examining it. A broken bone stuck out from the side of his calf, its splintered end red with gore. He swallowed. How the hell would he get out of there with a compound fracture?

But something about the bone's angle didn't look right. He moved the lighter's flame closer to the injury, then traced a finger gently down his shin, from the knee to the wound. Smooth. No break.

He gasped. The bone wasn't sticking out of his calf, it was sticking through his calf.

I'm impaled on a dead man's bone!

The lighter's flame blew out, plunging him into the graveyard's blackness. Leo groaned. He had to get free, but every movement brought a fresh wave of agony.

The rain stopped, but darkness remained. He wrapped his arms around himself, shivering. Sure, he was soaked from the rain and the pooled water in the pit, but how could he be so cold when sweat still poured down his face? Maybe he was in shock. If so, he was running out of time.

The wind died, leaving him with the putrid smell of thawing dead flesh. He tried breathing through his mouth, but that made it worse. Instead of just smelling the rot, the odor was so thick, it was like tasting it. Bile rose in Leo's throat and he choked it back. *Ignore it. Concentrate on getting out of here.*

He lit the lighter and held it closer to his wound. The calf didn't seem to be bleeding much, but that could change once he pulled it off the bone. He took his jackknife out of his pocket and cut his pant leg off. Not the best bandage, but it would have to do until he could get back to the village.

A scuffing sound came from the inky blackness beyond the lighter's weak glow. Leo's heart raced. His damn rifle was still with the four-wheeler. He raised the lighter and pointed the knife at the sound. Did spirits make sounds? Or was it the grizzly the elder had encountered, feeding on human carcasses? Either way, he was screwed.

Leo held his breath and tilted his head, listening. The sound didn't repeat, so he folded the knife and put it back in his pocket. He pulled his belt off. It'd be a serviceable tourniquet if he needed it, but he hoped that wouldn't be necessary. He had to catch a break at some point.

He peered over his shoulder. The edge of the grave, and his ATV, were a good ten feet away. From the way the four-wheeler's headlights shone over him, he figured he lay about three feet below ground level. The four-wheeler was still running, so it would likely be drivable. But how much fuel would it have left? Would he make it back, or die alone out there?

Don't think that way.

He steadied himself, his hands outstretched and propped on body parts. The damn things seemed to be thawing faster than when he'd first touched them. He pushed on the chest of a bearded man next to him, and it let out a belch. The stench gagged Leo and he turned away to keep his lunch from coming up again.

He waited for a minute, gathering his thoughts, then nodded. "Now or never."

Reaching out, he grasped just below his kneecap with one hand, and around the ankle with the other. *One, two, three.*

He pulled with his hands at the same time he pushed up with his leg. A wail welled from deep inside him, burning his throat and lungs with its intensity. His leg came halfway off the bone and stopped. Motes swam before his eyes and the world spun. *Stay awake. Please let me stay awake.*

Sobbing, Leo took great, heaving breaths and pulled again. The leg popped off the bone, but he didn't have the strength to ease it to the ground. Instead, it slammed down and all went black.

LEO'S EYES popped open to a light show in the sky. Streaks of lightning crisscrossed above him, bathing the area in flashes of daylight.

How long had he been out?

His back throbbed and he struggled to sit up, a groan escaping his lips. Blood oozed from the gaping hole in his leg. Leo tried to bend it to get a closer view of the calf, but his leg remained motionless.

Shit. I can't even feel the damn thing.

Leo wrapped the pant leg around the wound. Even if he was protected from the pain, it didn't mean it wouldn't start bleeding the minute he moved. He scooted backward, then pulled his wounded leg after him. Gritting his teeth, he concentrated on getting to the edge of the pit. Scoot. Drag. Scoot. Drag.

A heavy crack came from somewhere in the darkness before him. *Shit.* Whatever it was, the damn thing was huge.

A crashing sound to the left. *And it's got company.*

Leo strained to go faster, his breath coming in great gasps. Tears poured down his face, but he didn't stop as he imagined a pair of grizzlies bearing down on him, just out of sight. What would it feel like to be torn in half by two of those monsters?

The crunching, shuffling pursuers sounded closer. Leo's arms burned with his frantic pace. *Where's the edge of this fucking pit?*

He backed into a wall of earth. Wasting no time, he grasped the edge and pulled himself up. When his legs were all that remained in the shadows of the pit, he had a sudden vision of the unseen predators grabbing his ankles and pulling him down to his death.

Grabbing his left pant leg, he swung his legs over and pulled himself to the ATV. Through pure upper body strength fueled by adrenaline, he muscled himself up with the handlebars. The gas indicator showed the tank to be half full. He whooped and swung his right leg over the seat, hauling himself to a sitting position.

He looked around to get his bearings. Behind him lay home. He'd have to go slow all the way back. If he got thrown again, he might never get back on.

A rustle. A growl. *That was no grizzly growl.*

A gnarled hand thrust to the sky and a pair of yellow eyes reflected the ATV's lights. Leo's breath hitched, then an ungodly shriek split the night.

Leo screamed, opened the throttle, and spun the ATV toward home.

The de Havilland Otter shook as it banked over the Chukchi Sea. Jen Reed checked her seatbelt for the tenth time, then glanced across the aisle at Devin. He sat with his eyes half shut, the turbulence not making any impression. If her old man wasn't scared, then she'd be damned if she'd show it.

He glanced at her. She tried looking cool as the plane bounced again, but her knuckles turned white as she clung to the armrest.

The pilot's voice came over the speakers. "Getting a little rough. Just stay strapped down and we'll be on the ground in a few minutes."

Jen tried to tighten her belt, but it was already as snug as could be. Devin turned to her, one bushy white eyebrow raised. "You OK?"

Jen shrugged, an unnatural gesture since her hands still clenched the armrests. "You've been through one landing, you've been through them all."

Devin leaned into the aisle and lowered his voice even though there were no other passengers. "It's all right to be scared."

She turned toward him, a flash of annoyance heating her face. "I'm not afraid," she snapped.

Devin's expression didn't change, but he turned away and looked out the window. Jen could have kicked herself. One of the reasons she'd come on the assignment was to spend time with him. See if they could finally have a relationship. She pressed her lips together. She had to think more before she spoke, something she didn't have a lot of practice doing.

She peered out the rain-streaked window. They flew below the angry-looking black and gray clouds. Since it was July in northern Alaska, a time when the sun didn't set, she'd expected nothing but sunshine, but the weather patterns the past few years had been unusual. That, and there'd been historically high spikes in temperature. On the other hand, she wouldn't have been there if it weren't for the effects of the crazy weather.

The plane dropped a dozen feet, stabilizing with a slam that rattled the cabin. Jen waited for her stomach to catch up. She forced a smirk. "Next time I take a cab."

Devin made no reply. It was pretty obvious he wasn't used to her wisecracks. When not in the field, he'd spent his archaeology career in the stuffy halls of academia. It wouldn't surprise her that he'd never spent time around someone like her. But that's who she was, and he'd have to get used to it. Just like she'd have to get used to his lack of expression and periods of silence.

A village came into view, a cluster of houses huddled near the coast, with a large rectangular building in the middle and another on the inland edge of the town. A hill rose to the east, with a gravel runway on top and several large trailers on a flat area halfway up its slope. To the west was the sea and a smattering of boats.

The Otter swooped down, bucking and shuddering. Jen closed her eyes. *Let it be over.*

The plane bounced and swayed. Jen swallowed and let her head fall forward as if she'd dozed off. After several minutes she couldn't stand not knowing how close they were. She opened her eyes and did her best to fake a yawn just as the plane smoothed out, bounced once, and settled onto the runway. She was thrown against her seatbelt as the brakes squealed and the plane came to a stop ten yards short of the runway's end. *That's going to leave a bruise.*

The engines cut and the pilot came out of the cockpit, a smile painted on his face to complement a salt-and-pepper beard and mirror sunglasses. He opened the outside door. "Welcome to Point Wallace, Pearl of the Arctic. Watch your step while exiting."

Jen followed Devin down the short stairway to the ground. The wind had picked up and whistled across the hilltop, while the rain had eased into a steady drizzle. A slight break in the clouds offered a sliver of morning light. From where they stood, Jen couldn't see anything but the churning sea and endless tundra. She felt a pang of isolation.

A white crew cab pickup headed for them. It stopped, and a slender middle-aged man with receding gray hair stepped out from the driver's side.

Devin smiled and shook the man's hand. "Hal, good to see you."

He turned to Jen. "Jen, this is Dr. Parsons. Hal, this is my daughter, Jen."

Jen hesitated. Hearing Devin call her his daughter felt strange. But Dr. Parsons was the other reason she'd come on the trip. A chance for a young environmental scientist three years out of college to work with one of the legends of the field was an opportunity she couldn't pass up. She smiled and shook Parsons' hand. "It's an honor to meet you, Dr. Parsons. I wrote a term paper on your work on the effects of changing weather patterns on migratory animals."

Dr. Parsons chuckled. "Call me Hal." He raised an eyebrow. "I wasn't sure anyone had read that paper, so I'm honored. What have you been doing since you graduated?"

He wants me to call him by his first name? "I contract out doing fieldwork, mostly soil and water samples in remote areas."

Devin crossed his arms. "Contractor? I thought you worked for the state."

Jen shook her head. "I like to have control over my schedule."

Hal smiled. "We've only begun sampling, so we can certainly use your skills here. And I think we can expose you to some advanced analysis work, if you're willing."

"You bet."

The pilot carried their luggage over and placed it on the ground. "That should be all your baggage." He nodded at Hal. "I've got to get out of here, Doc. That cloud ceiling's coming down. National Weather Service says there's a hell of a storm coming in and aircraft will be grounded soon. I may be a crazy-ass bush pilot, but even I don't want to be up in this blow."

Hal clapped him on the back. "Have a safe trip back."

The pilot took two steps toward the plane and turned. "One other thing. There's a NOAA alert for increased sunspot activity. They expect moderate to severe communications interference for the next day."

"OK," Hal said. "We'll hunker down for now. See you in a few days."

The pilot saluted and strode off to the Otter as an older, rusted pickup rattled to a stop next to the plane. A thirty-something man with a trimmed beard and slick-backed hair climbed out and approached the pilot. Dressed in jeans and a flannel shirt with a big-ass gun strapped to his hip, the guy would've looked like a lumberjack if he weren't so thin.

"Who's that?" Devin asked.

Hal glanced at the man and frowned. "No one you want to know. He's our local bootlegger. Name's Griffin."

"Bootlegger?" Jen said. "He brews moonshine?"

"Point Wallace is a damp village. You can bring in alcohol for your own use, but can't sell it. Griffin brings in a lot more than one person can drink, but he always gets more."

Jen watched the pilot hand Griffin a box. Griffin laid it in his pickup bed and looked up, his gaze meeting hers. A half-smile broke out on his face. *Creepy.* Jen looked away.

Devin picked up his suitcase and reached for Jen's, but she grabbed it first. "I've got it," she said.

Devin hesitated, as if he were going to say something, but he stayed tight-lipped. He placed his bag in the truck bed and climbed into the front passenger seat without a word.

Jen frowned. She knew he wasn't capable of much emotion, but how could they establish a relationship if he didn't show it? *Or at least talk.* She tossed her suitcase next to his and took the back seat.

Griffin's starter chugged for a few seconds then started, and the engine roared to life. Black smoke belched out of the exhaust. Grinding the gears, he locked eyes with Jen and drove off, the truck disappearing over the hill's edge. A cloud of his exhaust whisked over Hal's truck. Jen wrinkled her nose at the stench.

Hal ignored it and started the crew cab pickup. He smiled at Devin. "It's been, what, twenty years?"

Devin grinned. Jen raised her eyebrows. Seemed he was capable of something more than a stone face after all.

"Twenty years," Devin said. "Ever since Gobekli Tepe in Turkey." He looked over his shoulder at Jen. "Hal was a medical doctor back then. Spent his time on archaeological digs, patching us up."

Hal shook his head. "I still can't believe I was able to fill my gravedigger position with the famous archaeologist, Devin Reed."

Jen squinted. "Gravedigger?"

"A term of endearment," Devin said. "The Chukchi Sea is eating away at the coast, and exposed an old native graveyard. I'm here to help the community relocate it to more stable ground. I don't usually work environmental studies, but I couldn't pass up time with an old friend."

Jen sighed. It took Devin talking to someone else for her to find out what the hell he was there for. When she'd asked him on the phone, he'd changed the conversation to the work he was doing then. She pressed her lips together. *This isn't going to be easy, but I'll make it work.*

Hal steered the truck down a dirt switchback road on the side of the hill. The village lay before them, sets of prefab houses patched with plywood and corrugated steel. Halfway down the hill sat three large white trailers outfitted with solar panels on a flat section of the slope. Hal pulled up in front of them and they all piled out of the truck.

Hal pointed to the middle trailer. "This is our headquarters and administrative offices. The trailer on the right holds our bunks and dining facility. You'll each be assigned a room." He nodded at the third trailer. "And this is a state-of-the-art lab. The best of its kind within the Arctic Circle."

Jen grinned. "Impressive. But do you have cable?"

Hal laughed. "A sense of humor, too? We'll get along just fine."

Devin pointed at a big gray tank that sat a hundred feet above them on the slope. "What's that? Water?"

"Fuel," Hal said. "We're mostly solar powered, but on days like today, we sometimes have to switch to generator."

He opened a door on the end of the headquarters trailer. "Come on. I'll give you the five-minute tour."

Devin and Jen followed him into a long, narrow corridor peppered with muddy shoe prints. Hal walked past a couple of rooms and led them into the third.

A cluttered room, it sported two desks and several bookcases stuffed with binders. The dense odor of old, burnt coffee hung in the air.

A thirty-something man with bleached blond hair and Clark Kent glasses sat behind one of the desks, hunched over a microphone while he moved dials on a radio panel. An older native man with a buzz cut stood in front of the desk, while a younger native man in jeans and a Grateful Dead T-shirt leaned against the wall next to him. He looked to be about Jen's age.

The radioman pressed a button on the microphone. "Wallace Science One to Wainwright Science One, do you copy?"

He released the microphone button, and loud static came from the speakers. The radioman adjusted another dial and repeated his request. He got the same answer.

The radioman shook his head. "Sorry. The solar activity is too great right now." He looked over at Devin and Jen and smiled. "You must be our new team members. I'm Pete Nance, Hal's assistant."

Devin nodded. "Devin and Jen Reed."

The older Native man offered his hand. "Raymond Kignak, and this is my nephew, Chris Nageak." Jen shook Raymond's hand, then stepped back so Devin could do the same. Raymond had a helluva strong grip for a guy who looked to be approaching seventy. She noted the Marine Corps tattoo on Raymond's forearm.

Chris nodded at Devin and Jen. "Good to meet you."

Hal cleared his throat. "What's going on?"

Raymond frowned. "Leo set out for Wainwright this morning. He was supposed to call when he arrived, but we haven't heard anything, and he should be there by now."

"None of our phones or radios in the village are working, but we thought yours might," Chris said.

Hal scratched his chin. "I wouldn't worry too much about it. He'll probably call as soon as the solar activity dies down." He shrugged. "After all, Leo was born and raised here. What kind of trouble would he likely get into between Point Wallace and Wainwright?"

H al pointed to the last door in the headquarters hallway. "Here's the final stop on the tour. Devin, this is your workspace."

Jen's stomach growled. "How about we catch lunch after this?"

Devin glanced at his watch. "I agree. It's almost two."

Hal smiled. "Sorry. I get carried away sometimes with what we've done with the facility. We'll do a quick look in the archaeologist's office and head to the dining hall."

He opened the door and flipped the light switch. Florescent lights flickered on to reveal a twenty-foot-wide, ten-foot-deep windowless room with shelves lining the back wall. An autopsy table sat in the middle.

Hal moved to one of the neatly arranged cardboard boxes on one of the shelves. "You should have ample supplies." He pointed to labels beneath each box. "Body bags, surgical masks, gloves."

Devin pulled a box out and rummaged through the contents. "Damn fine setup considering how remote we are."

Jen's stomach growled again. "Unless you've got a hamburger and fries in one of those boxes, I'd like to check out the cafeteria."

"Let's go then, shall we?" Hal said.

He led them out of the headquarters trailer just as Chris zoomed up on an ATV and hit the brakes. He skidded to a stop, sending gravel flying across the parking area. Cupping his hands to his mouth, he yelled over the engine, "Dr. Parsons, we need you right away at my uncle's house. Leo's back and he's in real bad shape."

Hal tossed his keys to Devin. "Start the truck. I'll get my bag and let Pete know what's going on." He ran into the trailer.

Chris sped off, spraying more gravel in his wake. Jen and Devin ran to the truck. She hopped in the back while Devin took the driver's seat. He pulled it up to the trailer just as Hal reappeared carrying a small satchel.

Hal jumped in and pointed to where Chris had disappeared over the lip of the hill. "Head there. The hill's slope is flatter from this point on, so it's a straight shot. Just take it easy."

Devin drove the truck over the lip and down toward the village. Jen rolled down her window, rain pelting her in the face, and took in the scene. The roads, nothing more than tire tracks between houses, were barely visible in the reduced light. They passed by a corrugated metal house with a dozen doghouses outside, a barking husky chained to each one. The truck's headlights picked up a handful of kids running after each other and weaving between buildings. They waved as the truck passed. Jen waved back.

Hal pointed to a large one-story building up ahead. The modern, flat-roofed structure stuck out like a sore thumb. It was as if someone had picked up a building from the city and dropped it in the middle of the village. "Turn right after the community center," Hal said. "Raymond's place will be the third house on the left."

Moments later, they pulled up in front of a larger house with an ATV parked outside. A pair of antlers hung above the front door, and a drenched American flag flapped on a short pole attached to the porch railing with duct tape.

Hal jumped out and ran into the house, leaving the front door open. Jen and Devin followed him inside just as the rain intensified and thunder rumbled overhead.

The front rooms consisted of a large, well-worn living room and a kitchen. The aroma of cooking meat filled the area. Jen couldn't identify the meal by its smell, but it made her mouth water and stomach grumble again.

Hal knelt next to a blanket-covered couch, talking to a young native man who writhed in pain, his eyes squeezed shut. Raymond stood at the head of the couch, arms crossed and worry lines creasing his face. Chris watched from the other end, his fists clenched by his side.

Jen stepped closer to get a better view of Leo. The man's clothes were soaked, and his left pant leg was crudely cut off and wrapped around his calf. Chest heaving with each raspy breath, his body spasmed, and something shiny fell from his pocket and bounced across the floor. Chris picked it up. He caught Jen watching him and showed her a worn lighter with the Marine Corps symbol embossed on the side. "Leo's lighter. My uncle gave it to him, and he'd hate to lose it."

Hal opened first one of Leo's eyes, then the other, and shined a light in them. Leo's pupils were so dilated, Jen couldn't see any part of the irises. Hal pursed his lips and untied the crude wrapping around Leo's calf. It dropped away and he gasped. Jen craned her neck to see. It looked like someone had drilled a half-inch hole through Leo's leg. The edges of the wound had turned black. Even with all that, there was only a little blood oozing. Hal turned away and coughed. A foul odor slapped Jen in the face. "Shit." She buried her nose in the crook of her arm and fought back the urge to puke. Devin made a disgusted noise next to her.

Hal looked up at Raymond. "Can we get some hot water?"

Raymond turned toward the kitchen, and an ancient native woman in a traditional kuspuk, a tunic-length hooded overshirt, shuffled out of the hallway. She looked a hundred if she looked a day. She said something to Raymond in Inupiaq, and he answered in kind. She nodded, limped into the kitchen, and took a glass pitcher out of the cupboard.

Hal pulled a stethoscope out of his bag and listened to Leo's chest. He shook his head and pulled out a blood pressure cuff. Leo jerked his arm away as Hal attempted to wrap it around his bicep.

With effort, Raymond held Leo's arm still. Hal wrapped the cuff and took the reading. He sat back on his haunches. "This is bad."

Raymond released Leo, who seemed to have settled down. "What is it?"

"His heart rate's increasing and his blood pressure's going through the roof."

"Islig," Leo moaned.

Jen furrowed her brow. "What'd he say?"

"Islig," Raymond said, his eyes on his sick nephew. "We call it a mountain, but it's more like a big hill. It's forbidden to go there."

Chris let out a loud breath. "Islig means fear. Fear Mountain. Where the spirits live."

Raymond leaned over Leo. "What about Islig? Were you there?"

Leo squirmed. "Bodies. Dozens. Hundreds. Death is in me. It calls to me."

A crash came from the kitchen. The old lady froze, her eyes wide. The pitcher lay broken at her feet. Lips trembling, she said, "Tuqunaragri."

Leo murmured something Jen couldn't make out. She leaned in closer. Raymond had bent down, and Hal cocked an ear. "What was that, Leo?"

Leo's eyes flew open, his irises huge and deep yellow. "It's in me!"

Jen stumbled back, stepping on Devin's foot, but he didn't seem to notice. His eyes were fixed on Leo, who kicked out and nearly connected with Chris's jaw.

Hal broke the spell first and fished around in his bag. "Hold him. I'll give him something to calm him down."

Raymond held Leo's shoulders while Chris and Devin restrained his legs. Leo's creepy eyes focused on Jen. Hair stood up on the back of her neck. What the hell had happened to the guy? She'd never heard of anyone with yellow irises before.

Hal injected something into Leo's arm. Within a minute, he relaxed and his eyes closed.

"He should sleep awhile." Hal listened to Leo's chest. "Better. Not great, but better."

Jen hugged herself. "What's wrong with him? And what the hell's up with his eyes? I'm going to have nightmares for months."

Removing a blood collection syringe from his bag, Hal shook his head. "I don't know yet. Whatever it is, it's moving fast, and he could lose the leg. We need to get him to a hospital."

Chris stared at the floor with his hands shoved in his pockets. "We can take him overland."

Hal frowned. "Normally, I'd agree. But his illness is too big of an unknown. He may not survive the trip."

"Maybe that bush pilot would go up in an emergency," Jen said.

Hal stuck the needle into Leo's arm. Dark red blood flowed into the collection tube. "He won't take the chance. Bush pilots are a bit crazy, but they're not suicidal."

"We've got to do something," Raymond said.

Packing away his equipment and the blood samples, Hal nodded. "I'll get these to the lab and see what I can find out."

Jen placed her hands on her hips. "We should go to the mountain and find out what happened there."

Hal stood. "No. We don't know what the hell's out there. It could be contagious."

Devin crossed his arms. "I'm with Jen."

Jen's eyebrows shot up. *He's agreeing with me?*

Devin continued. "If it's contagious, we already have it, so I'm going. I've been on several digs with biological hazards and can handle it. Time for me to be useful around here."

Chris stepped next to Devin. "I'm going, too. I know the way."

Jen straightened. "I came out here for a unique experience. If hunting corpses by a haunted mountain in the middle of nowhere doesn't check that off my bucket list, nothing will."

Hal's lips pressed tightly together, but he remained silent.

Jen strode to the door. "Time to find out what happened to Leo."

4

Jen stepped onto the porch. "So how do we get there?"

Devin turned to Chris. "We'll need equipment from the archaeologist's office. If we load it into the truck, will it make it out to the mountain?"

Chris shook his head. "Not a chance. You need a four-wheeler. I've got a buddy with an ATV trailer that'll hitch up to the back of mine. Unless you've got a ton of stuff, that should work."

Jen crossed her arms. "We're going to get real cozy if all of us ride your ATV together. Are there any others?"

Chris jogged down the steps and mounted his four-wheeler. "There are three more sitting in back of the headquarters trailer." He started the engine and raised his voice. "Keys are hanging on the wall of the admin office. Meet you there." He waved and rode off, disappearing behind a house.

"What's your plan, Gravedigger?" Jen asked.

Devin scratched his chin. "Chris and I will go see what's out there. If there are bodies, my job here may have gotten bigger."

Heat rose in Jen's face. "What do you mean you and Chris? You're not leaving me behind. I'm damn sure not taking another step in that house, and I won't sit around a stuffy science trailer on my ass. I'm going, too."

"We don't know what we'll run into out there. Besides, the tundra's no place for a city kid."

"City kid?" Jen glared at him. "You don't know me. That's the damn problem. If you'd brought your ass around a little more when I was growing up, you'd know I've spent a lot of time in the wilderness camping, hunting, and fishing. I know how to ride ATVs and snow machines, how to make shelters and snow caves, and where to find food and water."

Devin's face fell. Jen clamped her mouth shut. She had lost control and overdone it. Again. That was how she'd lost her last three boyfriends. The rain picked up and Jen wished it would just wash her away.

"OK," Devin said. "You're coming. Let's get moving."

Jen stammered. "I-I'm sorry. I didn't mean to—"

"It's all right. I should've remembered what you told Hal about spending a lot of time in the field." He gave her a grin. "And you're twenty-five. Far from a kid."

Jen opened her mouth to thank him, but Hal rushed out of the house and they piled into the truck. Jen sat in the back, wheels turning in her head. She'd expected Devin to be combative and too set in his ways to change, but he'd shown her different. Was there hope for them to establish a relationship after all the time they'd been estranged? While he certainly wouldn't be a 1950s' TV dad, maybe there was room for mutual respect.

"What's the story with Raymond and his nephews?" Devin asked. "They seem extremely close."

Hal kept his eyes on the rutted road. "Their father left the village when they were still toddlers and never returned. Their mother, Raymond's sister, died in an ATV accident when they were in their early teens. Raymond raised them as his own."

Hal parked in front of the lab trailer and stared out the windshield. "Look, I don't agree with what you're doing, but I can't stop you." He got out of the truck. "Just be careful." Without another word, he disappeared into the trailer.

Jen shrugged. "Isn't he Mr. Happy?"

"I'll go get the equipment," Devin said. "Can you get the ATVs?"

Jen hopped out of the truck. "Can do."

A peal of thunder boomed nearby as she hurried into the admin trailer. Still hunched over the radio in the office, Pete put a hand up as she walked in, then keyed his mic. "Wallace Science One to Barrow Control. Come in, please." He sat back and a garbled voice came over the speaker, but Jen couldn't make it out.

Pete wiped his hand down his face. "How's Leo?"

"Not good, but Hal's working on him." Jen scanned the wall. "Where are the ATV keys?"

Pete raised an eyebrow.

Jen sighed. "Hal knows. It's OK."

Pete hitched a thumb over his shoulder. "Next to Hal's desk. The gas tanks should be full, but check them just in case. Don't want to come up empty out there. Especially not in this weather."

"Do you have a couple of ponchos we can borrow?"

"Sure," Pete said. "That closet next to the file cabinet."

Jen grabbed the ponchos and two sets of keys and stepped into the hallway. She almost ran into Devin. She held the keys up and jingled them. "I'll check out the four-wheelers and pull them around."

He nodded. "I'll get the supplies and meet you out front."

Ten minutes later, Jen parked the second four-wheeler as Chris pulled up.

"How much stuff does your father have?" Chris asked.

Jen shrugged. "No idea. I've never been on one of the Great Corpse Hunter's safaris."

Chris grunted and went inside. He and Devin loaded the trailer on the back of Chris's four-wheeler.

Jen nodded at the ATV trailer. "There's still plenty of room on that thing."

"We'll need it," Devin said. "I plan to bring one of the bodies back for examination."

Jen and Devin started their ATVs. Chris cupped his hands around his mouth. "Stay close enough behind me to see my lights."

He took off down the hill. They followed him as he threaded his way through the village and out onto the tundra. The rain had slowed, and the thunder and lightning had stopped. A couple of miles out of town, Chris slowed to a halt and waved the others forward.

When they caught up with him, he pointed ahead. "See that ground there?"

Jen looked out where Chris's headlights shined. About ten feet ahead, the ground was pitted, and beyond that there appeared to be several large holes. "The heat is melting the permafrost," she said, "and the ground's collapsing."

"Would Leo have gone this way along the coast?" Devin asked.

Chris nodded. "This is where he would've turned toward the mountain."

Jen peered out into the tundra. A large shadow rose in the distance. "So what are we waiting for?"

Chris smiled and gave her a thumbs up, then gunned his throttle and headed toward Fear Mountain. Jen hesitated long enough to make sure Devin was coming, then she followed Chris, ignoring the queasy feeling in her gut.

5

They reached the base of the mountain without incident and turned right, their headlights exposing the tundra as they rode along. A few minutes later, Chris slowed and gestured for them to stop. "We need to take it easy here," he yelled over the engines. "Leo's been riding this tundra all his life, and something caught him off guard. Stay behind me."

Jen and Devin nodded, then followed Chris as he eased the throttle open. They drove at a slow speed for another hundred yards, their headlight beams sweeping the ground, before the tundra ended and blackness lay beyond.

They stopped and turned off their engines, but kept their headlights on. "What the hell is it?" Jen asked.

Chris hopped off his four-wheeler and shook his head. He picked up a flashlight from the trailer and shone it back and forth on the edge of the darkness. "It's a big pit. Looks like the tundra caved in here."

Devin opened a large box on the trailer. "Help me with these."

Jen and Chris joined him, and he pulled out a pair of cordless twin halogen lights on tripods. Jen and Chris both took one, and Devin grabbed another from the box. "I'll set mine up straight in front of the ATVs. Jen, plant yours twenty feet to my right, and Chris, plant yours twenty feet to my left."

Chris and Jen nodded, and Devin walked straight toward the pit. "Don't get too close to the edge, since we don't know how stable it is."

Jen set up her tripod a few feet back and waited for the others. When they'd finished, Devin pointed to the back of his light. "The switch is on the bar between the lights. Let's get these on."

Jen flipped the switch, and the halogens flooded the pit in bright light. Devin's and Chris's also came on. Jen peered into the pit and her heart skipped a beat.

The pit wasn't deep, maybe four feet, but was filled with hundreds of bodies. It reminded her of pictures she'd seen of mass graves, except the bodies weren't just lying there. They seemed to have been flash-frozen in the middle of some action, their arms askew and their legs ready to take a next step. She focused on a body just in front of her. Dressed in what looked like old-fashioned clothes, it had a chunk of its neck missing as if something had taken a bite out of it.

Devin hurried to the trailer and back. "Everyone puts these on now."

He put a surgeon's mask on his face and handed one each to Jen and Chris. Jen placed hers on and Devin tossed her a pair of latex gloves. "These, too."

Devin was the most animated she'd ever seen him. His brow furrowed and his posture stiffened. It took a minute before the reason hit her. The great Devin Reed was scared.

Devin picked up a shovel and handed it to Chris, who'd already donned his mask and gloves. "We have no idea what killed these men, but if it had anything to do with Leo's illness, we need to find out."

He headed back to the pit. "Jen, you're with me. Chris, bring the body bag out and spread it out on the ground."

He shined a flashlight at the edge of the pit, then stomped a foot along it. The ground remained solid. Jen peered into the grave. All of them had the same type of archaic clothes on. How long had they been there?

Devin pointed to the corpse of a bearded man in a cotton jacket and overalls. "Chris, point those two sidelights here."

When Chris had adjusted the lights, Devin lowered himself into the grave, almost tripping over a frozen leg. He waved Jen on. "Come."

She eased into the pit and placed her feet in the only two clear spots she could find. That's when the smell smacked her in the face. Nothing she'd ever encountered smelled as thick and as foul as the bodies and the thawing muck they lay in. She coughed and prayed she wouldn't puke in her mask.

Devin put a hand on her shoulder. "Easy. First time you've smelled something like this, isn't it?"

She nodded.

"It's the smell of death. Not the cleaned-up, funeral home kind of death, but the raw, unsanitized, natural version. It never leaves you once you experience it."

Jen breathed through her mouth. "Thanks for the warning."

Devin pointed at the bearded man. "What do you see?"

Jen coughed. "A smelly dead guy."

Devin sighed. "Get closer and look. You're a scientist, so act like one."

Jen frowned, but he was right. She took a deep breath and bent down to examine the man. He looked to have been in his early thirties and was short, about five and a half feet. The fabric of the coat was torn down his entire left arm. She moved the torn fabric to the side and found a wound on his shoulder. "He's got a hell of a hickey here."

Devin squatted next to her and ran a gloved finger over the wound. "A bite."

Jen looked at him. "Is it possible some animals fed on these bodies?"

Chris stood on the edge of the pit, just above Devin, watching them. "Sure could. Grizzlies have been active lately."

Devin examined the bite. "Not big enough for a bear. Besides, this bite isn't recent. It was made before he died."

"How do you know that?" Chris asked.

Devin pointed at dried blood around the wound. "Wounds inflicted on a frozen body don't bleed."

The bearded man appeared to be atop the frozen soil and not trapped in it, so Jen pulled on his petrified arm to see if she could roll him over. She braced her right boot against another corpse's leg and pulled. The damn thing wasn't moving.

"Next time wait until I tell you to touch a body," Devin said. "This is an archaeological site and needs to be treated as such."

Jen felt heat rise in her cheeks. *Why am I always screwing up around him?* "OK."

Devin attempted to roll the corpse, but it didn't move for him, either. "In a normal dig we'd take days or weeks to carefully unearth a body, but

Leo doesn't have that luxury, so we'll need to be a bit more brute force." He turned to Jen. "Grab a shovel. Chris, is that body bag ready?"

Chris's head popped up over the lip of the pit. He handed a shovel to Jen. "Ready when you are."

Jen tested the soil with the tip of her shovel. "Hard as a rock. We're not digging anybody out today."

Devin placed his shovel under the corpse's injured shoulder. "We don't have to get the shovels too far in, just enough to pry him up. Get yours under his upper thigh."

Jen jammed the tip of her shovel under the corpse's thigh. Devin pushed down on his shovel with his foot, driving the blade a couple inches into the permafrost. Jen did the same to hers, and it moved further under the body's thigh.

Devin wiped his brow. "You ready?"

Jen nodded.

Devin gripped the handle. "Ready, one, two, three."

Jen pushed down on her shovel. The corpse wasn't budging. Devin strained so much that tendons popped out in his neck.

The body raised a quarter inch. "Hold up," Devin said, letting go of his shovel.

"I think I have it." Jen grunted and pushed harder.

Just as she was about to give up, the body rolled over with a great ripping sound. The corpse's left arm tore off, still frozen into the ground.

Jen leaned on the shovel, panting. "Shit."

Devin threw his shovel down. "I told you to stop."

Jen took a deep breath and coughed. "If it helps, I don't think he felt a thing."

Devin put a hand to his forehead. "OK. OK. No big deal. Let's get him bagged and out of here."

Jen grabbed the corpse's legs. Devin had its upper body. They lifted and rolled it onto the body bag. Chris zipped it up while they climbed out of the pit. The three of them carried the body bag and placed it in the trailer, then threw in the shovels and went to get the lights.

Before turning hers off, Jen shined the lights further out into the pit. *What the hell?*

There were several body-shaped depressions, as if someone else had removed bodies, too. Who the hell would do that?

Devin called to her. "We've got everything packed except your lights."

Jen turned off the lights, plunging the pit back into darkness. She listened. Crackling and crunching like ice melting in a glass of tea. The tundra was thawing at an enormous rate.

She picked up the lamp and turned to bring it back to the trailer, but from somewhere not too far behind her came scratching sounds. She peered over her shoulder into the darkness, and the scratching stopped.

"Jen," Devin snapped. "Let's move."

Jen darted to the trailer and dropped the lamp off, then climbed onto her ATV and followed Chris the hell out of there.

6

A fter what seemed like hours, the shadowy outlines of Point Wallace houses appeared ahead. The sky had opened up again and the driving rain made it hard to see much detail beyond several yards. Jen adjusted her poncho hood in a doomed attempt at keeping the rain out of her eyes.

They wound their way through the village and climbed the hill, their tires working to gain traction.

"All this rain has softened the ground," Chris said. "There's more grass and less mud on the right side of the hill, so come up that way next time."

Lightning flashed, painting the trailers in momentary daylight.

Devin hopped off his ATV. "Let's get the body inside. Everything else can wait."

Devin held the science trailer door open as Jen and Chris stumbled inside with the body. He led them down the hallway to the archaeologist's room and gestured to the autopsy table. "On there."

He helped them lift the body onto the table and wiped his hands on his pants. Jen felt filthy and wanted nothing more than a hot drink and a shower. "I'll go see if Pete has any coffee brewed."

She stepped into the hallway and almost collided with Hal. He tried to look past her and into the room. "What did you find?"

Jen moved aside and Devin waved Hal in. "A mass grave. The bodies are well preserved, but old. Late nineteenth century is my guess. We brought one back for examination."

Jen slipped back into the room. No way would she miss the conversation.

Hal removed his glasses and wiped them with a handkerchief. "I've got something as well, but I'm not exactly sure what it is. Want to take a look? It's over in the lab."

Devin nodded.

Hal strode from the room without a word, Devin on his heels.

Chris passed by Jen. "I'm going for that coffee."

"Catch you later." She hurried from the room and over to the lab trailer.

The lab looked as clean and antiseptic as it had when Hal had given them the tour earlier. Hal and Devin hovered over a microscope in the corner. Hal gave Devin an arched eyebrow when Jen joined them. Her heart skipped a beat. They weren't going to throw her out, were they? She was a scientist, too. Not as experienced or lauded as them, but so what?

Devin met Hal's gaze with an unblinking one of his own. "Whatever I can see, Jen can see."

Hal shrugged, and Jen let out a breath. Devin was really trying to connect with her. It wasn't quite enough for her to forget his years of absences, but she felt a connection to him she hadn't before.

Hal pulled a vial of blood from a small refrigerator beneath the table. He tilted it so one drop landed on a glass slide, then pressed another slide onto it and placed them under the stage clips.

Hal peered into the eyepiece and adjusted the focus. "I wasn't sure what I was seeing at first." He straightened and stepped back. "Take a look."

Devin looked into the microscope. "Looks normal to me."

He straightened and motioned Jen over. She peered through the eyepiece and saw hundreds of donut-shaped red blood cells. "Same here."

"Watch closer," Hal said. "The outer boundaries of the cells."

Jen squinted and adjusted the focus. It took a minute, but she found a cell with a membrane that didn't look right. "Looks like it's blackening."

"Keep watching," Hal said. "Now that you've found one, you should see more."

He was right. She noticed dozens of cells in the same condition. The blackening of the membrane seemed to be spreading. She straightened and let Devin look. "What the hell is it?"

"It's not bacterial," Hal said. "We'd see that. My guess is some type of virus."

Devin looked up from the microscope. "You can't see it?"

Hal removed the slides, placed them in a plastic bag, and sealed it with tape. He tossed it in a biohazard waste bucket. "As well supplied as we are, we don't have an electron microscope." He rubbed his eyes. "Besides, I'm no virologist. We'll have to get the samples to Anchorage once the weather clears. There's an associate of mine, Dr. Wilson, who's staging labs for a new study on the effects of cold temperatures on the human body. He has contacts in the CDC." He sighed. "But for now I have nothing new to help Leo."

Devin clasped him on the shoulder. "You've done what you can."

"No." Hal strode toward the trailer door. "I haven't. Let's take a closer look at that body you brought in."

Jen jogged to keep up with Hal and Devin. "Not much you can do with a frozen body."

Hal ignored her. She followed them into the headquarters trailer. Hal stopped at the admin office door. Pete sat at his desk, shuffling papers, while Chris leaned against the wall, coffee mug in hand, talking to him.

"Still no radio?" Hal asked.

Pete shook his head. "I gave up for now."

"Keep trying," Hal said. "We may have a contagion, and need to let the state authorities know. They can contact the CDC and get the ball rolling."

Pete's eyebrows rose. "Contagion?"

Hal nodded. "Just a precaution, but Leo's blood may contain a virus, so we need to play it safe. And the logical place for him to have contracted it would be at the mass grave."

Chris frowned. "So are we infected, too?"

"Doubtful," Hal said. "I suspect Leo got it from his wound. Most likely, it's not airborne, but passed on through fluids."

Jen pursed her lips. Hal was making a lot of assumptions. Did he believe what he said, or was he just trying to keep everyone calm? "What good does it do to tell Wainwright? It's not like they can get the state troopers or anything."

"They might," Pete said. "They have newer and more powerful radio equipment and can cut through outages we don't have a hope to."

"And now I'm going to check our friend on the autopsy table," Hal said. "Devin, Jen. With me."

They returned to the archaeologist's office. Devin rummaged through the boxes, pulling supplies. He handed Jen and Hal long rubber aprons, masks, and gloves. He donned his own set and laid a selection of scalpels and syringes on the table next to the body bag.

Hal unzipped the bag and turned on the overhead surgical light. "Let's take a look at our mystery man."

Jen stood on the other side of the table as Hal pulled the bag back to reveal the corpse's face. Other than the slightly grayish tinge of the skin, he looked as if he were sleeping.

Hal tried to pry the eyelids open. "They're still frozen."

He looked at Devin. "What do you make of the clothes? Seen anything like this before?"

Devin looked closely at the corpse's coat. "Coarse wool. Almost like a pea coat." He unfastened a button. "Black glass buttons. Most likely this gentleman is from the late 1800s, as I thought." He unbuttoned the rest of the coat and opened it.

Piles of brown dust were stacked up on the man's shirt, his underarms, and in the inside folds of the coat. Jen reached out and pinched some between her gloved fingers.

"What is it?" Devin asked.

Jen rubbed the dust. She'd seen something similar a year before. It turned out to be tiny, almost microscopic, spores. *But where did they come from?* "It's very fine. Could be a lot of things, but I'd need to see it under a microscope to tell for sure."

Devin rummaged through a box on the shelf. He removed a small capped plastic vial, opened it, and held it out to Jen. She picked up more dust and dropped it into the vial. He closed it and handed it to her.

Hal felt the dead man's temples. "Not much we can do on this frozen end. Let's check the extremities."

He spread the bag more, exposing an arm. He lifted the wrist and flexed it. "Better." He moved the fingers. "Fingers thawed, pliable." He glanced over his shoulder. "Can you hand me the heavy scissors?"

Jen stepped next to him, selected the scissors from the array of tools, and handed them over.

Hal cut the heavy wool of the coat arm and then the cotton shirt sleeve, exposing a hairy arm with a crude tattoo of a woman in a grass skirt. "Definitely a sailor."

Devin nodded. "As far as I could see, all the other bodies were dressed the same."

Hal pressed on the underside of the forearm. "Hand me the syringe. I've found a spot thawed enough to penetrate."

Jen handed him a syringe, and he inserted its long needle into the arm and pulled the plunger back. Deep dark red blood filled the barrel. He placed it to the side and zipped up the body bag. Pulling down his mask, he let out a long breath. "Let's go to the lab and see what we can make of this."

He strode into the hallway, with Devin following.

Jen stepped out of the room and removed her mask. Chris leaned against the wall with his arms crossed. "So what do we have?"

She wiped a hand across her forehead. "Besides a hundred-and-twenty-year-old popsicle that smells like fish? We've got a bit of a mystery. Who were these guys and how did they get there?" She nodded at him. "How long has this village been here?"

Chris shrugged. "Thousands of years."

"And there's no mention of these sailors in your stories?"

"No. So they are sailors?"

"Yeah, from the late 1800s, most likely."

"We can ask my uncle. He might know, but I'd be surprised. Our stories are passed on from generation to generation. They aren't meant to be secret. On the contrary, it's important to us that they be shared."

"It could be important," Jen said. "I've got to get to the lab, but maybe you should find your uncle and join us there."

Chris nodded. "See you there." He ran off.

When Jen got to the lab, Hal was bent over the microscope. He sat up, removed his glasses, and rubbed the bridge of his nose. "Same thing as Leo."

Devin took a look. "Sure is. Guess that solves the puzzle of how Leo became infected."

Jen took a clean slide and spread some of the dust on it. "Let's see what we have here."

She sat at the microscope and swapped slides. Closing one eye, she squinted into the eyepiece and adjusted the focus. It zoomed in to show clusters of spiny shaped spores. "Scleroderma areolatum."

"What was that?" Devin asked.

Jen straightened. "Spiny spores."

"Is that significant?" Hal asked.

Jen dropped the capped vial of spores into her shirt pocket. "Not sure. Would love to study them on an electron microscope."

A metallic *chunk chunk* came from the doorway. Having spent a lot of time at the gun range, Jen knew exactly what that was.

She spun. A short elderly native man with salt-and-pepper hair hanging wildly down to his shoulders aimed a twelve gauge shotgun at them.

No one moved. The man pointed the gun at each one of them in turn. "Where is the Tuqunaragri?"

Jen and Devin looked at each other. What the hell was he talking about? Jen's pulse pounded her ears, but still her mouth opened before she knew it. "I'll bet we can find it for you on Google maps."

The wild man squinted at her.

Shit. When will I learn to shut up?

Hal's voice quivered. "We don't understand that word."

The man squeezed his eyes shut for a moment. "The body you brought back from Fear Mountain. The Tuqunaragri. Either you take it back now, or you'll join it."

7

J en stared at the shotgun, her mouth going dry. *Am I going to die in this place?*

Devin put his hands up and spoke in a calm, soothing voice. How he managed that, Jen would never know.

"Put the gun down and we can talk."

The man swung the shotgun to point at Devin. "The body must go back now, before it's too late."

Devin took a deep breath. "We can do that. Just put the gun down."

Raymond appeared in the doorway behind the man, towering over him. "What are you doing, Norman?"

Norman spun and spoke to Raymond in Inupiaq. Raymond answered him in kind and held his hands out. The man gave him the gun. Jen let out a breath she hadn't known she was holding.

Raymond stepped into the room. "What's this all about?"

Norman answered, again in Inupiaq. Raymond shook his head and put a hand up. "In English."

Norman looked from Raymond to the others, and back again, his lips a thin line across his face. For a few moments there was silence, then his shoulders sagged and he nodded. "It's time to tell the story."

Raymond laid the shotgun on a table. "What story?"

"The story of Fear Mountain."

Jen's heart rate had slowed to near normal, but her legs were wobbly, so she pulled out a stool and sat.

Norman closed his eyes for a moment, then spoke. "The story passes down that in the latter part of the 1800s, they came. I've since looked up some of the known facts on the Internet and found that in 1871 a fleet of thirty-three whaling ships was trapped in the ice. The sea had frozen all the way to land as close as a few miles north of here. We knew nothing of it at the time, until men walked off the ice and into our village. They staggered and moved very slowly, as if they had frozen limbs from their journey. Our elders approached them, but as they got closer and the strange men saw the elders, the strangers let forth a terrible sound. These men, these ice walkers, had deep yellow eyes, and they growled and gnashed their teeth as they came. Had their limbs not been half frozen, they surely would've caught the elders."

Raymond frowned. "And you're saying these ice walkers are the same men whose bodies Leo found?"

Norman nodded. He pointed at Devin. "The same as the one he brought back to the village. A Tuqunaragri."

Jen stood, but kept a steadying hand on the table next to her. "What does that mean?"

Raymond scratched his head and squinted. "The literal translation is one who acts dead."

A chill ran down Jen's spine and her mind flashed back to the scratching she'd heard in the pit. Maybe the old guy wasn't crazy.

Devin crossed his arms. "All legends have a grain of truth. Perhaps these men were just sick. If I recall, there was a large typhoid outbreak during that time."

Norman shrugged. "I don't know. I only tell you what has been passed down. In it was the warning that they would destroy the world if they were ever disturbed. This is why we have the stories of spirits at Fear Mountain —to keep everyone away."

Hal took off his glasses and wiped them on his shirt. "If those bodies at Fear Mountain are the same ones you describe, how did they get out there? How did they get buried?"

"Another ship docked, here at our village. Men from the government, Army men and men who were in charge that did not wear uniforms, came ashore. By then the bodies had frozen completely in the subzero temperatures and stood like statues all around the village and beyond. These men collected the bodies and moved them out to Fear Mountain. The tundra was hard to dig in, so they set up large tents and built fires underneath them to thaw the ground enough to dig. Many men worked in shifts for days and dug a trench, a pit. They tossed the bodies in and filled it. Because of the permafrost, these creatures would stay frozen forever."

Raymond shook his head. "Why have I not heard this before?"

Norman licked his lips. "When they had buried the bodies, the men from the government, the ones not in uniform, spoke to the elders. They said that no one must know of this, and if word ever got out, then our village would be destroyed. So the elders called a meeting and everyone pledged to silence. As the new generation was born, none knew about this, and the older generations died off. But they didn't want it completely forgotten in case the information was useful to our people someday, so there were always three elders who knew the story. When an elder that knew died off, the other two would pick a replacement and burden them with the secret."

"Who are the other two elders?" Raymond asked.

"Jacob Adams and your mother."

"My mother?"

Norman nodded. "We were all sworn to secrecy. When your mother passes, we plan on you taking her place."

"I see," Raymond said. "Norman, will you go to my house and help my mother take care of Leo?"

"What about the Tuqunaragri?"

"Let me talk it over with Hal and his friends. We'll figure out the best way to get the body back."

Norman stared at Raymond for a few moments, then turned and trudged out the door.

Raymond nodded at Hal. "So what have you been able to find out about Leo's illness?"

Hal cleared his throat. "Leo's blood has some anomalies."

"Anomalies? What does that mean?"

Jen crossed her arms. *Enough talking around it.* "There's something wrong with their blood cells, and Leo has the same problem. He was infected when he was impaled on the bone."

Raymond frowned. "Is that true? What is the cure?"

"I don't know." Hal's shoulders lowered. "It's something I've never seen before."

Jen sighed. "I know what to do. We need to get Leo to Wainwright. The weather is lightening up. Maybe the radio's working now?"

Chris walked into the room. "There you all are. I've been looking for you." He looked at Jen, then his gaze went to the shotgun on the table. "What's going on?"

Raymond put a hand on his shoulder. "We'll fill you in later, but we've got to get Leo to Wainwright."

"Wainwright's a long way," Chris said.

Hal cleared his throat. "This is way beyond me. He may not survive the trip, but it's his only hope."

Jen walked to the doorway. "I'll see if Pete's making progress."

"That's why I came over here," Chris said. "Pete made contact with Wainwright for less than a minute. He told them about the contagion, but isn't sure if they got it or not."

Hal pulled the truck keys out of his pocket. "I'd better get back and take a look at Leo. Anyone coming?"

Devin stood. "Let me check on our guest on the autopsy table, and I'll be right out. I just want to make sure Norman didn't do anything to him."

Jen followed him out.

THE CORPSE APPEARED UNDISTURBED. Devin and Jen put on gloves, and Jen unzipped the body bag. Devin lifted the sailor's arm and bent it, while Jen did the same with a leg.

"His arm has a lot more flexibility," Devin said.

Jen nodded. "So do his legs. In fact, he's pretty damn limber for a man who's been dead over a hundred years."

"He's thawing fast." Devin felt the sailor's head. "But the head's still frozen. It'll probably be the last part to thaw."

He zipped the bag closed and took off his gloves. Jen snapped hers off, tossed them in the biohazard box, and headed out to the truck. It was running and everyone else was in it when they arrived. Jen squeezed in next to Chris and Raymond in the back, while Devin hopped in the front. Jen caught Chris up with what he'd missed as they rode to Raymond's.

When they arrived, Hal jumped out, grabbed his bag, and jogged up the steps. He opened the door and froze. Jen stopped behind him. "What's wrong?"

When Hal didn't answer, she peered around him. Raymond's mother lay on the kitchen floor. Her chest looked like it had exploded, painting the walls and the floor around her in blood. Her entrails hung out of her abdominal cavity and were spread across the tiles. The place smelled like a freezer full of meat that'd gone bad.

"What the hell?" Devin's voice came from behind her.

Norman, the elder with the shotgun fetish, lay on the couch, a slack expression on his face. Leo leaned over him with his back to the front door. Ripping and chewing sounds came from him. Norman's hand rose weakly. "Help me," he moaned.

Jen's mind slipped gears as she tried to make sense of the scene in front of her, but Raymond broke her trance. "Mother."

Raymond pushed past the others and rushed to his mother. Slipping on the gore, he landed on his back beside her. He scrambled to his knees, sobbing.

Hal staggered backward onto the porch, his face bloodless.

Leo spun, his yellow eyes glowing with hate. Blood stained his face and dripped onto his chest, and he chewed what looked like a piece of intestine. He dropped it and screeched, "Scree!"

Jen cringed. It was the sound of nails running across a chalkboard, and it went right through her. Bile rose in her throat and she was frozen to the spot, clamping her hands over her ears.

With a primal growl, Leo leapt on her.

8

Leo slammed into Jen and drove her to the floor, knocking the air from her lungs. She managed to jam her elbow against his throat and kept his gnashing teeth inches away from her face. His breath had the rotten stink of the pit. She tried to catch her breath and gagged.

Devin kicked Leo's side. "Get off my daughter!"

Leo ignored him and pressed farther, his snapping jaw closer and closer to Jen. She had to do something or he would tear her face apart. She tried to raise her knees, get them underneath him so she could shove him off, but his weight was too much. He was going to eat her face.

The pressure on her elbow disappeared, and Leo was pulled off, Raymond and Chris each grasping one of his arms. Leo struggled like a feral cat, trying to bite them as they dragged him back to the couch.

Jen rolled up onto all fours, shuddering and coughing. Devin took her arm and helped her stand. Her knees buckled, and he kept her from falling by wrapping an arm around her. Raymond had Leo's arms pinned behind him, and while Leo kicked and growled, his yellow eyes drilled into Jen's.

"Everyone out," Raymond yelled. "Get ready to close the door once I've cleared it."

Devin led Jen out. Fresh air slapped her in the face, giving her strength. Hal leaned over the porch rail, puking onto the muddy road.

Chris stationed himself beside the open door. "Ready when you are, Uncle Raymond."

Raymond's voice came from the house. "I'm coming on the count of three. Close the door after I get through."

Devin leaned Jen against the rail. "Are you okay by yourself?"

Jen nodded, and Devin stationed himself next to Chris.

"One, two, three!" A crash came from inside the house, and Raymond streaked through the doorway. Devin and Chris rammed their shoulders into the door and slammed it shut. The door shuddered as a heavy weight hit it from the other side.

Raymond ran back to the door, his keys in hand, and locked the deadbolt. He leaned with his back against the house, breathing heavily, his arms and shirt stained with blood. "What the hell's wrong with him?"

Hal straightened, still clutching the railing. "Leo needs help."

Jen's legs felt less rubbery, and she stumbled toward the others. "Help? Leo needs a straitjacket."

Raymond shot her a dirty look. Chris put his hand on his uncle's shoulder. "You OK?"

Raymond nodded.

"We need to get out of here," Devin said.

Raymond's brow furrowed. "I'm not leaving my nephew or my village."

Hal frowned. "I don't want to bring the infection elsewhere."

"But Wainwright's radio equipment can get through when ours can't," Jen said. "Isn't that what Pete told us?"

"True." Hal tapped a finger on his chin and stared off into space. "And even if we have the virus, we'd get the CDC involved quicker from Wainwright, and prevent it from spreading any further."

Jen straightened, much steadier than before. "Then Devin and I can go to Wainwright and send the message."

"You'll never make it there alive," Raymond said. "Not by yourselves."

Chris raised his hand. "I can take them, then bring their medic back for Leo."

"It's probably our best chance," Hal said.

The banging stopped. Raymond pressed his ear against the door. "He's still there, but he's breathing awfully heavy. I hope he doesn't hurt himself."

Jen raised an eyebrow. "Not exactly on the top of my worry list."

Raymond looked at Hal and sighed. "You're probably right. It's the best chance we have."

Hal headed for the truck. "I'm going with you, since there's nothing I can do for Leo at this point. Let's get moving."

THIRTY MINUTES LATER, Jen and Devin stood next to four ATVs in front of the science trailers. Devin put a hand on Jen's shoulder, concern written on his face. She remembered how he'd attacked Leo to save her. "I'll get you out of here," he said. "I may not have been there for you when you were growing up, but I'm here now."

Jen's eyes searched his, her lips pressed tightly together and she swallowed. "We'll get each other out of here."

Devin smiled. "That's a deal."

Hal and Chris came out of the trailer with four backpacks. Chris handed one to Jen. "Food and water for the trip."

They loaded up and started off down the hill with Chris leading. As they weaved slowly through the village, they passed Raymond's house. He stood on the porch, his hands raised, and talked to a group of villagers gathered before him. It looked as if he were calming them down.

Outside of town Chris sped up, and the others kept pace, their headlights lighting up the terrain ahead of them. Even though the rain had stopped, the cloud cover had thickened, casting the tundra in a deeper gloom.

They stopped at the break in the trail. Jen looked toward the mountain. She couldn't see it in the dark, but she could feel it.

Chris turned to the others. "We need to go inland, but not all the way to the mountain."

Devin nodded. "That's good by me. I don't need to run into that place again in the dark."

Chris sped off with the others following. A few minutes in, he turned right. Although bumpy, the ground seemed more solid to Jen than it had during their last trip. They maintained a moderate speed, and Jen had already started wondering how long the trip would take when a man staggered into the headlight beams, directly in front of Chris. Chris swerved, missing the man by inches, and Jen got a flash of the man's face. Ashen skin, facial hair, yellow eyes. *Impossible.*

A dozen more men lumbered toward them from three sides. Chris signaled the others to stop.

The man Chris had nearly hit tilted his head to the sky and let out an ear-piercing screech. *Just like Leo.* The other men answered in kind and they all staggered in an almost-jog toward the riders.

Screeches echoed from the darkness around them. They seemed to come from hundreds of voices and from every direction. Jen screamed over the cacophony. "We need to get the hell out of here."

Hal yelled over the engines. "There's an opening in their ranks. If we can get through there, we'll have a clear path to Wainwright. Come on."

He gunned his throttle and roared between two groups of sailors. Just as he shot by them, his headlights lit up a dense wall of more sailors in front of him. Hal's brake lights flared, but he didn't stop in time and slammed into them, sending sailor bodies flying. Hal tried to turn the ATV around, but one of the creatures bear hugged him from behind and bit into his neck.

"Hal," Devin yelled.

Hal screamed. Blood spurted from his neck and sprayed other sailors, who pounced on him, dragging him to the ground as they fed.

An ashen hand clutched Jen's shoulder. *Oh, shit.* Jen accelerated, but the sailor hung on as the ATV shot out from under her. Slammed to the ground, she gasped.

The sailor bent down toward her, his mouth open and ready to bite. She kicked his chest with both legs, sending him flying back, then hopped to her feet. More sailors had locked onto her and weren't far away, and the guy she'd kicked was getting back up. *I should've at least knocked the wind out of him.*

A beeping horn caught her attention and she spun. Two sets of headlights zoomed toward her. Chris zipped past and ran into the nearest sailor, knocking him back. Devin came to a skidding stop and she jumped on behind him, wrapping her arms around his waist. "Let's get the hell out of here."

Devin followed Chris as they raced back the way they'd come. Jen glanced over her shoulder. The mass of sailors had turned and were lumbering after them. *We're leading them right to the village.*

9

Hal's death played over and over in Jen's mind. It had happened so fast. *What a gruesome way to die.* She clenched her jaw. She'd be damned if she and Devin would end up like him.

The village came into view, with some houses lit from a porch light or a glow through a window, and others nothing more than a black silhouette in the distance.

A figure ran from the village and onto the tundra. Another figure burst from behind a house, sprinted after the first one, and jumped on it like a lion bringing down its prey.

What the hell? No way the dead could've beat them back.

They entered the village and stopped in front of Raymond's house. The streets were deserted, and a quiet cloaked the scene. No rain. No thunder. No lightning. Just the wind and oppressing darkness.

Chris hopped off his four-wheeler and grabbed his rifle from the gun scabbard. Keeping his voice low, he said, "I need to find Uncle Raymond."

Jen dismounted. Sweat ran down the back of her neck. *Where is everyone?*

She followed Chris onto Raymond's porch. The front door was splintered open from the inside, and fresh blood had pooled on the rubber welcome mat. "I'll come with you," she said.

Devin grabbed her arm. "We don't know what's in there."

A woman's scream came from somewhere toward the hill, followed by a chorus of screeches from all directions.

Jen licked her lips. "I think we know what's out here. Besides, we should stick together."

Chris nodded. "You two come inside and watch the door. I'll search the house for Uncle Raymond."

"OK." Devin stepped inside and stood against the wall on one side of the doorway. Jen took the other side, wrinkling her nose at the overpowering smell of rancid meat. Chris crept into the shadows of the living room and disappeared.

A screech came from a house a block away. A woman ran out the front door, pursued by a child whose yellow eyes caught the light from an open door across the street. The little girl growled and snapped her teeth as she raced after the woman. She wrapped her arms around the woman's leg and bit into her calf, dragging her down. The girl crawled up the writhing woman's back and bit into her shoulder, pulling a chunk of flesh out and chewing it like a piece of steak.

A bang came from the back of the house. Jen pressed into the wall, peering into the blackness of the living room. *We're surrounded.*

The floor squeaked, and Chris stepped from the darkness of the hallway. "No one here."

Jen let out the lungful of air she hadn't realized she'd been holding in. "You scared the shit out of me."

Devin slumped into a sitting position and put a hand to his forehead. "Phew."

Rifle slung over his shoulder, Chris carried a handgun and a three-foot section of metal pipe. "Didn't find Uncle Raymond, but I did pick these up."

Chris handed Devin the gun. Devin held it away like it would explode at any second. "I don't know what to do with this."

"I do." Jen took it from Devin, and he gaped as she removed the magazine, slammed it back in, and pulled the slide back, letting it snap forward. "Sig .45. Nice."

"You know guns?" Devin asked.

Jen frowned. "You don't spend a lot of time in the Alaskan outdoors without one." She held the pistol up. "I'll take this."

Chris shrugged and handed Devin the pipe. "Low tech, but it packs a punch."

Chris handed two boxes of ammo to Jen. She opened them and dumped the rounds into her pockets. "I'm ready."

They stepped out of the house, and the zombie kid looked up from its dinner. Blood sprayed from its mouth as it screeched.

Chris aimed the rifle at it, but didn't pull the trigger. He lowered the barrel. "That's little Annie Brower. I've watched her for her folks a time or two. I can't shoot her. She's just a kid."

Annie streaked toward them, teeth bared and an animal growl rumbling in her throat. Devin raised the pipe over his head. Jen aimed the Sig and pulled the trigger. The bullet hit Annie in the chest and she staggered, then fell forward on her hands and knees. Heart hammering, Jen lowered the gun. *I just killed a little girl.*

Devin lowered the pipe. "God help us all."

Annie's head rose, her piercing yellow eyes fixed on Jen. She sprinted at her as if she'd never been shot. Annie reached the porch steps and leapt. Jen pumped two more shots into her, one in the chest and the other in the stomach. Annie dropped onto the steps, then sprung again. The pipe flashed by Jen and bashed Annie's temple—a hollow gong rang out when it connected. She dropped to the porch in a heap and lay still.

Jen kept the gun pointed at her. "Is the zombie dead?"

Devin squinted. "Zombie?"

Chris prodded Annie with the barrel of his rifle, rolling her over. "Might as well call it what it is." Annie's head was caved in at the left temple. "Seems to be really dead this time. Poor Annie."

A growl from the street behind them caused Jen to spin. Annie's victim had risen and glowered at them with predator's eyes. Two villagers streaked past the porch, followed by another raging zombie. The zombie's stomach was ripped open, frayed ends of its guts trailing behind it and flapping in the wind. The villagers disappeared behind a house. Just before he followed, the zombie looked back at Annie's victim and light splashed on him. His face was ashen, and his long hair even more scraggly than the last time Jen had seen him. *Norman.*

Norman screeched and ran off after his prey. Annie's victim followed.

Devin gripped the pipe tighter. "We've got to find a safe place. Get out of the open."

Jen shivered. "After what we've just seen, there might not be a safe place."

10

C hris wiped his forehead with the back of his hand. "Uncle Raymond would either go to the science trailers or the community center."

Jen checked her ammo. "I'm not feeling warm fuzzies that a trailer would keep those things out. Besides, the community center's that big building we passed, isn't it? It looked pretty sturdy, and it's only a couple of blocks away."

Chris stepped off the porch, his head on a swivel, looking back and forth. "Follow me."

Jen nodded toward Chris. "Follow him. I'll take up the rear. That'll keep the guns in front and back."

Devin hesitated. He looked like he would say something, but then hurried after Chris.

Chris led them to the shadows of the building across the street. He snuck to the corner and peered around, then whispered, "The door's closed, so that's a good sign, but there are four zombies milling around in front of it."

Devin rubbed his chin. "We need a diversion. If we can pull them away from the door, we have a chance."

"We should move up a building," Chris said. "That'll put us only twenty yards away. I think we can do it without being seen, just be real quiet."

He stepped around the corner and crept forward, staying in the shadows, Devin right behind him. Another zombie stumbled onto the road, but didn't turn Jen's way. She slipped around the corner and followed the others to the next house, glancing over her shoulder to make sure they weren't followed.

A zombie screech in the distance ripped through the night, followed by several gunshots. The zombies in front of the community center all tilted their heads back and returned the call. They ran off in the direction of the original screech.

Jen hugged the wall. Other screeches answered from all directions. Dozens of zombies streaked past the end of the road, oblivious to the prey nearby.

How many new zombies are there now?

One zombie turned its head and stared at her as it raced by. No doubt it had seen her. Why didn't it stop?

Jen put a hand to her pounding chest. "They swarm like bees."

Chris squatted and felt around, then stood, holding an empty bottle. "But did they all go? Let's see if there are any left close by."

Jen put an arm out to stop him. "Wait."

Chris stepped to the edge of the house and flung the bottle. It landed with a crash between two houses across the way. Nearby screeches echoed from several directions.

The blood drained from Jen's face. "Shit. That's going to bring a swarm. Go."

Chris raced toward the community center doors. Devin stumbled, caught his balance, and hurried after Chris. Jen swept the area with her gun. No targets yet. She darted toward the community center and was halfway there when Chris got to the doors and tried opening them.

Chris looked back at her, his face drawn. "Locked."

Devin arrived and pulled on the handle. No good.

A screech from close behind her sent chills over Jen's body. She dug in her heels and pumped her arms, giving it all she had. Chris and Devin banged on the door. "Let us in. It's Chris."

Several more screeches rang out. *Thanks for throwing the damn bottle, Chris.*

One of the double doors flew open, and Raymond stood in the doorway. He stepped back, raised a shotgun, and aimed it past Jen. She hoped he was a good shot.

Chris ducked into the building, but Devin stood, looking behind Jen, his eyes wide. "Run! They're right behind you."

Jen waved at him to go on. With a frown on his face, he backed into the building, holding the pipe at the ready. Raymond fired. The thump of a body hitting the ground behind her spurred Jen into one last burst of speed. She streaked through the doorway and tripped, falling and sliding across the shiny linoleum floor. She came to a stop on her back, panting. Her gaze snapped to the open door. A dozen zombies had almost reached it. Raymond and Chris slammed the door closed, and Raymond propped a bar against it. The door shuddered from the impact of the zombies, but it held.

An elderly villager with jumbled white hair and a vacant look in her eyes scuffled over to Jen. "Have you seen my sister Gwen? I've been looking all over for her."

Raymond put an arm around the woman's shoulder and led her away. "Come on, Tara. Let's get you a comfortable chair."

Chris held out a hand and helped Jen up. "What's with her?" Jen asked.

"Tara has dementia," Chris said. "Her sister takes care of her. She's lost without her."

"Where is her sister?" Jen asked.

Chris scanned the room. "I don't see her in here."

Raymond returned. "Can someone tell me what the hell's going on around here?"

Devin shook his head, panting. "Some type of contagion. Has to be what Leo has."

"Contagion?" Raymond let out a nervous laugh. "That turns people into monsters?"

Jen brushed her pants off. "They're zombies."

Raymond gawked at her.

Even with all that's happened, he's looking at me as if I'm crazy?

"Yes, Uncle," Chris said. "People die and come back to eat the living."

"Zombies?" Raymond looked at Devin. "I know what I've seen looks like zombies, but you're a scientist. Surely there's another explanation."

Devin sighed. "I don't know what to believe, but the creatures do act like zombies you'd see in books and movies, and since there's no scientific term for them, zombies will do."

Raymond scratched his head, then looked around. "Speaking of science, where's Hal?"

"He was eaten by the zombies you don't believe in," Jen said.

Raymond's eyebrows rose. "What?"

"The dead sailors in the pit," Jen said. "And they're heading this way."

"Oh, shit." Raymond paced. "How many?"

"If they all reanimated," Devin said, "a couple hundred at least, but we never saw the full extent of the pit."

Jen looked around the room at the clusters of villagers, most of whom had a blank look on their face, as if they'd just woken up from a nightmare. *Or to a nightmare.* "That would be more of them than the humans in here. What do we have? Fifty? Sixty?"

"Forty-eight at last count," Raymond said. "That's out of a population of two hundred seventy-one."

The banging on the door intensified, causing it to shudder. Raymond slammed a fist into his hand. "Another fifty of those things on that door and it'll crack like an eggshell. Two hundred more and there'll be no place to hide."

Chris cleared his throat. "What happened here, Uncle?"

"Leo broke through and attacked us," he said. "He bit a chunk out of old Simeon's neck, then ran off. Simeon was pumping blood all over the place and died. A couple minutes later, he jumped up and his eyes had turned yellow, just like Leo. He grabbed his sister and chewed on her arm." Raymond sighed. "It all went to shit from there. A bunch of us came here and locked the doors. We've been able to get a few people in, but only a few."

Chris put an arm around his uncle. "You saved people. That's what matters."

Raymond shrugged. "But for how long? These creatures keep finding people hiding in their houses and attack them. Their numbers are growing."

A shout came from across the room. Tara peered out a window and waved. "Gwen is out there. She looks hurt."

She ran to a side door. "I need to let her in."

"Tara! No!" Raymond sprinted toward her, with Devin, Jen, and Chris on his heels.

Tara flung the door open, her arms wide. "Gwen. Over here."

A chorus of screeches answered her.

11

Chris sprinted past the others and reached the door just as an obese middle-aged woman in a kuspuk darted in and leapt on Tara. Chris rammed his shoulder into the door and slammed it home.

Tara's screams cut off into a watery gurgle as Gwen bent down and clamped her mouth on Tara's lips. It looked like she was giving her mouth-to-mouth. But Gwen pulled back, shaking her head viciously, and ripped Tara's lips off her face. The zombie stood, chewing the flesh and swallowing as Raymond slid to a stop before her. Gritting his teeth, he leveled the shotgun and fired. The pellets shredded the kuspuk and turned the zombie's stomach to hamburger. She snarled at Raymond and lunged. He gripped the shotgun at both ends and barely kept her from his throat by pressing it against her chest.

Devin swung the pipe and it glanced off the zombie's head. The damn thing stumbled backward, releasing its grip on Raymond.

The head. That's how Dad killed Annie. "Hit her in the head," Jen yelled. "It's the only way to stop them."

Chris swung his rifle around and fired. Half of Gwen's head disintegrated in a red spray, and she fell in a heap.

Raymond wiped his brow. "How'd you know how to kill them?"

Devin panted, his hand on his chest. "Brilliant, Jen." He looked at

Raymond. "I killed one on your porch with a blow to the head. And that was after it had taken several bullets to the body."

Devin spun as a screech came from behind him. Tara came to her feet, her yellow eyes glaring at him. Tongue flicking from a ruined mouth, she crouched, ready to attack.

Jen only had one chance. She took the firing position she'd been taught in firearms class, aimed over her dad's shoulder, and squeezed the trigger. A hole appeared in Tara's forehead, and the back of her head exploded, spraying blood, flesh, and bone across the linoleum floor. She dropped like a marionette whose strings had been cut.

Devin whirled and said something to Jen. With a ringing in her ears, she yelled, "Can't hear."

He hugged her and spoke into her ear. "Thanks for the assist."

She squeezed him. "No charge for the first one. Besides, we're getting each other out of this, right?"

"That's right."

Chris's head hung. "Poor Tara. She deserved better."

Jen's gut ached. She'd been celebrating killing a zombie, while Chris considered it to still be Tara. She put a hand on his shoulder. "I'm sorry. I forgot these are people you grew up with. I didn't mean to be cruel."

"Not your fault," Chris said. "If I don't get over it and start taking these things out myself, more of my friends will die."

Devin nodded. "It's unfortunate, but you have to consider your friends gone once they turn."

Chris managed a weak smile. "You're right. Jen saved our lives. I shouldn't be whining." He gave Jen a thumbs up. "That was a heck of a shot."

Jen squeezed his shoulder. *Need to change the subject.* "Thanks, but did you notice that bitten people are turning faster? Leo took hours. This last one took a couple of minutes."

"The virus may be mutating," Devin said.

"Listen up," Raymond bellowed. "No doors get opened without my permission. I don't care who you see out there." The men and women who'd stood off to the side during the attack mumbled and nodded.

Raymond motioned to Chris. "Find those who still have their wits and station one person at each door." Chris ran off to a group of men gathered in front of the restrooms. A few of the men nodded and headed for the doors.

Chris jogged back over. "All the doors are covered."

Raymond walked to the middle of the room and clapped his hands sharply together. The villagers went silent, the constant banging and growling at the door the only sound. "Last we heard, the storm's supposed to break tonight. Our weekly supply plane is scheduled to arrive in the morning. So we just need to last the night."

The villagers murmured among themselves. Raymond went on. "But we need to be able to defend ourselves. So I want everyone to grab a weapon. Anything hefty that you can swing and knock these things in the head. That's the key. Any other damage doesn't bring them down, only the head."

Three men and a woman walked up to Raymond and pulled out hand-guns. Raymond nodded. "Good. I'd like each of you to double up with a door guard."

"What about me?"

Raymond spun. Griffin, the bootlegger, stood patting the grip of a long-barreled revolver holstered on his hip.

"What've you got?" Raymond asked.

".357 Magnum."

Chris's eyebrows rose. "Bad-ass gun." He pointed to Griffin's other hip. "What's that, a hatchet?"

Griffin removed the weapon from the sheath attached to his belt. "Tactical tomahawk. Small, but deadly."

"You're sober?" Raymond asked.

"As can be."

Arms crossed, Raymond stared into Griffin's eyes. "You stay here so you can back up any of the doors."

Griffin nodded. "You got it."

Villagers overturned chairs and broke the legs off. One man took the axe hanging next to the fire extinguisher and gave it a few practice swings. In the midst of all this, the banging and growling at the doors grew louder.

Shattering glass sounded from the women's room. Chris flung the door open. Three zombies had broken the window and were feasting on a woman lying on the floor, her throat ripped out and her glassy eyes staring at the ceiling. Another zombie lunged for Chris. Jen shot it in the face, blowing off its lower jaw, but not stopping it. *Shit.* Her second round went in its left eye, and it dropped. Chris slammed the door shut and pressed his back against it. Jen and Raymond helped him as the door shuddered under the zombie attack.

"Bring us something to brace this door," Chris yelled. A man rushed over with a two by four, jammed one end under the doorknob, and braced the other end against the floor. It slipped. Raymond grimaced. "The linoleum's too slick."

Jen waved to the man with the axe. "Bring that over here."

The man with the axe ran over. "Give it to Chris," she said. "Take his rifle and get back to the front door." Jen propped the piece of wood under the doorknob again, then pointed at where it met the floor. "We need a hole there now."

Chris nodded and raised the axe over his head. Jen stepped back, and Chris swung, creating a crack in the linoleum. With a few more deft strokes, there was a nice groove. Jen propped the piece of wood again, and it fit perfectly. The banging at the bathroom door continued.

Jen bent forward and propped her hands on her knees. Chris stepped back and let out a long breath. "They're not getting through there. It would take more of them than can fit in the bathroom."

Jen straightened and wiped her brow. "I'm exhausted. I think the adrenaline's beginning to wear off."

Chris pointed to a kitchen area. "Why don't you go get some coffee and sit for a bit. We're pretty secure right now."

"I might just do that." Jen walked over to the kitchen, where a pot of oily looking coffee sat. She poured a cup, leaned against the counter, and drank, the bitter liquid burning down her throat. The damn stuff must've been sitting there for hours.

Devin wandered over and stood next to her. She made a face and pointed to her cup. "Crappy, but it's the only game in town. Want a cup?"

Devin shook his head.

"Are all your expeditions this fun-filled?" Jen asked.

Devin gave her a weary smile. "Guess I saved the best for last." He took Jen's hand. "I know I was a shitty father, and I'm sorry."

Jen waved him off. "Not the time. We'll talk once we get out of here."

"That's the first thing we'll do when we get back to Anchorage," Devin said.

Raymond strode up to them. "I'm not sure this place will hold when those sailors get here, but I've got a plan."

"I'm all ears." Devin stood. "Is there anywhere more secure in the village?"

"I'm not talking about here. Wainwright."

Jen had been taking a drink and almost spit up the coffee. "Are you crazy? That's what we tried to do, and we lost Hal. Those things were as thick as flies out there."

"What's going on?" Chris asked as he joined the group.

"Your uncle is contemplating suicide," Jen said. "He wants to go to Wainwright." She crossed her arms. "What is it about that place? Everyone wants to go, but no one seems to get there."

Raymond frowned. "I've got a plan, and I've got twenty-seven other villagers willing to go."

"What's the plan?" Devin folded his arms.

Raymond took a deep breath and exhaled. "Since there are hundreds of the sailors coming from the south, we head east for about five miles, then swing out around them. They won't even know we're there. They'll keep coming here and we'll slip away."

Jen frowned. Sounded like a decent plan, but she remembered Hal's screams. She didn't want to be caught by the zombies out on the dark tundra. "Why not just wait here, and keep that as plan B if the community center looks like it'll be overrun?"

"By the time that happens," Raymond said, "it'll be too late. There'll be too many zombies for us to fight through to get out."

"You've got a point there," Jen said.

"So are you with me?" Raymond asked.

Jen looked at Devin. "What do you think?"

Devin frowned. "It's suicide." A loud bang came from the front door. It rattled.

Raymond crossed his arms. "It's suicide to stay. I learned in the corps that you have to adapt to the situation. This isn't the first solution I'd pick if we had other options, but we don't."

"This will be the first place rescue teams will look," Devin said.

"So you're staying?" Raymond asked.

Devin nodded.

Jen's heart fluttered. She liked Raymond's plan better, but she'd stick with Devin. "Then I'm staying."

Raymond looked at Chris. "And you?"

Chris stepped next to his uncle. "Gotta stick with family." He and Jen locked eyes for a moment. They weren't so different.

Raymond called out. "Clear the front door. We're going through."

He strode to the door, and other members of his group stood behind him, their faces somber.

Devin took Jen's arm and tugged. "We don't want to be too close."

She shook her head. "We should at least help them get clear of the building. Plus we'll need to make sure the door gets secured after they leave." She jogged toward the group at the front door.

Raymond locked eyes with Jen for a second, his jaw set. "On the count of three."

"One." He removed the iron bar from the door.

"Two." He unlocked the deadbolt.

"Three!"

The group slammed into the door, and it opened outward a couple of feet. The growls and snapping jaws grew louder, and a bloody, flesh-eaten hand grabbed for Raymond. He pointed his shotgun into the opening and fired.

"Again. Harder!" Raymond yelled. "Now."

The group pushed again, with help from villagers that were staying. The door opened halfway and the group pushed outside, guns booming and blunt weapons smashing into skulls. They moved through the zombies inches at a time, but they made progress.

Jen aimed at several zombies but couldn't get a clear shot.

Raymond's head rose above all, and fire spit from his shotgun barrel. The zombies swarmed them, but they slashed their way through the mob. Soon, all that could be seen was Raymond's head as the zombies encircled the group, but still they trudged their way forward. Jen's pulse raced. *They're going to make it.*

A cry of alarm turned Jen's attention to several zombies that had noticed the open community center door and all the fresh meat behind it.

A teenage zombie with a mangled arm rushed Devin, who wrestled him to the ground. Holding the creature down with one arm, he swung the pipe over his head and struck the zombie's forehead. Its head split and it went motionless.

Jen lined up her sights on one of the remaining zombies and shot it in the bridge of its nose. Another couple of quick shots and the remaining threat was gone.

A deafening boom came from behind Jen, and half of a zombie's head exploded in a gore-infused mist.

Jen ducked and looked behind her. Griffin stood, both hands holding the .357, a curl of smoke floating up from the end of the barrel. He smiled at Jen. "Not bad, huh?"

Asshole.

The group of escaping villagers made it across the street, almost through the zombie horde.

A scream came from the group, followed by a cacophony of screeches rising from the other side of the melee. Raymond looked back at the community center, his face slack and eyes wide. "Sailors," he mouthed.

A wave of the infected washed over the group. Several mottled hands grabbed Raymond's head and pulled him from sight.

12

J en reloaded and fired several rounds, making kill shots with most of them. "We need to open a hole on this side so they can come back."

Devin and several villagers rushed the back of the zombie horde, felling the creatures with deft blows to the head. The zombies were so intent on attacking Raymond's group, they mostly ignored Devin and the other villagers. And the few that tried to attack them were quickly dropped by one of Jen's bullets.

The wall of undead villagers broke down, and two of Raymond's group stumbled toward the community center. One, a young woman, had a gaping bite wound on her cheek. *God forgive me.* Jen sent a well-placed shot into the infected woman's forehead and she collapsed.

Jen kept the gun aimed at the other survivor, a man. His head down, he fell to his knees and looked up at her. *Chris.*

"Help Uncle Raymond," he breathed.

The zombie horde had turned their full attention to Devin and the villagers. "Fall back," Devin yelled as the man to his right was yanked into the mass of undead and disappeared.

Jen and Devin each took one of Chris's arms and half dragged him through the door. The last of the villagers ran into the building. Devin let go of Chris and slammed the door, but not before a withered hand shot through and prevented it from closing all the way.

Devin strained to keep the door from being pried open. "Need help here."

Two villagers rushed to join him, but five more hands shoved through the small opening, grasping for victims. One man holding the door screamed. A toddler had crawled through and bit his ankle. The man released the door and stumbled backward before tripping over a table and falling on his back. His head bounced off the floor and he lay still. The toddler crawled to the unconscious man and chewed on his thigh.

The door opened farther as another zombie pushed halfway through, almost grabbing Devin's arm. Jen lowered Chris onto a chair and pulled her gun back out, shooting the zombie. It went limp and wedged in the doorway, keeping Devin and the villagers from getting the door closed.

She looked around. Where the hell was Griffin?

Chris stood, shaking his head as if to clear it. "We need to get out of here. Those things are coming in whether we want them to or not." He cupped his hands to his mouth. "Devin, we've got to go."

Devin wrestled with a bearded seaman who kept trying to grab him by the neck.

"Devin," Chris shouted again, but he still didn't turn.

Jen took a few steps toward the door and bellowed, "Devin."

Devin looked back.

"Let's go."

A gnarled hand shot out from the doorway and grabbed a villager, who hacked at the arm with a knife. Two zombies climbed over their dead comrade in the doorway, and the rest of the villagers trying to shut the door fled. Devin pushed away an outstretched hand and ran to Jen and Chris. "What do we do now?"

Chris jerked a thumb over his shoulder. "All the zombies have been attracted to the front door, so we'll go out the back."

The front door was ripped off its hinges, and zombies, both fresh villagers and ancient seamen, rushed into the community center. Jen grabbed Devin by the arm and ran to the back of the building. Screams of anguish followed.

Jen stopped short. Damn door was chained and locked. "Are you freaking kidding me?"

Devin pulled on the chains. "Who has the key?"

Chris came to a sliding stop. "Uncle Raymond does." He hefted the fire axe. "But I have the master key. Stand back."

Chris swung the axe and it bounced off the lock. "Shit."

Two seamen zombies stumbled toward them. Devin took one out with a blow to the head, and Jen dropped the other with a bullet.

Chris hacked at the lock again. The damn thing dented, but didn't open.

Several of the villagers who had been attacked minutes before rose from the floor, their yellow eyes searching for a meal.

Jen squared off next to her father. "Chris, you better get that open now or we're the main course in an all-you-can-eat zombie buffet."

One of the zombie villagers sprinted toward them, and Jen raised the pistol. Devin stepped in front of her. "Save the bullets."

He timed his swing early and missed the zombie, who sprung on him, driving him to the floor.

A loud *clank* and a whoosh of fresh air came from behind Jen.

Devin held the zombie's snapping jaws inches away from his neck. "Need some help here."

Jen lined up the pistol on the zombie, but it was too close to her father.

Several zombie sailors stumbled toward them. *I have to take the shot.* Her finger pressed against the trigger, she followed the zombie's head as it snapped its jaws at her dad. If she could time it when its head was the furthest away from her father—

The axe sliced down and embedded in the zombie's skull with a thud. It fell to the side. Chris yanked the axe free, and Jen pulled Devin to his feet. "Out the door. Now."

The sailors were almost on them, with villagers pushing them from behind. The villagers would've already feasted on them if the slower sailors hadn't been in the way.

Jen and Devin stumbled outside, and Chris slammed the door closed. He put his back against it and held it shut.

"Where do we go?" Jen asked. "And if you say Wainwright, I'm kicking you in the nuts."

The door shuddered, but Chris held it closed. No way he'd be able to keep that up for long. Jen braced herself against the door and Devin joined them.

"We need to find somewhere to hide until the plane comes," Chris said.

Devin's eyebrows rose. "You think it's really coming?"

"I don't know, but it's our best hope."

Jen grunted as the door inched out. "What's the big building on the other side of the village?"

Chris pushed just as the door started to open. It closed again. "The school? Not a bad idea, but we'd have to go through those things out front to get there."

The door opened a few more inches. Jen strained to help keep it back. "We need to go somewhere now." The lights of the science trailers caught her eye. "Up there."

Devin glanced over his shoulder. "Perfect. We can see the whole village from there, then map a path to the school."

The door pushed out again. Jen gritted her teeth and gave it all she had, but it wouldn't budge. Arms shot out from the foot-wide opening, and she slid over to avoid them. "Devin," she yelled. "Get up the hill."

"But what about you two?"

"We'll follow, but you need a head start. Go!"

Devin ran.

"Take the right side," Chris called out.

Jen gasped. The door opened another couple of inches.

"These things will only follow us up the hill," Chris said.

Jen looked for her father and found him disappearing behind a building next to the hill. "The slower ones are in front. If we let the door open quickly, maybe they'll fall and stack up. It could slow the fast ones in the rear."

Chris nodded. "If we don't go straight toward the hill, we might throw them off. Let them see us go in a different direction, then circle back around."

Jen grunted. Her muscles burned. If they didn't go soon, she might not have the strength to run. "I'll follow you. On three. One, two, three."

They let the door go, and Chris dashed off to a house on the right. Jen sprinted after him, a chorus of screeches chasing her. She glanced over her shoulder. The plan had mostly worked. A half dozen of the slower zombies lay in the doorway, blocking the others. But two dead villagers pushed their way over the fallen sailors and chased after them. One of them was an overweight middle-aged man. He ran at no more than a jog. The other, a twenty-something woman in an I Heart Alaska T-shirt, had a chunk missing from her thigh. She limped and was only slightly faster than the man.

Twenty feet ahead, Chris disappeared around a corner. Jen followed a few seconds later and nearly ran into a bare-chested man in bloody jeans. He growled at her and gave chase. Chris was still ahead of her, but stopped and cocked the axe back. Jen dove for the ground at his feet as he swung. She rolled and came up on her knees. The zombie lay a few feet away, its head removed.

"I owe you one," she said.

"Let's hope you don't have to pay me back." Chris grabbed Jen's hand and pulled her up. She followed him in a zigzag pattern between the houses, finally coming to the bottom of the hill, below the science trailers.

Chris pointed up the slope. "There." Devin had made it halfway to the ledge the trailers sat on.

They climbed the slick grassy hill, slipping twice, but caught up with Devin. When he saw them, he sat, his lungs heaving. "Need a rest."

Jen took one arm. "Not here. We're too visible."

Chris took Devin's other arm, and they hauled him to his feet. Half carrying Devin, they climbed the rest of the way to the trailers.

Jen glanced down at the village. Dozens of zombies milled around outside the community center, while groups of two and three wandered between houses. A gunshot and a man's yell came from somewhere to her right, and the group outside the community center screeched as one and ran, stumbled, and crawled toward the sound.

Familiar growling came from below her. Two zombies lurched out of the shadows of a house, their eyes fixed on her. *Looks like they don't all leave when there's a swarm.*

"We're gonna have company," she said. "But they're the slow sailors, so it'll take them a while to get up here."

Devin and Chris joined her, peering down the hill. "Shit," Chris said. He pointed to the slope off to their left. Several figures scaled it like spiders on a web.

Jen's heart hammered. "Villagers."

A screech came from her left and a sailor shambled toward them. Chris lifted his axe. "I've got this one."

Another zombie joined the sailor. Its yellow eyes locked on Jen.

He looks familiar.
Jen's eyes grew wide. "Pete."

13

C hris swung his axe wildly at Zombie Pete and missed, nearly slicing into Jen's arm on the follow-through. She jumped back. "Hey!"

Devin gave Pete a glancing blow in the shoulder with the pipe. It was enough to knock him off course as Jen dodged to the side. Pete hit the ground and recovered, ready to spring.

The sailor rushed Chris, who sidestepped him and brought the axe blade down. He missed the sailor's head, but cleaved his remaining arm from his body.

Pete screeched, then leapt at Jen. She ducked and Pete sailed over her, his head meeting a well-timed swing from Devin. Pete's skull caved in just above his temple and he landed in the mud, sprawled and unmoving.

Chris charged the sailor and didn't miss as he drove the axe blade into its forehead, downing the creature. He propped the axe against the trailer and wiped the sweat from his brow. "That's becoming a workout. Why didn't you just shoot Pete?"

Jen straightened and cracked her neck. "I'm a great shot, but shooting leaping zombies in the head isn't something I've practiced." She pulled the magazine from the pistol and checked the rounds. Two in the magazine and one in the chamber. "Almost out of ammo. No use wasting it."

"Smart." Chris picked up the axe.

Devin smacked the pipe against his palm. "How do we get to the school from here?"

Snarls sounded closer from below. Jen tried to picture the village as she saw it when they landed.

Of course. "What if we go out and around the village."

Chris smiled. "Brilliant. We can follow this hill to the northern side of the village, then circle around and approach the school from the tundra."

Zombie screeches echoed from the village below. "No time to waste." Chris slung the axe over his shoulder and strode toward the north end of the hill.

Jen pulled Devin's arm. "Come on. No time to think about it." She let him go ahead of her while she kept watch from behind.

Chris kept from the edge of the flat part of the hill, but soon came to its end at a steep slope. "We'll have to go up to the runway to go the rest of the way. The slope at that side is more gradual."

"But if we go higher up the hill," Devin said, "we'll be out in the open and won't have that lip to hide us from the village."

Jen ran her fingers through her hair. "The zombies won't be able to get up the slope. And they're too stupid to think of going around."

"Right," Chris said. He pulled the axe off his shoulder and started climbing, using the axe like a walking stick.

Jen looked at Devin and gestured up the slope. "Age before beauty."

A slight grin broke out on his face for a moment, then he trudged up the hill after Chris.

Jen had made it halfway up when activity below caught her attention. She glanced down. Several dozen zombies stood at the base of the hill, attempting to climb it. One would get several feet up the steep slope, then slip and fall, knocking over the others.

More zombies gathered at the same spot, making it more difficult for them.

We work great as bait. If we could just get them to stay there, we'd have free rein of the village. She reached the runway. Chris and Devin stood on the edge. "Looks like we've attracted some attention," Chris said.

"How many do you think there are?" Devin asked.

Chris shrugged. "Two hundred and seventy-one souls in Point Wallace. If we assume most of them have been taken, that'd be at least two hundred.

Add a couple hundred sailors and what's down there looking at us isn't a lot of what's out there."

Jen walked across the runway and looked out over the Chukchi. The wind shot off it, blowing small raindrops into her face like tiny needles. Devin stopped next to her.

Chris ran over. "A small horde has made it to the trailer. Won't be long before they're here."

Jen swept hair out of her eyes and the wind blew it back over. "After you."

Chris hurried toward the northern end of the runway. He stopped at the edge, and Jen and Devin caught up with him.

"It's a gradual slope, but it's rocky and easy to slip on the small stones that litter it, so be careful." He started down, using the axe to help him balance.

"Why don't you go next?" Devin asked.

"I've got the gun. I can cover you guys from behind."

Devin frowned. "But who's going to cover you?"

A screech came from behind, and Jen glanced over her shoulder. "Shit. A couple of them are already here. We go together."

She grabbed Devin's arm and they stepped onto the slope. Jen slipped, but righted herself by holding onto him.

Chris had made it halfway down and his path looked to be clear. Jen and Devin hurried to catch up. Jen kept her eyes on the ground in front of them, trying to avoid any rocks. *Freaking impossible.*

They'd reached the halfway point when a zombie screech came from the top of the slope. Echoed by three more, it sent a shock down Jen's spine. Four villagers stood at the top of the slope. One sprinted toward them and the others followed a second later.

Devin stopped. "We won't beat them to the bottom."

Tight-lipped, Jen turned to face the oncoming horrors. "Then we make a stand here."

14

Jen and Devin stood shoulder to shoulder as the four zombies barreled toward them. A teenage girl was in the lead, with the others spread out behind her.

Jen wiped raindrops from her eyes and glanced down the hill. Chris had just reached the bottom.

She aimed her gun at the lead zombie, trying to keep the sight on its head. "It's moving too damn fast and its head keeps bobbing."

Devin tightened his grip on the pipe. "I've got this."

"The others aren't far behind," Jen said. "If we don't take them out quick as each one arrives, we could end up fighting all four at once."

Can't let Devin take them all himself.

Jen went down on one knee and aimed the gun at the lead zombie. Sure enough, its midsection bobbed as it bounded, but there was always a portion of it in her sight.

She took a deep breath, let half of it out, held it, and squeezed the trigger. The gun's recoil pushed it into her hand and the shot hit the zombie just under the ribcage.

It lost its footing and fell, growling and tumbling toward them. Jen tugged on Devin's arm. "Get out of the way."

She and Devin scooted aside and the zombie rolled by. Chris stood at the base of the hill, his axe drawn back.

"One down, three to go," Jen said. She lined up her sights on the next zombie. The round missed its midsection and hit it in the leg. It fell, but didn't roll. The two remaining zombies streaked past it.

"Shit," Jen said. "We'll still have to take care of three."

The two lead zombies bore down on them.

Devin dug his feet in and crouched. "I'll just have to get the rest. You should get down the slope with Chris."

"Always got to play superman, don't you?" Jen said. "I'm not going anywhere."

The zombie she'd shot in the leg had regained its feet and limped toward them, then its leg folded and it fell to the ground.

"Holy shit," Jen said. "I think the bullet shattered its bone."

She took aim at one of the lead zombies. "You take the one on the left. I'll at least slow down the one on the right. Give you some breathing room."

Devin licked his lips. "All right."

Sweat beaded on her forehead.

Twenty yards out. She lined up the sights on its chest.

Fifteen. Wounding it won't work. It'll be too close. I have to make a kill shot.

Ten yards. Jen lined up the sights on the creature's nose. Its head bobbed up and down. Holding her breath, she waited until its eyes disappeared below her sights and squeezed.

The bullet entered the zombie's head between the bridge of its nose and an eye. The creature dropped, the momentum rolling it down the hill straight at Jen. It took out her feet and she slammed to the ground, dozens of sharp rocks pressing into her back like ground glass. She gasped.

Devin grunted, and the hollow ringing sound of the pipe reverberated over Jen. A body hit the ground, rolled a few feet past her, and lay still, its stench slapping Jen in the face.

She groaned and pushed herself up into a sitting position. Devin reached down and pulled her to her feet. "I'm going to feel this one for a while," she said.

"Thanks to you," Devin said, "we made it out of this in one piece."

Chris called out. "No time to stand around. More can come at any time."

He stood over the first zombie. Its body lay at his feet and he yanked the pointed end of the axe from its head.

Jen and Devin stumbled down the rest of the slope, stopping at the base. Jen stretched her back. "Glad to get on flat ground again."

"No time to rest," Chris said. "Follow me." He and Devin hurried off. Jen looked back up the slope, then jogged to catch up.

They walked a couple hundred yards into the tundra before Chris stopped. "There's no telling if some of those sailors are still out here, so keep your eyes open."

Jen hadn't thought of that. She couldn't help but glance over her shoulder every thirty seconds or so.

The rain and wind picked up as Devin led them in an arc around the village, which was still in view. Screeches reached them several times, and a few shadows flitted around between the lights of the houses.

Chris stopped. "The school is straight in front of us, at the edge of town. It'll be the first thing we reach."

Jen swallowed. "Don't get me wrong, I'm glad we're not going into the middle of the village again, but those things can pop out anywhere."

"Even out here," Devin said.

Thanks for the warm and fuzzy thought. "Then what are we waiting for?"

The three of them walked toward the village.

A woman's shriek followed by the boom of a shotgun came from somewhere deep in the village. Answering screeches replied immediately.

"I think we should pick up the pace," Jen said. "Get in there while they're distracted."

"Agreed," Devin said.

They broke into a jog, feet splashing in pools of water collecting on the tundra. As they closed in on the school, screeches from the village became louder. The school loomed, a single-story solid looking structure. The side they approached had a number of windows, but no doors. *It could be in any small town in America and look like it belonged there.*

"There are two main double doors," Chris said. "One on each end."

"What if they're locked?" Devin asked.

Chris shook his head. "I've never seen them locked. This is a small village and it's hard to get away with anything, so the school's always been safe."

Screeching echoed from beyond the school on their left. They reached the school and Jen nodded toward the other end of the building. "I guess we take door number two."

Chris led them to the corner and peered around it. "Nothing moving."

Jen strode past him. "Then let's get the hell in there." She scooted to the double doors and pulled on a handle.

Locked.

"Shit."

15

Chris tried the other handle. It didn't move. "I've never seen this before."

Jen pressed her face against the window, peering past the thin crisscrossed wires in it. Shading her eyes, she gazed down a hallway. Nothing moved.

"Guess we'll have to go to the other door after all," Devin said. Tight-lipped, Chris pushed past them and around the building. Jen made sure Devin kept up, and hurried after Chris.

When they reached the other end, Devin put a hand up and they stopped. Jen cocked her head but heard nothing.

"Thought I heard a screech," Devin said.

Chris glanced around the corner and pulled back. He waved the other two over and whispered, "Three of them down the road, four buildings on the right. They're just wandering around."

"What should we do?" Devin asked.

Jen propped her hands on her hips. "We can't stay out here all night. We should try the doors."

"And what if they're locked and those zombies see us?" Devin asked.

"What other choice do we have?" Jen replied. "Besides, there's only three. We can take them."

Chris shrugged. "I agree—"

Jen ducked around the corner on the balls of her feet and crept to the doors. Glancing over her shoulder, she padded to the first door and pulled on the handle.

It didn't move.

Fuck.

She took a deep breath and pulled on the other door handle. Locked. Sweat broke out on her forehead and her heart kicked into overdrive.

A screech sounded behind her. She spun. One of the zombies had detected her, and the other zeroed in on her as well.

Devin and Chris rushed to her with questioning eyes. She shook her head. "Both locked."

More screeches came from somewhere ahead, no farther than a couple of buildings away. Answering calls came from all around them.

"There are more than three," Devin said. "We need to get out of here. Head back into the tundra."

More calls rolled in from the tundra. *What the hell?*

Chris looked the way they'd come. "There's at least two dozen sailors heading straight for us. They're not real close and they're not real fast, but they've cut us off that way."

"The school's our only chance," Jen said. "If the doors are locked then someone must be inside."

The three zombies down the road closed in.

Jen peered into the school. A corridor ran from the locked doors to the other exit fifty yards away. A second corridor split off halfway between them on the right.

Jen kicked the door. "Help. Let us in," she yelled.

Chris joined her, banging his fist on the window. Jen shook the handle and rattled the door in its frame. "Open up. They're coming."

"I need some help with the zombies," Devin said. He stood in a defensive stance, the pipe cocked over a shoulder.

Chris hefted his axe and joined him.

Jen glanced their way. The three zombies were almost on them and another dozen appeared in the distance.

A head stuck out from the side hallway and looked at her. *Griffin.* Jen's heart leapt and she banged her open palm on the window, the force sending a shock up her arm. "Open the doors!"

Griffin's head pulled back. *What the fuck?*

Jen turned to the others just as the three zombies reached them. Devin swung his pipe in a perfect golfing drive shot, slamming one zombie in the chin and knocking it backward. Another fell to Chris's blade. The third slammed into Devin and drove him to the ground. Jen grabbed it by the neck and pulled, but the damn thing was strong and only interested in Devin.

Devin struggled to keep it away from his face.

"Get back," Chris said. Jen stepped away and the axe came down in an arc, splitting the back half of the zombie's skull.

Jen helped Devin up. "Not done yet," Chris said.

Jen looked down the street. The dozen zombies had turned into two dozen. *Too many to handle.*

She pressed her face to the door. A woman's head peeked out from the middle corridor. "Open the door," Jen yelled.

The lady didn't move.

"Chris," Jen said, "there's a woman in here but she's just standing there."

Chris looked in the window. "Miss Janine," he yelled. "It's Chris. Chris Nageak. Open the door, please."

The lady made a few tentative steps into the hallway. She was a small thing, not much taller than five feet, and she moved like a scared mouse.

"Miss Janine," Chris yelled. "We don't have much time. Please. Open the door now."

The lady made a few more tentative steps.

"I'm going to die if you don't open the door now," Chris yelled.

"I need some help here," Devin said. Chris slammed his open fist on the frame, then joined Devin.

Miss Janine was almost at the door. Jen didn't want to break eye contact with her. "Just push the bar and open the door. We'll get in, but none of them will. We can help you. We can help each other."

"Get ready for incoming," Devin said. "Forget the door, Jen. We need your help."

The growling and sounds of rushing footsteps were almost upon them. Jen lined up one of the leading zombies in her sights. She squeezed the trigger.

The gun clicked empty.

16

A *clunk* came from behind Jen and something pressed into her back. She reached out as she turned, and Miss Janine disappeared into the side hallway. But Jen's arm held the door open.

She pulled it wider. "Get in!"

The wave of zombies was only yards away. Devin hurried through the door, but Chris didn't move.

"Chris," Jen yelled. "What the hell are you doing?"

He seemed in a trance as the horde bore down on him. Jen stretched out, grabbed his collar, and yanked him through the door. She pulled it closed and fell to the floor as the horde reached the building.

They pounded on the doors and windows, their drool mixed with blood and gore running down the pane.

Chris continued to stare at the horde, his mouth hanging open.

Jen picked herself up gingerly, her shoulder and hip throbbing. "What's wrong with you? You almost got yourself killed."

Chris pointed at the window. His lips moved, but nothing came out. Jen spun.

Towering over the zombie faces pressed to the window was Raymond.

He pushed his way to the front. Chunks of flesh were missing from both his arms and legs, and his eyes had a hunger she'd never seen in another human. He slobbered and reached out to grab her, but was denied. He screeched, and it went right through Jen.

"I'm sorry," she said.

"Uncle." Chris rushed to the window. Raymond took his eyes off Jen and looked at his nephew as if he were a thick, juicy steak.

A pang of sympathy rose in Jen's chest. She put a hand on Chris's shoulder. "It's not him anymore."

He shrugged her off. Devin moved to Chris's other side. "We need to get out of sight. Let these things calm down and disperse."

Chris glared at Devin. "My uncle isn't a thing."

Devin's eyes filled with empathy. "There's no time to be gentle. If more of them come, there's a chance they could break in. So I'm going to be blunt. Your uncle is dead and he's not coming back. What you see out there is a parasite that's taken over his body."

Chris stared at Raymond. "I can't leave him like that. He took care of me all these years, the least I can do is make sure he's at peace."

"Later," Jen said. "Now's not the time. When it is, I'll help you."

Chris studied her for a moment then nodded.

Jen walked him to the side corridor. Miss Janine stood at the other end. Jen strode toward her, and the short woman shrank, but stood her ground. When she reached her, Jen bent over and gave her a hug. "Thank you."

Miss Janine's face turned red. "I couldn't take a chance on them getting in, but I also couldn't let them kill you." Her voice came out soft, almost like a whisper.

Chris hugged her. "You're my hero, Miss Janine."

Devin stood back and nodded at her. "Thanks."

"He told me not to open it," Miss Janine said. "Said it would get the children killed."

"Who told you not to open the door?" Chris asked.

A throat cleared and Griffin stood in a doorway down the hall. "That'd be me. After all, she's got children here. Wouldn't want to put them at risk."

Miss Janine squeezed her hands into fists. "But I opened the door for you."

Jen stormed to Griffin, coming nose to nose. "You pull that kind of shit again and I'll feed you to the zombies myself, one piece at a time."

Griffin put his hands in the air and laughed. "Whoa there, spitfire. No need to be that way."

Jen's pulse pounded in her ears. "Why'd you disappear from the community center and leave us holding the bag?"

Devin put a hand on Jen's shoulder and gently pulled her back from Griffin. "I'd like to know that myself."

Griffin rested a hand on the butt of his holstered revolver. "I saw an opening and took it. Looks like you guys made it out all right."

Chris rushed Griffin, his fist cocked back. Miss Janine stepped in front of him. "I won't put up with any of this. There are children here."

She gestured to the room behind Griffin. "In there. They're already scared, so don't make it worse. Come in and help calm them."

Griffin moved aside and Jen entered the room, catching a whiff of alcohol and body odor as she passed the bootlegger.

The room was a small gym, its only windows near the ceiling. *Good.* Three children, who looked to be between six and ten, sat on a bench, quietly talking among themselves. They stood and bunched together when Jen entered.

"Children," Miss Janine said. "These are friends. They're here to help us."

Chris walked in and the oldest girl's face brightened. "Chris." She ran to him and wrapped her arms around his waist. Chris hugged her back, smiling. "Natalie. I'm so glad to see you're OK."

She took his hand and tears streamed down her face. She sniffled. "Oscar Johnson came in the house and he looked sick. His eyes were yellow and Dad asked him if he needed help."

She wiped her face. "Mom told me to go to my room. That's when Oscar jumped on Dad and they fell to the floor. Then Oscar bit Dad."

Chris knelt next to her. "It's OK, honey. You don't have to think about it anymore."

She shook her head. "And Oscar bit Mom, too. I ran outside. There were other people eating other people. I was so scared. I hid under the Nortons' house and couldn't think of a safe place to go, until I thought of school."

"When I got here," Miss Janine said, "Natalie was hiding in the girl's room. Bobby and Alexei came just after, and that's when I locked the doors."

"And you let in Griffin, too," Chris said.

Griffin sauntered into the gym. Jen eyed him.

"She did," he said. "She's an angel."

"Apparently we wouldn't have gotten in if it hadn't been for this angel," Devin said.

Griffin's eyes narrowed as he glared at Devin.

Jen frowned. *Got to keep my eye on this asshole.*

Devin eased into a chair and wiped his face with his soaked shirt sleeve. "Chris said a plane should be coming in the morning. We can rest here safely until then."

Miss Janine handed a roll of paper towels to Devin. He smiled, ripped a couple of sheets off, and dried his face.

Jen wandered into the hallway. Had Miss Janine checked all the rooms? *Could there be something hiding in here?*

She crept back up the hallway they'd come in and stopped at the intersection with the main corridor. There was still growling and some banging coming from the direction of the door they'd entered, but it had calmed.

She padded back to the room, and Miss Janine was handing out bottles of water. "Would you like one, too?" she asked.

"That would be great." Jen took the offered bottle and drank half of it without stopping. She accidentally let out a belch and the children giggled. Miss Janine gave her a stern look and Jen said, "Excuse me."

Chris leaned his axe against the wall. Jen nodded at it. "You might want to keep that close."

"Why?" Devin asked.

Jen took another swig of water, then put the bottle down. "Miss Janine, have you checked all the rooms in the school to make sure they're empty?"

Miss Janine looked from Jen to Chris then back again. "No. I couldn't leave the children alone."

Jen nodded at Griffin. "And I'll bet Mr. Spineless here hasn't set foot out of this room either."

Griffin gritted his teeth.

Miss Janine shook her head.

Jen cocked her hips to the side and gave Griffin a smirk. "Hoping the kids would protect you?"

The knuckles on his fists turned white, but the bootlegger didn't move. *Just what I thought. Won't do anything when he's outnumbered. What a tool.*

Chris picked up his axe. "I'll check the building." He strode out the door.

Devin sighed and stood, the pipe in his hand. "He shouldn't be doing that alone." He disappeared into the hallway.

Jen gestured to the door, inviting Griffin to leave. "Want to prove me wrong?"

Griffin slid the tomahawk from its sheath. A wicked-looking thing, it was all black except the blade's edge. Griffin handled it easily. "Got this for a bottle of vodka a month ago. Didn't know how handy it would come in."

He gave it a few practice swings, then mimicked Jen's gesture. "Ladies first."

Banging came from down the hallway. "Help," a female voice screamed.

Jen sprinted to the main corridor and glanced at the door they'd come in. There were still a few zombies, and they went bat shit crazy when they saw her, throwing themselves against the door and the windows.

"Open up." A woman stood outside the opposite doorway. "Please," she screamed. She looked behind her, then turned back. "They're coming!"

Griffin caught up with Jen. "Wait. You open that door and the zombies might get in."

"Then you better be ready to fight." Jen sprinted to the door. Four villagers were nearly on the woman.

"Stand to the side," Jen yelled. The woman moved, and Jen slammed into the bar, throwing the door open. The woman rushed in and disappeared down the corridor. Jen yanked the door to close it, but caught a twenty-something zombie with a shredded arm in the doorway. That gave the other zombies time to attack the opening, keeping Jen from closing the door. She strained to keep it from flying open, but the bar slipped a little at a time through her sweaty fingers. She made an attempt to grab the handle, but the shredded arm zombie snapped at her hand, just missing as Jen yanked it back.

Where are Chris and Devin? She glanced down the hall. *Where the hell did Griffin go?*

Yellow eyes pierced hers, boring into her, through her...almost hypnotic...bared teeth with chunks of meat stuck between them...clacking shut over and over...the death smell washing over Jen as the zombies lunged forward time and again.

She broke eye contact with them and stared at her fingertips turning white as they slipped farther and farther off the bar.

A boom from behind echoed painfully off the walls, and half of the twenty-something zombie's head disintegrated. Startled, Jen fell back and the door flew open.

A zombie leapt onto her and she grabbed it around the neck to keep it away, but her arms had little strength after holding the door closed and they trembled as she struggled. The zombie pushed closer. Jen turned her head and closed her eyes. *This is it.*

A sharp thunk and the zombie went limp. She was able to roll it off her. Devin stood over her, his hand out. She grabbed it and he pulled her up.

Chris and Griffin stood over the zombies, both wiping bloody blades off.

Jen lunged at Griffin. "Where they hell were you?"

Griffin put his hands up and backed away. "Easy there. I just helped save your life."

Jen's legs buckled, and Devin kept her on her feet. "Helped me?" she said. "By running off? Seems that's all you're good for."

"I'm not a big fan of Griffin's," Chris said, "but that's not fair. He came and got us. We didn't hear Marcia's screams from the back of the building."

Jen went cold and shivered so hard she could barely stand. "Adrenaline's leaving your body," Devin said. He led her to the gym and sat her down. Miss Janine handed her a bottle of water and she took a sip.

Devin sat next to her as the others spoke to the new girl. "Griffin shot the first zombie with that big gun of his, then took out the one on top of you with his tomahawk."

Jen swallowed a mouthful of water. "I still don't trust him. He runs too easy."

"It was the right thing to do this time," Devin said. "You were both outnumbered. And we would've never known you needed help."

Jen stood. "Let's go meet the new girl."

She stumbled, but recovered. Devin put an arm around her, steadying her, and they walked over to the others.

Chris gave Marcia a bottle of water. She drank part of it and seemed to be trying to catch her breath.

"Where were you?" Chris asked.

She swallowed. "Home. We need to go back. My dad's there and those creatures are beating on the door. It's only a matter of time before they get in."

"Why didn't he just come with you?" Devin asked.

Chris frowned. "Her father's wheelchair-bound."

Marcia stood. "I've got to go get him."

Chris took her arm. "Sit and rest. I'll get your father." Jen looked at Devin and his gaze met hers. *He's thinking the same thing I am. We're not letting Chris go alone.*

Marcia shifted her position and her pant leg rose for just a moment before it fell. But it was enough time for Jen to see the fresh bite wound on her ankle.

17

J en nudged Devin and Chris. "Can I talk to you two in the hallway just a second?" She strode out the door without waiting for an answer.

Devin stepped into the hallway with a curious look on his face, while Chris's expression was blank. "What's up?" he asked.

"It's Marcia. She's been bitten."

Chris glanced back into the room, then shook his head. "I didn't see anything."

Jen's heart sank. Chris had lost so many people he knew, even having to put some of them down. She didn't want to give him another one. "Left ankle. It's covered by her pants but they slid up for just a second."

Chris studied her for a minute, then made a beeline for Marcia. Something in his expression must have alarmed her, because she leaned away from him. "What's wrong?"

Chris crossed his arms. "Lift your pant legs."

Marcia slid down the bench a few inches. "What are you talking about?"

Jen and Devin took positions on either side of Chris. "Your ankle," Jen said. "You've been bitten."

"Son of a bitch." Griffin drew his revolver and stepped away from Marcia.

Miss Janine gasped. "Children, come to me."

Marcia's face fell and tears welled in her eyes. "Please don't kill me," she sobbed.

Jen's gut ached. She could only imagine how Chris felt.

Chris glanced at his axe propped against the wall, then at Jen. "If we lock her in a classroom and leave her until she turns, then she won't feel a thing when we have to..."

Devin frowned. "It's a big risk."

"You ain't shitting," Griffin said. "This is why I didn't want to let anyone in."

Miss Janine looked at Chris. "Why don't we just let her go outside?"

"Miss Janine," Jen said, "please take the children to another room."

Miss Janine herded the children out. Devin looked at Jen, his eyes searching hers. "What do you want to do?"

Jen stepped in front of Griffin and put her hand out. "I'll do it."

Griffin shrugged and handed her the .357 Magnum. The damn thing weighed a ton.

She turned to Marcia and the woman wailed. "You can't be serious," Chris said.

Jen pointed the gun at Marcia's head and Chris grabbed her wrist, pulling her arm up. "No more," he said. "There's been enough killing."

Jen's gaze seared his. "She's going to change and it's going to be soon. If we let her go, she's one more zombie between us and the plane. Maybe even the one zombie that infects another one of your neighbors."

Chris stared at her, then blinked. His eyes lowered to the floor and he gave a slight nod. Devin turned away and Griffin crossed his arms, watching her with a curious expression on his face.

Marcia lay on the floor in the fetal position, sobs racking her body. Her pant leg had pulled up again and the bite mark was there for all to see. The skin around it had turned black and the veins leading from it were discolored.

Jen aimed at Marcia's head. Her hands shook so much she struggled to keep the gun steady. Swallowing, she said, "We'll get your father and bring him back here." She took a deep breath and squeezed the trigger, the report of the blast deafening as it echoed off the close walls. The sweet aroma of burnt gunpowder invaded her nostrils and caused her to cough.

Marcia lay still, a bloody hole in the side of her skull and blood pooling around her head.

Devin cleared his throat. "I'll clean up. You go sit."

Jen walked slowly to the other side of the room and sat on a bench, facing the wall. She hadn't signed up to make those kinds of decisions. *But who the hell else is going to make them?*

Griffin put his hand over the revolver. "Someone had to do it."

Jen released the gun and stared at the floor. *Not someone. I had to do it, and I'll be damned for it.*

Her throat tightened. *But I'll make that sacrifice to get us out of here safely.*

Devin's voice broke her from her thoughts. "We should go get Marcia's father."

Jen stood. The body was gone. *How long have I been sitting here?*

Her father's eyes were filled with empathy. His arms went to encircle her, but he pulled back. *He's as confused about us as I am.*

Jen reached out and pulled him to her.

"I'm sorry I got you into this," he said.

She broke the embrace and wiped her eyes. "Not your fault, Dad."

Devin's eyebrows rose and Jen gave him a weak smile. "That's right. I said Dad, and I meant to."

He nodded, eyes watering. "I've wanted to hear that for a long time."

Chris stood at the doorway, his axe resting on his shoulder. "We should go. No telling when those zombies will break into Marcia's house."

Jen opened a cabinet door. Sports equipment was stored inside, and she rustled through it before picking up an aluminum baseball bat and giving it a few practice swings. "This should work fine."

Miss Janine brought the children back in, but she steered them away from the bloodstained part of the floor with a hole in it.

Griffin walked in wiping his hands together. "Body's wrapped and put in the janitor's closet."

Chris nodded. "Thanks for that."

Griffin shrugged.

Jen approached Chris. "I'm sorry about Marcia."

Chris gave her a fleeting smile. "You wouldn't have had to do that if I'd been strong enough to do it myself."

"When are we going to get the old man?" Griffin asked.

Jen raised an eyebrow. "You're volunteering?"

Griffin licked his lips. "You guys can't keep all the fun to yourselves."

Jen headed to the main corridor. "Then let's go."

She peered around the corner. No zombies in sight at either door. "All clear."

"How can that happen?" Devin asked. "The horde at the community center didn't go away."

"You have to be out of sight and quiet," Griffin said. "That's what made the community center a death trap. Too many people yapping."

Chris chewed his lip. "And the gym is far enough back from these doors that they couldn't hear us. Even the gunshot."

Devin interrupted. "Back to Marcia's father. How far away is his place?"

Chris pointed toward the door Marcia had come in. "Three blocks that way."

Jen strode to the door and pushed it open, keeping it from closing with her foot. Devin and Chris filed out. Griffin looked like he'd rather be anywhere else. "Looks clear," Chris said.

"I'm not seeing anything, either," Jen said.

Devin took a step away from the building. "What are we waiting for?"

Jen eased the door closed. *Locked out again.*

She ran to the first house and ducked underneath. With a height of three feet, the space under the house allowed her to crawl rapidly on her hands and knees.

Growling and banging could be heard somewhere ahead. Chris took the lead while Griffin lingered behind. Chris stopped at the edge of the house, then scurried under the next one. Jen made sure Devin made it before crossing herself.

Griffin ducked down next to her. The banging and growling were closer. "That must be the zombies trying to get into Marcia's father's house," Jen whispered.

Griffin pulled his .357. "Are you nuts?" Jen said. "That'll just bring more of them. Put it away."

Chris pointed to Griffin's sheathed tomahawk. The bootlegger holstered the gun and pulled the tomahawk out.

"How are we going to get in?" Devin asked. "Is there a back door that's clear?"

"One more house until we get there," Chris said. He hustled over and dove under the next house.

The others joined him, and they worked their way to the other side.

The damn zombies sounded like they were right on top of them. Jen crawled to the front of the house and looked over. She counted eight of them banging on the front door. She crawled back. "Front's covered pretty good. I don't know how the hell we get past them and then get a guy in a wheelchair out of there."

"Just follow me," Chris said. He ducked under Marcia's father's house and stopped dead in the center. "Watch this."

He reached up and fiddled with something before standing, his upper body disappearing into the house. "Holy shit," Jen said. "An escape door. I never would've guessed."

"In his younger days, Marcia's father was a bootlegger," Griffin said. "Not such a terrible occupation."

Chris pulled himself up and disappeared inside.

"Jen next," Devin said.

Jen hauled herself in. The house was pitch-black. She scooted away from the opening, and Devin climbed in and knelt beside her.

Griffin stuck his head in. "I'll keep the escape route open." He disappeared under the house.

"John," Chris said. "Where are you?"

A flashlight came on, and Chris pointed the beam around a living room and kitchen. It settled on an empty wheelchair lying on its side over by the front door.

"John," Chris whispered harshly. "We're here to take you to safety."

A groan came from behind them, barely audible with all the banging. Chris shined the light on the couch and padded toward it, while Jen crept around to the other side. Chris pointed the beam behind the couch and there an old man lay facedown, struggling to crawl. Chris rushed forward. "Let's get him in his wheelchair." He took one of the man's arms and Jen took the other. Chris held the light out to Devin. "Hold this."

They picked the man up and he struggled. *Damn, he's got some spunk.*

Once John was placed in the wheelchair, Devin shined the flashlight on him. John reared his head back and screeched. He lunged at Jen and fell onto her, knocking her to the floor and trapping her legs with his body. She lost her grip on the bat and it rolled out of reach.

Zombies at the door returned John's screech and doubled their efforts to get in. The door rattled in its frame, then bowed in with a resounding *crack.*

18

C hris wrapped his arms around the old man and pulled him off at the same time Devin grabbed Jen under the arms and yanked her backward.

"Get out," Chris yelled.

Jen scurried to the hole in the floor and dove through. She rolled away from the opening and Devin dropped next to her. Another huge *crack* echoed from the house and footsteps rumbled across the floor.

Chris fell through the opening and onto his stomach. He pushed up to his hands and knees. "Go. They're right behind me."

Jen scrambled back the way they had come, pausing under the house across the road. Devin ran across the gap between the houses, and Chris was hot on his heels. Several zombies were back at the trap door. One dropped to the ground and tried to stand under the house, blocking the others from getting out. *Stupid-ass things.*

"Where the hell's Griffin?" Chris asked.

Jen looked around. Nothing but zombies. She clenched her jaw. *That son of a bitch flaked out on us. Again.*

A screech went up a few houses away. They'd been spotted. Answering calls came from every direction. Jen paused in the middle of the house. "Where the hell do we go?"

"We've got to get back to the school," Chris said.

"Through this?" Devin asked.

Zombie feet rushed by in every direction. They'd be spotted as soon as they came out from under the house. "Maybe we just wait here," Devin said.

Chris pointed behind them. "No time."

The zombies chasing them had finally figured out how to crawl, but they were slow at it. *Can't count on that lasting.*

"How far's Raymond's house?" Jen asked.

"Couple blocks." Chris pointed. "That way. Away from the school."

"Why there?" Devin asked.

The zombies from the house had nearly reached its edge. "The four-wheelers," Jen said. "What better way to outrun these things?"

Chris scrambled forward. "Follow me."

They sprinted across the road and slid underneath another house, leaving several screeching zombies in their wake. Chris didn't stop, and they scrambled to the next house in record time. One more and Chris stopped and pointed. "There it is."

They were catty-cornered from Raymond's, the four-wheelers sitting out front. An old woman, the front of her kuspuk a bloody mess, wandered back and forth on the porch. Two teenage creatures stumbled around several feet from the ATVs.

Jen looked behind her. The pursuing zombies had reached the last house they'd crawled under. Her pulse beat double-time. The undead skittered under it like spiders. *Freaking things have definitely figured out how to move under buildings.*

"Zombies coming up on our ass. We have to get on those four-wheelers." She slid out from under the house and raced toward one of the teenage zombies. It noticed her and shrieked. The other one spun, and both sprinted for her. *Shit. Didn't want two at a time.*

"I've got the one on the right," Chris said from behind her.

Jen closed in and reared her bat back. Chris caught up and readied his axe. Five feet away, Jen's zombie leapt at her. Caught off guard, she clumsily swung the bat upward and ducked. She missed the zombie and fell to the ground, but it sailed overhead.

Scrambling to her feet, Jen faced the creature, its yellow eyes burning with hunger. It sprung again, but this time she was ready. She swung and stepped to the side at the same time, the bat connecting with the zombie's ear.

It fell to the ground rolling. When it came to a stop, it pushed itself up, but stumbled while trying to approach her. She ran up to it and bashed it in the nose, blood and bone fragments splattering the front of her shirt. It slumped to the ground.

Devin battled the old woman, while Chris was pulling his axe from the other teenager's skull. Thirty yards down the road in the direction they'd come from, a horde rumbled toward them, big enough to fill the space between houses.

Jen dashed to a four-wheeler, just as Devin took out the old lady. Jumping on, she had a sinking certainty it wouldn't start, but it roared to life as soon as she turned the key. Devin and Chris hopped on their ATVs and started them up.

"Where are we going?" Chris shouted over the engines.

"How long before the supply plane normally comes?" Jen asked.

Chris looked at his watch and held up two fingers. "Couple hours."

The damn horde was only twenty yards away. "Take us to the school," Jen said. "Long way around so we won't be followed."

Chris goosed his accelerator and put the ATV in gear. He shot down the road, heading for the outskirts of the village, with Jen and Devin behind him. They turned a corner, losing sight of the horde, and zoomed out onto the tundra.

Jen wiped moisture from her face. A light rain had started and the wind had eased. *And the clouds are breaking in the distance. Planes should be able to fly soon.*

Chris led them down the path they'd taken before. When they reached the spot where they'd broken off to go to Fear Mountain, he stopped and turned off his engine. Jen and Devin did the same. The silence was oppressive.

"Pretty sad that this is the safest place for us right now," Devin said.

Chris checked his gas level. "And about as far as we go if we don't want to run out of gas out here."

Jen sat back in her seat and closed her eyes for a moment. If she concentrated, she could pretend she was back in Anchorage, hiking in the Chugach Mountains.

The sound of the breeze in my ears.

The stillness.
A screech came from farther out in the tundra.
And fucking zombies trying to eat me.

19

J en peered out into the dusky tundra. A figure moved. Then another. As her eyes became accustomed to the low light, more and more zombies emerged. "Holy shit. Are the sailors still thawing from the pit?"

"Looks that way." Devin turned on his headlight and aimed it. The beam landed on a couple dozen sailors, their yellow eyes glowing in the light. He swept the beam left, then right.

"There are hundreds more," Chris said.

"So much for being safe." Jen started her engine. "We need to get to the school."

Chris and Devin started up, and the trio headed across the tundra to the far side of the village. Chris started to pull away, so Jen sped up just as a wind gust hit and took her breath away. Bouncing across the uneven ground, she was nearly thrown off her seat. "Slow it down," she yelled. "The sailors don't move that fast."

Chris let back on the throttle, allowing the others to catch up. "We need to get back quick. When these hundreds of sailors show up in town, the place will be thick with them. We won't be able to move."

They rode straight toward the school. Its lights were still on. *Hope Miss Janine and the kids are OK.*

Several yards out, a small horde rushed them from behind a house.

Eight strong, six were villagers. The riders had been heading for the far door, and the zombies would soon be between them and their destination.

Chris swung his four-wheeler toward the other door, and Jen and Chris mimicked him. The entrance was clear, but would Miss Janine unlock it in time?

Jen pulled up just as Chris dismounted. She turned off the engine and ran to the door. Chris took a defensive position with his axe and Devin arrived and joined him. "Bang on the door and get Miss Janine out here," he said.

Peering in the window, Jen raised her fist to slam it against the door, but paused. At first everything looked the same. *But that streak of blood at the corridor intersection wasn't there before, and it looks fresh.*

She reached for the door handle and paused. The damn thing wasn't closed all the way. She pulled it open.

Swinging it wide, she said, "Door's open. In now."

Devin and Chris ran in, and Jen pulled the door closed behind her with a *clunk*. The zombies didn't break stride and slammed into the door twenty seconds later.

Chris looked around. "Where's Miss Janine?"

"I don't know. The door was unlocked. In fact, it wasn't even closed all the way."

Devin frowned and peered down the corridor. "I don't like the sound of that."

"Miss Janine," Chris called.

Jen grabbed his arm. "Shh. If something's in here, we don't want to ring the dinner bell."

"We've got to get out of sight of the zombies outside," Devin said, "or they'll do all the ringing for us."

Jen crept down the corridor and stopped at the intersection. The blood streak was wider there. She pointed and whispered, "This wasn't here before."

Chris peeked around the corner. "It comes from down there."

Jen swallowed, a pang rising in her chest. She raised the bat and padded down the hallway to the gym, the noise of the zombies at the door fading.

Chris hugged the opposite wall and Devin stayed at her side. Jen stopped outside of the open gym door. The lights were off inside, cloaking who knew what. She took a deep breath and nearly gagged. It was as if she had stepped into the slaughter room of a busy ranch on a hot summer's day.

Devin covered his nose and Chris made a face. "I may be sick," he said.

Jen waited, but nothing stirred in the gym. *One, two, three.*

She reached in and flipped the light switch, then staggered backward into Devin.

Blood and entrails painted the floor and splattered the walls. The bloody streak started at the benches. Where the kids had been.

Jen turned her head away and staggered into the hallway. Nausea threatened, but she choked down the bile that rose to the back of her throat. *Little kids. They were just little kids.*

Devin rubbed her back.

It took a couple of minutes, but the wave of nausea passed, and tears flooded her eyes. She looked at Devin. "Those kids," she choked out.

Devin pulled her in and encircled her with his arms. "I know."

She laid her head on his shoulder and wept as he soothed her. She'd never had anyone who could console her like that since her mother died. She didn't want to let go.

Can't afford this now. Got to get us out of this first.

She raised her head and pulled back, wiping her eyes. "Sorry. I'm good."

Devin's eyes filled with sympathy. "It's OK to cry, you know."

She gave him a weak smile. "I know, Dad. But I can do that later. Right now we need to concentrate on getting the hell out of here alive."

Jen closed the gym door. Chris leaned against the wall, his face ashen. "The whole village is dead. I'm all that's left."

A bang came from up the corridor. The entrance door.

Were the zombies back? Jen raised the bat, ready to bash in some zombie heads. Devin and Chris closed ranks on her side.

Footsteps clomped down the hall, getting closer.

20

J en tried to swallow, but her mouth had no spit.

The footsteps still echoed down the hallway. *How the hell long is that walk?*

Griffin appeared at the end of the corridor, his chest heaving. He stumbled toward them.

Jen fought the urge to kick him in the balls.

"You're here," Griffin breathed.

The bootlegger bent forward with his hands on his knees. Chris pushed past Jen. "I'll check that the doors are secure."

Griffin straightened and leaned back against the wall with his eyes closed. His breathing had slowed. "Didn't think I'd make it. That was damn close."

"Where the hell did you go?" Jen asked. "You took off on us again."

His eyes opened and he stared at her, incredulous. "I led them away from you."

Jen scoffed.

"Forgive me," Devin said. "But that sounds like bullshit."

Chris returned. "Doors are good."

Griffin stood. "One of those things was crawling around and spotted me under the house. It made that high-pitched sound of theirs and others came. You guys were still inside and I figured if I joined you in the house then we'd all be trapped."

He crossed his arms. "So I ran and they followed me."

Chris raised his eyebrows and looked at Jen. "He tells a good story, I'll give him that," she said.

Red splotches appeared on the exposed parts of Griffin's face, and he spoke through gritted teeth. "I may be a lot of things, but I'm not a liar. I just went through hell and almost got bitten and now I get interrogated?"

"You didn't get chomped and neither did we," Jen said. "But we can't say the same about Miss Janine and the kids."

"What are you talking about?"

Jen stepped away from the gym door. Griffin looked at her, his head slightly turned and his eyebrows lowered. She nodded at the door. "Go ahead."

Griffin approached the door as if it were about to explode. He grasped the handle lightly and turned it, then looked back at the others. Chris gestured to the door.

Griffin opened it, and the thick odor of slaughter washed into the hallway. The bootlegger stepped back as if it had physically slapped him in the face. He stood still for thirty seconds, then closed the door. He didn't turn back to the others.

"Griffin?" Devin said.

"She saved me." Griffin's voice was thick. "And she was damned and determined to save those children. Babies. They were just babies."

A clattering sound came from the hallway behind them. Griffin whipped around. Devin and Chris went into defensive stances, and Jen's muscles tensed.

She craned her neck, but couldn't see to the end of the hallway where the sound came from. "What's down that way?"

"A couple of classrooms, janitor's closet, and the kitchen and cafeteria," Chris said.

"We better check it out," Devin said.

Chris straightened. "Doesn't have to be a zombie. Maybe Miss Janine and the kids hid down there."

Griffin drew his tomahawk. "Want odds on that?"

"It's possible," Devin said.

"Only one way to find out." Jen crept to the next doorway and scanned the room. "This one's clear."

Chris cleared a room across the hall, while Devin and Griffin took the next one.

The hallway took a bend to the right. Jen stopped there and peeked around the corner. A pair of swinging double doors stood closed twenty feet away. A crash of metal on metal came from behind the door. Jen pulled back and hugged the wall, her heart doing a drum solo. "Sounds like a drawer of forks and knives being dumped on the floor."

"I'm thinking less and less that it's caused by humans," Chris said.

"You think?" Griffin said.

Devin nodded. "Maybe we just block the door? Keep whatever it is in there?"

"Don't think I can stay in here knowing there's something creeping around back there," Chris said.

Jen took a deep breath and let it out slowly. "Then we better get in there and see what's on the menu." She crept around the corner and hugged a wall as she closed in on the kitchen doors. Devin kept up against the other wall, and Chris just plain walked down the middle of the corridor as if he were out on an after-dinner walk. *A stroll with an axe, no less.*

Stopping at the door, Jen looked back to find Griffin right behind her. He smiled and shrugged. *Definitely not counting on him being there when I need it.*

Each door had a two-foot-by-two-foot window at eye level. Jen took up position on one side and peeked in. The kitchen was a landscape of stainless-steel tables and appliances. Metal mixing bowls and utensils were scattered across the tables, range, and floor.

"I see a mess," Jen whispered, "but not what made it."

Devin looked through the other side. "Same here. There are two large stainless-steel doors. One is shut and the other is open about a foot."

Chris pushed a door open a few inches, then entered and moved to the left. Jen and Griffin slipped in behind him. Devin watched their rear.

The kitchen looked as if one of those asshole reality TV chefs had a fit and tossed the whole damn thing. Cabinets were empty and the floor was littered with cooking implements.

Jen nodded at the open stainless steel door. Chris nodded back and took a position on the open side. Devin stepped forward, a solid grip on his pipe, and Griffin held the tomahawk at the ready. Jen grasped the door handle and threw out one finger, then two, then three, and swung the door open.

Jen inched out from behind the door and looked inside a walk-in refrigerator. Boxes were stacked in the back and racks were filled with plastic wrap-covered bowls, large open cans, and condiments.

Damn thing wasn't big enough to hide much, but Jen stepped in and looked between the boxes and racks. She turned to the others. "Nothing."

Chris held a hand up, then waved for the others to follow him. He tiptoed to a wide opening in the wall with a metal blind pulled down over it. The serving line. Where the lunch ladies ladled out the slop.

Jen stood next to him and listened. It took a minute, but there was no doubt. Someone was eating, and doing it loudly.

Chris pointed to the metal blind, then pointed upwards. Griffin grasped one end and Chris the other. They pulled, but it didn't move. Jen reached over to the bottom of the blind and slid a latch back. They tried again, and the blind slid upward without a sound.

Jen gripped the bat. The blind stopped at the top, but Jen couldn't see the whole cafeteria from her vantage point. Even so, nothing seemed out of place. The chairs were placed upside down on the edges of the tables and the floor looked like it had been washed and swept.

She leaned out the window. The munching sounds drew her attention to the left. There, against the wall, lay Miss Janine, her eyes dull and staring at the ceiling. Four children squatted around her, filling their mouths with bloody meat and organs from her shredded abdomen.

Someone behind her let out a small gasp.

Heat rose in Jen's face and she squeezed the bat. *No more.*

She jumped through the opening and rushed the zombie feast.

21

T he kids turned around at the last second, their meals hanging from their mouths.

Swinging the bat underhand, Jen caught Natalie in the jaw. The girl fell back as the other three children jumped to their feet.

Jen's momentum took her past the kids and she skidded into a corner. Natalie rose, her jaw hanging limply and bloody drool spilling from her mouth. The other three children fanned out. Jen stepped out from the corner to give herself more swinging space. *You little shits are going down.*

Devin, Chris, and Griffin came running, and the two boys Miss Janine had cared for with Natalie broke off to meet them. Natalie and another boy Jen didn't recognize closed in on her from opposite sides.

"I'm all dressed up with nowhere to go," Jen said. "So let's dance."

Natalie growled, nothing in her movements indicating anything but a hungry predator.

She can't bite me with a broken jaw. She concentrated on the boy.

Just as sounds of battle came from the middle of the cafeteria, Natalie lunged. Jen feinted, and when the boy attacked a second later, she swung and caught him on the shoulder. *Shit.*

The two zombies backed up, then rushed straight at her as one. Jen raised the bat overhead and stepped into the attack, bringing the weapon down and stepping off to the side. The boy ran past, and the bat came square down on top of Natalie's skull, the crack sudden and brutal. Natalie slumped to the floor and the boy leapt at Jen. Without time for another swing, she rammed the end of the bat into the boy's chest. Knocked back into the corner, he scrambled to his feet and sprung again.

Too damn fast. She barely ducked in time, then stumbled back into the wall. The boy sprung as she turned, but Griffin appeared and buried the tomahawk blade in the back of the kid's head. The momentum slammed the kid into Jen, bouncing her off the wall and to the floor. She pushed the boy's limp body off her.

"Thanks," Jen said.

Griffin wiped off his blade with some napkins and sheathed it. "Do you always do that?"

Panting, Jen asked, "Do what?"

"Just run into the middle of shit." He put a hand out.

She grasped it, and he pulled her up. She smirked. "It's becoming my trademark."

The boy Jen recognized as Bobby lay in a pile in the middle of the cafeteria. Devin and Chris had outmaneuvered Alexei across the room and were closing in from separate sides.

Alexei swatted at Devin, who jumped back. Chris took the opportunity and swung the axe overhead, missing the boy's head, but carving a canyon down his back. The boy stumbled, and Devin bashed his forehead with the pipe. The boy collapsed.

Jen pulled a chair off a table and sat. "Those little buggers were a handful."

Devin stood next to her, bent over with his hands on his knees. "I was wondering who Miss Janine would open the door for after the incident with Marcia." He nodded to the unidentified boy. "Of course, she would for a child."

Chris joined them, giving each a bottle of water. "Found these in the fridge." He unscrewed his bottle and downed half of it. Wiping his mouth on his sleeve, he gave a satisfying belch.

After emptying his bottle, Griffin crushed it and threw it into a trash can ten feet away. He raised his hands in the air. "Score."

Jen took a sip. "I'm getting numb to all this killing. If I would've had to kill these zombie kids at the beginning, I don't think I could've done it. But after I saw them gnawing on Miss Janine in their own version of Mystery Meat Monday, I lost it."

Chris nodded. "I think we're all becoming numb to it, but that's good in a way. It may be the only way we survive."

Devin took a drink, then poured the rest of the water over his head. "I don't know if I can physically do much more of this. I'm not exactly young and in shape." He reached out to Chris. "What time is it? How close are we to the plane coming?"

Chris glanced at his watch. "If it comes at all and if it comes at its normal time, we have about an hour."

Jen walked over to one of the cafeteria's draped windows and pulled back a corner. *Shit.*

Turning back to the others, she said, "Those sailors we met on the tundra? They're about to make port here."

She peeked back out the window and watched as hundreds of zombie sailors lumbered toward the village.

"How are we going to get to the landing strip now?"

22

J en tipped the water bottle back, letting the last swig empty into her mouth. She swallowed. "The bottom line is we're screwed. The damn runway is on the other side of the village and we're about to have a zombie convention out there."

She picked up her bat and strode to the kitchen door. "We can't wait. Have to make our move before the rest of the undead navy gets here."

Devin rose from his seat. "Why don't we take a boat now that the sky's clearing?"

"Not our best option," Chris said. "Even though the clouds are letting up, it's still windy and the seas will be rough. As a last resort, I'd take it, and we might survive if we kept close to shore. But I still think the plane's our best bet."

"But we don't even know if a plane's coming," Jen snapped. "Even if we can get to the runway, it may be for nothing."

Chris threw the axe over his shoulder. "If the plane doesn't come, then we'll be at the top of the hill and can map a safe path to the boats from there. Just like we did to get to the school."

"I'm not sure about this plan," Griffin said.

"Then you can always stay here," Jen said. Griffin went silent and pursed his lips.

There were no great options, only shitty and shittier ones. How the hell could they get out alive?

Will we get out at all?

The question had bubbled up unbidden from Jen's subconscious. *No time for doubt.* She thrust her jaw out. "We need better weapons, more firearms, and transportation."

"And how do we get that?" Chris asked. "That's a lot to ask for while we try to keep from being eaten."

"We also need a diversion," Jen said. "These things seem to be easy to distract. Why not use that to give us the time to get across the village?"

Devin rubbed his chin. "That's a great idea, but what do we use for a distraction?"

"Something loud," she said. "Maybe something that moves. Lights seem to attract them, too."

Griffin smiled. "Then I'm your man."

"Let me guess," Jen said. "You want to give them booze and let them drink till they pass out."

"It's true I bring in booze," he said, "but it's not all I deal in. I have some top-notch fireworks in my house. You want noise and light? That'll do it."

Jen did a double take. *Damn good idea.* "That's step one. Once the creatures are distracted, where are we going to get weapons and ammo?"

"That's a bit harder," Chris said. "You'd find them in any house, but we don't know which houses have zombies trapped in them."

"What about the community center?" Devin asked. "There were villagers with guns who dropped them when they were bitten."

"And the doors are knocked down, so no zombies will be trapped there," Jen said.

Griffin pulled his tomahawk out. "Then let's get the hell out of here."

JEN LOOKED out onto the tundra. The sailors shambled along less than a hundred yards away. Between the driving rain and the light fog forming, she had no way to tell how many there were. But what she could see caused her breath to hitch. The damn zombies stretched across the horizon as far as she could see. "We need to move our asses."

"We can't stop once we get going," Griffin said. "So keep up."

Jen gripped her bat. "No crawling around under houses. Too slow."

Griffin took off, catching Jen by surprise. She grabbed Devin's arm and pulled him forward. "Let's go. Keep up, old man." She raced after Griffin, glancing back to make sure Devin and Chris followed.

Griffin had already made it to the next house. He stopped on the side, peering forward and waving for the others to catch up. Jen stopped behind him. "No screeches so far."

Devin and Chris approached from behind. A screech rose from the tundra.

"Me and my big mouth," Jen said.

A symphony of answering screeches roared from the tundra and the village.

"Time to go." Griffin sprinted forward.

Zombies woke up all around, their screeches piercing Jen's ears and sending a jolt down her spine.

When she caught up with Griffin, movement farther in the village caught her eye. A horde of a dozen or so streaked toward them. "We've got to move."

Griffin took off like a runner from a starting block. Jen turned to make sure Devin and Chris followed, but found no sign of them. She ran back into the road and scanned the area.

Another horde, twice as big as the first, stampeded her way.

Jen's breath came in short gasps and her heart threatened to burst. "Dad!"

No answer came.

23

Frozen with indecision, Jen scanned the surrounding area looking for any sign of Devin. *Where the hell'd he go?*

The larger horde was only a house and a half away. She'd have no chance if she didn't leave at once. She cupped her hands and yelled, "I'll be back for you."

She sprinted for Griffin and passed the next road only twenty yards ahead of the first horde. *Holy shit.*

Kicking it into high gear, she neared Griffin. He dashed past the house, then took a left. Jen followed, glancing over her shoulder. The first horde stayed with her and the second, larger one, roared right behind them.

Griffin took an immediate right. They should've been to his house by then. *He's trying to lose them.*

Jen raced around the corner, glancing back at the last second. The horde hadn't come into view yet.

Standing on the porch of an unremarkable, weather-beaten house, Griffin held the door open. Jen zoomed through it and Griffin closed it behind him. "Where are the others?"

Jen held back tears. "I don't know. I turned around and they were gone."

Griffin cracked the door open, then eased it closed. He put a finger to his lips. "The zombies are in front," he whispered.

A cacophony of screeches surrounded the house, penetrating the walls and drilling into Jen's head. She didn't dare move. Crouched and ready to spring into action, she stared at Griffin and the door as the stampede of footsteps rumbled by, then faded.

The bootlegger tip toed past her and into a back room. She crept to the room's doorway and watched. An eight-by-eight room practically stuffed with boxes, only one person could fit into it at a time. Griffin lifted a box, then shook his head and tried another.

After three boxes, he pulled one off of a high stack and smiled. He laid it on the floor and pulled the tucked flap open. "Bingo."

Jen didn't know much about fireworks, but recognized that the top package of sparklers wouldn't do them any good. Griffin put that package to the side. He did the same with the next two packages, but paused when he came to the fourth.

"What's that?" Jen asked.

He showed her the package. "M80s. Big-ass firecrackers."

"But don't those just blow up quick, then you have to light another? We'd have to stay in the area to keep those going."

Griffin handed them to her. "Those are the warm-ups."

He pulled another box off the stack, then shook his head and put it to the side. "Booze."

After several more boxes, he stood back with his hands on his hips. "Where the hell did I put it?"

Jen glanced at the door. Her father was still out there. "This is taking too long. What are you looking for?"

Griffin stepped out of the room. "The good stuff. Stuff I was keeping for myself. I hid it somewhere, but can't remember where."

He wandered into the cluttered living room, past the torn, stained couch, and into the kitchen.

Ignoring the piles of dirty dishes in the sink and the trash on the floor, he opened a cabinet and pushed cereal boxes and canned food aside. Shaking his head, he moved to the next cabinet and repeated the process.

Oh, for crying out loud. Jen opened a cabinet and mimicked his actions. *Don't know what the hell I'm looking for.* She found nothing but food.

They met at the last cabinet. Jen stepped back and gestured to it. "This is your treasure hunt."

Griffin checked the bottom shelf, then rifled through the middle one. With a sigh, he pulled a box of bread crackers out then felt behind it.

His eyebrows shot up, and he pulled a completely black box out. "This is it."

"This is what?"

"A cake." He flipped it over and read the writing on the back. "A two-minute one."

"We're in the middle of the apocalypse and you want to bake a fucking cake?"

Griffin cleared a spot on the counter and placed the box down. "You really don't know anything about fireworks, do you?"

When she didn't answer, he said, "It's got multiple rockets and shit in it. You light it and it gives you a whole show."

"And it lasts two minutes?"

He nodded. "We toss a few M80s over the next house. That'll draw them there. Then we head back to the school, light this thing, and book our asses over to the community center. Two minutes is a long time for us to get out of the area."

"One step you missed there," Jen said.

"What's that?"

Jen cleared her throat. "We find Chris and my dad on the way back to the school. We're not leaving them behind."

Griffin let out a long breath. "Look, I don't blame you for not trusting me, but I promise you we'll find them both before we set off the fireworks."

So there's a human being in there after all. Jen clapped him on the shoulder. "We'll all get out of here."

She ripped open the M80 package. "Now let's set off some fireworks."

24

J en cracked the front door and peeked out. The screeching had stopped. Sensing no movement, she opened it farther and scanned the area. "Clear."

Griffin handed her two M80s. "How's your throw?"

She shrugged. "I throw like a girl."

Griffin made a face.

"I throw like a girl who played softball for years. I can chuck something as small as an M80 far enough."

They stepped onto the porch and faced the house. The rain had died to a steady drizzle. "We need to get these over at least the next house. Don't want to draw the zombies too close to us," Griffin said.

Jen glanced up and down the road. Still clear. "I can do better than that. Mine'll go over the next two houses."

"Good." Griffin removed a box of matches from his pocket.

Jen held an M80 in her throwing hand. "How do you want these spaced? I say we throw one, wait for the explosions, then throw another."

"That'll work. Then we go back into the house and wait for things to calm down before heading to the school."

Jen nodded.

Griffin struck a match against the side of the box and produced a blue-

and-yellow flame. Jen lit her wick and threw the M80 high over the house. Two seconds later, Griffin's arced out of sight.

A boom, then another, echoed between the houses. The screeching began, several from close by.

Jen lit her second M80 and flung it, then ducked into the house. Griffin did the same and closed the door behind him, just before two more resounding booms penetrated the walls.

The screeches multiplied and footsteps pounded the ground. *Please let Dad be somewhere safe.*

Griffin opened the refrigerator door. "Want a beer?"

Jen nodded, and Griffin tossed her a can. She opened it and took a swig. No need to whisper with the racket from the zombie stampede outside. "Why?" she asked.

Griffin leaned against the counter and opened his can. "Why what?"

"The bootlegging," Jen said. "Doesn't seem like a good career choice."

Griffin shrugged. "My talents lie in a couple of specific areas." He took a mouthful of beer.

Looking around the kitchen, Jen said, "I'm betting housekeeping isn't in the top ten."

Griffin laughed, spewing beer onto the floor. "Shit."

He coughed and wiped his mouth. "You're a real ball buster." He took another swig and swallowed. "My talents are in flying and selling, and I've taken the best opportunity to do both."

"So you have a plane?" Jen asked.

He shook his head. "Had. Troopers caught me at a dry village with some vodka and my plane was confiscated. So now I just use mail order."

Something bumped into the house and Jen froze, her can of beer almost to her mouth. When no other sound followed, she took another gulp. "Don't get too big of a head, but you're not a dumb guy. Why not get a flying job that pays you?"

Griffin downed the last of the can and placed it on the counter. "I've got a problem with authority figures and I don't play well with others. If you find a company that'll hire me with all that, let me know."

Jen grinned. "Not something I've ever seen on a job description."

Griffin smiled back. He folded his arms and waited.

Things quieted little by little outside until Jen heard nothing else.

"Don't think we can wait much longer, or the plane might land before we get there."

A footstep clomped on the porch and Jen's eyes met Griffin's. "Could be my dad," she whispered. She tiptoed toward the door, but Griffin grasped her arm. "Peek out the window first."

Jen crept to the window and pulled back a sliver of the curtain.

Three sailors stumbled around on the porch.

You've got to be freaking kidding me.

25

J en looked down the road from both sides of the window, then straightened. "What do you see?" Griffin whispered.

"I don't see any others, but I can't see all of the road from this angle." She choked up on the bat. "There could be a horde just out of sight for all I know."

Griffin scratched his beard. "We don't have a choice. No time to wait. We have to take those three out before they can sound the alarm." He frowned. "If there are more out there and they attack, we'll have to fall back in here and figure something out."

Jen nodded. *I've got to get to Dad. What if he's injured?* "I'm with you."

Griffin peeked out the window, then backed away. "Two are just a few feet outside the door. It's the third one that worries me. It's halfway across the porch."

"You go for that one," Jen said. "I'll take care of the other two."

"How's that going to work?"

Jen licked her lips. "You run between the first two. Ignore them and get the other one. You'll have to be fast."

"And you?"

"I'll take care of mine. Don't you worry."

Griffin laid the cake package on the couch. "OK. Let's do it."

They huddled at the door and Griffin turned the knob slowly. He nodded, then breathed, "Three, two, one."

He burst out the door and rammed between the two closest sailors. Jen stepped out and swung at the head of one of them, hitting it square in the back of the head. It dropped, and Jen reared back while the other sailor turned on her, its eyes glittering. It tilted its head back and Jen jerked the bat around and smashed its nose. Teeth scattered on the porch.

Griffin rushed the other sailor. They'd lucked out; it had been facing away from them. But it heard him coming and spun to meet the threat. *Damn. A fast sailor zombie? What the hell?*

It leapt at Griffin, who jumped to the side and was able to take a chunk from its chest with a swing of the tomahawk.

Jen's remaining sailor stumbled backward, but managed to keep its feet. It tilted its head back, but all that came out was a weak whistling sound. Jen cocked the bat back and let it fly, crushing the sailor's skull at the temple. It fell to the porch.

Griffin's sailor pulled itself to its knees. Grunting, Griffin brought the tomahawk overhead and planted the pointed end into the top of the zombie's head. It slumped and lay still.

Jen backed to the door, her head swiveling left and right. No sounds. No movement. "I think we did it."

Griffin hurried into the house and returned with the cake package. "Maybe we have some luck after all."

He ran past the next house with Jen behind him, stopped and scouted the road, then continued to the other house. Jen caught up and grabbed his arm. "My dad."

"Where was he when you last saw him?"

She tried to get her bearings. The house they stood next to looked the same as any other, battered by the elements, with a four-wheeler outside and a snow machine with a tarp draped over half of it.

"It was either right where we're standing, or that next house closer to the school."

"I'll search the next house. You check out this one." Griffin peered beneath the house. "Nothing under there. Be quick." He ran across the road.

Jen climbed the stairs, her stomach dropping when she hit a squeaky step. She paused, then proceeded when nothing happened.

The door was closed and blankets hung on the inside of the windows. She turned the knob and eased the door open. Gripping the bat like her life depended on it, she stepped inside and closed the door, then fumbled on the wall for the light switch.

She flipped a switch. Dull light cast shadows over a tidy, but threadbare room. Family pictures hung on the wall alongside various skins and animal trophies. An ivory dream catcher hung from the ceiling in the center.

"Dad," Jen said.

Two doors stood at the back of the house. She pressed her ear against one. "Dad, are you there?"

Nothing stirred. She pushed the door open and flipped the light on. A lumpy bed on a rusted metal frame lay against a wall. A new-looking handmade blanket lay on it.

Jen opened the other room and lit it. Two single beds, a few toys, and children's clothes scattered about.

Shit. "Dad? Chris?"

Maybe they'd returned to the school. *I swear I'm not leaving this village without them.*

She left the house and stood on the porch, scanning for any sign of trouble. Griffin stood across the road. He held his hands up and shook his head.

Where the hell are they?

She walked toward Griffin, but stopped. A noise. *A rustle.*

The tarp on the snow machine moved in the wind. She let out a long breath. *Getting jumpy.*

But the tarp moved again, near the bottom. "That's not the wind."

She raised the bat over her head and stalked toward the tarp. It rustled again, but without a gust of wind blowing first. Something pressed against the inside of the tarp. *Not an animal. Too big.*

Swallowing, Jen leaned forward and grasped the end of the tarp with one hand. She glanced at Griffin, who hurried to join her.

She yanked the tarp off, and on the ground staring at her was Marcia's father. He tilted his head back and let out a blood curdling shriek.

26

J en brought the bat down on the old man's skull, silencing him in mid-screech. Griffin ran up. "Marcia's father?"

Shaking the blood off the bat, Jen said, "Yeah. He takes a licking, but keeps on ticking."

Several answering shrieks sounded from the direction of the M80 detonations. Griffin didn't need to tell her what to do. Jen raced toward the school. She beat Griffin there by seconds and pulled the door open.

"Where are you going?" he asked.

"My dad might be in here."

Griffin pointed back the way they'd come. "I don't think so."

Devin and Chris trotted toward them. Jen ran to her dad and clutched him to her. "I thought you were gone."

"Can't get rid of me that easy," he murmured.

She released him. "Where the hell were you?"

"We saw we weren't going to make it and didn't want you two coming back to get us, so we hid behind the house until the horde passed."

Chris nodded at the school. "Then we came back here until we heard the fireworks."

Griffin took the cake out of the package and laid it on the ground twenty feet from the school's entrance. "Get over here. I need to light this before the drizzle screws it up."

Jen pulled Devin over with her. When they reached Griffin, Devin bent over with his hands on his knees. Jen put a hand on his back. "You OK?"

"Just out of shape," he gasped. "I'm good to go."

"You're going to have to be," Griffin said. "We can't wait any longer."

Chris walked over, his eyes scanning the area. "Why don't the rest of us wait for Griffin on the other side of the school?"

Devin straightened. Jen took his hand and they followed Chris. By the time they reached the other entrance, Devin's breathing had slowed and become less raspy. Even his color seemed better.

Griffin streaked toward them, waving for them to get moving. The group raced from the school as a boom came from behind and the sky lit up in blues and greens. Another blast, then dozens of smaller explosions followed, as if a hundred firecrackers went off in the sky.

Zombie screeches rose but were drowned out by the fireworks.

Griffin zigzagged between buildings and almost ran into a sailor as he rounded a corner. The zombie let out a quick screech, but Jen's bat dropped the creature. No answering shrieks came.

They passed Raymond's house as the big finale—a cascading rainbow of colors with big explosions punctuating the show—burst over the village. Jen broke onto the road and headed for the community center. "Didn't think I'd be glad to see this place again."

Devin stumbled in and slumped onto a chair, his lungs heaving. Jen found water and brought him some. "You take it easy," she said. He nodded, unable to speak.

Pools of drying blood lay on the floor, especially near the doors. Half-eaten organs were strewn everywhere, clouds of flies buzzing above them. Jen checked the doorways for weapons, but found nothing more than pieces of wood suitable for clubs.

"Jen." Griffin stood in the kitchen area holding a revolver.

She hurried over and took it from him. Popping the cylinder open, she checked the rounds. "Only two left unfired."

Chris stood at the back door, looking out. He turned to the others. "The villagers are already coming back."

"Shit." Jen closed the cylinder and stuck the revolver in her belt. "We better get up that freaking hill."

They left the community center single file out the front door, with

Chris taking them in a wide arc to the base of the hill. He looked at his watch. "The plane should've been here twenty minutes ago."

"Then we should get to the boats," Devin said. "We can't stick around here any longer."

Chris looked up the hill. "Stay on the far edge. The middle is all mud." He clambered up the slope and didn't look back. Griffin followed.

Jen turned to Devin. "You first. I'll hold the rear."

"I'm supposed to protect you," Devin said.

Jen took his hand. "We're supposed to protect each other, and this climb'll take a lot out of you." She squeezed his hand. "My turn to take care of you."

Devin kissed her on the cheek. "I bought a condo in Anchorage before we flew out here."

Jen gave him a slight push on the back. "Come on, then, old man. Let's go home."

Devin trudged up the hill and Jen kept pace behind him, maintaining watch on the houses at their rear. A few minutes later, they climbed high enough to see over the roofs. Zombies gathered in clusters, wandering aimlessly about. Jen's heart raced as she and Devin worked their way higher and she had view of the whole village. Hundreds of zombies filled the streets. *Rush hour in Zombietown.*

Devin reached the lip of the flat section of the slope and stepped onto it with one foot, but lost his balance with the other. With a cry of surprise, he slid backward. Jen caught him from sliding farther. Chris and Griffin each grasped a hand and pulled him up.

A screech sounded behind Jen. A sailor outside the community center had seen them. The call was repeated across the village, and hundreds of zombies raced for the slope.

Jen pushed her father forward. "Get out of sight. Head for the trailers."

Chris sprinted for the trailers, but skidded to a halt.

A sailor lumbered into view, and Jen took a practice swing with her bat. "This is going to be almost too easy."

The sailor shambled toward her, but Jen caught her breath as another figure rushed them, its eyes burning into hers.

Raymond.

27

Raymond screeched. He zipped past the sailor and bore down on Jen. Chris took a swipe at him, but Raymond bowled him over and continued rumbling toward Jen.

Devin jumped in front of her and slammed the pipe into Raymond's chest. It might as well have been a pillow as much as it did to slow the huge zombie. Raymond knocked Devin to the side.

Jen ducked and cracked her bat across Raymond's shin. Raymond hit the ground and tumbled over the edge of the hill. Jen ran to the edge and watched him tumble all the way to the bottom.

Griffin put a round in the sailor's forehead, and it fell in a heap.

Jen joined the others, her pulse pounding in her ears. "Son of a bitch. Raymond's damn near unstoppable."

Chris leaned on his axe and wiped the sweat from his brow. "There are too many of them. We won't make it to the boats with all the undead flooding the streets, so what do we do now? Make a last stand in the trailers?"

"They won't hold," Devin said. "Too flimsy. Our only choice is to go up to the landing strip."

Snarls sounded closer from three sides. Griffin looked down the slope. "Most of them can't make it up through the mud. They keep slipping back down, but there's still a couple dozen or more on their way up the sides."

"What then?" Chris picked his axe up.

Jen's gaze fell on the fuel tank a hundred feet up the hill. "We burn them?"

Griffin jogged back to her. "What?"

"Chris can punch a hole in the side of the fuel tank with the axe. It empties down the hill and into the village, and we light it. Might not take them all out, but it could kill enough of them to give us a fighting chance to make it to the boats."

Chris smiled. "Brilliant." He ran around the trailer and toward the tank.

Jen pulled Devin's arm. "Let's go, Dad."

The first wave of zombies reached the trailer just as she arrived at the tank. One of the creatures spotted them and let out a screech that was echoed by the rest.

Chris reached in his pocket and tossed something to Jen. She caught it. It was the Marine Corps lighter. Leo's lighter.

He hefted the axe. "Be ready to light the fuel when I tell you, but you'd better stand back. You don't want to get any of it on you."

Griffin grabbed her wrist. "No. That tank'll explode. We have to be under cover first."

Shit. Jen looked around, her gaze falling on the trailers. Running downhill, they could reach them in seconds. And the fuel would flow right by. She pointed at the trailers. "We'll all take cover behind them."

Chris nodded. Jen joined Devin and Griffin a few yards to the side. She pulled the revolver from her belt, while Griffin's face hardened and he faced the incoming zombies with his .357. "Six rounds left," he said.

Devin's eyebrows lowered on his ashen face. "Make them count."

Chris grunted and attacked the tank with the axe. It bounced off the side, leaving a small dent. He reared back and swung again. The dent didn't seem to get deeper.

A teenage boy with a gaping chest wound reached them and Devin knocked him away with the pipe. The zombie regained its footing in seconds and rushed him. Jen aimed. *Got to time this right.* She led the zombie and squeezed the trigger. The gun clicked empty.

"Shit! I didn't line up the right fucking chamber."

The .357 Magnum boomed behind her and the teen's face imploded, spewing gore in an arc behind him.

Two more zombies reached them and Devin managed to jump out of a middle-aged man's way at the last second and whack it with the pipe. He missed the head and instead hit the back of its neck, adding a cracking sound to Chris's grunts as he swung the axe.

Griffin planted his tomahawk into the forehead of the other zombie and stepped in front of Devin as the middle-aged man counter-attacked. He didn't have time to recover from his last strike, but managed to push the zombie to the ground.

Jen turned to Chris. He hadn't made any headway. "Turn it around. Hit it with the pointy end."

Chris looked at the axe head and groaned. "Of course." He reared back and drove the point into the tank. Fuel trickled out of a small hole.

"That's it," Jen yelled.

Chris punctured the tank again, and the trickle became a stream. "Not enough. I've got to get it emptying faster than that."

Griffin shot the middle-aged zombie, then glanced down the slope. "Better hurry."

The second wave of zombies was nearly on them. Griffin lined up his sights on the horde climbing the slope and took a lead zombie down. Jen pulled her gun, popped the revolver's cylinder open, and lined up the chamber with the first live round. Griffin's gun boomed again.

Devin struggled to fight off a man with a bloody stump for an ear. He stumbled backward and fell. Jen shot the top of the zombie's skull off.

Chris widened the hole in the tank, and fuel gushed out. He backed up. "Let's take cover." A growl from behind got Jen's attention, and Raymond raced in and tackled Chris to the ground. Fuel splashed over them as Chris struggled to get him off. He managed to get up on one knee and keep Raymond's clacking jaws back, but he coughed and sputtered as the fuel poured over him.

Jen lined up her sights on Raymond's head, but he moved just as she fired, and the round went through his shoulder. *Shit. Out of ammo.* She dropped the gun and picked up her bat.

Chris pushed Raymond back and struggled to his feet, but two more zombies attacked.

"Get out of there," Jen yelled.

Chris put one zombie in a headlock, but the other jumped on his back and bit into his shoulder. Chris screamed. He grabbed at the zombie on his back and ducked, flipping it over. It landed on its back a couple of feet from Jen.

Raymond grabbed Chris from behind. A dozen more zombies closed in on him, only a few yards away.

"Get down there and light it," Chris yelled.

Jen's head spun. Lighting the fuel would kill Chris. *But I have no choice. He's been bitten.*

Raymond jumped on Chris's back, bent his head down, and tore his ear off. Chris reached around, but was unable to grasp him. He screamed and flailed at the zombie.

Devin threw off another attacker and caved in its head with the pipe. He turned and faced thirty more zombies slipping on the fuel, but nearly up the slope. "Let's go."

Raymond grabbed Chris's head and turned it toward him. Chris pushed against him, but the zombie drew his face toward its mouth. Jen couldn't see what he did, but it looked like Raymond was kissing Chris on his upper cheek. Chris shrieked and Raymond released him, chewing.

Chris turned toward Jen, his empty eye socket oozing gore. "Please, Jen!"

Jen glanced at Raymond as he slurped the last of Chris's optic nerve into his mouth like a strand of spaghetti. Griffin's gun barked, and a hole appeared where Raymond's nose had been. He wobbled, then dropped.

Two more zombies piled onto Chris. He wailed as they tore into his flesh. "Jeeennnn!"

Tears streaming down her face, she grabbed her father's arm. "We need to get under cover."

Her father caved in the face of a bearded zombie. "They're between us and the trailers."

Most of the zombies had peeled off toward Chris, but nine still raced toward them. "We run through them. Knock 'em over. Like bowling pins."

Griffin charged down the hill, waving his tomahawk over his head and screaming. Jen pulled her father behind her and darted down the hill after him.

Griffin swung, and his tomahawk embedded in the lead zombie's temple. It fell, and his weapon went with it. He rammed into another zombie, and it held onto him as they both rolled to the ground.

Jen aimed for a spot between a man with his neck torn open and a girl with an arm that looked like hamburger. Two steps before they collided, she lowered her shoulder and yelled.

She propelled the two zombies to the side, but another one was just behind them. She hit it full force, its open gut spraying her with blood and bits of innards. She stumbled, but her father pulled her along and behind the science lab trailer.

She wiped the gore from her eyes. The fuel had made it several yards past the trailers, but had pooled. "It's not going to the village," her father said. "It's seeping into the ground."

Griffin pushed himself to his knees, but three zombies piled on him. Griffin bellowed as they stripped the flesh from his arms and neck.

Jen's hands trembled as she struck the lighter's wheel. Sparks flew, but the wick didn't light.

She pressed her thumb against the wheel again. "Please light," she whimpered, and spun the wheel.

A yellow-blue flame appeared on the wick. Jen tossed it at the fuel trail, and it ignited with a *whomp*. A wall of heat drove her back and seared her skin.

Seconds later the world shook, throwing Jen and her father to the ground. The trailer tipped towards them, its roof peeling off and flying down the hill. She covered her head with her arms. The trailer wobbled, threatening to crush them, then slammed back down in an upright position. Its windows shattered and sprayed shards of glass on her and her dad.

Jen removed her arms from her face and brushed off glass. She watched a huge fireball rise in the sky, carrying glowing embers and pieces of debris with it.

Devin picked Jen up under the arms. "We need to get to the boat. This whole village is going up."

Pieces of the flaming debris rained down, sparking fires all over the village.

Jen hugged her father. "Chris." She sobbed. "Even Griffin came through in the end."

He patted her back. "I know. But you did them a kindness. I would rather someone kill me than live as a monster. Would you do that for me if the time came?"

Numbness flooded Jen's mind. Kill her own father? She peered into his eyes and saw nothing but sincerity. *We're OK and we're getting out of here, so what does it matter?* "I will," she murmured. "I promise."

They held each other for a minute, then Jen let go and wiped her eyes. "Which way?"

Devin pointed off to the left. "I don't see anything over there."

She nodded and climbed to the top of the hill, the crackling and popping from the fires echoing in her ears. The sweet stench of burnt flesh hung in the air.

She glanced back to make sure her dad was still with her. Only a few steps behind, he held his left arm close to his body.

"What happened? Did you get bit?"

He put his good hand on her shoulder. "Just a sprain. I'm a little old to be playing zombie slayer."

She put an arm around him. "Could be a second career."

He shook his head. "Let's hope not."

28

An hour out of Point Wallace, Jen looked back. The smoke column coming from the village looked tiny. The weather had cleared, but the sea remained choppy. Devin guided the eighteen-foot boat south and kept it about a hundred yards offshore.

Soaked from the waves crashing over the gunwale, Jen shivered and hugged herself. The hot weather did little to warm her when she was splashed with frigid sea water every thirty seconds.

Devin slumped and almost fell off the bench. Jen put an arm around his shoulder and steadied him.

"You OK?"

"Not feeling well."

She put a hand over his. "Why don't you lie down? I'll take the wheel."

"Keep it on course," he said, slurring his words.

She eased him to the floor. "I think I can handle the navigation. Not exactly rocket science."

He rolled into the fetal position.

She slid behind the wheel and kept it steady. Her mind raced. *How long will it take to get to Wainwright? Do we have enough gas? How the hell will we explain what happened?*

A whole village had gone up in smoke. People were going to demand answers, and she didn't want to give the ones they had.

A speck appeared in the sky ahead. It slowly grew larger. Her heart leapt. She recognized the sound, even from a distance. One of her ex-boyfriends had been an Army helicopter pilot and had taken her up in a civilian rental several times.

The helicopter flew toward them, following the coast. The *whup, whup* of its blades grew louder. Jen waved and whooped. "Over here. Please."

The helicopter veered from the coast and approached them, its military markings becoming clearer. A loudspeaker turned on with a squelch and a nasal voice said, "This is the Alaska National Guard. We're here to assist anyone from Point Wallace. Head to shore and we'll pick you up."

Thank God!

Jen steered the boat to a rocky beach and ran it aground. The helicopter landed fifty yards away and two soldiers jumped out.

As she helped her dad out of the boat, he slumped, his full weight on her. It took everything she had to keep from dropping him.

The soldiers were almost upon them. "We're rescued, Dad. We made it."

The men stopped short. "Are you OK, ma'am?"

"Yes. We're so glad to see you."

The other soldier pointed at her dad. "What about him?"

She smiled. "My dad. He's not feeling well. Been through a lot."

The soldiers looked at each other. Something passed between them.

"If we help him," the first soldier said, "can you make it to the chopper on your own?"

Jen nodded. "But I need to help my dad."

"We've got him. Go on." The soldiers moved in and each draped one of her father's arms over their shoulders. "Go ahead. We'll catch up."

Jen let go of her dad, and the men walked him toward the helicopter, his feet dragging on the ground. She ran ahead, remembering to duck as she approached the spinning blades.

A soldier with a visored helmet waved her forward. He pointed to a canvas-covered bench. "Sit there. Put on your harness."

She climbed in and he helped her with the straps. The other two soldiers walked her father up, and the three soldiers lifted him in and strapped him onto the bench across from her. His head still slumped forward. The soldier with the helmet examined him.

"Is he OK?" she asked.

He nodded and sidled over to her as the chopper lifted off. "How are you doing?"

"Tired. Worn out."

He reached into a bag and pulled out a syringe and a medicine vial. He stuck the needle in the bottle and drew out slightly yellow liquid into the syringe.

Uneasiness crept into her gut. "What's that?"

The soldier smiled. "Just something to relax you."

"I don't need it. I'm OK now that we're getting out of here."

He nodded at the other soldiers, and they held her down. She struggled. "I don't want it," she screamed. "Stop!"

There was a sting in her upper arm, then coldness seeped into her veins. The soldier who'd injected her checked her pulse. She already felt droopy.

He patted her shoulder. "You'll be asleep in another minute or so."

She wanted to tell him "no," but she couldn't get her mouth to work.

Her father's hands clenched and unclenched.

Jen's eyelids grew heavy. Just before she lost consciousness, her father straightened, raised his head, and opened his eyes.

His yellow eyes.

WHEN'S THE NEXT BOOK COMING OUT?

Get a free eBook and receive news and updates of coming releases, get recommendations, and enter giveaways at:

uprising.marobbins.com

AUTHOR'S NOTES

When I first decided to write post-apocalyptic fiction, I thought I'd start with a zombie story, since that was my favorite to read.

But when I looked at the number of zombie books available, I thought the genre was crowded and my series would get lost in the glut. So I wrote The Tilt which is a non-zombie post-apocalyptic story.

The Tilt was a great story to explore and write, and I'll finish the series in the future, but I found there are still a lot of readers out there like me—readers who read a lot of zombie fiction and still want more.

The result is the story you have just read. And there's much more coming as the zombie apocalypse strengthens and spreads. You can expect a lot of action, unique new characters, both ally and foe, and plenty of twists and turns.

Thanks for reading this book, and I hope you join me in this journey through the Zombie Uprising.

M.A.

ACKNOWLEDGMENTS

First, I want to thank my wife, Debbie, who puts up with me disappearing into my office for hours at a time. I also always appreciate my critique partners Brooke Hartman, Louise Goulet, Molly Gray, and Tam Linsey.

This book had a great group of beta readers. Thanks for making the book better: A.M. Ireland, Ellen Engelbrecht, Helen Zawacki, Katie Lee Cook, Leland Lydecker, Maureen R. Meyer, Natalie, Rachel Wagner, Shauna Joesten, 'The real Petrovich', Vinnyz, and Wayne Tripp.

My editor, Tamara Blain of A Closer Look Editing, did her usual bang-up job. I'm always amazed at the things she picks up that I missed. Domi of Inspired Cover Designs did a tremendous job on the eye-catching cover.

Mostly, I'd like to thank you, my readers. I ultimately write these books for you because I am one of you. Every email, review, and rating I get from readers is fuel for writing more books. I don't take you for granted. You're an important part of this process.

THE GAUNTLET

BOOK TWO IN THE ZOMBIE UPRISING
SERIES

CONTENTS

To Duane Jones, George Romero's first zombie-fighting hero.

1

Officer Dan Brunell pulled his cruiser into the neatly paved parking lot of the Wasilla Mountain View Funeral Home. The only building in sight, it looked almost idyllic. Surrounded on three sides by birch and fir trees, the building had a front facade that made it look like a homey log cabin.

Dan stopped beside an Escalade with a short, balding man in a flannel shirt and jeans leaning on it. The man tossed a lit cigarette on the asphalt and ground it under his shoe as Dan strode over.

"Mr. Greenberg. You report a burglar?"

Abe Greenberg blew out a cloud of smoke and glanced at the front door of the funeral home. "Sounds like it. I came in to pick up some papers, and before I could unlock the door, I heard a crash from inside. I waited, and there were more noises. Sounded like someone was tearing the place apart. They were loudest in the back."

Dan frowned and hitched his belt up. "And there's no one else in there?"

Greenberg shrugged. "No one alive. Just one client in the back who arrived today. Did you know One-Eyed Jack?"

"That skinny old guy with a patch over an eye? The bartender at the Loon?"

Greenberg nodded. "The same. I already opened him up and did initial prep, so he damn sure ain't wandering around in there."

Dan sighed and keyed the microphone attached to his shoulder. "Base, this is Officer Brunell. Made contact with the owner. I'm going to do an interior check."

"Roger. Need backup?"

Dan hesitated. His shift was over in a couple of hours, and his flight to Florida with Wendy and the kids was an hour and a half after that. He calculated how long he'd wait for backup, just to rouse some homeless guy who'd found an unlocked window. "No backup at this time."

"Roger. Make sure you check in at fifteen-minute intervals."

"Roger that." Dan held a hand out. "Keys."

Greenberg pulled a set of keys out of his pocket and dropped them in Dan's hand. "The square gold one fits the front and back doors."

Dan nodded. "You stay here. I'll get this guy out of your place. Won't take but a couple of minutes."

Dan walked to his cruiser and unlocked the shotgun mount. No need to take chances. The homeless guy could also be a meth head. He jacked a shell into the chamber and strode to the front door. Pausing, he pressed his ear against it. Nothing.

The key slid into the lock quietly enough, but when he turned it, the deadbolt made a loud *clunk* as it retracted.

He listened again. Satisfied there was no immediate danger, he eased the door open and pointed the shotgun in the doorway.

The midnight sun only shined five feet into the entryway, leaving the rest of the lobby in shadows. Dan leaned in and flicked the light switches. Arched doorways to his left and right displayed empty viewing areas, and a closed door across the lobby led to the embalming room.

Muffled banging came from behind the door. Dan inched to the door. Something slammed into it, and he jumped back. Heart pounding, he waited.

The banging stopped, but someone on the other side breathed heavily. Dan thought to announce himself as a police officer, but his mouth had gone dry, and he couldn't work up enough spit.

This is so not what I need tonight.

The breathing sounded close. The damn guy had to be inches from

Dan, with just the door between them. A low, guttural growl vibrated through the door.

What the hell? Sounds like a damn animal.

Dan backed away. Protocol required him to call for backup. He glanced at his watch. An hour until shift end. Backup would probably take most of that time. *Vacation.*

"Screw it," he said. "My shotgun will take down any human or animal."

He crept to the door. Keeping his shotgun pointed forward, he pulled the door open, and a chemical smell smacked him in the face. He sneezed. Light glinted off the empty steel embalming table in the middle of the large room, but most of the room remained in darkness. Dan swept the shotgun barrel from left to right. Nothing moved. *What the hell?*

Keeping his feet planted outside of the room he reached in and fumbled along the wall for the light switch. His hand grazed something cold and smooth, and he jerked it back. A shiver ran the length of his spine. He took a deep breath. *Stop spooking yourself.*

He pulled out a flashlight, switched it on, and trained the beam on the wall to his right. The light switch sat right where he expected, and a metal case stood just beneath it. *A cold, smooth metal case.*

He scoffed at his skittishness and flicked on the light. The room looked like a tornado had hit it, with papers strewn about, tables toppled, and instruments scattered over the floor.

A naked man stood in the corner, his back to Dan. *This is no homeless guy. This asshole's high on something.*

Dan pointed the gun at the man's back. "Police. Turn around slowly."

The man's head tilted to one side, then he shuffled back a step. A long, slow growl came from deep in his chest.

What the hell have I gotten into? He keyed his mic. "Base, this is Brunell. Request immediate back—"

The naked man turned and sprung at Dan in one fluid motion. Dan threw up his hands and managed to push the attacker to the side. The naked man crashed into the metal case, shattering its glass front, and bounced to the floor.

The radio squawked. "Officer Brunell. Repeat."

Dan aimed the shotgun at the man. "Another move like that and I'll blow a hole through you."

The man pulled himself to his feet and faced him. Dan gasped. The drugged-out man before him was One-Eyed Jack, his patch missing and his empty eye socket seeming to gape at him. *And his one eye. It's yellow? What the hell's with that?*

Jack straightened and bared his teeth at Dan. Rough stitches formed a "Y" over his chest and stomach. *This can't be real.* Bile rose in the back of his throat.

"Officer Brunell. What's your status?"

Dan keyed his mic but didn't know what to say. He muttered, "Help."

Jack tilted his head back and let loose with a shriek that made Dan cringe. Dan aimed at Jack's chest. Jack crouched as if he were about to spring again, and Dan pulled the trigger. The pellets hit Jack's chest dead center, knocking him onto his back.

Dan's training kicked in. He pressed the mic button. "Base, this is Brunell. Need immediate backup. Suspect down."

"Roger. What's suspect's condition?"

Oh, hell. What do I say to that? He's dead, but he attacked me anyway?

Jack pulled himself up and into a crouch, then leapt at Dan, knocking him back through the doorway and on his ass. Jack landed on him and drove him to the floor. The shotgun skittered across the entryway, and Dan held Jack back by grabbing his skinny upper arms and locking his elbows.

Jack snarled and pressed on Dan, snapping his jaws at his face. Dan rolled to the side and threw Jack into the wall. He scrambled to his feet as Jack sprung at him again. For a skinny little shit, One-Eye had a lot of energy.

Jack went for Dan's neck, but Dan grabbed his arms again. Jack strained forward, his mouth opening and closing, teeth clacking, and yellow eye glistening.

Dan's sweaty hands slipped. One-Eye got closer and closer. Dan let go with one hand and tried to flip Jack away, but Jack grabbed the arm that held him and sank his teeth into the bicep.

Dan screamed as flesh and muscle were torn from his arm and swallowed by the dead bartender. He struggled to get away but became weaker every second as his blood puddled on the floor and Jack ravaged his arm.

Within a minute, the pain dulled and he could no longer move. He lay there, listening to One-Eye snacking on his arm. His last thoughts were of his family and the vacation they'd never have.

2

Jen opened her eyes.

What happened? Where am I?

She took a deep breath. A rush of nausea flooded her stomach, but she lay still and it eased. She found herself staring at an unlit light fixture on a ceiling.

Dull yellow light shined from her left, and she turned toward it. A small desk and chair with a lamp sat against the wall.

She eased herself into a sitting position, her stomach roiling, and surveyed the room. The dim light didn't reach the corners, but she made out two doors and a small refrigerator next to the desk.

What the hell? No windows?

She searched her memory, thinking she had been at one hell of a party the night before. Maybe she'd passed out and was still there.

But then the memories flooded in. The village. The pit. The zombies, the blood, the gore.

Her dad.

Where is he?

Groggy, she swung her feet to the floor and caught herself as she almost kept going. Too unsteady to get up, she just sat there.

What's the last thing I remember?

The helicopter. The guardsmen helped Dad to it and strapped me in.

Beyond that, she drew a blank.

She took another deep breath and rose, steadying herself with her hand on the wall. One of the doors was near the foot of her bed, so she shuffled to it, figuring if she fell she could land on the bed.

She grasped the knob and eased the door open, then fumbled for a light switch. Bright white luminescent light blinded her, and she stepped backward before clutching the doorway. Her eyes adjusted and before her was a bathroom. Not a homey, fluffy-rug type of bathroom, but an institutional one. One with sparkling chrome fixtures, tile floors, and the stinging aroma of disinfectant.

She stumbled to the toilet, stepping as fast as she could. *Damn floor's made of ice.*

She dropped her pants and sat. *No underwear.* The pants and shirt had the same washed-out blue color.

That's it. I'm in a hospital. But where?

She finished, pulled up her pants and tied the string in front. After washing her hands, she splashed some water on her face.

Better.

She wandered into the bedroom and over to the other door, where she flicked the light switch on the wall. An LED overhead light shined, chasing away the shadows and bringing out the drab white-greenish colors of the walls and ceiling.

"Time to see where I am." She grasped the doorknob and twisted, but it didn't budge. Jiggling it didn't help. She examined the knob, but there was no locking mechanism visible. *The damn thing's locked from the outside.*

She knocked on the door. "Hey. Anyone there? Can you hear me?"

No answer. She pressed her ear to the door, but heard nothing. *What the hell?*

She banged her fists against the door. "Hey! Open up! I'm awake."

Nothing. Was she in a military hospital? Quarantine?

She kicked the door, stubbing her toe. "Shit!"

Hopping to the bed, she squeezed her eyes tight and repeated, "Shit, shit, shit, shit, shit."

She plopped onto the bed and held her foot, rocking back and forth. Five minutes later, the pain had dropped to a dull ache and she examined the room in the full light. A mounted TV hung in an upper corner, its screen black. Besides the bed, desk, chair, and small refrigerator, the room was devoid of any other furniture. No dresser or closet. Where were her clothes?

She limped to the desk and opened the refrigerator. Bottles of water and cans of soda lined the door and filled the racks. She shrugged, pulled out a can of soda, and popped it open. After gulping down half the can, she let out a deep belch and noticed a remote control on the desk. She picked it up and sat on the bed, taking another swig of soda. Pointing the remote at the TV, she pressed the power button and the TV popped on, displaying a national news channel.

Jen brought up the channel listing and looked up the lower number channels. Sure enough, they were local channels she recognized. She was in Anchorage. She smiled. "Just call me Sherlock."

The date and time on the channel listing showed it was just after 7 a.m. the day after she and her dad had fled Point Wallace.

Metal sliding into metal caught her attention. A click came from the door and it opened. A muscular thirty-something man in khaki pants and a polo shirt that accentuated his large biceps stood in the doorway. He reminded her of a younger Mike Tyson. His eyes met hers and something in them told her he wasn't anyone to mess with. He stepped into the room and to the side, and a large woman in a dirty white apron puttered in and placed a tray on the desk. She turned and left, never looking at Jen.

Jen jumped up. "Wait. Where am I? Who are you?"

The muscular man glanced her way, stone-faced, then stepped through the doorway. A short, older man in a suit stepped up beside him and stared at her, his arms crossed. His eyes creeped her out. Sunken into the shadows of his sockets, they stared emotionlessly at her as if they were independent beings. Jen stumbled toward him, but he closed the door before she made it. The click on the locking mechanism caused her heart to drop, but she tried the knob anyway. When it didn't move, she pounded the door with a fist. "Talk to me, dammit! Why am I a prisoner? Where's my dad?"

She pressed her ear to the door. The sound of a squeaky wheel moved farther away and disappeared.

"Shit!" She stomped to the bed and dropped onto it, folding her arms. How could someone treat someone else this way?

The smell of bacon filled the room, and her stomach grumbled. She approached the tray on the desk. It had a cup of coffee, creamer, sugar, a glass of orange juice, napkins, silverware, and a covered plate. She removed the cover and breathed in the aroma. Bacon and scrambled eggs, with toast.

Ravenous, she cleaned the plate off within minutes. At least they weren't going to starve her.

Picking up the remote, she sat back in the chair and brought up a local news channel. The screen showed a close-up of the news anchor. "Reports are still incomplete about the fire that devastated the small northwestern Alaskan village of Point Wallace."

The feed switched to video of helicopters landing on the Point Wallace airstrip. They looked just like the helicopter that had picked up her and her dad. "The governor has called up the Alaska National Guard to assist with the search for missing villagers. So far there are no reported survivors." Another shot displayed the guardsmen deploying from the helicopters. "We'll stay on top of this story and bring you updates as they occur."

Wait. Those guardsmen all carried M-4 carbines. Why would they need those for search and rescue?

She jumped up and paced the room. They weren't telling the public everything. How many of the zombies survived? Bile rose in the back of her throat. Maybe the fire hadn't wiped them out.

FOUR HOURS LATER, she sat on the bed flipping through channels when the lock clicked. She dropped the remote on the bed and stood. Muscle Guy opened the door and stood to one side as the server brought in another tray.

She took a step toward him. "Talk to me. What's going on?"

The man put a hand out and took a defensive stance. With his shaved head and large frame, he looked menacing. She froze. *He could break me in half without breaking a sweat.*

The server picked up the dirty breakfast tray, left the new tray, and scurried out the door. The guard stepped into the hallway and began closing the door.

Jen's heart sank. Someone had to talk to her. She'd go crazy if she didn't find out something soon. She licked her lips. "Please. Tell whoever's in charge I want to talk. I don't know what I did or why I'm here. I'll cooperate. I just want some answers."

The guard hesitated for a second before the door clicked shut.

Jen spent the next few hours switching TV channels, looking for more on Point Wallace, but it was like the story had never existed. No mention of it on national or local news. Were they covering it up? If so, it had to be by someone high up in the government.

She took a deep breath and exhaled. *They could make me disappear and no one would know it.* If it was a government coverup, she might never be seen again. They'd just report that she and her dad died in the Point Wallace fire, their remains so severely burned that identification of all body parts would be impossible.

Dinner came at 5:30 p.m. She sat on the bed, her arms folded and her burning gaze directed at the guard. He ignored her. The tray switch was made and she caught a glimpse of the sunken-eyed leprechaun in a suit just before the door clicked shut.

She dove into the meal. She had to keep her strength up. If someone didn't talk to her soon, she'd have to do something. Her mind raced through possible escape scenarios. She could stand off to the side with the chair when the next meal came. The big server lady would be no problem, so she'd take the guard out first. But what about the little guy? He didn't look like he'd be a problem, but looks can deceive.

The local news came on with a lead story of a disturbance in Wasilla. Forty minutes north of Anchorage, it was one of the fastest growing areas in the state. Jen turned the volume up.

The newscaster stared seriously into the camera. "A riot involving dozens of people is taking place in a strip mall on the northern outskirts of Wasilla tonight. Wasilla police and Alaska State Troopers are responding and are warning citizens to stay away from the still unfolding drama. Our own Quentin Kelly is there. Quentin?"

The screen changed to a man in a shirt and tie, his salt-and-pepper hair perfectly in place. He held a microphone and had one hand to his ear. "Thank you, Sandy. Police aren't saying much, but I've spoken to some witnesses who said a disheveled man entered a local barber shop and attacked the customers. Some of the wounded customers then joined the man and attacked others."

Screaming and yelling drowned out the newsman as panic-stricken people rushed past him. Several law enforcement officers, guns drawn, ran the other way. The newsman glanced over his shoulder, then back at the camera, his face slack. "The riot is getting close. We may have to—"

A screech cut him off and he cringed. Jen's heart skipped a beat and her breathing quickened. No mistaking that sound. How the hell did a zombie get all the way down to Wasilla from the Alaskan bush in a day?

The newsman's eyes grew wide. "Sandy, we're getting out of here."

Gunshots peppered the background sound as more people stampeded past the camera. One old man stumbled, and a middle-aged woman jumped on his back, driving him to the ground. The woman glanced at the camera just as it cut off. Jen only saw her for a few seconds, but it was long enough to see the yellow in her eyes.

3

Jen stayed up all night switching between channels, trying to get the latest on the zombie outbreak in Wasilla. There had been no more live reports, just updates from the newsroom. All communication with the responding troopers and police had been lost, and the local stations repeated warnings to residents to stay indoors. By early morning, the outbreak had spread to the nearby city of Palmer.

The governor declared the entire Matanuska-Susitna Valley a disaster area and ordered a full recall of all Army and Air Force National Guard. They, along with the Anchorage Police Department, set up a barrier on the Glenn Highway at the Knik River Bridge. Reports of unrest in Fairbanks hit the news by 6:00 am the next morning, and the President of the United States declared the State of Alaska a disaster area and ordered Air Force and Army troops on Joint Base Elmendorf Richardson in Anchorage to assist local forces.

And never was there a mention of the dead walking, attacking, eating, and infecting the living. Someone at some level of government had to know what was really going on. Jen suspected the people in charge of the building she sat in knew the situation precisely.

The door unlocked at seven the next morning, and the server loped in with a tray. Rings under her eyes, she picked up the old tray, nearly dropped it, and left. The damn security guy looked like he'd stayed in a five-star hotel, with pressed pants, a clean shave, and no sense of fatigue. Jen stood as he prepared to close the door. "Did you pass my message on? That I'd like to talk to whoever's in charge?"

His gaze met hers and he nodded, then he closed and locked the door.

Jen dug into her breakfast, keeping her attention on the TV. Just as she scooped the last of the scrambled eggs up, the power went out. With no windows, the room was pitch black. Somewhere in the distance, an alarm sounded, and footsteps pounded down the hall.

She sat still, not daring to move. After a few minutes, she detected a weak glow from beneath the door. Probably some sort of emergency lighting in the hallway.

A loud click came from the TV, and the lights came on. She powered the TV and surfed the channels for another news station.

What the hell happened?

She had just tuned into a local news station when the picture went out. The power light on the TV was still green, but the cable box showed red.

Shit.

She changed the TV's channel from the cable feed to the local airwaves. They were still up, but the picture was fuzzy and the audio filled with static.

"City officials ... downtown disturbances ... multiple injuries ... warn people to stay away from ... power down all over—"

Jen changed to another local channel. The picture had a little snow, but the audio was clear. A female reporter stood in front of the camera. "I'm here in Town Square in downtown Anchorage, where police have cordoned off much of Fourth and Fifth Avenues."

A line of police stood several yards behind her in full riot gear, their backs to the camera.

"Word is a crowd of rioters is heading this way down Fifth Avenue. As you can see behind me, the police are prepared to repel them."

A man's voice came from somewhere near the reporter. "Here they come. Prepare for contact."

The reporter looked over her shoulder and everything went quiet.

Great time for the sound to go out.

Jen turned the volume up all the way. The shuffling of the police officers came through the speakers, so the sound worked. It was as if they all held their breath.

A high-pitched shriek washed over the police line, followed by a chorus of answering shrieks. It sounded as if hundreds of sets of fingernails were being scratched across a giant chalkboard. How many were there?

Shrieks turned into a roar. A burly policeman strode into view just as the picture cleared. "Stand your ground!"

The reporter turned to the camera. "I think we should leave."

The first wave of yellow-eyed demons slammed into the police line, which bent but held, but only until the second wave hit several seconds later and washed over them. Two zombies tackled the sergeant, one ripping his throat out and the other clamping its jaws on his arm.

A zombie in a ripped shirt and dirty jeans grabbed the reporter and sank his teeth into her shoulder. She screamed as he ripped a chunk of flesh out and chewed it, looking into the camera just before its signal ended.

Jen sat, her hands clenched on the chair's seat and her breathing shallow, as the news anchor appeared on screen, his usually carefully coifed hair askew and his eyes wide. "Grab your guns, gather your loved ones, and lock yourselves in." He stood and ripped the mic off his lapel. "I'm going home."

A voice called out from somewhere in the studio. Jen couldn't make out what was said, but the anchor looked to his left and flipped the bird. "Fuck you. I'm out of here. I'm not sitting at a desk while the end of the world comes."

He strode out of view. The camera stayed on his empty chair for thirty seconds before the feed switched to commercials.

Jen charged the door, throwing her body against it. "What the hell's going on out there?" She slammed the door with the base of her palm. "The city's dying. They're coming."

When no one answered, she rammed her shoulder into the door. "Is there anyone out there? We're in danger."

Panting, she dropped onto the bed. What would she do when the zombies came? She had no weapons. She looked around. *And this damn room is a trap. One way in, one way out.*

The door opened and the guard stood with a tray in his hand. He stepped to the desk and set it down.

Jen rushed him and rammed him into the desk. He folded over at the waist with an *oof*. She pushed off him, ran out the door, and stopped. The hall went in both directions, each ending in a turn. There were no doors or windows. Just shiny tile and bright lights and that damn antiseptic smell.

The guard dashed out the door and slammed her against the wall. Her lungs emptied and she fell to the floor, gasping. He picked her up, tossed her onto the bed, and closed the door. The lock *clunked*.

Jen lay on the bed, her heart pounding and sweat trickling down her cheek. She had to get out of there and find her dad.

She sat up and screamed, "I want to see the person in charge. Now."

No answer. The damn guard was out there. He'd been out there the whole time. Did that dick ever sleep?

Soft whistling came from the other side of the door. A snippet of a tune, Jen couldn't quite place it. Something classical. By the fifth time he'd whistled it, she'd had enough, and trudged back to the bed and plopped down.

Exhausted, she lay back and closed her eyes. She'd need her rest. She'd think better, and fight better, with it.

THE LOCK CLICKED and Jen's eyes snapped open. No telling how long she'd been out, and the damn TV didn't work, so she couldn't get the time there.

The door opened and the guard stood in the doorway, knees slightly bent, arms apart, his eyes scanning the room. He looked like he expected to be jumped. *Not so dumb.*

He glanced at her and picked up the lunch tray. He frowned. "You didn't touch this."

So he does speak. Jen sat up slowly, trying to look as passive as possible. "Been sleeping."

He nodded. "Then I'll leave lunch and dinner both." He shrugged. "It's not much. Sandwiches. All I know how to make."

She raised an eyebrow. "You're making my food? What happened to the lunchroom lady?"

"Gone. All the locals are gone." He placed the second tray on the desk.

Jen took a deep breath and exhaled. "Please. I need to talk to someone in charge."

He stepped into the hallway and faced her. "I let him know. He'll see you when he has time."

He closed and locked the door.

Stomach growling, Jen sat at the desk and lifted the lunch tray's plate cover. A peanut butter and jelly sandwich and a bag of potato chips. "I guess cuisine is the first thing to go in an apocalypse."

She picked up the dinner tray's plate cover and groaned. "Of course. Another peanut butter and jelly sandwich. This guy's going to kill me with this crap."

She ate both sandwiches and inhaled the chips, then opened the refrigerator. Only two more cans of soda. She pulled a can out. Why save them when she could be a zombie by morning?

An hour later she was running through channels with the remote and having no luck picking up a signal, when the door lock clicked. She put the remote down and turned in the chair. "What now? A midnight snack of peanut butter and jelly?"

The guard stepped in and to the side. She raised her eyebrows at him, but he gave her no reaction.

A tall man in his late twenties wearing a white lab coat walked in and peered over his round wireframe glasses at Jen. "Hi, Jennifer," he said in a soft Southern drawl. "I'm Dr. Wilson, but most folks call me Doc. I hear you've been asking to see me." He smiled. "Let's chat."

4

J en jumped to her feet, and the guard stepped between her and Dr. Wilson. The doctor put his arm out. "It's OK, Mark. She just wants some answers, and I've a mind to give her some."

Mark moved back into the doorway, blocking off her escape. *This guy doesn't miss anything.*

Wilson gestured at the chair. "Please, Miss Reed. Have a seat." He glanced at Mark. "I think Mark'll feel a little better if you do."

Jen eased into the seat. "Where's my dad?"

"He's here," Dr. Wilson said. "Would you like to see him?"

Jen smiled. "Yes."

Dr. Wilson nodded. "Fine. I can make that happen, but I'll also need something from you."

"What's that?"

"I need to find out more about your experiences in Point Wallace."

So she had information he wanted? She had some leverage after all. "There was a fire. We got out."

Mark stood still as a statue, no expression on his face. *He's really soaking everything in. What else has he heard in this building?*

Dr. Wilson sighed. "Really, Miss Reed, I was hoping we could be reasonable. You and I both know what's going on. I'm trying to stop it, and your assistance could be invaluable."

"And I get to see my dad?"

He nodded.

"And we can leave?"

"If I had my druthers, you could leave right now, but—"

"But we have the authority to detain you to get the information we need." The sunken-eyed man in the suit sauntered into the room, his nasal voice irritating her. "Miss Reed, the President of the United States has declared martial law in Alaska, and we will do whatever is necessary to combat and contain the outbreak."

Dr. Wilson frowned. "Hatcher, why don't y'all chill?" He turned to Jen. "What he said is true, but my concern is you won't be safe. I understand you've seen the local news reports?"

She nodded. "I have, Dr. Wilson. But how did the zombies get down here? Weren't they all destroyed in the Point Wallace fire?"

Wilson put a hand up, palm out. "Doc. Please call me Doc. Not all of the zombies were destroyed, but that's not how the virus got here."

"How, then?"

"I'll answer your questions and let you see your father if you'll agree to help me. Let me mine your experiences in Point Wallace. Do we have an agreement?"

Hatcher crossed his arms. "She doesn't have the proper security clearance."

"I'm giving it to her right now," Doc said. "What do you say, Miss Reed?"

What did she have to lose? Besides, if it would piss Hatcher off, she was all for it. "OK, but cut the Miss Reed crap. I'm Jen."

"Good." Doc walked to the door. "Get some sleep and we'll talk in the morning."

Jen stood up and took a step toward him. Mark stepped in front of her and Jen put her hands up in a gesture of surrender. "No harm. Just want to see my dad."

Doc walked out the door. "Tomorrow, Miss Reed."

Mark closed and locked the door. "It's Jen," she yelled through the door.

Despite having had little sleep, Jen still had trouble dozing off. Funny how she'd lived without her father for all those years and suddenly she couldn't wait to see him again.

·   ·   ·

SHE WOKE the next morning when the door opened and Mark brought in her breakfast tray. She sat up and yawned. "If you made me peanut butter and jelly sandwiches for breakfast, I'm going to kick your ass."

The burly guard cracked a smile and answered, "I made eggs and bacon, but you're welcome to put PB and J on your toast."

Jen laughed. "I thought the standard food after an apocalypse was canned peaches." She stood and put a hand out. "What's your last name, Mark?"

Mark stared at her hand, his grin melting.

Jen sighed. "Oh, come on. Are you afraid of little old me? I just thought we could start over."

He gave a slight shrug and shook her hand. "Mark Colton."

"Now when do I get to see my dad?"

He sighed. "You have a one-track mind, don't you?"

"And I'm told I'm a little pushy, too. So when do I see him?"

"Doc will stop by this morning. He'll tell you."

Jen opened her mouth to protest, but he put a hand up. "He's a busy man, but if he says he'll see you, he'll see you."

Jen nodded. "Good enough. For now."

Mark left and Jen dug into her breakfast. She'd just finished when the door opened and there stood Doc. He carried an aura of calm about him. If she didn't already know about the virus, she would've never guessed he was trying to save humanity.

He leaned against the door frame. "I trust you've had plenty of rest."

Jen swiveled in the chair. "I got enough." She wasn't going to ask about her dad again. At least, not yet.

Doc cleared his throat. "Let me give you an abridged version of what's been happening, then you can answer some questions. Fair enough?"

"OK."

"The dead are being reanimated and are attacking, infecting, and eating the living. Zombies, some would call them, and it's not an altogether incorrect characterization."

Jen leaned forward. "Welcome to my world. What can you tell me that I don't know?"

"It's caused by a virus."

Jen crossed her arms. "So you get bitten, then you die and come back as one of them."

Doc squinted. "That's part of it. You don't need to be bitten to be infected, all you have to do is die. It takes a bit longer to reanimate that way, but the results are the same."

"Don't have to get bitten? How does that work?"

Dr. Wilson rubbed his eyes. "I'm not sure. But it's why I need your help. You're the only person who's observed these creatures up close and has the scientific training to report on them."

"I'm an environmental scientist. I'm familiar with viruses at a basic level, but not an expert."

"I need every scientist I can muster," Doc said. "We need to crack this soon, because later may be too late."

Help stop this nightmare or sit in a room eating peanut butter and jelly sandwiches until the world ends? Tough choice. "And my dad?"

"I'll take you to him in a moment," Doc said. "But I need to know something first. Other than with the explosion and fire, were you able to stop any of the infected from the pit?"

Jen thought back. "Yes, but you had to damage their head. Their brain. I shot some in the head, and other times caved in some skulls. It worked the same way with the locals who'd turned. They just moved faster."

"Did they?"

Jen pushed back a strand of her hair. "I think it was because they were fresher, if that makes any sense."

"It does, indeed."

Jen stood. "My father."

Doc stepped to the side and put his arm out. "Of course. After you."

Jen walked out the door and into the bright hallway lights. Mark stood next to her.

"You can take a break," she said.

Doc walked past her, heading down the left corridor. "Where you go, he goes. That's part of the deal I made with Hatcher."

"I thought you were in charge," Jen said.

"I am, but I still have to answer to the CDC, and they're the ones who sent Hatcher when this all started."

Jen shrugged and followed him. If it took having a shadow to get out of solitary confinement, then so be it.

A man and a woman dressed in scrubs and engaged in deep conversation walked past as Doc led Jen around a corner and to an elevator. The doors opened and she followed him in. The indicator showed they were on the third floor and Doc punched the four. He turned to her. "You'll have the run of the facility except for the first floor and any door marked authorized personnel only."

"Why the first floor? Don't want me making a run for it?"

Mark shook his head. "You'd never get out the first floor. We evacuated it and welded all the doors shut two days ago."

"What the hell for?"

"It's the only floor with windows," Mark said. "The creatures appear to be attracted by sight and sound. No people visible, no zombies."

The elevator stopped and the doors opened. Doc strode into the hall and to the right. Jen followed. Mark's footsteps echoed behind her as they walked down the hall.

Doc stopped at a door with a red sign that said "Authorized Personnel Only." To the right was a large window with blinds.

He turned to her. "Your dad—"

"My dad's in there? I want to see him now. No more delays."

Doc nodded, then gestured to Mark. Mark walked to the end of the window and opened the blinds.

Strapped in a standing position to a vertical table was her father, his head bowed, clothed in faded green hospital pants and a shirt.

Doc knocked on the glass and her dad's head jerked up, his yellow eyes burning into Jen's. She stepped back, covering her mouth with her hand, and let out a gasp.

Her dad let out an ear-piercing shriek.

5

Heart racing, Jen stumbled back from the window. Mark dropped the blinds into place.

Doc put out a hand. "Are you all right?"

"Dad? He—he was bitten?"

"No. He was infected, as you are, but he died and was reanimated."

Mark reached out as if he were going to put an arm around her shoulder, but hesitated and awkwardly dropped it to his side. "I didn't know that was your dad."

Jen's knees collapsed. Mark caught her and propped her against the wall. Her dad's shrieks died off. She closed her eyes, tears rolling down her cheeks and her body shaking. "What did he die from?"

"We did an MRI, and his left coronary artery was blocked. He died from a heart attack."

Recent memories flooded Jen's mind. Her dad holding his left arm close to his body. Him curled up at the bottom of the boat.

Doc's voice lowered. "I'm sorry, but I didn't know how else to tell you. My granny always said that the best way to remove a bandage is to just yank it off."

Jen took a deep breath and let it out. Wiping her eyes, she straightened. "Is there somewhere I can sit?"

"Of course," Doc said. "My lab." He led them down two doors and into a large room filled with expensive-looking electronic equipment Jen couldn't identify, as well as microscopes and Bunsen burners. A sixty-inch monitor, affixed to the wall above a cluttered desk, displayed updated time and weather information.

Doc led her to a desk near the door and Mark eased her into the chair. He filled a glass from a sink and gave it to her.

Grateful, she took a sip, then tilted her head back and emptied the glass. "So how the hell did my dad become infected without being bitten? Is the virus airborne?"

Doc leaned against a counter. "We believe so, although by what mechanism we're not sure. What we have learned is when the virus is transferred through saliva or blood, the effects are almost instantaneous. But when delivered through the lungs, the virus lies dormant until the host is deceased." He frowned. "It takes a little longer for them to turn, but I don't know why yet."

Something was niggling at the back of her mind. Something that happened recently, but she couldn't quite remember. "What are you doing with my dad?"

Doc straightened. "First off, we're keeping him as comfortable as possible. We feed him raw meat several times a day." He sighed. "But we needed him. We took blood samples and sent them back to the CDC, where they extracted the virus to use in researching a vaccine."

Mark took the empty glass from Jen. Her heart leapt. "So you think you can cure him?"

Doc shook his head. "Dead is dead. But the hope is we can cure the virus that's dormant in the living so they don't reanimate upon death."

"So you're a virologist?"

"I'm a behavioral scientist," Doc said. "More of an observer than a doer."

Jen's head swam. Her father was a zombie, and she would become one someday unless the CDC could find a cure. *What a damn nightmare.*

A beeping sound came from the cluttered desk. Doc logged onto the computer and clicked an icon. A blue light blinked above the monitor and the screen filled with the video image of a thin gray-haired woman with intense dark eyes. "Status report."

Doc rolled his chair back and looked up at the screen. "We have the infected survivors of Point Wallace. The father, Devin Reed, has transformed and is secured." He hitched a thumb over his shoulder. "This is Jen Reed, his daughter."

The gray-haired woman gave Jen a smile that didn't quite reach the corners of her eyes. "Miss Reed, I'm Dr. Cartwright, Director of Operations for the Center for Disease Control. I hope we can secure your cooperation."

Jen stepped closer. Even over video the lady reeked of bureaucracy. "I guess it depends on what cooperation you're looking for."

Dr. Cartwright's lips pressed together to form a thin line. Doc cut in. "I haven't had a chance to brief her yet."

"See that you do." Dr. Cartwright's face disappeared from the screen and the time and weather displayed.

Jen crossed her arms. "She isn't by chance searching for ruby slippers, is she?"

A grin crossed Mark's face.

Doc chuckled. "I heard you were a bit of a spitfire."

Jen wanted to like Doc. His laid-back attitude put her at ease. But first she had to get the full picture. "How about that briefing you mentioned?"

Doc fidgeted with a pen on the desk. "I need your blood, too."

"Mine? Why?"

"We suspect there are different properties of the virus when it's dormant, like it is with you, and active, like your father's. They need to study the differences to attempt a cure."

Jen rolled up her sleeve. "Then take my blood."

Doc opened a cabinet and pulled out a box of syringes. He selected one and placed it on the desk.

"What are the chances of finding the answer?" Jen asked.

Doc tied off her upper arm with a rubber tourniquet. "The virus isn't that sophisticated, it's just very efficient and arrived without warning. There are no guarantees, but they've already made good progress. With your blood, I expect they'll be able to do animal tests by next week."

Jen's eyes widened. "That's amazing."

Doc jabbed the needle in Jen's arm and untied the tourniquet. Blood flowed into the cylinder. "There's a lot of motivation," he said. "Normally, this process would be off like a herd of turtles, but all the FDA rules have been suspended."

He removed the needle from her arm and placed a small bandage on the wound. "You should go back to your room and rest. This will go out to the CDC immediately. It might be the last package out to Joint Base Elmendorf Richardson for transport. Things are getting mighty dicey out there."

Jen wasn't going to argue. The shock of seeing her father had taken a lot out of her. She stood, and Mark moved to her side. "I'll take you back," he said.

Doc filled a vial with the blood. "When you're rested, I'd like to talk to you about your experience in Point Wallace, if you've a mind to."

Jen nodded. "Sure, Doc."

Mark led her into the hallway. When they arrived at her room, Jen sat on the bed and Mark turned to leave, but Jen reached out and touched his arm. "Could you stay for a few minutes?"

Mark turned back. He towered over her, considering her with his soft brown eyes. "Sure."

Jen struggled with a question she had for him. She didn't want to piss him off, but she had to know. She looked him straight in the eye. "Why are you here? Why are you involved in this?"

Mark rubbed his chin. After a few seconds, he gave a slight nod as if he'd made a decision. "This was supposed to be an easy assignment. Doc and his team were setting up to perform winter experiments on human survival in the cold. They didn't need much for security, so I planned on being here for only a few days, then I could monitor the systems remotely from home."

"Where's that? Home, I mean."

"Biloxi, Mississippi."

Jen sighed. "So then Point Wallace happened."

"Yeah," Mark said. "Doc got a call and he brought his staff into his lab. Hatcher showed up and was assigned as second-in-command after Doc. My orders were to secure the building and follow Hatcher's directions. I had no idea what the hell was going on, but I did as I was told." He gestured toward her. "You came in the next day."

"And my dad."

"I didn't know about him until yesterday, the first time I saw him. And like I said, I had no idea he was your father until you said it."

Jen lay back in bed. Mark seemed sincere, but he was part of the whole government deal that was keeping her prisoner. And keeping her safe, it seemed.

Mark walked to the door. "You better get some rest. I'll be right outside."

He closed the door. Jen waited for the *clunk* of the lock's tumblers. It didn't come. A minute later soft whistling came from the other side of the door. The tune was slightly familiar. Something classical.

She laid her head on her arms and stared at the ceiling. *Even if Doc comes up with a cure, he can't help Dad. He has no future.*

His words from Point Wallace ran through her mind.

I would rather someone kill me than live as a monster. Would you do that for me if the time comes?

AFTER AN HOUR OF REST, she got up and tried the TV again. Nothing on the airwaves. She walked to the door and opened it just as the lights went out again. The dim emergency lighting in the hall let her see a shadowed figure to the right of the door.

"You OK?" Mark asked.

"I'm good."

They stood there in the dark and said nothing. A few minutes later the lights came back on.

"That took a while," Jen said.

Mark looked up at the fluorescent overheads. "The Anchorage power grid is out."

"Then why do we have lights?"

"We have arrays of batteries in the basement. They've taken over."

Jen frowned. "It's got to be a real mess out there if the power's out. How long will the batteries last?"

"We've got solar panels on the roof. They'll keep the batteries charged until we hit the short days in winter."

I'll be damned if I'm staying that long. I'll help Doc and take care of Dad, then I'm out of here. "I'd like to see my dad."

Mark searched her eyes. "You sure?"

She nodded. "The first time was a shock. I'm ready this time."

He shrugged. "OK." He led her upstairs to the window with the blinds. "Want me to open them?"

"No." She lifted a blind and peeked through. Her father was still strapped upright to the table as she'd first seen him, his head down.

Again, the memory of her promise flooded in. She pressed her lips tightly together and tears burned her eyes. *I'll keep my promise, Dad.*

6

Jen stood in the hallway the next day, peeking through a blind at her father again. He had his head raised and sniffed the air as if he knew someone was nearby. Low, rumbling growls came from his lips. Jen squelched the urge to lift the blind higher and make it easier to watch him. No doubt he'd see her and go apeshit.

It was getting harder and harder for her to see her father in the face of the undead monster before her. Her resolve to kill the creature and release her father continued to grow. *Is he trapped in there, or is he already gone?* No matter, she'd make sure he had the chance to rest in peace.

She glanced behind her. Mark leaned against the wall, studying his cell phone and whistling that tune again. It was beginning to play in her head when he wasn't around.

Thanks, Mark.

She lowered the blind and turned. "Have you been able to talk to your family?"

Mark shrugged without looking up. "Not yet. But I'm sure they're OK."

Clipped footsteps echoed down the hallway from the direction of the elevator. *Hatcher.*

"What are you doing out of your room?" he said.

I've had enough of this asshole. "None of your damn business."

Mark moved to her side and faced Hatcher. "Doc said it was OK."

Doc sauntered down the hallway behind Hatcher. "Is there a problem here?"

Hatcher pointed at Jen. "She's a security risk. She shouldn't be anywhere near the dead subject."

"Dead subject?" Jen said. "That's my father."

"Oh, no." Hatcher crossed his arms. "He was no longer your father the minute he turned. He's now government property."

Jen balled her hands into fists and took a step toward Hatcher. "Like hell."

Mark grabbed her arm and held her back. "This isn't the time," he whispered into her ear.

Doc stopped beside Hatcher. "We have no need for the zombie. His blood's been collected and shipped to the CDC." He nodded at Jen. "She's next of kin and should be allowed to determine what happens to him."

"And I'm going to give him peace," she said.

Hatcher's face grew red. He faced Doc. "I understand you're in charge here, but you have to answer to your superiors, too. I'm not trying to be the bad guy here, but the country's in a deadly situation and if it isn't handled properly, it could mean the end of everything."

Doc's voice softened, and he put a hand on Hatcher's shoulder. "I know you're doing your best under sorry circumstances, but being a hard-ass with Jen won't accomplish anything. The loss of one zombie won't hurt the cause." He peered over his glasses. "Let her give her father peace."

Hatcher looked at Jen, then back at Doc. "I can't stop you, but I will make a full report once we're evacuated. I would be derelict in my duties if I didn't."

Doc nodded. "Yes, you would. I understand your position, but Jen gets to determine what happens to her father, and she gets the freedom to move around. So I suggest y'all chill."

Hatcher glared, then strode off down the hallway.

Doc smiled at Jen. "Well, now that that's over, would you mind coming to my office and assisting me?"

"Sure," Jen said.

She and Mark followed Doc to his lab. He pointed to a faux leather swivel chair. "Please have a seat."

Jen sat, and Doc pulled up a chair. Mark leaned on the counter behind her. Doc reached into his coat pocket and pulled out a small capped plastic vial half filled with brown powder.

"The spores," Jen said. "Where'd you get them?"

Doc placed the vial on the desk. "Your pants pocket, when they brought you in. So you know about the spores. What about the mycovirus?"

Jen tilted her head. "Mycovirus? What? On those spores?"

Doc nodded.

"We didn't have the equipment to magnify them enough to see the virus," she said.

"What's a mycovirus?" Mark asked.

Jen turned in her chair. "It's a virus that infects fungi." She swung back to Doc. "What do they have to do with anything?"

"Where'd you find the spores?" Doc asked.

"Inside the coat of one of the sailors. Why?"

Doc waved his hand dismissively. "I'll get to that. Please just answer my questions for now."

Jen shrugged. "OK."

"How much did you find in the coat?" Doc asked.

"It was full of spores. There had to be billions of them."

Doc sighed, removed his glasses, and rubbed the bridge of his nose. "Did the other sailors have the spores as well?"

Jen thought back. She'd run into plenty of the sailors and had killed more than a few, but none of their coats had been open. "I don't know. The only reason we discovered them was we examined that one seamen before he thawed."

Doc stood and paced. "And there was severe weather when the sailors rose. Wind gusts to seventy miles an hour according to the weather reports."

Jen nodded.

"What do you think that did to the spores?" Doc asked.

Jen squinted. What the hell was Doc getting at? A mycovirus and the spores being blown into the air and carried away? "Oh, shit."

"Are you saying the zombie virus is a mycovirus?" Jen asked. "But they only infect fungi."

"True," Doc said. "Normally. But what we're dealing with here has been far from normal."

"So that's how the virus has spread," Mark said.

Doc placed a hand on Mark's shoulder. "I believe so." He turned back to the desk and opened a drawer, retrieving a thumb drive. "I've done as much research and analysis on it as I can here. Our data link with the CDC went down this morning and I've had only limited satellite communications with them. When we leave, I'll take this data with me so it can be studied further with their state-of-the-art equipment."

He put the drive and vial in the drawer. "But there's something else I need your help with, Jen." Doc pulled the computer keyboard toward him. "We've been running drones, both from here and Joint Base Elmendorf Richardson."

"We just call it JBER," Jen said. "It's easier."

"Jay Bear?"

"Yeah. J-B-E-R. JBER."

Doc shrugged. "OK. So we've been running a couple of drones from here, and the Air Force has been running a dozen or so from JBER. I've merged all the footage and have been analyzing it."

"For what?" Jen asked.

Doc smiled. "I'm a behavioral scientist. Even if we had a cure in place right now, we'd still need to figure out how to deal with the zombies we already have."

Jen glanced at Mark. He raised an eyebrow, but remained silent. "OK, Doc," Jen said. "Let's see what you have."

Doc hit a key on the keyboard and the video began. It was a shot from the sky looking straight down. Buildings, roads, and trees zipped by before it seemed to slow.

"Watch for it," Doc said.

The drone hovered over a group of three humans. They picked their way through a parking lot of abandoned cars.

The picture widened, and Jen recognized a midtown bookstore. The lot was half full of abandoned cars and the survivors ducked down and weaved their way between them.

The picture widened further. Jen wasn't sure if it was the camera widening its angle or the drone climbing higher.

When it showed the whole parking lot and building, a half dozen figures shambled at the top of the screen. Jen's muscles tensed as the group of humans slowly made their way toward the zombies.

"Watch the zombies," Doc said.

First one, then all of the zombies sniffed the air and turned toward the humans. When one of the humans stood to look over a car, the zombies all tilted their heads back and opened their mouths. Seconds later, they streaked for the humans.

The picture switched to another view. It took Jen a second to realize it was of a department store parking lot across the street from the bookstore.

There had to be thirty zombies spread across it, and they all raised their heads and opened their mouths, before sprinting in the direction of the humans.

"Wait for it," Doc said.

When the zombies disappeared from the shot, movement at the side of a car caught Jen's attention. A zombie milled around the lot as if it hadn't heard the call.

Doc paused the video. "We know the zombies shriek when they spot prey, and that other zombies who hear the shriek respond with shrieks of their own."

"Other than the sound being different, it reminds me of wolves howling," Jen said.

"That's a great observation," Doc said. "A zombie howl."

Mark grunted. "That's a good term for it."

Doc nodded. "So at least one zombie spots a human and calls the others. They respond with howls of their own and run off to the chase."

"Sure," Jen said. "Same as Point Wallace. Like swarming wasps."

"Y'all are just great at naming things," Doc said. "A zombie howl and a zombie swarm. I'll be sure to attribute you in my notes." He rubbed his chin. "But what about that one that didn't howl, and didn't chase after the humans?" He cleared his throat. "I mean, didn't join the swarm?"

Jen studied the picture on the screen. "That happened in Point Wallace, too. Almost like the zombies that didn't run off were deaf."

"Or left behind in case any humans made a break for it," Mark said.

Doc pointed at Mark. "That's what I think. While it could be because they don't hear, I'd have to assume that the rate of zombie deafness is roughly equivalent to the rate of human deafness."

"Makes sense," Jen said.

Doc put a forefinger in the air. "But, the rate of human deafness is less than one half of one percent. And yet, we see it in this video, and Jen reported the same at Point Wallace. That would be a far higher rate than humans."

Jen's heart skipped a beat. "So you're saying these things are smarter than we've thought."

"They are," Doc said. "But I think it's more of an instinctual intelligence than any real smarts. Problem is, I can't be sure without more data because we need to eliminate the possibility that the virus itself is mutating and making them smarter."

"Holy shit," Mark said. "Bad enough these things have overwhelming numbers and are hard to take down, but if they're getting smarter, too..."

Jen took a deep breath. "You're just full of sunshine, Doc. Any other good news?"

He turned to the screen. "Watch this."

He unpaused the video, and it switched to an overhead view of an area Jen couldn't identify. The drone flew over industrial buildings backed up to a green belt of fir trees.

Two people ran full tilt from the trees and toward a building. Seconds later, four smaller dark figures burst from the trees in pursuit.

"What the hell are those?" Jen asked.

Doc said nothing.

The camera zoomed in on the small figures, then brought them into focus.

"Dogs?" Jen said.

Mark leaned closer to the screen, squinting. "They look like huskies to me."

Doc froze the picture and zoomed in. One of the dogs must've sensed the drone because it looked up in mid-stride.

Its eyes were yellow.

7

A week later Jen sat back in her chair and rubbed her eyes while Doc loaded another video. "So once the zombie swarm has attacked the victim, it slowly disperses, but not all of them. Other than that, I don't think I know much more today than a week ago after we watched the first drone videos."

"You're as right as rain," Doc said. "But here's the latest footage we have. You'll find it interesting."

The video displayed a treeless greenbelt. "It looks like the park strip downtown," Jen said.

The drone had zoomed out to capture three blocks. Zombies wandered alone and in groups at the far left and right of the footage.

Doc pointed to the top middle of the screen at the entrance to an alley. "Watch here."

Two figures appeared there. They peered out, then walked slowly across the park strip in plain view of the zombies. The zombies continued to wander around.

"What the hell?" Jen said. "They should be zombie poop by now."

The figures reached the other side of the strip and disappeared into a backyard.

Doc paused the video. "Best I can tell is that the zombies have a limited distance where they can detect prey. I think the two people we saw there weren't detected because they were far enough away, and because they moved slowly and didn't attract attention."

"How far away do you have to be?" Mark stood by the door and had been so quiet Jen had forgotten he was there.

"I don't have enough data to make that determination," Doc said. "I wish we could send more drones up, but we don't have the time."

"What do you mean we don't have time?" Jen asked.

Doc stood and stretched. "Spoke to Cartwright on the satellite phone this morning. They're sending a convoy to pick us up and take us to JBER tomorrow morning. Seems she's anxious to get my research into the spores and the mycovirus. Imagine that."

Jen grinned. She'd become used to Doc's laid-back ways. He sounded a bit like a hick, but he was smarter than any professor she'd had at college. "Sounds like it's time to ask for a raise."

"If you don't mind, I need to collect all my data and get it ready for transport." Doc gathered the strewn papers on his desk and stacked them.

"Oh, sure." Jen stood and turned to Mark. "How about some time on the roof?"

Doc chuckled. "Hatcher's going to bust a vein if he catches you up there."

Jen shrugged. "Then that'll be one problem solved."

Mark opened the door and led Jen into the hallway. They passed by an open doorway a minute later where Hatcher sat at a desk, studying a sheaf of papers. "I swear that man wears the same damn suit every day," Jen whispered to Mark.

"Or maybe he has a bunch of the same suit," Mark said.

Jen's laughter echoed down the hallway.

They exited the elevator on the fifth floor, and strode down the hall, rounded the corner, and stopped at a door with a security card reader next to a sign that said Authorized Personnel Only. Mark looked up and down the hall, then ran his card through the reader. A loud *clunk* came from the door and he pulled it open.

Jen hurried in and climbed the stairs in front of her. She waited at a door with a small wired window until Mark ran his card through another reader and pushed the door open.

She stepped onto the roof, spread her arms, and took a deep breath.

Ever since coming to the roof almost a week before, it had become the highlight of her day.

High clouds passed overhead, but the sun peeked out every few minutes. Late July was Jen's favorite time in Anchorage. Still plenty of sun and the rainy season still off by a few weeks. She walked past the solar panels and sat on a wooden bench, then patted the spot next to her. "Take a load off."

Mark sat and leaned forward, planting his elbows on his thighs. "Guess we'll be out of here by this time tomorrow."

"You knew about the convoy?" Jen asked.

"Found out just before I went to your room this morning."

A little pang of disappointment stung her. *Why not tell me?* She frowned. She'd let herself think these people were becoming her friends and that she belonged to the group. She shook her head. *But no one takes care of number one better than number one, herself.*

The breeze picked up and with it the rank smell that had been there every time Jen had been on the roof. A mixture of burned wood and something else she couldn't place her finger on, it had become fainter as the columns of smoke in the distance had died.

"Where will they take us?" Jen asked.

"They have a setup at Fairchild Air Force Base near Spokane. Doc said they'll probably quarantine us for a short while, then he'll head to the CDC and you and I can go wherever we want."

A gunshot sounded in the distance, followed by zombie howls. *The dinner bell has been rung.* "So you'll head to Biloxi?"

Mark nodded. "Check in on my folks and my sister and check out the situation. See if I need to get them someplace safer."

He leaned back on his arms. "How about you?"

"I don't have any relatives left that I've ever met. Besides, I've pretty much been on my own since I was a kid, so why mess with what works?"

"Everyone needs help." Mark glanced back at the door to the stairs. "We shouldn't stay up here too long. It may be funny, but I still don't want Hatcher popping through that door. He can make a lot of trouble for us."

I need more time out of the damn suffocating building. "What'd you do before this? I mean, before you did security for the government?"

Mark's jaw tightened and he stared into the distance.

"Did I say something wrong?" she asked.

Mark chewed his lower lip, then his shoulders relaxed. "No. You didn't. My past is just something I don't talk about."

Jen grinned. "As long as you're not a serial killer or something."

Mark's eyebrows shot up.

"You're shitting me." She slid away from him.

He put out a hand. "Not in the way you think."

"You need to explain right now." No way she could fight him. Too damn big and strong. She eyed a three-foot-long two-by-four laying next to a solar panel.

Mark closed his eyes and tilted his head back. He took a deep breath and exhaled it. "I'd spent a few years in Army infantry, but was eventually accepted to fly drones in the Middle East. I'd sit safely back at an air base, recon for ground troops, and take out terrorists with missiles."

He straightened his head and opened his eyes, staring in the distance. "I was able to get the position because I'd already been certified for light planes and so the transition was simpler."

Jen leaned forward and looked at him. "That was war, not serial killing."

Mark squeezed his eyes shut and opened them again. "It was, until a particular mission. Intel reported a convoy of Al Qaeda taking place. They believed top leadership were in the vehicles."

He cracked his knuckles and wrung his hands. "I was given the mission. The convoy stuck out like a sore thumb as it traveled across the desert between towns. I identified the vehicles and was given the clearance to engage. I sent three Hellfire missiles at that convoy, keeping the last one for any cleanup. I didn't need it. Those cars and trucks were blown to shit."

Jen sat entranced by Mark's story. For the first time since the shit had hit the fan, she'd forgotten about zombies and the end of the world. Her breathing slowed and her heartbeat quickened as the story went on.

"At the end of my shift," Mark said, "I stopped and had a couple beers, then hit my bunk. The next morning, it was all over the news. That convoy had no terrorists. It was families, women and children, fleeing for their lives. None of them survived."

Jen put a hand on his shoulder. "It's not your fault. You didn't know."

He shrugged. "Doesn't matter. I still did it. But then it got worse. My major called me in and congratulated me on a job well done. I'd followed my orders. He said there were unfortunate casualties, but I did my duty."

Mark turned toward Jen with watery eyes. "Unfortunate casualties?

There were eighteen dead children and five dead women." He jerked a thumb to his chest and raised his voice. "And I killed them. No one else."

Jen softened her voice. "What happened then?"

"I beat the shit out of that major and was court martialed. I got busted down in rank and assigned to convoys. Guess they thought I'd never make it home. Problem is I did, but eleven of my buddies didn't." He rolled up his shirtsleeve, exposing a ragged scar across his forearm. "One piece of shrapnel was all I got. Doesn't seem fair that I killed those innocents and this was all that happened to me."

Jen squeezed his shoulder. "I'm sorry I asked. I didn't mean to bring this all back up for you."

Mark stood and wiped his eyes. "I live with it every day. I think that I can't make it up to the ones I killed, but maybe I can keep others alive. With my court martial on record, I couldn't get into any law enforcement, so I went with security."

"You can't save everyone, Mark. No one can."

"I know," he said. "I've had to become hardened to that fact to keep my sanity, but I will at least protect my family and those I'm hired to protect."

A screech of tires came from nearby. Jen jumped to her feet. "That sounds like the front of the building, on the Old Seward Highway."

They ran to the highway side of the building, where a stand of trees kept it hidden from the road. Jen stood at the four-foot wall that ringed the rooftop.

A zombie howl came from the same direction as the tire squeal. Two people burst from the trees and made a beeline to the building's front door. A man and a woman, who both looked to be in their twenties. The woman held something to her chest. Jen squinted to get a better look.

A baby.

Multiple howls came from the trees. Jen leaned on the wall. The door was right beneath her, six floors away. The man beat on it and yelled, "Let us in. Please!"

The baby wailed as the mother tried to calm it. "We've got a baby," the man screamed.

Jen grabbed Mark's arm. "We've got to open the door."

Mark swallowed. "I'm sorry, but there's nothing we can do. The doors are welded shut. Even if we were down there right now with all the equipment, we couldn't get it open in time."

The zombie howls grew louder, and Jen turned back to the tragedy unfolding before her. Five zombies raced from the trees. The man pushed the woman behind him. Bare-handed, he attacked the lead zombie, a thirty-something man in bloody jeans and a shredded flannel shirt.

The man swung and knocked the zombie back. Before he could recover, a female zombie tackled him to the ground. The thirty-something zombie and the female zombie leapt onto him and ripped the flesh from his chest as he struggled and screamed.

The woman screeched. "Why didn't you help us?"

Jen tore her eyes from the dying man and looked to the woman and baby. The woman glared at her. "Why didn't you help?"

Jen's mouth went dry and her lower lip trembled. Speechless, all she could do was watch as three zombies slammed into the woman, knocking her into the door. The woman turned her back to them and wrapped her arms around her screaming child.

The other two zombies joined in as they tore her shirt off, clamped their jaws on her, and ripped chunks of skin and muscle off her back. The baby cried and the woman shrieked as they feasted. She never took her eyes off Jen.

The woman staggered, then fell to her knees. The zombies piled onto her, and she disappeared beneath them. The baby let loose with a long keening wail that felt like a knife slicing down Jen's spine.

Jen stumbled back from the roof's edge, tears streaming down her cheeks. Mark caught her and led her to the door. Just as she was about to step through the doorway, the child's scream cut off.

8

J en spent the next morning watching her father through the blinds and wondering what it would've been like to have had the chance to get to know him better.

She wept. Not just for him, but for the couple and their baby. She couldn't do anything for them, and she couldn't save her father. But she'd make sure she granted him his final peace.

Hatcher strode by, no doubt checking to make sure Mark watched over her. *What an asshole.*

Mark stood in his normal position, leaning against the far wall and whistling his tune over and over. Jen had begun to hear the damn thing in her sleep. She'd asked him to stop earlier and he had, but he'd picked it back up within minutes. He didn't even know he had.

Doc walked up the hallway. "The convoy will be here in an hour." He stopped in front of Mark. "I want you to lead the evacuation coordination."

"Me?" Mark said. "Isn't that Hatcher's job?"

Doc leaned in to Mark and whispered something Jen couldn't hear. Mark nodded. "OK. I'll be right down."

Doc nodded at Jen and walked at a clipped pace to his office.

"Let's go." Mark hitched a thumb over his shoulder. "I'm needed in the lobby."

"What did Doc say about you taking over Hatcher's duties?"

Mark's gaze was intense as it met hers. "Doc doesn't trust him. This trip will be dangerous enough without that bureaucrat screwing things up."

"Doc's smart in a lot of ways," Jen said. She glanced back at the blinds. "You know what I have to do, and the quickest, most painless way would be with a gun."

Mark looked in both directions, then spoke softly in her ear. "We'll each be armed when the convoy gets here. You can come back up and take care of business."

That's an interesting way to put it. "OK, but don't leave without me."

Mark smiled. "Never. I figure it's my job to get you and Doc safely to JBER. This is a mission I won't fail."

Jen swallowed. He'd said it like he'd risk his life for her and Doc. She followed him to the elevator.

When they arrived in the lobby, a tech in a white coat jogged up to Mark and held out a walkie-talkie. "It's the convoy commander. He says they're twenty minutes out."

Mark took the radio. "This is Mark Colton. Copy you're twenty minutes out from my position."

The radio crackled. "Roger. Have all passengers and supplies ready to go on the first floor."

"Roger that," Mark said. "Have you run into any unfriendlies?"

"Had a good battle at Girdwood, but we got through with no casualties."

Jen smiled at Mark. She couldn't wait to get out of there.

"Roger," Mark said. "Out."

He handed the radio back to the tech. "Sound the alarm so everyone knows it's time to muster."

The tech nodded and ran off. Moments later, the alarm blared. Mark raised his voice. "Stay with me."

He approached a group of men at the front door. "Can we get out the door now?"

A man in overalls with a stomach the size of a watermelon scratched the back of his bald head. "Yup. But it also means those things can get in, so I hope that convoy's here soon."

"Does the door open inside or out?" Jen asked.

The bald man shrugged. "Out. Why?"

"The zombies aren't smart enough to pull on a door. They only go forward when they're after humans."

Mark gave the bald man a pat on the back. "Just spoke with the convoy. They'll be here soon and we won't have to worry about the door."

The tech with the radio ran over. "Ten minutes out."

Mark nodded. "Where's Doc?"

The tech pointed to the elevator. The doors had just opened. Doc stepped out and loped over to Mark and Jen. "Everything set?"

"So far, so good," Mark said.

Doc turned to Jen. "There are four important things that need to get through to Fairchild: our data store, the vial of spores, you, and me."

"Me?" Jen asked. "What do you need me for?"

"You're the only person who experienced what happened at ground zero. Plus, you and I are the only scientists who have studied the creatures' behavior. I believe that will be critical in defeating them."

Two Humvees, two SUVs, and a bus rumbled down the drive and pulled up in front of the building. Several soldiers deployed around the vehicles, and three others entered the lobby.

The lead soldier stopped. "Dr. Wilson."

Doc raised his hand. "That's me."

The soldier walked over and shook his hand. "Captain Lupone, Alaska National Guard. We're here to escort you to the flight line at JBER, sir."

Doc gestured to Mark. "Mark Colton. He's coordinating the evacuation."

The men shook hands.

"And this is Jen Reed. She's the only survivor of Point Wallace."

Lupone nodded, but didn't offer his hand.

He can treat me the same as them. She thrust out her hand. "Pleased to meet you, Captain."

Startled, Lupone shook her hand. "Likewise."

He turned toward his men. "Get these people some weapons."

The soldiers jogged out to the bus and returned with a wooden crate. Captain Lupone opened it, revealing rifles and pistols. "I objected when my superiors told me to arm civilians, but I was overruled. I just hope none of you shoot me or my men."

He gestured to the open crate. "Who's first?"

Doc nodded at Mark. "Why don't you start?"

Mark picked up a rifle, pulled back the bolt, and peered into the chamber. "M4, nice. Got some 5.56 NATO rounds?"

Captain Lupone nodded at his men and they opened the second crate. Mark picked a couple of thirty round magazines from it and a sling of 5.56 rounds.

Jen was next and picked up an M9 Beretta and a full magazine. She inserted the magazine and pulled the slide back to load a round into the chamber. She moved to Mark's side as Lupone called out, "Form a line here and take one weapon. It is not optional; all convoy members will be armed."

Lupone handed Doc a pistol. "You, too, sir."

Doc removed the magazine, checked the rounds, and slapped it back in. "Y'all wouldn't happen to have a holster?"

"Sorry, Doctor."

"Shame."

Jen glanced at the stairs and elevator. No one was near them. She had to go take care of her dad and get back in time to leave.

Mark gave her a side glance and whispered in her ear. "Go take care of business, but there'll be one more alarm. When you hear it, haul ass back here because we'll be leaving soon after."

Jen nodded and walked as normally as possible to the elevator and pressed the button. It opened and she stepped in.

As she approached her father's room, her steps were the only sound in the hallway. Her father stood as he had before, his head down. What had they planned for him since they were leaving? Just let him rot there?

No way Doc would do that. He wouldn't let him loose, but wouldn't leave him to suffer, either. *If a zombie's capable of suffering.*

She opened the door, pistol at the ready. Her father lifted his head and glared at her, his yellow eyes boring into hers with a mixture of anger and hunger. He reared his head back and shrieked.

She aimed the pistol at his forehead, her hands trembling. *Calm down. Breathe.*

Arms grabbed her in a bear hug and pulled her back into the hallway. Her hand reflexively squeezed the trigger, sending a bullet into the wall. Struggling to wrest herself from her assailant's grip and keep hold of the gun, she shot several rounds into the room. One of the arms around her loosened, then a hand darted out and knocked the gun from her grip. Hatcher's nasal voice came from just behind her ear. "What the hell do you think you're doing?"

She struggled and loosened his hold enough to plant an elbow in his stomach. Hatcher gasped and released his grip. Backing up to the far wall, Jen searched for the gun. "I'm keeping my promise to my dad and you're not going to stop me."

Hatcher stood, bent over, at the doorway. The gun lay on the floor just to his right. He scooped it up and pointed it at her. Still doubled over, he said, "I told you he's government property."

"What are you going to do with him? You're leaving him anyway. Let me put him to rest."

He shook his head. "We may be back. We may find we need him. I won't be responsible for losing a government resource."

Angry tears stung her eyes. "I'm keeping my promise." She rushed him and rammed him in the chest, sending him stumbling backward. His arms windmilled, but he overcompensated and fell back into Jen's father, who clamped his teeth on Hatcher's neck and tore off a mangled piece of flesh. Blood pumped from the wound in time with his heartbeat, and he slid to the floor.

"Help." He sat, propped against her father's legs, his eyes wide with fear.

His hands were empty, so Jen searched the room and found the pistol under a desk. She picked it up and took position in the doorway again. Her father chewed and swallowed his meal. His yellow eyes were unfocused, giving the appearance of ecstasy. Jen aimed at his forehead. *This is for you, Dad.* Her hands steady, she squeezed the trigger. The pistol pushed back into her palm. A hole appeared in her father's head, and the back of his head exploded, painting the table and wall behind him in a crimson spray. His head fell forward and he was still.

Jen closed her eyes. Tears welled and trickled down her cheeks. "Good-bye, Dad. Your pain is over."

A gurgling sound came from Hatcher. She glared down at him. His eyes half-closed, he croaked, "Me, too. Please. Don't want to be like them."

Jen lowered the pistol. "Sorry, Hatcher, but you're government property now."

She took a step back into the hallway. Hatcher gaped and struggled to speak, but only gasps and croaks came out.

Shit. I can't do it.

Jen squatted in front of Hatcher and placed the gun to his forehead. "I'll show you the mercy you tried to deny my father."

Hatcher closed his eyes and she squeezed the trigger.

Click.

Empty. Hatcher's eyes popped open, pleading, while he gurgled and coughed.

Jen bit her lower lip. In such a hurry to take care of her dad, she'd grabbed the gun and forgotten to take any extra ammo.

The alarm went off again. They were leaving. *It's now or never.*

Hatcher went silent, and his head dropped to his chest. Jen left the room and closed the door. Hatcher would reanimate soon.

She took one last look at her father and ran to the elevator, wiping her eyes.

9

When Jen stepped out of the elevator on the first floor Mark stood with his arms crossed, a frown on his face. "Just in time. I was gonna go look for you. Did anyone else hear the shot?"

Jen shook her head. "No one else on the floor."

"Good." He handed her two boxes of ammo and guided her to where Doc and Captain Lupone stood.

"Ah," Doc said. "There we are. Time to load up. Y'all are riding with me."

Lupone spoke into a radio. "Commence loading. Perimeter watch, keep your eyes peeled and report if you see anything. Even if it's only one zulu."

"Anyone seen Hatcher?" Doc asked.

Jen's heart skipped a beat. "He's on his way. Said he had to take care of something and it'll only be a minute."

"Fine." Doc grinned. "He's been assigned a seat in the bus. At the back."

Lupone opened the door and held it. "Dr. Wilson, you and your group have the first SUV."

Jen kept her empty pistol in her hand and followed Doc and Mark out the door. She tried not to look down as she crossed the threshold, but couldn't help herself. She stepped over the dried blood and bits of flesh, but stumbled as she nearly stepped on the brown-stained baby blanket.

Bile rose in the back of her throat and she swallowed it back down. *No time for that. Shit is getting real.*

She and Mark climbed into the back of the SUV, while Doc sat in the front next to the soldier at the wheel, who turned to look at each of them. "Welcome aboard. I'm Specialist Grant. My orders are to get you safely to your plane at JBER."

Doc shook his hand. "Dr. Wilson, but please call me Doc."

Grant looked back. Mark put his hand up. "I'm Mark."

Grant's gaze swept to Jen. He looked like a kid dressed up to play Army. *What is he, twelve?* "I'm Jen. Where are you from, Specialist Grant?"

"Kodiak."

Jen hadn't thought much about anywhere else in Alaska. The kid had to be worried about his family. "Any word on how they're doing?"

Grant shook his head. "Nothing for a few days. They had a few zombies pop up when I was last able to check in, and they kept ahead of them. But who knows now? It didn't take long for Anchorage to become infested."

Jen nodded. Infested was an interesting word choice. She took out empty magazines and loaded them. "I hope they're doing OK."

"I'm heading out on that plane with you. Then I plan on finding a way back home."

Doc smiled. "Now that's the spirit. I truly like a positive attitude."

The radio squawked. "This is Captain Lupone. From now on, I'll be addressed by my call sign Whiskey One. That's the lead Humvee. Whiskey Two is the Humvee that will take up the rear of the convoy. Both Humvees are armed with Mark 19 forty millimeter auto grenade launchers. They'll clear the way if we run into a horde."

"Grant, have you used those grenade launchers yet?" Jen pushed a magazine into her pistol and jacked a round into the chamber.

He smiled, and his eyes glistened in the light. "We took out a horde of over a hundred just outside Girdwood. It was a hell of a battle and was over in a couple of minutes."

Mark nodded at Jen. "What are you thinking?"

Jen frowned. "Girdwood's isolated down the highway and has a population of less than two thousand."

"So, what's your point?" Grant snapped.

Someone's a little touchy. "So if you get a horde of a hundred from a population of two thousand, then with Anchorage's population, the equivalent would be about fifteen thousand. Something tells me those grenade launchers won't be too effective against something like that."

Grant scowled and faced forward. "Captain Lupone knows what he's doing. I served a tour in the Middle East with him and he got the whole unit home safe. My money's on him."

Jen shrugged. "Just saying."

Mark gave her a sideways glance. *He hasn't experienced a swarm, but I'll bet his convoy experience is setting his radar off about now.*

Lupone spoke again. "The first SUV with Dr. Wilson in it is designated Bravo One, while the other is Bravo Two."

Another voice came over the radio. "Sir, what's the designation of the bus?"

"Bus," Lupone deadpanned.

Grant laughed. "That's how the captain is, serious when the situation needs it, but he's one of us."

"Let's move out," Lupone said.

The vehicles started and the convoy rolled onto the Old Seward Highway.

Jen's pulse quickened. She scanned the abandoned cars and silent buildings. No sign of zombies.

Vibrations from the Humvee in front of them traveled through the SUV. *Damn thing is loud, and there's two of them.* "I don't think this will work."

"Huh?" Grant said. "What are you talking about?"

"The vehicles, especially those Humvees, make too much noise. Noise attracts the creatures. We'll never make it."

Grant shrugged. "Captain says we can do it, so we can."

He's just blowing me off. Asshole. "I'll bet Custer's men said the same thing."

Lupone's voice came over the radio. "Whiskey One to convoy. Our intent is to move at the fastest speed possible. From what we see up front, Old Seward is littered with abandoned vehicles, so our speed will be limited as we navigate around them. If this continues, we may cut over to the New Seward Highway."

Jen watched the scenery pass by. She guessed they were going no more than twenty-five miles per hour. All of the cars they passed were empty, some with doors left open, and some with blood spatters on the windows and finish.

"Whiskey Two to Whiskey One. We have zulus coming onto the road in the rear. Count three—no, four."

"Roger, Whiskey Two. Don't use the Mk on them. Have your gunner take them out with a rifle."

"Roger, Whiskey One."

Jen leaned up behind the driver's seat. "Can I talk on the radio?"

"Are you kidding?" Grant said.

"Then you talk. Tell them not to shoot."

"Why the hell not?"

Doc coughed. "I believe she's concerned that the noise will draw more zombies." He wiped his mouth with a handkerchief. "She's surely right."

Grant scoffed, picked up the mic, and keyed it. "Bravo One to Whiskey One. Dr. Wilson suggests we not fire. He says it will attract more zulus."

There was silence for a minute, then, "Whiskey One to Whiskey Two. You have your orders. Bravo One, tell Dr. Wilson that I appreciate his concern, but we have a time line to adhere to, and I'm confident we can handle more zulus."

Jen put her head in her hands. "Even if they don't swarm us, you'll run out of bullets before we get to the plane."

Grant chuckled. "You've never seen an Mk 19. Effective firing range is over fifteen hundred yards. We shot a few at Gridwood, then took the rest out with small arms fire."

Jen looked out the window. They were in the roundabout at Huffman Road. The businesses down Huffman were quiet, and only a few zombies stumbled around.

"Whiskey One to convoy. We have five Zulus ahead and the road is clearing up. We're going to pick up speed and run them down. How is the rear, Whiskey Two?"

"Whiskey Two to Whiskey One. "Threat neutralized."

Grant glanced over his shoulder. "See? What'd I tell you?"

The SUV picked up speed. Jen held onto the armrest. No way the trip would be that easy, just running over zombies like they were roadkill.

The SUV jumped and bounced. Jen didn't want to ask what they were running over.

"Woo hoo," Grant yelled. "Five more zulus down."

The bus's brake lights went hard red, and Jen was thrown against her seat belt as their SUV screeched to a stop. She glanced at Mark. His face had gone hard and his eyes kept moving. He leaned slightly forward as if ready to jump out at any time. *I don't want to know what memory he's reliving.*

Jen looked ahead, and all she saw was the fat-ass back of the bus. She pressed her head against the window, trying to see around it, but it was a waste of effort. She looked outside her window at an old video store parallel with the SUV. The single-story building had peeling paint and looked as if it might fall over in a strong wind. Its windows covered in old movie posters, it added to the eeriness of the day. She'd been there a couple of times with her mother when she was young, renting kids' movies. It was a dump back then, too.

A chorus of high-pitched shrieks came from ahead of them, beyond the bus. "Holy shit," Jen said. "There's got to be a ton of them."

"Whiskey One to convoy. We have a mob of zulus converging rapidly on our position from one o'clock. Estimate one hundred. We took out the same number in Girdwood, we'll do it again. Stay calm and stay in your vehicles. Whiskey One is deploying the Mk."

A *chunk, chunk, chunk* followed by *boom, boom, boom* came from ahead.

"More damn noise," she whispered to Mark.

Mark nodded, beads of sweat forming on his forehead. "This isn't going to end well."

Jen looked at the other buildings nearby. A warehouse with large open doors was the closest place to run to. *Too open.*

"Whiskey Two to Whiskey One. Zulus approaching the rear at a run."

"Whiskey One to Whiskey Two. How many?"

"Damn. Two, three hundred."

"Whiskey One to Whiskey Two. Deploy Mk. We cleared the hundred up here, but more are attacking. Whiskey One to convoy. Stay in your vehicles and keep them locked."

Jen grabbed Mark's arm. "We need to get the hell out of here. They're swarming."

Grant's head jerked around. "Didn't you hear the captain? We need to stay put."

Doc began to speak, but was cut off by a chorus of shrieks. They were coming not only from ahead and behind but also from the Huffman side to their right. The only open direction was toward the video store.

Jen threw the door open. "Follow me if you want to live."

10

J en sprinted across the road to the video store, pistol in hand. The door was nailed shut, and she yanked on it, but it wouldn't give.

A second set of hands grasped the handle. *Mark.*

They wrenched the door open a few feet and ducked into the building. Doc and Grant followed moments later.

Mark pulled the door shut.

Jen eyed Grant. "Thought you'd go down with the ship."

The soldier glared at her. "I'm not abandoning my post. My orders are to protect the three of you and get you to JBER. I can't do that if I'm not with you."

The zombie howls stopped, but the ground vibrated and the windows rattled. It sounded like a damn stampede. Jen put a finger to her lips and knelt behind the window, peeling back the corner of a movie poster.

The Whiskey One gunner continued to shoot grenades at the horde attacking from the front, keeping them back, but just barely. Whiskey Two did the same, but the sheer number attacking from the rear had the horde creeping closer.

A tidal wave of undead gushed out from between the buildings on the other side of the road, washing over the two SUVs and the bus. All three vehicles were toppled and covered with the zombies ripping at doors and windows. The screams of those trapped inside were muted, but clear.

The Whiskey One gunner glanced back and yelled something down to the Humvee crew. A mob of zombies climbed the back of the Humvee, and two of them pulled the gunner out and sank their teeth into his flesh while he screamed for help. He managed to rip an arm away and grab his pistol. Bellowing, he put it to his temple and pulled the trigger.

A skinny bare-chested teen zombie dove into the open gunner hatch, followed seconds later by two more. Gunshots rang out and muzzle flashes painted the inside of the hatch.

Whiskey Two had fared worse. The horde pushing in from the front had made it to the Humvee's hood when another wave attacked from the back. The gunner unloaded his pistol and tried to duck into the hatch, but a tall woman with a breast chewed off grabbed his head and pulled. The gunner held on and seemed to be winning the battle when two more undead grabbed his arms and jerked him out. The tall woman bit into his neck, sending a plume of blood over the horde.

The driver's door flung open. A soldier jumped out and raced toward the video store, but only made it ten feet before a mob of zombies tackled him and he disappeared beneath the feeding frenzy.

The undead rushed the open door. Gunfire erupted inside the vehicle, but bullets were ineffective against the mob. Within seconds, the gunfire had ceased.

Jen's heart raced. The whole damn convoy was gone.

A zombie streaked by an inch in front of her window. She dropped the poster corner and fell back. Did those monsters know they were in there?

Mark stood next to her, his face pale in the gloomy store. Doc had his arms crossed and mumbled to himself, while Grant turned away from the window, his hands closing and opening.

Jen waved to get their attention, then put a finger to her lips. They had to be quiet and stay out of sight. If the horde knew they were there, they'd bust down the shabby old store's walls in a heartbeat. She gestured for the others to follow her.

She led them to the lone back room and pulled the curtain over the entrance. A sliver of light shone from the top of a poster-covered window and provided enough light for her to know where each of the others stood. "We have to be quiet and wait for them to disperse," she whispered in the dark.

No one answered. *Good. They get it.*

Something banged into the wall next to her and she flinched. Other thumps came from around the building. So many zombies out there, they were walking into buildings.

Three hours after they'd hidden in the room, the thumps finally died off, and Jen dared hope the zombies had moved on.

SOMETHING BANGED into the front door. Jen held her breath and aimed her pistol at the curtain. The others tensed up too, but they all relaxed after another hour passed and they heard nothing else.

Grant whispered, "We'll stay here the night. Move out in the morning." He stood next to the curtain. "I'll keep watch."

Jen sat in a corner and leaned back. Hours passed, and the occasional growls stopped. The sun set and they were blanketed with darkness.

Exhaustion conquered fear, and Jen fell asleep.

11

Light filtered into the room, landing on the curtain. Awake the past few hours, Jen had kept her pistol pointed at the curtain.

Tilting her head, she listened. Nothing but the normal creaking of a piece of crap building.

Jen slid over to the curtain and pulled a corner of it aside. The store lay quiet and empty in the dingy light filtering in through the movie posters.

She stuck her head out and scanned the room, then padded between the rows of empty, dusty video display cases to the window she'd peeked out from the day before. She stepped on a loose board and it squeaked. Her pulse pounded in her ears, drowning out any slight noise.

Taking a deep breath, she eased her foot off the board and peeked outside. The vehicles stood silent and bloody, the Humvee doors open and the SUVs and bus lying on their sides with smashed and shattered windows. Dried blood stains streaked and spattered the asphalt.

She turned, and Mark stood beside her. "We should check the other windows," he said. "Don't want one of those things to pop out from around the corner."

Grant walked out of the room bleary-eyed and looked out a window on the far side, his M4 strapped over his shoulder. "Nothing here."

Doc joined them, peeled back a poster on another side, and let an array of sunlight hit the floor. He peered out. Shaking his head, he looked back at Mark. "Nothing here either."

Grant had his hand on the front door. "Wait," Jen said. He paused.

She continued, "They seem to detect us by either sight or sound. So stay under as much cover you can, and for crying out loud keep quiet."

"One other thing," Mark said. "Guns are a last resort. If we run into any zombies, we need to try to take them out without firing a shot."

Grant scoffed. "So we're supposed to box them?"

Jen glared at Grant. "You shoot when you don't have to and you'll bring a swarm down on us. Or maybe you'd like to go it alone?"

"A sound tactic, indeed," Doc said.

"That's OK," Grant said. "Mark and I can knock their skulls in with our rifle butts." He winked at Jen. "We'll protect you."

Jen propped her hands on her hips. "I've had more than one of these things on top of me, nasty breath and all, and I've survived. How close have you been?"

Grant mumbled, "Just saying."

He eased the door open and stepped out of the building. Jen followed, then waited for Mark and Doc. The sun blazed and she had to cover her eyes to see through the glare. Nothing came charging at her. *So far, so good.*

Hunched over, Grant slowly stalked toward the lead Humvee, each foot carefully placed onto the gravel in front of the other.

Jen mimicked his movements. Although she made more noise than him, she surprised herself with how quiet she moved.

Grant reached the open driver's door and pulled his rifle off his shoulder. He leaned inside and checked the interior. His nose wrinkled, then he coughed, turned away, and puked on the ground.

I remember the first time I smelled death, not so long ago. Jen patted him on the back. "Deep breaths."

He straightened and inhaled. "I saw some things in Afghanistan, but nothing like that." He coughed. "And that smell."

Jen ducked her head into the Humvee. By the looks of it, the interior could've been painted rusty brown. The smell hit her: the death smell she'd first whiffed in the pit by Fear Mountain. It reminded her of the time her freezer went out while she was on vacation. Two weeks the meat had sat in there, and when she got home and opened it the smell knocked her over.

She backed away from the vehicle and the cloud of flies that hovered over it. "No bodies, just a lot of blood."

"Any weapons?" Mark asked.

She shook her head. "Didn't see any. Of course if they were covered in blood, I might've missed them."

Grant had regained some of his color. "I need to call and check in," he said. "The walkies we have won't reach JBER, but the radios in the Humvees will."

He leaned into the driver side and ducked back out with the radio mic in his hand. He keyed it.

"Whiskey One to Command One. Do you read me?"

Soft static buzzed from the Humvee's speakers. Grant reached in. "Need to turn it up a little and try another channel."

He straightened and brought the mic to his face. "Whiskey One to Command One. Do you read?"

A voice blasted over the speakers. "Whiskey One, this is Command One. Where the hell are you?"

Grant scrambled headfirst into the Humvee, while Jen cringed and pressed herself against the side of the vehicle, expecting to hear a chorus of shrieks at any second. Mark raised his rifle and took a shooter's stance, while Doc's eyes grew big and he froze in place.

No shrieks came.

Grant stepped back. "Damn volume was up too high."

Jen frowned. "What was your first clue?"

The voice came from the radio. "Command One to Whiskey One. This is Colonel Butler. What is your location?"

"Two miles north of the labs," Grant said.

"Repeat, Whiskey One. It sounded like you said two miles from where you started."

"That is correct, Command One. Two miles north."

"What is your sit rep, Whiskey One?"

"We were attacked by a swarm. Four survivors. I'm the only military member left."

The radio went silent.

Doc tilted his head and leaned toward the Humvee door. "Is the radio still on?"

As if to answer him the voice came back over the radio. "Please confirm.

Is Dr. Wilson one of the survivors?"

"Roger."

"Whiskey One, is Captain Lupone KIA?"

"Roger. This is Specialist Grant. Myself, Dr. Wilson, Mark Colton, and Jen Reed are the only survivors."

"Whiskey One, your mission is to escort Dr. Wilson safely to the flight line at JBER. The last C-130 is standing by to transport him to Fairchild Air Force Base."

Doc put his hand out, and Grant gave him the mic. "This is Dr. Wilson. I trust there's room on the plane for the rest of my group."

"Affirmative."

He handed it back to Grant.

Jen nudged Mark. "I guess he's our golden ticket."

Mark smiled.

Grant keyed the mic. "Whiskey One to Command One, any chance of getting a chopper?"

"Negative, Whiskey One. The base has been evacuated and the only asset remaining is the C-130."

Grant spit on the ground. "Fucking great."

"Command One to Whiskey One, cell phone coverage is spotty in the Anchorage Bowl. Some towers are operating on backup and some are inoperative. You are expected to call in with your sitrep every hour if you have a signal. Use command cell number Whiskey Tango Foxtrot."

Grant sighed. "Copy. Out."

"Good luck, Whiskey One."

Grant tossed the mic on the driver's seat. "Yeah, good luck."

Jen glanced up and down the road. "We've been lucky so far, standing out here in the open. Better get a move on."

"We should scavenge the vehicles for supplies, weapons, and ammo before we go," Mark said.

Grant puffed his cheeks and blew out a breath. "Can someone else take the Humvees? Don't think I can do them. Those were all my buddies."

Doc put a hand on his shoulder. "I'll take this one."

"I'll take the rear one," Jen said.

"Looks like Grant and I have the bus and SUVs," Mark said.

Jen walked with Mark and Grant as far as the bus, her eyes moving, looking for any sign of zombies. "I really don't like being out in the open like this."

"We're right here if you need us," Mark said. He and Grant climbed onto the bus.

Jen approached the SUVs in a crouch. *Don't want one of those things popping out at me like a jack-in-the-box.*

She kept the pistol pointed forward and checked each of the SUVs before passing them. Except for a ringed finger on the dashboard of the second SUV, all that remained was blood and weapons.

The Humvee stood silent, its open doors seeming to beckon her. She paused and scanned the surrounding area again, but there were no signs of movement. Doc's feet hung out of the other Humvee's door and Mark and Grant looked to be halfway through their sweep of the bus.

Leaning in and kneeling on the driver's seat, she pointed her pistol at the rear of the vehicle and swept it with her gaze. Empty. While there were splashes of blood and a pile of entrails on the front passenger floorboard that had already drawn flies, the interior wasn't as bad as the first Humvee's. A couple of rifles lay in the back.

Something yanked her left ankle and she went down, her forehead slamming into the center console. She lost her grip on her pistol and it fell onto the driver's floorboard. Fighting the motes swimming in her eyes, she grabbed for the gun, but was jerked clear out of the vehicle. She landed chest down on the asphalt just before her attacker let out a shrill zombie shriek.

12

Jen rolled over and pushed herself into a sitting position. A soldier with the nametag Williams, stood over her, half his face missing and an eyeball hanging out.

Jen scrambled back against the open Humvee door. "Mark!"

A chorus of muted shrieks came from somewhere behind her. *Shit.*

Still wobbly, she pulled her feet in, but was too slow. Williams grabbed her foot.

"Mark!"

Where the hell is he?

She lashed out with her free foot, connecting with Williams' jaw and splattering blood and drool over herself. He released her and stumbled backward, but lurched at her again. Feeling around on the Humvee's floorboard with one hand, Jen kicked at Williams again and missed. The chorus of shrieks became louder.

"Mark!" She screamed as loud as she could. She had to get the hell out of there. *Did they leave me?*

Her scrambling hand touched the barrel of her pistol. She felt down to the grip and grasped it just as Williams jerked on her ankles again and pulled her away from the vehicle. Her shirt had come up and her bare back screamed from being dragged across the asphalt, but she brought the pistol around to aim at Williams' face. His yellow eyes locked on hers and a saliva-and-blood mix drooled out the ruined side of his mouth as he bent over her. *Gawd. His breath.*

"Do you kiss your mother with that mouth?" Jen squeezed the trigger, smiling at the satisfying kick and the way Williams' nose disappeared. The screeches sounded again.

She pulled herself up using the Humvee's door and shook her head to clear the fog. *No time to screw around.*

Mark was the first to get to her. "What happened? Why'd you fire?"

Jen gestured at Williams. "Guess he didn't want to leave his post. Where the hell were you while I was getting groped by zombie GI Joe? I called for help."

Grant ran up and almost tripped over Williams. "Shit." He looked away. "We were pulling supplies out of the back of the SUV and didn't see what was going on."

"We've got to get back to the video store and hide," Jen said.

Mark looped her arm over his shoulder and she shook him off. "I'm good."

Mark frowned, but said nothing.

"Grant." Jen hitched a thumb over her shoulder at the Humvee. "There's at least one rifle in there. Grab any you find and don't forget ammo."

Grant jumped into the Humvee while Doc jogged over to them. "As much as I'm a proponent of staying calm, I'd prefer to see a tad more urgency."

Still a bit dizzy, Jen jogged to the video store with Doc at her side and paused at the doorway. Grant exited the Humvee with two more rifles and handed one to Mark.

A zombie with a half-eaten leg limped into view between the two SUVs and screeched. The answering calls come without a pause.

"They're almost on top of us," Jen said.

Grant raised his rifle and aimed at the zombie. "I've got it."

Mark pushed the barrel down. "No time. We've got to leave this area."

"What do you mean?" Grant asked.

Mark pointed to the lead Humvee. Another slow zombie limped into view. "These were probably the ones too slow to get far away after the last swarm."

Jen checked the road for more. "Mark's right. If these things see us go into the store, we're toast. Who knows how many are coming? Our best chance is to outrun those two and hide. Follow me."

She jogged behind the store and into the trees. Her head had almost cleared. Just out of sight of the road, she waited until the others had caught up. Mark handed her his extra rifle and Grant shoved another into Doc's hands, then pushed past her. "Follow me," he said.

"Why you?" Jen asked.

"I'm trained. I'm the only military person here."

"We don't have time for this shit," Mark said. "We need to put some distance between us and them. Jen, get us out of here."

Jen nodded. She pushed through the trees and tall grass, trying to not make noise, but it was hopeless. They sounded like a stampede.

The screeches faded a bit behind them, but growls came from ahead. She stopped and held up her hand. The others froze.

The growling sounds came closer, and Jen ducked into some brush, signaling the others to do the same. Ten seconds later, two zombies rustled through the undergrowth, heading in the direction of the convoy.

A minute passed. Then two. Mark looked at her and shrugged. She stood and whispered, "Need to be quieter or we won't hear them."

Doc gave her a thumbs-up, and Mark nodded. Grant looked at her, but didn't react. *Guess who's going to be a pain in the ass?*

She led them through the foliage and stopped when it ended at a set of railroad tracks. "Which way?" Doc asked.

Jen closed her eyes and pictured a map of Anchorage in her mind. "The tracks run north and south, so going north will take us in the right direction. The tracks are mostly out of sight of the roads." She added, "I think."

She leaned out from the trees and peered up and down the track. Nothing moving. "But we can at least follow them for now. We just need to stay near the trees so we can take cover if we spot any trouble."

She stepped out of the brush.

Grant frowned. "Who put you in charge?"

Jen sighed. *Not again.* "Are you from Anchorage?"

"Kodiak," Grant said.

"Then maybe Jen's the right person to lead us since she knows the city," Mark said.

Grant frowned. "But I'm the authority here. I'm a solider. I know tactics."

Jen crossed her arms. "How many zombies have you fought?"

Grant looked away. "None."

"Then I think we should let Jen lead, son," Doc said. "We're wasting time here."

Grant kept his mouth shut.

We need him, so take it easy, Jen. Don't say something smartass and piss him off more. "We can't do this without you, Grant," she said.

Grant adjusted the rifle in his arms. "I'm good. Let's go."

"We can't keep using guns," Mark said. "We need weapons that don't make noise and bring swarms."

"Melee weapons," Grant added.

"Right," Mark said. "Melee weapons. Car jacks, bats, anything that can bash a head."

Jen smiled. "Just so happens these tracks run behind one of those big box hardware stores. Think we can find what you want in there?"

"Now you're talking," Mark said.

Grant stood off by himself, not saying anything. Jen walked over to him. "How do you think we should travel down the tracks?"

Grant straightened, his features hard. "Single file. Makes a smaller profile. I'll take point. The rear guard needs to keep an eye behind us." He nodded at Mark. "How about you?"

Mark shot Jen an amused look. "Happy to take the rear."

"Good," Grant said. "Jen, you're behind me since you know the city. Doc is behind her."

They followed the tracks, pausing at every muffled screech or branch snap, but they remained unseen. Thirty minutes later, Grant raised his hand and they came to a halt. He took a knee and gestured for everyone to join him. "The trees are thinning out up ahead."

Jen knelt next to Grant. The back of a strip mall peeked through a break in the trees. "The hardware store is next to a strip mall. I think that's the one."

Mark took a couple of steps toward the track and craned his neck. "Our concealment thins out quite a bit before we get to the store, but there's a train wreck on the tracks that will give us some cover—"

Grant stood. "Follow my lead." He crept forward.

Jen and Mark exchanged a glance. When was Mark going to let Grant know who the real soldier in the group was?

They crept to the edge of the trees. A few zombies wandered on the far side of the parking lot, too far away to be attracted by anything but a loud noise.

"Only ten yards to that wreckage," Doc said. "Best we get going."

Grant nodded. "I'll go first."

"Can we quit playing G.I. Joe and just all go?" Jen asked.

"That's not standard procedure," Grant said. "You have no idea what—"

Jen sprinted to the train. She didn't look back to see if the others were coming and didn't really give a shit.

Reaching the train, she pressed her back against it. Mark and Doc darted across the open space, with Grant on their heels.

"Dammit, Jen," Grant said when he arrived. "This isn't a fucking game. I'm OK with you taking charge when it comes to navigating the city, but I'm more qualified in combat."

Jen opened her mouth to reply, but caught Mark's expression. He gave her a slight shake of his head.

I'll bet he doesn't want me spilling the beans on him. Nodding, Jen said, "OK. What do we do next?"

Grant peered around the wreckage, toward the back of the store. "We'll go in the same order as we did on the tracks."

He led them past the wreckage and through a broken section of fence. The loading dock's overhead door stood open like a giant mouth. They stopped in front of it.

"Can't say it looks welcoming," Doc said.

Grant pulled a flashlight from his belt and turned it on. "Anyone else have one?" The others shook their heads.

"That's the first thing we should find," Mark said. "That, and batteries."

Jen nodded at Grant. "Looks like you're still the lead."

Grant shouldered his rifle and took out his pistol. Shining the light into the loading bay, he swept the beam from one side to the other. "All clear. Stay close."

He led them between stacked boxes and a forklift to a door. Looking back to the others, he shined the light on his face and put a finger to his lips.

The door opened outward without making a sound. The light shined up and down the back aisle. Nothing stirred, undead or alive.

Grant led them down the aisle that lay in front of them, its shelves stacked with cables and electrical gear. He swung the light back and forth in front of him. Jen clasped him on the shoulder and he stopped. "Back to the right," she whispered.

The beam swung to the right and rested on a display of flashlights next to a rack of batteries.

Jen took three flashlights and handed one each to Mark and Doc, then gave them each batteries. Loading her flashlight, she strained to hear anything in the huge store, but it remained quiet. She turned the flashlight on. *Perfect.*

Grant crept down to the main aisle. Jen joined him, and her beam lit up a large poster at the end of the aisle they'd just left. It had a guy in overalls carrying lumber on his shoulder and looking happy about it. *Like hauling wood is fun.* Mark and Doc joined them, and four beams of light moved across shelves and displays.

Jen whispered, "How about the gardening section?"

Mark nodded and Doc gave a thumbs up. Grant led the way down the main aisle, with Jen pointing her light down each side aisle they passed. Damn place was as dead as a morgue.

Something hit the floor and bounced twice. They all stopped. With the echoing, Jen couldn't tell the exact direction it came from. She tilted her head, listening over the pulse pounding in her ears.

A bang came from an aisle two or three rows ahead. All the flashlights pointed that way.

"I believe that discretion is the better part of valor," Doc whispered. "I suggest we take our leave."

Grant took a couple steps forward and shined his light down the next aisle. "No growls. No screeches. Let's get what we came for." He pointed his beam at the end of the next aisle, which was labeled Garden Equipment.

Jen liked Doc's idea, but she wasn't going to leave anyone on their own. She readied her pistol and took position beside Grant at the same time Mark and Doc did. Together they crept to the Garden Equipment aisle.

Pointing their flashlights down it at the same time, they lit up a half dozen milling zombies, who turned as one and let loose with a screech that bounced off the floor and ceiling. The whole bunch raced toward Jen and the others.

"We've got to get out of here," Jen yelled. "Back the way we came."

Screeches rose from every direction. They'd walked into a hornet's nest.

13

Jen aimed at the lead zombie, a bearded guy in a ripped flannel shirt heading straight for Grant. A squeeze of the trigger and a solid kickback and the zombie went down, his momentum sliding him across the floor to stop just in front of Grant. Grant shook off his shock and aimed his pistol at the group of zombies. Other shots went off, and the zombies in the aisle were dropped before they could reach them.

"Follow me," Jen yelled. She pointed her flashlight down the main aisle they'd come down. Several zombies rushed toward her and were eliminated by the group.

Growls came from behind her. Mark yelled over them. "Five more on our asses."

Jen turned and took out two of them. More growling came from all sides. "There's a shit-load more in here. We can't stay and fight."

Doc fired over Jen's shoulder. "Damn, Doc. My ear." She didn't hear his reply.

Jen spun and lined up her sights on an old lady zombie who came at her so slowly that Jen almost felt sorry for her. She took off half the back of her skull with a shot.

The way back was clear. She grabbed Doc by the arm and pulled him along. "Go."

Jen shined her light down aisles as they passed. The first two were empty, but the next one had a mob of zombies heading up it. She didn't take the time to fire.

Grant took position in front of her. "Where the hell is the aisle that leads to the door? Anyone remember?"

Mark fired to the rear. "I think it was aisle fourteen."

"No," Grant yelled. "It was a single digit aisle."

Jen pointed her light at the end display of each aisle they came to. *Must've passed it. Couldn't have been this far away.*

Two aisles down, she caught the grinning face of the guy in the overalls. "Aisle ten," she yelled. "Take it."

Mark made several rapid shots. Jen glanced over her shoulder. The main aisle overflowed with undead.

"Are you sure that's the right way?" Grant asked.

With no time to answer him, Jen dashed around the corner to aisle ten, then stopped short. Another mob of zombies stood in front of the door leading to outside. Her flashlight beam hit them and they screeched, then ran, limped, and hobbled toward her. There had to be twenty of them.

Holding the flashlight pointed at them with one hand, she lined up her sights on the lead zombie and dropped it with one shot. *Too many. Too fast.*

She aimed and squeezed the trigger again, but it wouldn't move. "Shit." The magazine was empty. She hit the eject button, stuck the flashlight under her arm, and pulled another magazine from her front pocket. She slapped it in, released the bolt, and fired.

More of the zombies fell as Grant and Doc stood alongside her. Someone backed into her and Mark yelled, "We're about thirty seconds from being overrun in the rear. There's at least a hundred of them closing in."

Half the zombies in front of the door were down. Jen holstered her pistol and pulled the rifle from her shoulder. "We've got to push through. Follow me!"

She sprinted toward the zombies, holding her rifle with both hands, ready to strike. Another fell when its head exploded, leaving a twenty-something girl zombie in her path.

The zombie ran at her full tilt, and Jen held the rifle so the butt faced outward. As soon as the zombie leapt at her, Jen cocked the gun back and slammed it into the girl's face.

The zombie went down, but wasn't out. Didn't matter. Jen sidestepped it and aimed the butt at the ear of a middle-aged man in white painter's overalls. He grabbed her arm as she got close, but lost his grip when the rifle butt slammed home.

Grant leapt in front of her and took out another zombie with some fancy close quarters rifle work. *Damn, he's good.*

Doc hit one in the shoulder, knocking it off balance. Jen bull-rushed it and took it to the floor.

She scrambled to her feet and glanced over her shoulder. Mark still faced the rear and launched a constant barrage at the horde behind them at the entrance to aisle ten. They were running out of time.

Four zombies remained between them and escape. Jen launched herself at one and pushed it back into a light bulb display. It tripped and flipped over onto its stomach.

She twirled and brought the rifle butt crashing down on another zombie's nose. It crumpled. Doc struggled with one remaining zombie, and Grant shot it through the forehead.

"Way's clear," Jen yelled. She pulled the door open and prayed there weren't any outside waiting for them.

Mark sent a fusillade of bullets at the incoming zombies, grabbed Doc by the collar, and yanked him through the door. Grant followed, and Jen jumped through, pulling the door shut.

Undead fists pounded on the door. Jen stood, bent over with her hands on her knees, and panted. Mark put a hand on her shoulder. "We should go. I don't think they can get through that door, but there's been a whole lot of things happening lately that I would've thought impossible."

Jen nodded and straightened. Grant led them back through the loading dock and to the train cars. "Let's take ten," he said. "Need to figure where we're going from here."

Jen sat on the ground. "Grant."

He turned to her. "Yeah?"

"You kicked some ass in there."

He nodded at her. "And you're a nut. You ran right at those zombies." He grinned. "You'd make a good soldier."

She shook her head. "No, thanks. I just want to get somewhere normal. Get back to the internet, lattes, and hiking in the mountains without a corpse trying to eat me."

Doc patted her on the back. "If you hadn't rushed the zombies, we wouldn't have made it out. Sometimes crazy is the only thing we have."

"How about you, Doc?" Mark said. "This is a little more strenuous than what you're used to."

Doc wiped his forehead with the back of his hand. "I may work in a lab, but I run a half marathon once a year. Don't worry about me."

Grant walked out from the train cars and peered up and down the track. "Better take this chance to reload. How's everyone's ammo?"

Jen checked her pistol. "Two more magazines for the pistol. Haven't touched the rifle."

"I'm low on rifle rounds," Mark said. Jen tossed him a full magazine and he caught it. "Thanks."

Grant frowned. "We can't take many more situations like that or we'll be without ammo before we get halfway to the base."

"And we still need the close-combat weapons," Mark said. "The rifles are better than nothing, but not by much."

Jen put her head in her hands. There wasn't another hardware store in the direction of the base for miles, and she didn't want to veer off course if she didn't have to.

"Jen?" Doc said. "Any ideas?"

Jen took a deep breath and eased it out, puffing her cheeks. It would have to be some place other than a hardware store, but where?

She stood and glanced up the tracks. The tracks went north across 100th Avenue then on to Dimond Boulevard, where they crossed it on a bridge. Plenty of stores along the way, including a mall, but no hardware.

That's it. She turned to the others. "I know exactly where we can find the weapons we need."

14

Thirty minutes later, Jen lay on her stomach across the train tracks, scoping out the mall. Big and multilevel, it stood like a silent monument to the old world.

Packs of zombies gathered at every entrance visible, except one. But to get to that door, they'd have to cross the huge parking lot without being seen.

Next to her, Mark pointed to a double line of campers. "Looks like the dealer had a sale going on when the shit hit the fan. We can get halfway to the entrance without being seen if we use them as cover. Just go in between the rows."

Jen bit her lip. Groups of three to twenty zombies wandered through the parking lot. She watched them, trying to predict their routes, but they'd turn at random, sometimes doubling back the way they'd come. "There are a couple hundred of them that are visible. Who knows how many are on the sides of the mall we can't see."

"I don't know if it's worth the risk," Grant said.

Jen had always been good at maze puzzles, but none of them had pieces that moved. This looked more like a 1980's arcade game. "It's worth the risk, unless you want to go miles and hours out of the way, and maybe find there's a worse situation when we get there."

"You never did say what store we're going to," Grant said. "How do we know if it's worth it?"

She eyed Grant. He was no dummy. She'd be asking the same question. She squelched the urge to say "trust me" since she didn't trust him just yet, either. So far he'd shown up and fought when he was supposed to, but the stakes were too high to take any chances.

"It's worth it," she said. "Besides, I see an easier way in."

Grant frowned, looking out over the parking lot. "Where?"

She pointed to the RVs. "We follow Mark's suggestion of the campers. That gets us halfway. But there's no route the rest of the way that doesn't expose us at some point." She pointed to a row of Armed Forces Recruiter vehicles. "Twenty feet from the RVs to those. We can use them as cover, which will leave us twenty feet in the open to get to the door."

"I don't know how they don't see us then," Doc said.

Jen shrugged. "Then I guess it's a good thing you trained for those marathons."

"What if the doors are locked?" Mark asked.

"What?" Jen asked.

He got up on one elbow. "The doors. What if we run, attract all that attention and bring a horde down on us, and the mall door is locked? Then we're trapped."

Shit.

Grant snorted. "Yeah. Just what I thought. Look at her. She hadn't thought of it. Would've led us into a trap. Why don't you just let me make the tactical decisions? I'm trained for it."

Mark glared at him. "We don't need your macho bullshit right now, Mr. Communications Specialist. Her idea's still good, we just have to assess the risk."

"Assess the risk? And why the hell do you think you have room to talk? You're just a rent-a-cop."

Mark's face turned red, and Jen hoped he'd blow up at Grant, maybe even kick his ass. But he took a deep breath and the red disappeared from his face.

"Yeah, that's what I thought," Grant said.

Doc cleared his throat. "Let's look at this logically. We need close-combat weapons or we have to use the firearms and draw more swarms. If we survive that, we'll be out of ammo before you know it. If we have to go somewhere else to find the weapons, that increases the risk we'll run into just that situation, plus it's taking precious time we don't have."

"I don't remember the colonel saying we have a time limit," Grant said.

Doc cleaned his glasses with his shirttail. "They left behind one plane with its crew and some support. They can't guard the whole base, so they probably have a perimeter around the flight line. Even then, they're stretched thin. How long do you think they can hold it?"

Grant pounded a fist into the ground. "Shit."

Jen slid back until she was in a depression behind the tracks and stood. "So I guess that means we go in. Right, Mr. Tactical Decision?"

Grant mumbled something under his breath as he crawled back to the depression with the others. "Everyone check your gear and your ammo. Make sure you're ready for anything."

"Firearms are a last resort," Mark said.

Jen double-checked her pistol and stuck it in her belt, then pulled the magazine out of the rifle. Full. She slid the bolt back enough to see the chambered round. *Ready.*

Her heart rate picked up and she rubbed her sweaty palms on her pants. Every encounter with zombies had given them something new to deal with. *What the hell will this one bring?*

"Here we go." Grant slipped over the tracks and down into the parking lot. Jen followed and joined him behind a shiny new Chevy pickup. Doc slid in next to her, with Mark bringing up the rear.

Grant crept forward to the edge of the truck. Jen peeked over the truck bed. The closest zombies she saw were at least thirty yards away. *What about the ones I can't see?*

Grant ducked and ran past two more vehicles and stopped beside a monster RV. Damn thing was bigger than some houses. He signaled Jen to follow.

She sprinted for the RV, her eyes on Grant as he moved to the front of it. Panting, she took a knee behind the rear of the vehicle. She shouldn't have been so winded from such a short run. *Must be adrenaline. Or fear.*

She waited for Grant to signal an all clear, then waved Doc in, and then Mark. They gathered at Grant's position.

"So far, so good," Doc said.

Grant pointed down the line of RVs. "It's clear ahead and we have cover to the sides."

He stood and walked between the lines of RVs. Jen followed, but moved cautiously, checking underneath the vehicles and in the small gaps between them. It'd been too easy so far, just like in the hardware store, and that had gone to shit.

She reached the end of the lines of RVs and took a deep breath. Her mouth had gone dry and her gut ached. *How do soldiers in combat do this time after time?*

Grant turned back to the others. "There's a group of a dozen zekes about two hundred yards to the right and another twenty about twice that distance to the left."

"Zekes?" Jen scrunched her nose. "This isn't a damn video game. Next thing you know, you'll be talking about distances in clicks."

Grant ignored her. "The recruiter vehicles are almost straight ahead, just to the right."

Jen edged to the end of the RV and peered left and right.

"What the hell are you doing?" Grant asked, raising his voice.

Jen turned to him and put a finger to her lips. "Keep it down. I was just taking a look for myself, no need to come unglued."

"You don't trust my judgment?" Grant stuck his chin out.

"Enough." Mark got between them. "We don't have to like each other, but we need to cooperate to survive."

Grant pushed on Mark's chest. "I don't need you to—"

Mark grabbed Grant's hand and put it in a lock. The specialist's eyes got big. "Don't," he said.

"Doesn't hurt yet, does it?" Mark asked. "But you can feel the tension in the joint."

Grant nodded.

"We've got a problem," Doc said.

Jen looked in the direction he pointed. A zombie stood in the doorway of an RV two vehicles back.

Mark let go of Grant. The zombie shuffled out of the RV and wandered in the other direction. Jen started to breathe again. *That was close.*

Mark's stiff posture loosened, and even Doc looked relieved. The experience was testing his chill factor.

The zombie reached the end of the RVs and stopped. It wandered to the vehicle across from it, then turned toward them.

Oh, shit.

It walked closer, then turned again.

If we get out of this, I'll never call myself unlucky again.

The zombie stopped cold. Its head cocked as if listening for something. Doc's eyes watered and he held his mouth closed tightly. What the hell was wrong with him?

He sniffed, then sniffed again and put his face in the crook of his elbow before letting out a quiet snort. *He's trying to hold in a sneeze. Are you shitting me?*

The zombie turned around and its yellow eyes locked on Doc. It faced the sky and let out a screech.

Answering calls came from across the parking lot, some distant and others much closer.

"We need to go back," Grant said. "I can take out this one."

Jen grabbed his arm. "No, we go forward. To the mall. We go back with them all chasing us and there's no place to hide."

"I say we go back," Grant yelled.

Jen and Mark exchanged a glance. "Oh, no, not again," Mark said.

Jen spun and sprinted for the mall door.

15

The screeching grew louder, almost an angry roar, as she ran from behind the cover. A group of about thirty zombies on her left were in a full run, heading for her. She glanced to her right. Another dozen ran at her from that side. She did a double take. Two of the zombies, both younger men, had broken off from the group and streaked toward the mall door. *What the hell? If I didn't know better, I'd say they're trying to cut me off.*

She didn't dare look behind her to see if the others were coming. If they weren't, then at the very least she'd distracted the zombies so they could get away. Either way, she had to get through that door.

She passed an old SUV and a zombie slammed against the window from the inside, startling the shit out of her. It slowed her for a second. *Damn.* She needed all the time she could get.

Most of the zombies changed direction and headed behind her. That meant someone else followed her. *Good old Mark.*

Coming to the end of the parking row, Jen checked the zombies on her left. They'd closed the distance on her, but she'd still make it to the door before them. Barely.

She made sure there were no obstacles in front of her as she ran, then glanced behind her. Doc was only ten feet back, followed by Mark, with Grant taking up the rear. The zombies from the right side had nearly caught up with him, but he must've sensed it because he kicked in the afterburners and ran side by side with Mark.

Jen dashed up the steps at full speed, slammed into one of the double doors, and bounced off. Huffing, she grabbed the door handle and pulled. *Dammit!*

It didn't move. She jerked on it again and again, but it didn't change the fact the damn thing was locked. She shaded her eyes with her hand and pressed her face to the window. If anyone was there...

Doc clomped up the stairs. "Don't tell me it's locked."

Jen pulled on the handle again. "Won't budge."

"What about the other door?"

"What?"

He grabbed the handle of the other door and pulled it open. *Shit.* Jen pushed him inside and held the door open for Mark and Grant. She'd feel stupid about the door later.

While Mark and Grant were ahead of the horde, the two young zombies heading for the mall door would get there at the same time as them. If they delayed Mark and Grant even a few seconds, the horde would catch up.

Time slowed and Jen pulled the rifle off her shoulder.

Can't shoot. What if there are zombies inside?

I can knock them down with the rifle butt.

But then I won't get inside in time.

She laid her rifle inside the mall and picked up the trash can next to the entry. *Thank God it's not full.*

She waited until the two zombies were only several feet from Mark and Grant, then heaved the trash can at the zombies' feet, turned, and dashed into the mall and held the door open.

The two zombies fell on the stairs as the trash can took their feet out from under them. Mark and Grant burst through the doorway, and Jen yanked the door closed. Zombies hit the door one after another like birds flying into a window. They piled up, snarling and clawing at the glass.

Grant leaned against the wall, his lungs heaving, while Mark walked in a little circle, his hands propped against his back.

Doc whispered, "We should get out of their sight. They're making a racket and it could draw any zombies inside."

Jen tugged on a door to a beauty salon, but it was locked. "Come on."

She picked up her rifle and ran into the mall, stopping around the corner, out of sight of the zombies.

Sunlight invaded the darkness wherever there was a door, but the rest of the mall was pitch-black. The zombies outside the door had already started to quiet.

"Doc," Jen said.

"Yes?"

"Did you see those two zombies? The ones that broke off chasing our tails and made a beeline for the door?"

"That I did," Doc said. "Could be an aberration."

Mark cleared his throat. "And if it isn't?"

"Then our problems just got a damn sight worse," Doc said. "But for now we should get what we came for. Which way?"

Jen listened, but could hear nothing other than the few zombies still banging the door they'd just escaped through. She switched on her flashlight.

"What are you doing?" Grant whispered. "You'll bring any zombies inside right to us."

Jen shined the flashlight down the row of storefronts. *Now I know where I am.*

She turned off the flashlight. "Unless you want to stumble around in the dark, I'll have to turn it on a few times to get where we're going."

Mark's voice came from beside her, and she jumped. "Jen leads. Grant, take rear. Doc behind me. Put your hand on the shoulder of the person in front of you. And have a weapon ready."

Mark's strong hand gently grasped her shoulder.

"Everyone ready?" she asked.

When they all answered, she walked slowly ahead. The store she wanted was across from the barber shop and next to the arcade. If she was right, the barber shop was just a few shops ahead.

She strained to hear anything beyond their soft footsteps. The zombies banging at the door faded into the distance.

Jen stopped and pointed the flashlight toward the store fronts before turning it on. The light hurt her eyes, and it took a few seconds for her to focus. She'd gotten disoriented, and the light shined into the mall, instead of into the storefronts to her left. She held her breath, expecting a high-pitched screech any second. But nothing came.

She let out her breath, her heart hammering, and swung the light to her side. There, two stores up, was the barbershop. She kept the light on, expecting Grant to bitch at any second, and headed for the shop, turning once she reached it and facing the other side of the mall.

Benches, chairs, and plants were scattered around the middle of the mall. She'd have to keep the light on while crossing it. She turned to the others. "We'll all have to use our lights here. Too many obstacles to make it across safely."

"This is starting to remind me of the hardware store," Grant said.

The four beams cut through the blackness, revealing a food court in the middle of the mall. It was a shambles, as if a riot had taken place. Jen walked to the edge of the food court, then hesitated.

"What's wrong?" Mark asked.

Jen tried to answer, but she didn't have enough spit in her mouth to form words, so she shook her head. Her mind ran through all the possibilities of escape should they run into a swarm. They couldn't go back the way they came in, but who the hell knew the situation at the other doors? They might not have time to worry about it.

Something crackled in the food court and the four light beams darted to the right. Jen squinted, but couldn't make any movement out.

"Probably just the building settling," Grant said.

"Mmm hmm," Doc said. "Bless your heart if it is."

Mark pointed his light back to the middle of the food court. "No screeches, no zombies. Nothing good will come from us standing out here."

Doubt ate at Jen's gut. She was the one who brought them all there. Was it a good idea after all?

There are no good choices, this was just the best one.

Still, uneasiness gripped her.

She picked her way into the food court, stepping over furniture and debris. Mark joined her on her left, while Doc and Grant paced her on the right. Blocked by an overturned table, she shined her flashlight to the storefronts before them. The beam landed on the sign for the Arcade. She pointed it to the shop on its right. "That's where we're going."

"A comic book shop?" Grant said. "Are you fucking kidding me? You plan on hitting the zombies with a rolled-up copy of *Superman*?"

"I'm curious to see what we've come all the way here for," Mark said.

Jen stepped over a fallen chair. "I'll show you."

She weaved her way through the broken furniture and dried blood, at one point stepping on something still squishy, and waited at the comic book store entrance for the others to catch up. Still no sign of zombies.

Doc peered in through the store window and shined his light inside. He turned around as Grant arrived. "I hope we come out of this with weapons," Doc said. "So far, we're off like a herd of turtles."

Jen opened the glass door and went inside. The place looked as if it hadn't been touched since the zombies rose. She passed displays of comics, posters, and board games to get to the glass case counter.

Grant pointed his beam at the display case, which contained action figures and game cards. "So where are the weapons?"

Jen stepped behind the case. "Look up."

The wall lit up with the beams and showed nothing but empty hooks. "What?" Jen's heart sank. "They had all kinds of swords, axes, and spiked bats." She pointed at the hooks on the wall. "That's what they hung them from."

Grant scowled. "So we risked this for nothing."

Jen felt like an ass. She tried to search Mark's eyes for any support, but his face was hidden in shadows.

A clunk came from the back of the store. *That wasn't the building settling.*

Jen turned toward the direction of the sound. Mark aimed his pistol and flashlight at the back of the store. "Doc, Grant," he said. "Watch our backs."

"You got it." Grant had his pistol ready.

Jen and Mark crept toward the back of the store. Mark shined the light down each side aisle, while Jen kept her flashlight and pistol pointed in the direction of the sound. She swallowed. Her beam fell on a wooden door.

Mark gestured her to go forward and positioned himself to the side of the door. When Jen was five feet from the door, Mark put his hand out and she stopped. He mimicked opening the door and she stood ready, aiming down the pistol's sight. Mark grasped the door handle and mouthed "Three, two, one." He swung the door open, and her light beam fell on a skinny ninja with his hands up, shading his eyes from the light.

16

The ninja froze, eyes blinking through the slit in his hood. "Please don't kill me. I can be a big help to you."

He sounds like a kid. "Who are you and what are you doing here?" Jen lowered the flashlight from the ninja's eyes, but kept the pistol aimed at him. "No one's going to kill you, but we reserve the right to make cracks about your costume."

The ninja blinked and rubbed his eyes. "Can I stand?"

"Sure," Mark said, then added, "Do you have any weapons on you?"

The ninja stood, revealing a scabbard beneath him. "Just my katana."

"What's going on back there?" Grant asked. Jen glanced at him. He had moved halfway through the store.

"We're good," Mark said. "Get back to the front and keep an eye out."

Grant's shadow dissolved into the gloom.

The ninja watched Mark closely, particularly the pistol in his hand. "You're not from upstairs?"

Jen and Mark looked at each other. Jen gave him a shrug. "No. Who's upstairs?"

Mark cut in. "Before we get to that, I want to know who you are and what you're doing here."

"I'm Zeke. This was my mall until those others came." He hesitated. "We really should get back in this room before one of the gang's guards find us."

"Take your hood off, Zeke," Mark said.

Zeke didn't move, and Mark raised his gun. Zeke pulled the black hood off, revealing a late teen-early twenties face with a long nose, acne, and a half-shaved head with green hair. Various piercings adorned his ears, nose, and lip.

"Just a kid," Mark muttered.

Zeke eyebrows lowered. "Just a kid who's survived."

Jen smiled. "He's got a point there." She gestured to Zeke. "Let me see if I've got this right. You hid out in the mall when the shit hit the fan and survived, but some other people came in that you're afraid of and they camp out upstairs. Sound right?"

Zeke nodded. "Other people have come since. The gang upstairs either gets them to join up, or kills them."

Mark gestured with his pistol. "Why don't you move back into that room and we'll follow you. Leave your sword. We'll pick it up."

Zeke kept his hands up and backed into the room. From the outside it had looked like it was no bigger than a closet, but inside it would fit a couple dozen people.

Zeke pointed to a battery-powered camping lantern. "Close the door so the light doesn't give us away and I'll turn this on."

"I should get the others first," Mark said.

"Go ahead," Jen said. "I've got this."

Mark left and returned a minute later with Grant and Doc. He closed the door. "How about that light, Zeke?"

Zeke flipped on three battery-powered camping lamps. "Found these while rummaging through the mall."

The room lit up, everyone's shadows high up the walls. Cardboard boxes were stacked along one wall, while a long worktable with an assortment of action figures and other knickknacks lined another wall. Shelves with drinks and snacks stood at the end.

Mark switched off his flashlight. "Not bad."

"Why the ninja getup?" Doc asked.

Zeke put his arms out and smiled. "Like it? I used to almost live in this shop. I was here at least three or four times a week. I always wanted this costume, ever since they put it up on display six months ago, but I couldn't afford it." He spread his arms out. "Now I can afford anything in the store. Besides, it's great for sneaking around in the shadows."

"And the katana?" Grant asked. "It looks a little light to be useful for bashing in zombie heads."

Zeke picked up the scabbard and Mark raised his pistol. Zeke put his hands in the air. "I'm just going to show you."

Mark nodded at him. "Go ahead, but it'll take less than a second for me to put a bullet into you."

Zeke's hands shook as he slowly removed the sword from the scabbard. Long, thin, and curved, it reflected the light along a sharp looking blade.

Jen held out a hand. "Can I see it?"

Zeke hesitated. Jen kept her face neutral. "I'll give it back."

Zeke leaned forward with the sword. Mark cleared his throat. "Give it to her hilt first."

"Right." Zeke gave a weak smile and slid the sword into the scabbard and held it out so the hilt faced Jen.

Jen slid the sword out and gave it a few practice swings. She examined the blade. Damn thing looked sharp, but comic book shops don't sell swords with an edge. *Must be the light making it look that way.* She traced the edge lightly with a finger.

"Shit!" She pulled her finger back. Blood oozed from the cut. She slid the sword back into the scabbard Zeke still held, grabbed a t-shirt with a dragon imprint from the worktable, and used it to put pressure on the wound. "Where'd you get that thing?"

"On the wall over the display case." Zeke smiled. "Of course, a katana won't do much damage without an edge on it, so I broke into the knife shop around the corner and sharpened the blade."

"Where are the other weapons from the wall?" Mark asked. "The gang get them?"

Zeke laughed and pulled a stack of boxes away from the wall. He used the blade of his sword to dig between two pieces of sheetrock and pulled the bottom piece from the wall. An assortment of knives, helmets, chain mail, and weapons lay in the cavity.

Reaching in, Jen picked up a double-headed axe. "This will do quite nicely." She looked at Zeke. "Are these sharpened, too?"

Zeke shook his head. "But they don't need to be. Those can still lop off zombie parts, and all you really have to do is bash their heads anyway."

Grant took a huge broadsword. "This one's mine."

Mark hefted a mace and gave it a few practice swings. "You sure about that? You've gotta carry that heavy-ass thing around."

"True enough." Grant put the broadsword back and chose a solid, but lighter blade. "What about you, Doc?"

Doc put a finger to the corner of his mouth as he looked over the cache of weapons. "I do believe..." He bent down and lifted a spiked bat. "I played peewee league as a boy back in Georgia." He swung slowly, following through like a baseball batter. "Balance isn't bad. It's enough for me to smack a zombie upside the head."

Grant sheathed his sword in his belt and pointed his pistol at Zeke again. "How do you know the gang can't hear us in here?"

Zeke placed his scabbard on a table next to him. "As long as we don't yell, they'd have to be standing in the store to hear. Out there, it can echo depending on where you're at." He crossed his arms. "Can you guys stop pointing guns at me now? Haven't I proven I'm no threat to you?"

Jen holstered her gun in her belt. "He's OK. Just a kid." She thrust out her hand. "I'm Jen."

Zeke smiled and shook her hand, then he held it out to the others, who introduced themselves in turn. Zeke gestured to a shelf loaded with energy drinks and snacks. "Anyone hungry or thirsty?"

"No, thanks," Jen said. "Now that we've got the weapons we came for, we'll be on our way."

Zeke's face fell. "What's the rush? It's been weeks since I talked to anyone."

Jen bit her lip. The poor kid was lonely, but they had to get to the plane.

"We need to get to the base and catch a plane out," Doc said.

Zeke's face lit up. "There's still a plane out? Where's it going? I have a brother in Rhode Island I could stay with."

Grant put a hand up. "Whoa. This is a military plane and it's there to get Doc out."

"And Jen and Mark," Doc said.

Zeke grabbed Doc's arm. "Can I go, too? I won't take much room."

Doc looked at Jen and Mark. "What do y'all think?"

"Wait." Grant pushed between Doc and Zeke. "He's not authorized."

Doc put an arm out and guided Grant to the side. "You just made up my mind. I'm authorizing Zeke."

Grant's face turned red. "What the fuck? Are we going to pick up every damn stray on the way?"

Jen tried not to laugh at Grant, but a chuckle escaped her lips. Mark said, "I guess that's up to Doc, isn't it?"

Grant said nothing and walked back to the door. He pulled a cell phone out of his pocket. "Need to check in if we can."

Jen turned to Zeke. "Better get loaded up. You have a gun?"

Zeke shook his head. "My katana's enough."

"Have you ever shot a gun?" Mark asked.

"Sure," Zeke said. "I kick ass in all the top first-person shooters."

Doc frowned. "What's a first-person shooter?"

Jen sighed. "Kung Fu Nerd here is talking about video games."

"Right," Zeke said. "I'm a nerd and proud of it."

"Doc." Grant pushed through, holding out the cell phone. "The colonel wants you."

Doc reached for the phone. "What has he said so far?"

"Nothing. As soon as we connected, he told me to hand it to you."

Doc put the phone to his ear. "Hello?"

He nodded. "Yes, it's me."

He listened, then pulled the phone from his ear. "Exactly where in the city are we?"

"100th Avenue and Old Seward," Jen said.

He put the phone back to his ear. "Did you hear that?"

His eyes narrowed as he listened. "Wait. Just a minute." He pulled the phone from his ear, then pressed a finger to the screen. "OK. You're on speaker. Repeat what you said." He placed the phone on the workbench.

The colonel's voice came over the phone. "Not a good idea, Doctor. This information is on a need-to-know basis. You're the only one who needs to know."

Doc frowned. "I truly disagree. This affects us all. Besides, I'll tell them anyway. I'd rather they hear it from y'all so nothing's lost in the translation."

Jen could imagine this colonel sitting behind a desk and seething at having to give in to Doc. *It'll do him some good to realize he doesn't have control anymore. None of us do.*

The colonel cleared his throat. "We are being attacked by the creatures."

"Zombies," Jen said.

The colonel paused, then continued. "The base is too big for our skeleton crew to defend, so we've set up a perimeter around the flight line. Even that's a stretch. We can't hold on forever."

"How long do we have?" Mark asked.

"There's something else," the colonel said. "Protocol 159.37 has been implemented."

Doc's face flushed. "159.37? That's—"

"Yes, Doctor."

"What's protocol one five whatever?" Grant asked.

Doc removed his glasses and cleaned them with the tail of his shirt. "The protocol deals with stopping a pandemic in the most absolute way possible."

"Bottom line, Doc," Jen said. "Make it simple for my small brain."

"The area of infection will be cleansed with nuclear weapons."

Jen's breath hitched. "Area of infection?"

Doc nodded. "That would be Anchorage."

17

"Are you shitting me? We're nuking our own city?" Jen's head throbbed.

"Not city," the colonel said. "Cities. Anchorage, Wasilla, and Fairbanks. The president has given the order to implement the protocol in"—he paused—"fourteen hours."

Mark put a hand to his forehead, his eyes focused on the floor. "That's until the nuke drops. How long do we have until the C-130 leaves?"

"Twelve hours. That's the best we can do. Protocol is to be out two hours prior to detonation."

"Screw your protocol," Jen said. "You're our only way out."

Everyone started talking at the same time. The colonel's voice barked from the speaker. "Enough!" They all went silent.

"Good," the colonel said. "We don't have time for this horseshit. It took a day and a half for you to get less than a third of the way here. You need to pick up the pace. We need Dr. Wilson and his data."

Mark clapped his hands together once. "He's right. We need to go."

"Check in with me," the colonel said. "As often as you can. Once you hit the base perimeter, I might be able to send a team in a vehicle to bring you in, but we can't help you any more than that."

"Yes, sir," Grant said. He pressed his lips together so tight they turned white. *He's doing that hoo-rah stuff and gearing himself up.*

"Good bye, Colonel," Doc said.

"Good luck," the colonel answered.

Doc hung up the phone and handed it back to Grant.

Jen put her hands on her hips. "We should check our weapons loads, grab some food and water, and get the hell on the road."

"Wait." Grant stepped up nose-to-nose with her. "Who the hell do you think you are? I'm in charge here."

Doc put an arm between the two. "We don't have time for this."

"I disagree, Doc," Mark said. "Better to waste a little time now than waste lives later." He nodded at Jen.

She drew herself up, her stomach fluttering. "I never was much good at following, and now that the shit's gotten real, my patience for it is gone. I know the city and I'm the best hope we have in getting to the plane in time. Besides, if I want military experience, I'll rely on Mark."

Grant's jaw dropped. "Him? The rent-a-cop?"

Mark glared at Grant. "I spent six years in the infantry with tours in Iraq and Afghanistan. Bronze Star. I know how to survive."

"You're bullshitting," Grant said. When Mark didn't answer, he asked, "Aren't you?"

Jen patted Grant on the back. "Not a bit, but don't worry, the rear guard position's all yours."

"I agree that Jen should direct our movements from here on out," Doc said. "Are y'all done here, or do we need more discussion while the clock keeps ticking?"

Grant shook his head. Mark clasped him on the shoulder. "Look, we need you. We all have to work together or we die."

"Yeah, sure." Grant turned away, grabbed some beef jerky, and topped off his canteen with bottled water.

After they'd taken their supplies, Jen grasped the doorknob. "Mark takes lead. Then me, Doc, and Zeke. Grant, we need your skill covering our rear."

Grant nodded.

"Wait," Zeke said. "I almost forgot something." He went to a desk and rustled through a pile of papers.

Jen rolled her eyes. *This leading shit isn't going to be easy.* "Come on. We need to go."

"Go on," Zeke said. "I'll catch up. It'll only take me a minute."

Jen looked at Mark and he shrugged. "You're not out in front of the shop in a minute and you'll miss the bus. We can't wait any more."

Zeke waved him off. "I'll be there." He opened a desk drawer.

Mark opened the door into the shop, and the light from the lamps spilled out a few feet. He crept past racks of comics and paraphernalia to the front door.

Jen followed, but couldn't see anything more than his shadow. *Don't want to wake the boogeymen upstairs.*

She glanced over her shoulder. Either the door to the storeroom had been closed, or the lights turned off. An amorphous shadow followed her. Had to be Doc.

Mark left the store and took a knee. Jen ducked down next to him. "We should find a different door to leave. Those zombies are probably still at the one we came through."

"Good idea," Mark said.

She scanned the open food court. With the ambient light filtering in from the entrances, she made out jumbles of shapes, but nothing distinctive. Rustling came from a couple of feet next to her, and her pulse went into overdrive.

"Are you there?" Doc whispered.

Jen let out a deep breath and lowered the axe she'd unconsciously cocked back. She whispered, "Right here, Doc. Grant, you there?"

"Affirmative."

Creaking and settling sounds came from the darkness. There could be a hundred zombies out there and she wouldn't know it unless they growled or howled. She held her axe at the ready and the seconds ticked by.

Mark leaned in front of her and whispered, "Any sign of Zeke?"

Grant raised his voice. "Zeke? You here?"

No one answered.

"We don't have time to wait," Grant said.

Jen frowned. Zeke was just a kid, and she sure as shit didn't want to leave him to melt in a nuclear storm if they didn't need to. "One more minute won't hurt."

"Agreed," Doc said.

Something moved across the food court. Didn't sound accidental. It sounded...stealthy.

Jen slid the axe into a belt loop and pulled her pistol out. Did any of the others hear it? She didn't dare to risk making enough noise to ask.

It seemed to her that they stayed there, motionless, for another five minutes. Twinges in her calves warned her they were about to cramp. Maybe Zeke had changed his mind.

Mark whispered even lower than he had before. "Zeke here yet?"

"No," came Grant's reply.

Mark rose, and Jen followed his lead. *Too bad about Zeke.* She liked him, but they couldn't wait.

She put a hand on Mark's shoulder and Doc's hand clasped hers. Mark eased down the row of storefronts. *He's not crossing the food court. Must've heard the same thing I did.*

Steady and slow, Mark led them toward another entrance, the light from the glass doors spilling into the mall. Several yards from the short hall that ran to the entrance, he kicked a piece of debris. The group froze.

Jen tilted her head, straining to hear anything, and she picked up muffled growling. Not a zombie in pursuit of its prey, but one that probably wandered around outside.

Mark continued on, and the growling grew louder as they approached the doors. They reached the corner to the hallway that led to the doors and Mark peered around it. His shoulders sagged and he turned back to the group. "At least a dozen zombies at this one."

"Shit," Grant said. "How about we cross to the other side?"

"Thought I heard something over there earlier," Mark said.

Jen nodded. "Me, too. But what choice do we have?"

"Where are the stairs?" Grant asked.

Jen closed her eyes and ran through the layout as she knew it. "A set at either end, next to the elevators."

"So if we keep going in the same direction we'll hit them?" Grant asked.

"Yeah."

"Good point," Mark said. "We're more likely to run into the gang around the stairs. We'll go across here, but first we'll backtrack to get away from the light coming in from the doors. We'll be harder to spot that way. Hands on shoulders, people." He crept past the others, turning the team around.

Maybe we'll run into Zeke on the way back.

Ten yards in, Mark stopped. "We cross here. It'll be slow. Secure your weapons and use your free hand to feel for obstacles. Silence is more important right now than having your weapons ready. And stay low. No sense in making a bigger target than you need."

Jen slid her pistol back in her belt and held her hands in front of her and to the side. Mark moved one step at a time, paused, then another. She used the pause to feel for anything in the way. Ten steps in she felt a cold metal bar. Feeling up and down, she found it attached to more bars and flat wood. *A chair.* She stepped around it.

Sweat beaded on her forehead and a drop ran into her eye. She blinked, and wiped it away at the next pause. Judging by the light coming from the outside doors, they appeared to be no more than a quarter of the way across.

Mark stopped. A cough came from somewhere off in the darkness to their left. Jen slipped her pistol from her belt.

Several blinding white lights shined on them from three sides, and the echo of multiple guns being cocked had Jen's heart doing double time. She released Mark's shoulder and shaded her eyes with a hand, but couldn't make anything out.

A gravelly voice chuckled, "Welcome to our house. I insist you stay for a while."

18

J en blinked, trying to catch a glimpse of anything, but the lights had burned into her retinas. Judging from the sounds of the guns being cocked, there had to be at least a dozen of them.

The gravelly voice said, "Before we go on, I want you to lay all your weapons down. It'd be bad manners for a guest to walk around our house with them."

"Put them down," Mark said.

Jen placed her pistol on the floor, then unslung her rifle and laid it down.

"That cool-looking axe, too," the voice said.

Jen pulled the axe from her belt loop and eased it down next to her. She straightened and raised her arms. She had nothing left to fight with, not even a knife. She expected Grant to give them lip, but he said nothing as he complied. Doc and Mark followed suit, then raised their hands.

The lights pointed away from their eyes and at the floor, illuminating the weapons. A man in a dirty, torn pair of khaki pants and a blue dress shirt collected the weapons and disappeared back into the light.

A man in an expensive-looking suit coat and pants, with a black T-shirt stepped into the light. "My name is Trip," he said in the gravelly voice. He waved his hand like a magician taking a bow. "And these are my people, and this is my property."

Jen bit her lip. Trip's getup, along with his shaved head, goatee, and beady black eyes was ripe for a half dozen smartass comments. *Need to let Mark handle this. Don't think this asshole would take an insult very well.*

Mark glanced at her. Was he thinking the same thing? "We apologize for intruding. We didn't know the mall was already occupied."

"Well, that's a start," Trip said.

Grant spoke up. "If you'll just return our weapons, we'll be on our way."

Trip chuckled and laughter came from the darkness around them. "I don't think that'll work for us. In fact, to pay us back, you'll have to work for us."

"Work?" Jen said.

"Nothing's free, girl." He leered at her. "And I know exactly how you can work it off."

Jen's mouth went dry. *No damn way. They'll have to kill me.*

"I'm afraid there's somewhere we must be," Doc said.

"Oh, did you hear that?" Trip mocked. "They have an appointment." Laughter rolled off the walls and storefronts.

"We're due at the base," Doc said. "And if we aren't there soon, they'll come looking for us and I wouldn't want to be in y'all's shoes when they do."

The laughter grew even more. *Poor Doc gave it a good try.*

When the laughter settled, Trip said, "What's your name, girl?"

Jen glowered at him.

"So we have attitude, do we? Good. I like that, but only to a point." Trip pulled a pistol from inside his suit coat and pointed it at her. "What's your fucking name?"

Jen's hands trembled. She tried to get enough spit in her mouth to talk. She thought of giving him a fake name, but what did it really matter? "Jen."

"There now. That wasn't so hard. Pleased to meet you, Jen. Aren't you pleased to meet me?"

She gave a curt nod.

"Now that we're friends, I'd like you to do something for me."

"W-what's that?" Jen asked.

"Strip."

Jen's heart pounded. *Is this shit for real?* "What?"

"Take off your clothes, Jen."

"No," Mark yelled. He took a step toward Trip.

Trip pointed his pistol at Mark. "No, no, no. That's not acting like a good guest." He raised his voice. "If any of the others move so much as an inch, shoot them. But not in the head."

Jen found her voice. "The day I take off my clothes for a creepy little troll is the day I lie down and die."

Trip swung the pistol back at her. "I don't mind doing you after you've turned. It'll be a lot less back talk. Now strip!"

Jen clenched her teeth, jutting her chin out, and stared at him.

"Strip," Trip said, and he chanted, "Strip, strip, strip." The other disembodied voices joined in, the word hitting her from all sides, almost like a physical force.

Trip yelled above the others as they kept up the chant. "Strip, Jen, or you'll be shot."

This is it, then. I'll get a chance to see what it's like to be a zombie.

"Once we shoot you, we'll cut your friends up real slow," Trip said. "Make 'em feel it for hours. You can avoid all that by doing what I say."

Jen squeezed her eyes shut and clamped her hands over her ears. The chanting made it through and vibrated in her head like a heavy bass. She looked at Mark. He gave her a slight head shake. Doc peered back at her with sad eyes. Grant's jaw was set and anger brewed behind his eyes.

Jen removed her hands from her ears. The chanting continued.

"Running out of time, Jen," Trip said. "I'll cut up that big strong guy first."

Jen unbuttoned the top button of her shirt. The chanting grew in intensity. "Attagirl," Trip said.

The shaking in her hands had spread to her whole body. *Calm down, dammit. Buy more time. Look for an opening.*

She unbuttoned the second button. Several male voices yelled out, "Yeah."

Maybe she could get hold of a gun and shoot herself in the head before they did anything to her.

She unbuttoned the last three buttons and her shirt hung open, revealing her bra. A raucous cheer went up, causing her to shrink back.

A woman's high-pitched scream reduced the cheer to confused mumblings. Several of the lights turned away and multiple zombie shrieks filled the mall.

More lights turned toward the other side of the food court. Jen tried to see what they shined on, but Trip's people blocked her view. Shouts and gunshots rang out, then more screams.

A zombie dashed into the light and tackled one of Trip's people. The group exploded into chaos.

Mark grabbed Jen's arm. "We need to get the hell out of here."

"What about weapons?" she asked. "We can't go out there empty-handed."

She blinked as the shrieks, gunshots, and screams escalated. "Which way do we go?"

"Back to the comic store," Grant said.

A dark figure rushed to them. Mark stepped in front of Jen, his arm cocked back to strike.

"Wait," the figure said. "It's me. Zeke."

Dressed head to toe in his black ninja costume, he blended in with the shadows of the mall. *He really is a damn ninja.*

Doc grabbed Zeke's shoulder. "Which way do we go? We'll be in the middle of it in a few seconds."

Zeke pulled his hood off and smiled. "Follow me."

He led them back the way he'd come. Jen grasped Doc's shoulder and another hand grabbed hers.

They followed Zeke blindly as the gunshots slowed and the screaming and yelling increased. He stopped. "I'm holding a glass door open. Go on through."

They filed in and Zeke took the lead. "Hands on shoulders. Almost there."

Jen hung on and brushed against racks with clothes on them.

They paused and a door squeaked open. "Go in. Quick. Don't want the zombies to hear us."

Jen followed Doc in and stopped. The door closed and a match came to life. Zeke lit several candles and a warm glow filled the room. A small office with a couple of desks and computers, it had a second door on the outside wall.

Jen gave Zeke a bear hug. "You saved our asses."

Zeke shuffled his feet.

Mark pumped Zeke's hand. "I won't hug you, but I owe you one. We all do."

Even Grant smiled at Zeke. "But where'd the zombies come from?"

Zeke had a shit-eating grin on his face. "I propped open a couple of doors. The gang's yelling brought the zombies right to them."

"But now we're stuck in here without weapons," Grant said.

Zeke's smile got wider. He walked over to a large cardboard box standing in the corner and pulled it aside. There lay their weapons. Guns, sword, axe, everything.

Jen's jaw dropped. "How did you get those?"

"Easy," Zeke said. "They were busy with you and being pretty noisy. I even dropped one of the swords on the floor and no one turned around."

"And even if they had," Doc said, "your costume blended into the shadows."

Zeke nodded.

Mark let out a laugh. "And I thought it was just a costume."

"It was highly fortunate you stayed behind in the comic shop to get something," Doc said. "But what was so fired-up important that you couldn't leave without it?"

Zeke fished something out of his costume and held up a laminated card.

"What the hell is that?" Grant asked.

"A rare character card for my favorite game."

Doc laughed.

Jen picked up a pistol, ejected the magazine, and slapped it back in. "Let's load up and get out of here. Anyone know how much time we have?"

Doc looked at his watch. "Eleven hours, three minutes."

"Damn," Grant said. "That went by quick."

Mark hefted his mace. "So we go back out through the mall?"

Zeke walked to the door on the other end of the room. "Nope. This goes outside. Since it's not a glass door where they can see in, zombies don't seem to stop here as much. And it's got a peephole so we can see what we're up against."

Grant nodded, one eyebrow raised. "You knew this was here?"

"I've had my escape route planned for weeks," Zeke said. "Just in case."

Jen strode to the door and peered through the peephole. The fish-eye lens distorted the front end of a mini van parked against the curb, its driver still belted in and growling.

Four zombies stumbled through the parking lot, swaying between the cars and avoiding each other. Jen pursed her lips. *Do they ever fight each other?* She'd have to ask Doc about that.

She turned to the others. "I see five zombies, and one is trapped in a car."

Mark looked through the peephole. "This isn't an especially wide view. There could be a hundred more just out of sight."

Jen pulled the bolt back on the door. "Only one way to find out." She held her axe up with a smile, then swung the door open and stepped into the sunshine.

19

The zombie in the car reacted, snarling and snapping its jaws until it let forth a zombie howl. Jen ignored it and turned to face a tall, fat man in a torn and bloody jogging suit racing toward her at full speed. She swallowed and grasped the axe with both hands, holding it back like a baseball bat. A silver cross on a chain around Jogging Suit Zombie's neck caught the sun as it swung back and forth.

Closer. Almost there.

Six feet from her, the zombie opened its mouth, showing several gold teeth. Jen stepped forward and swung with all she had, aiming for its head. She missed, but bashed in its shoulder. The zombie stumbled to the side and attacked again, knocking her back into the car.

He dove for her and Jen rolled to her left. Jogging Suit Zombie slammed into the car, driving the creature in the car wild.

Jen staggered several steps away and caught a glimpse of Grant driving the point of his sword into a bearded zombie's eyes.

Jogging Suit Zombie roared and rushed her. She had just enough time to deflect it again with the axe, knocking it to the ground. Her damn arms felt like lead, but she planted a foot on the zombie's chest and let out a grunt as she swung the axe down and into the zombie's forehead. He fell still. Jen moved her foot to his neck and yanked the axe out.

Mark stood between two women zombies, ducking away from one and swinging his mace into the temple of the other. Doc buried a couple of spikes from his bat into the back of the other woman's head, dropping her.

Jen leaned on the car, panting. "That was a workout. Maybe I'll make an exercise video called 'Zombie Aerobics.'"

Zeke laughed.

Oh, great. Now I have a fan.

The zombie trapped in the car shrieked. Zeke put his face against the window. "She's still strapped in."

"We should shut her up," Mark said, "before she alerts any more."

Zeke held his katana in one hand and opened the door with the other. The zombie strained against the seatbelt, its head out of the car and jaws snapping. Zeke stepped to the side and swung the katana in a downward arc, lopping off the zombie's head.

"Nice," Jen said. "You made it look easy."

Zeke shrugged. "Not the first zombie to fall from my sword."

Grant leaned on his bloody sword. A zombie in a cop's uniform lay at his feet. "We can't keep doing this."

"We should be fixing to avoid zombies as best we can, and especially avoid fighting them," Doc said.

Jen stretched. "I'm for that. How much time have we got left?"

"Ten hours, fifty-eight minutes," Doc said.

"Are you kidding?" she asked. "The fight only lasted five minutes? Feels like it's been at least thirty."

Mark stood watching the others breathing heavily. He looked like he hadn't broken a sweat. *Showoff.*

"Don't we need to be going?" he asked.

Jen wiped the blade of her axe on the jogging suit. "Why do you look so damn rested?"

Mark shook the blood off his mace. "Which way?"

"Back to the tracks." Jen pointed to a bridge that crossed the road. "They go over there and keep heading north."

She jogged toward the tracks, zigzagging between cars to keep from stirring up the thirty or so zombies in the parking lot. The others followed, Grant and Doc looking ragged. When she reached the tracks, Jen turned back toward the mall. Mark and Zeke stood next to her, but Doc and Grant were still climbing the slope.

A group of ten people burst out of the mall. Even from that distance, Trip stood out. If anyone deserved to be zombie food, that asshole did.

Trip shouted and pointed at Jen. His group fired and Jen dropped to her stomach. "Shit."

A zombie howl went up and was joined by more across the parking lot. Three groups of zombies swarmed toward Trip and his people. They switched to targeting the undead.

Jen jumped up. "Let's get to the bridge while these guys are busy. If we're lucky, the zombies will get them. But if they don't, I want to get a head start. I've got a feeling old Trip isn't one to let things go."

Doc and Grant reached the tracks and Jen ran, leading them to the bridge. She took one last look back before crossing it. Trip's group had taken out several zombies. *Why couldn't they be shitty shots?*

Reaching the halfway point over the bridge, Jen looked west toward King Street, about two hundred yards away. Ten zombies milled around, but none reacted to the humans on the bridge.

Jen took cover in the trees on the other side of the bridge. Mark took up position next to her. A minute later Grant and Doc arrived. "No time to rest," Mark said.

"We just follow the tracks for now," Jen said. "Mark, can you take point?"

"Sure."

She pointed to Grant. "You OK on rear?"

Panting, Grant nodded.

They walked at a good clip, covered by trees on their right and industrial buildings on the left. Mark kept them close to the trees.

Doc moved to Jen's side, his hands on his back. "Notice the zombies up the road as we crossed the bridge?"

Jen nodded. "Not a peep out of them."

Doc pulled a bottle of water out of his pack. He took a sip and put it back. "Remember that last drone footage I showed you? Seems we were far enough away, and quiet enough, to keep from attracting their attention."

Mark glanced back. "So how far away do we need to be?"

"I wouldn't want to put that fine a guess on it," Doc said. "I imagine it depends on how quiet you are. Maybe even depends on the zombie." He shrugged. "Just something to stick in your back pocket for now."

Twenty minutes later, the tracks crossed Campbell Creek Trail. Jen stopped. "We have a choice to make. If we follow the tracks, they'll take us downtown and cross over Ship Creek to the base. Problem is, the tracks will cross a lot of roads, and those are always open areas."

"Downtown was overrun with zombies at the beginning," Zeke said. "I saw it on TV. A lot of downtown burned."

Mark gestured to the trail. "What about this way?"

"It takes us more east, but near enough to Boniface Parkway, which runs right into the base. Best part is we have a lot more cover taking the trail."

"If I had my druthers," Doc said. "I'd prefer to stay hidden as much as possible."

"I agree," Grant said.

Jen looked at Mark and Zeke. "I'm with Doc and Grant. Anyone against?"

Zeke shook his head. Mark shrugged. "You should take point. I'll be right behind you."

Jen led them onto the trail. It wound through the greenbelt with trees on both sides. They came to a fork and Jen took the left one. The trees grew thinner on the right and a neighborhood of duplexes appeared through occasional breaks in the foliage. Woodsmoke hung heavy in the air. Jen caught a breath of it and coughed. Was it just wood, or were there more organic things being burned?

A rapid series of gunshots came from the duplexes. Jen ducked. "That sounded damn close."

Zombie howls rose from several directions. Mark dashed for the tall undergrowth across the trail from the duplexes. "In the bushes."

Jen wasn't about to question Mark and was right on his tail, diving under cover. Zeke, Grant, and Doc tumbled in next to them. Zombie howls drifted closer, and Jen gripped her axe so tightly her knuckles turned white.

A group of three zombies burst from the trees a few yards away. Jen's heart hammered and she stifled a gasp. Even expecting them, their appearance was sudden.

The zombies sprinted across the trail and disappeared into the trees on the duplex side. The whole thing had taken fifteen seconds.

Doc went to rise, but Mark grabbed his arm. "Not yet," he whispered.

An unearthly guttural howl came from down the path. The trees in that direction shook and branches cracked. *What the hell is that?*

A moose galloped out onto the trail and headed straight toward them. Jen couldn't move. They would be stomped to death.

Ten feet away, it made a sharp turn toward the duplexes. It disappeared in seconds, but not before Jen's mind snapped a picture of its side missing several chunks of fur and meat. *Not to mention its yellow eyes.*

Jen squeezed her eyes shut. What a nightmare this had turned into.

Another series of gunshots came from the duplexes, followed by a long scream that cut off, and then silence.

"Best we get to where we're going before the zombies start wandering back this way," Doc said.

Jen stepped onto the trail. She wondered how much time they had left, but didn't dare ask. "I don't know about you, but I'm not waiting for Frankenmoose to come back."

Grant shook his head. "Can you beat that? I've never even dreamed of something like that, much less seen it."

"I'd surely love to study that creature," Doc said.

"Screw that," Mark said. "That thing looked bad enough, but can you imagine if there's a bear out there that's been turned?"

Jen's skin prickled at the thought. She shook it off. "Mark, point. Everyone else, you know where you are. And let's pick up the pace. We've been sitting too long."

Mark jogged down the path with the others close behind. They continued in silence, and Jen kept her eyes moving. After that moose coming out of nowhere, even the tree coverage didn't feel safe. They made good time, following the trail under Dowling Road and as it threaded between neighborhoods and industrial areas.

Mark stopped. "Road ahead."

"Old Seward." Jen pulled up behind him. "The trail should follow Campbell Creek under the road again."

"Not gonna help us," Mark said.

She crept up beside him. A damn burned-out car blocked the path under the bridge. No signs of movement. "Shit. We'll have to cross in the open."

She turned to Grant and Zeke. "We need you two to stay here and watch our flank. Mark, Doc, and I are going to scout out ahead."

Zeke gave her a smile, and Grant nodded.

Jen ran with Mark and Doc to the edge of the road and popped her head up, scanning the area. A large horde of thirty or so milled around at the intersection of International Airport Road, and another group of a dozen gathered to their right in front of an RV dealer.

"What do you think, Doc?" Jen asked. "Are they far enough away for us to cross?"

Doc cleaned his glasses with his shirttail. "I'd estimate they're about two hundred yards away on either side, give or take ten yards." He shrugged. "As I said before, I don't have enough data to tell for sure. Two hundred yards might be enough, or it might not."

Mark pointed across the road. "And we've got another problem."

Two zombies stumbled around the parking lot across the road. "If they see us and howl," Jen said, "we're screwed."

"Maybe we should go further up the road and find another place to cross," Doc said.

"But do we have time for that?" Mark asked.

Running feet approached from behind. Jen spun, cocking her axe back. Grant and Zeke scrambled up the embankment next to them. Breathing heavily, Zeke said, "Trip and nine of his people are coming. They'll be here in a few minutes."

Jen looked at Mark. "Looks like the decision is made for us. You and I have a couple of zombies to kill across the road."

"And hope we're far enough away from the two hordes," Doc added.

Jen sighed. "Why did the zombie killer cross the road?"

"I give up," Zeke said. "Why?"

"I guess we'll find out." Adrenaline flooded Jen's veins, giving her a rush. *I think I'm getting used to this.* She hunched over and crept onto the road, her axe ready for more zombie blood.

20

J en and Mark had made it to the solid lines dividing the road lanes when Mark grabbed her wrist. She stopped and followed his gaze. A zombie in the horde at the intersection had stopped milling around and faced them, its head tilted back. *Shit. Can they smell us, too?*

Jen's breathing slowed. She glanced at Doc and the others waiting at the roadside. Doc watched the zombie's actions, then shrugged at her.

Her attention went back to the sniffing zombie. She didn't dare turn around to check out the other horde in front of the RV dealership. All it would take was for one zombie to howl and she and Mark would be stuck in the middle of two converging hordes. Not to mention the two zombies they were on their way to kill.

The sniffing zombie lowered its nose and turned away. Jen let out an audible sigh, then clamped her hand over her mouth. Her eyes snapped to the two zombies on the other side. One of them was a middle-aged man dressed in bloodied mechanics overalls, and the other was a twenty-something woman with long blonde hair dressed in a torn pair of medical scrubs. They stumbled around aimlessly, their heads down and backs to Jen and Mark.

Mark tapped her shoulder. He pointed to her and then the mechanic, then to himself and the blonde. Jen nodded. She moved forward on the pads of her feet, the axe heavy in her hand.

Reaching the grass, she raised the axe over her head. The remaining ten feet to the zombie were covered in gravel. She took her first step on it and the stones ground together. It sounded as loud as a gunshot. The zombies turned and Jen sprinted to the mechanic. Before he faced her, she buried the axe into his temple. Mark slammed the mace onto the forehead of the blonde a second later. She fell, blood trickling onto the gravel.

Jen blew out a breath and waved the others over. Zeke jumped onto the road, and Jen waved at him to slow down. They weren't out of danger yet. Zeke nodded and tip toed across in an almost exaggerated way. Doc kept his eyes on the two hordes as he crossed, and Grant kept glancing back over his shoulder. *I almost forgot Trip and his gang.*

When they caught up, Jen led everyone down to the trail and north into the greenbelt. She walked with a quickened pace. Five minutes later, Doc said, "That was uncomfortable. What do y'all think?"

"I was about to piss my pants," Zeke said.

Grant glanced over his shoulder. "I think we got out of sight just in time. Trip and his people had to be close to the curve in the trail."

"That's good," Mark said. "That way they can't be sure we went this way."

Jen frowned. "I don't know. I think they do."

"How do you figure that?" Mark asked.

"They know we're heading for the base," Jen said, "and unless they all came off some tourist bus, they know the area. So they'd know we'd either go through downtown or up Boniface to get to the base."

Doc shoved his hands in his pockets and hung his head. "I shouldn't have told them we were heading to the base."

"Not your fault," Jen said. "It was a good bluff to tell them the military would come looking for us."

Grant pulled out the cell phone. "Speaking of the military, we should check in."

"Not here," Mark said. "We need a place to hole up."

Jen rounded a curve in the trail, then stopped and pointed ahead. "What about there?"

A couple hundred yards down the trail, on the outside of another curve, a three-story office building loomed over the trees.

"Nice," Mark said. "From the top floor, you can see all the way down here. If we spot Trip, it gives us plenty of time to move on without him being the wiser."

Mark broke into a jog, and Jen and the others followed suit. They broke through the trees in front of the building and came out the other side in a parking lot that surrounded the building on three sides. A large sign in front advertised a dentist, orthodontist, and physical therapist.

Jen pulled on the front door and it opened. She turned to Mark. "What do you suggest? Do we clear the whole building?"

Grant frowned. "We don't have time."

Jen raised an eyebrow at Mark.

"He's right," Mark said. "We should go straight upstairs to the back corner room, take out anything in our way, and then block the door."

"Couldn't we get boxed in?" Jen asked.

Mark's eyes pierced hers. "Absolutely."

Well, I asked. Jen entered, her axe cocked and ready to swing. Mark went up the stairs first, followed by Zeke and then Doc. Grant gestured for Jen to follow. She thought to drop a smart-ass remark, but Grant had done his part and she saw no reason to mess with him.

A zombie howl echoed from upstairs, and an answering howl came from the downstairs hallway just before a thirty-something woman with a missing ear and yellow eyes darted from the hallway and sprang at Jen. In an awkward reaction, Jen swung the axe early and the zombie slammed into her chest, driving her to the floor and knocking the wind out of her. She pushed on the zombie's chest, staving it off for a moment, but her arms collapsed. A flash of steel and the zombie's head cracked. The damn thing fell limp on Jen, bleeding onto her clothes.

Grant pulled the zombie off her and threw it to the side. He reached out a hand. "You OK?"

Jen grabbed his hand, coughing, and he pulled her into a sitting position. She stayed bent over, pulling in lungfuls of air until the dizziness went away.

Grant stood over her. "That piece of shit hit you pretty hard."

Jen pushed herself to her feet and wiped her sticky red hands on her pants. "Thanks. It would've had me if you hadn't been there."

Mark appeared at the top of the stairs. "Everything OK down here? We took out a couple on this floor."

"Thanks to Grant, I'm fine," Jen said. "He saved my ass."

Grant grinned at Jen. "I've been told I'm good at rear guard."

Another smart-ass. Great.

She plodded up the stairs and followed Mark to the last room on the right. An exam room, it had a desk and chair in one corner and an exam table in the middle of the room. Zeke stood at the window, peeking through the blinds.

"How's the view?" she asked.

"Perfect." Zeke glanced at her, then did a double take. "What happened to you?"

"Just a normal day in zombie world."

Zeke laughed.

Grant entered the room and closed the door behind him. He handed the cell phone to Doc.

"Zeke, can you keep watch on that trail while we check in?" Doc asked.

"Sure enough. I can stand like a statue for hours. I even once had a dog pee on my—"

"Just watch the damn trail," Grant snapped.

Zeke frowned and turned back to the window.

Doc pressed the buttons on the phone and it picked up immediately. "Where are you?" the colonel's haggard voice came over the phone speaker.

Everyone looked at Jen. "Midtown," she said.

"Not fast enough," the colonel snapped.

"How much time do we have left?" Jen asked.

"Nine hours and seventeen minutes," Doc said.

The cell phone cut out, then back in. "...is all you have."

Mark leaned toward the phone. "You'll have to repeat that, Colonel. You cut out."

"Can you hear me now?" the colonel asked.

"Yes," Jen said.

"The situation's getting worse on base. We've lost a few men already, and the only reason we haven't lost more is we've erected higher barriers around the flight line. But even that is just stalling the inevitable."

Doc rubbed his eyes. "How much time do we have?"

"Three hours. Four at the outside."

The air went out of Jen. They'd been busting their asses to get across the god-forsaken city and they were still behind the curve.

"If we're in danger of being overrun," the colonel said, "we'll have to leave."

Grant's face darkened and he crossed his arms. "We'll get there in time, Colonel."

"Yes," Doc said. "We'll tend to it."

"Roger," the colonel said. "Out."

Jen kicked the wall. "Are you shitting me? Three hours? How do we make that kind of time?"

"We'll have to drive," Grant said.

"Right." Jen pointed at him. "You remember what happened the last time we did that, don't you?"

Grant gritted his teeth, his jaw muscles flexing.

There I go again. He lost his friends and I just dug into that wound. "Look, I didn't mean that."

"You're both right," Doc said. "We'll need a vehicle, but we don't want a repeat of the convoy. A big extended cab pickup would be better. It's solid enough to run through a small horde and nimble enough to avoid the big ones."

"And what happens when we get to the base gate?" Jen said. "Don't you think there'll be a big horde there? And we can't just go around it."

Mark smiled. "We don't drive to the base gate."

"And where do we go?" Doc asked.

"I recall there's a small airport somewhere in north Anchorage," Mark said.

Jen nodded. "Merrill Field. So what?"

Mark shrugged. "We drive to Merrill Field and fly a plane to the base."

"Who's going to fly it?" Grant asked.

Jen snapped her fingers. "Mark can! He's rated for small planes."

Mark smiled at her. "That's a fact."

Zeke turned from the window. "They're coming."

"What?" Jen said.

"Trip and his gang. They're headed this way."

21

Jen peeked between the blinds. "There are only nine of them. Maybe the zombies took one out."

"Still too many," Mark said. "Let's put some distance between them and us."

"These guys are a pain in the ass." Jen followed Mark out of the building and joined everyone in front.

"We'll continue on the trail, but we're not far from the highway," she said. "We should have a good view of what's around us when we get there."

Zeke walked toward the trail. "I'll sneak back and slow them up."

"Hold your horses," Doc said. "There's no need for that."

"I'll hide in the brush and take out one or two in the rear," Zeke said. "If I can't do that, at least I'll get their attention and duck on out. It'll slow them down and give you a better head start."

Jen put her hands on her hips. "You'll just get yourself killed."

Zeke smiled. "I'm a ninja. We don't get killed." He ran into the trees and disappeared.

Stupid kid. Jen went to go after him but Mark grabbed her arm. "Our mission is to get Doc to the base."

"And since you're the one who's supposed to lead us," Grant said, "You can't chase after a crazy kid in a ninja costume."

Jen shot Grant a nasty look, but dropped her gaze when he looked back at her with concern in his eyes and not the scorn she expected. She sighed and led them onto the path, heading north.

It took only a few minutes to arrive at International Airport Road. After scanning the area and seeing no immediate danger, they jogged toward the highway. Multiple muffled gunshots came from behind them, stopping Jen in her tracks. *Zeke.*

Mark put a hand on her shoulder. "I'm sure he's all right, but we can't waste the extra time he's giving us."

She nodded and continued on. Nothing she could do for him.

When they reached the Seward Highway frontage road, she stopped at the edge of the slope up to the highway and crawled up to the guardrail. Keeping low, she peered over it and watched for movement. At least thirty cars were stranded on both sides of the highway, but there looked to be plenty of room to maneuver around them. Jen grinned. "Kind of like rush hour in the winter, but without the ice and snow."

Mark sidled up next to her. "Doesn't look too bad." He pointed to the right. "Two zombies by that tourist bus, but that's it."

Jen's gaze swept to the bus and the two zombies stumbling alongside it. One, a middle-aged man, tilted to one side and shuffled along. The other, a young teen girl with blue and red hair, shambled back and forth in front of the bus.

"That's south," Jen said. "We're heading the other way."

Grant joined them. "Problem is, you don't know if there are others hidden behind any of the vehicles."

Doc stood and shaded his eyes as he watched the two zombies. "Man's got a good point."

Mark grabbed Doc's arm and pulled him down. "How about we don't let them see us just yet."

Jen pointed at a Hummer. "There. That'll be the most heavy-duty vehicle we'll find here."

"Not a damn chance," Grant said. "Too close to the Humvees. There's no way I'll step foot in anything like that again."

Jen swallowed. For all Grant's bluster, he had still witnessed his friends' deaths and deserved a lot of credit for keeping himself focused on the mission. She looked past the Hummer, and her gaze landed on a Tundra truck. "That." She pointed. "Sturdy, and a lot faster than a Hummer. We need its speed to avoid and outrun the zombies, but it's solid enough for us to run through a decent-sized crowd of them."

Grant smiled. "Looks like a winner. How do we get to it without setting off zombie alarms?"

Mark unslung his rifle. "Follow me."

He crept up the frontage road, the others following him. Stopping parallel to the Tundra, he waited for the others to catch up, then snuck onto the road and hid behind a red minivan lying on its side against the guardrail. Jen stayed with him and signaled the others to wait.

Mark scoped out the zombies, then gestured for her to follow him. He darted across ten feet of open asphalt and knelt behind a police car. Jen followed his lead and peeked inside the squad car, looking for a shotgun. The rack was empty.

She waved Doc and Grant over, and they ducked and ran to the cop car. The two zombies still wandered aimlessly. They turned their backs to the group, and Mark dashed the twenty feet to the Tundra. Jen ran after him and made it to the truck just as the girl zombie turned back their way.

Doc and Grant froze halfway to the truck, looking like big kids playing red light, green light. Were the zombies far enough away to ignore them?

The zombie girl tilted her head and shuffled a few steps closer. She turned back as the zombie man lumbered toward the Tundra. He, too, stopped and sniffed the air. *There goes that sniffing shit again.*

Doc took that moment to swat at something on his face. The zombies shrieked and took off for him.

"Run," Jen yelled. She yanked the driver's door open and checked the ignition. No keys. *Dammit.*

Grant and Doc sprinted for the truck. More zombie howls rose up around them.

Mark jumped into the passenger side. "Start it up."

"No keys." Jen checked the sun visor, and Mark rummaged through the glove box.

Grant pushed Doc into the back and jumped in behind him. "Let's get the hell out of here. What are you waiting for?"

"No keys." Jen held her empty hands up.

A series of shrieks rang out from the east side of the highway. "Here they come," Doc said. "We'd best be getting a move on."

Mark pulled Jen's leg to the side. *What the hell?*

"There." He pointed to the floorboard. A set of keys lay there. Her damn foot had been covering them.

She ducked to grab the keys. A gunshot went off and a hole appeared in her window. She glanced to her side, and several of the gang stood at the edge of the highway, their guns aimed at her.

Jen stuck a key in the ignition, but it didn't turn. "Fuck!"

22

Two keys left.

A shot blew out the back windshield. Grant and Doc scrambled to the floor. "Get us out of here," Grant roared.

Jen tried the square key, but the damn thing wouldn't go into the slot. She pulled it back. *Upside down.* Flipping it over, she jammed it into the ignition and turned it. The engine jumped to life.

The two zombies climbed into the truck bed. A wave of twenty or more streaked to them from their right. Bullets peppered the outside of the truck.

"They're trying to shoot out the tires," Mark yelled.

Jen threw the truck into gear and slammed her foot on the gas. The truck screeched and jumped forward, its back end fishtailing. One of the zombies did a backward flip off the back. The other grasped the back window frame just behind Doc.

Jen swerved around an overturned bus, then crossed the road and passed a pile of burnt bodies before spinning the wheel to turn north.

The zombie hanging on to the window frame made a grab for Doc. Grant stabbed at it with his sword, knocking it to the truck bed.

"Keep this truck steady." Grant climbed through the broken window as the zombie scrambled to get to its feet.

Jen slowed and took wider turns to thread her way through the abandoned vehicles.

The zombie pulled itself to its feet just as Grant swung his sword. The dulled blade slammed into the zombie's temple. It stumbled, still alive, but disoriented. Grant kicked it in the stomach, knocking it out of the bed. He let out a whoop.

"Get back in," Mark said.

The wave of zombies in pursuit were closing in. Jen had to get their speed back up.

Grant jumped headfirst back into the cab, and Jen slammed the gas pedal to the floor. She passed several vehicles and zoomed onto the Tudor Road off-ramp.

Jen continued speeding down Tudor Road, but slowed as she approached the intersection with Lake Otis Boulevard. A semi lay on its side, partially blocking the intersection.

"Looks like you can get around it on the right," Mark said.

Jen frowned. "I don't like this. Can't see what's on the other side of the damn thing."

Grant whistled. "That must've been one hell of a crash."

Jen steered the truck to the right and slowed down, creeping forward. The other side of the truck came into view slowly.

A zombie in a mail carrier's uniform stumbled toward them, bloodstains on his chin and shirt.

Jen sped up. "This'll be easy." She swung the truck around the semi, making everyone lean to the right. The left side of the bumper knocked the mail carrier into the overturned trailer.

They cleared the pile, and the way forward opened up. Twenty yards ahead more than forty zombies milled about in the road.

"Back up," Grant said.

"No," Doc said. "Take a deep breath and get us going as fast as you can."

Jen tried to see past the horde in case there were stalled cars or debris behind them, but the zombies were too thick to see anything.

Fuck it. She slammed on the accelerator. "Hang on."

The zombies in front turned toward them, no doubt alerted by the shriekers behind the truck. Jen leaned forward and gripped the steering wheel with both hands, her knuckles turning white.

She aimed for the right side of the horde. If they got stuck and had to bail out, she didn't want it to be right in the middle of them.

The horde ran directly at them. She veered to the right, and they angled toward the truck. They weren't giving her a choice—she had to go right through the middle.

She squinted as they hit the first three zombies. Two of them bounced to the side, but the other went under. The truck shuddered and Jen struggled to keep it straight.

Running into the first wave slowed them down. Jen pressed the gas pedal to the floor. The front wheels spun, creating black smoke and the smell of burnt rubber. "What the hell are we stuck on?"

A zombie slammed into Mark's door. Mark shoved the door outward, sending the damn thing flying. Mark peeked out and under the truck before he leaned back in and slammed the door shut. "We're lodged on a couple of their bodies."

Grant leaned forward and twisted a knob on the dashboard. "We weren't in four-wheel drive. Try it now."

Jen pressed the gas pedal and the truck jumped forward, just as the zombies from behind reached it. Two of them managed to grab the tailgate and were dragged behind while the truck ran into the middle of the rest of the horde. Mangled hands grasped at the windows and doors, and rotted faces pressed against the glass, their yellow eyes filled with hunger.

The truck bounced and twisted, rumbling over undead bodies. They passed the last of them and Jen steered to the middle of the road. It looked as if it had been cleared at some point, with broken-down vehicles pushed to the side.

Grant aimed his pistol at the one remaining zombie holding on to the tailgate. A round in the head and their last hitchhiker was gone.

Doc ran his hands through his hair and smiled. "Now that was intense."

The zombies faded away in the rearview mirror, but Jen wasn't slowing down. She got them to Boniface Parkway in minutes and took the turn on two wheels.

Mark put a hand on her arm. "Do you want me to take it?"

Her heart hammered. "Sorry. Didn't mean to take it so sharp. Just want to get to the plane."

Boniface was clear enough that Jen could increase speed, and she only had to make small adjustments to avoid abandoned vehicles.

A chorus of shrieks rose to their right, and a tidal wave of zombies spilled onto the road behind them.

"Shit!" Jen pressed the accelerator to the floor. They were almost to Northern Lights Boulevard.

Another horde ran onto the road ahead of them, about a hundred feet past Northern Lights. There had to be a couple hundred. *Too damn many to run through.*

The tires squealed as Jen braked and turned left onto Northern Lights. The zombies still chased them from behind, with the horde they'd just avoided joining them.

The road curved right. "We can take Bragaw Street north just after the high school," Jen said. "A little further up from there we take a left and it takes us to the airport."

She came out of the curve, barely missing a huge dump truck that lay on its side. Ahead of them, just past Bragaw, there had to be a hundred more of the undead. Three zombie dogs in their group turned toward the truck and howled. The other zombies answered the call, and the horde streaked toward them.

Jen glanced in the rearview mirror. The zombies already chasing them filled the back window of the truck. Thousands of them.

Can't go back. Can't make it to Bragaw. A replay of the zombies washing over the Humvees flashed through her mind.

We're so screwed.

23

The zombies behind the truck fell back as the truck raced down Northern Lights Boulevard, but that meant the horde running at them from the front was closing in fast.

A high school came up on their right and dense woods on their left. The horde ahead crossed the intersection. *No chance making that road.* Jen jerked the steering wheel to the right.

"Head for that set of double doors," Mark said. "We just have to hope they're not locked."

Screw that. Jen had learned her lesson about locked doors at the mall. The truck jumped the curb and bounced across the grass. She aimed it right at the seam between the two school doors.

Glancing to her left, she did a double take. Like the two zombies at the mall, a group of about thirty zombies no longer chased them. They'd changed direction and raced straight for the door. *What the hell?*

"Slow down," Grant yelled. "You won't be able to stop."

Jen leaned over the wheel and double-checked her seat belt. "Better make sure you're buckled in, 'cause we ain't stopping."

A dozen of the zombies reached the door, spun, and ran at the truck. *Just when I started to believe they had some smarts.*

"Hang on," she yelled. They hit the zombies. Several bounced off to the sides and a few slipped under the truck. Two smashed against the grill like bugs, their teeth gnashing and arms reaching out toward the windshield. Another, a female firefighter still in her yellow suit, was tossed in the air and landed on the hood, her drooling, bloody face pressed against the windshield.

Blinded by her, Jen concentrated on keeping the truck on course despite the bouncing and shaking as it rolled over the undead. If she was off by even a couple of feet, they'd slam head-on into a wall.

The truck shuddered and its rear wheels came off the ground. It hesitated for a second, then found traction again and the zombie on the hood slid off. The truck rocketed through the doorway, the doors ripping off their hinges and slamming to the side.

"Whoo-hoo," Doc yelled. "That's mighty fine driving, young lady."

Jen slowed the truck down. The damn hall didn't go straight through the school. She'd have to make some turns.

Mark glanced over his shoulder. "They're right behind us." He turned to her. "Do you know where you're going?"

Jen kept her eyes on the hallway. A turn was coming up. "I spent a few years in this school after my mother died."

She spun the wheel to the left, and the truck screeched on the tile floor, its rear end bouncing off the wall. No sooner had the truck straightened than she hooked it right. She passed two more corridors and turned hard left.

She stopped before a set of double doors with a sign that said *No Street Shoes on the Gym Floor*. "Get them open, and close them after I get the truck in."

"What?" Grant said. "Are you fucking crazy?"

Mark jumped out and ran to the doors. He pulled one open and braced it, then opened the other. Jen drove the truck in. Mark closed the doors and jumped back in the truck.

"Damn, Jen," Doc said. "You're like Wonder Woman."

Jen smiled. "Those doors open out, so pushing on them won't get them open." She zoomed to the doors on the other side, stopping under a basketball hoop.

Mark and Grant hopped out and held the outside doors open. They closed them after the car was through and got back in.

The roar of the combined horde, even though it was on the other side of the building, drowned out any sound the truck made. "Holy shit," Grant said. "How many thousands of them does there have to be to make that racket?"

Jen hit the gas and the wheels sent dirt and grass flying into the school walls. She raced the truck over the football field, bounced through the parking lot, and ran through a gate with stop signs on it. The truck zoomed across the road and in between two eight-plexes.

She slammed on the brakes, stopping just before running into another apartment building. Grant craned his neck and looked left and right. "It's a dead end. I thought you knew this town."

Jen glared at him. "I don't know every damn inch of it."

Several zombies ran out of one of the apartments behind them, screeching into the air. The screeches were echoed by thousands of zombies back at the school.

Mark threw his door open. "No way to back out of here now. We'd run right into that big group."

Jen grabbed her axe and exited the truck. "We need to find a place to hide."

The zombies from the apartments chased after them. Jen and Mark stood at the rear of the truck and were joined by Doc and Grant. A ten-year-old girl zombie with her nose chewed off made a beeline for Jen. Jen hoisted the axe backward and timed the swing precisely, an uppercut that split the zombie's jaw and skull in half. The girl flew back and landed on the asphalt.

Grant slammed his sword into the side of an old woman, knocking her over. But she struggled to her feet, and he had to give her another whack to put her down for good.

Doc stood on the bed of the truck and let a twenty-something man with half his face flayed off scramble to climb up the tailgate, then he gave a mighty swing, splitting the zombie's head open and sending bloody splatter over Grant.

"What the hell, Doc? Watch out."

"Sorry."

Mark had positioned himself three feet in front of Jen. The next two zombies closed in, and Mark stepped between them. He brought the mace down to crush one zombie's skull, then spun and crashed it into the back of the other zombie's head.

"Damn impressive," Jen said. She readied herself for the last two. She timed the swing to take out the one on the right, but before they got close enough they stopped and split, one to her right and one to her left.

What the hell?

They came at her at the same time. The damn things were coordinating their attack?

She swung for the one on the left and gave it a glancing blow on the shoulder knocking it off course. It ran into the other one just before it reached her and kept it from tackling her.

"Need some help here," she yelled.

Mark bashed in the head of one of the zombies as the other turned and leapt at Jen. She slammed the axe's blade into the top of his head. He fell to the ground, lifeless.

Jen freed the axe. "Did you freaking see that? Those two damn zombies were working together."

Doc nodded. "That is so not cool. That's not the first time they've coordinated movements, so it's not a rarity. Seems the virus is mutating even faster than we initially thought."

Mark stepped around the truck. "No time for scientific discussions. We need to get moving. That big horde will come around that corner any second now."

Jen ran to the side of the eight-plex in front of the truck. "Follow me."

She threaded between the buildings, then turned left and ran past several more. They would have to hole up somewhere, but she wanted to be at least a little closer to the base.

She ran right past another couple of buildings and stopped. The others caught up with her. "Where are we going?" Grant asked. "We aren't going to outrun them."

She pointed to the building on their right. "Grant, you and Doc check for an unlocked door on that side. Mark and I will try this side." She ran to the first door to her left without waiting for an answer.

Locked. She moved to the next one and it was, too. When she tried the fourth one, she began getting nervous. Mark stood in front of another one and shook his head.

"Over here," Doc called. He stood at the open door for the middle apartment in the building across the street.

The roar of the zombie horde had become so loud, it felt like a tidal wave about to crash over them. Jen expected to see them blasting around the building at any second. She and Mark sprinted to the door Doc held open. Grant streaked in just before Jen and Mark. Doc ducked in and closed and locked the door.

"Everyone upstairs," Mark said.

They ran up the darkened carpeted stairway. Mark flipped on a flashlight. "End of the hallway and stop."

They huddled underneath an old clock on the wall. "Everybody quiet," Mark hushed.

The floor vibrated as thousands of feet pounded the pavement outside the building. Jen held her breath.

Something banged into an outside wall downstairs. Startled, Jen jumped. More thumps came, like when a rainstorm was just picking up speed. *The damn zombies are running into the building.*

"Even that many won't penetrate a wall," Doc said.

Another sound, a hollow thumping, came from downstairs. *That doesn't sound good.*

Jen ran halfway down the stairs and looked down the front hallway. The front door shook with the impact of undead bodies slamming into it. As she watched, a crack spidered down the length of the door frame.

Jen rushed back upstairs to the others. "I think we're about to have company."

24

The stampede of undead had ceased shrieking and roaring, with nothing but the pounding of their feet marking their passage by the building.

Jen opened the last door at the end of the hall and entered. "Come on."

She closed it after the others joined her and sat on the floor, leaning against the door. If the zombies came upstairs, the flimsy-ass door was their last hope.

The pounding, both of the feet and on the building, slowed until the last of it faded into the distance. Jen turned on her flashlight. Its beam fell on an empty crib.

Where's the baby now? Is it a zombie, or did the parents get it to safety?

One corner of the crib had a dark brown stain on it. Jen pointed the light to the floor below. It showed a larger stain about the size of a dinner plate, with parts of it so dry it had begun flaking off. A crushed pink rattle lay next to it. Her mind flashed back to the young couple with the baby that were torn apart.

Jen swallowed. She shoved the image to the back of her mind and continued to the window. Pulling out the edge of the shade, she watched the street.

A zombie shambled past the apartment, seemingly aimless as it zigzagged down the road.

Movement to her left caught her attention. Another three zombies lurched out from an open garage. Their movements seemed more purposeful. *Holy shit.* They changed directions together, perfectly synchronized.

Jen leaned back and whispered. "Doc. You need to see this."

Doc joined her. She pulled the shade back a few more inches and pointed to the trio. "Look."

Doc's left eyebrow rose. "Well, I'll be dipped in dog shit."

"That one in front of the other two seems to be leading them," Jen said. "Watch. As soon as it changes directions, the other two follow its lead."

The lead zombie, a middle-aged woman with an afro and a bloody hole in her chest, angled toward the door of an apartment across the road. The two zombies behind her changed direction as soon as she did.

"Is this another one of those mutation things, Doc?" Jen asked. "Are these things getting smarter?"

Doc stepped back. "I don't know. Could be. They're acting almost like a flock, where they fly in a vee formation and all the other birds follow the lead."

Jen dropped the shade. "So do we have to worry about these things tracking us down, or opening doors?"

They slipped back into the hallway.

"I don't know," Doc said. "So far it doesn't rise above instinct. But who knows how far it could go?"

"What are you two talking about?" Mark asked.

Jen turned her flashlight off since Mark had his on. "There are only a few zombies that I can see, but some of them are acting strangely. Like they're learning things."

Grant wiped the back of his hand across his forehead. "What kind of things?"

"There's a small group of them out there sticking together, staying in a formation. First time I've seen that."

Mark frowned. "We don't have the luxury of time." He looked at his watch. "Down to just under two hours. I don't think we can worry about evolving zombies. We need to get the hell out of here."

Doc put his hand out to Grant. "Let me see the phone."

Grant handed it over, and Doc turned it on. It rang almost immediately, the loud sound rattling Jen. "Lower the damn thing."

Doc reduced the volume, then pressed the speaker button. "Colonel?"

"Where are you?"

"Just north of the high school on Bragaw," Jen said.

The phone crackled. "Where's the doctor? I want to speak to him."

"Right here, Colonel."

"Doctor, I don't think we have more than thirty or forty minutes before we're overrun. I'll stay as long as possible, but you need to get your ass over here."

"Roger," Mark said. "We're on our way."

Automatic gunfire sounded from the phone. "Shit," the colonel's voice said. "Got to go. Just get here." The phone went dead.

Doc handed the phone back to Grant. "How are we supposed to get there? We're pretty much trapped."

Jen crossed her arms. "There are a few zombies out there, but we can take them."

"Before they set off the alarm?" Grant asked.

Jen sighed. They'd have a thousand more zombies on their asses before they could finish off the few out front.

"We'll drive out," Mark said.

Jen scowled. "There are a lot of cars out there, but the zombies will send out an alarm before we could—" She snapped her fingers. "The attached garage downstairs. If there's a working car in there, we're set."

"Guess it's another road trip," Doc said.

Mark led the way downstairs, shining his flashlight in the kitchen. "I'll check in there for keys. Jen, why don't you look in the garage? Doc and Grant can split up and rummage through the bedrooms."

Jen turned on her flashlight and shined it down the hallway. As she approached the door to the garage, she bit her lower lip. If the garage was empty, they'd have to come up with something else.

Two vehicles sat side by side in the garage, a shiny late model SUV that looked like it had been driven off the dealer's lot that morning, and a dented green truck with rust stains and a missing front fender. She checked inside each for keys and came away empty-handed.

Built-in shelving lined the two of the walls, and a workbench sat opposite the garage door. Jen rustled through the loose screws and bolts lying on the bench, the smell of old grease and oil making her sneeze.

The door to the apartment popped open and Mark stepped through, jingling a set of keys on a ring. "Kitchen drawer, for the win."

He strode to the SUV and hopped in the driver's seat. "I'll just turn it enough to make sure the battery's still good. No need alerting the zombies before we're ready to leave."

Doc stuck his head through the door. "There you two are. Grant and I struck out."

"Mark found some keys. He's about to try them."

Grant pushed past Doc. "Don't start the car. It'll get attention we don't want right now."

Mark nodded. "Thanks, Grant. Hadn't thought of that." He winked at Jen.

Mark slipped the key into the ignition and tried to turn it. It didn't move. He pulled it out. "Maybe that's the key for the back hatch. Let me try this other one." He slid the other key in and twisted. "No dice."

Jen's eyes went to the junker truck. "You've gotta be kidding me."

Mark shrugged and got out of the SUV. "Beggars can't be choosers." He opened the truck's door, and it let out a cringe-inducing squeal.

"Not sure that thing's gonna stay together," Jen said. "Even without trying to ram it through a horde."

Mark sat in the driver's seat and pushed the key into the slot. He twisted it and the lights came on.

"Looks like we've got a winner," Grant said.

Jen frowned. "All four of us won't fit in the cab. Someone will have to sit in the bed."

Grant raised his hand. "Guess that'll be me."

"Why do you think that?" Jen asked.

"You need to drive. You know the area and can react quicker than me if our way gets blocked." Grant nodded at Doc. "Doc has to stay protected. And Mark's the one with the real combat experience." Grant shrugged. "Just thinking about it tactically."

Mark stuck out his hand and Grant shook it. "What's this for?" Grant asked.

"Don't let anyone ever tell you that you aren't a real soldier," Mark said. "Now get in the back."

Grant smiled and hauled himself into the truck bed.

Mark unlatched the garage door. "Everybody in. Don't start the truck until I raise the door. I'll jump in and then you need to get us the hell out of here quick."

Jen stood at the driver's door. "What if it doesn't start?"

"I'll close the doors and we'll have to figure something else out. We don't have time for experiments."

Jen nodded. "Let's load up." She slid into the driver's seat.

Doc climbed in the other side and slid next to Jen. Jen tried to ease her door shut without having it squeak, which was a lost cause. It latched with a *clunk* and the door didn't close flush. She pulled on it and it rattled. *Will this damn thing stay closed?* She put her hand on the key and looked at Mark.

"Ready?" he asked.

She gave a thumbs-up. Mark rolled the garage door up. A half dozen zombies screeched and sprinted for them and a bloodied biker zombie that had been just outside the door grabbed Mark's collar and yanked him out of the garage.

Adrenaline kicked in and Jen flipped the handle on the truck door, but it didn't open. "What a piece of shit."

Mark smashed the mace into the biker's face and kicked it back, knocking it into two other zombies. They collapsed into a pile.

Doc put a hand on Jen's arm. "Take it easy and try the ignition again."

His calm and serene shit pissed her off sometimes, but she twisted the key. The engine went *whir, whir,* then nothing. "Do any of you know how to get this damn thing going?" she screamed.

"I can," Grant yelled through the window. "I had to baby that Humvee on the way up here. I can do it with this thing, too."

"Then get in here and do it." Jen rolled down the window and yanked on the outer handle. She pulled her axe as she exited the truck and ran to Mark. He'd just dispatched a skinny zombie in a pair of shorts that drooped to its knees.

Jen slashed at a balding, middle-aged man with half his face missing, and caught him under the jaw, knocking him backward and splitting what remained of his face.

The truck engine ground behind her. *Guess Grant isn't having any better luck.*

At least two dozen zombies ran onto the street from between two buildings down the road.

"We're going to have to close the door," Mark yelled.

Jen reached up and grabbed the handle, but the door was stuck. "Help me."

Mark dropped a teenage girl who wore a pair of sunglasses that hid her yellow eyes. "Shit's getting worse."

Jen followed his pointed finger. A pack of zombie dogs streaked onto the road. There had to be ten or more. *How the hell do we fight them?*

The truck's engine sputtered and roared. She glanced back and Grant smiled and gave her a thumbs-up. He stuck his head out the window. "Hop in."

"Mark," Jen yelled. "In the back."

Mark ran to the back of the truck and vaulted over the side. Jen dove into the bed headfirst, and Mark banged on the side of the truck. "Let's go."

The truck jerked forward, slamming Jen against the tailgate. *Thank god that thing didn't fly open.*

She tried to get to her hands and knees, but the truck made a sharp turn and threw her into the side of the bed. Mark grabbed her under her arms and pulled her up. "Stay away from the sides and be ready."

She got up on one knee, still holding the axe in a firm grip.

The cab's back window opened. "Grant needs to know which way to go," Doc said.

Jen stood and leaned on the top of the truck cab. Zombies flowed out from between buildings, and Grant ran the truck right through them. One grasped the grill and pulled itself to the hood. Jen pulled out her pistol and sent a bullet through its left eye. It disappeared under the truck.

Jen leaned down to the window. "Go straight until you hit the main street. That's Bragaw. Then turn right and don't let anything stop you. We don't have time to go another way."

"Jen!"

She spun. Mark knelt on both knees. A German Shepherd, its fur matted with blood and yellow hate in its eyes, crouched on the bed, ready to pounce. Mark swung at it, but it leapt over the mace and snapped at him, its teeth barely missing his face.

Damn, that thing's fast.

Mark backed against one side of the cab, and Jen knelt at the other. The dog sprung at Mark, avoided his mace, and dodged to Jen's side of the bed. She brought the axe down, and it leapt back barely in time.

The truck's speed had picked up. Jen glanced to see where they were. Twenty feet from the turn. She held the axe handle with both hands and cocked it back over her shoulder. Mark continued to battle the dog. It attacked, retreated, and attacked again in one fluid motion. Mark wouldn't be able to keep up with it for long.

Just a few more seconds.

The truck made a hard turn, catching the dog off guard. Knocked off its feet, it was flung into Jen's side of the bed. She brought the axe over her head as fast as she could and hit the dog in the forehead, cracking its skull. It fell to the bed, its legs splayed and tongue draped out of its mouth.

Mark lay back and blew out a breath while puffing his cheeks. "Holy shit. Nice shot. Can you imagine facing a whole pack of them?"

Jen looked behind them. The zombies, dogs and humans, fell farther behind. She leaned into the cab's back window. "Nice driving, Grant."

He beamed.

"The next major road is Debarr," she said. "Hang a left. We're almost there."

"You got it."

She sat down next to Mark. "You OK? No bites?"

He shook his head. "Damn good thing you were here. I never would've survived that thing."

"Just luck," she said.

Mark let out a short laugh. "I've noticed you tend to do things your own way. You were supposed to stay in the cab and drive, but you didn't and it worked out this time. But one of these times, it's going to bite you in the ass." He rubbed his mouth with the back of his hand. "Anyway, thanks."

The truck wound around a broken-down police cruiser. Its doors were open and dried blood and bits of flesh decorated its windshield. Mark was right. She'd grown up taking care of herself, and had a hard time trusting people she didn't know. But of everyone in their group, she trusted Mark the most, and that's why she'd jumped out to help him. She couldn't afford to lose him.

The truck slowed and Jen stood to look ahead over the cab. The Debarr intersection was littered with twisted metal and burned corpses. Grant picked his way between the wreckage, the truck jerking and bumping over charred flesh and bone. The smell of burnt meat hung heavy in the air.

The zombies chasing them seemed to have given up, but as they turned onto Debarr, several more wandered into the road in front of them. The truck cleared the wreckage and Grant gunned it, mowing down three of the zombies in mid-screech. Debarr was almost totally clear, and despite the responding screeches around them, the zombies that poured into the road were too far behind to catch up.

Jen knocked on the back window. "Keep going straight past the hospital —the road curves—then look for an access road to Merrill Field on your right at the stoplight."

"How much farther?" Mark asked.

"If the roads are open, a couple minutes," she said.

A pileup just past the hospital blocked their way. Grant slowed down and eased the truck over the sidewalk and onto the grass. They reached the access road to Merrill Field a few minutes later and followed the winding road up to the aircraft parking area. When they reached the top of the hill, Grant stopped.

Jen stood to take in the devastation. It looked like the place had been bombed. Of the few buildings still standing, they were mostly hollowed-out wrecks. The rest were nothing more than blackened ruins. The breeze washed the smell of burnt wood over her.

Jen's heart sank. "What the hell are we going to do now?"

few zombies staggered through the distant charred ruins, but were far enough away that they took no notice of the truck and its occupants.

Doc shook his head. "The whole place? The whole damn place is gone?"

Grant got out of the truck and slammed his fist against the side. "I don't fucking believe this. We did everything. We never gave up. And what did we get for it?"

Doc looked at Jen. "Maybe we shouldn't give up now. Is this all of the field?"

Jen shaded her eyes and scanned the area. She'd passed Merrill Field a million times on the highway, but had never been on it.

She tried to find landmarks that were near the highway, but couldn't. The piles of debris were too high. Could there still be undamaged planes they couldn't see from their position?

"Grant," she said. "Take us around this mess."

"For what?"

"We're looking at the flight line, but there may have been some aircraft parked by the buildings near the highway."

Mark raised his head. "Hell, yeah. They could be parked for maintenance, or loading and unloading. Why didn't I think of that?"

Grant swung his door open and jumped into the truck. Doc hopped in the other side. "Never give up hope," he said.

God, I wish he'd quit that.

Grant put the truck in gear and steered it to the left, past the charred remains of several planes and a helicopter. A zombie ran at them from behind a pile of debris. When he grasped the tailgate, Jen knocked his head in with the axe.

They drove up a rise and around a collapsed building, and the rest of the airfield opened before them.

Most of it was in the same condition as what they'd already seen— destroyed buildings and planes. Burned bodies and vehicles.

"There," Mark yelled. He pointed to a small building near the highway. All that remained on one side of it was the foundation, but the other side of the building looked untouched.

In front of it stood five planes. The two nearest the wrecked side of the building were non-flying, with one missing a wing that looked like it had snapped off, and another that was missing a wheel and tilted to the side.

The other three looked untouched.

Grant jammed the gas pedal to the floor, and Jen fell on her ass in the bed. Mark thrust out a hand and pulled her back to her feet.

"I'm not even pissed," she said. "Things are finally going our way."

"Don't get your hopes up too far," Mark said. "We still have to find keys, and the engines have to turn over."

Jen nodded. "And in good repair, right?"

"We may have to accept some risk," he said. "We've got minutes to get up and fly to JBER. If there's a sticky control or something else I think I can handle for the short flight, I'll take her up."

The truck came to a stop several feet from the single-engine plane on the end. Mark jumped out of the bed and jogged to it.

He opened a door and leaned in. "Everything looks good so far."

"Not that I'm one to worry," Doc said, "but aren't you supposed to do some type of preflight?"

"No time to do a detailed look," Mark said. "Besides, I don't want to take too long with each of them. I'd rather find the keys and see which one we're getting before I spend the time."

Mark checked out the next plane, another single-engine plane with the wings overhead. The door stood open and he poked his head in. "Same here."

He turned toward the last plane, an older looking two-engine model. He propped his hands on his hips. "Don't bother with that one."

Jen stepped next to him. "Why?"

He pointed to a puddle beneath it. "Oil. We don't have time to troubleshoot."

Grant had walked toward the building, rifle slung over his back and sword in hand. "Any keys should be in there, no? Let's hope they weren't all in that part that was blown away."

Jen squinted at the building. The side that still stood was dark and at an angle where the sun didn't penetrate very far. "I don't think Doc should be going anywhere near that."

Mark looked at the building, then Doc. "Agreed. Grant and I will go in. You stay here with Doc and keep him safe."

"Me? How about Grant sits this one out."

"I don't trust his judgment and abilities as much as I do yours."

Jen stood chest-to-chest with Mark. "All the more reason I should have your back."

Mark shook his head. "Getting Doc to the base is our mission. Besides, do you think the military will take us without him?"

Damn, if he doesn't make sense. I freaking hate it, but he's right.

Mark ran over to Grant and together they jogged to the building. Jen approached the truck where Doc waited. "You and I will hang out here. Watch their backs."

Doc leaned against the truck and laid his rifle in the bed. "We're not watching anything. Y'all are just trying to keep me bubble-wrapped."

"Does that bother you?"

Doc laughed. "Not a bit." His face got serious and he said, "Dammit, Jim. I'm a bio scientist, not a warrior."

Jen laughed. For the first time since all hell had broken loose, she thought about a future. She'd love to work with Doc once they got the hell out of there. *And I'll bet he'd go for it, too.*

Mark and Grant disappeared into the building, their flashlight beams playing on the walls.

Jen leaned against the side of the truck, crossed her arms on top of it, and laid her head down. When had she last slept? She'd been so hyped up, she hadn't felt tired. But the adrenaline level had to be dropping. Her eyelids grew heavy.

Someone shook her arm. Had she fallen asleep? She straightened. Doc pointed to the highway, not far from the building. A dozen zombies shambled down the road and were on track to pass right by the building. If Mark or Grant made too much noise, it would attract them. Maybe even their flashlight beams would do it.

They had to be warned. Jen spotted a door at the other end of the building. She could enter there unseen by the horde and warn Mark and Grant.

She bit her lip. But what would she do with Doc? She'd stayed back with him to keep him safe. None of the buildings were closer than thirty yards or so, and nothing stirred within or between them.

"Doc," she said, "I need you to get in the truck and wait for me."

"Where are y'all going?"

She pointed to the building door. "I'll slip in there, let the guys know what's coming, and be right back here before you know it."

"I'll come with you."

She shook her head. "No way. You're our ace in the hole for getting out of here. Plus, you have info that might help with a cure. You're too important."

Doc sighed. "OK. But take it easy and be careful. I was hoping when this is over that you might come work with me."

Jen's mouth opened, but she couldn't think of a thing to say. He wanted to work with her? She nodded and pointed to the truck. Doc smiled and climbed in the driver's side.

The zombies on the highway had staggered closer. Jen would have to take a wide angle to get to the door so they wouldn't detect her. She ran to the ruins of a firetruck ten yards away, then darted behind a bent and twisted pair of dumpsters. From that spot, she was blocked from the zombies' view.

She sprinted for the door and pressed her back to the wall beside it. Doc sat in the truck and gave her a wave. She waved back. She had her rifle slung across her back and the axe ready to swing. She twisted the knob.

Locked.

Shit.

The door had a window, but its blinds were down. She tried to peek through them, but saw nothing but darkness.

Smashing the window would make too much noise and probably alert the zombies she was trying to warn the others about.

Only one other choice.

She raised the axe overhead and brought it down on the door knob. It popped off and spun away on the asphalt. She pushed on the door, but it didn't budge. *Damn dead bolt.*

She cocked an ear. Shuffling, but no growls.

Time was running out fast. The zombies would be at the building any second, and the C-130 could take off any minute.

She reared her arm back and smashed the door's window. The sound echoed over the airfield. She whispered through the window. "Mark. Grant. You hear me?"

A growl answered her, and a woman in a print dress with an arm that dangled by a thread of flesh slammed into the door, knocking the blinds off. Her mouth snapped inches from Jen's face, her fetid breath causing Jen to gag.

Regaining her composure, Jen buried the axe into the woman's head. The creature collapsed.

A chorus of screeches rose from the other side of the building. She hadn't gotten to Mark and Grant in time. She flicked on her flashlight and raced through the room, catching glimpses of lockers and benches before bursting through an open doorway into a hall.

Light beams played over the walls and ceiling at the other end of the hallway. The zombie howls were louder in that direction.

"Mark. Grant."

"Jen, what are you doing here?"

They stood at a closed door. It shuddered with the force of several bodies.

"I came to warn you about the zombies coming up the highway," she said.

"Nice timing," Grant said.

Mark put up a hand. "Wait. What's that?"

Jen tilted her head, listening. Over the zombie noise, she heard the faint sounds of a car horn. Her eyes grew wide. *Doc.*

27

The horn blared again.

Mark craned his neck and peered past Jen. "Where's Doc?"

"He's in the truck." Jen sprinted for the door.

"You left him alone?" Grant yelled after her.

She looked out the broken window to make sure it was clear, then opened the door and stepped out. No zombies on that end of the building.

Weapons fire echoed down the hallway. The zombies were breaching the door. Jen hesitated. *Who do I help?*

A truck horn sounded. Jen's eyes snapped to their truck. Fifteen zombies surrounded it. *Shit.*

The zombies screeched, growled, and banged on the doors and windows. Another six rushed out from behind a pile of rubble and joined them.

Doc would be safe for a while if he kept his head. Jen slipped the rifle off her shoulder and took a firing position. If she could take them out from where she was, she'd still be close enough to help Mark and Grant. She aimed at a zombie that stood on the hood, stomping its feet on the windshield. It was only a matter of time before it caved in the glass.

She aimed for its ear, took a breath and held it, then squeezed the trigger. The light recoil pushed the butt into her shoulder, and the zombie's head split. It slid to the hood, and then onto the asphalt. The smell of spent powder stung her nostrils.

A screech to her left caused her to spin. Some of the highway zombies must've heard the commotion and abandoned the inside of the building. A half dozen of them sprinted for her.

Gunshots rang out from the truck. *I'll get back to you as soon as I can, Doc.*

She swung her rifle toward the highway zombies and shot two of them, but only killed one. The creatures were too close for a rifle, so she pulled her axe and crushed the skull of the first zombie to reach her, while ducking out of the way of the second one. She spun and brought the axe down on the back of the second zombie's head after it passed her, and it sank to the ground.

Mark would be proud of that move.

The last three zombies were slower than the others. Jen risked a glance at the truck. Two more zombies lay dead next to it, but another one stood on the truck bed and reached in the broken back window, trying to grab Doc.

More gunfire came from inside the building, then stopped. "Could use some help out here," she screamed.

Jen kicked the chest of one zombie, knocking it to the ground. She brought the axe blade down on its neck, almost severing the head from the body. A second swing completed the job. The head continued to snap its jaws silently at her.

Doc screamed, "Jen!"

The zombie had Doc's head pulled out of the truck's back window. Jen picked up her rifle and aimed at the son of a bitch, a husky guy in a gore-soaked flannel shirt and jeans. Her finger went to the trigger. She took a deep breath and held it, then slowly squeezed the trigger.

Her head jerked back by her hair and her feet flew out from beneath her, sending her rifle shot into the sky. She slammed down on her back and the air rushed from her lungs.

A tall blonde woman with one side of her face de-skinned silently bent over Jen, her mouth wide open and heading for Jen's throat.

A shot sounded, and the top half of the zombie's head disintegrated. The lifeless hand lost its grip on Jen's hair and the zombie fell. Grant stood at the doorway, his rifle aimed her way.

"Doc," she croaked.

Jen pushed herself to her knees and pointed toward the truck. She looked back at Grant. "Doc."

Grant brought his rifle to his shoulder and shot. The zombie disappeared over the side of the truck, and Doc pulled himself back into the cab.

Jen caught her breath and stood. Another couple of zombies climbed into the truck bed and attacked the back window. Grant took out one, but the remaining one dove headfirst into the cab and had Doc in its grip. The other zombies roared as if being fed by bloodlust.

Gripping her axe tight, Jen staggered for the truck. Shots rang out from behind her, and the zombies attacking the truck fell one by one. Two zombies still remained when she reached the truck. The one in the cab was on top of Doc, who fought it bare-handed, barely managing to keep it from biting. The other zombie, a large man who looked as if he had been a bodybuilder, stood between Jen and the truck, his yellow eyes glaring at her.

Got to get to Doc.

She ducked just before reaching the bodybuilder. He reached out, but grabbed nothing more than air, sending himself off-balance. Jen gave him a glancing blow to the shoulder and sent him to the ground.

Jen grabbed the passenger door handle and yanked it open, her axe getting caught on the frame as she swung. She dropped it and grabbed the zombie's shoulders and pulled.

Doc screamed and the zombie fell onto Jen, blood splashing the windshield.

Jen rolled backward, tossing the zombie out the door. She grabbed the door and slammed it shut.

"Doc."

Doc's shirt was ripped open. Jen pulled the fabric back. His shoulder had a chunk of flesh missing and it bled steadily.

Doc gasped for breath and grabbed her hand. "Have to get this to Dr. Cartwright."

"What?"

Doc pushed a thumb drive and the vial of spores into her hand. "Has data on spores and how they spread virus. All my research. Promise me you'll get them to Fairchild and Dr. Cartwright."

Jen nodded and shoved the drive and vial into her pants pocket. She cradled Doc's head. "I'm sorry, Doc. I should've stayed with you."

He shook his head. "Not your fault." He coughed. "And tell Dr. Cartwright that I wanted to make you my assistant, and that I think she'd be right smart to take you under her wing."

"She won't believe me." Jen's eyes watered.

He coughed and closed his eyes. "Tell her I said I'd eat a bug if it wasn't true. Tell her just like that and she'll know it came from me."

"OK, Doc."

"I've wondered what the change would feel like."

"How does it feel, Doc?"

He opened his eyes. "Hurts like a bitch." His brown irises had lightened, but he smiled. "Chill, dude."

It wouldn't be long.

The remaining zombie banged on the truck door, but slumped to the ground when Mark's mace crushed the back of its skull. He opened the door. "Doc?"

Jen shook her head.

"Take care of me," Doc said.

Jen frowned. "What?"

"Like you did for your father. Will you take care of me, too?"

She caressed his head with one hand while she pulled her pistol with the other. Tears flowed down her face. "Of course, Doc. I'll take care of you."

28

J en and Mark lowered Doc's body to the ground. Jen crossed his arms and closed his eyelids. "I'm going to miss you," she whispered.

The phone rang. Grant scrambled to get it out of his pocket. He pressed the answer and speaker buttons. "Yes, Colonel."

"This will be my last call. We're wheels up in ten minutes, with or without you. The situation here has become untenable."

Mark faced the others. "We can make that time. I've got three sets of keys in my pocket. We just need to find a plane that matches one of them."

The phone crackled. "Then I'll expect you here before we leave."

"We will be," Jen said. "See you then."

"Wait," the colonel said. "Dr. Wilson, the lab at Fairchild wants to know if you have any special equipment requests they can set up now so you won't have to wait once we arrive."

Jen held her breath. Grant pressed the mute button. "What do we say?"

"The truth." Mark pressed the mute button to clear it. "Colonel, I'm afraid we've lost Doc."

"Lost?"

Jen sucked in her lower lip. "He's dead."

Silence. Jen squinted at Grant. "Did we lose connection?"

The colonel's voice came over the speaker. "Then our mission is done here. We'll leave immediately."

"What about us?" Jen asked.

"You failed in your mission. I have no use for you."

"But Doc gave me the spores and a thumb drive with his notes on it."

The colonel's voice lowered an octave. "I never put much stock in what Dr. Wilson was to contribute, and I can't verify that you're not just saying things to save your skin. I won't risk my men any further."

Mark grabbed the phone from Grant. "Wait. What about the nukes? When will they fall?"

A light clicking sound came from the phone. "Colonel?" Grant asked.

"Standard operating procedure is two hours after we're wheels up. I suggest you get in a vehicle and get as far north on the other side of the mountains as you can. Good luck."

The phone went silent.

Grant flung the phone to the pavement, and it broke into several pieces and scattered. "If I ever catch up with him, I'll give him his good luck."

Jen hung her head. "So what do we do?"

Mark pulled the keys out of his pocket and jingled them. "We find the plane that matches one of these keys and fly south."

Jen looked at Doc's body and her chest ached. "No time to bury Doc."

Mark put a hand on her shoulder and guided her to the truck bed. "Come on."

When they reached the planes, Mark pulled out one set of keys and gazed at the tag attached to it. Jen peeked over his shoulder. The tag said "Mountain View Aviation," then underneath that was handwritten N400204.

"That's the tail number?" she asked.

Mark nodded as he scanned the planes before them. "Don't see it."

Jen pointed to one of the piles of plane debris. "There." She ran over to it and lifted what was left of the tail. It had three numbers visible, and they matched the last three numbers of the key tag.

Mark tossed the keys to the ground. "Guess that one's not flying." He pulled out another set.

The number on that tag didn't match any of the surviving aircraft, either.

"You sure there aren't any more keys in that building?" Jen asked.

Grant frowned. "We didn't have time to go through every drawer and pile of shit. These were the only keys on the board that was marked 'Keys.'"

"We did check in the desk beneath the board and around that area in case any of them fell off," Mark said.

Jen's heart thudded against her chest. Outrunning the nuke in the truck seemed like a long shot. And who knew what kinds of hordes they'd have to fight through to get there?

Mark took out the last pair of keys and read it. He looked at the three undamaged planes and shook his head. "Not here."

Jen stuck her hand out. "Can I see?"

He dropped the keys into her hand and she looked at the tag. Like the other tags, it had the name of the air service and a tail number. The damn number didn't match any of the three planes before them. "Shit."

She flipped the tag over.

"Guess we better load up, then," Grant said. "But I'd like to find something bigger than this truck."

Jen brought the tag closer and squinted. In faded ink, it said, "Ted Stevens."

Ted Stevens? The late senator?

Grant climbed into the truck and started it. Mark stood, holding the passenger door open. "Jen?"

"I know where this plane is."

29

M ark peered at the tag. "Where does it say its location?"
She pointed out the faded writing. "It says Ted Stevens."
Grant turned the truck off and ran over. "What's going on? We need to get out of here."

Mark took the airplane keys from Jen. "She says she knows where this plane is, but all it says is Ted Stevens."

Grant's eyebrows lowered. "Ted Stevens? He was Alaska's senator, but he's dead. What would he have to do with a plane?"

"Who's Anchorage International Airport named after?" Jen asked.

Grant snapped his fingers. "Of course. So the plane's out there?"

"Why not?" Jen said. "There are a ton of small planes parked out there."

Mark shook his head slowly. "I don't know. How can we be sure?"

"You can't," Jen said. "But even if this plane isn't there, a hundred more are."

Grant crossed his arms. "But that's back across town, and we have less than two hours. The drive out of town will be quicker." He jerked a thumb at the highway. "The way out's right there."

"Sure," Jen said. "And where are we going to go after we get out of town? Canada? Do you think they'll let us in? How do we know the virus hasn't spread there?"

Mark slid the keys into his pocket. "Either way's a risk."

Jen pulled the thumb drive and vial from her pocket. "Here are two good reasons to fly."

"What's that?" Grant asked.

"Doc gave them to me before he died. The drive has all his data on the zombies, and the vial contains the original spores that spread it. They don't have these at the CDC. It could be important in stopping this shit."

"We could fly right to Fairchild," Mark said, "and get the information there faster. It could make a big difference."

Grant patted the truck's hood. "If we're going back across town, we need something better than this. Something bigger, more solid."

Jen put her hands on her hips and scanned the area. *Where can we find something bigger than a pickup?* She snapped her fingers. "I know."

"What?" Mark asked.

She pointed past the Glenn Highway. "Two blocks that way. I had a friend who worked for the city's street maintenance department. They have a storage facility over there where they keep the dump trucks and snow plows during the summer. Those bad boys are huge and heavy."

Grant smiled. "That'll be perfect."

They loaded in the truck and Grant drove onto the highway. A few zombies staggered across the road in the distance.

Jen pointed in the air. "Look."

A C-130 climbed into the sky over JBER. "There goes our ride," Mark said. "I guess the clock starts ticking."

Jen directed Grant across the highway. "Take a right there."

They drove along a road with a fifty-foot drop-off to Ship Creek on one side and warehouses on the other. The warehouses ended with a fenced-in equipment yard containing dozens of heavy vehicles.

"This is it," Jen said.

Grant stopped the truck next to a double gate and they got out. Mark grabbed the padlock and chain locking the gate. "Well that sucks."

"Use your mace," Grant said.

Jen slipped her axe into a belt loop. "Might as well ring the dinner bell." She hauled herself onto the chain link fence and scaled it ten feet to the top. "Try to keep up, fellas."

She dropped to the ground and crouched as she scanned the lot. Mark and Grant landed next to her, and she led them between a road grader and a sand spreader. There, backed up to the rear of the lot, was a row of big-ass yellow dump trucks.

"I think those might work," Mark said.

Grant's eyes got big. "Beautiful."

Jen grabbed his arm. "Wait." She pointed to a truck in the corner with a huge V-shaped plow on front. "Just what the doctor ordered."

"Are you fucking kidding me?" Grant ran up to it. "You could plow through almost anything with that. Damn thing has to be at least sixty thousand pounds."

He climbed into the cab, looking like a kid at Christmas. Rolling down the window, he stuck his head out. "The keys are in it."

A whirring sound came from under the hood and it broke into a full-throated roar, with black smoke shooting from the pipes.

A chill-inducing grinding of gears echoed over the lot, and the truck lurched forward, stopping next to Jen and Mark. Grant turned off the truck and climbed out. "I think we've got our transportation."

"How's the fuel level?" Mark asked.

"About three fourths of the tank."

A single screech sounded from behind them. Jen whirled to face a thirty-something zombie with a heavy beard and overalls. He streaked toward her. In one motion, she pulled her axe, sidestepped the zombie, and swung the blade around, taking a chunk of the zombie's skull off. "How about a little off the top?"

Mark nodded, smiling. "You're getting pretty good with that thing."

"I've gotten a lot of practice lately."

A series of screeches sounded from several directions. Mark opened the passenger side door. "Let's see how well this thing works."

Grant started the truck as Jen hopped in and sat next to Mark. A half dozen zombies had reached the outside of the gate and pressed against it.

Jen laughed. "I forgot the gate was chained and locked. They're not getting in here soon."

Grant put the truck in gear. "That's our way out. We have to go through the gate and the zombies." The truck shuddered and bounced, the engine rumbling. A dozen zombies stared back at them from the gate.

"Damn things are multiplying," Grant said. "Better hang on."

He got the truck rolling and the point of the blade hit right between the two gates. It snapped the chain and shoved the gates to either side, knocking the zombies away.

"Stee—rike," Jen said.

The truck rumbled onto the road and Grant took a hard right, the force of the move pressing Jen against the door. She caught a glance of Grant's face, and he looked the happiest she'd seen him. "Yee haw," he yelled.

Jen ran through the possible routes to the airport in her head. The most straightforward route would be to follow the highway to downtown and take Minnesota Drive south to International Airport Road. But the smoke from downtown still rose thick into the air and the narrow roads and close buildings would make it difficult to avoid hordes.

"Better go back the way we came," she said. "At least we know the roads aren't too bad up to Northern Lights."

Mark nodded. "Good idea."

Grant drove the truck through Merrill Field and onto Debarr. A few stray zombies charged them and were crushed beneath the truck's wheels.

He turned onto Bragaw and drove down the middle of the road, the V blade parting wreckage and debris like the Red Sea. Grant pumped his fist when the truck's blade tipped a school bus out of the way. "This is working better than I expected."

Mark waved his hand in front of Grant.

"What?" Grant asked.

"We can do a lot in this truck," Mark said, "but we're not invincible. We still need to avoid hordes and pileups if we can."

Grant waved him off. "I got it. I got it."

Jen sighed. Just when she'd started trusting Grant to not screw up, he was making her nervous again. *But who am I to talk? I made the biggest screwup yet.*

Grant slowed the truck and eased around the big pile of blackened, twisted metal at the intersection of Bragaw and Northern Lights. A few zombies screeched and jumped onto the truck, two climbing up the back of the bed and another on the running board outside Jen's door.

Mark nodded at the door. "Sit back and open the window." He took out his pistol.

Jen leaned back and slid the window down. The zombie, a dark man with an eye missing, held onto the side view mirror with one hand and clawed at her with the other. Jen plugged her ears, and Mark's gun went off in front of her. When she looked out the window, the zombie was gone. She raised the window. "Thanks."

Mark smiled. "I haven't had many easy targets like that."

Screeching rose around them. Grant switched gears and the truck rumbled on.

"Take this road to the Seward Highway," Jen said. "We'll have more room to maneuver there. Then we'll take the Old Seward to International. It's a straight shot to the airport from there."

Grant gave her a salute. "Didn't we come through there on foot earlier?"

"Exactly," Jen said. "The intersection was clear and the zombies were only moderately heavy."

They plowed through a dozen more zombies before hitting the Seward Highway. "This ain't right," Mark said. "Where the hell are all the zombies?"

"They're out there," Jen said. "I'll be happy to avoid them."

A dead semi lay ahead under the sign indicating that the Old Seward turnoff was the next exit. Grant downshifted and eased the truck around the wreckage.

"Oh, shit," he said.

A milling horde of hundreds of zombies blocked their off-ramp. The mob turned as one and let out one hell of a zombie howl.

30

G rant let off the gas. "Shit. That's a lot of them."

"Gun it," Mark yelled.

Jen's breath hitched. This would be the real test to see if they'd picked the right vehicle. "Go right down the off-ramp, then keep straight."

Jen braced herself. Grant got the truck up to forty before it plowed into the screeching crowd and decelerated as bodies flew to the sides. Blood and body parts shot over the plow and painted the windshield in gore.

Grant downshifted, and the truck pushed through the crowd. More zombies streamed from between buildings, jumping onto the truck. *Just like the damn convoy.* They were going to be overwhelmed by sheer numbers.

Yellow eyes glared at her through the window as bloody hands grasped at the glass and slipped away.

Zombies on the hood blocked their view. A trickle of sweat rolled down Grant's cheek. "What do we do now?"

"Whatever you do, don't stop," Jen yelled over the growls of the undead inches from her face.

A muscular zombie on the hood slammed his fists against the windshield, and others followed his lead.

"Get us the fuck out of here," Mark said.

Jen checked the magazine in her pistol as Grant shifted gears. The damn truck bounced so much, she'd have a hard time hitting her targets, even at that close distance.

She pointed the gun at the windshield. "They get through and I'm going down fighting."

Mark leaned against her, his pistol in hand. "Save the last bullet for yourself."

"I can't see shit," Grant yelled. He turned the wheel, and the truck ran over something on the right side. Jen grabbed the door handle to keep from falling into Mark. The truck tilted to the left and wavered for a second before slamming down, which knocked half of the zombies off the hood.

"We're on the Old Seward," Jen yelled. "Speed this piece of shit up and go straight."

The truck rumbled over fallen bodies, causing it to buck and more zombies to fall off. A half dozen zombies remained on the hood, the muscular one still slamming its ham-sized fists into the windshield.

A crack appeared and spidered out.

"We can't wait," Mark said. He aimed at the zombie.

Jen glanced out her window. Only one remained on the running board. She brought the window down. "Don't shoot the glass. I've got this."

A teenage girl in a midriff-baring crop top, her intestines hanging from a gaping hole in her belly, flailed her arms, trying to grasp Jen. Jen pulled the trigger and the zombie's head snapped back as it tumbled from the truck.

Jen wriggled out the window.

"What the hell are you doing?" Mark asked.

She held her left arm out to him. "Hold on to me."

He grasped her arm and she leaned back, her ass on the door, and aimed the gun at Muscle Man's forehead. She squeezed the trigger just as the truck bucked. Her round shredded his left shoulder and he lost use of that arm, but continued pounding with the other fist.

Jen took a deep breath and lined up the sights on the creature's forehead. Sticking her tongue out of the side of her mouth, she squeezed the trigger. A hole appeared right where she'd aimed, and Muscle Man's yellow eyes rolled up into his head just before he took a swan dive off the hood. Jen took aim at each of the other zombies in turn and cleared the hood.

Mark pulled her back into the cab. She fell into the seat and closed the window. "Take that, Clint Eastwood."

"We're pulling away from them," Grant said. "Kicked their asses."

Mark handed Jen a new magazine. "There weren't that many."

Jen frowned. "There had to be a couple hundred, at least."

"I figured four hundred, give or take," Mark said. "But there's almost half a million in the city. We could easily run into a swarm of thousands, and we barely escaped this bunch."

Jen leaned forward and stared at the side view mirror. The remaining zombies had stopped chasing them. They were clear for the moment.

The truck rumbled toward the intersection with International Airport Road. A mass of vehicles blocked the road, just past the intersection. Uneasiness crept into her gut.

"Let's take this turn a little slower than the last," Jen said. "Just in case there's another horde waiting for us."

Grant shot her a dirty look, but downshifted. He leaned forward. "Hey, this is where we crossed before, right?"

Jen nodded. "We crossed this road to get to the highway where we picked up the Tundra."

Grant slapped the dashboard. "That's it." He leaned forward. "But there's something different about it. Were those cars there before?"

Mark pulled out his pistol. "Stop the truck!"

A shot rang out and a muzzle flash came from the cars in the intersection. The truck's windshield shattered and fell in. Several more firearms blazed in front of them, rounds peppering the truck.

Jen ducked, and a hole appeared in the back of her seat.

Mark hit the floorboard. "Ambush."

31

Jen fell to the floor as Grant jammed the brake pedal. The truck's brakes squealed and it shuddered to a stop.

Bullets flew through the glass and into the front of the truck, the sound of each round hitting causing her to flinch.

Jen's mouth went dry and her heart hammered her chest. "I know what to do with zombies, but what the hell do we do with this?"

Mark hunched over next to her. "Keep your head down for starters."

Grant raised his pistol above the dashboard and fired a few rounds. Mark put a hand on Grant's wrist and lowered it. "You're just wasting ammo."

This noise is going to bring a swarm and then we'll really be trapped. Images of the carnage at the convoy played unbidden in her mind.

"Open your doors," Mark said. "Let's see what cover we may have."

"What if they're on the side of us, too?" Grant asked.

Mark shook his head. "They would've already attacked us from there. All the gunfire we're taking is from the front."

Jen unlatched the door and pushed it open. It bounced back and she pushed it out again with her foot, using less force. It stayed open. The gunfire picked up and the door's window shattered. She pressed back against Mark.

Grant got his door open. On his side was a car dealership with an open parking lot, but the damn building was too far away to make a run for it. On Jen's side stood a motorcycle shop much closer to the truck.

Jen covered her head as chips of glass rained down. "What do we do?"

Mark chewed his lip and peered out her door. "Grant, can you drive this thing over to the cycle shop without getting your head shot off?"

Grant pulled his door shut. "Just watch me." He scooted up on the seat, but kept bent over, and put the truck into gear. It rumbled forward and he turned the wheel, keeping his hands below the dashboard. The firing stopped for a few seconds, then picked back up. Rounds tore into his door and hit the seat back. Grant hit the brakes. "If we turn any more, those bullets will be flying right into this cab."

"What we need is a diversion," Mark said.

The gunshots slowed down again. *Are they reloading? Now would be the time to move.*

"Cover me." Jen jumped to the ground and scampered toward the motorcycle shop. She pumped off a few rounds from her pistol in the general direction of the shooters. Mark and Grant leaned out from the doors and laid down fire.

Almost there. Bullets whizzed overhead and the glass windows of the cycle shop shattered. Jen dove for safety behind the outer wall. She pressed against the wall, panting.

The shooting stopped.

A syrupy voice called out from the intersection. "Well, darling. Looks like we do get to play again."

Trip? Is this for real?

"Don't be rude," Trip called out. "You can at least say hello back."

Jen stood and edged to the corner of the building. Mark and Grant crouched behind the dashboard, shoving new magazines into their rifles. She looked at Mark, spread her hands, and shrugged. *What do I do?*

Mark pointed toward the shooters and mimicked someone talking with his hand.

Jen yelled. "What do you want?"

Trip laughed. "You, baby."

Bile backed up into Jen's throat. *Freaking creep.* "We don't want any trouble. Why don't you just let us go by?"

"Not a chance. You still haven't paid your trespassing fine. And now you're trespassing on my intersection."

A burst of gunfire punctuated his sentence, and the impact chipped the corner of the building, inches from Jen's face. She backpedaled and fell on her ass.

Picking herself up, she turned to the truck. Mark had his rifle aimed at her. Before she could process it, the gun fired and something behind her hit the ground with a thud. She whirled, and a balding zombie that had to weigh three hundred pounds lay still a couple of feet away.

Trip's gang started firing again. *Probably think Mark shot at them.*

She gave Mark a thumbs-up and his eyes went wide. *What the hell?* She spun, and there stood Zeke in full ninja garb.

"Hi, Jen," he said.

She pulled him into a back-crushing hug. "I thought I'd never see you again. What the hell happened?"

He pulled his hood off. "I took out two of them and they chased me all over, but never saw me. I followed them out here and stuck close. They'd given up on following you, but figured they could ambush anyone passing through the intersection. I was just leaving to go find you guys when they started shooting." He smiled. "Glad I came back to check it out."

The gunfire slowed down. "I'll tell you what," Trip yelled. "You come over here, Girly, and the others can move on."

Mark shook his head, his teeth gritted.

Jen looked down at the fat zombie. "With all this gunfire, you'd think there'd be a ton of zombies swarming us."

"They picked the right place for a firefight," Zeke said. "There are trees lining this whole intersection, and hundreds of cars in the lots that break up the sound and keep it from traveling too far. Any zombie more than a block or two away probably doesn't hear much, and Trip's gang cleared three blocks out before they settled in."

Jen scratched her chin. "So we just need to draw a horde close enough for those assholes to attract them with their guns."

"Yeah," Zeke said. "There are a ton of zombies not too far from here."

"What direction?"

He pointed toward the gunmen. "Past them."

Jen smiled. "Perfect. You and I are going zombie wrangling."

32

Jen waved to Mark, then put up her hands, palms up, indicating for them to stay where they were. Mark's eyebrows furrowed, but he nodded.

Jen holstered her pistol. "Take me to the horde."

Zeke pulled his hood on and unsheathed his katana. Jen grabbed her axe and followed him to the back of the building.

After looking both ways, Zeke sprinted across the back parking lot and into the brush. Jen followed him, glancing over her shoulder toward the intersection. The building concealed her from Trip's men until the last second. Hopefully, they were too busy with Mark and Grant, and hadn't noticed her streaking by.

Zeke cut through the bushes and covered the rocky ground to a strip club without making a sound. Jen followed him and slipped on loose rocks, nearly taking a tumble. But she righted herself and joined Zeke on the back side of the building.

They slipped around to the side of the building and stopped. International Airport Road lay in front of them. "We cross here," Zeke said. "Fast as you can. They probably won't see us, but if they do, they won't have time to get a good shot."

Jen nodded. "Ready."

Zeke peered around the corner toward the intersection. He raised his right hand, then dropped it. Jen took off and sprinted straight for a warehouse. The firefight continued unbroken at the intersection, and she pulled up at the warehouse, panting.

This is the easy part and I'm already breathing heavy. Need to pace myself.

"How much farther?" she asked.

Zeke pointed ahead. "A couple of blocks that way."

He threaded his way around shipping containers and abandoned vehicles. More industrial buildings appeared on their right, while a greenbelt, thick with fir and birch trees, lined their left. The greenbelt muffled the sounds of battle to almost nothing.

Zeke stopped and put a finger to his mask where his lips were. "We're close," he whispered. "Some of them may have strayed since I was here a half hour ago."

He pressed against a warehouse wall and crept to a set of metal stairs that ran to the roof. Rushing up the stairs, Zeke didn't make a sound. Jen took three steps up and stopped. She sounded like a freaking stampede.

How the hell does he do it?

She looked up and Zeke stepped onto the roof. She took the steps slow to keep the noise down, but took two at a time. The noon sun beat down as she stepped onto the roof and joined Zeke at the other end, where he lay on his stomach looking over the edge. Her breath hitched.

Between the group of industrial buildings, thousands of zombies milled around, packed shoulder to shoulder in some places. A giant warehouse stood across the way, its huge double doors wide open and more of the zombies lumbering inside.

The growling of so many undead had merged into a hum. "You weren't shitting," Jen whispered. "Trip will shit his pants and run when he sees this many coming."

"The only way to lure them there is to use ourselves as bait," Zeke said.

Jen swallowed. "Yeah. Let's figure out our route."

She slipped to the back of the building and stood, looking out over the greenbelt. They'd need a route that they could easily run through, but one that would slow down such a big swarm. She turned to say something and found herself nose-to-nose with Zeke. Startled, she stepped back. He grabbed her arm. "Don't fall off the roof."

Heart pounding, she took a deep breath. "I wish you'd quit doing that sneaky shit."

Zeke shrugged. "Sorry."

She pointed at the trees. "The trail we came through earlier runs right through this greenbelt. I say we go for it."

Zeke pulled his hood off. "Good idea. If we can get through the trees and onto the path quickly, we'll be running the trail with no obstacles. Most of the zombies will have to run through the trees and brush since the trail won't hold them all."

Kid is smarter than I thought. "Right. And we come onto the Old Seward behind Trip and his gang." Jen frowned. "But it won't be easy. We'll have to run straight at them in the open."

Zeke smiled. "Once they see the horde, they'll stop shooting and take off. I think we'll be OK."

Jen put her fist out and Zeke bumped it with his. "Let's get down there and stir up a hornet's nest," she said.

She led him down the stairs and to the corner of the building. She pointed toward the trees. "See those two birch trees right past that old blue Dodge truck?"

Zeke nodded.

"That's where we head. I lined it up from the roof. If we go straight through there, we'll hit the trail several yards in. Follow it to the left and we'll end up on the Old Seward."

"Got it," Zeke said. "How do you want to get them moving?"

"All we've got to do is find one and make it screech." Jen crept out from the building, past a few cars. Zeke stayed by her side. She crouched by the car and scanned the area. A half dozen zombies staggered back and forth.

She whispered to Zeke. "This is going to be easy." She stood and strode out from behind the car. The zombies wandered, not noticing her. Jumping up and down she yelled, "Hey, zombie assholes. Over here. Fresh brains."

The six zombies spun toward her at exactly the same time. *What the hell?*

They paused for a moment, then sprinted at her. Hundreds more zombies stampeded from behind the building.

Holy shit. Jen streaked to the tree line. *What the hell was that? No screeches and they all still knew to attack?*

Zeke darted ahead and she followed him into the trees, pushing past needled branches and underbrush. The sound of thousands of footsteps behind her.

Her shoes hit asphalt and she turned left just as a ninja-shaped figure disappeared around a curve ahead of her. Already breathing heavy, she pressed on, a stitch stabbing her side. She reached the curve and glanced back. Zombies poured onto the trail, hot on her ass. Not one grunt, not one screech. It was creepy as shit.

She caught a flash of Zeke ahead and pushed to keep up, the muscles in her thighs burning. She dared another glance behind her and was relieved to see the horde wasn't catching up. But it wasn't falling back, either. One stumble, one fall, and she'd be zombie chow.

She zipped around another curve and Zeke stood several yards ahead. He pointed down the trail. "Old Seward."

He joined her as she caught up. Freaking kid ran as if he'd just woken up from a nap. Didn't anything faze him?

The sounds of gunfire smacked them in the face as they burst onto the road and turned left. Trip and five others with him crouched behind the blockading vehicles, their backs to Jen and Zeke.

The shooting stopped and the thrum of thousands of feet pounding the asphalt had Trip and his gang turning around. Two of his men took off running toward a restaurant at the intersection. Trip stood, his mouth hanging open as if he couldn't comprehend the scene before him. But it lasted only a few seconds as he shouted orders. He and his remaining crew reloaded and fired in Jen's direction.

Jen glanced back and was sorry she did. Zombies covered both lanes of the road and more poured out from the trail, the trees, and between buildings. It was a silent flood of undead that would tear apart anyone in its path.

A bullet kicked up the asphalt a few feet in front of Jen and her attention went back to Trip. A muzzle flash flared from the crazy asshole's barrel and the sharp whine of a bullet zipped just above Jen's head.

I'm so screwed.

33

Zeke yelled, "I'll go around them on the right. You go left."

She nodded and angled left. The thought of zigzagging to throw off Trip's aim flashed briefly in her mind, but that would slow her down and bring the swarm closer to her ass.

The dump truck started up and rolled through the intersection toward the airport. Her breath coming in gasps, Jen changed direction and headed straight for the truck. Zeke raced ahead of her.

Trip was now the only one of his gang not in flight. He gritted his teeth, took aim at Jen with his rifle, and fired. The bullet passed somewhere in front of her. She kicked it up a gear and sprinted around the truck. Zeke was already in the cab. She jumped on the running board and peered back at the intersection. Trip had abandoned his spot and was running toward the restaurant. His men stood at the entrance holding the door open.

Jen braced her rifle against the shuddering dump truck door and took aim at Trip's back. *Bastard won't get away.*

The truck bounced over something as she squeezed the trigger, and the shot went wild. She grabbed the door to keep from flying off, barely hanging onto the rifle with the other hand. Recovering, she took aim again. Trip was only a few yards from the restaurant. Most of the swarm was on his tail.

She lined up the sights on his back, took a deep breath, and held it. A drop of sweat rolled down her nose as she squeezed the trigger and the rifle's butt recoiled into her shoulder. Trip fell, holding his leg. She'd missed his back, but he was screwed anyway. He rolled onto his back and emptied his rifle at the oncoming horde, which washed over him like a tidal wave and smashed into the restaurant's door, knocking it down. Scores of zombies flooded into the building.

Jen opened the cab door and pushed in, jamming Zeke into Mark.

Mark reached over and placed a hand on her arm. "I thought you were dead."

Jen rolled her eyes. "Easy there, big guy. Let's not get emotional."

"We're not out of the woods yet," Grant said.

He worked the clutch and glanced at the side view mirror. Jen looked out her side. A good portion of the horde had turned and were pursuing them. They trailed the truck by a couple hundred feet at most.

"How about putting this thing in turbo?" Jen asked.

Grant shook his head. "Oil pressure's down. Black smoke coming out the exhaust. I've got it up to almost thirty, but it isn't going any faster."

Mark frowned. "A lot of rounds went into this thing. We're lucky it even runs."

Jen looked at her watch. "Just over an hour before the government turns Anchorage into a glowing crater. We can't afford to go this slow."

Grant slammed a fist on the dashboard. "Pressure and speed are still dropping. At this rate we've only got a few minutes before that swarm catches up."

34

Zeke pointed ahead to the side of the road, where a building ended and dense trees and underbrush lined the sidewalk. "If Grant can slide the truck over to pass close by that building, we can jump into the bushes and wait until the horde passes."

Grant eased the truck to the right side of the road. "It's our best chance. Everyone out when we pass it. Looks like the road slopes down after that, so I can put the truck in neutral and let it go."

"But what happens when they catch up with the truck?" Jen asked. "They'll be between us and the airport. We'll never make it out of here in time."

"We'll have to figure that out later," Mark said. "Right now, we have to survive this swarm."

There has to be a better way. Jen looked ahead on the road, her gaze resting on a line of vehicles several hundred feet ahead. *Perfect. If I can find one that starts and has keys.*

Branches from the large bushes scratched the truck. "Get out now," Grant yelled.

"Can't take a chance on the zombies seeing us as they go by, so we've got to get through the brush on one jump." Jen pushed the door open and stepped onto the running board. Branches scratched her arms and neck, leaving red lines, with some oozing blood. She stuck her hand out to Zeke. "Give me your hand."

He looked puzzled, but extended his hand. Jen clasped it. "Don't forget to go into a roll." Zeke nodded, and Jen tugged him out of the truck. He disappeared into the brush.

Mark slid to the door and grasped her hand. "Good idea." She held onto the door frame and heaved him out as he pushed off with his legs.

Grant positioned himself at the doorway and she grabbed his arm. "Ready," he said.

"You guys lay low," Jen said. "I'll lead the swarm away."

"What?" Grant said.

"We're a team, and it's my turn up to bat. Just meet me at the airport. Follow this road and you'll run into it." She yanked Grant out and he disappeared into the brush.

The truck had crested the road and picked up speed on the down slope. She needed to get off, but the damn thing was going too fast. She eased her foot down on the brake and when the speedometer dropped to fifteen miles per hour, she threw the driver's door open and climbed onto the running board. One glance at the swarm told her she'd have to hit the road running. If she tripped or slowed too much she'd be a stinky-ass zombie in no time. At least till the nuke dropped.

One. Two. Three.

She jumped to the road and pumped her legs as soon as her feet hit the asphalt. Her balance off, she leaned forward and her arms windmilled. *I'm going to fall on my face.*

She grabbed the truck door and straightened, matching pace with the vehicle. Her stride stabilized and she ran to the left. Several vehicles lined the road fifty feet ahead.

Coming up to the first vehicle, a shiny new Subaru, she gave it a once-over. *Flat tire.*

She bypassed it and moved on to a minivan. She pulled the door open and felt the ignition. *Keys!* She jumped in and turned the key. Nothing. *Fuck!*

She jumped back out and darted for the next car, a puke green Ford coupe. Grabbing its door handle, she pulled. Locked. *Dammit.*

The lead zombies were almost on her. She had one more chance. The next vehicle had to work. She was running out of time and stamina. She sprinted forward and almost stopped in her tracks. *You've got to be shitting me.*

The closest vehicle, and the only one within twenty yards, was a dinky rusted ice cream truck.

35

Jen dashed to the ice cream truck, the sound of thousands of running feet reverberating in the road.

The truck leaned to its left side, but all the tires were full. A sliding door with the paint-peeled picture of a clown lay open, and she jumped into the seat.

Her hand went to the ignition. Empty.

That's it. I'm going to die surrounded by melted ice cream sandwiches and nutty bars.

She felt in the change tray and came away with empty candy bar wrappers. Leaning over, she popped the glove box open and pulled out registration paperwork, owners manuals, and maps. *Who the hell uses those anymore?*

A bump in the back sent a vibration through the truck. Jen's eyes snapped to the side view mirror. A middle-aged man with black plastic glasses hanging askew and a shredded fast food uniform rushed around the back of the truck and toward the driver's door. Jen grabbed the handle and slammed the door closed. The zombie pressed his hands and face against the window, bloody drool dripping down his chest.

"Sorry, sir," Jen said. "But we're all out of brain-flavored ice cream. Do come back again tomorrow."

She searched between the seat and the center console, coming up with hair, gum, and more wrappers. "What a damn pig."

A thump on the passenger side caught her attention. A small girl with half a tongue left banged on the window. More pounding came from the rear of the truck.

Jen licked her lips. Another thirty seconds and she'd be surrounded and unable to move, even if she could start the truck. Pulse pounding in her ears, she checked the seat pocket, then pulled down the sun visors. Something dropped to the floor with a metallic rustle.

She felt on the floorboards and picked up a set of keys. Heart pounding, she tried first one key in the ignition, then another. *Fit, Dammit. Fit.*

The passenger side glass exploded and three zombies leaned through the window, pawing at her.

Checking to make sure she had the last key right side up, Jen inserted it into the ignition. It slid right in. She turned the key and the engine turned twice and stopped. *FUCK!*

She pulled her pistol and shot two of the zombies grabbing for her. Dead weight clogging the window, they kept others from climbing in.

Two zombies climbed on the hood and smashed their fists against the already cracked windshield. Jen took a deep breath. *If this fucking thing doesn't start this time, I'm putting the barrel to my head and finishing it.*

She twisted the key. The engine turned once, then twice. She pressed the gas pedal and it coughed, then caught.

Jen threw the truck into gear and jammed the pedal down. The truck lurched forward. The zombies on the hood fell off and the two hanging in the window came along for the ride. She checked the side view mirrors, and a sea of undead filled them.

The truck's acceleration sucked, but she did get it up to thirty miles an hour. A glance in the mirrors showed that she'd pulled away from the horde and was putting more distance between them.

Got to slow down. Need to lead them out of the way so the others can get to the airport. Kind of like the Pied Piper.

She eased up on the gas pedal and allowed the horde to get within ten yards of her, then kept the pace steady. A few zombies slowed down or veered off.

Scanning the dashboard, she found a toggle switch and flipped it. "Pop Goes the Weasel" played. Jen found a volume knob and turned it to the max setting. The music blared from the roof and the zombies picked up their pace. Jen sped up to compensate, and watched the horde. None of the zombies wandered off.

"Got it." She pumped her fist.

She drove up International Airport Road, drawing more zombies from the surrounding buildings. She kept watch as some filled in the front ranks of the swarm and edged closer to the truck, causing her to reposition farther ahead.

The urge to go faster and get the hell out of there ate at her. Seemed it damn near took forever to pass the next intersection, where more zombies joined the horde. There had to be a couple thousand of them following her and hundreds more approaching from in front.

Got to get them off International so the others have a clear way to the airport. The first intersection was too small, but the next one, the Minnesota Drive offramp, would work. Six lanes on Minnesota, there was room to bring them all in after her.

She turned onto the offramp and led the macabre parade the wrong way down the northbound lane, weaving between broken-down vehicles. Like ants, the zombies flowed down the ramp and through the grassy berms on the side of the highway. Almost a quarter mile down the road, they still came.

Jen scratched her head. She'd have to get off Minnesota and take the back roads to the airport before long. The next exit was a half-mile away in the southbound lanes. That should be far enough to get the whole horde away from the airport route.

She drove over the median to the southbound lanes and the swarm flowed around obstacles, maintaining its distance behind her. "Pop Goes the Weasel" started over again for what had to be the fiftieth time. Jen groaned. "I hear that freaking song one more time and I'm gonna let those things put me out of my misery."

Jen's breath hitched. Another horde raced at her from ahead. She had to get to the exit before she ran into them.

She checked the rear view mirror. The horde flowing over the ridge from International had thinned. "Yes!" She'd cleared the way for the others.

Now to save my own ass. She pushed the accelerator to the floor and began to pull away from the horde behind her.

She passed the sign for the exit. "Just in time. Thank God this thing had some pickup when I hit the gas." *Gas.* She looked at the gas gauge. The red needle vibrated over the E. She slammed her fist on the dashboard. "Really? What the hell did I ever do to deserve this shit? Can't just one thing be easy?"

The off-ramp lay only ten feet to her right. She flipped the toggle switch and the music stopped. No need to attract any more.

The beat of pounding feet sounded like someone's bass was cranked up to the max. The leading edge of the mob ahead reached the exit ramp just before her. She dodged several zombies, then hit two others, which slowed the truck. She sideswiped a few more as she navigated the curve. One more jumped in front of her. She gritted her teeth and plowed right into it, the truck bumping over the undead body.

The road ahead was clear. Jen looked back, and she was pulling away from them. Pumping her fist, she screamed, "Yeah!"

She lost sight of them as she went around the next curve. Just before popping back out on International Airport Road, the ice cream truck sputtered, jerked, and died.

The horde could still be coming. Jen got out and ran to the intersection, counting at least seven abandoned vehicles there.

She checked two with no luck and had just kicked the door closed on the third one when a throaty roar from behind made her heart jump. She ducked behind the car and unshouldered her rifle. The roar grew louder, but it wasn't the roar of a swarm. More like an engine.

A bright red Camaro shot into view from behind a pile of burned-out cars. It swerved and wove around the junk and debris in the road.

Jen stayed hidden. Trip was dead, but there could've been more Trips out there.

The last quarter mile to the intersection was clear, and the Camaro kicked it into to overdrive and zoomed down the road, then braked hard, the tires leaving black streaks on the road and the smell of burnt rubber in the air. It came to a stop in front of Jen's hiding place.

The driver's window rolled down. "Hop in." Jen peeked over the hood. Grant waved and beamed at her. "It looks clear from here and we've got a plane to catch."

36

Thirty minutes later, Jen watched out the window as the plane broke over the Chugach Mountains. Prince William Sound lay ahead, and the small town of Whittier to the right. A flash of light burst from behind the plane. Mark took the plane into a dive and straightened it out a few hundred feet over the water.

Jen squeezed the armrest and peered out at Whittier. Scattered groups of figures ambled about the streets and docks. *Another dead town.*

Mark let out a loud breath. "Looks like we made it out of range."

"When will we need fuel?" Grant asked.

"Range on this Piper Cherokee Lance is about a thousand miles," Mark said. "But I wouldn't push it. We should stop every couple hundred miles if there's a place to fuel up. Never know when one of those little towns will be out of fuel or overrun with undead. Who knows how far the virus has spread?"

A whale breached the water's surface a few hundred yards away. Jen pressed her face against the window and squinted. Just before the whale disappeared beneath the waves, she thought she caught a yellow tint to its eyes.

An elbow dug into her ribs. She turned. "What?"

Zeke jerked a thumb at Mark.

"I'm heading to Biloxi to check on my family," Mark said. "Want to tag along? I could use you."

Jen placed her hand over her pants pocket and traced the outline of Doc's thumb drive. "Got one stop to make first."

"Where?"

Jen looked back out the window. "Fairchild Air Force Base. I've got a promise to keep and a colonel's ass to kick."

AUTHOR'S NOTES

Thank you for following me on this adventure. If you liked The Gauntlet, please leave a review on Amazon. This will help the book reach more people who like the kind of stories you and I do.

The Gauntlet was an interesting story to write. I normally start off with a premise, then put together a high level outline. Often, these outlines have gaps that I fill in as I go.

I've found that some of my best secondary characters are created after the outline is set and I'm spilling the story out of my subconscious. That's exactly how Zeke showed up.

I love quirky, unique characters, and Zeke has fast become one of my favorites. I'm actually writing these notes after completing the drafts of Book 3, The Citadel. I can tell you that Zeke takes it up a notch in that book.

If you'd like to keep up with what I've got coming out, sign up for my email list at uprising.marobbins.com. You'll get a **free** eBook, new release announcements, updates, and even some drawings to win prizes like signed paperbacks and other unique items. In fact, I recently had a drawing where I'll use the winner's name for a character in Book 4 of the series.

I appreciate every reader of my work. Without you, I'd just be telling stories to myself.

Till next time.

M.A. Robbins

ACKNOWLEDGMENTS

I couldn't do any of this without the support of my wife, Debbie. I know how lucky I am to have her. Much appreciation goes out to Domi at Inspired Cover Designs for another great cover. This was the first time ever that I felt the first version was perfect. Thanks to Tamara Blain of A Closer Look Editing for making my prose look much better. And special thanks to a great group of beta readers who caught plot holes and patiently answered my questions: Helen Zawacki, Leland Lydecker, Maureen Meyer, 'The real Petrovich', and Wayne Tripp.

THE CITADEL

BOOK THREE IN THE ZOMBIE UPRISING
SERIES

CONTENTS

To F. Gary Newton, Simon of Simon's Sanctorum. He made late night horror movies fun for a teenager in the early 70's.

1

The Cessna flew smoothly beneath the blue Washington sky. Jen looked around at her fellow bedraggled passengers. Finding out Seattle was a dead city had taken the wind out of all of them. *That and almost getting wasted at Klawock. Took two damn weeks to get out of there.*

Grant moved in the back, sending a breeze of body odor in her direction.

"Damn," she said. "Want to keep your funk back there? You'd knock out a zombie at a hundred yards."

Grant scowled. "You don't exactly smell like sugar and spice."

Jen ignored him. They'd been stuck in close quarters for so long, it was no wonder they were snapping at each other.

She watched out the window. *Haven't seen a moving vehicle in the past hour. Lots of ant people, but they all stumbled around.*

"Fifteen miles out," Mark said. "Time to try and raise someone." He reached for the mic and keyed it. "Fairchild Control, this is N400204. Do you read?"

The radio remained quiet.

"They're probably all dead, too," Grant said.

"Tell us what you really think, Eeyore." Jen caught Mark's eye. "Took less than two weeks for that crud to get down here and take out Seattle. Wonder how far it's gone?"

"For all we know, it's everywhere." Mark raised the mic. "Fairchild Tower, do you read? This is N400204. Come in."

Zeke sat in the back, reading a manga he'd somehow stashed in his ninja costume. He looked up. "What do we do if they don't answer?"

Mark sighed. "Guess we'll fly by and see what's going on. If it looks clear, we can land and forage. They're bound to have fuel, just hoping it isn't all jet fuel."

"N400204, this is Fairchild Control. Can barely hear you through the static. What's your location?"

Mark straightened in his seat. "About fifteen miles due west of your position."

"N400204. Repeat."

"Piece of shit radio." Jen hit it with her open fist.

"Fairchild Control," Mark said, "our location is approximately fifteen miles due west of your position."

"Roger, N400204. You are ordered to change course. There is a ten-mile no-fly zone around our location."

"Negative, Control," Mark said. "Your location is our destination."

The radio remained quiet.

"Fairchild Control," Mark said. "Your location is our destination. Do you read?"

"You are ordered to change course, N400204. There is a ten-mile no-fly zone around my location."

Mark looked at the others. "Can you believe this shit?"

Jen put out her hand. "Let me try."

Grant put a hand over his face. "This never turns out good."

Mark handed her the mic and she made a face at Grant. She keyed the mic. "Fairchild Control. This is N400204. We've flown all the way from Anchorage. We're running out of fuel and need to land at your location. Do you read?"

"N400204. Did you say Anchorage? Confirm."

"Yes. Roger. Affirmative. Whatever the right word is."

"Change your heading, N400204, or you'll be shot down."

Zeke looked up from his manga, a hoop earring swinging from his ear. "He sounds serious. Do you think he'll do it?"

The plane shook as a jet roared past them from behind. Jen jumped, Grant swore, and Mark held on to the wheel as the plane bucked in the back draft. Zeke leaned forward, peering out the front window. "Now that was some awesome sauce. Where'd it go?"

"N400204. You are nearing the no-fly zone. Turn back immediately or you will be downed."

Jen clicked the mic. "Shoot us down and Dr. Cartwright won't get the data we brought from Dr. Wilson."

Silence.

"Did you hear me, Fairchild? We have the shit to save the world."

"N400204, stand by."

Jen wriggled her eyebrows. "You've just got to know what makes them tick."

Mark grinned and shook his head. "The shit to save the world, huh?"

Two jets maneuvered into position off each of the Cessna's wingtips.

"N400204, proceed to my location and land from the southwest. Our fighters will escort you."

Jen handed the mic back to Mark. "See, that's the way it's done."

The jets moved farther to the side, the sun glinting off their canopies.

"I don't get it," Grant said. "What do they think we're gonna do with a little plane like this?"

"They want to make sure we're not zombies," Zeke said, his eyes still on his manga.

Mark banked the plane. "Everyone buckle in. We'll be on the ground in a minute." He picked up the mic. "N400204 to Control. Preparing for landing."

"Roger, N400204. You may proceed. Park at the northeast end of the runway and turn off your engines."

"Roger."

Grant coughed. "Guess there'll be a welcoming committee."

The plane slowed and its nose dipped. The base came into view, its runway lined with hangars and other buildings. A concrete wall encircled the entire base except a couple hundred yards of the southwest corner.

"Holy shit," Jen said. "I've never heard of an Air Force base with a wall before."

"That's because there's never been one," Mark said. "They got that damn thing up in record time."

Grant leaned forward. "That wall's got to be at least twenty feet tall." He pointed. "And look. Guard towers."

"And that open part's got all that construction equipment," Jen said. "Looks like they plan to finish it, but I don't see anyone there."

Zeke sat up and yawned. "Maybe they're all at breakfast."

The Cessna descended toward the runway. A fire truck with its lights flashing was parked at the northeast end of the runway. Several Humvees sped toward the same spot.

The plane settled on the tarmac and Mark hit the brakes, guiding the aircraft to stop near the fire truck. He turned off the engine. "Leave the weapons. We don't need them on base, and I don't want to give anyone an excuse to get nervous and shoot."

Zeke gently put his scabbard on the seat. "I don't like leaving Betty unsecured."

"Betty?" Jen asked. "You've named your sword?"

"Of course," Zeke said. "All great men have named their swords. Haven't you heard of Stormbringer, Oathkeeper, and Excalibur?"

"And now Betty," Jen said. "Sure rolls off the tongue."

Mark opened the door. "Let's get out there before they come in and get us."

They exited the plane. Mark put his hands up and the others followed suit.

Two Humvees flanked the fire truck. Gunners with machine guns aimed their weapons at them from atop the Humvees, the vehicles' throaty engines idling.

Jen waved at them. "Hey. You want to come out and play?"

The fire engine rumbled off, revealing two squads lined up in hazmat suits and carrying M4s. One soldier stood to the side, pistol holstered on his hip.

Jen cupped her hands to the sides of her mouth and yelled over the roar of the receding fire truck, which had black smoke belching from its exhaust. "Are those rifles in your hands or are you just happy to see us?"

The pistol soldier barked an unintelligible order, and seventeen rifles snapped to and pointed at the newcomers.

2

Mark raised his hands in the air, a gesture copied by Jen and the others.

The soldier with the pistol stepped forward. "I'm Sergeant Howell. Are you armed?"

"No," Mark said. "We left our weapons on board the plane."

Howell nodded. "Is the data for Dr. Cartwright on the plane, too?"

Jen stepped forward, and half the rifles pointed at her. She froze. "I have it. In my pants pocket."

"Your name?" Howell asked.

"Jen. Jen Reed."

"Jen Reed," Howell said. "Slowly remove the items from your pocket."

She eased her right hand into the pocket, grasped the thumb drive and vial, and removed her hand. She held her hand out and opened it. Howell strode to her side, his hazmat suit crinkling with each step. He pointed his pistol at her chest, then nodded at the vial. "What's that?"

"The original spores carrying the virus."

Howell stepped back, holstered his pistol, and removed a plastic bag from a pouch in his suit. He took the thumb drive and vial and placed them in the bag before sealing it.

He turned and Jen said, "Wait."

Howell paused, then continued back to his position beside his men. "What is it, Jen Reed?"

"Can I see Dr. Cartwright?"

"She's not here. She's in CDC Headquarters in Atlanta. We'll transfer the digital data and send the vial on a military transport."

Jen frowned. She needed to talk to Cartwright. "Then I guess we'll just be moving on. You wouldn't be able to spare some fuel, would you?"

"I'm afraid you won't be going anywhere just yet," Howell said. "You'll be put in quarantine for twenty-four hours, just to be safe."

"Why?" Grant said. "If you're worried about us turning, you'd be better off letting us go."

Howell put a hand out, palm down, and lowered it. The soldiers shouldered their weapons. He gestured to Mark. "You can all put your hands down."

Zeke made an exaggerated showing of wringing his arms out. "My arms were getting sore."

"You can't leave yet," Howell said. "Dr. Cartwright may have some questions for you once she gets the data. Besides, it's Colonel Butler's orders."

"Butler?" Jen said. "You mean the same dickhead that abandoned us in Anchorage and flew off with his tail between his legs?"

A few of the soldiers looked at each other and scuffled their feet. Howell remained still. "Colonel Butler is the commander of this installation and he answers directly to Dr. Cartwright. Orders are you all stay in quarantine for twenty-four hours."

He pointed to a one-story, nondescript building twenty yards behind him. "That's the quarantine facility. You'll have showers, beds, and food." When no one moved, he said, "I assure you it's only for a day."

Jen frowned. "Not giving us much of a choice." She shuffled toward the building, her friends following.

The front door opened into a long hallway down the side of the building. On the right was a door and a long window. Howell opened the door. "In here, please."

Five sets of bunk beds lined the walls, while a long table and chairs sat in the middle of the room. A door marked "Bathroom/Showers" stood on the back wall. An acrid odor stung Jen's nostrils, causing her to sneeze. The place smelled like it had just been scrubbed down with every cleaning chemical known to man.

"Cozy," Jen said. "I'd like to take a shower and not have to get back into these nasty clothes."

"We'll find you some fresh clothes," Howell said.

Zeke raised his hand. "I have extra clothes on the plane."

Howell appraised him for a moment, then nodded and closed the door. The lock tumblers clinked.

Howell appeared at the window, and his voice came from the speaker above it. "I'll inform Colonel Butler that you're here."

Jen waited until he left to speak. "I don't like living in a damn fishbowl."

Grant went into the bathroom and came out a minute later. "Facilities look good."

Mark stretched out on a bottom bunk. "Might as well get some rest. We'll be back in the air in twenty-four hours."

Zeke stood in front of a case of MREs. He opened it, lifted one out, and examined the package. "Veggie omelet. Wonder how this tastes?"

Grant made a retching sound. "I got one of those on deployment. I'd rather eat sand. There's a reason everyone called it a 'Vomelet.'"

"I could use something to eat, too," Jen said. She picked out an MRE and plopped onto a bed. "I hope they get those clothes here soon. I can't stand my own smell."

Grant rummaged through the MREs. "It's all shit."

Mark had lain back on the bed with his hands behind his head. "Pretty much the definition of MREs."

Zeke opened his package and shoveled food into his mouth like there was no tomorrow. Grant watched him, disgust and disbelief alternating on his face.

A click came over the speaker. Howell stood to one side of the window in BDUs and with his hazmat suit removed. Beside him stood a barrel-chested man with close-cropped red hair that thinned in the front. He had a neutral look on his face and eagles on his collar. *Butler.*

"I trust you're comfortable," he said.

Jen scowled. "Trust isn't a word you should be using with us."

Mark gave her an imperceptible headshake.

Butler acted as if he hadn't heard her. "You're the scientist." He pointed at Grant. "And the guardsman."

Grant stood at attention. "Yes, sir."

Kiss ass.

"Once you pass quarantine, you'll join one of my units."

"Sir?"

"The president has nationalized the guard and reserves."

Grant's face dropped. *Poor guy will never get back to Kodiak now.*

Butler pointed at Mark, whose jaw tightened. "Who are you?"

"Mark Colton. I was security for Doc."

Butler's eyebrows rose. "Bang-up job you did."

Mark's face grew dark. *I wouldn't want to be Butler if Mark gets pissed at him.*

Butler put his hands on his hips. "We have the scientist of the group, the guardsman, and the security man." He nodded at Zeke, who still sat at the table stuffing his face and getting half of it on his ninja costume. "Who the hell is he?"

Jen shrugged. "He's our ninja."

"Colonel," Mark said, "we delivered the data to you for Dr. Cartwright. We'd like to move on. How about we just get our plane fueled and fly out of here?"

Jen tilted her head to the side. Mark's jaw muscles were still tight and his voice was clipped.

The door's deadbolt clunked and it opened. Two soldiers stood there, one holding a gun aimed at Jen and the others, the other walking in with a pile of clothes. He dropped them on the floor. The two soldiers backed out and closed the door.

Howell pointed to the clothes pile. "BDUs in various sizes. One is bound to fit each of you."

Zeke stood. "What about my—"

"We got one of your extra costumes from the plane," Howell said. "It's at the bottom of the pile."

Zeke pulled his shirt over his head, revealing a thin, but muscled body covered in tattoos. "Awesome. I'm ready for a change."

Jen put a hand to her eyes. "Don't ever do that again, Nerd Boy. And go take a shower first. You smell like a fresh turd in the middle of summer."

There was a click. Butler spoke to Howell, but it didn't come over the speaker. Howell saluted and strode off.

Another click and Butler said, "If there's nothing else, then I have plenty of other issues to tend to."

He turned.

"Wait," Mark said.

Butler turned back, his eyebrows raised.

"What about the plane and the fuel? We'd be out of your hair in no time."

The colonel leaned forward and the speaker clicked. "The plane is ours. Specialist Grant there is ours. The rest of you will leave once your quarantine is up, but you'll leave on foot."

3

J en walked out of the bathroom with her hair wet and her new BDUs snug, but comfortable.

The door clicked, then opened. Sergeant Howell stood there.

"Been a change of plans," he said. "Cartwright wants to speak to you."

Finally get to speak to someone with some sense.

Howell had his pistol holstered. No other soldiers were in sight.

"I'm up for it." Jen nodded at her friends. "But they come with me."

Howell held the door open. "Absolutely."

He led them down a plain-looking hallway, their footsteps on the tiles loud and echoing. Outside the building, Jen took a deep breath of the breezy air. She'd been locked up for less than a day and it felt like a month.

Howell led them to an awaiting Humvee and paused as a helicopter rose from a nearby helipad. When its sound receded, Howell said, "You'll find an M4 and M9 Beretta with holster and ammo inside the Humvee for each of you. No one goes unarmed, even on base."

"What about my katana?" Zeke asked.

"Your melee weapons are in there, too."

"Solid." Zeke jumped in and grabbed his katana, cradling it like a lover. Jen shoved her axe into her belt and strapped on the 9mm.

Howell put the Humvee into gear and took off, navigating past troop formations and heavy vehicle traffic. A helicopter passed overhead as the Humvee stopped in front a long one-story building with a sign that said "Headquarters" on it.

Howell led them inside at a clipped pace. He stopped at a natural wood door and rapped his knuckles on it.

"Enter."

Howell opened the door and gestured for the others to go in.

Jen entered the room. A long conference table lay in the middle, chairs around it. Blackout curtains kept the room dim, with overhead LEDs providing light. Butler sat at the head of the table and the other seats were empty.

A sixty-inch video monitor hung on the wall across from the door. Dr. Cartwright's curt face was displayed on it.

"Come in and have a seat," she said. "Quickly now, I have a lot to do."

Jen sat and leaned forward on her elbows while the others took seats around her. Jen glanced at Butler. He sat ramrod straight, his eyes focusing on some unknown point on the wall.

Jen said, "Dr. Cartwright—"

"First, let me thank you for delivering the vial and data," Cartwright said. "We've received the data digitally and are processing it. The vial should arrive later today by military transport."

She paused, staring at Jen.

Jen cleared her throat. "You're welcome."

Cartwright gave a short nod. "I would like to know about Dr. Wilson." The muscles in her face loosened and she blinked several times.

Is she going to cry?

"I'd like—no, I need to know about his final minutes."

Jen's pulse picked up. She'd shoved Doc's death into the back of her mind with all the other bad crap, and now she had to pull it out and relive it.

I got him killed.

She took a deep breath. "He wondered what turning would be like."

"And?"

Jen lowered her voice. "It was painful."

Mark's head lowered. Cartwright visibly swallowed, but her expression remained the same. Her glasses had slid to the tip of her nose, and she tilted her head forward and peered over them at Jen. "What else...what else did he say?"

"He gave me the thumb drive and vial and asked me to get it here. To get it to you."

Cartwright nodded. "Even then, his last thoughts were on helping others."

She took her glasses off and rubbed her eyes before putting them back on. "And there was nothing else?"

Jen squared her shoulders. That was her opening. "He said to tell you he recommends I work with you. He'd planned on making me his assistant, and he thought I should work for you once he was gone."

Butler scoffed.

"Did he?" Cartwright asked.

Jen narrowed her eyes. "Yes."

"Colonel Butler, can you and your sergeant give us a moment, please?" Cartwright said.

Butler shook his head like he hadn't heard correctly. "You want me to leave?"

"Yes, Colonel. Please."

Butler stood, tight-lipped, and stalked out the door.

Cartwright picked a paper up from her desk. "I printed out all of Doc's notes and reports, and this letter jumped out at me. It's addressed to me. Besides other, more personal things, he mentions just what you said. That you should work for me."

Jen looked at Mark, who raised an eyebrow, then back at Cartwright. "OK. So is there a problem?"

"How do I know you didn't add that to his letter after he died?"

Jen shot out of her seat. "What? Why would I do that?"

Cartwright looked over her glasses at Jen. Jen waited for her to say something, but she just stared. Jen sat down.

"If you worked for me," Cartwright said, "you'd have resources available to you like food, transportation, and shelter. That's a lot more than most survivors."

"When would I have changed it? Doc gave it to me right before he died. We were out in the city and on the run."

Cartwright's eyes never left Jen's. "How do I know that? He could've given it to you before you left the lab. Plenty of computers there to hop on. Or maybe you found one in the city."

Jen laughed. "Sure. In a totaled city with zombies and asshole humans trying to kill us at every turn, we stopped somewhere that miraculously had power, just so I could see what was on a thumb drive."

Mark interrupted. "What Jen says is true. I was there when Doc died."

"Me, too," Grant said.

Cartwright's unflinching gaze swept over each of them in turn and landed on Zeke, who was examining the ninja hood in his hands. "What about the man in black?"

"Nope. I was busy with those assholes Jen mentioned."

"I see." Cartwright adjusted her glasses and sighed. "Until I have more proof than that, I'm afraid I can't honor the request. I therefore must release you to Colonel Butler."

"Wait," Jen said.

Cartwright's hand had moved to the bottom of the screen. She pulled it back. "Yes?"

"Something Doc said. It's on the tip of my tongue."

"Please don't waste my time, Miss Reed."

"It's not Miss Reed. It's Jen." She had to remember. What was it Doc said? *Think. Bug. Something about a bug.*

"I'll eat a bug if it isn't true," she blurted out.

Cartwright leaned closer to the camera, her mouth hanging slightly open. "What did you say?"

"Doc told me to tell you that he'd eat a bug if it isn't true."

A smile spread across Cartwright's face, and her eyes glistened. "That son of a bitch."

Cartwright sat back. "I believe you, Jen. There's never been a person on this earth I've trusted more than John Wilson."

Cartwright's smile faded. "Back to business. Jen, I'd like to offer you that assistant position. Will you take it?"

Jen glanced at Mark, who grinned and shook his head like he couldn't believe it. Grant sat, nodding at her. Zeke gazed at a wall.

Jen straightened in her chair. "Yes, Dr. Cartwright. I do accept."

"Good," Cartwright said. "Young man?"

Zeke looked around. "Me?"

"Yes. Please ask the colonel and sergeant to step back in."

Zeke walked to the door, opened it, and said, "She wants you back."

Colonel Butler strode in and took a position by the door. Sergeant Howell stood a few feet to his left, his hands clasped behind his back.

"Colonel."

"Yes, Doctor."

"Jen answers only to me, and will receive all cooperation and support needed for her to perform her mission."

To his credit, Butler didn't strangle on the words, but he looked like he'd just swallowed a shit sandwich. "Yes, Doctor."

Jen glanced at Mark. What about him? "My first request is to have Mark, Grant, and Zeke assist me."

Cartwright sighed. "I can authorize the big guy and the skinny ninja. But the president activated the National Guard, and your friend there is under Colonel Butler's command."

Grant looked at Jen with a hangdog expression. She'd figure a way to spring him.

"When do we get out of here?" Mark asked.

Cartwright steepled her fingers. "A week. I need you to go outside the base and record observations of zombie behavior. Dr. Wilson's notes mention a possible mutation and behavior changes. We need current data."

Butler grunted. "They're just a bunch of dumb meat bags."

Mark glared at Butler. *Yeah, Mark. I'm still pissed he left us in Anchorage, too.*

"Why stay here and study them? Hasn't the virus made it to Atlanta?" Jen asked.

Cartwright frowned and looked to her side for a moment. Was someone else there with her?

"It has made it to almost every corner of the globe," Cartwright said. "We lost the west coast before we could do anything. But the government initiated protocols to more closely monitor population deaths to neutralize the deceased before they can turn."

Mark squinted his eyes. "Protocols?"

Cartwright ignored him. "So there are very few zombies here to study, while Fairchild is at the front lines." She locked eyes with Jen. "That is why I need you there for now."

"And then we go to Atlanta," Jen stated. "Makes sense. I'll get the data you need."

"Good," Cartwright said. She reached for the screen and paused. "Doc didn't give false praise. The way he described you tells me we'll make great strides together. I'll be in touch."

The screen went blank. Butler crossed his arms. "I expect you'll complete your mission and get the hell off my base. We're in a war zone, and I don't need civilians running around and getting in the way."

Mark's hands clenched, his knuckles turning white. "You didn't do too well in Afghanistan with your military troops, either."

Butler glared at him. "Sergeant," he barked. "Show them to their rooms and the dining hall." He pointed at Grant. "Except the specialist. Assign him to a recon unit. He's been in the middle of the shit already. Might as well take advantage of his experience."

An alarm blared from speakers on the wall. Jen flinched and covered her ears.

Howell grabbed a phone that had no dial buttons. The alarm stopped, and Howell barked into the mouthpiece, "What direction? How many?"

He slammed the phone into the cradle. "Sir, attack from the southwest. Estimated strength in the thousands."

4

Jen piled into the idling Humvee outside the Headquarters building, sitting between Mark and Zeke. Butler sat up front while Howell jumped into the driver's seat. Looking glum, Grant sat in back.

Howell put the vehicle in gear and drove like a bat out of hell, arriving at the unfinished southwest wall in minutes.

Twenty yards past where they parked, the wall ended. Construction equipment sat quiet as soldiers took up firing positions back from the perimeter.

Butler strode toward a platform against the wall on a hydraulic lift. "Stay with me," he barked.

When the last of them boarded, Howell hit a button on a control box and the platform rose in the air. Other platforms with armed men were already in the air, just above the wall.

Howell handed Butler a radio and he keyed the mic. "Where's the damn Apache? And I haven't seen that C-130 take off yet."

Static burst from the radio, then a voice said, "Hotel Four on the way, sir. Fully loaded. C-130 is taxiing for takeoff."

They reached the top of the wall and Jen's heart skipped. Zombies raced toward the base, as far as she could see.

The helicopter swooped behind their platform and hovered, facing the perimeter.

Jen spoke into Mark's ear. "Is that helicopter the Apache he asked for?"

Mark nodded. "It's a two-seater that's armed for bear. I saw a Blackhawk parked on the tarmac on the way over here. They carry a punch, too, but are also good for transport."

Howell yelled over the thumping of the rotor blades. "One of our recon planes spotted them heading this way. Some will hit the wall and we'll wipe them up, but others will stumble into the gap in the wall."

The lead wave of zombies crashed against the wall to Jen's right, and the soldiers stationed there opened fire.

Zombies went down, but more filled their spots faster than the soldiers could keep up.

Machine gun bursts from her left had Jen ducking and looking that way. A sea of zombies had breached the open perimeter and the helicopter had opened fire, along with a couple hundred soldiers and several Humvee-mounted .50 cal machine guns.

They were barely keeping up. What the hell would happen when they had to reload?

Colonel Butler pointed to the sky. "There it is."

A C-130 gunship appeared and flew high over the distant trees. It banked and spit fire from its side. Hundreds of zombies fell.

"I've gotta get me one of those," Mark said.

Grant watched the plane bank and come around for another run. "You're not kidding."

Jen grinned. "What do you think, Zeke?"

She glanced behind her, then turned. Zeke wasn't on the platform. "Shit."

"What?" Howell asked.

"Zeke is doing his ninja shit again," she said.

Mark pointed down to the line of soldiers holding back the horde. Zeke stood behind them, his hood on and his katana ready. When the soldiers in front of him reloaded, Zeke jumped out and sliced through the lead zombies, felling several and keeping the others back. When the next shots fired, he ducked behind the line.

They stopped to reload again, and like a dancer, Zeke sprung forward, his katana singing through the air and into undead flesh. Sunlight glinted off the blade as he stepped forward, sliced, spun, and beheaded another zombie. Then he ducked and stepped back to take out another.

Entranced, Jen could only watch. *That little shit really is a ninja.*

The C-130 burped another storm of death, and hundreds more zombies bit the big one.

Butler put his hands on his hips. "Damn good job." He keyed the radio mic. "Order ground units forward on mop-up. Have Hotel One fly cover and the gunship return home."

"Yes, sir," came from the radio.

"And transition to cleanup operations as soon as the all clear is reported."

"Yes, Colonel."

The Humvees and ground troops pushed past the perimeter. The occasional gunshot barked, but it seemed as if the horde had been destroyed.

More troops moved forward with flamethrower tanks on their backs.

Mark pointed at them. "Clean up?"

Howell nodded. "Too many to bury. Too many to stack and burn. Who knows what other diseases they're carrying?"

"Sergeant, take us down and back to Headquarters," Butler said.

Howell pushed a button and the platform lowered to the ground. Zeke stood off to the side, talking with a soldier. He'd cleaned off his katana blade, but his costume was splattered with blood and innards.

Jen waved to him as she walked to the Humvee. "Come on, Zeke. We're heading back."

Zeke was the last to get in. He pulled his hood off and had the biggest shit-eating grin Jen had seen on his face.

"That was a blast," he said.

"You did a hell of a job," Grant said.

Zeke shrugged. "That was only the first level. Can't wait to move up to the second level."

"What does that even mean?" Grant asked.

Jen grinned. "It's a nerd thing."

Zeke winked. "Damn straight."

Howell parked at the Headquarters building and Butler stepped out. "Show them to their rooms and the chow hall, then get Specialist Grant to his new unit. I want them done with their mission and out of my hair." He strode into the building.

Howell guided them inside and down a long hallway to a T intersection. A sign in front of them pointed left to the dining facility.

"Dining facility?" Jen said. "Sounds fancy."

Mark shrugged. "It's a chow hall with a fancy name."

Howell pointed down the hallway to the right. "Rooms are down here."

He led them past two more hallways, and they came to lobby with a
soldier behind a desk.

"Smitty," Howell said. "You have the keys for those rooms?"

The soldier reached under the counter and handed Howell three sets
of keys. "Fresh linen, cleaned, and aired out."

"Thanks." Howell handed the keys out. "I suggest the first thing you do
is go get some chow. You never know when the shit'll hit the fan around
here and you'll go without until it's over."

"Specialist Grant, you're with me." Howell strode away, Grant by his
side.

Zeke sniffed. "I'm starving."

Jen looked at Mark and raised her eyebrows. "I could eat," he said.

Ten minutes later, they sat in the empty chow hall, a tray of food in
front of each of them.

Jen cut her roast beef and gave Mark a sidelong glance. "What's with
you and Butler? I mean, other than him leaving us high and dry in Anchorage, the asshole."

Mark paused mid-chew, then swallowed. He took a sip of coffee. "Was it
that obvious?"

"It was obvious you don't like him." Zeke slurped soup off his spoon.

Jen shrugged. "You said something about Afghanistan."

Mark put his coffee cup down and wiped his mouth with a napkin. He
looked around and dropped his voice. "I'll tell you what I know. But you
have to keep it to yourself."

Jen nodded. Mark turned to Zeke. He'd given up on the spoon and had
picked up the bowl and slurped even louder from there.

"How about you?" Mark asked.

Zeke put the bowl down and wiped his mouth with his sleeve. "I can
keep a secret."

"I didn't make the connection when we heard his name back in
Anchorage," Mark said. "But the minute I saw that flat-top carrot head, I
had no doubt it was him."

"What about him?" Jen asked.

Mark leaned on the table and clasped his hands together. "I never served directly with him, but did serve with some that did. Butler had a reputation of risking his men's lives for a mission."

"Isn't that what all commanders do?" Jen asked. "Isn't it a risk any time they go out?"

Mark scowled. "Not like this guy. He'd send them out when he could've waited for more troops and kept the death count down. No, all he cared about was the objective."

"Kinda like the Joker," Zeke said.

Mark ignored him and continued. "It wasn't just the grunts. He had a major who pushed back and argued with him. The major stuck up for his men and Butler didn't like it."

"So they're out on a mission, and when it came time for extraction, the major and three of his men stayed in the rear to cover everyone else."

Mark paused and took a drink. "The Taliban attacked, but the colonel and his men made it to the helicopters. All he had to do was have his men lay down cover fire while the major and his men beat feet to join them. Instead he ordered the helicopters to leave."

Jen clenched her teeth. The same damn thing he'd done to them in Anchorage. "What happened to the major?"

Mark faced her, his upper lip curled back as he spat out the words. "Remember those four soldiers that were kept hostage by the Taliban and were beheaded one at a time over six months?"

Jen's stomach soured. "No telling what that asshole would do to us."

Zeke finished his soup and put the bowl down. He let out an exaggerated sigh. "Lucky for us we'll be gone in a week." His face clouded. "But not Grant."

"Don't you worry about that," Jen said. "I've got leverage with Cartwright and I'm going to use it. I'll get Grant out of here."

Howell strode into the chow hall. "I'm glad you took my advice."

Jen caught Mark's eyes. They'd have to be more careful where they talked freely. Howell could've walked in during their conversation.

Mark gestured to an empty chair pulled up to the table. "Join us, Sergeant?"

Howell put his hands on his hips. "Not this time. You're going to join me and Colonel Butler."

"What for?" Jen asked.

"Colonel's taking you on a mission. We're to meet him at the helipad in ten minutes."

"We get to ride in a chopper?" Zeke asked.

Jen winced. *Yeah, we'll ride out in it, but will we come back in it?*

5

Howell stopped at a metal door just inside the lobby. He banged his fist on it and yelled, "Howell here. Need ammo loads now."

A small door opened and closed, then the metal door swung open. A shirtless soldier stepped to the side and let them in. "Whatcha lookin' for, Sarge?"

Howell positioned himself at the center of the room and Jen stopped next to him. Weapons lined every wall. Racks of M4 Carbines against one wall, with pistols and machine guns along another.

"Need M4 and 9mm loads for each of these folks," Howell said. "Going shopping in the city."

Jen walked over to the machine guns. "These look pretty nice."

"M60s," Howell said. "Sorry, but you're not authorized."

The armorer stacked the ammo on a desk. "Here ya go."

Zeke stood across the room admiring the flamethrowers. He glanced back and jerked a thumb at the rack in front of him. "Mind if I take one of these instead?"

The armorer looked at Howell.

"Fuck, no," Howell said. "You all get standard load out. Get your ass over here and grab your rounds."

Zeke shrugged. "Can't blame me for trying." He took a sling of 5.56 ammo for his rifle.

"You know how to handle that weapon?" the armorer asked.

"I have a master badge on my M4 Carbine. I love this gun."

"Master badge?" The armorer squinted. "Never heard of that before. Where'd you get it?"

"FPS," Zeke said.

"FPS?"

Zeke slung the rifle over his shoulder. "First Person Shooter."

Mark took pistol ammo from the armorer. "You don't want to know."

"Load it all up," Howell said.

Jen followed Howell outside. It had cooled and dark clouds had rolled in, covering the base in a dusk-like shadow.

Howell climbed into the driver's seat of an extended cab pickup. Jen and the others joined him.

As much as it was an understatement, Zeke looked awkward—a skinny kid with a rifle, pistol, and sword. "How are you going to manage all of those weapons?" she asked.

Zeke winked at her and lowered his voice. "Once we get into any real action, I'll hide the rifle and take out Betty." He patted the scabbard.

Jen rubbed her face. "For your sake, I hope this zombie apocalypse doesn't end too soon. I don't know if there's room for you in the place called normal."

Howell put the truck in gear and took off.

The muffled *whump whump* of helicopter blades signaled they'd arrived at the helipad. The truck stopped ten yards from the helicopter and they all got out.

"Follow me," Howell yelled. He hurried to the helicopter, bending over as he got closer. Jen mimicked his movements.

"This is a Blackhawk," Mark said to Jen.

The colonel sat in the front seat with the pilot, his headset on. Howell seated each of them and made sure their belts were secure, then gave the pilot a thumbs-up.

The helicopter lifted a few feet off the ground, then tilted and flew forward while it gained altitude.

Butler turned and yelled over the helicopter's racket to Jen. "Dr. Cartwright wants you to observe. We've got a roundup in progress and I thought it'd give you a chance to see what we've been doing. At the same time you can observe the zombies."

They flew over the wall and across countryside to the highway. Nothing moved below, the cars and trucks parked at weird angles and looking like toys.

"What's a roundup?" Jen yelled back.

"You'll see, Miss Reed. You'll see."

Jen didn't remind him to call her by her first name like she'd done with everyone else.

The helicopter flew over the city. Abandoned cars littered the streets, along with a few shuffling undead, but it was mostly just a graveyard. Butler pointed off in the distance and looked at the pilot. The pilot nodded and the chopper shifted to fly in that direction.

Mark sat quiet, almost trance-like. *He's flown these things plenty of times, so it's no big deal to him.*

They slowed as they came to the larger buildings in the city. The helicopter descended toward the top of the tallest building ahead of them. Jen braced herself for it to hit hard, but it landed so smoothly she almost couldn't feel it.

The pilot flipped some switches on his console and the blades slowed down. "You can remove your restraints at this time."

Howell unlatched his belt, pulled the door open, and stepped onto the rooftop. Jen and the others followed him out.

Butler led them to the edge of the roof and pointed below. Several shorter buildings flanked the one they stood on, lining up to create a U shape, with their building at the bottom of the U.

Jen looked at Mark, but he didn't break his eyes away from the troops assembled on top of the other buildings. Set up with machine guns and other small arms, they faced the inner part of the U.

"This is our roundup," Butler said. "We had a recon unit go out and stir up the meat bags. They're leading them here as we speak."

He pointed to the streets below. "Every side street is blocked off with vehicles, except for that one directly below us. That's where the recon vehicle gets out after luring them here."

"What keeps them from following your men out of there?" Mark asked.

Butler shaded his eyes and scanned the area. "You'll see."

Jen shifted the rifle on her shoulder. "Then it's shooting-fish-in-a-barrel time."

Butler smiled. "Exactly. So you see that we're taking care of business here. Eliminating the threat a few hundred and a few thousand at a time."

"Sir." Howell pointed to the left. A Humvee drove up a two-lane street bordered by an open park on one side and a lake on the other. A horde raced after it. Several zombies strayed, and the Humvee honked its horn, keeping them locked on the vehicle. The deluge of zombies kept coming. There had to be several hundred.

Butler pulled a handheld radio from his belt and brought it to his mouth. "Command One to all units. Targets in sight. Prepare to engage."

The soldiers on the rooftops, who had been lounging and smoking, gathered their weapons and set up.

Zeke had wandered off, exploring. *He gets bored easy.*

The Humvee paused at the opening of the trap, then traveled down the street between the buildings, the hungry horde clamoring behind it. Just before it would've hit her building, the vehicle took a sharp left and zoomed down the open road. A moving van parked on the side of the road roared to life and pulled across the road, blocking it. A soldier hopped out and scurried away.

The horde hit the dead end and stopped. Having no prey in sight, they milled around.

Butler put the radio to his mouth. "Commence firing."

The immediate blast of gunfire made Jen cringe and take a step back. The troops on both sides poured rifle and machine gun fire into the zombies and they fell like flies.

Five minutes later, commanders shouted to cease fire. Not a zombie moved.

"Shit," Jen said, her ears ringing. "There had to be five or six hundred of them."

Butler turned to her. "This is what we do, Miss Reed. We take out the enemy. It's just a matter of time before we have them all."

"But you still have the virus to deal with," Mark said.

"Dr. Cartwright and her team will take care of that." Butler smirked at Jen. "Did you observe any behavior you need to report back?"

Pompous asshole. "Not much to observe if they're all dead."

"Precisely why you're wasting your time here," Butler said.

Would it be too obvious if I accidentally tripped and knocked him off the roof?

"Jen," Zeke called from behind.

She glanced over her shoulder, then spun. Zeke stood over two headless zombies. "Where the hell did they come from?"

Zeke wiped his katana off on their ragged clothes. "Door on the other side of the roof. It opens facing the other way, so we didn't see it when we got here."

Howell pushed the corpses with his toe. "Good job, soldier."

Zeke pulled his hood off. "I'm a ninja. If I was a soldier, I would've been over there with you guys, not hearing these zombies coming because of all the gunfire."

Mark smiled. "He's got a point."

Butler grunted and stalked to the helicopter. "Back to base. Cleanup crews will take care of the bodies."

Jen peered down to the street. Dozens of soldiers with flamethrowers had already begun.

AFTER LANDING AT THE BASE, Butler drove off in a staff car without a word.

Fine with me.

Howell dropped them off at the HQ building. "You're safe to get some rest for a while, unless there's an attack on the base."

"Are we free to walk around?" Mark asked.

Howell shrugged. "Sure. Everywhere except the restricted areas designated by Colonel Butler."

"Where are those?" Jen asked.

"Here and there," Howell said. "They're clearly marked and have guards posted."

Zeke squinted at Howell. "Why would you have restricted areas here? There's only soldiers on the base and the zombies aren't going to try sneaking in."

Jen chuckled. He sometimes acted odd, but Zeke had it together.

"Even soldiers have varying security clearance levels," Howell said. He climbed into the truck, rolled down the window, and stuck his head out. "Just stay away from those areas. The guards are armed and take their jobs seriously."

He put the truck in gear and drove off.

Jen propped her hands on her hips and raised her eyebrows. "If it's something Colonel Butthead doesn't want us to know about, then it must be worth looking at, if only to piss him off. Who wants to go find some restricted areas with me?"

6

J en stopped on a corner. Several soldiers and an airman passed her, ignored Mark, and stared at Zeke.

Jen nudged Zeke. "I guess that sneaky ninja stuff works better at night."

Zeke sniffed. "I could make myself invisible during the day, too. Just no reason to do it now."

Mark shook his head, smiling.

Jen frowned. A large, square building stood on the corner lot behind them, its sign indicating it was the supply warehouse. Across the street from it lay an identical building, its large doors open. Armed soldiers drove forklifts amid stacked pallets.

The base fire department sat on the third corner, and on the last one was a small medical clinic.

"Haven't seen anything restricted," Jen said. "Were they just screwing with us?"

Mark shaded his eyes and peered down the street. He pointed. "There. See that?"

Several buildings down there was a gap, then barbwire-topped fencing wrapped around a building. "Ah. Where there's a fence, there's something interesting," Jen said.

She strode down the sidewalk, with Mark at her side and Zeke trailing behind. As they got closer, the full building came into view. Square, five stories, and with no windows, it seemed familiar.

"Looks a bit like our facility in Anchorage," Mark said.

Jen nodded. That was it. But the Anchorage building didn't have a fence.

The only visible door faced the sidewalk they walked along. A gate with an armed guard stood between the door and the road.

As they neared, a car stopped and a short man with balding gray hair and glasses hopped out. His cheap-looking suit was a size too big and the jacket fluttered in a gust of wind.

"Wonder who that is," Jen said. "First non-soldier I've seen here." *Didn't Butler rant about not wanting civilians on base?*

The guard opened the gate, nodded at the man, and closed it after he entered.

Jen slowed as she passed. The man put his hand in a box next to the door and a green light came on as the door opened. Before it closed, she caught sight of a long lit hallway with several soldiers standing along it.

"You need to move along," the guard said.

His voice grabbed Jen's attention. She looked at him, then realized she wasn't moving. Mark and Zeke had gone a few yards past the gate and turned around.

"Sorry," she murmured. "Lost in my thoughts."

The guard glared as she caught up with Mark and Zeke. When they were out of earshot, Mark nudged her. "What did you see?"

She shook her head. "A hallway and some guards. No telling what the hell's going on in there."

They turned at the corner, heading back toward the HQ building.

"Who do you think that guy in the suit was?" Zeke asked.

Mark stopped and put out his arms, causing Jen and Zeke to halt.

"Let's not get all tinfoil hat about this." He pointed past them. Jen turned. On the roof of the restricted building stood a tall, heavy antenna.

"Communications," Mark said. "Always restricted."

Jen put her hands on her hips. *Was that all it was?* She felt like an ass.

She pushed past Mark. "I don't know about you guys, but I could use another meal and some sleep."

. . .

A WEEK later she turned off the shower and toweled off. *Funny how you miss the little things when you don't have them.*

Her dresser had more military clothing her size, so she put on a fresh set and headed to the chow hall.

The place was almost full, but she spotted Zeke at a corner table with one plate stacked with pancakes and another brimming with eggs, bacon, and home fries. The smell of the bacon made her mouth water.

She grabbed some scrambled eggs and bacon and joined Zeke. He had just drowned his pancakes in half a bottle of fake maple syrup. "What's our plan today?" he asked.

Jen swallowed a mouthful of eggs and picked up a piece of bacon. "I figure I better check in with Cartwright. But after that we need to get out in the field. I'll talk to Howell about getting us a vehicle."

Mark strode into the chow hall looking more relaxed than she'd seen him before.

He made a beeline straight to them and sat down. Leaning forward, he lowered his voice, barely audible over the mixture of conversations and clinking silverware. "Found out more about that restricted area."

Jen swallowed what she had in her mouth, then downed her juice. She glanced at a nearby table, then whispered, "What do you have?"

"I got up early this morning," Mark said, "and went for my run. When I was done, I went to the gym and lifted some weights. There was a guy next to me and we spotted for each other. We started talking, and I just happened to mention the restricted area."

He scooted his chair up a bit and looked around before continuing. "Guy said his barracks roommate was picked for duty at the restricted area. The troops call it Area 51. His roommate moved over to the special barracks for people who work in Area 51. He didn't see the guy for a month."

Mark licked his lips. "When he ran into his buddy again, all he could get out of him was a 'Hey, how are ya doing?' The guy kept his mouth shut and walked away."

Zeke stabbed a sausage patty and held it up, examining it. "Definitely sounds like something strange is going on there."

"It does," Jen said. "And everyone here knows it. Why else call it Area 51?"

Mark shrugged. "Could mean nothing. There's no place on Earth where rumors fly more freely than a military base."

"I'd ask Cartwright about it," Jen said, "but I need to feel her out a little bit more. I'm not sure yet what I can trust her with." She pushed her plate away. "In the meantime, we need to get into the city and see what our zombie friends have been up to."

Zeke pointed his fork at two greasy pieces of bacon on Jen's plate. "You going to eat those?"

Jen shook her head. He stabbed the bacon and shoved it into his mouth. *Where the hell does this skinny kid put all that food?*

"How do we get to the city?" Mark asked.

Jen put a finger in the air. "For that, we need to see the good Sergeant Howell. Rather than getting a vehicle, I think it's safer if we can hitch a ride on the helicopter. Ready?"

Mark stood. Zeke let a quiet belch out and pushed his chair back from the table.

Jen led them out of the chow hall and to the HQ building's lobby, where a disinterested looking guard sat at a desk.

"Where can we find Sergeant Howell?" she asked.

The guard looked them over, then jacked a thumb over his shoulder at a hallway. "Fourth door on your right. Word to the wise: if his door isn't open, make sure you knock."

Jen strode past him and into the hallway. The fourth door stood open, and Howell sat at a desk studying a sheaf of papers.

"Sergeant Howell?" she said.

He looked up and laid the papers down. "Miss Reed and company. What can I do for you?"

"It's Jen," she said. "Do you have any roundups scheduled for today?"

He leaned back in his chair and pointed to a whiteboard. "Schedule's there. Got one in about two hours, and another midafternoon. Why? You didn't get enough of them yesterday?"

Jen raised an eyebrow. "As entertaining as it is to see hundreds of dead people torn apart, we do have to move on to other things. I'd like to get a ride into the city on the helicopter."

Howell rubbed his chin. "Sure. Do you know where you want to go?"

"Not where your troops will be," Mark said.

Howell stood and stepped to a map of the city next to the whiteboard. "This morning we'll be hitting the northeast section of the city. This afternoon it'll be the western section."

Jen looked at the western section on the map. "What do you think, Mark? We take the west this morning, before they go in and clean it out?"

Mark frowned and inspected the map. He pointed to the northeast. "If the hordes are coming from Seattle and Portland, they'll hit the west first, so I think that's a good call."

Howell folded his arms. "You'll be out there all alone. We'll have no troops in that area until this afternoon, so you'll be stuck in the middle of a ton of zombies and have no immediate backup."

Jen smiled. "Just what I wanted to hear."

7

Crouching, Jen crept to the north end of the rooftop. The thumping of helicopter rotor blades faded in the distance.

A facade on the front of the building rose three feet above the roof's edge and helped her keep a low profile from the thirty or so zombies wandering aimlessly on the railroad tracks twenty yards ahead.

Mark and Zeke took positions on either side of her. "Looks like they didn't take notice of the Blackhawk," Mark said. "How can that be? Damn thing should be drawing every walking corpse within a couple of miles."

Jen shook her head. The undead were still changing. Evolving. "It's like there's something new with them every day."

Zeke tapped her on the shoulder. "I'll check for rooftop entries."

"Good idea," she said. "No surprises. Why don't you also walk the perimeter of the roof and see what we have on all sides? With the way they're acting, we may need all the notice we can get if they attack."

Zeke nodded and stalked off. Muted gunfire came from the northeast. "Guess the roundup has started," Mark said.

Jen grunted. Hopefully, the noise from the roundup would draw any huge hordes away.

She looked down the tracks to the left. A group of nine zombies lumbered in their direction, with one in the lead and the others spread out behind it.

She tapped Mark on the shoulder and nodded toward the incoming zombies. "They're still using formations."

He nodded. "Like geese. Do you notice something else?"

"No," Jen said. "What's that?"

"Listen."

Jen lowered her chin and concentrated on sounds. Other than the distant gunfire and her own breathing, it was pretty quiet. "Not much to hear."

"Exactly," Mark said. "We're close enough to those zombies straight ahead to hear their growling, but there's nothing."

Shit. She listened for any sound from them, but there was still nothing. "That sucks. When they stopped screeching, that took away our main warning system. Even then, we could hear their growling if they were close enough."

Mark wiped a hand down his face. "Now they'll be ninjas, like Zeke."

Zeke slid next to Mark. "There's no ninja like me."

"What'd you find, Grasshopper?" Jen asked.

"Pretty light for zombies. Anywhere from two on one side to five on another." He pointed to the door on the roof. "One point of entry, unless they start scaling walls or flying helicopters."

"Don't laugh," Jen said. "The way they're going, that might be coming."

Mark scoffed. "That's a bit much. I can see them evolving some instinctual practices, but real thinking? Their brains died."

Jen watched the zombie group in the V formation getting closer. "Who knows what that virus does to the brain?"

Mark's eyebrows rose, but he said nothing.

Zeke pointed to the zombies in formation. "The guy leading them has no visible wounds. Kind of looks like my grandpa at his funeral."

Jen studied the leader, an older man in a dirtied suit. *Looks like he wasn't bitten. Need to remember that for Cartwright.*

Zeke shifted the rifle strapped to his back. "Is this all we're gonna do? Camp up here? Pretty boring, if you ask me."

The kid was right. So far all they'd seen was passive behavior. The information was good, but they'd need to see more of the aggressive, predatory behavior to see if and how it had changed.

"Zeke," she said, "let's stir some shit up, but quietly." She jumped to her feet and waved. Zeke stood next to her, jumping up and down, holding back laughter.

The milling zombies turned as one and streaked straight for them. They hit the rail on the side of the bridge, flipped over, and landed on the street below. A few lay still, but the rest pulled themselves up and hobbled out of sight.

The other group stopped, its leader staring at the rail the first bunch fell over.

Holy shit! Is it thinking?

It turned its head toward Jen, regarding her with yellow eyes. *Damn. He's giving me the creeps.* It sprinted back the way it had come, the others in the group staying in formation.

Jen's mouth hung open and she turned to Mark. "Did you see that? Freaking thing gave me goosebumps."

He swallowed. "Yeah. It's like it learned not to do what the others had."

"Now we've got smart zombie leaders?" Jen said. "What the hell's next?"

Something ran into the inside of the rooftop door. Zeke drew his katana.

Jen and Mark walked toward him. "That's a pretty heavy looking door," Mark said. "One zombie isn't coming through there."

The pounding became more rapid and intense. "That's not just one," Zeke said. "The numbers are going up."

Jen looked around the roof. "Having one entry point is great because you only have to defend one point, but it sucks when you need more escape routes."

"Zeke," Mark said. "Are there other buildings nearby? Anywhere we can escape to?"

The door shuddered from another attack. Zeke pointed to the south side. "One there, but the roof's got a ton of air vents and shit on it, so it would be hard to land there without hitting something." He jerked a thumb to the east. "That one has only one or two. That'd be the best bet."

The doorframe let out a loud crack.

"East side it is." Jen sprinted to that section of the roof. She and Mark peered down as Zeke arrived. The other rooftop was at least a floor lower than the one they stood on. It had no lip on the edge and just a few pipes and vents sticking up.

"Damn," Jen said. "That's a freaking mile across."

Another crack came from the doorframe, and a corner of it pushed out.

Mark took her by her shoulders. "We can jump it." He looked at Zeke, then back at Jen. "Just remember, go into a roll when you hit the roof. It'll dissipate the energy."

"That's true," Zeke said. "It's a sacred ninja technique."

Jen squinted at him. "You do make me wonder sometimes."

Mark handed Jen his rifle and ran back to the center of the roof. "I'll go first. Show you how to do it. Toss the rifles to me, then make your jumps. Just don't hesitate to come. One at a time."

He sprinted toward the roof's edge, pushed off with a foot and sailed through the air. He landed on a shoulder and rolled a couple of times. He jumped up and ran back to the edge. "Toss the rifles."

Jen heaved his M4 across the alley. He caught it and laid it down. She did the same with hers, then Zeke threw his. Mark took the rifles to the middle of the roof and waved at them. "Come on."

Jen and Zeke ran back to the center where Mark had started. "You go first," Jen said.

"Oh, no," Zeke said. "I know what I'm doing. I can make it easy, no worries. But someone needs to stay on this side when you jump, in case something happens and you need help."

Jen took a deep breath. "Yeah. OK."

Mark yelled, "What are you waiting for?"

Jen crouched in a runner's stance. *You've got it. You've done long jumps before; it's no different. Except the six-story death drop.*

The door burst open and zombies poured onto the roof.

"We both go," Jen yelled. "Now."

A zombie cop streaked for them. Zeke took off and Jen followed. Her pulse pounded in her ears and all she heard above it was her ragged breath and thumping footsteps close behind her.

Zeke made the edge and leapt, his arms windmilling as he soared through the air. He dropped out of sight. *Did he make it?*

The footsteps were almost on her. *Shit shit shit shit shit.*

Five feet from the edge, the other roof came into view. A hand grazed her back. She concentrated on the roof's edge. Somewhere a gunshot boomed. Something heavy hit the roof behind her.

Jen jumped into nothingness.

8

T he gaping chasm loomed below as she sailed through the air. *Too slow, I'm moving too slow.* Images and sounds assaulted her senses. The blast of a gun. Zeke rolling across the roof and bouncing to his feet. The beat of footsteps on the roof behind her. Mark aiming his rifle at her. Zeke's laugh as he rushed forward, waving his katana over his head. The edge of the roof barreling up to meet her.

Not going to make it.

Jen tucked her head and slammed into the rooftop inches from the edge. She tumbled forward a few revolutions and ended up flat on her back with her arms and legs splayed. Zeke stood over her. "You OK?" he yelled over the crack of another gunshot.

Jen took a deep breath and waited for the pain to come. She flexed her hands and bent her legs, but they seemed fine. Even her back wasn't complaining. "Looks like I got lucky."

Zeke stepped past her, swinging the katana. A head rolled by. Zombies streamed over the edge of the hotel roof and most disappeared in the gap. A few leapt for the roof and missed, all except the one that Zeke had taken care of before it could do any damage.

She placed her hands flat on the roof and pushed. Mark reached for her right hand. "We can't stay here." He pulled and she rose to her feet.

Another zombie made it across, and Zeke dispatched it before it could gather itself.

Stuck in the middle of a zombie-infested city with no transportation. Got to get out of this shit and get to Atlanta where it's safe.

The deluge of zombies ended. Zeke kept his katana at the ready. "Why do you want to move? This position's pretty easy to defend."

"They know we're here," Mark said. "We're supposed to be observing, not engaging."

Jen cracked her neck. "I agree with Mark, but not because the zombies that ran off the roof know that we're here. I'm more concerned with how many zombies that we haven't seen know we're here."

"Come again?" Mark asked.

"How the hell did all those zombies know we were there? We made no noise. When we waved at the zombies on the tracks, there were no others in sight. So why would they rush the roof in a big group so suddenly?"

"That zombie that led the others," Zeke said. "It was like he spotted us and let the others know."

Mark put his hands on his hips. "Come on. You're not saying that they're communicating with each other, are you? They didn't even shriek like they used to."

"I agree with Zeke," Jen said. "I know it sounds insane, but how many times in the past few weeks have we thought something couldn't happen, only to find out the impossible had become routine?"

She sighed. "We can talk about that later. We need to get to somewhere safe. Another rooftop. They're probably on their way up here now."

She went to the building door, turned the handle, and pushed it in. Stairs led down fifteen feet to another door. A zombie girl darted out from beneath the stairs and rushed Jen. She jumped backward out of the doorway and pulled the door closed with a loud click.

The zombie banged on the door.

A confused look crossed Zeke's face. "It's only one zombie. Why didn't you kill it?"

"I got sloppy and wasn't ready." She drew her axe.

The door clicked and opened into the building. Jen's heart skipped a beat. *What the hell?*

The zombie girl stood inside the doorway, her hand still on the door handle.

"What the fuck?" Mark said.

The zombie leapt for Jen, who slammed the axe into the base of its skull. Zeke finished it off with one slash.

"We're out of time." Jen hurried down the stairs and rushed into the hallway. She strained to pick up any sound beyond the rustling of Mark and Zeke behind her.

Pushing the door beneath an Exit sign, she entered the stairwell. Zeke eased the door closed and Jen held up a hand. She closed her eyes and listened.

"Nothing obvious," she whispered. "We can't get trapped in a stairwell, so whatever we run into, we fight through."

Mark stepped in front of her. "I go first and Zeke takes the rear."

She opened her mouth to argue, but remembered how she'd insisted that Doc stay in the middle of the group in Anchorage. "OK."

Mark kept his rifle pointed down the stairs as he took the steps at double time. Stopping at every floor, they listened for a few seconds, then continued.

When they reached the bottom of the stairwell, Mark pushed the door open, and they stepped into a coffee shop.

Undisturbed, everything lay in its place. Jen pointed to the front door, which had a picture window next to it. "Let's get on that street and the hell out of here. If those zombies were able to let others know we're here, it shouldn't be long before they show up."

Mark knelt next to the window and looked up and down the road. "Nothing I can see, but my angles aren't good here." He turned to Jen. "We need a rooftop that's not far away so we can signal the helicopter when it comes for pickup."

Jen bit her lip. "But it has to be far enough away so anything on this rooftop or the hotel's can't see us."

Mark looked at her and sighed. There was something different in his expression.

He's afraid. He could deal with an enemy that he knows. But if I'm right, then how much more don't we know about the zombies?

Mark pushed the door open and stepped onto the sidewalk. Jen crowded behind him. The street stood deserted.

They crept to the right, staying against the building, and surveyed the streets when they reached a convenience store on the corner. *Not a damn thing.*

"Where the hell are they all?" Jen asked.

Mark shook his head. "Not seeing any makes me more nervous than seeing a few."

Zeke pointed across the street. "There. That office building. Five stories and taller than any of the buildings on the block."

"Good," Jen said. "Need to get off the streets."

Zeke touched her arm. His eyes squinted and he cocked his head. "Listen," he whispered.

Jen froze and concentrated. Something in the distance. Soft, but getting louder fast. Reminded her of a cattle stampede in an old Western. *Shit.* "Horde."

She grabbed the convenience store's door handle and pulled, but it didn't budge. Mark yanked on the other door with the same result.

The stampede grew louder, the sound bouncing off the buildings.

"I can't even tell what direction it's coming from," Jen said. Heart pumping a mile a minute, she looked around for cover.

"No time to think about it," Mark said. "We have to make a break for the office building."

Her mouth dry, Jen nodded.

Mark gestured for them to follow, then streaked across the road and into a small parking lot next to the office building.

The thundering footsteps seemed to come from everywhere, building to a crescendo about to burst like a swollen dam.

Jen raced after Mark, with Zeke zipping past her.

Mark ducked in between two trucks and Jen dove in with him. He had taken a knee and gestured for Jen and Zeke to do the same.

Vibrations from the stampede traveled through the asphalt. A flash of movement caught Jen's eye and she looked out into the parking lot. A flood of zombies rushed by.

Her stomach fluttering and taking shallow breaths, she froze. *Don't give them a reason to look this way.*

The stampede seemed to never end. She had a fleeting thought that they were running circles around them and she was seeing the same zombies over and over. But the number began to trickle down. A few minutes later, the stragglers passed, their footsteps fading in the distance.

Mark put his hand out. Jen nodded. She wasn't moving anytime soon.

When another two minutes went by, she gave Mark a thumbs-up. He nodded, and she peered over the back of a truck.

Quiet. No movement. "I think we're OK," she whispered.

"I wonder where they were going," Zeke said.

Mark licked his lips. "They headed in the direction of the hotel."

"Oh, shit," Jen said. "We would've been overrun."

Mark straightened. "Let's get in the office building and out of sight."

They raced into the building, piling into the lobby.

"Wait," Jen said. She clicked the door's deadbolt into place. "Let's see if they're smart enough to pick a lock."

"We should clear the building and check all the doors and ground floor windows," Mark said.

"I'll take the second floor," Zeke said.

Jen frowned. "Maybe we should just stick together."

Zeke pulled his katana and gave it a practice swing. "This has been a boring mission. Betty and I could use a little fun."

Jen glanced at Mark. *Can you believe this guy?*

Mark gave her a slight shrug. "We'll meet you at the stairway on the second floor."

A half hour later, they pushed open the door to the roof and stepped into the sunlight. Jen ducked and positioned herself at the southern edge. Not a zombie in sight. *Good.*

Mark waved her over. "We need to stay out of sight."

"This mission's shit," Zeke said. "Not one damn zombie in the building."

Jen sat down next to the ninja. "It's a good thing. How many zombies were in that horde that rumbled by us earlier? Think you could kill all of them?"

Zeke smiled. "Dunno, but it'd be a lot of fun to try."

Mark shook his head and sat on the roof, his back against the door.

Two hours later, Jen was about to doze off when Zeke said, "Listen."

The thumping of helicopter rotors came closer, and Jen scrambled to her feet. "Where's it coming from?"

Zeke pointed south. "There."

The tiny helicopter grew larger and louder as it approached. It hovered a couple of blocks away. "They're over the hotel," Zeke said. "We need to get their attention."

He jumped and waved. "Over here," he screamed.

Mark tackled him and Jen put a hand over his mouth. "Just wave," she said, "but do it back from the edge of the roof where the helicopter can see you, but the zombies on the street can't."

Zeke looked at her with big eyes and nodded his head. Jen removed her hand.

Mark released Zeke and he stood, wiping off his ninja outfit. "We're OK. They didn't hear me over the rotor blades."

Something crashed below them, and Jen's breath hitched. She inched toward the front of the building and peeked over the edge. The front door she'd secured had been smashed in and scores of zombies rushed in through the breach.

They'll be here any minute.

9

J en pulled her pistol. "They've broken into the building."
"Shit." Mark held his handgun with one hand and took his mace in the other. "We need that helicopter now."
It still hovered over the hotel. *What the hell is it doing?* Jen pointed the pistol in the air and fired a round. Damn thing didn't move. "Next time we make sure we get a radio."

The first zombie ran into the door to the roof.

Have to find someplace defensible.

More thumps from the door. It rattled in its frame.

"There." Mark pointed to the door.

Zeke's eyebrows lowered. "There what?"

"The raised rooftop entry. We can get on top."

"Brilliant." Jen ran to the side of the entry.

Mark laced his hands together. "You first, Zeke. Then Jen."

Zeke stepped on Mark's hands and pulled himself onto the roof. Mark boosted Jen, and she grabbed Zeke's outstretched hand.

The door burst open and zombies poured onto the roof, rushing away from them. Jen and Zeke reached down, each taking one of Mark's hands, and strained to pull him up. One of the zombies turned and rushed for Mark. It grabbed for his dangling leg and Mark lashed out with his foot, bashing the zombie's head with his boot heel. Jen and Zeke dug in, the tendons in Zeke's neck standing out. Teeth gritted, Mark rolled onto the roof on his stomach.

Jen bent over, hands on her knees, panting.

Zeke slashed at the zombies trying to climb onto their perch. Jen aimed and fired at their heads while Mark swung his mace in great arcs to keep them back.

Even though they climbed and groped at the humans, the zombies uttered no sound. *Not even a damn grunt. Creepy shit.*

The thump of helicopter rotors caught Jen's attention. Their rescuers headed their way.

"It's coming," she yelled.

The draft from the rotor blades nearly blew Jen over. She emptied her magazine and reloaded.

A rope lowered from the chopper. "Jen goes first," Mark yelled.

She shook her head and Mark glared, then pointed to the rope.

The zombies were stacking up, and one grabbed Mark's pant leg, throwing him off balance. His arms windmilled as he tipped toward the ravenous horde. Jen grabbed his arm and Zeke sliced through the zombie's arm. With Jen's help, Mark righted himself. "Go now," he yelled, and clubbed a hairy, bearded zombie on the temple. "The longer you take, the longer before I can get out of here."

Jen grabbed the rope and looked up at the soldier visible in the helicopter's door. He made a wind up gesture and she rose to the helicopter.

It had probably taken only a minute to get there, but still seemed too slow. Mark and Zeke swung and shot, and chopped and hacked at the undead closing in on them.

Jen crouched next to the soldier and he pointed at the seat. She shook her head and pulled the rifle off her shoulder. Propping it against the door, she aimed at the head of a zombie reaching out for Zeke while he dealt with another one. Holding her breath, she pulled the trigger and the back of the zombie's head blew out.

The rope reached Mark and Zeke. Mark nudged Zeke and nodded to the rope. Zeke cleared his side of the raised rooftop entry and grabbed the rope. Jen concentrated on keeping the zombies from climbing up behind Mark. Without taking time to control her breathing, she killed a half dozen zombies before she missed. She pulled the trigger and nothing happened. The action was open. *Shit. Empty.*

She scrambled to grab a fresh magazine. The zombie she'd missed had climbed up behind Mark. "Mark. Behind you," she screamed.

Mark's attention stayed on the horde before him. Barely keeping them back, he'd stopped using his pistol and battered them with his mace.

Jen ejected the empty magazine and slammed the new one in. Zeke climbed in the helicopter beside her and aimed his rifle downward.

Jen jacked a round into the chamber. The zombie grabbed Mark's collar and pulled him backward.

Jen shot and the zombie fell into the horde below. With that small pause, the undead in front of Mark pulled themselves up.

Zeke killed them as fast as they came. Jen continued raining down lead on the creatures behind Mark. Still a few got through, but Mark made quick work of them with the mace.

Mark stumbled. *He has to be exhausted.*

The rope dangled behind him. *He doesn't see it.*

She yelled, "Mark. The rope."

Zeke aimed his rifle. "I've got this." He slowly squeezed the trigger. The bullet hit right behind Mark.

Mark jumped and glanced behind him. Grabbing the rope, he swung the mace wildly. The damn zombies were too close to him. Jen couldn't risk hitting him.

Mark bashed and kicked as he rose. Dozens of zombies had made it to the entry roof and all reached for him. The helicopter ascended and pulled Mark out of the horde's reach. He plopped onto the floor a minute later.

The soldier said something into his mic and the helicopter flew toward base.

HOWELL STOOD by a Humvee several yards from the helipad. Jen jumped out and stumbled over to him. "Hope you don't expect us to tip you for these rides."

Howell grinned. "They're on the house."

The helicopter rotors slowed as Mark and Zeke walked up.

"Heard you folks had your hands full out there," Howell said.

"You could say that." Mark cracked his neck. "All I want right now is a hot shower, some chow, and a nap. What do you say, Zeke?"

Zeke looked at Mark as if he had grown another head. "I'm just getting started." He smiled at Howell. "But this last mission was freaking epic."

Jen opened the Humvee door. "Let's get back to the rooms, Mr. Epic."

Five minutes later, they piled out at Headquarters. Howell lowered his window. "Colonel's gonna want to debrief you."

"I'll keep my briefs on, if you don't mind," Jen said. "Colonel or no colonel."

Mark ignored her. "Why does he need a debriefing? Jen's working for Dr. Cartwright."

Howell shrugged. "His base. His rules."

"How did he become in charge of this base, anyway?" Mark said. "I've never seen an Army officer in command of an Air Force base."

Howell scratched his chin. "The wing commander was killed in the first horde attack. That was the day after Colonel Butler arrived. Guess the brass figured he was already here, so they might as well give him the command."

"Sounds convenient," Mark said. "For Butler."

Howell studied Mark's face, then said, "Not sure I'd call it that. Anyway, I arrived a couple days later. Most of the Air Force folks are gone. All except a few flight line personnel."

He closed the window halfway, then turned back to Jen. "Colonel's on a post inspection for the next forty minutes, so you should be ready for the debrief by then." He drove off.

"That gives you enough time to conference with Dr. Cartwright," Zeke said.

Mark slapped Zeke's back. "Not a bad idea. Get the findings to Cartwright now. Who knows what Butler may do? In fact, I wouldn't tell him shit. Just say the zombies acted the same."

"That's a hell of a dangerous game to play," Jen said.

"Not as dangerous as trusting Butler," Mark said. "Have you already forgotten how he left us in Anchorage to die?"

"But what about the innocent soldiers?" Jen asked. "Shouldn't they know?"

Mark's eyes narrowed. She'd hit a sore spot. "How will we turn on the video conferencing equipment?"

"Leave that to me," Zeke said. "I helped set up audiovisual equipment in high school."

Jen grinned. "Should've known."

Zeke led the way to the room. He walked in, flipped a switch on a console on the table, then pushed a button. The TV came on but remained blank until the word *Connecting* displayed.

"Can't wait to get the hell out of here," Jen said.

Mark leaned into the hallway and peered up and down the passage before closing the door.

The monitor filled with Dr. Cartwright's upper body, leaning on a desk. She peered over her glasses, a curt expression pasted on her face. "Jen. What do you have for me?"

Jen licked her lips. How much should she tell her?

In the end she told her everything: their mission and how the zombies seemed to communicate without speaking, how they suspected that the zombies that turned without being bitten seemed smarter than the others.

Cartwright took her glasses off and let them dangle from the chain looped around her neck. "We have some specimens here, but all have been bitten. Our strict protocols have kept the newly dead from rising. We may have to make some exceptions."

She frowned. "What did you call them again? Leaders and what?"

"Drones," Jen said. "Leaders and drones."

"Can we leave this place now?" Mark asked. "She's given you the information you need."

The door burst open and Butler marched in. "How dare you start a debrief without me?"

Howell strode in and closed the door behind him.

"Colonel Butler," Dr. Cartwright said. "You will be given information as I see fit. Jen works for me, not you."

"I suppose I'll be rid of her now that she's reported back to you."

Jen stood. *I can't believe I'm doing this, but there's more to learn here and I'm in the best position to learn it. Besides, Butler wants us gone too badly. He's up to something.* "I'm staying for a while longer. I believe there's more to learn about the new zombie behaviors." She shrugged. "It could end up meaning nothing in the long run, but it could also be a game-changer in this war. In the memory of my father and Doc, and so many others, I have to risk staying in the field for this."

10

Butler's face flushed. "What the hell do you mean you're staying? The deal was a week."

Jen clenched her fists. *I'd love to kick this asshole in the nuts...if he had any.*

Mark stepped between Butler and Jen, and Zeke pressed in on her side.

"There's no need to shout." Cartwright's face had the same placid expression as if she were placing a dinner order.

Butler stopped in front of Mark and turned toward the monitor. "I've got the defense of the United States on my shoulders, and I don't have the time to babysit civilians."

"Babysit?" Jen leaned around Mark to glower at Butler. "Listen, Colonel Butthead. We can take care of ourselves."

"Really?" Butler sneered. "And who had to be airlifted just today before they were overrun?"

Mark's jaw muscles tightened and Jen gently pulled him to her side. Butler glared down at her.

"So when you airlift your own troops, do you consider it babysitting?" Jen asked.

Butler sputtered, "They're soldiers. They're supposed to be supported."

Cartwright cleared her throat and everyone's attention shifted to her.

"So you're saying that airlifting assets from the field is support?" Cartwright gave a slight smile. "And not babysitting?"

Butler puffed his chest. "Our agreement was for these civilians to stay for a week. The week is up and they need to leave."

"But there's more work to be done," Cartwright said. "I'm proud and thankful that Jen has volunteered to stay and follow up on her recent findings."

"What findings?" Butler asked. "And why wasn't I informed?"

Cartwright gestured to the monitor. "Jen?"

Jen licked her lips, but her mouth had gone dry. "The zombies"—she gave a slight shake of her head—"or the virus, have evolved. We observed behavior that indicates the zombies' cognitive abilities have increased."

"Cut with all the flowery language and tell me what you saw."

"A zombie opened a door that was latched."

Butler stared at her for a moment, then chuckled. "Are you shitting me? Those meat bags are dumb as shit."

"I know what I saw," Jen said.

Mark thrust his jaw forward. "I saw it, too."

"Me, too," Zeke said.

"Look," Butler said. "Maybe one of them opened a door, but I'll bet it was already partly open and the damn thing stumbled into it at the right angle and knocked it open." He looked at Cartwright. "You're a scientist. Don't you have to have more evidence? A bigger number of them?"

"A larger sampling size?" Cartwright steepled her fingers before her. "That's a good point, Colonel."

Butler put his hands on his hips and nodded. The red was receding from his face. "That's what I mean. I'm glad someone here has some sense."

Jen smiled. "Then we agree."

"About what?" Butler growled.

"We need a larger sample size. Of course, that means we need more observation, and in order to do that, we'll have to stay here for a while longer."

"What?" Butler said. "No."

"I'm briefing General Lewis on our status in about an hour," Cartwright said. "I'll pass on that Jen and her team are staying, and that you agree."

Butler's lips pressed together, drawing a thin line across his face. He closed his eyes and his nostrils flared, then he took a deep breath and exhaled. "Agreed."

He opened his eyes and lowered his brow, staring at Cartwright. "But I will be briefed on all activities. This team will not leave this base without either me or Sergeant Howell knowing where they're going, what they're doing, and when they'll return."

Fat chance, asshole. Jen waited for Cartwright to knock him down to size.

Cartwright stared at the monitor then reached forward, her hand disappearing below the picture. "Agreed." The connection closed.

What the Holy Hell?

Butler scowled. "Give your outside itineraries to Sergeant Howell and coordinate all activities with him."

He marched toward the door and stopped when he stepped into the hallway. He glanced over his shoulder. "And this room is off-limits. You will not have any communication with Dr. Cartwright unless and until I authorize it."

He disappeared down the hall, with Howell following in his wake.

Jen kicked a chair, sending it slamming into the wall. "That asshole. What the hell does he hope to get from all this bullshit?"

"He's hiding something," Zeke said.

"What?" Jen asked.

Mark nodded. "I agree with Zeke. He is hiding something and he doesn't want it to get out. I'll bet the brass would replace him if they knew, and that's what he's trying to avoid."

"So we've got an asshole colonel who's supposed to be trying to save the world, but he's doing something underhanded?"

Zeke sat on the conference table. "He's an asshole all right, but I think in his mind he's a patriot that will do anything he thinks he needs to do for his country."

"Great," Jen mumbled.

Mark clapped his hands together. "I'm pretty hungry and you two smell like zombie shit. How about we clean up and get something to eat?"

Thirty minutes later they sat at a corner table in the chow hall.

Jen made a face when she swallowed a mouthful of mashed potatoes. They had an off taste. *Probably dehydrated.* "We should target different sections of the city each time we go out."

"Maybe we can get hold of some night vision gear and go out at night," Mark said. "Unless they can see in the dark, it'd give us a clear advantage."

Zeke pushed his chair back and stood. Jen looked up. "You leaving?"

Zeke ignored her and walked toward the exit door for the serving line. Grant walked out, holding a tray.

"Grant," Zeke called.

Grant's gaze snapped to Zeke, and his eyes grew wide. He glanced at a table of soldiers to his right. Several of them had stopped eating and turned to look at him.

Grant ignored Zeke and continued toward the soldiers' table.

Zeke put a hand on Grant's arm. "Hey, Grant."

Grant dropped his tray, the dishes cracking and the food splattering as it hit the floor.

"Now look what you've done," Grant roared.

Zeke stepped back, his mouth working like a fish out of water. "Sorry. Didn't mean to startle you."

Grant grabbed Zeke by the front of his costume. "Startle? You knocked my tray down."

Mark jumped to his feet and took a couple of steps toward Zeke.

More and more heads turned to witness the argument. The table of soldiers had all turned and watched with keen interest.

Grant grabbed Zeke's hands and used them to mimic a push. "This. This is what you did. Why? What the hell do you want?"

"I—I was going to invite you to join us." Zeke gestured to the table where Jen sat. Her mouth hung open. *What the hell's wrong with Grant?*

"You're all civilians," Grant yelled. "I'm going to sit with my battle buddies. I don't have time for you."

Zeke turned back to the table. Jen's heart broke. Zeke looked crushed. Mark walked Zeke back to the table.

"It's OK," Jen said. "He's always been an asshole to you. That's all he is. Now that he's back with the military and doesn't need us to save his ass, we see his true colors."

Mark patted Zeke's back. "I should've kicked that guy's ass a long time ago."

Zeke's shocked face slowly transformed and he smiled.

Jen's eyes narrowed. "What the hell's wrong with you?"

"Grant's OK," Zeke said. "He's still our friend."

"What do you mean?" Mark asked.

Zeke put his closed left hand to his chest and looked around. With a satisfied grin, he turned his hand palm up and opened it, revealing a folded slip of paper.

11

J en looked up and down the hallway, then closed the door to her room. "So what's Grant's note say?"

Zeke unfolded the paper and squinted. "You're being watched by everyone. Colonel's orders. I need to speak to Jen. Tonight behind the base motor pool two blocks to the west of Headquarters at ten o'clock."

"Who'd've taken Grant as a James Bond type?" Jen said.

Mark rubbed his face. "Could be a trap."

"No." Zeke handed the paper to Jen. "Grant's a good guy."

Jen read the message and tore it up. "Why do you say he's a good guy? He gave you a lot of shit in Anchorage."

Zeke shrugged. "He was scared. But he came through for us when we needed him, didn't he?"

Jen walked into the bathroom, dropped the torn pieces of paper into the toilet, and flushed it.

"He did come through in Anchorage and Klawock," Mark said. "I know I'd be dead if not for him." He pointed at Jen. "You, too."

Jen pursed her lips. *Maybe Grant knows what the hell's going on around here.* "I think it's worth the chance. I'm going."

. . .

AT NINE O'CLOCK, Jen stood in the empty lobby with Mark and Zeke.

"Let's go over it one more time," she said. "At nine thirty, you both leave your rooms and head in opposite directions, and I'll scoot out at nine forty."

"So you're just going to walk out the front door?" Mark asked.

Jen smirked. "You know me better than that, but I'm not telling you how I'm leaving. Better that you don't know."

"This is going to be epic," Zeke said. "I'll head to the east, then I'll melt into the shadows and tail anyone that's following me."

"Don't get caught," Mark said.

"Shit." Zeke smiled. "I made it around that mall in Anchorage and never got caught. I've got a much bigger playground here."

Jen laughed. "I'll talk to you both in the morning. No sense making anyone suspicious by getting together late at night."

"OK." Zeke walked down the hall that led to his room.

Mark stood silent for a moment, staring at Jen. "Be careful. I know you can take care of yourself, but if you see or hear anything that's not right when you get there, get the hell out. Grant's a soldier, and he may prize that more than the bond we all share from survival."

Jen gave Mark a hug, and he seemed taken aback. After a minute, he put his arms around her and squeezed gently, then broke the hug.

"Remember, anything unusual and you get out of there." He turned and took the hallway that led to his room.

Jen called after him. "OK, big brother. I will."

She whistled and sauntered across the lobby and into the hallway leading to the chow hall.

As she'd hoped, it was empty. She opened the cold case and pulled a soda out. Popping it open, she sat at the table closest to the women's rest room. The clock on the wall read nine ten p.m.

She wasn't worried about a trap. After all, if Grant had set her up, he knew she'd get to him eventually. *And he wants to keep his balls.*

A pair of soldiers walked by in the hallway, talking. Neither paid her any attention.

Did Grant know what Butler was hiding? Or maybe there was something else, something important enough for him to risk the meeting.

At nine thirty, she tipped the soda can, downing the last of the drink.

She stood, crushed the can, and shot it like a basketball into a trash can ten feet away. She raised her arms when it went in. "Score."

No one had come into the chow hall the whole time she'd been there. She looked around at the walls, vents, and light fixtures, searching for anything that looked like a camera. *Damn, I'm really getting paranoid.*

The clock said nine thirty-five. She pushed the ladies' room door open and walked in. After checking the stalls to make sure they were empty, she unlatched the window and waited.

When her watch flashed nine forty, she tip toed to the door and hit the light switch, plunging the bathroom into darkness. A soft glow from the frosted window guided her there, and she slid it up a quarter inch at a time, praying it made no noise.

She stuck her head out. No movement. Nothing but crickets and the sound of an engine starting in the distance.

A slight breeze washed over Jen as she climbed through the window and lowered herself to the ground. Praying no one would enter the bathroom while she was gone, she crouched and snuck to the edge of the building.

All was quiet, so she darted across the grass to the next building and slipped between it and a warehouse. Across the next road stood a darkened field. Down the road to her left, light spilled out of a short, one-story building, and the sound of metal hitting metal echoed from it. Voices spoke every minute or so, but no one came out.

She'd have to make it across the street and across the field without being seen. *Got to go. Grant may not wait if I don't show up on time.*

She dashed across the road, her footsteps sounding as loud as gunshots to her. They muffled when she hit the grass. She glanced left at the occupied building, but no one ran out pointing at her and calling for help. *Or shooting.*

Jen raced to the back of a shadowy building and crouched beside it, her heart racing.

Standing hunched over, she crept to the side of the building and paused to listen for any movement. A helicopter rose in the distance, its lights heading away from base.

She peered around the side of the building. Pools of light from the street lamps splashed onto the asphalt.

Taking time to place each foot solidly on the ground so as not to crunch the gravel, she made her way to the front.

The motor pool stood across the street, one of its overhead doors open and looking like a huge, dark mouth waiting for someone to enter so it could close and swallow them.

Jen sprinted across the road, her boots scuffing on the asphalt. The sound echoed off the buildings.

She slipped inside the door and hugged the wall. As her eyes got used to the darkness, shadows emerged. A large one several feet in front of her had the outline of a truck. Other lumps to her left could've been anything.

She took a deep breath. "Grant?"

She cringed. Even though she'd spoken in a near whisper, it sounded like a shout in the stillness.

"Grant. You there?"

A rustle from deep in the garage put her in a defensive crouch. Without thinking, her axe appeared in her hand.

"Jen?" Grant whispered.

"Over here."

A shadow detached from the back and moved toward her. "Where?" Grant asked.

"Keep coming straight forward."

The shadow stopped in front of her, its breathing shallow and fast. A hand touched her chest.

"Hey," Jen said. "Watch it with that. You didn't bring me out here just to cop a feel, did you?"

"No. No. Oh, God. I didn't mean it. I was just trying to figure out where you were."

"Relax, soldier boy. I know it was an accident. You should, too. After all, your hand's still attached to your arm."

Grant chuckled. "Always a hot shit."

"Enough old home days," Jen said. "What have you got for me?"

"Like I wrote. Everyone's watching you. They're watching me some, too, because I came in with you. It's obvious they don't totally trust me yet."

"So what?"

"Something's not right here," Grant said. "I heard you're staying. I wanted to warn you to go. I don't think you're safe here. Hell, I don't think I'm safe here."

Jen scoffed. "Out in the middle of nowhere with millions of zombies probably on their way? What's not to feel safe about?"

"Not the zombies. Butler. There's something going on at Area 51."

"What?" Jen asked. "What's going on?"

Headlights swung around a corner and bathed them in LED light for a moment. Grant grabbed Jen's arm and pulled her behind the truck. "Shit. It's them."

12

The large truck rumbled by, the throaty roar of its engine fading into the distance.

Grant's heavy breathing was the only sound remaining.

"I think we're OK," Jen said.

Grant stood. "We better leave."

"Drag me all the way out here and leave me hanging?" Jen said. "Bullshit. You're not going anywhere until I hear what you have to say."

A streetlight's beam fell across half of Grant's face. He licked his lips. "Area 51. Those trucks, they're what's wrong."

"What trucks?" Jen pointed to the street. "You mean that one that just passed?"

Grant nodded. "My job is to drive trucks, and every day at three a.m. I bring one to the supply building on the flight line. It gets loaded with supplies."

"What kind of supplies?"

"Don't know. I'm supposed to sit in the truck and wait for it to be loaded. Once it is, a sergeant tells me I'm good to go, and I drive to Area 51."

Jen folded her arms. "What's in there?"

Grant shrugged. "I back into the loading bay and turn it off. There's always an empty truck parked there. I take that one back to the supply building."

"Come on, Grant. You brought me all the way the hell out here for that?"

He shook his head. "The trucks at night—like the one that just passed —are different."

"Different how?"

"They told me to drive one of them once when the regular driver was on sick call. They brought me to a warehouse on the edge of the base, told me to drive the truck to Area 51 as normal and bring back the unloaded truck.

"I backed into the loading dock," Grant said, "and there was no one around. I shut off the engine and had just opened the door when it happened."

"You're really stretching this out," Jen said. "What the hell happened?"

"Something in the back of the truck banged on the side."

Jen frowned. "Loose cargo."

"No. The truck had been stopped for a minute, and it was the first time I'd heard anything. I walked to the other truck and heard it from the back of the first truck again. There was someone or something moving in the back of that truck."

"Why didn't you open the back and see?"

Grant shivered. "I had this feeling of being watched. No one in sight, but I could've sworn someone had eyes on me. I jumped into that other truck and lit out of there."

Another set of lights came down the road. The vehicle stopped under a streetlight. "An MP truck," Grant said.

The truck's passenger shined a spotlight into the building behind the streetlight.

"Shit," Jen said. "We've got to get out of here."

"Come on. There's a back door."

Jen followed Grant into the cool night air. The spotlight shined through the motor pool's windows. They waited for the truck to move on, then Jen let out a breath. "So why are you telling me all this? What am I going to do about it?"

"You need to leave. But you can tell Dr. Cartwright what I told you. Something is going on and it's tied to Butler. No one talks about it. They go all quiet and ignore you if you mention it."

Jen bit her lower lip. Area 51 had tripped her radar the minute she'd

seen it. Why an armed guard? The security door and scanner should be
enough protection for a communications building. And why the armed
soldiers lining the hallway? And the secret deliveries?

"Jen?"

She broke away from her thoughts. "I'll talk to Cartwright, but I can't
leave yet. Not only is there more to do, but it'd look suspicious if I left just
after I said I needed to stay."

"Then watch your back." Grant took a few steps from the building and
looked both ways. "We better get out of here before the MPs come back.
Take care of yourself." He slipped off into the shadows.

SOMEONE BANGED on Jen's door. She sprung from bed and reached for
her axe.

"Miss Reed. Colonel Butler wants to see you."

Jen put her hand on her chest, afraid her heart would burst from it.
"Hold on."

Throwing a robe on, she noted the five a.m. time on the digital clock.

She jerked the door open. An MP stood in the hallway.

"Five in the morning?" she said. "Who the hell gets up at five in the
freaking morning?"

"Sorry, ma'am." He looked anything but sorry. "Colonel Butler wants to
see you now." His eyes dipped to her cleavage and Jen pulled the robe
tighter around herself.

"Give me a minute." She closed the door and damn near jumped into
her clothes. Opening the door, she pushed past the MP. "Let's go."

Butler sat behind a desk, a cup of black coffee against his lips. He took
a sip and put the cup down. "Miss Reed. Got something for you. In light of
our mutual goal of getting you and your civvie friends out of here, I'm
taking you out this morning for some observing."

Jen took a seat and swung one leg over the side. Butler's jaw tightened.
Good.

"I'm game. Another roundup?"

"Not for you," Butler said. "We'll drop you and your friends off on our
way to a roundup."

"No."

Butler's eyebrows shot up. "No? You said no to me?"

"Last time we did that the chopper was too far off when we ran into trouble."

Butler shrugged. "We'll drop you off only a block or two from the roundup. You'll have all the firepower close by."

Jen scowled. She couldn't say no and not seem unreasonable.

"I'll even throw your friend, Specialist Grant, in. I'll bet you two have lots to talk about."

Jen's heart skipped a beat. Did he know?

Butler sat back in his chair and laced his fingers behind his head. "Been a while since you've talked, no?"

Son of a bitch does know.

Change the subject back. "It's a deal," she said. "But we get a radio."

Butler smiled. "That'll work. You and your team need to be in the lobby at oh-six-thirty hours. Sergeant Howell will shuttle you to the helicopter."

Jen gave him a curt nod and walked out.

TWO HOURS LATER, Jen jumped onto the roof of an office building. Mark, Grant, and Zeke hopped off the Blackhawk and landed next to her. The pilot waved and took off.

Jen surveyed the roof. "Zeke, wanna check out that door?"

Zeke popped her a salute and jogged to the door.

"Why am I here?" Grant asked.

Jen went to one knee and pulled Grant with her. "Butler knows we met. He offered to have you come with us. I had no other way to warn you that he knows."

"So you two were caught last night?" Mark turned his gaze on Jen. "Why didn't you tell us when you came to get us this morning?"

"We weren't caught last night," Jen said. "At least no one confronted us last night."

Zeke jerked a thumb over his shoulder. "Door's secure as long as we don't have a horde storm it, or run into one of those smart zombies."

The radio on Jen's belt squawked. "Command One to all units. Commence firing."

Gunfire broke out nearby. Jen shaded her eyes and looked toward the sound. Sure enough, the Blackhawk had landed on a building four blocks away.

"Let's get observing." She walked to the edge of the roof overlooking West Main Avenue.

Mark joined her. "I'd like to get this observing shit done and get out of here. I feel better that the zombies haven't taken over the rest of the country, but I still need to check on my family."

"I'm with you," Jen said. "But if we find something that helps Cartwright and the CDC crack this thing, your family may never be in danger."

Deserted, the street reminded Jen of one of those Hollywood end-of-the-world movies.

Mark pointed to their right. "I'll go watch this side."

"Good idea," Jen said. "Grant, why don't you take the side across the roof, and Zeke, take the last one."

Grant nodded and jogged to his post.

I remember when he wanted to be in charge back in Anchorage. I like him better now.

Zeke stood there for a moment. "Is this all we're going to do? Just stand up here?"

"That's the plan. Unless something goes to shit."

He huffed and lumbered to his side of the building. Jen peered back onto the street. It hadn't changed.

"Command One to all units. Zulus have broken through. Use all available firepower."

Explosions echoed down the streets, and black smoke rose above the buildings, blocking the helicopter from view. *What the hell?*

She looked at Mark, who turned toward her and shrugged. Zeke danced and clapped. Grant had taken a knee and watched the smoke with a frown.

Jen pointed at each of them in turn. Every one of them scanned their side of the building and shook their head. *We're not going to see shit here. All the zombies are corralled and being wiped out.*

"Command One to all units. Cease fire. I repeat, cease fire. Let the smoke clear so we can assess the situation."

The smoke had drifted almost to Jen's position. The acrid sulfur-laden cloud probed her nostrils and caused her to sneeze. She shoved her face into the crook of her arm.

Another helicopter swooped in overhead. Mark ran over. "That's an Apache Longbow and it's armed for bear."

The smoke swirled beneath the Apache's spinning blades.

"Echo One to Command One."

"Go, Echo One."

"The smoke's cleared on our position, east building. Zulus are escaping down side street, heading for West Main Avenue."

"Roger, Echo One. Hotel Three, do you copy?"

"Copy."

The Apache swooped past Butler's position and descended until it disappeared behind the building.

"Hotel Three to command. We have eyes on Zulus. They've hit West Main Avenue and are heading west."

A horde dashed out from behind the building and flowed Jen's way. *If they keep their course, they'll pass right by us.*

"Command One to Hotel Three. Engage. Command One to Hotel One."

Explosions came from the other side of the building. The horde kept a straight course.

A Blackhawk swept in from the west and fired on the horde. Dozens of zombies fell in the street.

Movement on a building across the street caught Jen's eye. A zombie stood on the roof like a statue, staring at the oncoming horde.

"Hotel Three to Command One. Have engaged targets. Be advised they're splitting up and finding cover in buildings."

"Holy shit," Mark said. "They are taking cover. No leaders, they're just going."

Jen pointed at a group disappearing into a movie theater on the other side of the street. "And they're splitting up evenly. What the hell?" *The zombie on the roof.*

Jen's gaze snapped to the roof. The zombie stood there, expressionless, its yellow eyes boring into hers.

13

Zeke raced over. "A bunch of undead just ran into this building."

"Shit." Jen waved Grant over. "We need to watch that damn door."

"Command One to Hotel One and Three. Disengage."

"Roger, Command One. Hotel One Disengaging."

"Hotel Three disengaged."

Grant joined them. "What's up?"

"We may be getting company," Mark said. "Zombies have entered this building."

"How many?"

Zeke wrinkled his nose. "I lost count. They were coming in too fast."

"Then make an educated guess," Mark said.

Zeke closed his eyes and held a finger up. Mark looked at Jen and rolled his eyes.

"Maybe fifty, but could be as much as a hundred," Zeke said.

"Command One to Alpha One. Target grids Victor Tango Zulu eight to fourteen."

"Oh, shit," Mark said. "We need to get out of here."

"What?" Jen asked. "What is it?"

Mark sprinted for the door. "When they talk about targeting, they're talking artillery. And since all the zombies are in our area..."

"Command One to Alpha One. Commence firing."

Mark grabbed Jen's arm. "Come on, Zeke."

Explosions on the street rattled the building. Jen lost her footing on the vibrating roof, but Mark kept her upright.

Grant had the door open and they all ducked inside. Mark let go of Jen and whipped out his flashlight. "The zombies went into the buildings, so Butler's going to destroy the buildings to take them out."

He shined the light on a door to the stairway. "Grant, take point."

"Butler knows we're here," Jen said.

Mark pointed at her. "Exactly."

Grant had his flashlight out and entered the stairs. "Zeke, you're next."

The building rocked, and Jen fell backward into a wall. Dust and debris fell from the ceiling.

Butler's going to raze these damn buildings to the ground. If he can't get us to leave, he'll just kill us and claim the zombies got us. The asshole.

Jen ran onto the stairs, with Mark behind her. She drew her pistol and followed Zeke. Grant had already made it to the first landing.

"Don't get too far ahead," Mark called out.

Grant waited, peering down the stairs. Just as Jen reached the landing, he looked up, his eyes wide. "They're coming. Three floors down."

Another blast hit the building. This time Jen kept her balance, but just barely.

She opened the door to a hallway and shooed the others in. Closing the door, she pushed past the others and opened the first door she found.

A copier room. Several plotters and printers stood against a wall, while metal cabinets lined another. She waved the others over. "Plenty of room in here."

Mark was the last in and closed the door. "Everyone in the corner."

They set up shoulder to shoulder, firearms aimed at the door. Jen peeked out the window next to her. The movie theater on the other side of the intersection was gone, and in its place lay an enormous pile of rubble. Across the street, the building where she'd seen the leader had lost its top two floors. Flames licked its sides. Down the road, the smoke was so thick, she couldn't see crap, but the chunks of wood and stone in the road gave her a clue to what she'd find there.

Another strike on their building hit below them.

"Command One to Alpha Two. Zero in on coordinates given to Alpha

One and let go with everything you have. I don't want a building left standing in that area."

"Roger, Command One."

Jen keyed the radio. "Jen Reed to Command One. Come in."

No answer.

"Jen Reed to any unit. Please respond."

"Echo Three to Control. Northeast perimeter is secure."

"Control to Echo Three. Copy."

"Dammit. This is Jen Reed. We're in the area you're about to bomb. Cease fire."

"Alpha One to Command One. Coordinates input."

Jen sprung to her feet. "Fucking radio isn't transmitting. Either we go now or we end up buried under this damn thing."

Grant cracked the door open. "All clear." He turned around. "I'm with Jen. At least we have a chance with the zombies."

"OK," Mark said. "Let's get back on the stairs, same setup with Grant at point. We don't stop. If we hit a horde, we fight our way through it or die."

Grant flung the door open and darted down the stairs, with Zeke on his heels. Jen entered the stairwell and glanced above. Two zombies had turned and headed their way. She nudged Mark and took a shot at one of the zombies just as the building took a hit. *Shit.*

Mark took out both zombies with head shots, but missed one on his first try.

"You're still handy to have around," she said.

He gave her a little push. "Go."

Grant and Zeke had made it to the next landing. Holding onto the rail, Jen took the stairs two at a time. Grant and Zeke continued pulling away and she picked up her pace. *Don't want to get separated.*

Her breath came in ragged gasps by the time they reached the third floor and the building took another hit. Somewhere in the darkness the stressed structure emitted a low groan.

Grant and Zeke stopped halfway down to the second floor. They had their rifles up and firing. A flood of zombies ran up the stairs. Jen took out several, but even with all of them shooting, there were too many targets. *Fifty zombies? More like a couple hundred.*

Grant and Zeke backed up until they stood on the landing with the others.

"No way we can take them all," Grant yelled.

Another barrage hit the building, knocking down several zombies. Pieces of wall fell on the stairs.

Mark opened the hallway door. "In here."

"What the hell?" Jen said. "We'll be trapped there."

"We'll take the stairs on the other side," Mark said.

"How do you know there are stairs on that side?"

He pointed to a sign on the wall for emergency evacuation procedures. *Sure enough.*

Jen raced down the hallway, a stitch in her side. She reached the other stairway door, readied her pistol, and shoved the door open.

Nothing.

She waved the others over. "It's clear."

Zeke and Grant sprinted to her, while Mark closed the door and joined them. "Let's hope there's not a leader with them."

Grant hesitated. "Where do we go when we get to the first floor?"

"What?" Zeke asked.

"Where do we go?" Grant repeated. "We can't stay in the building or we'll be buried, and we can't go outside with the shells hitting out there and buildings collapsing into the street."

"Shit," Jen said.

Zeke clapped his hands together. "I know. The basement."

"Are you fucking crazy?" Grant yelled.

"We'll be crushed down there," Jen said.

"Not if we take the sewers out of here." Zeke smiled.

Grant planted his hands on his hips. "How the hell do you know there's a sewer?"

"While all of you were asleep last night, I found a computer in an office, pulled up the internet, and read everything I could about this city." He pointed to his head. "A good ninja gathers all the information about the enemy and the battlefield that he can."

Mark laughed. "You're a genius."

Grant clapped Zeke on the shoulder. "Let's go, buddy." He raced down the stairs. Zeke gave Jen a thumbs-up and followed.

Jen reached the first floor just as Grant opened the door to the basement stairway. He shined his light down it. "Dreary looking."

"Not as dreary as it'll look when the building comes down," Mark said.

Another hit shook the building. Jen braced herself and stayed on her feet. The hits were coming every minute or so.

Two more strikes came moments apart—one not far above them and one in the street.

"Down," Mark yelled.

Something knocked Jen off her feet and onto her back. Her pistol skittered across the floor.

Her reflexes kicked in and she put her hands out in front of her just as a thirty-something zombie in a shredded business pantsuit landed on top of her. It opened its mouth and snapped its jaws.

Jen coughed at the smell. It had been over a week since she'd been hit with that stench.

A shot went off close by, and the side of the zombie's head exploded, spraying blood and bone across the floor. *And on my shirt.* Jen rolled the corpse off her and grabbed Mark's outstretched hand. "Thanks for the save."

Mark handed her pistol over. "Let's go."

Zeke appeared at the door. "What happened? We heard a gunshot."

Jen waved him back. "We're OK." She brushed past him and stood at the top of the stairway. Pulling her flashlight out, she turned it on then shined it down the stairs.

Musty and narrow, the concrete stairway went ten feet down, then took a ninety-degree angle to the left.

"Where's Grant?" Jen asked.

Zeke stood behind her. "Bottom of the stairs."

Mark pulled the door closed. "You go first, Zeke. You know the way."

They joined Grant at the bottom. He and Zeke shined their flashlight beams across a large basement. Shelves jutted out from the walls on one side, while boxes were stacked on another.

"Let's split up and find the damn sewer entrance," Jen said. "I'll go straight. Zeke and Grant, can you take the right side and check around those shelves?"

They spread out and approached the shelves.

Jen looked at Mark. "The left work for you?"

He grunted and nodded. "Keep your eyes open. If you see anything, sound out."

Jen swung her beam back and forth in front of her and eased forward.

They had to get out of there fast, but it wasn't the time to take chances either. The strikes on the building were muffled down there, but it wouldn't be that way for long.

Zeke and Grant talked as they wound through the shelves. Mark moved boxes around, but otherwise stayed silent.

Jen reached the far wall. Office furniture and equipment were stacked in a far corner, and Jen walked that way.

Grant yelled and several shelves tipped over. Jen shined her flashlight that way. "You guys all right?"

Grunts, crashes, and scuffing feet came from their direction. Jen holstered her pistol and drew her axe, then stepped toward the noise.

Something grabbed her free arm and yanked her back.

14

The hand let go as Jen spun and swung the axe. Damn thing sliced through air, the action knocking her off balance and onto the floor.

"Wait," a voice above her screamed. "We're human. Don't hurt us."

Jen turned her flashlight toward the voice, illuminating a woman in a dirty business skirt and jacket, her eyes wild.

Zeke's voice called out. "I've got one."

Jen glanced to where another beam glowed by the shelves.

Mark appeared next to the woman. He had his mace in hand. "Who are you and why did you attack?"

The girl shivered and wrapped her arms around herself. "I'm Sharon Watson. I used to work here. Pridger's Accounting on the fifth floor." Her voice squeaked as she said, "Please don't hurt us."

Grant and Zeke arrived escorting a man in a shabby suit between them. Zeke had the man's arm locked behind his back. "And you?" Jen asked.

"John Dormand," he said. "Senior partner at Pridger's."

"Why'd you attack us?" Mark asked.

"I didn't," Dormand said. "I was hiding and this one"—he pointed at Grant—"tripped over me."

Mark swung his gaze to Sharon. "And you?"

"I-I didn't attack anyone," she said. "I heard you talking and knew you weren't one of the creatures. Then I saw your lights. I didn't want to startle you by speaking, so I touched your arm."

Jen lowered her axe. "Is it just you two, or is anyone else gonna jump out at us?"

"Just us," Dormand said. "We've been down here for weeks." He added, "I think."

"You think?" Grant asked.

Dormand shrugged. "At first, there were four of us and we'd go upstairs and scavenge the building. But it became more dangerous. We lost the other two. Sharon and I decided to stay here until we ran out of food. We haven't seen the sun since."

Another explosion rocked the building. A large crash came from up the stairway.

"What's going on out there?" Sharon asked.

"The army's bombing us," Grant said.

Jen wiped dust from her eyes. "We need to get to the sewer system. Do you know where the entrance is?"

"Will you bring us with you?" Sharon asked.

"Of course." Mark's voice softened. "Where's the sewer entrance?"

Sharon pointed to a pile of desks. "I'm pretty sure it's underneath them. They've been there for months, but I noticed a manhole cover in the floor before they were stacked there."

Jen ran to the desks and pulled one off the top. It bounced on the floor, breaking a leg off in the process.

Grant and Zeke joined in. Jen handed her flashlight to Sharon. "Can you hold that for us?"

Sharon nodded and lit the desk pile.

Jen and Mark worked together to pull desks off the pile and out of the way.

Another strike on the building caused the pile of desks to fall over. Jen smiled. "Butler doesn't know he's helping us now."

In minutes they uncovered a four-foot-wide manhole.

Grant stuck two fingers in the manhole cover's notch and pulled. His face squinched and arms strained, but the damn thing didn't move. He straightened, puffing. "Weighs a ton."

"We need a lever," Mark said. "Crowbar or something like it."

"I found a metal bar when we first came down here," Dormand said.

"Was going to use it as a weapon in case any of those things got down here, but it was too heavy."

Mark tossed him a flashlight. "Show us."

The building shook and something heavy slammed the floor above them, causing Jen to duck. "Shit. I thought it was coming through."

Dormand led Mark to the stairs and pointed the beam to the side. "There."

Mark picked up and returned with a four-foot piece of rebar.

Another strike and the floor above collapsed at the stairs. Debris flew into the basement, followed by a cloud of dust. Jen coughed. "We're out of time."

Mark stuck the rebar in the notch and rubbed his hands together. He grasped the end and pushed down. The cover didn't move. Jen grabbed the bar in front of Mark, and Zeke and Grant ahead of her.

Dust made it difficult to see the cover. Grant sounded like he was coughing up a lung.

"Get those lights closer to the manhole," Jen yelled.

Seconds later, she could just make out the cover.

"On three," Mark yelled. "Give it all you've got. If we get it up, roll it to the right." He choked and went into a coughing fit.

Another crash. This one close. *The damn thing's about to come down on our heads.*

"One, two, three!"

Jen pushed down, grunting. It moved, but barely. The bar rose as the others released it.

The ceiling collapsed not more than ten feet from her. A piece of solid debris struck her foot. *Damn, that hurts.*

"This is it," she yelled. "Give it more than you've got."

Two more sets of hands joined them. "One, two, three," Mark yelled.

The bar dipped lower and the cover teetered on the other end. "Roll it to the right," Mark gasped.

Sweat poured down Jen's face and her arm muscles trembled. Teeth gritted, she strained to keep the cover up. It moved, but how much she couldn't tell. Someone let go and the bar rose. Then someone else let go and the weight and strain on Jen's arms were too much. She lost her sweaty grip and the cover slammed down.

Jen dropped to her knees. She grabbed one of the flashlights and pointed it at the manhole. The cover partially covered the opening, leaving a three-foot gap.

"We can get through," she yelled.

A dark figure swept past her and shined a light down the hole. "There are rungs," Zeke said. "I'll go first." He disappeared down the hole.

The building shivered under another strike. It was in its dying throes.

Jen grabbed Sharon's arm and led her to the manhole. "Hurry down."

Sharon nodded and climbed down out of sight. Dormand was next. He hesitated. "What if those things are down there?"

Jen pulled her pistol and pointed it at his face. "Down. Now!"

Dormand hurried down the rungs.

She coughed. *Can barely breathe in this shit.* "Mark, you and Grant next."

"What?" Mark said. "No way."

"No time to argue. We need you both down there in case there are zombies. Go."

Mark slid onto his stomach and disappeared over the edge. Grant followed.

The ceiling above Jen let out a deafening crack. Jen jumped into the hole as the ceiling caved in. Pieces of concrete struck her in the head and shoulder as she fell. She slammed into someone and knocked them off the rungs, both of them landing in ankle-deep water.

Someone grabbed her arms and pulled her away as a ton of concrete and plaster poured from the hole.

Jen was lifted to her feet and guided farther into the sewer. "This way," Zeke said. She stumbled alongside him, hacking. His flashlight barely penetrated the dust.

They reached a turn in the tunnel and the dust cleared. Mark stumbled in front of her, Grant's arm over his shoulder. Grant looked as bad as she felt. Sharon stood off to the side with her flashlight on the others.

Mark let Grant go and the soldier stood, bent over, with his hands on his knees, vomiting. Mark's eyes teared, leaving streaks in the dust on his face. Jen pushed off gently from Zeke. "I can stand." Zeke stepped back as she leaned against the wall. She wiped her face with her arm and gagged. "What the hell did I land in? I reek."

Grant straightened. "Thanks for falling and knocking me into that shit. And I mean it literally. I think I swallowed a turd."

"Wait," Mark said. "Where's Dormand?"

"He went the other way. Said he knew a safe place in that direction." Sharon put her head in her hands and sobbed.

"What's our next step?" Grant asked.

Mark examined Jen. "Your head's bleeding pretty good." He cut off one of his sleeves and pressed it to her forehead. "Hold this."

Jen held the cloth to her forehead and Mark pulled the ends of the sleeve behind her head and tied it. "You'll be OK. Scalp wounds look worse than they are."

He turned to the others. "I say we try to find an exit to the street and see where we are."

Grant nodded. "Good idea. Figure out what direction we need to go. We could be moving farther away from the base for all we know."

"We should at least find some shelter before night comes," Jen said.

Zeke brushed himself off. Covered in dust, his ninja uniform made him look more like a ghost than an assassin. He shined his flashlight down the sewer tunnel. "Follow me."

Twenty minutes later, the air became more breathable and the sounds of destruction faded into the distance.

"There." Grant pointed to a smaller manhole. Thin beams of light broke through the cover's holes.

Mark moved beneath it and put his foot on a rung. "I'll check it out. Stay here and I'll let you know if it's clear."

He climbed, the heels of his boots making each rung give off a muffled *ring*.

When he reached the cover, he pressed his shoulder against it. It lifted and sunlight hit his face, causing him to squint.

Sliding the cover out of his way, he stuck his head out of the manhole and looked around. Seconds later, he ducked his head inside. "All clear up here. Everybody up." He pulled himself up.

After everyone got out, Jen helped Grant slide the cover back into place. Zeke had his katana out and gave it a few practice swings. "How about I go scout?"

"I think we're better off sticking together." Mark had his mace in his hand. "Only close-combat weapons. No firearms."

Jen's watch showed ten minutes to noon. *Can't tell direction from the sun yet.* "Need to get our bearings. Follow me."

"How are we going to tell where we are?" Grant asked. "We don't know this city."

"I do." Sharon stepped forward.

Jen led the way to the alley entrance and peered out into the street. No sign of zombies. *And no artillery.* She waved Sharon forward and pointed to a street sign. "Second Street. What direction is the base?"

Sharon pointed behind them and to the left. "Interstate 90 is a couple of blocks behind us. If we follow it west to Highway 2, it'll take us to the base."

"Sounds like a plan," Mark said. "Let's head toward the interstate and grab a vehicle on the way."

Jen jogged to the other end of the alley and popped her head out just as a dozen zombies rushed by in a V formation. The leader, an unusually tall shirtless man with coarse autopsy stitches across his chest, whirled around and rushed at her with the rest on his heels.

15

Jen backpedaled into the alley. "Horde coming!"

A hand pressed on her back. "We're with you." Mark stepped next to her.

The zombies rushed into the alley, the leader nowhere in sight. *Where the hell is he?*

Jen reared her arm back, grasping the axe tight enough to turn her knuckles white. She timed her overhead swing and brought the blade down on the first zombie's head. A man in mechanic's overalls with the name Brad stitched over the pocket, he dropped at her feet.

Mark's mace was a blur as he bashed first one zombie, then another. One of them fell and the other staggered. Mark gave the second one another lick and it went down.

Zeke jumped past them, his katana blade slashing. "Leave some for me and Betty."

He spun and took out the next three in seconds.

Still the horde pushed forward. The narrowness of the alley prevented more than three from attacking at once.

Grant tapped Jen on the shoulder. "Fall back. I'll take a few."

Jen dropped back and Grant drove the tip of his sword under a fat zombie's jaw and into his brain. The zombie fell before Grant could pull his blade out, and the tall man took the sword down with him.

Jen grabbed Grant's collar and yanked him back just as an old woman sprung at him. Jen followed through with her axe and hit the zombie in the shoulder, knocking it over.

She stepped forward, split the skull of the next zombie in line, then planted the blade in the old woman's forehead.

Only three zombies left. Jen zeroed in on the leader, who stood back from the others and watched the battle.

Jen shoved past the other two undead and bulled her way to him. At the last second, he ducked and Jen's axe sailed over his head. She lost her balance, slammed against the wall, and fell to the ground. Her axe flew out of her grasp. The leader stood over her, his yellow eyes sizing her up.

Zeke finished off the last of the attackers and sprang for the leader, who sidestepped him and dashed out of the alley.

"Zeke," Mark yelled. "Hold up."

Zeke stopped at the end of the alley. "I can catch him."

Jen sat up and Grant helped her to her feet. "That was a leader," she said. "He'll probably take you right to another horde."

"And will probably bring them back here," Mark said.

Jen turned to see how Sharon was, but she'd disappeared. "Sharon?"

Grant looked back. "Shit." He ran to the other end of the alley and peered up and down the street. Walking back to Jen, he shook his head. "No sign of her."

"Must've gotten scared and took off," Mark said.

"We've got to go find her," Grant said.

"Can't," Jen said. "No time. We got lucky this was a small horde and they stacked up in the alley. We won't get that lucky a second time."

Mark sighed. "We did what we could. She survived long enough for us to find her. She might find a place to lay low and wait things out."

Jen patted Grant on the back. "Come on."

Grant nodded and they walked out onto the deserted street.

"She said the highway's a couple of blocks this way," Jen said. "Let's find a vehicle."

Cars were parked every which way along the street, with some crowding the middle. Jen opened the door of a large SUV and checked for keys. None.

An engine started and a minivan pulled out from the curb. Zeke stuck his head out of the driver's window. "Got one. Almost a full tank, too. Come on."

Jen raced to the van and slid the side door open. "You know how to drive?"

"Hell, yeah," Zeke said. He gunned the engine.

"I'm not talking about driving in a freaking computer game," Jen said.

Grant ran up. "Maybe I should drive. That's what I do."

Dashing over from the other side of the road, Mark yelled, "Get in. They're coming."

Sure enough, a huge horde zeroed in on them from two blocks away. They filled the whole damn street.

Jen jumped into the back and slid over. Grant took the passenger seat next to Zeke.

Mark dived in. "Go!"

Zeke hit the accelerator and left tire marks and black smoke in his wake.

Mark slammed the door closed and sat up. He glanced over his shoulder. "Keep going. We need to lose them."

Jen sat forward and pointed to the next street. "Take a right there."

The tires screeched as Zeke threw the van into a tight turn. It sideswiped a police car, tearing off its side-view mirror.

Zeke laughed. "Couldn't have gotten away with that a month ago."

Jen glanced behind them. The horde hadn't stopped, but had fallen back. "Take it easy, Zeke. We're outdistancing them, but if you get us in an accident, we're toast."

"There." Grant pointed at the interstate on-ramp.

Zeke took the van into the turn without Jen's heart jumping into her throat, and they entered the interstate. Abandoned vehicles littered the highway, and Zeke did a great job avoiding them and keeping speed. Jen watched the rear, but saw no sign of the horde.

Two miles farther, Grant pointed ahead. "Look at that. It's the cavalry."

A convoy of five Humvees headed their way. Mark tapped Zeke on the shoulder. "Pull over."

Zeke slowed the van and stopped. Mark and Jen got out and waved their arms. A gunner on the lead Humvee waved back, and the Humvees pulled up several yards in front of them.

The lead gunner yelled, "Who are you?"

Grant got out. "I'm assigned to Supply. These people are a scientific team studying the zombies. They report to Colonel Butler."

The lead vehicle's driver's door opened and a sergeant stepped out. "Load up. One of you in each vehicle. I'll radio in and let them know we're coming."

Jen took the lead vehicle. The sergeant put the radio mic to his lips. "Echo Eight to Control. We've picked up one of our Supply Specialists and three civilians. Please inform Control One."

"Echo Eight, this is Control One. Bring them to my location immediately."

"Roger, Control One. En route."

The Humvee made a U turn and the convoy sped back to the base.

Sergeant Howell met them at the Headquarters building. "The colonel wants to see you right away."

Jen scowled. "I'd like to see him, too."

Howell led them into the building and to Butler's office door. He knocked.

"Enter," Butler said.

Howell opened the door and waved the group in. He closed the door, staying out in the hall.

Butler's desk stood in the corner. Made of an expensive-looking dark wood, the damn thing shined. *Probably has some poor private first class wax it every day.* The rest of the office was spartan, with a second door next to the desk, but not much else.

Mark stood with his fists clenched, while Grant stood at attention. Zeke studied the ceiling tiles.

Butler leaned back in his leather chair, with the American and Army flags flanking him. "I'm glad to see you've made it back in one piece. When are you leaving?"

Jen clenched her jaw. *What an asshole.* "Why? Don't want another chance to kill us?"

Butler's face turned bright crimson in an instant. "How dare you accuse me."

Mark bent forward with his fists on Butler's desk. "It wouldn't be the first time. How about Major Morris and his men in Afghanistan? Same thing, except this time you didn't just leave us, you tried to bomb the shit out of us."

Butler rose, his voice trembling. "I want you out of here now. All of you." He pointed at Grant. "Get back to your damn unit."

He turned to Jen. "And you're the worst of the bunch. I've half a mind to place you into custody."

Time to play the trump card. "What do you think Dr. Cartwright would have to say about that?"

Butler's lips pressed together and he said nothing.

Jen propped her hands on her hips. *Let's make this even better.* "Fuck you, Butler. We're going to finish our mission and you're going to support us. Screw with us again, and I'll recommend to Dr. Cartwright that you're removed from your position." She had no idea if Cartwright would support her on that, but neither did he.

Butler's eyes narrowed and he clenched his fists. "I will follow my orders." He pointed a finger at Jen. "But any of you step out of line and I'll lock your asses up and ship you out."

Jen patted Zeke on the shoulder. "I'm hungry. Anyone ready for lunch?" She glanced at Butler as she left the room. His face was turning color again.

16

J en scooped a mouthful of mashed potatoes into her mouth. Zeke and Mark had been silent since they left Butler's office, only offering comments about the food selection in the chow hall.

Grant separated himself as soon as they walked in and sat with some soldiers on the other side of the hall.

Jen swallowed and took a sip of water. "I have an idea for next steps."

Mark wiped his mouth with a paper napkin. "If it's got something to do with taking Butler down, then I'm in."

Zeke picked up the top of his hamburger bun and examined the contents. "Two pickles? Cheap bastards."

"Zeke," Jen said. "Focus. Eat the damn burger as it is and listen up."

Zeke sighed and placed the top of the bun back in place. "I think we should go kill more zombies. Find their leaders and take them out."

Mark's eyebrow rose. "Not a bad tactical idea."

Jen leaned forward. "I need to talk to Cartwright first. Give her a full report."

"And then?" Mark asked.

"Butler's hiding something. Otherwise, why try to kill us? He doesn't want us around, and we won't leave."

Zeke took a bite of his hamburger. "So what's he hiding?" Pieces of chewed food fell onto his plate.

Jen made a face at him. "Don't ninjas have some sort of reputation for being neat and orderly?"

Zeke shook his head.

"Anyway," Jen said, "I don't know what he's up to, but it's pretty obvious it has to do with Area 51."

Mark shrugged. "Agreed. So what—" His face slackened. "You want to break into a guarded, probably alarmed, restricted area on a military base."

Jen grinned. "Glad we're on the same track."

"Look, Jen," Mark said. "I'm all for taking Butler down, but I want to get to my family."

"I'm in," Zeke said.

Jen stared at Mark. "I promised you I'd go with you to make sure your family's OK, and I plan on keeping that promise. But I'd feel a lot better if you joined me on this. I wouldn't have gotten out of Anchorage without you." She patted his arm. "You're like my good luck charm."

Mark squeezed his eyes shut and sighed. "You've saved me, too. But keeping up with you is a pain in the ass."

"This is the asshole that let soldiers die in Afghanistan and left us out to dry in Anchorage. I think the sky's the limit for his next backstab. Don't you?"

Mark opened his eyes. "Yeah, I'll do it. But on one condition."

"What's that?"

"You tell Cartwright what you're planning. If she tells you not to do it, then we don't."

No idea what Cartwright will say. "It's a deal."

Thirty minutes later, Jen stood in front of the conference room monitor, the screen filled with Cartwright sitting at her desk.

"Your observations about the leader zombies is intriguing," Cartwright said. "It leads me to believe the virus does something to the live human brain that it doesn't get a chance to do to a bitten victim before he dies. This adds a worrisome dimension to the situation. We'll begin experiments on that theory immediately."

She leaned forward. "I also agree with your assessment of Colonel Butler. He's shown signs of instability and the military hierarchy is concerned. My apprehension is that he'll try to kill you again. And if he really is unstable, he may not care if I find out. I think my influence with him is hanging by a thread."

"Do you think we should just cut our losses and get out of here?" Mark asked.

Jen shot him a glare.

Cartwright put a finger to the corner of her mouth and looked off camera. "It's a risk I don't want you to take." She peered over her glasses at the screen. "Tell me again about the restricted area."

"There's a guard at the front gate and another at the back gate that controls entry into the loading dock."

Cartwright waved her hand as if to shoo a fly. "No. The man. The civilian you saw. Describe him."

"Short, older guy," Jen said. "Big round glasses, what hair he still had is gray."

Typing sounds came from the speakers. "Just a minute," Cartwright said, turning her back to the monitor.

"Was this the man?" she asked, facing them again. She held up a sheet of paper with the picture of the civilian they'd seen.

"That's him," Jen said.

Cartwright looked at the monitor and lowered her voice. "Who's in the room with you?"

"Just me, Mark, and Zeke."

"His name is Dr. Jeffrey Morgan. He was once a respected research neurologist."

"Once?" Mark asked.

"Yes. Once, but no more. Not after being arrested for experimenting on humans."

"Shit," Jen said. "What kind of experiments?"

"Mind control, implanting memories, that kind of thing." Cartwright straightened. "I had information he was there, but not what he was up to."

"Information?" Mark said. "From who?"

"Another time," Cartwright said. "Just understand that whatever Dr. Morgan's working on is guaranteed to be a threat."

"How did he end up here?" Jen asked.

Cartwright adjusted her glasses. "Exactly what I'd like to know. He disappeared while out on bail awaiting trial, and there's been no trace of him until now."

Zeke cleared his throat. "Sounds like we need a ninja infiltration of Area 51 to see what's going on in there."

Jen jerked a thumb at Zeke. "Kung Fu Panda here is right. Someone has to see what's going on."

Cartwright sighed. "I have an asset on base who reports only to me, and has been in Area 51. There's a top floor that's heavily secured that Morgan disappears into. My asset doesn't have access to that floor."

"Who's the asset?" Jen asked.

Cartwright ignored her question and peered over her glasses. "And there's another issue. I need you back here to get more of your blood."

"You didn't get enough the first time?"

"We're running out of what Doc sent, and you're the only survivor of Point Wallace."

Mark cleared his throat. "What difference does that make? Pretty much everyone has been infected."

Cartwright steepled her fingers. "Jen received a higher concentration than anyone else, and I need to see if it affects her differently over time." She sat back. "It could lead to a dead end, or a significant breakthrough. I can't tell at this point, but I'm leaving no stone unturned."

"So we break into the top floor of Area 51, find out what's going on, and get Jen down to you," Zeke said. "Sounds simple enough to me."

"No," Cartwright said. "My asset can pursue Butler's plans. I need Jen here."

Mark sighed. "As much as I want to get out of here, your plan doesn't make sense, Doctor. Unless your asset is willing to blow his or her cover, we're the best shot you have of finding out what the hell's going on here."

Jen crossed her arms and stared at the floor. If they just left, who knows what Butler could pull? He'd already shown many times over that he'd sacrifice others for what he wanted. *Besides, it's not guaranteed that studying my blood will actually help stop the zombies.*

She looked up. "I think I can do both. A quick try to see what Butler's got up his sleeve, and then we leave. I'm tired of just reacting to shit. Time to go on the offensive."

"That would be unadvisable." Cartwright removed her glasses and rubbed her eyes. "But also valuable."

Jen patted Zeke on the back. "Looks like we're in the spy business."

"We?" Zeke said.

Jen grinned. "You don't think I'm letting you have all the fun yourself, do you?"

Mark sighed.

"Jen." Cartwright's face softened. "I won't give you orders; Doc made it clear to me that doing so would create the opposite effect. But as someone who cares about what happens to you, I urge you to reconsider. There's little I can do to help you from here."

Jen wavered. *Not fair. She brought up Doc. My biggest failure.* She jutted her jaw forward. "I'm going to do this for Doc. And everyone else."

Cartwright leaned forward and the monitor went black.

"Are you nuts?" Mark asked. "You've done some crazy shit, but this is in another ballpark. A restricted area with armed guards and an insane commander?"

Jen smiled, but inwardly cringed. She'd gotten caught up in the moment, and Mark was bringing her back to earth. "We need to get out of this room before we get caught. Zeke, check the hallway."

Zeke opened the door. "All clear."

Jen strode into the hallway and to her room. Mark and Zeke joined her.

"All right," Mark said. "What's the plan? How are you going to infiltrate Area 51?"

"I can sneak in there at night," Zeke said. "I blend in with the shadows."

Jen waved him off. "There's a better way. Who do we know with access to the loading dock?"

"Grant?" Mark said.

Jen shrugged. "Every day at three a.m. And there are some quiet buildings along his route where no one would notice him stopping for a minute and taking on an extra load."

"And that would be you," Mark said.

Jen grinned. "Exactly. Zeke, think you can get another note to Grant?"

"Easy," Zeke said. "But do you think Grant will go along with it?"

"I don't know," she said. "But either way I'm getting into Area 51 to find out what the hell Butler's trying to hide."

17

Kneeling behind some old barrels on the side of the rec center, Jen shivered in the early morning darkness.

"I still think I should go with you," Mark said, his voice startling her.

"It'll be easier to sneak around if it's just me."

"At least bring me along," Zeke said. "Sneaking is what I do."

Jen nudged him. "You would be the person they'd expect to try something like this. Besides, I need both of you out here in case I run into trouble."

A truck rumbled in the near distance. Jen's pulse picked up. The truck drew closer. *Will Grant risk himself to help out?*

The sigh of hydraulics and the squeak of brakes signaled it had stopped out front. A door opened and closed.

Jen gave Mark and Zeke a thumbs-up and dashed around the side of the building. The truck blocked her from the road and the back of it faced her. *Good job, Grant.*

She pulled the door up and rolled into the back, pulling the handle down behind her.

She turned on her flashlight. Surrounded by crates and boxes, she stumbled as the truck started moving with a jerk.

Have to find somewhere to hide.

She squeezed between two pallets and ducked behind a third. She'd had an idea of jumping into a box and letting the soldiers carry her off, but all the damn boxes were secure and the crates nailed shut.

The truck slowed, then stopped. Voices came from outside. Grant's was one, but she couldn't make out the words. The truck moved forward, continued for a couple of minutes, then turned and backed up, the warning beeps loud enough for her to hear them clearly.

With the squeal of brakes, it stopped and the engine went silent. A door opened and closed. Seconds later, another truck started and pulled out, its engine noise dimming in the distance.

The door rolled up, spilling light into the back. Jen pushed back behind a pallet.

"What've we got today?" a deep voice asked.

A woman's voice answered, "Same old shit, I'll bet. Steak and wine for the colonel and his civilian, and canned spaghetti for us."

Deep Voice laughed. "Butler says we're the elite troops, but we get fed worse than the others going to the chow hall."

Someone jumped onto the back and a banging came from that direction. Jen peeked out. A burly soldier had jammed a crowbar beneath a crate's lid and was trying to pry it up.

"Gimme a hand, Jonesy," he said.

A buffed up female soldier with short black hair joined him. "One, two, three."

They pushed, and with a ripping sound, the crate lid rose on one side.

Jonesy reached a hand in. "Holy shit, if this is what I think it is..."

She pulled on something then removed her hand. It held a can of beer.

"Are you kidding?" Deep Voice said. "That must've been a mistake."

Jonesy popped the top and downed a swallow. "Mmmm."

Deep Voice pulled another can from the crate. "This damn thing is full of them."

Jonesy swallowed and smacked her lips. "Are you thinking what I'm thinking?"

Deep Voice tilted his head. "No. What?"

She swatted him on the shoulder. "Sometimes I wonder just how dumb you can get."

He shrugged.

"If this crate goes to the food stores, the supply clowns will drink it all."

"So what do we do?" Deep Voice asked.

Jonesy rolled her eyes. "We grab a case for ourselves and go rat-hole it right now."

Deep Voice smiled. "Good idea." He reached in and hauled out a case.

Jonesy grabbed another one. "One for you and one for me." She slapped Deep Voice's hand as he went to get a third. "No more," she said. "They won't report a couple missing, but might if we take too many."

The back of the truck shuddered. Jen peeked out. Deep Voice and Jonesy stood on the dock. Deep Voice picked up both cases and put one on each shoulder. "You stay here and I'll go hide them."

"Like hell," Jonesy said. "I'm going with you. I want to know where mine is."

"But what if someone comes by and sees us gone?"

Jonesy strode to a door, punched numbers in a keypad, and held it open. "Then we better be quick about it."

I need to get through that door.

Deep Voice stepped through and Jonesy followed him, releasing the door.

Jen dashed out of the truck and to the door. She reached out as it closed and caught the handle before the door clicked shut. She puffed her cheeks and let out a breath. *Close.*

Sticking her head into the hallway, she looked right, peering down a long corridor that ended in a door with a meshed window. Jonesy had just walked through the doorway.

Down the other direction, two doors stood on the right side of the hallway. No sign of anyone there.

Those doors probably lead to the front of the building. Not what I'm looking for.

She stepped into the hallway, eased the door closed with a click, and padded to the meshed doorway, where she peeked through the window at a stairway. Voices came from above and were getting closer. She slipped beneath the bottom stairs and held her breath while footsteps scuffed above her.

The door to the hallway opened and Jonesy said, "See. Told you it'd only take a minute."

After the door closed Jen crept to the window. Deep Voice and Jonesy disappeared through the doorway to the loading dock.

Stepping softly, Jen climbed the first flight of stairs and then the second, where a door marked with the number two stood at the landing.

She peeked through the mesh window and ducked back down. Soldiers walked up and down the hall, some with papers in their hands and others fully armed.

She climbed to the third floor. Fewer soldiers there, but still too risky to try. *Dammit.*

The fourth floor had multiple doors along the hallway on either side, but no soldiers in sight. Jen grasped the door handle and turned it. A soldier walked out of an office that stood five feet in front of her, and headed the opposite way down the hall.

Jen released the handle and ducked. Pulse pounding in her ears, she peeked through the window. The soldier disappeared out the door at the other end of the hall. She got a flash of another stairway before the door closed.

Clasping her hand to her chest, she willed her heart to slow down. She looked down to see she'd gripped her axe's handle involuntarily.

She snuck up the stairs to the fifth floor, where a metal door with no windows greeted her. A keypad lay on the wall to the side.

This would be the place that Cartwright's asset couldn't penetrate. Definitely something going on in there.

"Looks like it's door number four," she said.

Jen crept down the stairs to the fourth floor. She watched through the window for a minute and detected no one. Voices came from below her on the stairs.

Shit.

Cracking the door open, she slipped inside the hallway.

The top of a head appeared down the stairs. Mouth dry, she ducked and hurried to the first office but the knob wouldn't turn. *Dammit.*

She rushed to the next door across the hall, and it, too, was locked. Voices from the stairs grew louder, and Jen's mouth went dry. The third door open easily and she ducked into the darkened room, closing the door behind her with a clunk that sounded like a gunshot. Her breath came in shallow gasps as she waited in the dark.

The voices approached and stopped in front of the door. A drop of sweat ran down her cheek. *Don't come in here. Don't come in here.*

"Colonel Butler wants that report by the end of the day," a man's voice with the hint of a Boston accent said.

Another voice grunted and a door across the hall squeaked. "Yeah, yeah. I know the drill."

The door closed and one set of footsteps echoed down the hall. Another door opened and closed, and then there was silence.

Jen fumbled along the wall and flipped a switch. The sudden light blinded her and she squinted.

When her eyes adjusted, she took inventory of the room. Shelves laden with cleaning supplies lined one wall. A mop and bucket stood next to a sink, and several sizes of brooms lay stacked in a corner.

Her mind searched for a way to the fifth floor. A pair of janitor overalls hung from a hook. *I could dress as a janitor and fake my way in.*

She scoffed. *Stupid. How would I get past a keypad?*

A clock on the wall showed she'd already been inside for almost twenty minutes. Mark and Zeke would be wondering what she'd found.

Maybe I should just find a way out and get to Atlanta.

Rubbing her shoulder, she tipped her head back to stretch her neck muscles and her attention settled on a large ventilation grate on the wall.

Bingo.

18

T he step stool squeaked and tilted to one side as Jen balanced herself on the top step. She caught her breath and put a hand against the wall to steady herself.

Don't tell me after all this I'm going to get taken out by a shitty piece of janitorial equipment.

She pulled the screwdriver she'd found in a toolbox from her pocket and removed the four screws holding the cover on. Holding the screwdriver between her teeth, she used both hands to pry the cover off the wall. A dusty breeze hit her in the face and she turned her head to sneeze.

Her flashlight beam showed dust bunnies as big as rats in the shaft. *Great thought, Jen. Thanks.*

The shaft went left and right. To the left there were other openings farther down until the light could reach no more. To the right, it went several feet until it met a vertical shaft.

Jen laid the flashlight in the vent and tried to jiggle the vent. Three feet by three feet, it was made of thick metal and didn't move.

Satisfied, she clicked the flashlight off, stuck it in her belt, and climbed down the ladder.

A door opened and closed nearby. Jen readied her axe and stood to the side of the door. Footsteps clicked on the tile past her door. Another door opened and closed, and there was silence.

She considered locking the door, but it might draw suspicion. She had to find a way to avoid alarm while she was in the vent. Her eyes roved over the contents of the room and settled on a plastic placard leaning against the mop bucket. It said "Caution Wet Floor." She smiled.

Two minutes later, she'd taped a piece of paper underneath the vent opening that said "Vent Repairs in Progress by Order of Colonel Butler." Butler had the soldiers so cowed they wouldn't dare to question him on it.

She secured her axe on her back. If she was going to be sliding around on her stomach, she didn't want that thing scratching the vent and bringing unwanted attention. She climbed the ladder and pulled herself into the vent, sliding to the right. Once she was fully in, she took out her flashlight and shined it toward the vertical shaft.

It only took a minute to reach it. She pointed the beam down and saw where it split off into the next two floors below her.

She rolled onto her back to look up and regretted it when the axe dug into her back. Shit. *No good place for that thing.*

Gritting her teeth, she pointed the light upward. The opening for the next floor lay twelve feet away.

Jen slid her upper body into the shaft and grabbed onto a two-inch outcropping where two sections of vents were fastened together. *Not going to be easy.*

She pulled her upper body up while sliding her lower extremities farther out. Her fingers burned with the effort. Worse still, they became slick with sweat. Raising herself again, she grasped the next outcropping with one hand, then repeated the process.

Only her feet remained in the horizontal vent. She strained to pull them out. They slid slowly and stopped. Her breath came in short gasps.

One, two, three. Pull.

Her feet slipped out and banged the side of the shaft. Jen's slick fingers lost their grip and she fell, feet first down the shaft, her hands desperately clutching for something, anything to hold on to.

She spread her legs, her feet hit an outcropping, and she stopped with a bang that echoed through the vents. She thrust her arms up and grabbed an outcropping above her.

Jen's head drooped forward and sweat ran down her face. *Too close to quit. Come on, finish this shit.*

She wiped first one hand, then the other on her shirt, then

reached for the next outcropping. Moving slowly, but methodically, she climbed her way back up to the horizontal vent she'd come from. She stopped and listened, but there was no shouting, no signs of pursuit.

Gulping air, she continued upward, arriving at the fifth-floor vent a few minutes later. She pulled herself inside and collapsed, her heart racing and muscles burning.

On her elbows and knees, she inched toward the first vent opening and stopped at the grate. Bile spilled into the back of her throat. *The smell. The graveyard smell.*

It was dark as pitch, but Jen sensed something moving just beneath the vent, and she leaned back from the grate. *They're keeping zombies up here? For what?*

Another movement came from across the room, along with the clinking of chains.

Jen crawled to the next vent opening and the death smell faded. Unlike the previous room, this one—an office with a cluttered desk—was well lit. A computer on the desk was on and had a document displayed, but Jen couldn't read it from her position. Several stocked bookshelves ran along one wall.

Voices came from farther down the vent. She crawled closer to it and froze when Butler said, "You better have made progress."

She slid up to the vent opening. The room was a cross between a lab and a surgery. Computers, beakers, and other instruments lined counters against the walls, while an operating table stood in the middle of the room. Strapped to that table lay a soldier, the top of his skull removed and wires running to some type of probes inserted into his brain. His eyes were open, but he showed no signs of life.

Jen squinted to get a good look. Yellow eyes.

The wires ran to a machine on the counter, and Morgan stood next to it, adjusting a slider.

Butler towered next to him, his hands on his hips. "We're out of time, Doctor. My superiors are asking too many questions."

Dr. Morgan didn't reply and continued working the controls.

Butler's face reddened. "Doctor," he yelled.

Morgan looked up at Butler and blinked as if coming out of a dream. "What is it, Colonel?"

Butler clenched his fists, but answered calmly. "I need to know when you expect a successful test."

Morgan removed his small, round wire-framed glasses and blew on them before replacing them. "Science doesn't run on timelines, Colonel." Butler scowled, and Morgan raised a hand. "But in this case, I've made some headway.

"As you recall, my plan was to control the undead electronically. Watch Corporal Stennings there on the table."

Holy shit. Dr. Frankenstein stuff.

Morgan turned a dial. The zombie soldier didn't move. Butler grunted and his jaw clenched.

Morgan adjusted a slider, then said, "I think we have it now." He turned the dial again.

The zombie kicked a leg out.

Butler grinned. "What else can he do?"

Morgan stretched his back. "That's it so far."

Butler's eyebrows rose. "Are you fucking kidding? You made a dead man's leg move? I did that with a frog in high school."

Morgan frowned. "Of course, the results of electronic control hasn't been what I'd hoped."

"So what's Plan B?"

Morgan put a finger up. "I've found a way for you to start controlling the zombies today. Soon, you'll have your own army and no one will be able to stop you from marching on Washington."

19

J en squinted. *Butler controlling zombies? His own army? Against Washington? This shit can't be real.*

Morgan adjusted his glasses. "Do you remember the recording you provided me of the conversation between Dr. Cartwright and those refugees from Anchorage?"

Jen clenched her fists. *They taped us?*

Butler nodded. "Wish I'd started tapping their conversations sooner. So far, we only have their call from yesterday, and even then, only the first twenty minutes. My comm folks are new at that, but have assured me the tap won't drop again."

"I gleaned some interesting information from them," Morgan said. "A case in point is what they called leader zombies. These are humans that die without being bitten first. When they're reanimated they have the ability to communicate with, and control, zombies who were created from being bitten, which are called drones."

"Nice science lesson," Butler said. "What does that mean to me?"

Morgan stepped past Butler and pulled back a drape at the end of the room. Behind a large window, three zombies were chained to the wall. They strained uselessly to attack Morgan, their yellow eyes gleaming.

"Another demonstration," Morgan said. "I trust you recognize the zombie in the middle."

The zombie he pointed to wore military BDUs with several bullet holes in the chest. Jen couldn't make out his name tape because of a bloodstain.

Butler sauntered over to the window. "Captain Beal. You're looking a little worn." He chuckled at his own joke.

"Observe." Morgan pointed at Beal's head, where a bulky plastic helmet was strapped.

Morgan picked up a microphone and turned it on. "Captain Beal."

Beal went apeshit, flinging himself against his chains.

"Captain Beal," Morgan repeated. "Sit on the floor."

The zombie captain continued to flail against his restraints.

Morgan took a small device from his pocket. Black, with a red button, it fit snugly in his hand. He pressed the button.

Captain Beal's back arched and his arms flung out, fingers splayed. A mournful moan came from deep in his chest.

Morgan released the button, and Beal came out of his convulsions. Morgan spoke into the mic. "Captain Beal. Sit on the floor."

Chains rattling, the zombie captain lowered himself to the floor.

No freaking way.

The other two zombies, both with various chunks of flesh missing from their bodies, continued to lunge at the windows.

Butler clapped Morgan on the shoulder. "Now you're talking. Screw the fancy wires and shit. Discipline has always worked for me." He frowned. "How many of those helmets do you have and how do we control them from a distance? We'd need a couple million of them."

Morgan's face broke into a Cheshire grin. "We only have the one helmet at this time, but more can be manufactured within the week."

"One?" Butler yelled. "How many can we have within a week?"

"Thirty to fifty."

"What the fuck, Morgan? How the hell does that help me now?"

Morgan pushed his glasses up. "These helmets are fairly complex. It has a speaker, GPS tracker, and the circuitry to send a powerful localized EMP pulse into the zombie's brain."

Butler stepped nose-to-nose with Morgan. "I don't want a fucking science lesson. I want results, and I want them now."

Morgan calmly stared back at Butler. "If you'll step aside, I'll demonstrate."

Butler backed away, his face a bright crimson.

I've got a feeling I'm not going to like this.

"As I reported," Morgan said, "the EMP signal is what causes the zombie to feel pain. In fact, it's the only thing I've found that will do so. And the beauty of it is that it has to be powerful and concentrated, so the Pentagon can't just set up a huge EMP pulse to stop your army."

"Results, Doctor. Now."

Morgan sighed. "Observe. Remember, Captain Beal is a leader." He spoke into the microphone. "Captain Beal, tell your two zombie friends to sit."

Beal sat still, his yellow eyes searching the floor in front of him.

Morgan held up the torture device. "Captain Beal, do as I ask or I'll use this again."

Beal's gaze rose and focused on Morgan. Jen swallowed. That wasn't just a look of hunger. Beal's eyes held raw, pure hate.

As if on cue, the zombies on either side of Beal sat and became still.

"Holy shit," Butler yelled. "Just like that. Morgan, you're a genius."

Morgan beamed. "Control the leaders and you control them all."

"When can we get the other leaders fitted for their helmets?" Butler asked.

"My recommendation is to have as few leaders as possible." Morgan pulled the drapes back over the windows. "By reviewing drone footage, my preliminary analysis is that the average leader can control up to ten thousand drones. I recommend two hundred leaders. As I said earlier, we have the one helmet now and could have thirty to fifty more by next week."

Butler closed his eyes for a minute. "That's a half million loyal troops by next week." He slapped the doctor on the shoulder. "Now that's results." He frowned. "But I have to find forty-nine more leaders. And I want them with military experience."

"Why's that a problem?" Morgan asked.

Butler scowled. "Those are good men out there, some with families." Closing his eyes, he rubbed the bridge of his nose. "Maybe the cost of saving this country is too high."

Morgan removed his glasses. "Aren't you the one who will lead us to take back this country from the politicians? To weed out and destroy the un-American influences in the halls of power?"

"Yes," Butler said. "I take no joy in the bloodshed that's to come. But once Washington falls, I believe we can get this great nation back to its roots. Back to its destiny." He straightened. "Then we'll move on to destroy our foreign enemies. Our undead army will be unstoppable."

This fucking guy is nuts. Enough observation bullshit. We've got to take him out.

Jen slid backward, past the office and the darkened room. *Where they probably have more poor saps chained up. Are they murdered soldiers, too?*

She shifted to her side and shined the flashlight behind her to the vertical shaft. *Another ten feet.*

Her axe slid on her back and she reached around to grab it, but missed. It hit the metal vent with a clatter, and Jen's heart stopped.

"What the hell was that?" Butler's voice came from ahead of her.

She stuck the axe in her belt and scurried backward, the damn thing banging with every move.

"Who's there?" Butler's head appeared through the vent opening. "Whoever you are, stop or you'll be shot."

Jen pressed on.

Butler's head disappeared, then reappeared with his arm. "I said stop." A muzzle flash illuminated him as an earsplitting bang rolled down the shaft. A bullet hit the side of the vent a foot in front of Jen.

Shit!

Doubling her efforts, Jen scrambled backward and her breath came in shallow pants. Seconds later, her feet dangled into the vertical shaft. Butler fired again and the round hit above Jen.

She lowered her feet until they hit an outcropping. She slid her upper body out of the vent just as Butler fired a third time. The bullet ricocheted off the vent an inch from her hand. She almost lost her grip on the vent, then disappeared down the shaft.

Not too fast. Don't slip.

She made it to the fourth-floor vent, crawled to the janitor's closet, and dropped to the floor.

A klaxon sounded, its blaring deafening. Shouting and footsteps came from the hallway.

Trapped.

20

The damn alarm gave her a freaking headache. How to get out? Being aggressive had always worked for her before. *If it ain't broke, don't fix it.*

She found a blue ball cap and placed it on her head, pulled the brim down, and secured her axe to her back. Pulling down the overalls on the hook, she shook them out then threw them on.

Someone banged into the door, startling her. When the door remained closed, she picked up a broom with a wide brush and put her other hand on the doorknob. With a deep breath, she pulled the door open.

The alarm sounded ten times louder in the hall. Armed soldiers ran by shouting. She couldn't hear a damn thing they said. Backing into the room, she hesitated. It'd look more suspicious if anyone saw her trying to hide, so she stepped out into the hallway and ran to the stairway door. *Look like you belong here.*

A soldier had pushed the stairway door open and looked back at her. He held it and waved her through.

She ran down the steps to the next floor. When no one stopped her, she kept going. Maybe she could get to the dock undetected and hide in the back of an empty truck. *Get out the same way I got in.*

She hit the first floor in a dead run and went to push the hallway door, when it opened and she stood face-to-face with Sergeant Howell.

They stared at each other for a moment, then he grabbed her arm. "Come with me."

Jen pulled her arm back and scrambled to pull her pistol, but the damn thing was under the overalls.

Howell let go and glanced over his shoulder. "We don't have time. If the wrong person sees you, you're screwed."

Jen flexed her arm. "And you're the right person?"

"I'm one that's not trying to kill you at the moment."

What the hell was she going to do? If he was telling the truth, he was her way out. If not, there wasn't much she could do to stop him.

What the hell. "I'll follow."

Howell strode down the hall. Jen kept pace.

Other soldiers, their rifles at the ready, ran by them and toward the stairs. Jen kept her head down and stayed behind Howell.

He took the door that led to the front of the building.

Passing empty offices on each side, they walked into the front lobby. *Still dark out.* Howell pulled back from the glass doors and stopped.

"Butler's standing out front," he said. "He's got two armed guards with him and he's watching everyone come out."

He peeked out and turned back to her. "Stay right behind me. I'll distract him and you keep on going."

"Why?" she asked. "Why are you doing this?"

He smiled. "We'll talk later. Get your friends and go to the conference room. Don't call Dr. Cartwright. Wait for me."

Jen licked her lips. "OK."

"When I stop to talk to him, you keep going."

"Got it."

Howell followed several soldiers out the door, and Jen stayed in his shadow. Butler couldn't see her, but she couldn't see how close they were to him either.

Howell raised a hand. "Colonel, they think they have someone cornered on the fourth floor."

He stopped, and Jen walked around him and through the gate.

"Is there just the one?" Butler asked. "Do we know who it is?"

"No, sir."

"I'll bet it's those assholes working for Cartwright."

Jen wanted to run. Wanted to find Mark and Zeke. But she couldn't afford to bring any attention to herself.

She made a beeline toward the rec center. It stood dark and still. Slipping into the shadows, she put down the broom, leaned against the wall, placed a hand on her knee, and barfed.

"Jen." A soft voice in her ear. She spun.

"Jen," Zeke repeated.

Jen reached out and pulled the skinny ninja into a hug. "I'm so glad to see you."

"You OK?" Mark's voice came from behind Zeke.

Jen chuckled. "I am now."

"What did you find out?" Zeke asked.

Butler. Howell had lured him off the scent, but it wouldn't be long before that shit head was looking for her.

"We're in deep shit. I need to talk to Cartwright. Now." She peeled off the overalls and hurried across the road.

Mark jogged to her side. "Did Butler see you? Is that why we have to hurry?"

Jen shook her head. "I'll tell you everything when we get to the conference room." She broke into a run.

They arrived at the conference room and entered. Zeke closed the door and Jen flipped the light switch.

Howell stood by the monitor, a pistol pointed at them. "Glad you could make it."

21

J en stepped toward Howell. He aimed the gun at her chest. "Not a good idea."

"Why the hell did you help me get out of Area 51 if you're doing this?" Jen asked.

"He helped you get out of there?" Mark leaned forward on the balls of his feet, his hands clenched into fists.

Howell swung the barrel towards him. "Why don't you all have a seat on that side of the table while I explain?"

Jen hesitated. If the three of them attacked at once, they might get him. But someone was sure to get hurt, or worse.

As if reading her thoughts, Howell said, "Please. Just hear me out. No need for anyone to get hurt."

Zeke took a seat and laid his scabbard on the table in front of him. *He's not fooling me. He could have that katana out and swinging in half a second.*

Jen pulled a chair out next to him and sat. Mark didn't move.

"I'll explain everything," Howell said. "We're on the same side."

Mark's jaw muscles clenched, but he sat next to Jen.

"As long as your hands stay on the table and you keep your seats, there's no need for this." Howell holstered his pistol. "My name is Lance Howell; however, I'm not who you think I am."

Jen smirked. "I'll bet you're really one of the Lost Boys. Or is it Tinkerbell?"

Howell grinned. "It'd take a lot more than that to get a rise out of me." He leaned over and set his hands on the tabletop. "I'm a CID Special Agent."

"CID?" Zeke said. "Are you a spy?"

"No." Howell straightened. "Army Criminal Investigation Division. More like an FBI Agent."

"So, Mr. Super Secret Agent," Jen said, "are you here because of us? Or because of Butler?"

Howell nodded. "I was told you're sharp as a tack, but with a bit of a mouth."

Jen frowned.

Howell held a hand up. "Let's not get off track. I'm here to investigate Colonel Butler and what's going on in Area 51."

"Cartwright said she had an asset here," Mark said. "How do we know it's you?"

Howell looked into Jen's eyes. "I'll eat a bug if I'm lying."

Jen glanced at Mark and Zeke. They looked back at her with raised eyebrows.

"Dr. Cartwright told me to tell you that," Howell said.

Jen leaned back in her seat and let out a loud breath. "I believe you."

Mark visibly relaxed. "I agree."

"And you?" Howell looked at Zeke.

"I'm cool if they are," Zeke said.

Howell nodded. "Let's call Dr. Cartwright and brief her. Then we need to get you to your plane."

Zeke pressed the console button on the conference table. The monitor screen remained dark. "What's up with this?" Zeke pressed it again.

"Let me," Howell said. He pressed it. Nothing.

Zeke turned the controller over and checked the wiring. "Looks good here. Is the monitor plugged in?"

Howell looked behind the monitor. "Shit." He turned it around. All the wires had been yanked from the back. He picked up a phone on the table and put it to his ear. "Dead. Someone didn't want us using this again."

"Doesn't matter," Jen said. "Butler's got the thing bugged. He said they started listening in on our last call with Dr. Cartwright."

"What?" Mark said.

Something bumped into the wall by the door. Zeke jumped up and positioned himself beside the door, drawing his katana. Mark put a finger to his lips and pulled his pistol.

No more bumps on the wall, but stealthy footsteps instead.

Jen moved to the window and peeked through the blinds. Trucks with flashing red and blue lights were parked at the curb. Several shadowy figures ran toward the window. "Cops out here."

Howell reached under the conference table and stood up with a shotgun. He holstered his pistol and jacked a shell into the shotgun's chamber. "We're going to have to fight our way out of here."

"Damn," Jen said. "Got any more shit stashed around here?"

Howell shrugged. "Planted it there before you came in. Just in case."

Zeke looked back at Mark and whispered, "I don't want to kill humans, especially soldiers."

A lump settled in Jen's gut. "I'm with Zeke, but it's either we go all-out, or get captured and let Butler turn us into his undead shock troops. We'll kill a lot more people then."

"He's turning people into zombies?" Howell asked.

Jen nodded. "You know Captain Beal?"

"Beal went missing on patrol." Howell's face hardened. "We kill a few MPs or kill thousands or millions of civilians because we didn't get the information to Dr. Cartwright. It sucks, but I know what I'm going to do."

Mark chewed his lower lip. *This is hitting him where he lives—killing innocents.*

Mark nodded slowly. "So we escape from here. Then what?"

"I've got a blue crew cab truck parked by the chow hall's outside exit. Keys are in it and the tank's full. When we get out of this room, go right and get your asses to the chow hall."

"You leave your keys in your truck?" Zeke asked.

Howell nodded. "By Colonel Butler's order, keys are left in all vehicles on base in case there's an attack and the vehicle is needed."

"Are you coming with us?" Jen asked.

"I've still got a job to do here," Howell said. "I need to relay your information to Dr. Cartwright and keep an eye on Morgan." He licked his lips. "As long as none of these MP's survive, my cover's intact."

"How can you watch Morgan when he's locked up on the fifth floor?" Zeke asked.

Howell shrugged. "He's either there or at his residence across from the base chapel. I bugged it. He hasn't said shit yet, but he'll slip up. It's only a matter of time."

Jen drew her Beretta. "I think we're out of time." A drop of sweat rolled down her cheek. "How do we get this party going?"

Something banged against the door twice. "This is the military police. By order of Colonel Butler, base commander, all civilians are to surrender to us and be placed in protective custody."

Protective, my ass. Jen opened her mouth to tell them so, but Howell shoved his hand over her mouth. "Not the time for a smart-ass comment," he whispered.

Jen nodded and he removed his hand.

"This is Sergeant Howell, Colonel Butler's adjutant. I have the suspects in custody and could use your help in walking them out."

Howell nodded to Mark, who opened the dead bolt and stepped back.

"I've got their weapons secured," Howell said, raising the shotgun to his shoulder. "Request your assistance in moving the prisoners."

Jen knelt behind the conference table, propping her arms on it. She lined up the sights with the door, took a deep breath, then slowly exhaled.

The door burst open.

22

Jen fired at the MP in the doorway. He fell to the hallway floor, clamping his hands on his neck, blood spurting between his fingers. Two more MPs rushed through the doorway and Howell's shotgun went off. One of them staggered backward with a shredded chest. The other aimed her pistol at Jen.

Standing behind the door, Zeke stepped out and brought his katana down in an overhead swing, severing the MP's hands. The MP screamed and fell back into the hallway.

Gunfire shattered the window behind Jen. She hit the floor, facing the window. A pistol poked through the blinds, and she fired six rounds in a diagonal pattern. An MP flopped into the room, bringing the blinds down with him. He looked dead, so Jen put a bullet in the back of his head.

Yelling came from the hallway. The first two MPs to be shot had turned. Gunshots went wild, chipping wood from the doorway trim and shattering a ceiling light.

"Now," Jen said. "While they're busy with their friends." She leapt onto the conference room table and jumped off the other side. Streaking out of the room, she went right. A zombie MP had already ripped the throat out of one of his buddies and pressed against the other. The human MP screamed for help. Jen ran past him.

She reached a T intersection in the hall and took a left toward the chow hall. She glanced back just before she went around the corner. Howell was a few feet behind her, and Mark and Zeke had just passed the MPs. The screaming MP had gone silent as his buddy chowed down on his shoulder.

Jen and Howell burst into the chow hall at the same time. Half the tables were occupied, with most of the soldiers on their feet and watching the doorway in alarm. All eyes swiveled to the newcomers. Howell stopped and held out his arm, causing Jen to halt. "What the hell are we waiting for?" she asked.

She turned back to the hallway. *Where the hell are Mark and Zeke?*

A sergeant at a table near the entrance stood. "Sergeant Howell, what's with the shotgun?"

Other soldiers murmured.

Mark rushed into the chow hall, his breathing heavy. "What are you waiting for? Go."

Zeke backed in through the doorway as his katana danced in front of him, keeping a zombie MP back.

Jen yelled, "This way." She took off for the exit, but a stout soldier stepped out in front of her. She aimed at his crotch and fired. The shot missed, but it was enough to make the soldier rethink his strategy as he dived out of the way.

Jen hit the glass doors and pushed them open. Mark and Howell slipped out.

"Where's the truck?" Mark asked.

Howell pointed to the right. "There."

The zombie MPs spilled into the chow hall, with Zeke still battling one of them.

"You two go and get it started," Jen said. "I'll get Zeke."

Jen sprinted for the ninja. "Zeke!"

The zombies had split up and attacked diners. Zeke still sparred with the zombie MP with the shredded chest. The zombie stayed just out of range of the katana, looking for an opening.

Jen aimed at the damned thing's head and pulled the trigger. It dropped to the floor with a hole just behind its temple. Zeke spun around. "That one was mine and Betty's."

She pulled on his arm. "Come on, D'Artagnan. Your carriage awaits."

Soldiers attacked in the dining hall were beginning to turn as Jen and Zeke dashed through the crowd. Jen ran into the back of a zombie. When it lunged at her, its head burst in a spray of blood, brains, and bone. Howell stood at the door, smoke coming from the shotgun's barrel. A zombie soldier charged at him. "Howell," Jen yelled. "Look out."

Howell brought up the shotgun just as the zombie leapt on him, driving him to the floor. He kept its snapping jaws from his face. Jen pulled her axe and swung, cleaving its head just above an ear.

She pushed it to the side and gave Howell a hand up. "I owe you one," he said.

A squad of armed soldiers burst into the chow hall and took down several zombies.

"Get out of here," Howell said.

"Call Cartwright," Jen said. "Tell her Butler plans to attack Washington."

Howell waved her off. "Go."

Jen dashed to the idling truck a few yards outside the door. Zeke held the door open and she dove in. Zeke landed on her a second later. The vehicle took off, the force of it closing the door.

Jen pushed on Zeke. "Want to give me some space?"

Zeke took a seat and helped Jen up.

The truck sped toward the flight line. "Where are we going?" Jen asked.

Mark glanced at her. "Our plane. We're getting the hell out of here."

The sun peeked over the horizon, bathing the base in light and shadows. Mark drove the truck to the flight line and steered it toward the northeast end, where they'd left the plane.

As they got closer, a dozen blue and red flashing lights showed up behind them. "Shit," Mark said. "We've got half the base chasing us."

Jen pointed ahead. "Then there's the other half." Another eight sets of lights approached them from ahead.

"Where the hell do we go?" Mark asked.

"Ram the front gate," Zeke said.

Mark turned the wheel and the truck careened across the runway. "We'll never make it that far."

"What about the opening in the unfinished wall?" Jen said.

"But aren't there fences there to keep zombies out?" Mark asked.

"You got a better idea?"

Sirens blared from behind them. Jen looked back. Two pickup trucks and a Humvee raced after them. The Humvee had a gunner. "They've got a machine gun on that Humvee."

Mark glanced in the mirror. "M-60. It could be a lot worse. Could be a .50 cal."

"Right," Jen said. "So I die from a big bullet up my ass instead of a huge bullet up my ass. Sounds like a deal."

They hit the grass on the other side of the runway and bounced toward the wall opening. The construction crews still had lights on the wall and their equipment in action. Jen checked their pursuers. Not falling back, but not getting closer.

Mark jerked the steering wheel to weave between a front-end loader and a dump truck. He pulled it back to avoid a group of workers, then straightened it out. "They won't shoot with all these construction workers around."

He pointed through the windshield. "Look at the fence. See the opening for the first fence on the far left? We go in there, hang a right, and the second fence's opening is about seventy-five percent of the way across. It's like a maze."

"I'll trust you," Jen said. "But I say we just ram through it."

The truck rattled over the uneven ground. "Here we go." Mark hit the brakes and slowed to a crawl, then made a hard right turn. The engine roared as he accelerated, then slowed and made a left before speeding up again.

The M60 on the Humvee opened up.

"Hold on," Mark said. "One more to go."

Bullets sang as they passed over the truck. Mark slammed on the brakes for the last opening and took the turn, ripping the passenger's side-view mirror off on the gate. The back window shattered and he floored the accelerator, breaking out into clear, flat land.

Jen and Zeke bumped fists. "We made it," Zeke said.

"Don't celebrate yet," Jen said. "We escaped Butler only to end up in a zombie war zone."

23

The truck bounced over the uneven ground. Mark could barely keep the wheel straight. He steered for a road several yards away, where the truck jumped the curb and the ride smoothed out. "Damn," Jen said. "My ass is going to hurt for the next week."

Mark steered around an abandoned vehicle. "So what the hell did you find out? What's Butler up to that's so dangerous?"

"I'm not sure you'll believe me."

Zeke settled back into the seat. "I'd believe you if you told me Butler was going to raise Godzilla from the sea."

Snickering, Jen said, "Thanks. But it's not that far off."

Zeke straightened.

"Just tell us," Mark said. "After all we've been through and the crazy shit we've seen, I'm not sure more crazy shit wouldn't make sense."

"Morgan has been experimenting on zombies." Jen cleared her throat. "Butler wants to build himself an undead army that he commands to march on Washington, D.C., and take over the government."

Mark raised an eyebrow. "Based on the way you've acted since you found that out, I'm guessing you think that's possible."

"I saw it with my own eyes. They tapped our last conversation with Cartwright and heard our observations about the leaders. The plan is to control the leaders, which allows them to control the drones."

Zeke sat up. "I saw a movie like that. They put collars on them and made them do stuff."

"They have a helmet," Jen said. "It's like a bike helmet. They put it on the leader and they hit a remote control button that hurts the zombie. I've never seen one cringe before."

"A zombie in pain?" Mark asked. "How?"

"Morgan said the helmet emits localized EMP waves or something like that," Jen said. "But the bottom line is he can get the leader to do what he wants, and he says the leader can control ten thousand drones."

Mark whistled. "We need to find a way to call Cartwright."

Jen frowned. A dozen zombies stumbled around at the intersection ahead. Beyond it lay a subdivision. "We're the only ones who can prevent Butler's plans. It'll be too late for anyone else to act."

Mark swerved around two zombies. Another ran at the truck and bounced off the bumper. "I still think we should try to get word to Cartwright."

"Why not do both?" Zeke said. "Contact her, then go kick Butler's ass. I'm up for that."

"What do you say?" Mark asked.

Jen shrugged. "OK. We try one place to see if we can call out. But it's got to be somewhere we can hide for now. Tonight, we go after Butler, no matter if we've contacted Cartwright or not."

"OK," Mark said. "We want to find a place that's likely to have a generator and some other form of communication, like a radio."

Zeke held up a walkie-talkie. "Here's a radio."

"Need a stronger one than that to reach Atlanta," Jen said.

They'd arrived at Route 902, and Mark stopped at the intersection. "Which direction?"

A sign ahead told them to go left for Spokane and right for Medical Lake. Mark jabbed a finger at the sign. "There's a good place. A hospital. Bet we find a generator and radio there."

Jen squinted. A smaller sign below the other one said Eastern Hospital and had an arrow that pointed right. "Good idea. A hospital should be defensible and have some food."

Mark turned onto Route 902 and followed the signs. As they passed Lefevre Street, Jen pointed past him. "Look."

A thousand or more zombies milled around in front of a school two blocks down. A sign for the high school stood on the corner. "I've had enough of high schools," Jen said.

Mark laughed. "That was pretty intense."

"What?" Zeke asked.

"In Anchorage," Jen said. "When you were babysitting Trip and his gang. We had to lose a mega horde by driving through a high school."

"Damn," Zeke said. "I missed some fun stuff."

They came to the intersection of North Howard Street. A sign for Eastern Hospital pointed them to the left. Mark followed the road down to a lake.

Jen pointed across the lake. "I'll bet that's the hospital."

A long multistoried brown building, partially hidden by trees, stood atop a small hill.

Mark rubbed the stubble on his chin. "Looks a bit institutional. Even for a hospital."

He turned onto the road and followed it around the lake and up a gradual slope through the trees. It led to a series of buildings, the largest being the brown one they'd spotted across the lake. "Eastern State Hospital" was engraved over the main doorway. Most of the buildings were brick, and it looked like one of those places you'd see the ghost chaser shows on TV investigate.

Zeke smiled. "Pretty creepy place."

"I don't think this is your typical hospital." Mark pointed to a fenced-in area. "That looks like some kind of recreation area."

"Are they trying to keep people out, or in?" Jen asked.

Mark pulled into a parking lot. "If nothing else, it's huge and Butler would have a hard time finding us here."

He parked between a green-and-tan jeep and a shiny black minivan. "No zombies so far."

He turned off the truck and hopped out. "But there's a lot of room inside that building to hold them. Don't get complacent."

Jen climbed out of the truck and checked her weapons' loads. She switched out magazines on her pistol and shoved it back in the holster.

"Can I get some help?" Zeke pulled two stuffed backpacks from the back seat.

"What are those?" Jen asked.

Zeke plopped them down on the asphalt. "Goodie bags. This is where I got the radio. They've got extra ammo and food and shit." He jerked a thumb to the canopy on the back of the truck. "I looked back there and found a few more."

Mark unzipped one and rifled through the contents. "Nice. We'll have to thank Howell for this."

"We should move with the bare essentials for now," Jen said. "We can lock the truck and this stuff'll be here when we want it."

Zeke and Mark tossed the packs back in and locked the doors. Jen crossed to the nearest building entrance, two tall doors in an imposing entryway. She waited for Mark and Zeke to catch up, then pressed the old-style thumb latch and pulled the door open.

Light spilled into the entry way, across a dirty tile floor. A flight of stairs with an old-fashioned scrolled railing led to a landing and another flight of steps. The hallway extended into the gloom on either side.

A counter that reminded Jen of a hotel reception desk in old Westerns stood off to the side. Jen ducked behind it, shining her light on the paper-work sitting on a shelf. She picked some up. One was a doctor's note on a patient. Next to diagnosis, it said Paranoid Schizophrenia.

Jen straightened and laid the papers on the counter. "I know why this place looks so creepy and unhospital-like."

Zeke slid his katana from the sheath strapped to his back and faced the darkness of the corridor on their left.

"You see something?" Mark asked.

"Not sure," Zeke said. "Maybe."

Jen cleared her throat and Mark turned toward her. "This is a mental hospital," she said.

Zeke put a hand up. "Listen."

Jen strained to hear anything from the hallways. The stairs. She shook her head. "Don't hear anything in here."

Zeke raced to the door. "Not in here. Out there."

Jen and Mark joined him at the door. The unmistakable *thup thup* of helicopter rotors came closer. Jen pulled the door closed, plunging the lobby into darkness. Each of them turned on a flashlight.

"Think they're looking for us?" she asked.

Mark grunted. "I never heard of them coming this way before. Always to Spokane. And since we escaped heading south, I think it's a good bet they aren't just sightseeing."

The muffled sound of the rotors got louder. *Are they going to land here?*

Jen cracked the door open. The helicopter hovered above a small building a couple hundred yards away. "Why would they think we're here? Are they checking out the whole town?"

The helicopter rose and flew over them toward the lake and the town. Jen opened both doors and set the doorstop. "At least this will give us a little light in here. Let's check this place out. Medical or mental hospital, they could both have a generator and maybe a radio."

She pulled out her axe. "I'll take lead."

"I've got rear." Zeke took a couple of practice swings with his katana.

Jen led them to the right, the lights from her beam and Mark's tracing across the walls and floor. The first door on their right stood open. Standing back from it, she shined her beam inside. Desks, chairs, and computers. Nothing looked disturbed.

Moving on, they cleared all the first floor rooms on that side of the building, ending up in a small break room with soda and snack machines. Jen plopped down on a chair. "It'd take us a couple of days to clear this whole damn building. We don't have that kind of time."

Mark bit his lip. "Agreed. Although I don't like it, we'll have to take more of a risk."

He shined his light on the snack machine. "Potato chips. I could use a few of those." He swung the beam to the soda machine. "And a cola. Even warm, it'd hit the spot."

Zeke pointed to a high energy drink. "I down those things like water when I'm in an all-nighter RPG binge with my friends."

"RPG?" Mark said. "Is that like your FPS?"

Jen groaned. "Let's get back to business. There's no power, so the machines won't work."

"I'm sure your axe could shatter the glass," Mark said. "Then we can take what we want."

"Are you nuts? That racket would bring every zombie hiding in this wing."

Mark smiled. "Exactly. Flush them out at one time. Like you said, we don't have time to go door to door."

Why didn't I think of that?

"Stand back." Jen stood in front of the snack machine and cocked the axe back. *One, two, three.* She swung the blade, shattering the glass into big chunks that fell away. She repeated her actions on the soda machine.

Mark ran to the doorway and cocked his head. "We've got company. And a lot of it."

24

Mark eased the door closed and Jen pushed the fallen soda machine toward it. Zeke and Mark helped and they had it blocking the door in seconds.

Jen found a corner table and laid her weapons out on it. The footsteps seemed like they were everywhere—in the hall, the floor above, and on the other side of the walls behind her. It was like the building was infested with big-ass mice.

Zeke and Mark joined her in the corner. Mark knelt and had his rife to his shoulder. Zeke took a defensive stance and had his katana ready to taste zombie blood.

The stampede continued and gave no signs of stopping. Jen's watch told her it'd been ten minutes. *Are they just running around in circles out there?*

One of them ran into the door every minute or so. It would rattle and Jen would aim at it, but no effort was made to breach the room. The zombies had no idea they were there.

Thirty minutes passed, and Zeke and Mark sat down, deciding the risk of attack was low. Even at rest, though, they kept their weapons close and were ready to jump into action.

Jen leaned against the wall, the vibrations helping her keep track of the zombies' tempo. It seemed to her it had slowed a bit.

She stood, and Mark and Zeke looked at her, Mark with his trademark one eyebrow raised, and Zeke with his smirk and curious eyes.

Jen crept to the window and peeked through the blinds. A number of the zombies had made it outside, where some continued to run as if they chased something, and others had slowed and wandered.

She went back to the table. "It's slowing," she whispered. "It reminds me of when you disturb a wasp's nest. They'll go batshit for a while, then calm down."

She leaned against the wall. The vibrations had died to where she could make out individual footsteps. She closed her eyes and concentrated. *Another one dropped out. And another.*

Five minutes later, one set of footsteps was all that remained.

"It's pretty much done," she whispered.

Mark kept his voice low. "That's all well and good, but how many are just standing around in the hallway, ready to sound the alarm?"

Zeke stood. "With no window on the door, there's only one way to tell."

Jen snuck to the window and scanned the road and parking lot. *Damn.* "All the ones that were out here a while ago are gone."

Mark joined her. "If your analogy of the wasp's nest is right, then they're all back in here." He sighed. "This building won't work. Too many."

Jen raised the blinds and pointed across the road to a smaller one-story building. "How about that?"

"Easier to clear and control," Mark said.

Zeke opened the window and hopped onto the grass beneath it. He crouched, his hand on the katana's handle, and scanned the area. "All clear."

Jen crawled through the window and walked with him to the smaller building's door. A plaque next to it read "Auxiliary Supply."

She turned the knob and pulled the door open, rearing the axe over her shoulder.

Mark rushed in and shined his flashlight beam to the left, while Zeke pointed his to the right.

Boxes and office furniture lined the walls. "Guess this is their equivalent to a junk drawer," Jen said. She walked past Zeke and pointed her beam at a closed wooden door painted institutional green.

"Might as well start here." She turned the knob and cracked the door open, shining the light through the slit opening.

"More damn furniture." The beam caught a desk with a cushy faux leather chair behind it. Nothing moved, so she pushed the door wider and played the beam over the room. A couple of desks, computers, and phones gathered dust, while stacks of paper flowed from inboxes and a sorry-looking coffee maker sat on a counter next to a sink. "That's got to be one of the dreariest things I've ever seen," Jen said.

Zeke pushed past her. "I swore I'd never have a nine-to-five desk job. Now you know why."

Mark sat in the plushy chair, leaned back, and rested his feet on the desk. "I don't know. Doesn't feel too bad to me."

Jen and Zeke laughed. *Nice to see Mark let his hair down for once.*

A bump came from the far wall. All the light beams shined on it. Nothing but a short bookcase.

The bump sounded again. "Guess we have a wasp's nest here, too," Mark said.

"Can't be as many," Zeke said. "This place wouldn't hold them."

Jen had her ear pressed to the wall. "More than one. They're in the next room."

She crept into the hallway and to the next door down. The damn things bumped against the door, rattling it in its frame.

Mark appeared next to her. "If we're quiet, they shouldn't get too stirred up."

Jen studied the furniture crowding the hallway. "I've got a better idea. Help me out."

She grabbed a chair and placed it next to another just outside the door where the zombies stumbled around. "Keep the path wide at this end, then make it more narrow further down the corridor."

Mark placed a desk next to the chair. He smiled. "Brilliant."

Zeke pitched in, and soon Jen stood back and studied their work. The piles of furniture against the wall were stacked five feet high and created a funnel with the wide end next to the door and the narrow end twenty feet down the hall. "I think we're ready," Jen said.

She pulled her axe from her belt and approached the door. She nodded at Zeke and Mark at the other end of the funnel. "Get ready. I'll be running my ass off."

Mark stood on one side of the hallway with his mace and Zeke took the other, his katana at the ready. Jen grasped the doorknob. Something bumped it and she pulled the door open.

A zombie in a lab coat with a tie glared at her, his yellow eyes piercing. She caught a glance of multiple pairs of yellow eyes in the darkness of the room before she sprinted down the hall.

The lab coat zombie dashed after her. He nearly grabbed the back of her shirt just as she reached Zeke and Mark. "Duck," Mark yelled.

Jen dove for the floor behind Mark, who swung his mace upward and connected with the zombie's jaw, shattering it. It stumbled, giving Zeke enough time to cleanly behead it.

The undead poured out of the room and raced for the humans, but jammed up at the funnel's end. With only room for one at a time, they couldn't overwhelm their prey.

Jen, Mark, and Zeke got into a rhythm. Jen would crack a skull open with her axe, then drag it forward as Mark caved in another's head. As it fell, Zeke stepped in and separated the next zombie from its head. When the last one stumbled forward, Zeke raised his katana. "Me and Betty have this one." He waited until the zombie was within range and sliced, but only got the blade halfway through its neck. It stumbled back, its head tilted to the side.

Zeke raised his sword and paused. "What the hell?"

The blade had snapped in half. "Betty!"

The zombie lunged for him, and Mark pulled him back. "Keep your head in the game."

Jen planted her blade in the zombie's scalp and it dropped to the floor with a thud. "Damn, Zeke. You've got to pay attention."

"Looked like about fifty of them," Mark said.

Zeke picked up the broken-off blade and held it and the katana up. "I knew it wouldn't last." He looked at Jen. "It wasn't a real katana, you know."

No shit. Jen put her hand up. "Listen."

Mark tilted his head, then smiled. "Nothing."

"Let's check this place out." Jen stepped over a body and strode down the hall.

Twenty minutes later they had cleared the building, finding only one more zombie, a janitor stuck in his closet.

"I think the break room's a good place to set up," Mark said. "Two doors, easily defensible, plus it has water and food."

Jen nodded. "We should get those backpacks in here and plan our next move."

"You get those," Mark said. "I'm going to check all the phones."

Ten minutes later Mark lumbered into the break room. "Any luck?" Zeke asked.

Mark collapsed in a chair. "No, I checked every damn phone." He looked at a wall phone situated next to a silent refrigerator. "Except that one."

Jen picked it up and shook her head. "Sorry."

Zeke pushed past her and grabbed the refrigerator handle. "Wonder what's in here?"

Jen put a hand across his chest. "Don't you dare. Whatever's in there is guaranteed to knock us over with its stench."

Mark dumped one of the backpacks onto a table. He picked up two walkie-talkies. "Jen, Zeke."

They walked over and he tossed one to each of them. "Why do we need these?" Zeke asked. "I thought we were going to stick together."

Mark emptied the other backpack and fished another radio out of the pile. "You never know if we'll get separated." He turned his radio on and adjusted the channel until voices came from the speaker. "Besides, we can listen in on Butler."

"Hotel One to Command One. No sign of targets in sector twelve."

Butler's voice came over the airwaves, the noise of a helicopter's interior in the background. "Roger, Hotel One. Proceed to sector twenty-one."

"Roger."

"Command One to all units. This mission will continue until the targets are located and neutralized. If this has not been done by nightfall, we'll pick right back up in the morning."

A series of "Rogers" followed.

"Hotel Four to Command One. Request permission to deviate and recon for Zulus in the west."

"Negative, Hotel Four. You have your orders."

Zeke found a bag of chips in the cupboard, tore it open, and stuffed a few in his mouth.

Mark turned off the radio. "Butler's taking a risk not sending out his recon. If a huge horde from Seattle or Portland heads this way, he may not have much warning."

"Wish I had a map with the sectors identified," Jen said. "Then I'd know where his men were." She kicked the wall. "But it wouldn't matter. How can we lure him in without his entire army coming along?"

"Mmff-crir." Bits of potato chips fell out of Zeke's mouth.

"Wait," Jen said. "I think the great Oracle is about to grace us with his wisdom."

Zeke swallowed, making exaggerated expressions. "I said, you just need to have something he wants and doesn't want to lose."

"What the hell would that be?" Mark asked. "He wants us, but he'd be just as happy if we killed ourselves."

Jen snapped her fingers. "You're a genius, Zeke. I know exactly what he'd want."

"I know I'm going to regret asking this," Mark said, "but what would that be?"

"Dr. Morgan. We're going to kidnap him tonight."

25

C louds slid in front of the quarter moon as Jen parked the black minivan between the last two houses at the end of the road.

"This is the dumbest idea I've ever heard," Mark said. "Break into the base we just escaped from."

"That's why it's perfect," Jen said. "Who would expect someone to be dumb enough to try it?"

Zeke slid the side door open and jumped out. "I love using my ninja skills. This'll be a blast."

Mark sighed and opened his door. "If they make me a zombie, I'm going to eat your face off."

"Deal," Jen said.

Zeke was harder to spot in the shadows than normal. In addition to his black ninja costume, Mark had applied some camo face paint around Zeke's eyes that he'd found in one of the packs.

Jen raised a pair of binoculars and scanned the wall. Two guards stood on the other side of the fence. Lights on the outside of the wall lit up the area twenty yards out from the fence.

She handed the binoculars to Mark. "Just as I'd hoped." She pointed to the gap. "Look there."

Mark adjusted the focus, then gave a low whistle. "Butler's pulled all the combat engineers from finishing the wall. Bet he's got them out looking for us, too. But only two guards? What if a horde attacks?"

"Who knows what that crazy ass is thinking?" Jen said. "Maybe they're just there to raise the alarm. The fence could hold back a decent horde long enough for reinforcements." Jen stretched her arms and shook them out. "Either way, if we make a straight line to it from here, there's a narrow dark strip where we can get almost all the way to the wall."

"And if we're caught out there in the open," Mark said, "we're screwed."

Jen pulled the rifle off her shoulder. "Let's go. In and out."

"What if he's not at his quarters?" Mark asked. "What if he's in Area 51?"

Jen shrugged. "Then we think up a plan B." She crouched and crept onto the field, the dead grass crunching under her feet. Mark caught up with her and she glanced back to find Zeke, but he'd disappeared. *Freaking ninja.*

Halfway across the field, Mark's arm shot out across her chest. "Get down," he whispered.

Jen dropped prone on the ground and had her rifle to her shoulder. She scanned the field in front of her through the rifle's iron sights, but nothing moved.

"Why are we lying here?" she whispered.

"Listen," Mark said. "Ahead and to the right."

Irregular footsteps crunching the grass came from that direction, and they headed their way. *Zombie.*

She pulled her axe from her belt. "You got your mace?"

"Yup," Mark whispered. "You ready to go?"

"Always."

"On three," Mark said. "One, two, three."

Jen hopped to her feet and dashed into the shadows, staying low. If she ran into the zombie in the dark, it would be harder for it to bite her if it had to bend over to do it.

A *thud* and an *oof* that reminded Jen of a football player making a tackle came from her right.

"Go high," Mark said.

A solid shadow stood in front of her. Jen wound her arm back and rushed it, swinging toward the top of the shadow as she passed.

The axe bit into bone. After all the zombies she'd sent to hell, she could tell what she hit just by the feel of it.

The zombie fell, taking her axe with it.

"Mark," she said. "Where are you?"

His voice came from beside her. "I ran into the damn thing. Thanks for taking it out."

"No problem." She felt around on the ground until she found the zombie. She held her breath and fumbled for the axe handle, then yanked it out.

Jen rose away from the dead creature and started breathing again. "Hope there aren't any more."

She peered toward the wall opening. The two guards walked their post, making no indication they'd heard the scuffle. "Where the hell is Zeke?" she asked.

Mark cleared his throat. "Hard to see shit out here. Better stay close."

"Those guards are easy to see," Jen said. Something moved in the shadows a few yards from the guard shack. *What the hell?*

The guards huddled and one lit a match, pressing it to the end of a cigarette in the other guard's mouth. A shadow broke away from the gloom just outside the light's reach and crept to the edge of the fence. The guards took no notice as one of them laughed while the other talked.

Jen squinted. *Is that...?* "Zeke?"

Mark groaned. "What the hell is he doing?"

Jen jogged toward the gap, well out of the light's range. Ninja or no, Zeke was pushing it.

Zeke picked something up from the ground and climbed halfway up the fence. Only several yards away, the guards were so involved in conversation, neither had noticed the ninja.

When Zeke reached the top of the fence, he tossed an object toward the other end of the fence. The laughter stopped and both guards raised their weapons, pointing them into the gloom and away from Zeke.

Jen slowed, and Mark caught up to her. "We're getting too close to the light," she said.

Zeke jumped from the top of the fence and landed like a cat. The soldiers still had their backs to him. One of them said something to the other, who shook his head.

Zeke removed the scabbard from his back as he approached the guards like a leopard ready to leap on its prey.

"Come on. Come on," Mark said.

One of the guards turned halfway toward Zeke.

Shit. They see him and he'll be gunned down in the open. Jen lit out toward the light.

Mark let out a soft "What the hell?"

Jen yelled, "Hey, Asshole. I'm over here."

Awash in the bright lights, she shielded her eyes with her hand.

"Stop," one of the guards yelled. "Hands up."

Jen slowed, but kept walking. *Got to give Zeke time.*

A distinct *click click* of chambers being loaded made her heart skip a beat.

"One more step and we shoot."

26

J en threw her hands in the air and froze in place, her breath coming in shallow gasps.

"Come forward slowly," a soldier said.

Jen took a step, paused, then took another. She squinted. Best as she could see, the guards' attention was fully on her. *Good.*

Ten yards away, a shadow raced toward the soldiers. One of them glanced over his shoulder and yelled. Zeke had the katana's handle in both hands and swung it, scabbard and all, slamming it into the first guard's temple. He collapsed. As the other soldier swung his gun around, Zeke slid in low, taking the guard out at his knees. The soldier fell, losing his grip on the rifle, and it clattered to the ground. Zeke swept it up and pounded the fallen guard in the forehead with the butt.

Jen broke into a run, and Mark raced past her seconds later. Zeke opened a gate in the fence and stood there as calm as could be, waiting for the others to catch up.

Mark grabbed Zeke as he passed through the gate and dragged him into the shadows.

Jen closed the gate behind her and joined them. "What the hell was that?"

"Mark said we shouldn't kill any of the soldiers if we don't have to, right? But we had to get in here, didn't we? I just took care of it."

"Dammit, Zeke," Mark said. "You can't—"

"Wait," Jen said. "Why be surprised? This is who Zeke is, and he did get us in without having to seriously hurt anyone."

Mark grunted. "Still, we need to work as a team."

"Zeke," Jen said, "promise us you won't pull this bullshit again."

Zeke sighed. "OK."

"Good enough," Jen said. "We don't have time to sit here and talk about it. Let's go around the flight line."

"I'm lead." Mark hustled off.

Zeke tapped her on the shoulder. "I've got it back here."

Catching up with Mark, Jen stayed a few feet behind him. Zeke didn't make a sound, and she had to glance back every couple of minutes to make sure he was still there.

The flight line had minimal lights, which made it easy to skirt around without being seen.

Mark stopped on the side of a dark maintenance hangar. "Should we get transportation now?" He pointed at a Humvee parked across the access road.

"Perfect." Jen climbed into the driver's side. "And thanks to Butler, the keys are in it." Mark and Zeke hopped in. Jen started the engine and put the truck in gear, pulling out. "Anyone know where the chapel is?"

"Take your second left," Zeke said.

Mark glanced at him. "How do you know where it is?"

"I've gone out every night and scouted the whole base."

Mark looked at Jen and raised an eyebrow. *Zeke never fails to surprise.*

Jen made the turn. "Go two more blocks and take a right," Zeke said. "Morgan's place will be two blocks past that on the left."

The truck turned onto a street with single-family houses. All were dark, except one up on the left. A single guard stood watch out front. "Were there any guards before?" Jen asked.

"Just the one up front," Zeke answered. "We should come in from the rear, though, in case security's been increased."

As they passed the front of the house, the guard raised a hand. Jen did the same. She drove a few more blocks then turned off the road and approached the house from the rear, turning the truck around before stopping. "Just in case we need to get out of here quick."

They gathered in the shadows of a tall hedge. "Zeke should go first," Mark said. "Just scouting. Then report back."

Zeke gave them a thumbs-up, then padded off. He disappeared like a ghost between two trees.

Jen pulled her pistol. "Hope I don't have to use this."

"If you do, it means all hell's broken loose."

Minutes passed and all Jen heard were crickets chirping and her own shallow breathing.

A shadow detached from a fence and crept their way. Jen raised the pistol. *Probably Zeke, but just in case...*

The shadow disappeared ten yards out. Mark cleared his throat. "Zeke," he said. "Answer now, or I'll shoot."

"It's me." Zeke's voice came from beside Jen and she jumped back, nearly tripping. "Holy shit, you scared the piss out of me."

"Sorry."

"What's the scoop?" Mark asked.

"Only the one guard," Zeke said. "House is completely dark inside, but the bathroom window on the first floor is unlocked. Doesn't move real smooth, but I can get it all the way up without making noise."

Damn. He's handy to have around.

"First thing is to take out the guard," Mark said. "Then we go inside."

"I've got a plan," Jen said.

Ten minutes later, Jen pulled the Humvee to a stop in front of the house. She rolled down the window and the guard walked over.

"Kinda cold out here," Jen said. "I'm heading in for some coffee. Can I bring you a cup?"

Still a few yards away, the guard smiled. "Thanks. I appreciate..." He squinted at her and drew his pistol. "Why are you wearing camo paint?"

A beefy arm wrapped around the guard's neck, causing him to drop the gun. Mark kept the pressure on until the guard stopped struggling. He dragged the unconscious soldier into the bushes. Jen looked around. "Where's Zeke?" she whispered.

"Right here." Zeke stood in the open doorway. "Let's go," he whispered. "Morgan's asleep. Guy snores like a freight train."

Jen and Mark followed him inside and down a hallway. Snorting sounds came from behind the last door. *Zeke wasn't kidding.*

Mark eased the door open and crept to the side of the bed. Zeke joined him. Mark nodded at Jen and she flipped the light switch.

Morgan cried out. Blinking from the sudden light, Jen pointed her gun in his general direction. "I'd just as soon kill you right here, so if you do anything other than what you're told, you die. And the bullet won't go in your head, so you could be one of Butler's puppets."

"I'll do what you want," Morgan said in a shaky voice.

Jen's eyes adjusted to the light. Morgan had curled up at the head of the bed. Mark grabbed his arm and yanked him to his feet. "Get dressed."

Morgan looked at Jen.

"Oh, for shit's sake." Jen backed into the hallway and closed the door, then snuck to the living room and peered out the front window.

An MP truck approached and slowed down. The passenger shined a flashlight beam on the truck they'd left out front, then at the house. Jen ducked just in time. She looked back out and the truck took off, turning a block down the road. Steady red brake lights reflected off a house window. *They're not leaving.*

Jen ran to the room and flung the door open. "We've got an MP patrol outside and I'll bet they've called for backup."

27

Mark pushed Morgan's face into the bed and pulled his arms behind him. Morgan cried out, "Don't break my arms."

Zeke held up a pair of zip tie handcuffs. "Found these in the truck."

Mark put them on Morgan and pulled him to his feet. "Come on."

Jen led them to the front window. Red and blue lights flashed down the street. MPs, their guns drawn, took cover a block over. "We've got a bunch of MPs on the right." She looked down the other end of the street. No movement. "But the left looks clear."

Zeke opened the door and Mark walked out, pushing Morgan in front of him. He held his pistol to the doctor's head.

An MP shouted, "Drop your weapons."

"You're going to let us leave," Mark yelled. "Or Morgan's dead."

Jen and Zeke stayed behind Mark as they moved toward the truck.

"I repeat. Drop your weapons or we'll open fire."

The lights of two more MP trucks turned a corner in the distance. "Shit," Mark said. "New plan."

"What new plan?" Jen asked.

"You take Morgan in the truck. Zeke and I will cover you and keep these guys busy."

"Bullshit," Jen said.

"I don't want to die," Morgan moaned.

"Mark's right," Zeke said. "It's the only way. We'll distract them so you can get Morgan somewhere secure, then we'll meet up with you later."

This whole thing's going to shit. "Where?"

"That first building downtown they left us on," Mark said. "Now take Morgan. No time for chitchat."

Jen grasped Morgan's upper arm and pulled him toward the truck.

"This is your last warning," the MP yelled. "Drop your weapons and release Dr. Morgan."

Mark and Zeke ran back to the house, firing several shots toward the MPs. Jen yanked Morgan to the truck and flung the back door open. "Move it, asshole." She shoved him onto the seat and slammed the door.

Bullets pinged off the back of the Humvee as Jen jumped into the driver's seat. A voice called out. "Do not fire on the vehicle. Dr. Morgan is in it."

The front window of the house was already gone. Zeke and Mark fired steadily from the shadows.

Jen started the engine and peeled out. She glanced back at the house. *You assholes better escape or I'll kick your butts.*

She took the next turn hard and heard a thump in the back. "Ow," Morgan said.

Straightening the truck, she floored it, blowing through stop signs and heading for the flight line. Flashing lights pulled out several blocks back.

"Better hold on, Morgan. It's gonna get rocky."

"I'm still on the floor. Let me get up."

They flew across the flight line, bouncing and shuddering on the uneven ground on the other side. Morgan screamed as he was thrown around in the back. Jen grinned. "Ooo. I bet that's gonna bruise."

The gap fence was lit up like a theater stage, and several soldiers milled around. They looked up as the Humvee zoomed down the slope toward the fence. Jen honked the horn and kept the pedal to the floor. "Hang on, Morgan. We've got a Humvee this time and we're going through that freaking fence."

The soldiers scattered, one diving out of the Humvee's way at the last second. The vehicle hit the fence and the chain link tore right off the posts.

The Humvee slowed as it went through the second fence and damn near didn't make it through the third.

Jen goosed the accelerator, turned off her lights, and drove into the darkness. Her pursuers stopped at the ruined fence.

A few minutes later, she turned onto South Graham Road, speeding for the 902 into Spokane. She slammed her fist on the dash.

No way they didn't get caught. And a damn good chance they were shot.

She took the on ramp to the 902. When she checked her rearview mirror, Morgan's face filled it. He had a good bruise on his forehead and his glasses were missing. "What do you think of me so far?" Jen asked. He remained tight-lipped.

She sped up, dodging abandoned vehicles and the occasional zombie. Glancing out the windows and in the rearview mirror every couple of minutes, she strained to hear the sound of approaching rotors. But none came.

Reaching Highway 90, she slowed as the obstacles increased. The sky had gone into a deep blue pre-dawn. *Got to find a place to hole up.*

When they reached the Route 2 interchange, the road cleared. It looked as if someone had gone through with plows and pushed everything to the side.

Morgan leaned back in the seat. "You know the colonel will move heaven and earth to free me."

Jen took the exit to South Division Street and turned north. "I'm counting on it."

Small groups of zombies wandered about. All drones. *All they need is one leader to pick up the thousands wandering the city.*

Morgan straightened in the seat and peered out the window. His voice trembled. "Do you know how many zombies are out here? You can turn a corner and be surrounded by ten thousand."

Jen chuckled. "Wouldn't that be karma if they chewed on the asshole experimenting on them."

"We can't keep driving around the city like this," Morgan said. "We'll draw the wrong kind of attention."

Jen stopped the Humvee. "Shush."

"Don't shush me."

Jen drew her Beretta and pointed it at Morgan's face. "Then shut the fuck up instead."

Morgan went silent. Jen turned off the engine and opened her window. Loose garbage and leaves skittered down the street in the wind. But another sound rose above it. Still in the distance, it grew louder.

Helicopter.

28

Jen started the engine and threw it into gear. She knew where she wanted to hide out, and it wasn't far.

They zoomed down South Division Street, barely missing an overturned van and plowing over a zombie dog that rushed in front of them. At Second Avenue, Jen took a sharp left and turned off her lights.

She pulled up in front of a long tall building off South Madison Street, turned off the Humvee, and hopped out with her axe in hand. The helicopter was so loud, she expected to see it hovering over her.

Opening the back door, she grabbed Morgan by the upper arm and yanked him out of the vehicle. "Stay right here. I'm your only protection."

Leaning into the front seat, Jen picked up the M4 Zeke had left and threw it over her shoulder.

"You can't do this to me," Morgan said. "I was just following orders."

Jen guided him through a set of glass doors and pulled him toward the stairs. "I suggest you shut the hell up unless you want to attract some of your friendly neighborhood drones."

Morgan's lips tightened.

They stopped on the third floor landing. Had she heard something? Jen pressed an ear against the door. Shambling footsteps. A few, just a few. She put a finger to her lips and jerked her thumb at the door. Morgan nodded. He understood.

Keeping hold of his upper arm, she guided him up the next few flights to the top floor, where a sign welcomed them to the top-rated insurance company in the state. Jen dragged him into an office and sat him behind a desk. "You can cool your heels here while I check things out."

"You can't leave me tied up and alone," Morgan whined. "What if a zombie comes by while you're gone?"

Jen stepped into the hallway. "If you're quiet, they won't know you're here." She closed the door. *Dumbass.*

Methodically working her way from office to office, it took her twenty minutes to clear the floor. She had half a mind to jerk the office door open and see if Morgan would shit his pants, but decided against it. *Don't want to be stuck up here with that and no ventilation.*

She pulled the desk out of the office and shoved it against the door to the stairway. *Won't stop a horde, but it'll keep anything from sneaking up on me.*

Morgan glared at her as she plopped down on a chair next to him. "Butler's going to tear your friends apart if you don't let me go."

Jen's gut ached. *I got them into it and I'll get them back.*

Feeling anything but happy, she nonetheless smiled at Morgan. "As long as I have you, he won't do shit." She pulled the radio off her belt and switched it on.

Nothing came across. She changed the channel. Still nothing. "What channels do they use?"

Morgan slumped back in his seat and shrugged. "How the hell do I know? I need something and I pick up the phone."

Jen scoffed. *Asshole's as useful as a solar-powered flashlight.*

She continued changing the channel. A voice came from the radio on the third try. "Echo Twenty-three to base. Entering Medical Lake."

Keying the mic, she said, "This is a message for Command One. Command One, do you read?"

Silence, then, "Base to unidentified personnel. This is a military-restricted channel. Identify yourself."

"I want to talk to Command One."

"Negative. Identify yourself. You are in violation of emergency martial law orders and will be held accountable."

Jen stood. "Look, asswipe. Butler's already trying to kill me, so I'm not particularly worried about some regulations. I suggest you get that excuse of a colonel on here because I have something he wants."

Weaker voices came across, patrols communicating directly with each other. Then a burst of static. "Base to unidentified personnel. Switch to channel thirty-two."

"Ten-four, good buddy. Keep them smokies off your tail."

Jen moved the dial to the new channel and listened. Nothing but light static. A clear channel? *Doesn't want any of his men hearing this.*

She keyed the mic. "I'm here."

"Seems you and I have a problem." Butler's voice seemed strained, even over the airwaves.

"Yup. How about we make a trade? Give me my folks back and you get Doctor Frankenstein here."

Morgan scowled at her. She kept the mic keyed and kicked him in the shin.

"Ow. Bitch. Get me out of here, Butler."

Jen brought the mic to her lips. "Your guy's still up and kicking. How about I talk to mine?"

"Jen."

"Mark? You and Zeke OK?"

"Yeah. Listen, don't trust—"

"Mark? Can you hear me? Mark?"

Butler's voice came on. She could hear the sneer in it. "Your friends are fine. Where do we make the exchange?"

Morgan gave Jen a puzzled look as she strode from the room and down the hall.

"Where do we make the exchange?" Butler repeated.

Jen peered out a window at the end of the hall. "Remember the hotel roof you dropped us off at?"

"Yes."

The hotel's roof was visible. *Just a block away.* "Bring Mark and Zeke, and you'll get Morgan."

"When?"

"How long will it take you to get here?"

Butler paused.

"An hour."

Shouldn't take more than twenty minutes for him to get here. Son of a bitch is up to something. "Agreed."

The channel went silent. Jen turned the radio off and clipped it back to her belt.

She'd set it up so Butler would land on the hotel and she could see if he was alone, then have him fly over to the building she was in.

Morgan looked up when she entered the office. "So?"

Jen shrugged. "Your boss said he'll be here in an hour. I've got plans to throw him off his game."

Morgan laughed. "You think you're going to outthink a soldier? Little girl, he's already ten moves ahead of you."

Jen sighed. *What a dick.* She turned her back to him and strolled out of the office. She'd found a snack room with a cupboard full of goodies on the other side of the floor when she'd cleared it. Her stomach growled at the thought of food.

Chomping on a bag of chips, she turned the radio back on. Was Butler listening for something from her?

She changed the channel back to the active one she'd first found. Still some traffic about Medical Lake. Sounded like they'd caught a significant horde and were busy clearing it out.

"Base to all units. Base to all units. Zulu activity increasing in Spokane. All units directed to evacuate from Spokane and back to base. Do not engage. Repeat. Return to base and do not engage."

What the hell?

An Apache helicopter flew overhead, heading back to base. Jen ran back to the office. Morgan looked up at her as she entered. Something on her face got his attention.

"What's wrong?" he asked.

Sunrays shot like laser beams across the room. Jen peeked through the blinds and onto the street below. It was flooded with zombies, both human and the occasional canine. They looked like ants swarming a dropped ice cream cone on a summer's day.

Jen's heart raced. *Where the hell'd they all come from? And so fast?*

The zombies froze. Jen blinked her eyes. *Did that just happen?*

The radio squawked. "Base to all military units. Stay on this channel. Base to Jen. Switch to channel thirty-two."

"What the hell's your boss up to, now?" She turned to channel thirty-two and keyed the mic. "Butler. You there?"

"Have you looked onto the street lately?" Butler sounded proud of himself.

"Bunch of zombies. Same shit, different day."

"Oh, I think there's some different shit today," Butler said. "Leader One, disperse your troops to search the buildings for Jen Reed. You and your drones have explicit orders to kill, but not infect her. You also have explicit orders to deliver Dr. Morgan safely to me. If any of your drones fail, you will be punished."

Jen chewed the edge of her lip. *Is this shit for real?*

The zombies parted a block away, and a single figure, wearing a plastic helmet and a uniform, walked through them.

"So you've got a leader looking for us? Good luck with that."

The uniformed figure stopped, and the zombies split into groups and poured into buildings.

Butler laughed. "I've got the numbers. They'll find you. And I've been thinking that I'll let the drones capture you and hold you for the leader to kill."

There's something more here. Something he's dying to tell me. "I'll bite. What's the big surprise?"

Butler chuckled. "I guess the leader's not close enough to make out well. But when you do meet face-to-face, why don't you give my regards to Corporal Grant?"

29

J en squinted and tried to make out features of the lone figure, but he disappeared into the financial building across the street. *Could be Grant. Could be a hundred other guys from the base.*

"I guess you're screwed," Morgan said.

Jen blinked. Grant or not, she was in the shit.

She raced to the stairway door and pressed her ear against it. Dozens of footsteps echoed from below. She pushed on her blockade. It'd keep dozens back, but they'd just call for reinforcements and get through, anyhow.

She hiked her rifle on her shoulder and pulled Morgan from the chair.

"There's no place to run," he said.

She pushed him in front of her. "Move. Down the hall."

He shrugged and lumbered down the hallway and around the corner. She stopped him at a door with a sign that read "Roof Access."

Morgan laughed. "This is your plan? What are you going to do, jump?"

She pulled his cuffed hands up, stretching the ligaments in his shoulders. He cried out.

"Maybe I'm going up there to push you off. Ever think of that?"

Pulling the door open, she shoved him through. *Truth is, I have no idea what I'm doing. But one thing I've learned in the last month is there are always ways out if you look for them.*

They reached the roof and the door slammed shut behind them. "Sit," she said.

Morgan sat, cross-legged, watching her with interest, but keeping his mouth shut.

Jen ran to the far corner. No roofs close enough to jump onto. She checked out each corner in turn, with the same result.

I really screwed this one up. Should've made sure I had an escape route when I chose the building. Mark would've done that.

Movement caught her attention. The figure in uniform walked, head down, across the roof of the financial building. It took slow, purposeful steps, and stopped opposite from Jen. She walked to the edge of the roof to get a better look. It lifted its head.

Grant.

Grant's yellow eyes bore into hers. Without a movement or a word from him, the other buildings emptied and the zombies dashed into hers.

Jen unslung the rifle from her shoulder and aimed it at Grant. He stood unmoving, but quivered in her sights as she fought to control her breathing.

It's not Grant anymore. It's Butler's tool.

Banging came from the door. *Not much time.* She dropped to a knee, propping an elbow on a kneecap to steady herself. She took a deep breath, aimed, and let out half her breath. Faces flashed through her mind: her father, Doc, Chris. Tears welled in her eyes. *I'm sorry, Grant.* She squeezed the trigger and the bullet went through Grant's left eye and blew his zombie brains and pieces of the shattered helmet across the rooftop. He wavered for a second, then flopped onto his back, disappearing behind the roof's raised edge.

She swallowed. *All he wanted was to get back to Kodiak to check on his family.*

Zombies in the street stopped in their tracks, then shuffled aimlessly. Many wandered onto the street from her building.

She turned toward Morgan, who sat with his head hung. "Guess you assholes didn't think about someone taking out your leaders," she said. "Pretty easy fix."

Jen keyed the mic. "Uh, Butler. I think your dastardly plan to conquer the world has hit a snag."

The radio remained silent. Jen shoved the mic toward Morgan. "Maybe you better tell him."

She keyed the mic. "Butler, this is Morgan. She shot the leader. All the drones will return to their default behavior."

"What the hell does that mean?" Butler's voice was laced with fury.

"They'll wander around until they spot a meal, or there's some other disturbance," Morgan said.

Jen took the mic. "Not too smart, Butt head. Should've kept your general in the rear, where he was safe."

Morgan's head drooped forward. *Time to press the advantage.* "How about that prisoner swap? Seems like you're out of options."

Come on, Butler. Come on.

"One hour," Butler said. "Hotel. I'll be there."

"Roger Dodger." Jen switched back to the main radio channel to hear the normal chatter. She grinned at Morgan. "Let's listen in for a while."

Something banged against the rooftop door. Jen pulled her axe. The door rattled with the next blow, and Jen pressed her ear to it. One, maybe two zombies. Better to take them out before they drew a crowd.

Morgan scooted away from the door, his eyes wide.

Jen took several steps backward and laid her rifle on the ground before taking a stance next to the door. Grasping the handle, she took a deep breath. *One, two, three.*

She swung the door open and four zombies fell onto the roof. She glanced inside and confirmed none remained, so she slammed the door shut and spun to face the threat.

A middle-aged man in a business suit charged her. She swung, but missed his head, the axe biting into his neck and knocking him down.

Two other zombies approached from opposite sides. She feinted at one, using the momentum to bury the axe into the bridge of the other zombie's nose. It stumbled backward, but didn't fall.

Shit.

Morgan screamed. Jen glanced his way. The fourth zombie shambled toward him as he slid his ass across the rooftop.

The businessman had regained his feet and raced toward her, the other two zombies coming at her again from the sides.

On pure instinct, she swung and caught the businessman in the temple at the same time she ducked and spun, causing one of her attackers to rush by and slam into the other one.

The businessman fell to the ground and lay still. The other two attempted to untangle their limbs, but Jen made quick work of them.

Morgan's screams went up an octave. The last zombie had him by the leg and pulled him toward his snapping jaws.

Jen dashed toward the zombie and tackled it just as it lifted Morgan's leg to its mouth. Jen lost her grip on the axe and it skittered away. She jumped to her feet and scrambled for it as the zombie gave chase a few feet behind. Jen leapt for the axe, rolled, and swung it upward, catching the zombie on the chin and ruining its jaw.

It grasped her leg and went for the meal. Jen kicked at it with her other leg, loosening its grip. Jumping to her feet, she swung and split the zombie's forehead. It flopped to the ground.

Panting, Jen stumbled to Morgan, who lay on his side facing away from her.

"I took care of it," she said. "Now you and I need to get ready for the trade."

Morgan rolled over and glowered at her with yellow eyes.

30

J en kicked Morgan onto his stomach and pulled him up by his cuffed hands. His pant leg rolled up, exposing an oozing bite wound on his ankle. Morgan kicked and twisted, but was no match for her. "You're still a little guy. It's not like the movies where zombies have super strength and shit."

She brought him to the edge of the roof and scoped out the street. A few groups of zombies bunched together and wandered, but most of them had left in search of food.

She pulled him back. "What the hell am I going to to do with you now? Butler will never make the trade."

A pipe ran up the side of the raised rooftop entry, leaving an inch between it and the wall. Jen slammed Morgan into it and removed her belt. She looped it through Morgan's cuffed hands and around the pipe before fastening it tightly.

She stepped back to admire her handiwork. Morgan growled and snapped his jaws, but stayed put. Jen left him and walked down the stairs to the top floor.

The desks she'd piled in front of the stairway door lay askew like a child's blocks. A single zombie rushed out of the doorway and bore down on her. Its silky blonde hair, missing tufts from its bloody scalp, flew in the breeze.

Jen stepped into its path, brought the axe down, and sent the zombie to its rest. She closed the stairway door and restacked the desks.

In one office, she found a huge purse sitting on a desk lined with pictures of children, old people, and cats. Lots of cats. Jen emptied the purse on the desk. A wallet with an ID of a gray-haired lady with deep dimples fell out. Jen left it all and headed for the roof with the purse in hand.

Morgan still struggled against his bonds, and moaned pitifully. "I need to keep you a secret just long enough to make the trade," Jen said. "Then I don't give a shit if he knows you're dead."

She pulled the upside-down purse over Morgan's head. It covered him down to his chest. Morgan stopped struggling and stood silently.

"I've seen you assholes get quieter in the dark," she said, "but I didn't expect this to work that good."

She tuned the radio to the main military frequency. Chatter erupted from it. "Echo Five to base. Copy we're downtown Spokane. Setting up position as ordered."

Jen looked up and down the street. *There.* A Humvee idled three blocks away.

She wandered back to Morgan. "Looks like your boss thinks he's smart."

More voices on the radio reported positions. *Did he bring his whole army?*

All of the signals were strong. They were all around her. Butler had laid a trap.

The distant sound of rotors came from the west. Jen stood on the eastern side of the raised rooftop entry and watched a dot in the distance. She changed the channel back to thirty-two.

"Command One to Jen. Do you read?"

"Copy," she said.

"Approaching the hotel rooftop with your friends. ETA three minutes."

Jen checked her weapons' loads and the rooftop door. *Secure.*

She scanned the neighboring rooftops for leaders or snipers, but found no sign of either.

The soft *thup thup* of the rotors got louder as the helicopter grew in size. It approached the hotel building.

Jen keyed her mic. "Two buildings to your right."

She stepped out from cover and waved at the Blackhawk. It changed course and landed on the far side of the roof. Only the pilot was visible. He hit some switches and the rotors slowed. Jen took cover behind Morgan and aimed at the helicopter's door as it slid open.

Butler climbed out, his pistol to the head of a bound and gagged Mark, the visible parts of his face crimson. Zeke jumped down next to them, his legs tied as well as his hands.

Not so dumb. Zeke could probably kick the shit out of him with his hands tied.

"No bullshit," she called out. "I'll put a bullet in his head if I even think you're going to pull something."

Butler pushed Mark forward and Zeke hopped next to him. "I don't need tricks. Once I get Morgan back, he'll work up another helmet. I've got plenty of leaders to send out and I'll have ten thousand zombies out here tracking you down."

Jen pressed the pistol barrel into Morgan's head. He stirred. She let off on the pressure. "Then maybe I should just take Morgan out now."

Butler shrugged, then licked his lips. *Son of a bitch wants me to think he doesn't give a shit, but he can't hide it.*

"You could do that," he said. "But I'm betting you won't. Your odds of escaping suck, but at least you have a chance if you make the exchange."

And your mad scientist is useless to you now.

Jen cut Morgan's zip ties, praying that he didn't start grabbing at her. "Untie them and we'll send them over at the same time."

A knife appeared in Butler's hand. "Back up to me," he said to Zeke. Zeke hopped backward and Butler leaned down and sawed through the ropes around his ankles, but kept his pistol pressed into Mark's back. "Don't try shit or your buddy here dies."

He cut Zeke's wrists loose and the ninja removed his gag. Butler pointed the knife to a spot twenty feet to his side. "Move your ass."

Zeke sauntered over to the spot and turned back, rubbing his wrists. *Of all of us up here, he's got the biggest balls.*

Butler freed Mark and shoved him forward. "Let's get this done."

Jen guided Morgan forward while Mark and Zeke walked toward her.

"Not you, girl." Butler pointed his pistol at Mark. "Just the hostages."

Shit. What if Morgan just stands there? She released Morgan's arm and backed away. Mark and Zeke continued toward her, but Morgan didn't move.

"What's wrong with him?" Butler asked. "Morgan?"

"I had to sedate him," Jen said. "He was freaking out and attracting zombie attention, so I found some pills and gave him a couple."

Butler stepped forward, waving his gun at her. "All of you get back."

Jen nodded at Mark and Zeke, and they moved back to the rooftop door.

Butler approached Morgan. "Come on, Morgan. Our ride's waiting."

He pulled the purse off Morgan's head and froze. Jen couldn't see Morgan's face, but Butler's bug-eyed expression told her all she needed to know.

Mark and Zeke looked at her, their eyes questioning. She shrugged. "Morgan got bit."

Morgan sprung at Butler, who pushed him to the side.

Jen knelt into a firing position and put a round in Butler's midsection. He stumbled backward, his arms splayed.

The helicopter started up. Jen aimed at the pilot through the glass. "Shut it down," she yelled.

The pilot ignored her and the rotors sped up. She moved closer. "Last chance," she yelled.

A hand grabbed hers and pulled upward, the pistol aiming to the sky. "No," Mark said. "We don't kill soldiers that aren't trying to kill us."

"Butler," Jen said. Mark released her. She aimed her pistol back at Butler. He teetered on the edge of the roof, a red stain spreading over his shirt. Morgan crept toward him like a leopard stalking its prey.

"This is for Grant, you asshole." Jen squeezed the trigger and the gun fired just as Morgan leapt at Butler. The bullet slammed into Butler's chest and he tumbled off the roof. Morgan couldn't stop his leap and disappeared over the side.

The Blackhawk hovered over the hotel as Jen rushed to where Butler and Morgan had fallen. Butler's body lay across the crumpled roof of a car, his head hanging over the side. Morgan lay unmoving on the sidewalk, a dark red splat on the pavement around his head.

Mark grabbed her arm. "We've got to go. I don't know what's going on, but that damn helicopter is tracking us."

Jen handed Mark her rifle. "You're a better shot than me. I might actually shoot the pilot."

Mark jacked a round into the chamber, took aim, and fired at the helicopter. A crack appeared in the windshield a foot from the pilot. The helicopter spun and raced back in the direction of base.

Zeke ran up, Jen's radio in his hand. "Listen to this."

Broken chatter came from the radio, mostly units reporting readiness and being in position. A voice broke through. "This is Hotel Three to all units. Command One is down. I repeat, Command One is down and unrecoverable. His last orders are to implement Operation Smoke Out. I repeat. All ground and air units are to implement Operation Smoke Out immediately."

Crackles and more broken voices came over the air before one broke through. "Echo Two to Echo teams, let's go get the bastards that killed the colonel."

Mark frowned. "We're in the shit."

Jen let out a mirthless chuckle. "I think we're permanent residents."

"Guys," Zeke said. "Come here."

Jen turned to Zeke, who stood at the roof's edge looking down. "What?"

Zeke pointed to the sidewalk. "I see Morgan, but where's Butler?"

Jen squinted at the empty indent in the car's roof. "Are you shitting me?"

31

J en looked at Mark. "That son of a bitch didn't damage his head." She stalked toward the door.

Mark grabbed her arm. "What the hell are you doing?"

"Let me go. I'm going to finish what I started."

Mark released her. "We've got bigger things to worry about than your revenge against Butler."

She poked him in the chest. "You didn't have to shoot Grant."

Zeke's mouth dropped open. "You shot Grant? Did you kill him?"

Jen squeezed her eyes shut and pressed the heels of her hands into her temples. "No. I mean, yes. But really Butler did." She opened her eyes and tears raced down her face. "They made him a leader and sent him after me. There were thousands of drones in this building, and Grant stood over there." She pointed at the roof across the road, Grant's body out of sight behind the raised edge. "Only way I could stop them was to take Grant out."

Mark's voice softened. "We didn't know that, but it doesn't change anything. We need to get to Atlanta and brief Dr. Cartwright on the latest mutations."

"He's right," Zeke said. "If we destroy the zombies, that'll mean Butler, too."

Jen bit her lip. *It's not like Butler's downstairs waiting for me.* "OK. Let's get to the Humvee."

Mark put up a hand. "Wait." He tilted his head, then ran to the roof's edge. He ducked and clambered back to them.

"Ground troops coming down the road. Humvees, armored carriers, and ground pounders. Looks to be five, six hundred."

"They know where we are." Jen clasped the door handle. "Come on."

Mark ran to her, but Zeke stood, overlooking the street. "You're gonna want to see this."

Jen joined Zeke and her legs almost gave out. Everywhere for two square blocks, the street and sidewalk had filled with zombies.

"How the hell did that happen so fast?" Mark asked.

Jen pointed below. The zombies pushed into their building. "They know we're here, too. Are these damn things evolving again? It's like they don't need Butler pulling the strings anymore."

"Where do we go?" Zeke asked.

Mark raced to the door and opened it. "They're coming up. There's a ton of them."

Nowhere to jump. Can't fight them. And no way down while they're on the stairs.

Jen snapped her fingers. "Why didn't I think of it before? Follow me."

She ran down the stairs to the sixth floor with Zeke and Mark on her heels and dashed into the hallway, stopping at the elevator doors. She tried to pull them apart. Damn doors didn't move. "Help."

Mark and Zeke stepped up and together the three of them pulled the doors open a few feet.

Jen turned on her flashlight and shined it down the shaft. The top of the elevator sat three floors below.

"You're not thinking what I think you're thinking, are you?" Mark asked.

Zeke stood in the doorway, rocked his arms a few times, and leapt into the shaft, grabbing the cable. Like a natural, he shimmied his way down to the car.

"OK, now you're just showing off," Jen said.

A crash in the stairway nearly stopped her heart. She stepped inside the elevator doors, balancing on the narrow ledge. "Unless you have a better idea, it's now or never."

Mark slid in next to her and shined his light on the cable. "You first. When you get to the elevator car, you can give me light."

Jen nodded. She tried to follow Zeke's example the best she could and leapt into the murky shaft.

She lost sight of the cable mid-jump and hit it with her chest. Wrapping her arms around it, she slid down the braided line.

Coming in too fast.

Her arms grew hot from the friction. Wrapping her legs around the cable, she squeezed. She still dropped, but at a slower pace.

Zeke stood on the car and reached out to her. She hopped down next to Zeke and wobbled, her arms windmilling. He grabbed her shirt and pulled her back.

"Isn't that a kick in the ass?" he said.

"Not exactly the phrase I'd use."

She whipped out her flashlight and pointed the beam at Mark. Tromping footsteps thudded through the walls. Vibrations from the swarming zombies made their way up through her shoes. *There's got to be a thousand in this building alone and they'll be on Mark's floor at any minute.*

Mark jumped and caught the cable like it was a move he'd practiced. He slid down, stepping onto the car with a light step.

"You made that look easy," Jen whispered.

He shrugged. "Army. Rappelling."

Zeke lifted a small door in the top of the car. "Let's get out of sight." He dropped into the car and Jen landed next to him. Mark closed the door as he joined them.

Jen shined her light on Zeke. "You look different."

Zeke turned around in the light. "Only thing different is I don't have my katana. I feel naked."

"That's it," she said. She pulled her pistol and axe. "Which one do you want? Mark has my rifle."

Zeke took the axe and balanced it in his hand, then lay it down and picked up the pistol. "I'm too used to the katana as my melee weapon. I'll take the pistol."

An explosion from below shook the car.

"What the hell?" Mark said.

Jen's pulse raced. "Don't tell me they're sending artillery again."

Another explosion, this one closer, nearly knocked her to her knees.

Mark sat on the floor. "We can't leave the elevator until the zombies are gone, and you're more likely to get hurt if you fall. So you might as well take a seat."

Jen grumbled, but lowered herself to the floor. "I wonder if those ground troops have engaged the horde."

Zeke pointed to her belt. "What about your radio?"

Jen pulled the radio out. She turned the volume down before turning it on.

"Echo Four to Control. Multiple Zulu units encountered. Repeat. These things are organized They're attacking in a tactical manner."

"Control to Hotel Two. Request assistance at Echo Two's location."

"Roger Base. This is Hotel Two. I have enough fuel and ammo to make one more run then need to return for resupply."

"Roger. All units, this is base. Our ground forces have met extreme resistance. Thousands of Zulus are attacking. Our units are defeating them and have nearly captured Second Avenue."

"Sounds like they're right outside this building," Jen said. "Artillery should slacken off now, shouldn't it?"

Mark nodded and put his head against the elevator doors. "Still a bunch of zombies running around out there."

The radio chatter increased. They announced that the zombies had been routed. "Clear the building and find the civilians."

"Command One to all units. Those civilians are important to national security. Find them and get them back here safely."

Mark raised an eyebrow. "Who's that?"

"One way to find out," Jen said. Mark's eyes widened and he tried to grab the radio from her, but she pulled it away.

"Command One, this is the civilians. Who am I talking to?"

"Civilian radio operator, switch to channel thirty-two."

Jen adjusted the radio. "This is Jen Reed. Who's this?"

"Miss Reed, this is General Lewis. I arrived on base a short while ago to relieve Colonel Butler of his command. What's your location?"

"Not so fast. Who sent you?"

"Dr. Cartwright."

Jen looked at Mark. He shrugged. "Sorry, General. We've been lied to enough that we're not taking any chances."

"Jen, Dr. Cartwright sent me. Now give me your location. We have teams in your area that can get you back safely."

"I'm afraid you'll have to give me more than that, General."

The radio remained silent. Jen keyed the mic. "General?"

"Jen, this is Sergeant Howell."

Mark's eyes went wide. "Well, what do you know?"

Jen held a hand up. "Go ahead."

"General Lewis is the real deal. We need you to come in."

"Damn," Zeke said. "Just when things are heating up."

Jen keyed the mic. "I still haven't heard the magic phrase."

"I'll eat a bug if I'm lying," said Howell.

Gunshots came from below. Men shouted. The staccato sound of automatic weapons came from just outside the elevator doors.

Jen looked at Zeke and he said, "Them's the code words."

Mark frowned. "It's the right thing to say, but I'm still hesitant. What if he's under duress?"

"Cartwright mentioned the other day that she had a meeting with General Lewis," Jen said.

"Command One to Miss Reed. Did you copy?"

Mark put his hands up. *He's letting me make the decision.* She keyed the mic. "General, we're hidden in the same building Colonel Butler landed on."

"Roger that. Hold tight. A unit is clearing that building now. I'll contact you when it's safe."

Twenty minutes later, footsteps tromped up and down the hall. Voices murmured.

"Command One to Jen Reed. Your building is secure. What's your location?"

Here goes nothing. "Elevator. Third floor."

She switched the radio back to the default channel just in time to hear Lewis. "Command One to Echo Three."

"Echo Three here."

"Roger, Echo Three. The package is in the elevator, third floor."

"Copy."

Someone banged on the door and yelled, "This is Echo Three. We're opening the doors. The building is clear, so put down your weapons."

Mark nodded and laid his gun on the floor. "Don't want anyone to accidentally get shot."

Jen placed her axe in her belt, and Zeke put his gun down.

The door opened and light streamed in. Jen squinted and shaded her eyes. "You our ride?"

A soldier offered her a hand and she took it. He pulled her to her feet. "Sergeant Washington, ma'am."

Another soldier had a radio to his lips. "Echo Three to Command One. We have the civilians and all look healthy."

"Roger, Echo Three. Get them back here."

The soldier helped Mark and Zeke up. "Let's go."

Mark hesitated. "If it's all the same to you, I'd like to keep my weapon."

"Me, too," Zeke said.

The soldier nodded. "Agreed. Get 'em and follow us."

"Hotel One to all units. Reports of Zulu buildup six blocks north of your location. Prepare to advance and engage."

"Base to all units. Aerial recon reports a horde of one thousand Zulus in sector twenty-three. All units are to advance to that location and engage."

A smattering of responses followed, then the channel went silent.

Sergeant Washington jogged to the stairs with two of his men. Zombie bodies and parts lay strewn over the hallway. Jen avoided what she could and tread carefully over what she couldn't.

They reached the double glass doors and walked outside. Jen nearly gagged and covered her nose and mouth. More bodies littered the landscaping and the streets, and flies hovered over the corpses.

The rumbling of Humvees and APCs echoed between the buildings as they raced north. An Apache zipped by in the same direction.

"Looks like a battle brewing," Jen said.

Washington looked at one of his corporals. "Shit. And we're gonna miss it."

Jen gave him a smile. "You don't have to."

32

Sergeant Washington shook his head. "No motherfucking way. I have my orders. And from a damn general."

"Your buddies need you," Mark said. "I was army. I know how that feels. We'll just drive the Humvee we took back to the base and you can join the battle."

The corporal stepped next to Sergeant Washington. "Come on, Wash. The way back's clear. We all just came that way. If any of my friends get wasted out there, I won't be able to handle it if I didn't at least try to help."

Another corporal nodded. "Same here, Wash. Besides, what's this general know? Probably been a pencil pusher his whole career."

Sergeant Washington glared at Jen from under a lowered brow. "We have our orders."

"You're absolutely right, Sergeant." Mark pointed to the Humvee Jen had escaped in the night before. "But we should drive this back out. You can cover our rear. It's safer."

"Safer how?"

"If one of the vehicles goes Tango Uniform, then we have another. It also gives us two mounted M60s instead of one."

Washington scratched his neck. "Then one of my crew will drive it."

"Not a good idea," Mark said. "You need your team to stay as one cohesive unit. I can drive it. Spent a lot of time doing that a few years back in the sandbox."

"And if you take off on us, my ass is grass."

Mark stuck out his hand. "From one soldier to another, you have my word we won't."

Washington squinted. "I will kick your ass if you fuck me over."

"I'd expect nothing less."

"All right," Washington said. "Mount up, everyone."

The radio came to life.

"Echo Fourteen to Control. Request immediate assistance in sector twenty-three. We underestimated the enemy strength and are trapped between hordes."

Washington put his hand up. "Wait a second."

"Control to Hotel One. Proceed to sector twenty-three and relay sitrep."

"Hotel One to Control. Already at location. Situation is grim. Four hordes of two thousand Zulus and up are attacking sector twenty-three from different directions. Multiple friendly units are engaging, but have no way to retreat."

"Roger. All units attack sector twenty-three from the south. Make a hole and get those units free."

Mark pounded his fist on the Humvee's hood. "They're throwing everything they have at them. They could lose all of their ground forces."

"It almost sounds like a trap," Zeke said.

Jen's eyes went wide. "Shit. I think you're right." She jumped into the Humvee and keyed the mic. "Control, order a full retreat."

"What the hell are you doing?" Washington ran to Jen. "Are you crazy, woman?"

"Control to unauthorized transmission. Stand down. You're interfering with national security operations."

"No," Jen yelled into the mic. "The buildup of zombies is a trap."

"Echo Two to Control. We're attacking the enemy's southern flank, but there's a massive movement on our flank. Large numbers of combatants are pouring out of an underground garage and attacking our rear."

"Command One to all ground units. Retreat. I say again. Retreat to highway. All air units provide cover."

Zeke tilted his head. "Something coming."

Jen strained to listen and picked up the first rumblings of engines.

Several Humvees and APCs zoomed past them.

"Let's get the fuck out of here," Washington yelled. "You people head for the highway and stay with our units until we get there. We'll cover your asses."

Mark jumped into the driver's seat and started the vehicle. Zeke hopped into the back, behind Jen's seat. Mark crushed the accelerator. "Dammit. Wish we had the acceleration of the truck right now."

They turned onto South Division Street and headed for the highway. Washington's crew were a hundred feet behind.

"If those other units passed us that fast," Jen said, "the horde can't be far behind."

Washington's Humvee drove up their ass. Jen glanced back, and Washington waved at them to go faster. Movement farther back caught her eye. "Oh my God."

A tidal wave of zombies chased them from a few blocks back. The mass of silent monsters ran at full tilt, filling the street, sidewalks, everything.

Mark had slowed to weave around stalled cars. "No slowing down for anything," he said. The engine growled and he sped up.

"The on-ramp's there." Jen pointed ahead.

Mark screeched onto the ramp. The surviving Humvees and APCs had parked in the middle of the road. Soldiers lined the guard rail, their guns aimed to the north.

Mark pulled beside an APC and stopped. They climbed out of the Humvee and grouped at the guard rail.

Washington pulled up next to them. "Get back in your vehicle and stay with us. We're going back to base."

A lieutenant approached them. "Sergeant, I just spoke with Command One on an alternate channel. The civilians are to stay here until this whole convoy goes back to base."

"Yes, sir," Washington said. "Where do you want us to set up?"

"Take your unit to our right flank. There's indication of enemy forces gathering in that direction."

"But, sir, we're supposed to stay with the civilians."

"We'll take over that responsibility." The lieutenant banged a fist against the side of the Humvee. "Now go."

Without another word, Washington's crew sped off to the other end of the line.

The lieutenant pointed at Mark. "You people stay here until and unless you hear different from me."

"Yes, Lieutenant," Mark said. The lieutenant strode off.

"Hotel Two to all units. Prepare to engage."

Jen put a hand out to Zeke. "Give me the rifle."

He handed it over. "What am I going to use?"

Jen pointed at the M60 atop their Humvee. Zeke's mouth dropped. "Jen, I love you." He scampered off to the vehicle.

Jen and Mark knelt behind the guard rail and aimed north. An Apache swooped overhead and back toward base.

Rumbling came from between the buildings in the distance. It reminded Jen of the sounds in a bowling alley.

Waves of undead pulsed down the road four blocks away. Jen's heart thudded. She looked from the thousands in the horde to the hundreds of defenders on the highway. *This is going to be a slaughter.*

Dozens of radios were on, the voices echoing across them. "Echo One to Alpha Two. Dial in to sector twelve and open fire."

A deafening boom, like a roll of thunder, came from somewhere in the distance behind Jen. The horde saw their prey. They surged forward, and a whistling came from overhead. The city exploded, the concussion knocking Jen onto her ass.

She crawled to her knees and slapped her hands over her ears. Oranges, yellows, and reds burned into her retinas. Black smoke rose and the blistering artillery attacks seemed to go on forever.

Until it didn't. Buildings were flattened and others stood in ruins, their remains ablaze. Thick black smoke curled into the sky.

Jen glanced back. Zeke raised his hands in victory, yelling something she couldn't hear. He stopped, his eyes widening, and pointed into the city. Jen turned back around. The black smoke had parted and thousands more figures poured though it and toward the highway.

Soldiers fired. Jen hadn't heard an order, but fired anyway. The mounted .50 cal behind her boomed as it tore into the wave of undead.

But still the horde gained ground. *We'd need double or triple our number to keep them back.*

A jet fighter streaked low over the city, dropping canisters over the horde. They broke open and burst into hellfire as they spread across the landscape.

Mark yelled into her ear. "Napalm. It'll stop them."

Jen shook her head. She remembered the zombies at Point Wallace. They caught on fire, sure, but it didn't stop them.

As if to prove her case, the fires died down, but the flaming figures pressed forward. She glanced at Mark and his face held sheer terror.

Voices came over the radio, but she couldn't make them out. She dialed the radio to maximum volume and pressed it to her ear.

"All units. Take cover. Bombers coming in close."

Far above, the outline of several B52s swept across the sky like ghosts. Again the whistling sound seemed all around her.

She grabbed Mark's arm and he looked at her. Pulling him toward the ground, she pointed upward. He got the message and flattened next to her on the asphalt. She covered her ears just before the ground shook.

A flash of heat hit her side and she thought she'd burst into flame. Her teeth rattled as bomb after bomb exploded several hundred yards away. When the explosions stopped twenty minutes later, Jen used the rail to pull herself to her feet.

For a mile in front of her, the ground was flattened. Buildings burned and black smoke roiled into the sky, blotting out the sun. Mark stood next to her. "Looks like we got them."

Jen nodded. "What I don't get is why they charged right at us."

"What do you mean?"

"If they're getting smarter leaders," she said, "then you'd think they'd be a bit more tactical than just running their drones into a meat grinder."

Mark shrugged. "They've got millions more. Guess they can sacrifice a few thousand."

Shouting came from farther down the line. Jen leaned over the rail to look, but couldn't see a thing.

"Jen. Mark."

Jen spun around. Zeke stood on the Humvee's hood, waving wildly. "They're coming up the highway."

Jen climbed up beside him and shielded her eyes. About a mile past the last military vehicle, an undulating mass pushed forward. "Shit. There's got to be ten thousand of them."

She caught movement from the corner of her eye and turned. A wave of zombies roared up the highway embankment behind the vehicles. They were outflanked.

33

J en fired to the rear. "Behind us!"

The soldiers reacted to the scores of zombies leaping over the railing and streaking toward them.

Zeke jumped into the gunner position and let off three-round bursts from the M60. One zombie went down, its head a stump on its shoulders, and another fell to the side as its knees were blown out.

"Echo Two to Alpha One. Concentrate fire twenty yards south of our position and fire for effect."

Mark pulled Jen behind a Humvee. "This is going to be harsh."

Jen lay beneath the Humvee, firing at the advancing undead. "If we don't take these assholes out quick, the ones running up the highway will be on us."

Distant thunder boomed. When she heard the whistling, Jen plugged her fingers in her ears.

The artillery rounds hit the embankment on the other side, throwing chunks of earth and pieces of zombies into the air. The odor of burnt dead flesh became overpowering.

Four volleys and the artillery ended. Jen pulled herself to her feet. Mark straightened next to her, and Zeke popped his head up in the Humvee's gunner position.

"Something's definitely pulling strings," Jen said. "This is all too coordinated."

The radio crackled. "Echo Seven to Control. Advancing horde is one hundred yards to engagement."

"Control to all units. Return to base. I say again. Return to base."

The Humvees were loaded and took off one-by-one. Jen looked around for Washington and his crew. She elbowed Mark. "Where's Washington?"

Mark pointed down the road. "There."

Washington and two of his crew sprinted up the highway toward them, the tidal wave of undead at their heels.

Jen jumped into the driver's seat and started the Humvee. Mark slid in next to her. "What the hell are you doing?"

Zeke called down. "There are still some of those flanking zombies. They're going to cut those soldiers off."

"Like hell." Jen threw the vehicle into gear and goosed the gas pedal. The three soldiers still ran, but had also noticed the flanking zombies. They shot at them as their paths came closer.

The chatter of the M60 cut through the air and mixed with Zeke's cries of delight as he cut down zombie after zombie.

Jen swung the Humvee to the side where the flankers were and knocked several over while running over even more. She brought the Humvee in an arc while Mark threw the back door open. Washington threw one of his men in and dove in behind him. A zombie grabbed the third soldier's shirt collar, yanking him back into the horde.

Jen gunned the accelerator while Zeke's M60 chattered away and Washington pulled the door shut. The Humvee pulled away from the horde and down the highway toward the base.

"Shit," Washington said. "You came back for us."

The corporal clapped Jen on the shoulder. "You guys are lifesavers. We owe you."

"Sorry about the other two," Jen said.

Washington's head bowed. "Mitchell and Johnson. Both good soldiers."

The other vehicles were long gone, but the road was clear and the horde fell back into the distance.

Zeke called down. "We've got a problem. Look off to the right."

Jen craned her neck and took in the northern part of the city. Fires still burned to their rear, but the rest remained untouched.

She steered the Humvee farther to the right to get a better view and her breath hitched. Zombies poured out from between every damn building in sight. "Holy shit."

Mark's eyes stayed on the extended horde. "There's not just ten thousand of those fuckers out there. There's got to be a million or more."

Washington leaned forward. "Hand me the mic and keep the pedal down."

Jen tossed the mic to the sergeant and he keyed it. "Echo Three to Base. We're bringing up the rear on the retreat and there's a huge horde coming in from the north. Estimated number is in the millions."

"Command One to Echo Three. This is General Lewis. Confirm the number."

"Yes, sir. The number is estimated to be in the millions, and they're swarming south."

"Roger. Command One to all air units. Proceed to the north and engage the enemy. Alpha One coordinate artillery with Alpha Two and additional air units from Minot and Grand Forks. Put up a wall of death those bastards can't pass."

"Alpha One acknowledges."

The highway curved south and the horde was soon out of sight.

"Command One to Echo Three. Do you have the location of the civilians?"

"Roger, Command One. They're with this unit. All three accounted for and unharmed."

"Bring them to me as soon as you arrive."

"Yes, sir."

THEY ARRIVED at the main gate ten minutes later. While the wall looked foreboding, Jen imagined a million zombies attacking it at once and could think of no scenario in which it kept them out.

She pulled the vehicle through the gate. "I suppose the general's at Headquarters."

"Good guess," Washington said.

Humvees sped by, and fully armed troops ran in formation toward the front gate. A jet launched from the flight line, fire roaring from its engines.

Jen parked in front of Headquarters a few minutes later. A short, stocky soldier with close-cropped salt-and-pepper hair marched out, followed by a trio of NCOs and Sergeant Howell. The older soldier had two stars sewn in his lapel.

Washington and his crewman snapped to attention and saluted. "Echo Three reporting mission accomplished, sir."

General Lewis popped a salute back and stopped in front of Jen. "Dr. Cartwright seems to think you're essential to the war effort."

"I'm not sure about that," Jen said. "She sent me a two-star general. If I was that important, wouldn't she have sent someone with a five star rating instead of two?"

Lewis stared at her while the NCOs behind him turned various shades of red. All except Howell, who struggled to keep a straight face. "Cartwright warned me about you. She was spot-on. Follow me." He flashed a grin, then turned and marched into the building. Jen winked at Mark as they followed the general.

The general led them to the conference room. One of the NCOs turned on the video conference system. "Guess it wasn't too screwed up if they got it fixed already," Zeke said.

The screen displayed Cartwright with dark circles under her eyes. A tired smile tugged at the corners of her mouth. "Jen."

A soldier burst into the room. "General, you're needed in the war room."

"Sergeant Howell, you stay with the civilians. The rest of you come with me." Lewis hurried out of the room, the NCOs trailing in his wake.

Cartwright put a hand up. "I'm sure you have a lot to tell me, but that can wait till you get here. I understand there's a major attack in progress, and with Colonel Butler dead, the urgency is getting you out of there and not on your report. General Lewis has ordered your plane to be refueled and ready for immediate takeoff. I also asked the general's permission for Specialist Grant to accompany you to Atlanta."

Jen swallowed. "Butler killed Grant and turned him into a leader. He sent him after me. Grant controlled thousands of drones, so I had to kill him. Once he died, the drones went back to wandering around."

Cartwright's face softened. "I'm sorry about Grant." She straightened. "But you must leave immediately. That includes you, Sergeant Howell."

"But I could be useful here," Howell said.

"I have more use for you here, Sergeant," Cartwright said. "You will return immediately."

Howell nodded, but remained silent.

Mark cleared his throat. "I'm not going yet."

"What?" Jen said. "What about your family?"

Mark shrugged. "All indications are that things are fine in Biloxi. Would that be right, Doctor?"

Cartwright frowned, but nodded.

"My other family needs me here," Mark said. "You saw what's out there."

Zeke stood. "I'm with Mark. This is where the battle is. Not back east."

Jen sighed. "I'm all for pitching in for God and country and all that bullshit, but what difference can we make? At best, we're three more guns."

"Recon," Mark said. "We can take the plane up. Butler diverted all the recon to the city the past few days and they're now all involved in the northern attack. What if there are more coming from the rear?"

"I could have you arrested and transported here," Cartwright said. "And it would take an additional aircraft out of service." She steepled her fingers. "How about a compromise?"

"I'm listening," Mark said.

"You use your plane to scout until you've covered the rear directions fifty miles out," Cartwright said. "Once you've completed that, you fly directly to Grand Forks Air Force Base in North Dakota, where I have a military transport waiting that will bring you here."

Mark rubbed his chin. "Whether we find anything or not, the general will have information he can use to deploy his troops."

"Deal," Jen said. "We're leaving immediately."

Cartwright nodded. "I'll inform General Lewis." The monitor went blank.

They piled into the Humvee and headed for the flight line. "What are they going to do if we find something?" Zeke said.

"Probably divert some air units to try to keep them back," Howell said.

Jen sighed. "If this base falls, it'll open up everything from North Dakota to Colorado. I don't think we can recover from that."

34

Mark started the Cessna and gave Jen the mic. "How about you be my comm?"

Zeke leaned forward from the backseat. "I can do it."

Jen smiled. *Zeke's the best zombie killer on the team, but when you get right down to it, he's still a big kid.*

She handed him the mic. "Why don't you go ahead and ask for permission to take off?"

He took the mic. "But once we're up," Jen said, "we need your eyes on the ground. I can watch my side and still use the mic, but it's not long enough for you back there."

Zeke nodded. "Are we ready?"

Mark grinned. "The radio's yours, big guy."

Zeke keyed the mic. "Attention, Fairchild Tower, this is..." He lowered the mic. "What's our call sign again?"

Jen looked at the paper the airman handed her before she boarded. "Romeo One."

"Oh, right." Zeke brought the mic to his mouth. "Fairchild Tower, this is Romeo One requesting permission to take off, good buddy."

He released the key. "How was that?"

"I think you could've left the 'good buddy' part off," Howell said.

Mark fiddled with the radio dial. "No answer. I forgot about this crappy radio." He glanced back at Zeke. "Try again."

"Fairchild Tower, this is Romeo One requesting permission for takeoff."

"Romeo One, you have permission for takeoff."

Zeke grinned and handed the mic to Jen. "Not bad, huh?"

Mark engaged the throttle. "You could do it for a living."

Mark guided the plane onto the end of the runway and increased the speed. Other aircraft and buildings sped by in a blur and the Cessna lifted into the air, flying over the wall.

Jen pressed against the window. "They're finally working on that gap in the wall."

"Butler had the combat engineers out looking for you instead of finishing their job," Howell said. "He put the whole base in jeopardy."

Mark craned his neck to get a look. "They're moving fast. The wall's as high as the men working on it."

The plane banked to the right and climbed higher. Black smoke hung over the base and as far north as Jen could see. It looked like it cleared farther south, with a layer of big fluffy clouds blocking the sun.

The radio crackled. "Romeo...status...by General Lewis's order."

Jen keyed the mic. "Fairchild Tower, this is Romeo One. Please repeat. You're breaking up."

"Status update...before...Lewis."

"Dammit," Jen said. "This radio's still a piece of shit."

The plane headed due south. Jen watched Medical Lake pass by beneath them. "Looks pretty clear on my side. Zeke?"

"Same here."

Jen tried the radio again. "Romeo One to Fairchild Tower, do you read?"

A loud buzz from the speakers startled her, and she scrambled to lower the volume.

Zeke stretched his arms. "This is kind of boring. I'd rather be down on the ground killing more zombies."

Howell had his face pressed to the window. "I see a couple zombies below. What about your side, Zeke?"

Zeke quieted and peered out his window.

"What's the first waypoint again?" Mark asked.

Jen consulted the paper. "St. John. Forty-five miles south of base."

"Should be just a ways ahead," Mark said. "Keep your eyes peeled for any hordes."

Jen studied the green-and-brown landscape beneath her. "I've got a horde of about fifty heading south, and another couple of onesies and twosies going in different directions."

"I've got less than that," Zeke said. "Maybe twenty in all."

"So far, so good," Howell said. "No major buildups."

Mark pointed ahead at a small town coming up. "Must be St. John."

They flew over it. "Nothing here," Zeke said.

Jen looked at Mark and shook her head. "Same."

"On to Ritzville." Mark banked the plane to the right.

Jen put the mic to her mouth. "Romeo One to Fairchild. Do you read?"

"This is Fairchild Tower. Command One is requesting your sitrep, Romeo One."

"Roger. Have reached St. John with minimal enemy activity. Now proceeding to Ritzville."

"Roger, Romeo One. Be advised to stay clear of our airspace on your way to Grand Forks. Increased contact with enemy forces in the area has required artillery and air support. Repeat. Stay out of the theater of operations."

"Roger, Fairchild Tower. Romeo One out."

Howell whistled. "There must be a ton of ordnance dropping there."

"Damn," Zeke said. "Where did all those freaking northern zombies come from?"

"Maybe they're from Canada," Mark said. "I don't remember anyone saying what was going on up there."

"Canadian zombies," Jen said. "Great. At least they'll be polite while they're gnawing your face off."

Zeke sat back in his seat. "This is a waste of time. There's nothing out here. They're all coming from up north."

"Keep your eyes on the ground," Mark snapped.

Jen raised an eyebrow at him and he sighed. "Sorry, Zeke. Didn't mean it that way. But what you're doing's important. If we can clear the other directions, they can fully commit troops to the zombies coming from the north."

"And if anything is coming from the south," Jen said, "they need to know now."

A goofy smile spread across Zeke's face. "No worries. You can count on me."

Jen noted ten different small hordes heading northwest. "So far I've seen a total of a few hundred since St. John, but they're all heading northwest, away from the base."

Mark cracked his neck. "Coming up on Ritzville. Let Fairchild know."

"What's our next waypoint?" Jen asked.

"Fort Spokane."

"Romeo One to Fairchild Tower. Do you read?"

The speakers let out a slight crackle and nothing else.

Jen tried again. "Fairchild Tower, this is Romeo One. Do you read?"

A burst of static, then nothing. Jen slapped the dash. "So are they not hearing us, or are we not hearing their reply?"

Mark banked the plane. "Give them the report. Hopefully they'll hear it."

"Romeo One to Fairchild Tower. Be advised we're not hearing you. Our sitrep is once again minimal enemy activity to Ritzville. Now proceeding to last waypoint at Fort Spokane."

The speakers remained silent. Jen slammed the mic into its holder. "Let's just get this shit done and head to Grand Forks."

Mark straightened. "Hey, I think I see something ahead."

Jen leaned against the dash and peered out the window. A shadow spread across the land that reminded her of bees swarming a hive. *Or more like hornets.*

They approached the area. "I see it out this side, too," Zeke said. "What the heck is it?"

"Oh my God," Howell said. "I hope it isn't what I think it is."

Jen looked out her window. "Mark, bring us down."

"How low?"

"As low as it takes to make this out."

The plane's nose dipped and dropped closer to the ground before leveling off. "How about now?" Mark asked.

"Can you circle here?" Jen asked.

"Got it." The plane banked.

No longer a blur flashing by, the mass came into perfect focus. Jen gasped. "Zombies. Millions of them, and they're heading straight for Fairchild."

35

J en snatched the mic from its holder. *Please work.*

"Romeo One to Fairchild Tower. This is an emergency. Do you read?"

Nothing.

"Romeo One to Fairchild Tower. There's a huge horde heading your way from the west. Do you read?"

"They're coming from the southwest, too," Zeke said. "Look."

Jen peered out the window. The darkness flooded the land as far as she could see. "Oh. My. God."

"And those things are running at full tilt," Mark said. He righted the plane and increased the throttle.

"We've got to go back to Fairchild and warn them," Howell said.

Mark nodded. "Heading back at full speed."

Jen brought the mic to her lips. "Romeo One to Fairchild Tower. There are millions of zombies moving quickly to your location from the west and southwest."

She turned to Mark. "They're going to hit the wall at the break. They only have that thing up to six feet or so. This horde will wash over it."

"And if they haven't heard your transmissions," Mark said, "Fairchild won't have a chance to reinforce that portion of the wall."

Zeke whistled. "It's like they're doing it on purpose."

"What?" Howell asked.

"The attack from the north is drawing all the firepower there while this larger group moves in from behind. Me and my gaming group did the same thing on this crazy map—"

"Romeo One to Fairchild Tower. Do you read?"

A crackle came from the speaker and Jen threw the mic to the floor. "How much longer?"

Mark hunched over the wheel, biting his lower lip. "Look ahead."

Jen peered out the front window. They were only a couple of miles from the base.

Howell looked down. "We're just clearing the leading edge of that horde. There won't be a lot of time once we land."

Mark shook his head. "I don't know what the hell they can do to plug that hole. If they divert the artillery and air units to the southwest, they might keep the horde from breaching the gap, but then the northern approach is open."

"The general's a smart guy," Howell said. "I don't know if it'll matter, but the base is in the best hands available."

The plane slowed and the nose dipped. "I'm not cleared for landing, so I'm going to buzz the tower to get their attention. Then we're going in."

A Blackhawk lifted off from the runway and flew north. Several bombers streaked high overhead.

The Cessna zipped by the tower, causing several of the air traffic controllers to duck. "I think we have their attention," Mark said.

Mark took the plane in a wide turn then straightened for the runway. He lowered the flaps and decreased speed. The runway came up to meet them and the plane bounced once, twice, then settled.

Emergency vehicles, their lights flashing, sped toward them.

"Don't stop," Jen said. "Get us to our parking spot. We can jump in the truck and get to HQ faster."

Mark pulled up near the pumps and cut the engine. Without waiting for the props to stop, they hopped out of the plane and ran to the truck. A maintenance crew member looked at them curiously. Jen pointed at him. "Get the plane refueled quickly. We're under orders from General Lewis."

The crewman nodded and ran off.

Howell hopped into the driver's seat and started the truck. The others boarded and the tires left rubber on the tarmac as they tore down the road.

A fire truck roared down the runway and stopped at the Cessna. The MP vehicle made a sharp turn and chased the truck.

Heavy vehicle and troop traffic forced Howell to slow and stop for others. The MP truck pulled up behind and they got out, but the traffic cleared and Howell sped off, causing the MPs to scramble back into their truck and give chase.

The truck arrived at HQ with a screech. Howell threw the truck into park. Jen jumped out just as the MP vehicle pulled up.

"Halt," a bearish-looking MP said, his pistol aimed at her.

Jen ignored him and ran into the building. The MP chased after her, but Howell tackled him into a wall, knocking the air out of him. Mark disarmed the second MP and followed Jen.

She burst into Lewis's office. Surrounded by soldiers in full combat gear, he looked up from his desk. "Where the hell have you been? We haven't heard from you since Ritzville."

Howell burst in.

Jen leaned on the general's desk, panting. "Radio problems. Huge horde coming from the south and west. Millions of them. The northern attack is a diversion."

"They're heading here at full tilt, sir," Howell said.

Lewis stood. "Divert all air units to the southwest. Keep half the artillery pounding the north and divert the other half to the southwest. And I want a helicopter out there on recon. We need eyes."

The men scattered and Lewis faced the wall, his head down and hands pressed against his back. "Millions, you say?"

"There had to be," Mark said. "We couldn't see the end of them. I think we found the expected surge from Seattle and Portland."

The general sighed. "There's no way we can hold that back."

Jen swallowed. "I don't think so."

The general turned around. "It's time for you to leave. Cartwright needs you. Our only hope is for some kind of cure, and she needs your blood and the information you have."

Zeke scratched his head. "It'd be a great battle. Imagine how many zombies I could take out."

Lewis sat on the edge of his desk. "We all have our role, and this isn't yours." He cast a steely gaze at Jen. "You go take care of business."

Jen's throat tightened. She nodded.

The MP burst in. "Sorry, General. I'll get them out of here."

"You see that you do." He pointed at the MP. "Escort them back to their aircraft, Code One. Radio the tower on the way and get them cleared for takeoff. Highest priority."

The MP looked at Jen, then back at the general. "Yes, sir."

Howell saluted Lewis. "Honor to serve with you, sir."

The general returned his salute. "Sergeant, your mission is to get these people safe to Atlanta."

"Yes, sir."

HOWELL FOLLOWED THE MP TRUCK, its lights flashing and siren wailing, through the traffic and to the flight line. "Look," Zeke said.

The zombies had reached the gap. No artillery hits sounded in the south. "I don't think they've re-aimed the artillery yet."

An Apache zoomed over them and sprayed gunfire at the zombies climbing over the wall. "It's too damn late," Mark said. "They can keep some back, but can't bomb the horde at the wall without taking the wall out."

Humvees, APCs, and trucks streaked toward the gap. Ground troops rushed in and took cover, then opened fire.

The zombie wave crashed over the wall, overwhelming the forces lined against them. Soldiers continued pouring fire into the mob, but one by one they disappeared under the wall of undead.

Howell pulled up to the plane. The crewman had a rifle and fired at zombies washing over an APC. "You're fueled up," he said. "Get the hell out of here."

They piled in and Mark started the engine. "We may not have a clear runway. Hang on."

The MP rolled down his window and gestured for them to follow. Mark nodded.

The leading edge of the mob had reached the runway. A zombie here and a zombie there, it wouldn't be another minute before it was flooded with the main body of the attack.

The MP sped ahead, swerving from side to side and knocking zombies out of the way. Mark pushed the throttle forward. Even with the help, it'd be close.

M.A. ROBBINS

A mass of zombies poured onto the end of the runway. "Shit," Mark said. "They're shortening the damn runway. Hang on."

He pressed the throttle to the max. The MP truck accelerated, knocking zombies aside, clearing a narrow path for the plane.

The plane lifted as the MP truck plowed into a thick wall of undead and came to a stop. Zombies washed over it.

Mark had the wheel pulled back as far as he could. A drop of sweat tracked down his cheek. "Come on. Come on."

The plane shuddered, then soared over the wall.

"We hit something," Mark said, "but we made it. We'll need to do a tower flyby at Grand Forks and have them check our landing gear for damage."

The plane continued climbing. Mark banked it in a wide circle, and Jen pressed her face to the window.

The undead had penetrated halfway into the base. Gunfire erupted everywhere. Squads of soldiers held their ground and were swept over by the horde.

The battle for Fairchild was over in minutes.

36

J en's heart sank. All those brave men gone. *Turned into drones.*

Howell held his head in his hands. "I don't know how we can stop that."

"We should head to Grand Forks," Mark said. "Report what we've seen."

Zeke had his nose pressed to the window. "Wait. Look there." He pointed to the west.

Howell raised himself up and looked past Zeke. "What the hell is that?"

Jen tried to look. "I can't see shit. What is it?"

"I think we found a leader," Mark said. "Going in for a closer look."

He banked the plane and descended to a couple hundred feet. The base was completely overrun and yet there were still miles of zombies outside its walls.

Mark pointed out the windshield. "Look at that, Jen."

She squinted. Ahead in the sea of undead, one stood alone, the horde flowing around it like a river around a boulder. "Can you circle it?"

Mark put the Cessna into a tight turn, and Jen took out a pair of binoculars. Pressing them to her eyes, she adjusted the focus until the figure came into focus. She hissed as she drew in a sharp breath.

"What is it?" Howell asked.

Zeke leaned forward. "I want to see."

"You won't believe it," Jen said.

"Say it," Mark snapped.

"That's Butler."

Butler threw his hands into the air and every zombie froze. "Holy shit," Mark said. "He's controlling them all. Look, even on the base they're all still."

"My God," Howell said.

Jen peered down at Butler, whose head moved to follow the plane with his yellow eyes. "Let's get the hell out of here and report."

"Agreed," Howell said. "The sooner the better."

Jen pressed both middle fingers against the window. *You'll see me again, you son of a bitch, and then I'll finish the job.*

AUTHOR'S NOTES

So the plot thickens in the Zombie Uprising world. If you liked The Citadel, *please leave a review on Amazon.* This will help the book reach more people who like the kind of stories you and I do.

I had someone ask me if I know what's going to happen in the next book before I write it. Well, I do to a point. I have certain milestones that I plan on meeting, but for some reason, Jen, Zeke, and the others seem to come up with a way to send the story in a whole other direction.

But that's what makes writing so fun to me. I love letting the characters loose to wreak havoc. Sometimes it ends up as nothing but outtakes from the book, and other times it takes it to a whole new level.

That's why I can't wait to write the next book. I want to see what's going to happen!

If you'd like to keep up with what I've got coming out, sign up for my email list at uprising.marobbins.com. You'll get a **free** eBook, new release announcements, updates, and even some drawings to win prizes like signed paperbacks and other unique items.

Thank you so much for reading the Citadel. Know that I take no reader for granted and I'm truly humbled that you spent your time reading my book.

Till next time.

M.A. Robbins

ACKNOWLEDGMENTS

I couldn't write enough books to give my wife, Debbie, the acknowledgment she deserves. Thanks to Domi at Inspired Cover Designs for her talent, patience, and quick turnarounds. To Tamara Blain of A Closer Look Editing, who goes beyond the grammar and spelling, and finds other gremlins I've missed. And to the core beta readers who took their time to read the first three books of this series and provide their two cents: Maureen Meyer and Wayne Tripp. Last but not least, I have to acknowledge TBone for ~~his patience~~ not whining too loudly while waiting for me to finish a chapter before I take him outside to play.

THE HYBRID

BOOK FOUR IN THE ZOMBIE UPRISING
SERIES

CONTENTS

To zombie readers everywhere. Some people may think we're weird, but they'll eat their words when the zombies are making hors d'oeuvres out of their intestines.

1

The C130 came to a stop, the tail door opened, and the ramp lowered.

Jen stepped onto the ramp and took a deep breath. She coughed and wheezed in another breath. "Holy shit, what's the humidity here?"

Mark walked past her with his arms spread. "Good old Southern air. Humidity's probably around ninety percent."

Zeke bounded down the ramp in his black ninja costume. *He's got to be burning up.*

"Need to get off the ramp," the crew chief said. "We've got to get going."

Jen scanned the airport. Commercial aircraft from small Beechcraft to national airline 747s were parked, dark and silent. No baggage handlers or their tractors. No guys waving planes to or from gates. The place was dead. "Where are we supposed to go?"

The crew chief adjusted his headset and shrugged. "No idea. Our orders were to drop you off at Hartsfield-Jackson airport and we've completed our mission. Now, move back, please."

Howell jogged down the ramp and to a stairway underneath a gate. "Can't change their orders, so let's see what we've got."

Jen adjusted the double-bladed axe on her belt and followed Howell and Zeke up the stairs. Mark stayed close behind her, scanning the area.

None of the schedule boards were lit and all the snack and news outlets were shuttered.

"Reminds me of a Stephen King novel," Zeke said. "Had a scene that described this perfectly."

"And where was everyone in that one?" Mark asked.

Zeke smiled. "I don't do spoilers."

"I say we head for the baggage area," Jen said.

A sound echoed from farther down the terminal hallway. Jen lifted the axe from her belt, while Howell and Zeke pulled their pistols and Mark's mace appeared in his hands.

"Isn't that the direction of the baggage area?" Zeke asked.

"Screw it." Jen wiped sweat from her forehead with the back of her hand and strode across the shiny tiles of the terminal. "I want to get to the CDC, give them my blood, then reload and go after Butler."

Mark hurried to keep up with her. "How are you going to find one zombie in the middle of millions of them?"

"Don't know. Don't care." Jen sniffed. "All I know is I won't find him by sitting on my ass here."

Two men in black suits appeared from around a corner fifty yards away. Jen stopped and reared back with the axe from pure instinct. The suited men reached into their suit jackets but froze when Howell and Zeke aimed at them.

"Who are you?" Howell asked.

One of them removed his hand from his jacket and raised it, displaying a badge. "Homeland Security. If you're the survivors from Fairchild, then we're here to take you to CDC Headquarters."

Jen relaxed and lowered the axe. "I hope you're taking us there in something with air conditioning."

Zeke and Howell lowered their weapons. One of the Homeland Security men, a blond with windswept hair who gave off a surfer vibe, stepped forward. "Agent Daniels." He nodded toward the other agent, a thirty-something man with dark features and piercing brown eyes. "Agent Rodriguez."

Rodriguez flashed his badge. "Pleasure. We've got transportation out front. We were going to pick you up at the drop-off point, but all entry to the flight line is blocked."

Mark slid his mace into his belt. "Let's get the show on the road."

Daniels led the way through the concourse and to baggage claim. Outside, a black limousine with government plates was parked at the curb. Rodriguez opened the back door.

Jen climbed in and nearly passed out. "It's like an oven in here."

Rodriguez climbed into the driver's seat and started the vehicle. Seconds later cold air blasted into Jen's face. "Ahh."

Zeke sat next to her, while Howell and Mark took the seat across from them. Daniels jumped into the passenger seat and the limo took off.

Jen leaned back, enjoying the arctic air flowing over her face. *I don't remember ever being this hot in my life.*

Howell peered out the windshield. They were just leaving the airport.

"Not much traffic," he said.

Daniels shifted in his seat and turned to the passengers. "You'll get a full debriefing I'm sure, but we have a fuel crisis. With several refineries down and others in danger from the horde, all commercial aircraft have been grounded and gasoline is being rationed."

Mark frowned. "Any attacks since Fairchild?"

"Smaller towns," Rodriguez said. "Nothing big. But the military is pouring into the front line bases like Mountain Home Air Force Base in Idaho and Nellis Air Force Base in Nevada."

They came to a stoplight, and Rodriguez slowed as the light turned red. Several cars passed through, each one loaded with people. A cop car went the other way. Jen caught a glimpse of a cop in the passenger side in full riot gear. *Smart idea. Makes it harder for the zombies to bite through.*

The light changed and Rodriguez turned onto Norman Berry Drive. They passed a strip mall with a smattering of cars and trucks in the parking lot. Two cabbies stood outside their parked cabs, talking.

Goosebumps formed on Jen's arms. "You can turn the AC down a little. Even an Alaskan girl has her limits."

Daniels adjusted the fan speed as the limo entered an intersection. A pickup flashed by mere feet in front of them and Rodriguez slammed on the brakes, spilling Jen onto the floor. Tires squealed, followed by a sickening crunch.

Doors opened as Jen pulled herself up. A late-model truck, its front end pushed in, rested against the folded side of a minivan. Jen hopped out of the limo and joined the others running to the crash site.

The truck's driver's door popped open. A thin, middle-age man in worn jeans and a straw cowboy hat stepped out and collapsed to his knees.

"You OK?" Jen dashed to his side.

He shook his head as though to clear it. "Just a little dizzy."

She put a hand on his back. "Why don't you sit down. I'm sure an ambulance is on its way." She eased him to the ground.

She stuck her head in the truck. An older woman sat on the passenger seat, her head lying against her window, a star pattern radiating from the impact point of her head. Jen checked her pulse. *Weak and fluttering.*

"What you got?" Mark's voice came from behind her.

She backed up and straightened, cracking her neck. "This lady needs an ambulance sooner rather than later." She nodded at the man in the straw hat. "He's shaken up, but should be OK."

Daniels jogged over. "Ambulance and backup on the way. Three minutes out."

"Backup?" Jen asked.

Rodriguez joined them. "New protocols. Everyone needs to get back to the limo."

"But there are people hurt over here," Zeke called out. He stood next to the ruined minivan, his face pinched. "There are eight people crammed in here."

Howell leaned over the minivan's driver, a thirtyish brunette with a gash on her forehead that bled like a stream. "Some of these people will die if they don't get help now."

Two other vehicles stopped on the side of the road and four men came running. "Need any help?"

"No." Daniels waved them away. "Everyone away from the vehicles, Now."

Howell gestured to the others. "Come on. Orders are orders." He herded them to the limo.

One of the civilians, a bear of a man with a shock of red hair, unbuckled the old lady from the truck and gently lifted her. "I'm not leaving someone's grandmama to die." He bent down to lay her next to the Straw Hat Man, and she wrapped her arms around his neck.

"Bless your heart," the redheaded man said. "Strong enough to hang on."

The old lady clenched his neck and pulled him closer. "What the hell?"

He struggled to keep his balance before letting out a scream and pummeling the woman with his fists.

She fell back, a chunk of bloody flesh in her mouth. The redhead stumbled away, holding onto his gushing wound.

The old lady swallowed her prize whole and fell upon Straw Hat Man, who struggled against her.

Yelling came from the minivan. Two of the other men raced back to their vehicle and peeled out. A pair of legs stuck out of the driver's door and kicked in the air as a desperate scream came from inside.

Jen pulled her axe and sprinted for Grandma Zombie. She'd just torn Straw Hat Man's soft abdomen open and had her face pressed into his guts like a kid bobbing for apples at a Halloween party. Jen drove her axe blade deep into the back of Grandma's head and she went limp.

Shots came from the limo. Zeke leaned across its hood and aimed at the minivan, smoke coming from the end of his barrel. The thirtyish woman lay facedown by the minivan, the back of her head blown out.

Zeke and Mark ran to the van. Mark cracked the skull of a teenage boy as he leapt from the vehicle, and Zeke shot through a window several times.

A growl made Jen spin. Straw Hat Man's yellow eyes locked on her. Her axe still buried in the old lady's head, she backpedaled out of the zombie's grasp. Another shot came from behind and a bullet hole appeared in the zombie's eye. He collapsed in a heap.

Sirens approached, and Jen wiped blood from around her eyes. *Some of these freaking things splatter like a bitch.*

She jerked the axe from grandma's skull and wiped it off on the old lady's dress before slipping it back into her belt.

An ambulance screamed to a stop, its siren cutting off. Two police cars stopped behind it and four cops in riot gear and weapons jumped out. Jen stumbled toward them. "You guys can relax. We took care of it for you."

A cop with a shotgun aimed it at her. "Let's clean this up, men."

Three other rifles swung her way.

2

Jen froze. *The hell?*

Zeke aimed his pistol at the cop with the shotgun. "Anyone shoots and you get it first. In the face."

The other cops swung their rifles toward Zeke. Howell aimed at them.

"You're outnumbered," a young black cop said. "Might as well drop it."

Daniels and Rodriguez pulled their handguns. "Homeland Security," Daniels said. "The safety of these people is a national security priority."

One of the cops looked at the one with the shotgun. "What do we do, Sarge?"

The sergeant kept the shotgun pointed at Jen. "If you're Homeland Security, then you know the protocol and why we need to follow it."

Mark had his hands up and his mace in his belt. "What protocol is the one where you pull guns on us?"

"Anyone in contact with the reanimated dead has to be put down," the sergeant said. "Anyone who is terminally ill will be put down." He glanced at Mark. "A bullet to the head."

"I thought everything was supposed to be OK back here," Jen said. Mark flashed a frown. *Now he's not so sure his family is safe.*

"Things are under control," Daniels said. "But it comes at a price. That's why every ambulance has a police backup."

"But what if you're shooting uninfected people?" Zeke said. "Ever think about that?" He blinked, and for the first time Jen noticed the dark bags under his eyes. She'd slept on the plane and assumed the others had, too. *Did Zeke stay awake to watch over me?*

"Sorry, kid," the sergeant said. "Can't take the chance."

Jen slipped her axe into her belt, the movement causing the sergeant to stiffen. She put her arms up. "I'm not gonna do anything. But let me ask you something."

The sergeant nodded.

Jen gestured to Zeke and Howell. "Put your weapons down."

Howell lowered his pistol. Zeke hesitated, but dropped his arm to his side when Jen glared at him.

"That's better." She turned her attention to the sergeant. "How long is it taking for someone infected with a bite to turn?"

He shrugged. "Couple of minutes."

She looked at her watch. "You've been here for five minutes. She pulled her lower eyelids down. "No yellow. See?"

The sergeant pursed his lips and looked at his men. One of them shrugged. "She's right, Sarge."

"What if it's a new strain?" the sergeant asked. "Could be one that takes longer."

"Strain my ass." Jen walked toward the limo. "I'm out of here. You want to stop me, you'll have to shoot me from behind."

"Wait."

Jen halted and glanced back. The sergeant lowered the shotgun and gestured at the others to do the same. "Stand down."

Jen let out a breath she hadn't realized she'd been holding. Growling came from inside the minivan. "Looks like you have some cleaning up to do."

The sergeant nodded. "Let's go." The cops circled the minivan.

Jen puffed her cheeks and let out a breath. "Can we go now?"

Mark put an arm around her shoulder and led her to the limo. "How the hell do you keep getting away with calling a bluff?"

She gave him a quick hug. "Charmed, I guess."

Rodriguez started the limo and they all jumped in.

A cascade of gunfire came from the minivan as they pulled away.

Broken only by wisps of clouds, the blue sky looked gorgeous as long as

Jen was in the air conditioning. *I hope the CDC keeps it cool.*

The limo pulled onto Interstate 85 and the amount of traffic picked up. Still, it wasn't anything like she'd heard about Atlanta's congestion.

Staring out the window at the vehicles passing by, she nudged Zeke.

"What's up?" he asked.

"Notice all these cars are full? You don't see any with just the driver."

The faux leather seat squeaked as Daniels turned around. "Not only has rationing been ordered, but it's against protocol to have fewer than half the capacity of a vehicle."

"Is it like this everywhere?" Mark asked. "How safe is it?"

Daniels shrugged. "These are national protocols. They're everywhere."

"How about safety?" Mark asked. "Heard anything about Birmingham?"

"Alabama?" Rodriguez asked. "Nothing specific there. There've been a few outbreaks, and only two of them became nasty. One was Dayton, Ohio. Lost a hundred and twenty people before it was brought under control."

"Another in Connecticut took a few dozen," Daniels said. "And you know what the common thread ran through both of these?"

"Let me guess," Jen said. "Protocols weren't followed."

Daniels pointed a finger at her. "Bingo."

They exited onto Route 78, passing pedestrians and bicyclists crowding the sidewalks.

Jen lay back and closed her eyes. She pulled her bloodied shirt away from her chest to get air under it, and it stuck to one side. "Freaking zombie guts. I should do a detergent commercial. 'Just a cup in the wash gets the zombie goop off.'"

She leaned back and drifted off.

JEN WOKE WITH A START, her hand going to the axe on her hip. The limo slowed as it approached a gate with a guard shack. Iron bar fencing on a brick base stood ten feet high and separated several high-rise type buildings from the street. The tallest, a concave-shaped silver building covered in windows, glinted in the sunlight.

The limo stopped next to the guard shack and Rodriguez rolled down his window. "These people are here at Dr. Cartwright's request. They have no credentials, so I'm vouching for them."

The guard lifted a piece of paper on a clipboard and peered into the back of the limo. His gaze settled on Howell. "Name?"

"Sergeant Howell."

The guard peered at Mark. "And you?"

"Mark Colton."

The guard nodded as he consulted the clipboard. "You two. Names."

"Jen Reed."

"OK."

"Zeke."

The guard squinted. "Zeke what?"

"Zeke Tripp."

Jen laughed. "Your last name's Tripp?"

Zeke looked hurt. "Yeah. What's wrong with that?"

"Nothing," Jen said, stifling another laugh. "It's just not the name I'd come up with for someone who's so stealthy on their feet."

The guard wrote something on the clipboard. "Good to go. I'll notify Dr. Cartwright you're on your way." He stepped away from the limo and gestured to another guard, who rolled the gate open.

Rodriguez put the limo in gear and drove into the compound. He pulled up to the main doors of the concave building.

Jen followed the agents in and sighed when a blast of cold air brushed her face. "Heaven."

An older guard just inside the door waved them all by. "Dr. Cartwright is waiting for you in her office."

An elevator ride to the eighth floor took seconds, and they stepped out into a carpeted hallway with soft lighting. Jazzy instrumental music played through speakers in the ceiling.

Daniels led them twenty yards down the hallway and into a reception area. A receptionist with a headset looked up and pressed something on her desk. "They're here, Doctor." She nodded and looked at Agent Daniels. "She'll be just a minute."

Thirty seconds later a buzz and a click came from a set of double doors to the receptionist's side. "You can go in," she said.

Rodriguez held one of the doors open and ushered everyone in. A large, spacious room with floor-to-ceiling windows, Cartwright's office was filled with sunlight. Framed artwork hung on one of the walls, while another had pictures and plaques. One that caught Jen's eye showed

Cartwright and the President next to each other in what looked like a serious conversation.

From what I've seen of Cartwright, everything's a serious conversation.

Cartwright sat at her desk facing them. She stood. "Jen, good to meet you." She made eye contact with each of the others in turn. "Good to meet you all."

She gestured to a comfy looking sofa and a set of chairs. "Please have a seat."

Jen took one of the chairs, while Howell took the other. Mark and Zeke plopped down on the sofa.

Cartwright took her seat. "I received the message you passed along at Grand Forks. I have to say, it left me wondering if the message wasn't misunderstood by the airman who communicated it to me. Would you mind filling me in?"

Jen leaned forward, her elbows resting on her knees. "Butler died and came back a leader."

"But a super leader," Zeke said. "Kinda like a top-level Boss on one of my video games."

Cartwright's eyes stayed on Jen. "And so it's true that he controlled a horde that numbered in the millions?"

"It's a fact, Doctor," Howell said. "Threw his hands in the air and every damn one of those things froze in place."

Cartwright rubbed her chin. "That gives me a lot to think about."

Jen fidgeted in her seat. "I'd like you to take my blood so I can go back out there and find Butler."

Mark's eyebrows rose. "I don't think that's a good idea."

Cartwright frowned. "We don't know where he is. Besides, I need you here with me. There's much to be done." She tilted her head forward and peered at Jen over the top of her glasses. "And I need you for more than your blood."

Jen stood. "All due respect, Doctor, but I was there at the beginning of this thing. I lost my Dad, Chris, Doc, and too many other people to count. I want to end it."

Cartwright sighed. "And you will. But as my assistant where you'll do more to end this catastrophe than you could by charging to your death."

Her face softened. "It may make you feel better to go after Butler, but your impact will help many more people if you stay and work with me."

Jen rubbed the heels of her palms into her eyes. *Feel like I haven't slept in days.*

She took a deep breath and let it out while puffing her cheeks. "OK, Doctor. I'll sleep on it."

Mark stood and stretched. "Come to think of it, I think we could all use a shower, some food, and a good sleep."

Cartwright pressed a button on her desk. "Amy, please send Agents Rodriguez and Daniels back in."

The two agents appeared immediately. "Take them to the hotel and get them settled," Cartwright said.

"Yes, ma'am," Rodriguez replied.

A young woman in a pant suit burst into the room like an eager intern. "Dr. Cartwright. News from the front."

"What is it?" Cartwright asked.

"There are multiple coordinated attacks against Boise, Las Vegas, and Malmstrom Air Force Base in Montana."

"How many?" Zeke asked.

"Tens of millions." The woman turned to Cartwright. "General Loomis said all three locations could fall within a day."

Cartwright pointed to the window-length blinds. "Close those. Let's get Colonel Rogers on video at once."

"Ma'am," the woman said, "I'm sure he's tied up with the attacks at the moment."

Cartwright stared at her. There was no anger in her face, but the woman hurried to close the blinds. Cartwright typed on her keyboard and a section of the wall behind her slid over and revealed a fifty-five-inch flat screen. The word "Connecting..." displayed on it.

An older soldier's face appeared on the screen. Silver eagles adorned the collar of a wrinkled uniform shirt. His lower eyelids drooped and his eyes had red blood vessels crossing the white sclera like a lightning strike.

"Dr. Cartwright," he said. "We're in emergency mode—"

"I want details," Cartwright snapped. "Some very important decisions may need to be made based on the situation."

The colonel's shoulders drooped. *This guy looks like shit.*

"Evacuation of Malmstrom AFB in Montana to Grand Forks AFB is in process. We estimate forty percent of the personnel and eighty percent of the equipment will make it out before the base is overrun."

"Shit," Mark breathed.

Cartwright's expression remained unchanged. "And Las Vegas?"

"It's going to fall." Rogers rubbed a knuckle in each eye. "And it'll be soon. There's a line of traffic heading east all the way to the Arizona border. Hordes have broken off and are flanking the city on the north and south. It's obvious they plan to attack the refugees and encircle the city."

Howell cleared his throat. "What about Nellis AFB?"

"Overrun an hour ago, but we evacuated all personnel and essential resources."

Zeke looked up from studying his fingernails. "What about Area 51? Did you fly the UFOs out of there?"

Jen clasped his forearm and shook her head. "Not the time."

Rogers ignored Zeke. "Boise is fifty-fifty. We've launched constant air strikes from Mountain Home AFB. It seems to have kept the horde at bay for now."

Cartwright sniffed. "Keep me updated, Colonel."

The screen went blank.

"Butler's behind it," Jen said. "I need to find him and finish what I started."

"Don't be foolish," Cartwright said.

"Excuse me?" Heat flooded Jen's face.

Mark turned toward her. "I wouldn't put it that way, but what are you going to do? Just walk through the horde looking for him?"

Zeke slapped the table. "I'm with you, Jen."

Jen sat back and let out a long breath. "I don't see me doing any good here."

"Why?" Cartwright asked. "Because you can't be out there acting like a hero?"

Jen frowned. "Wait a minute—"

"You are the only living person on Earth who received a fully concentrated inhalation of the spores," Cartwright said. "That makes you unique, and a superb test subject to find a cure."

"But we don't even know if that will help," Jen said.

"But if it does?" Cartwright asked. She raised a hand, the thumb and forefinger a half-inch apart. "We're this close to a cure. If you want to do something to stop this scourge, then help us with that."

Jen stared at the floor. *She's right. And so is Mark. How the hell would I find Butler without becoming a zombie snack? Still, I'd rather do something more than get poked with needles.*

Jen sighed. "Where do I go to donate blood?"

Cartwright gestured to the young woman. "This is Cindy Hirt. Cindy, please escort Miss Reed to the phlebotomy office and bring her back to me when she's done."

"Yes, Doctor." Cindy turned to Jen. "Miss Reed?"

Jen stood. "Lead on."

"I'll go with you." Zeke stepped to her side.

I love this guy. The little brother I never had. "I think I'll be safe in the building. Why don't you stay here? I won't be gone long."

Zeke pursed his lips and nodded.

She followed Cindy into the hallway and onto the elevator, where the assistant put a key in the panel and turned it, then punched the lowest button. Lower Level Four.

The elevator dropped quickly and quietly, stopping at their destination in seconds. The doors slid open with a slight *whoosh*, revealing a set of double doors with the words "Authorized Personnel Only" stenciled on them.

Cindy took an access card that hung from her hip and swiped it through a reader on the wall. A blip and green light from the reader and Cindy pulled the door open.

The room was thirty feet wide and almost that long. A rack of stainless steel morgue refrigerators lined part of one wall, while two stainless steel autopsy tables sat in the middle of the room, under large operating room lights hanging from the ceiling. Jen squinted. All the refrigerator doors had keyholes. *Keeping someone out or something in?*

Cindy strode through the room, pushed open a door on the other side, and walked through. Jen gave a refrigerator door handle a tug as she passed it. It didn't move.

She hurried after Cindy and into a hallway with a dozen doors, six on either side. She went to the first door and peeked into the small eye-level window. An old lady lay in a hospital bed with her eyes closed. A respirator mask fitted on her face, her chest rose and fell rhythmically.

What the hell are they doing down here?

She hurried to keep up with the assistant and followed right on her heels as she pushed through a pair of swinging double doors and into a large cavernous room. Buzzing lights hung from a high ceiling, casting a bright glow that reached into every corner of the room.

Jen stopped in her tracks. Lining both sides of the room were a dozen large cages, each with a snarling zombie inside. As if on cue, they strained at their chains as Jen and the assistant entered.

The assistant glanced over her shoulder and stopped. "They're very secure."

Jen blinked. "I'm not afraid, just surprised."

A door opened at the far end of the room. A balding middle-aged man with a blond handlebar mustache stepped out with a clipboard in his hand. "What do you have for me?" His gaze swung to Jen. "And who is this? Why is she in a restricted area?"

Jen followed Cindy to the man. His white lab coat had "O'Connor" embroidered over the pocket. "I'm Jen Reed. I'm guessing you're the vampire who's going to suck me dry."

The man looked at Cindy then back at Jen before he put his hand out. "Dr. O'Connor. I work with Dr. Cartwright."

Jen shook his hand. "Why don't we get on with this? These zombies are giving me a headache."

O'Connor looked at the zombies as if he'd just noticed they were there. "Of course. I'm so used to them, I've mentally blocked them out." He turned. "Follow me."

Jen followed him and Cindy into the room he'd appeared from. Two other people in lab coats sat at separate tables, one working on a computer and the other peering into a microscope. Shelves of vials and jars, as well as equipment like a centrifuge, lined the counters.

The door closed, cutting off the growls of the zombies.

"Please, have a seat." O'Connor gestured to a blood drawing chair. She sat as O'Connor rustled through drawers, pulling out a plastic open-ended tube with a nasty-looking needle at the end and several glass tubes with rubber at one end. Jen flipped the padded arm of the chair across her lap and rested her arm on it.

"Have you found out where the virus came from?" she asked.

O'Connor froze and glanced at her, then went back to rummaging in the drawer. "We're working on it."

He turned around and wiped down the crook of her arm with a swab. The sting of alcohol fumes made Jen crinkle her nose. "What have you found out so far?"

O'Connor stabbed her arm and Jen flinched. She looked away. She didn't mind shots or needles as long as she didn't have to look at them stuck into her body.

Cindy had wandered over to the lab tech on the computer, and they spoke in hushed tones.

Jen looked around at the well-equipped lab. Doc would've liked it there. *Doc.* His name still brought a twinge of guilt. *I'll never forgive myself for his death.*

A sharp jab in her arm caused her to pull in a breath.

"Just another minute," O'Connor said.

Jen looked down. A full tube lay next to two more. A fourth one was in the vacutainer and filling up fast. He pulled that one out, shook it, and laid it down, before slipping another in.

Looking away, Jen said, "Looks like a lot of blood."

"You'll be fine," O'Connor said. "But I want you to sit here for ten minutes afterward just to make sure you don't feel faint."

He removed the needle and pressed a cotton ball over the wound. "Hold this here, please."

Jen pressed a finger onto it as O'Connor taped it down. "I'll pass on the ten minutes," she said. *If I haven't passed out from anything that's happened in the last month, then I won't pass out from this.*

O'Connor shrugged.

Jen eased out of the chair and straightened. "Cindy, can we get going?"

Cindy looked over from the computer, said something to the lab tech, and walked to the door. Jen joined her, and as soon as the door opened, the zombies came alive again.

They'd made it several feet from the lab when Dr. O'Connor appeared in the doorway. "Ms. Hirt, Dr. Cartwright is on the phone for you."

Cindy put out a hand. "Wait here." She hurried into the lab.

"Shit," Jen said. "And I have to stay out here and listen to this?"

The door eased shut and the zombies went silent as if someone had flipped a switch.

Jen peered at each of them. All of their eyes were on her. *What the fuck?*

She took a few steps toward the exit, and the zombies straightened like soldiers at attention, their heads swiveling to keep their gazes latched on her. Jen approached one, a young redhead, and its soulless eyes locked on hers. *Nothing. Not even a spark of life in them.*

The lab door opened and the zombies went wild, gnashing their teeth and growling at Cindy.

Well, well. If this ain't some creepy shit.

4

J en followed Cindy back into Cartwright's office. What was going on with those zombies? Why did they quiet down when only she was there? Could it be another mutation in the virus? *Should I tell Cartwright?*

"Just in time," Cartwright said.

Jen broke from her thoughts. "Just in time for what?"

Howell stood next to Cartwright. He put his hand out. "Dr. Cartwright has assigned me to be her liaison with the Pentagon. I'm taking tonight's train to Washington."

Jen shook his hand, then pulled him into a hug. "Sorry to see you go." She broke the embrace. "You saved our asses more than once."

Howell smiled. "And you've saved a lot more with your observations and reports."

"And she'll save even more by helping us find a vaccine," Cartwright said.

Howell stopped in the doorway. "I think it'll take all of us to save humanity."

He disappeared into the hallway just as Mark and Zeke walked in.

"Where have you two been while I was getting stabbed?" Jen asked.

Zeke smacked his lips. "Got a bite to eat."

"Knowing you, it was enough to feed a bear," Jen said.

Mark laughed. "Don't you know it."

Cartwright's phone rang and she put on a headset. After listening for a few seconds, she said, "Yes. Bring them up."

Mark and Jen exchanged puzzled glances. Zeke examined a spot on the rug and scuffed it with his foot.

A knock came from the door a few minutes later. "Enter," Cartwright said.

An older woman with gray streaks in her curly black hair walked in with a younger version of herself. The younger woman's eyes grew big and a smile broke across her face as she yelled, "Mark." She raced to Mark and threw herself into his arms.

"Michelle," Mark said, his voice muffled as he held her close. He loosened his grip on her and put an arm out toward the older woman. "Mama."

The older woman shuffled to him, her eyes glistening, and buried herself in his arms.

Jen watched the reunion, half-fascinated at the emotional display and half-jealous there would be no such experience waiting for her. She glanced away, a little embarrassed about her feelings.

Cartwright sat behind her desk, her face neutral. *Is she really like that, or does she have to practice that look?*

Mark looked up. "Thank you, Dr. Cartwright. It's so good to know they're safe, and now I can escort them back to Biloxi."

"About that," Cartwright said, "I have an offer for you."

Mark frowned. "What offer? I'm not leaving them alone again."

Cartwright adjusted her glasses. "Precisely. I'd like you to become CDC Headquarters' Chief of Physical Security."

"But wouldn't I have to stay here for that?"

Cartwright nodded. "Yes. But part of the offer is that your mother and sister can stay here free of charge. Room, board, security. And that security will be provided by you."

Mark's mouth dropped open. He looked at his mother. "What do you think, Mama?"

Michelle nodded. "Take it. Things are getting weird out there. I know we'll be safer here with you."

"OK," Mark said. "I'll take it."

"Excellent," Cartwright said. "You can go through inprocessing tomorrow." She pressed a button on the phone. "Please come in."

The door opened and Cindy appeared. "Take our new Chief of Physical Security and his family to their quarters, and show them where to eat."

Cindy ushered the family through the door. Mark stopped and looked back at Jen. "I'll introduce you and Zeke later. I really want them to meet you."

Jen waved him on. "Looking forward to it. Just enjoy the time with your family." Her thoughts went unbidden to her mother and father.

Cartwright clasped her hands and laid her elbows on her desk. "Miss Reed and Mr. Tripp."

Jen turned to her. "So what've you got in your black bag for us?"

Cartwright frowned. "Bag?"

"Sorry," Jen said. "Wizard of Oz reference."

Cartwright sniffed and her phone buzzed. She pressed her earphone and listened. "Very well. Send him in."

What next?

The door opened and a man stepped in. He looked a couple years older than Jen and wore a pair of snug jeans and a T-shirt that showed every muscle. While not a bodybuilder, he either worked out or had a physical job.

Jen's pulse picked up. *I hope this one's for me.*

Zeke yelled, "Wayne." He rushed the man, who caught his skinny frame in a crushing hug.

"Zeke, I've been worried about you. I thought you died when they nuked Anchorage."

Zeke released Wayne and gestured to Jen. "Jen and Mark saved me."

Wayne's gaze fell on Jen and she swallowed. *Hazel eyes.*

"Uh," she said, "Zeke saved us more than once, too."

Wayne's eyebrows rose and he looked at Zeke. "Really? How?"

"I had this great katana." Zeke mimicked slashing the air with a sword. "It wasn't real, but it was close enough. It broke on a zombie."

Wayne glanced at Jen and she nodded. "He's amazing with a katana."

"Then we'll have to find you a new one," Wayne said. "We're heading back to Rhode Island tomorrow."

Zeke froze. "But I can't go back. I have to watch over Jen." He turned to her. "What would she do without me?"

Wayne glanced at her and winked. "She can come with us."

Jen's face grew hot. *Is he coming on to me?*

"Impossible," Cartwright said. "Jen must remain here."

"Then I have to stay," Zeke said. "Sorry."

Wayne sighed. "I couldn't get you to leave Anchorage a few years back when I did, so I'm not surprised I can't get you to join me now."

The door opened and Cindy stumbled in carrying two wooden boxes, one about four feet long and the other half that. She placed the boxes heavily on the table, arranged them side-by-side, and left without a word.

"What's that?" Zeke asked.

Cartwright approached the table. "I'm offering the two of you positions in Homeland Security."

"I'm not into groping passengers at the airport," Jen said.

Wayne snickered, catching Jen by surprise. *A sense of humor, too. Take me now.*

Cartwright's face hardened more than usual, if that were possible. "Homeland Security, not TSA. You'll both work for me—Jen on the cure and virus mutations, and Zeke as protection for Jen."

Zeke hovered by the table. "But the boxes. What's in them?"

Jen caught Wayne's eye. "He must've been a riot at Christmas."

"You have no idea."

"The boxes," Cartwright said, "are part of your equipment. You'll receive firearms, a badge, and these."

"A badge?" Zeke said. "Do we get a car with a siren and lights?"

Cartwright's pushing too hard. "And what do the badges get us other than a discount at the donut shop?" Jen asked.

"You'll be federal agents. They'll get you access and assistance from pretty much any agency."

Zeke's eyes shined. "Come on, Jen. Sounds fun to me."

Jen frowned. *I'm getting boxed in.* "Will it get me military assistance when I go after Butler?"

Cartwright ignored her and pointed to the long box. "That's yours, Mr. Tripp."

Zeke pulled the box toward him and lifted it, testing its weight. "What can it be?"

He flipped three latches on it and tilted the top back. An audible gasp escaped his mouth. "Oh. My. God."

Zeke reached in and lifted a deadly, beautiful katana. "Stainless steel, thirty-six-inch blade." He stepped back from the others and gave it a practice swing. "The balance is perfect. I could take out a ton of zombies with this." His eyes met Jen's. "And this one won't break."

Cartwright's face wore the glimmer of a smile. She had Zeke. *And she knows that's one way to get to me.*

Jen pointed at the remaining box as Zeke removed a scabbard from his. "I suppose this is for me."

Cartwright nodded.

Jen opened the box and reached in, pulling out a tactical tomahawk. *Like the one Griffin had in Point Wallace.*

"The blade is eight inches and the length with the handle is almost eighteen," Cartwright said. "Doc told me you admired this weapon that someone had in Point Wallace."

Jen hefted it. "Damn this is light and balanced well." The sinister blade looked like it would cut through bone, and the sharpened steel point on the other end would no doubt pierce skulls.

She removed a sheath from the box looped her belt through it before inserting the tomahawk. "I suppose this is mine only if I stay."

Cartwright leaned against her desk and crossed her arms. "I understand why you want to go after Butler, and you could do that, but you would be dooming many people."

"Not if I kill him."

"Killing him won't stop the virus," Cartwright said. "We've got to stop the dead from coming back. Emergency protocols have been put in place, but they aren't enough."

"We heard about the protocols on the way here," Jen said. "I'm not surprised that killing people who may not be infected doesn't work well."

Cartwright took her seat. "There are more than that. Armed personnel are stationed at all hospitals to make sure the recently deceased don't reanimate EMTs go out armed. All pet mammals have been quarantined."

Jen lowered her eyebrows. "Just the mammals?"

Cartwright nodded. "We've determined that the virus only infects mammals. But even with the quarantine, there are plenty of strays and other wildlife that die of natural causes, then reanimate and infect others."

She clasped her hands together and leaned forward, her elbows resting on the desk. "The truth is we're just barely staying ahead of it. There have already been multiple outbreaks that could have spread out of control. With the military and national guard committed to the threat in the west, we rely on federal, state, and local law enforcement agencies, and it isn't enough. Local militias have been formed to help fill the gap."

Jen swallowed. *Two threats, Butler and the virus, and I can't battle them both at once.*

"OK," Jen said. "I'll stay and help with the vaccine." She walked to the door. "But once it's ready, I'm out of here and on Butler's ass. And I expect your help in getting to him." *And in the meantime I'm going to find out what's going on with those whacked-out zombies downstairs.*

5

The next morning Jen and Zeke strolled out of the administrative office. A shower, a good night's sleep, and fresh clothes had done Jen wonders. She stopped in the lobby and pulled her access card out. "I wonder how much of this place we can get into?"

Zeke scratched the shaved side of his head. No longer in a ninja costume, he wore a T-shirt with sleeves he'd carefully ripped off, and a pair of black cargo pants. Somewhere he'd found gel and had turned the hair on the unshaven side of his head into a series of spikes. "We should be able to go anywhere." He pulled his Homeland Security Agent badge from his pocket. "Bad boys. Whatcha gonna do?"

"Put that thing away, Dirty Harry. I don't think it's going to do much for you while we're here." She smiled. "But once we're on the road again, we'll travel like a boss."

Zeke shrugged and dropped the badge back into his pocket. "So what are we going to do? I'm already bored." He adjusted the katana scabbard on his back.

Jen strode to the elevators. "Cartwright's supposed to be in some meeting for the next few hours, so let me take you on a tour of the basement."

Zeke followed her into the car. "That doesn't sound very exciting."

Jen punched the bottom button. "It's right up your alley."

"Why?"

"They've got zombies down there."

Zeke's face lit up like a Christmas tree. "Can I kill some?"

When they arrived on the lowest level, Jen made a beeline to the card reader by the door. *Let's see how much Cartwright trusts me.*

She slid her card through the reader and the door answered with a buzz and a clunk. She pulled it open and stepped into the hallway.

It looked the same as it had the night before. Buzzing lights hung overhead, glinting off the tile floor. Not a speck of dust lurked in the corners, and the air held a slight tinge of ammonia.

"What's this?" Zeke asked.

Jen peeked in the first door's window. A young man lay in a bed with an IV in his arm. His sunken eyes stared at Jen. "Not sure. I don't know if they're treating them here, or using them to test the vaccine. I'm guessing they're guinea pigs."

She led Zeke to the windowless swinging doors that led to the zombies and pushed one open.

The zombies went into a frenzy, straining at their chains as soon as Zeke and Jen entered the room. Zeke reached back and gripped his katana's handle, ready to pull it into action.

Looks like they're only quiet when one of us is out here.

She strode to the lab door and pointed at Zeke. "Wait out here for a minute."

Zeke shrugged and leaned up against the wall with his arms folded.

Jen pushed the door open and eased it shut behind her. She didn't even need to press her ear to the door to know the zombies were still going apeshit. *Guess that disproves that theory.*

"Miss Reed," Dr. O'Connor's voice came from behind her. She spun. He sat on a stool, loading a syringe with an off-color liquid. "You're just in time."

Jen pulled the door open and waved Zeke in, then gestured to O'Connor as Zeke entered. "Dr. O'Connor. Doctor, this is Zeke."

O'Connor nodded at Zeke, then turned to a thirty-something lab tech with Clark Kent glasses. "Randy."

The lab tech looked up. "Yes, Doctor."

"You're with me on this one."

Randy wiped his hands on his lab coat. "Yes, sir."

O'Connor swept past Jen and Zeke and paused as he opened the door. "You'll want to see this, Miss Reed."

He led them to one of the cages. Inside, on a gurney, lay the older woman Jen had seen in one of the rooms the day before. *Why do they have her in a cage now?*

Randy removed the padlock from the cage door and held it open as O'Connor stepped inside. An IV drip ran into the woman's arm and a mask covered her mouth and nose while a machine on a wheeled table next to her made wheezing sounds.

O'Connor waved Jen in. The zombies raised their din to another level. O'Connor leaned toward Jen and Zeke. "Mrs. Jawolski volunteered to be a test subject for the vaccine. In return, her family is living in a government-secured location."

"What's wrong with her?" Zeke asked.

"COPD," O'Connor said. "She's at the end. That ventilator is the only reason she's still alive." He inserted the needle into a rubber stopper halfway up the IV line and pushed the plunger until the contents were emptied. "Randy?"

Randy looked at his watch. "Injection at 8:41 a.m."

Jen watched the old lady's face. Was she supposed to turn? To die?

O'Connor herded them out of the cage. "Now, we wait. Ten minutes." He strode into the lab.

Randy locked the cage door and followed the doctor.

"This science stuff is pretty lame," Zeke said. "I expected something more interesting."

Jen gave him a playful slap on the back. "Now that I think about it, damn near every time you say you're bored, it suddenly gets un-boring and we're up to our necks in zombie shit. How about wishing for something else for once?"

Zeke sighed. "I've got to take a leak."

Jen pointed to the lab. "Saw an open door in the back of the lab with a toilet."

"Be right back." Zeke disappeared into the lab.

The door closed behind him, and the zombie racket cut off. *Shit. So it wasn't my imagination last time.*

Jen walked up and down the rows of cages. Every zombie stood quiet and followed her with their eyes.

She stopped at one, a fresh-looking woman with a pinched face and wide shoulders. She reminded Jen of her sixth grade teacher, Mrs. Curling.

Jen stood right up to the bars and stared into the yellow eyes. No hunger. No hate. Just blank.

The zombie's eyes flickered and startled Jen. "What the hell was that?"

The lab door opened, and Mrs. Curling flung herself at the cage door. Jen tripped and landed on her ass.

Zeke stood in the doorway, laughing. He rushed over. "Sorry." He chuckled again and wiped tears from his eyes as he pulled her to her feet. "After all we've been through, I never expected you to get freaked out by a zombie in a cage."

Jen put a hand to her chest. Her heart felt like it was going to explode through her ribs. She took deep breaths until it calmed.

Zeke stopped laughing and put an arm around her. "Are you OK? I didn't mean to laugh."

Jen managed a smile. "Why not? I would've laughed at you."

He chuckled. "It was funny."

"Miss Reed." Dr. O'Connor and Randy stood at the old lady's cage. "Time to complete the experiment."

Randy unlocked the door, and O'Connor examined the old lady. "Blood pressure and heart rate unchanged. EEG shows decreased brain activity."

"What does that mean?" Jen asked.

"We believe the more active the virus becomes, the more it stimulates the brain," Randy said. "It's a good sign that the activity is down in the test subject."

"Significant," O'Connor agreed. "This is the first vaccine to achieve it."

He removed the IV from the old lady's arm. "Everyone leave the cell, please."

Jen stepped outside the cage with Zeke. Randy held the door open.

O'Connor turned off the ventilator and removed the old lady's mask. "Life support removed at 8:53 a.m." He rushed from the cage and Randy slammed it shut, securing it with the lock.

The ECG showed a continued heartbeat. The old lady's chest rose, and a startling gasp came from her lips. Her eyes opened, showing only the whites, and the old lady took a huge wheezy breath, then went still. The ECG flatlined.

"Time of death," O'Connor said. "8:55 a.m."

"How long before she turns?" Jen asked.

Randy kept his eyes on his watch. "Between forty and sixty seconds."

"Twenty seconds," Randy said. "Thirty...forty...fifty...sixty."

Jen watched the old lady. She hadn't moved.

"Seventy...eighty...ninety."

O'Connor licked his lips. "I think we may have done it."

"One hundred...one hundred ten...one hundred eleven."

"Randy, unlock the door."

Randy looked up from his watch. "Are you sure? Shouldn't we wait a little longer?"

O'Connor held out his hand. "Nonsense. The poor woman's been dead for more than twice the time of any other reanimation. Give me the key."

Randy handed O'Connor the key, and the doctor removed the lock. Jen and Zeke exchanged a glance. Zeke already had his hand on the hilt of the katana.

Jen slipped her tomahawk from its sheath. "Not sure that's a good idea."

O'Connor bent over the woman with a stethoscope in his ears, listening to her chest. "Remove the monitoring equipment from her."

Randy hurried to the other side of the bed and removed the blood pressure cuff from the old lady's arm.

O'Connor straightened with a smile. "I do believe we've done it."

The old lady's yellow eyes shot open and fixed on O'Connor.

6

The zombie rolled off the table and landed cat-like on the floor. Jen grabbed O'Connor by the collar and yanked him behind her. Randy turned to run but the zombie sprung onto his back, knocking him to the floor. Jen shoved O'Connor at Zeke and reared the tomahawk over her head. She brought it in a wide overhead arc and drilled the point into the old lady's skull. The zombie slumped and Jen pulled her off Randy.

Randy's lab coat was torn and bloodied. *Is that his blood or the zombie's?*

He scrambled to his feet, breathing harshly, and bent over with a hand on his back.

"Are you bit?" Jen yelled.

He shook his head. "I've got a bad back and the test subject just made it worse, but I'll be OK."

"Jen!" Zeke held O'Connor on his feet outside of the cage. The doctor's head sagged.

Jen pointed the tomahawk at Randy. "Stay where you are."

"What do you mean? I just told you I'm OK."

Jen backed out of the cage, shut the door, and locked it. "No time to argue. If you still have those baby blues in a half hour, then I'll let you out."

"Let me the hell out of here now." The lab tech rattled the cage door.

Jen sheathed the tomahawk and put an arm around O'Connor. "Let's get him in his lab."

The caged zombies continued with their racket. *That shit's getting old. I'm with Zeke. We should drop them.*

"Wait." Randy stood at the cage door. "He's got a heart condition. There are pills in his bottom right-hand desk drawer. Keys are in his pocket."

Zeke held the lab door open while Jen walked O'Connor inside and lowered him to the floor. O'Connor's complexion had gone pale and his breathing shallow. "Call for help," she said.

Zeke closed the lab door then picked up a phone and pressed a button. Seconds later, he said, "Emergency in Dr. O'Connor's lab. He doesn't look well." He paused. "Right."

Jen rummaged through O'Connor's pockets and pulled out a ring of keys. She rushed to the desk and tried one. It didn't turn. "Dammit."

The next key she tried didn't fit. She glanced at O'Connor. Zeke hovered over him. "Is he still breathing?" she asked.

Zeke's eyebrows knitted. "Barely."

Jen picked a small worn key and shoved it into the lock. She turned it and jerked the drawer open. Hanging files took up most of the drawer, but a small prescription bottle lay in the front. She snatched it up and ran back to O'Connor. Zeke had folded up a lab coat and placed it underneath his head.

Jen opened the bottle and shook out two pills. "Need water."

Zeke dashed to a water cooler and returned seconds later with a cup.

"Hold his head up," Jen said. She placed the two pills in O'Connor's mouth and tipped the cup to his lips. "Come on, Doctor. This'll make you feel a lot better."

The lab door burst open and two emergency medical technicians rushed in. Jen backed away next to Zeke.

The EMTs took O'Connor's vitals, then placed him on a wheeled gurney and rolled him out the door, the growls of the caged zombies filtering into the lab.

Jen sank into the chair at O'Connor's desk and leaned back. "Guess that vaccine didn't work."

Zeke poured himself a cup of water. "But it delayed the change. Maybe O'Connor's on the right track."

Jen grunted in agreement. *How much time do they have to get it right?*

She opened the drawer she'd found the pills in and replaced them. A name on a file folder tab caught her attention and she pulled it up. In scrawling handwriting, the tab had "Dr. Jeffrey Morgan, Project Svengali" written on it. She pried the folder open. It contained a half-inch-thick stack of papers. The first was a progress report from Morgan on CDC letterhead. *What the hell? That asshole actually worked here? Why didn't Cartwright tell me?*

The lab door opened and Rodriguez and Daniels strode in. "Dr. Cartwright wants to see you."

Jen eased the drawer closed with her foot and pocketed O'Connor's keys. She pushed past the agents and out the door. *Were the human experiments Morgan was charged with performed here as part of Project Svengali?*

Zeke nudged her and pointed to Randy's cage. The lab tech stood at the cage door watching them with his arms folded. "Think I can get out now?"

Jen strode up to the cage and looked him in the eye. "No yellow. Looks like you're clean."

Zeke opened the door and Randy stepped out. "How's Dr. O'Connor?"

Jen shrugged. "We gave him the pills and the EMTs took him away. They didn't tell us squat."

Randy ran a hand through his hair. "I came here to work with Dr. O'Connor. He's had these attacks a few times before, and each one seems to be worse."

He thrust out his hand to Jen. "Thanks for being so quick to help him out."

Jen shook his hand. "He'll be OK."

"I hope so." Randy shook hands with Zeke, then trudged toward the lab, stopping at the door.

"I owe you one," he said and disappeared into the lab.

CARTWRIGHT STOOD BEHIND HER DESK, staring out the window when Jen walked in. The doctor broke her trance and sat, then waved Rodriguez and Daniels away. "Dr. O'Connor is stable for now. Please tell me what happened."

"He gave the old lady the vaccine, waited ten minutes, then pulled the plug," Jen said. "She died and didn't come back within two minutes, so Dr. O'Connor assumed she wasn't coming back at all."

Zeke sat on the couch. "Dr. O'Connor went in to check her out and she popped up like a jack-in-the-box. Jen pushed the doctor through the cell door to me and took care of the zombie. Dr. O'Connor's face had paled and he couldn't stand on his own."

"We got him in the lab and gave him his pills," Jen said. "Before we knew it, the EMTs were there."

Cartwright steepled her fingers. "Two minutes? We're getting closer." She slammed a fist on her desk. "But not close enough." She leaned back in her chair and rubbed her eyes with the heels of her hands. "We're running out of time."

"It's not that bad, is it?" Jen asked.

"When the outbreak started in Alaska, we had time to rally the troops in most of the rest of the states," Cartwright said. "Thanks to you and Doc, we had information up front on how the zombies behaved and how best to kill them. And on top of that, we had troops deployed to most larger cities to avoid major outbreaks."

Cartwright sighed. "But with all the federal and National Guard troops now on the front lines, we're entrusting local law enforcement and civilian militias. Training videos on how to spot and suppress outbreaks and how to fight the zombies are playing constantly on TV stations, cable stations, and the internet. Despite this, more and more incidents are occurring. I fear we're on borrowed time."

Zeke moved closer to Cartwright's desk, a definite gleam in his eyes. "Sounds like we should get out there and kick some zombie ass."

Cartwright shook her head. "Not a chance. I need Jen here until we have a vaccine."

"I'm betting the mammals are causing the outbreaks," Jen said.

"Quite probable," Cartwright said.

Zeke cracked his neck. "We've seen zombie dogs."

"And a moose," Jen added.

Zeke's mouth dropped open. "Really? I would've loved to have seen that."

Cartwright plopped her open hand on the desk, a ring on her middle finger making a loud noise. Jen and Zeke looked at her.

"We've quarantined all pets," Cartwright said. "But how many squirrels die in a day? Skunks? Beavers?"

Shit. "It only takes one," Jen said.

"Exactly," Cartwright said. "That's why perfecting the serum is so critical. Dr. O'Connor believes that once he perfects it, he can make it deliverable by spraying from the air. That'll immunize the wildlife as well as humans. The military will send back aircraft to undertake that mission when we're ready."

Agent Rodriguez hurried into the room.

"What is it?" Cartwright asked.

Rodriguez glanced at Jen and Zeke. "That task you gave me this morning. I have an update."

Cartwright stood. "Would you two excuse us, please? I'll let you know if there's any news."

Jen led Zeke into the reception area. Rodriguez closed the door behind them.

Cindy walked in. Her pantsuit looked like it had been ironed only moments before. "Is there anything I can help you with?"

"We're good," Jen said as she continued into the hallway.

Zeke followed her onto the elevator. "Where are we going?"

"Outside," she said. "I need some air. Starting to get claustrophobic in here."

Jen pressed the "L" button, and the elevator doors slid closed.

I need to tell Zeke what I found out about Morgan, but not here. Once we're away from the buildings and any interruptions.

The elevator slowed and stopped. The floor indicator showed they were at the fifth floor.

The doors opened and a crowd of screaming CDC employees pressed inside.

"What the hell?" Jen yelled.

A woman with wild eyes shrank against the elevator wall. "Hurry! Close the doors before the zombies get in."

7

The crowd pinned Jen to the wall of the elevator. "Out of my way," she screamed.

She squirmed and pushed off the wall, but didn't go anywhere. "Zeke, we need to get out."

"Over here," he yelled. He'd been trapped in a corner by the panicked mass. Even as skinny as he was, he wasn't able to squeeze out.

He raised an arm above his head. Jen notice the gun in his hand just before he pulled the trigger. The discharge was explosive in the tight confines of the elevator and the babbling group of employees was stunned into a momentary silence.

"Get off this fucking elevator and let us out or we start shooting," Jen bellowed.

The employees blocking the entrance piled out, and Jen muscled a man in a cheap suit aside. She broke into the corridor, where a swell of humanity pressed back into the elevator as it complained with an earsplitting buzz.

The doors closed on three people still trying to get inside. Jen pulled a younger man back. "There isn't room."

He swung his fist at her face and she ducked. His momentum threw him into a tech, who pushed him off.

Zeke pulled the other two people from the elevator doorway and the doors slid shut.

"Now look what you did," a gray-haired woman with thick glasses shouted. Tears streamed down her face.

Jen pulled her pistol and raised it into the air. Zeke followed suit. The crowd quieted.

"Homeland Security Agents," Jen said. Zeke pulled his badge and raised it next to his gun. He had an odd grin on his face and his eyes gleamed.

Little shit's having a ball.

Jen lowered the gun. "I want two answers and I want them fast. Which way are the zombies and how many of them are there?"

A woman in a nurse's uniform pointed down the hall. "Medical wing. I saw at least eight, but there are a lot of people missing. They may have been bitten."

Jen removed the tomahawk from its holster. "I suggest the rest of you find the damn stairs instead of waiting around here. Now, out of our way."

The crowd parted and Jen and Zeke hurried down the hallway. When Jen glanced back, everyone had disappeared. *Good. Fewer people we have to worry about becoming zombies.*

The tactical tomahawk was much lighter than the axe she'd previously had, but she'd seen Griffin tear zombies apart with his. *I'll just have to get used to it fast.*

She stopped at the end of the hall and Zeke peered around the corner, his katana ready to strike. "Nothing."

Jen stepped into the corridor. A nurses' station stood empty, but an overturned cart of food and paper scattered across the tile floor told her the zombies had been through. Blood streaks decorated the walls like some gruesome avant-garde art.

A dripping sound came from the station. Slow and heavy. *Drip. Drip. Drip.*

Jen motioned Zeke to take the far wall and she huddled against the near one. She took a step and listened.

Another step and waited.

She and Zeke were in tune. As much as they'd faced together the previous few weeks, they'd learned each other's tendencies and had become a dangerous team.

Zeke motioned to the right. Jen nodded. They reached the station.

Corridors went off in four directions from the nurses' station. A set of double doors was closed on one, but the others were propped open.

The constant dripping grated on Jen's nerves. Jen stepped behind the counter and stopped. Blood pooled around a half-eaten heart on a shelf. It ran down the side until it ran out of shelving and dripped steadily on an upturned bedpan. Jen took a towel lying on the floor and tossed it over the bedpan. The dripping continued, but much quieter.

"Which way?" Zeke asked.

Jen considered the corridors. No use going into the closed one. *But which of the other three? Wish I knew the layout.*

Something flashed down the corridor on her left. Her peripheral vision picked it up, but it had disappeared by the time her eyes had snapped that way. Zeke looked in that direction, too.

"As good a choice as any." Jen entered the corridor. Zeke took the opposite side of the hallway and together they made their way down the hall. The doors they passed were solid, with no windows, and all closed. Jen opened the first one she came to. Baskets of laundry crowded the room, but there were no signs of anything, living or dead.

A clattering came from an intersection ahead. Something metallic hit the floor and spun, making a racket. Jen put a finger to her lips and motioned Zeke to move ahead with her.

She reached the intersection and scanned both ways down the corridor. A pan, like the type used to hold surgical instruments, lay on the floor several feet away.

"We're getting too deep in here," Jen said. "If there were zombies down here, they should've attacked by now."

O'Connor stepped into view at the next intersection. His glasses gone and his mouth stained red, he glared at Jen.

"So that's how this shit started." Jen sprinted toward him and O'Connor darted out of sight.

"Wait for me," Zeke yelled.

Double doors on Jen's right burst open as she passed them, and two dozen zombies spilled into the hallway between her and Zeke, who skidded to a halt and took a defensive position.

Five of the zombies turned toward Jen. She gave the tomahawk a hefty swing at the first one, but its light weight threw off her timing and the blade zipped inches from the creature's face.

Shit. She pulled her pistol and dropped the zombie with a shot to the forehead.

More zombies flowed from other doors. "Zeke. Run!"

Jen took off the other way down the hall and around a corner. She had ten yards of corridor before it became a dead end. "Are you shitting me?"

The last door on the left stood open. Jen sprinted through it, slammed the door shut, and locked the large deadbolt.

Zombie fists pounded on it, but the thick wood barely shuddered. *I'll be safe in here.*

She turned to survey the room and her mouth went dry. O'Connor stood in a corner several feet away, his yellow gaze fixed on her. Jen aimed the handgun at O'Connor's nose.

"Sorry, Doctor. Consider this your termination notice."

O'Connor continued to stare. *Like the zombies downstairs.*

Jen lowered the gun just enough for a better view of the undead doctor. She stepped to the right and O'Connor's eyes followed her. She moved to the left and he never broke eye contact.

"What the hell's going on?" she asked.

O'Connor tilted his head back like he was going to let loose with a screech, but he swallowed, his Adam's apple bobbing. He lowered his chin and reconnected his gaze with Jen.

A drop of sweat rolled down her cheek. *This is something new. Are they evolving again?*

O'Connor's mouth opened, then closed. *Damn thing looks like it's trying to talk.*

Entranced, Jen lowered the pistol to her side. "What are you trying to say?"

The doctor's jaw worked up and down. He looked like a fish out of water struggling for a breath.

"Jiinn."

The blood rushed from Jen's face. *Did he just say...*

O'Connor shook his head like a dog with a toy. He glared at her. "Jin."

You're telling me these fucking things are going to start talking now?

"Are you saying my name? Jen?"

O'Connor's head jerked forward, then back.

Jen gasped. "What the hell?"

Muffled gunshots came from the distance, getting closer. Jen took a step toward O'Connor. "Dr. O'Connor, is that you?"

O'Connor's head jerked to one side, and then to the other.

Jen took a deep breath. Her pulse raced and a rock settled in the pit of her stomach as an unbelievable thought rose in her mind.

It can't be.

"Butler?"

The corners of O'Connor's mouth pulled back in a grotesque leer.

8

Jen raised the pistol, her hand shaking. "I'm going to find you and enjoy killing you again, you son of a bitch."

The blast of a gun came from just outside the door.

O'Connor raised his arms in a surrender gesture.

"How are you going to surrender when you're not really here?" Jen aimed at his forehead.

"Help," O'Connor grunted.

Jen licked her lips. *How'd I get stuck talking to a dead man who's talking through a dead man?*

"Why the hell would I help you?"

O'Connor's mouth worked, but no sound came out.

The door burst open and three security officers rushed in, their handguns cocked and ready. The largest stepped in front of Jen and fired.

"Hey," she said, "I can take care of myself." She pushed the security officer to the side.

O'Connor lay flopped over a chair, the top of his skull missing.

Shit. Now I'll never find out what the hell is going on.

Jen spun. "Who asked you to do that?"

She looked up into Mark Colton's soft brown eyes.

He smiled. "You're welcome."

"Why'd you kill him?" she asked.

His brow furrowed. "What? What else do you do with a zombie?"

She bit her lip. *Shut up, Jen.* She shook her head. "Think I banged my head on the wall when you shoved me. I'm all right now."

"You should have someone look at that," Mark said.

Jen gave him a half smile. "Like I said, I'm fine. Besides, looks like the medical department's become a bit short-staffed."

A security officer with her blonde hair in a bun approached. "Chief, looks like we're clean."

"I want all security personnel not on perimeter duty to clear every room in every building on the campus. Start with this one," Mark said.

The security officer nodded and rushed out of the room, barking instructions on a radio.

Zeke jogged into the room, relief flooding his blood-specked face when his eyes met Jen's. "There you are," he said.

Jen pulled his lanky frame into a bear hug. "I don't know why zombies go after you. You wouldn't even make a quick snack."

Zeke gave her an awkward pat on the back and stepped back. "Except for worrying about you, that was a hell of a lot of fun for me and Crusher."

"Crusher?" Jen said. "As names go, it's better than Betty, but your katana slices. Wouldn't Crusher be a better name for a mace or a bat?"

"It's named after a character on TNG," Zeke said.

"TNG?"

"*Star Trek Next Generation.*" Zeke beamed. "Wesley Crusher."

Jen sighed. "If nerdism was a super power, you'd rule the world."

Mark rolled his eyes. "Let's get you two somewhere safe."

TWO HOURS LATER, Jen and Zeke walked into Dr. Cartwright's reception area. Cindy looked up from her computer. "Go right in." Without waiting for an acknowledgment, she went back to work.

O'Connor's assistant, Randy, leaned forward in a chair in front of Cartwright's desk, while the doctor faced a large monitor with a split screen. On one side was Howell's somber face and on the other was a young woman about Jen's age. She wore wire-frame glasses and sported short frosted hair. Cartwright glanced over her shoulder. "Good timing. Have a seat." She gestured to the empty seats in front of her desk.

Turning back to the monitor, she said, "Sergeant, I need a transport aircraft immediately. This is a matter of the highest national security."

"That's what I told the general, ma'am, but he shot me down. There's a fierce battle in Boise and all transport aircraft are needed there."

Jen took her seat. *I hate coming in on the middle of conversations.*

"What do we need the plane for?" she asked.

The woman on the screen said, "Is this Jen?"

Cartwright nodded and pointed at the screen. "Jen, this is Dr. Preston. Donna, this is Jen Reed."

Donna offered a petite smile. "Good to meet you, Jen."

"Pleasure," Jen said. "What do we need the plane for?"

"To bring Donna here," Cartwright said. "She works in a CDC-affiliated lab in Boston and is our next best option after Dr. O'Connor."

"I thought the train ran to Boston," Zeke said. "Why can't she take that?"

Donna rolled back from the screen so her wheelchair was in view. "Before the disaster, I would've had no problem taking the train," she said. "But now that it's the sole method of mass transportation, it's filled to capacity, which makes it very difficult to navigate in my chair."

Howell looked off camera. "Be right there." He turned to the screen. "Boise is critical and there's been another major attack. This time it's Phoenix."

He disappeared from the monitor and Donna's face filled it.

"Can't Randy work on it here?" Jen asked. "He worked with O'Connor."

Randy scoffed. "That's like asking an operating room nurse to perform brain surgery."

"Clearly that's not our best option," Cartwright said. She adjusted her glasses and looked at the ceiling. "We're out of best options, and now we're down to the best of the worst."

"Donna," she said, "if we can't get you down to our lab, we'll get our lab to you."

Randy frowned. "So I'm going to Boston? Not sure that's a safe trip."

Cartwright shot him a withering glare. "Relax, we need you here in case O'Connor left any written notes that haven't been transcribed into the system. You're the only one who will know where they are."

Randy's shoulders relaxed.

"No." Cartwright stood. "I'll send the serum on the train with some agents."

"Serum?" Zeke asked.

"Dr. O'Connor had two doses of the latest iteration of his serum," Donna said. "He used one in his last experiment."

"But it didn't work," Jen said. "So why do you want it?"

"It's the result of all his research," Donna said, "and I don't want to start from scratch if I can help it."

"Fine," Cartwright said. "I'll have two agents leave on tomorrow's train with the serum."

Donna stared from the screen. "As long as one of those agents is Jen."

"What?" Jen said.

Cartwright scowled. "I need Jen here."

"And Dr. O'Connor's lab notes are adamant that a component of Jen's blood is essential for the serum," Donna said. "I don't know how much I'll need."

"So the human pincushion needs to go along with the serum." Jen leaned back in the chair. "Great." *And it'll get me farther away from Butler.*

Cartwright stared at the wall. And uncomfortable silence fell over the room.

Cartwright turned back to the monitor. "I don't like this at all, but I don't see another solution. At least, not unless the military would shake some air transport loose."

Zeke jumped to his feet. "I go where Jen goes."

Jen smiled. *My hero.*

Cartwright sighed. "We'll set it up on this end. I'll send you the specifics."

Donna nodded. "Looking forward to it. And looking forward to meeting you, Jen."

Jen waved at the camera. "Same here. How about some of that famous clam chowder when we get there?"

"You've got it." The monitor went blank.

Cartwright swiveled the chair around. "Things are getting dicey out there, even on the east coast."

"I thought the protocols were keeping things under control?" Zeke asked.

"Go ask O'Connor how well that's turning out," Jen said.

Cartwright stood. "You'll leave on tomorrow morning's train. Jen will carry the serum, and Agents Rodriguez and Daniels will accompany you."

"My brother's heading home on that train," Zeke said. "Can he travel with us?"

"I think that's a great idea," Jen interjected. Zeke and Cartwright looked at her. Cartwright's eyebrows were raised.

Jen shrugged. "Safety in numbers, right?"

"Very well. Have him report with you to the armory to be equipped for the trip. Then muster outside the front entrance of this building by 6:00 a.m."

Zeke smiled. "Back into action."

Cartwright frowned. "Let's hope there's not too much of that."

9

J en yawned as the SUV wound through the Atlanta streets the next
morning. She felt the pouch threaded onto her belt for the
hundredth time. She unzipped it and pulled out the stoppered
syringe. *Can't believe this freaking thing is humanity's last hope.* She
returned it, making sure the padding inside was wrapped completely
around it.

They'd passed only a few pedestrians and bicyclists, and even fewer
vehicles. It had rained overnight and the sun baked the streets, evaporating
the puddles.

"I'll be glad to get out of this freaking humidity." Jen pulled her shirt
away from her chest.

"Where are all the people?" Zeke asked. "It's like a ghost town."

Agent Rodriguez glanced at him from the front passenger seat. "It's
getting worse every day." He cracked his neck. "A week ago we'd had our
first major outbreak in Atlanta, but now there are several every day."

"We had a couple in Providence," Wayne said, "but the rest of Rhode
Island has been pretty calm."

Zeke examined the cell phone he'd been given at the armory. "No social
media. No games. How can they call this a phone?"

"It's for calls only," Wayne said. He sat between Jen and Zeke and his
shoulder kept rubbing Jen's as the vehicle bounced over uneven roads.

Jen pulled her phone out. In a hardened case, it was pre-programmed with numbers for Cartwright, Howell, and everyone in the SUV. She rapped her knuckles on the case. "Could run this thing over with a tank and not hurt it."

The SUV swerved and Jen pressed into Wayne. She pulled back and murmured, "Sorry."

Wayne gave her a smile. "No worries."

Stop it, Jen. You've got a job to do. Don't start getting all gooey like in a bad novel. There's still an apocalypse going on.

A breeze caught discarded papers and they flew down the empty street. "Doesn't look like there's anyone left in the city," Wayne said.

"Everyone's holed up in their houses," Daniels said.

The SUV swung around a curve and Jen held onto the door handle to keep from tumbling into Wayne again. Two blocks ahead, a crowd filled the street.

"Looks like we found the party," she said.

"Shit," Rodriguez said. "Everyone stay close to me when we get out. We'll have to get through that mess."

Jen frowned. "I'm not comfortable with crowds right now."

Daniels looked at Rodriguez. "They're all trying to get on the train. It's the only reliable long-distance transportation unless you walk or bike." Rodriguez put a hand on the SUV driver's arm. "Stop here, Stan."

The vehicle pulled to the curb. The crowd's edge lay a hundred feet ahead.

Rodriguez turned to the others. "There's no time to be polite. We'll have to bull through. I'll lead and Daniels will take the rear. Stay with us and have your badges out when we get to the train."

"I don't have a badge," Wayne said.

"Stick close. We'll get you in," Daniels said.

Jen lined up behind Rodriguez, followed by Zeke and Wayne. Daniels called out from behind her. "Ready."

Rodriguez stepped into the milling crowd, holding his badge up. "Excuse me. Homeland Security. Let us pass."

Jen stayed on his ass as he wove through the mass of humanity. Halfway there, she glanced over her shoulder and was reassured that the others still followed close behind.

A woman's scream came from the top of the wide gradual steps leading into the terminal. Yelling and cursing followed, and the crowd converged on the spot, jostling and shoving. A fight broke out.

Someone slammed into Jen from her left and she stumbled, but managed to stay upright. *Don't want to fall in this mess.*

Rodriguez yelled over his shoulder, "We're gonna have to take a detour. This way."

He pushed to the left, and Jen glimpsed the crowd ten yards ahead. The people appeared calmer.

The fighting spilled down the steps like a wave washing over the mass of hot, sweaty Atlantans. Rammed again, Jen was shoved into a tall, beefy man who glared at her. He grabbed her arm and pulled her toward him. "Who the hell do you think you are?"

"You'll find out when I knee your balls up into your throat," Jen said. She tried to follow through on the threat but the mob was pressed so close together, she had no room to act.

Someone grabbed her other arm. Jen glanced over. Wayne had stretched out and clenched her upper arm. Zeke peered at her over his shoulder. He reached back and pulled his katana, but he might as well have left it in its scabbard for all the good he could do with it.

The beefy man wrapped one ham-sized hand around Jen's throat. "Just 'cause you're government doesn't make you special."

Jen choked and tried again to knee the asshole, but she was immobilized by the bodies pressing in on her. Dots speckled her vision as she struggled to breathe.

"Jen," Zeke yelled.

An explosion came from nearby and the hand released her. Jen's legs gave out and she collapsed to the ground, her lungs heaving for air.

Wayne lifted her to her feet. "Come on."

Everyone outside the station had hit the ground except the agents, Wayne, Zeke, and Jen. Daniels stood with his gun pointed into the air.

The beefy man stood and pulled a handgun from the small of his back. Rodriguez and Daniels put three bullets each in him before he dropped.

Zeke drew his katana and stepped over cowering civilians. "Can't let him turn."

The beefy man grabbed a young woman's arm and clamped it in his jaw. She screamed, and a two-year-old girl at her side cried.

Jen stepped on people to get to the child and snatched her up. Zeke sliced halfway through the beefy man's neck, but not before he'd bitten two more people.

The crowd panicked and fled for the street. Zeke lopped off the beefy man's head with his next stroke, and Wayne took position next to him with his bat. A teen zombie rushed him and he swung, but his timing was off and the zombie crashed into him, knocking him to the ground.

A well-placed bullet from Agent Daniels exploded out the back of the teen zombie's head. "We can't stay here to help. Our mission is too important."

With the toddler in one arm and her pistol in the other, Jen shot one of the yellow-eyed monsters sizing Wayne up. The baby screamed, tears pouring down its cheeks. "He's right," she yelled. "Zeke. Wayne. I need you with me."

The brothers backed toward her. Zombies sprung on humans in panicked flight.

Shots came from the terminal. Militia members stood in the doorways firing.

Jen followed Rodriguez as he dashed toward the terminal. Chaos reigned. A few gunshots boomed within the crowd, but they were quickly silenced.

The path up the terminal steps cleared as the mob rushed for the streets. Rodriguez bull-rushed up the steps and slammed into a thin middle-aged man with luminescent yellow eyes, knocking him to the side. Jen side-stepped a zombie and its throatless victim and ducked through the terminal door behind Rodriguez.

The train's doors were still open, but a line of armed men, in police uniforms and civilian clothes, blocked the only way through a makeshift fence. Panicked people pushed against it, threatening to knock it down.

Daniels zipped past the others, his badge held high. "Homeland Security. We need to get on this train."

The first of the zombies entered the terminal and clamped its teeth on an older man's shoulder. The crowd inside surged away from them, and many rushed the side entrances in a desperate attempt to escape.

"Path is clear," Rodriguez yelled.

Jen hugged the child tightly and sprinted for the gate.

Several rifles pointed at the group as they made the gate.

Rodriguez and Daniels shoved their badges against the chain links. "Homeland Security," Rodriguez said. "We have to be on that train."

A state trooper jogged over and glanced at the badges. "Let 'em in."

A man in cammies with no insignia lifted the latch and opened the gate.

More zombies surged through the doors. The men protecting the train opened fire. Jen cringed. The explosive sounds echoed off the walls.

Civilians behind the fence were lined up to enter the train. Rodriguez barreled through them, and Jen panted, trying to keep up.

The guard at the head of the line looked up as they approached. "Back in line."

Rodriguez showed his badge. "We're going on. You have thirty seconds to get as many of these people as you can on board and then this train is leaving."

Jen pushed past the guard and ran into the first car. A few startled passengers looked up.

"When are we going?" asked a thirty-something woman with short platinum-blonde hair and a Georgia twang.

Jen took a seat. The child, a girl, kept her face buried into Jen's shoulder.

Zeke and Wayne hopped on and took positions at the door. Both had their rifles aimed toward the gate. Zeke fired. Wayne glanced at him. "Now?" he asked.

"You don't wait for orcs to be slicing you up before you start swinging your sword," Zeke yelled.

Rodriguez zipped into the car, his eyes searching for something.

Daniels backed into the car, his pistol out and firing. "They're breaching the damn fence."

Got to help.

Jen tried to lower the child to the seat, but she whimpered and clamped her arms around Jen's neck.

Three figures darted into the car just as the doors closed. One barreled into Zeke, knocking him to the floor, another attacked the platinum blonde, and the third landed face-down in the aisle next to Jen.

The zombie in the aisle sprung to its feet and gaped at Jen and the girl with its hungry yellow eyes.

10

The zombie on top of Zeke was almost a mirror image of him. Its hair half dyed in blue and half in red made its yellow eyes seem almost stylish.

Jen pulled the little girl's arms from her neck and pushed her away from the aisle. The zombie from the aisle hit Jen full force before she could fire. Her gun hand flung back, slamming into the wall. Pain exploded in her wrist and the gun dropped to the floor.

Jen held the zombie back with a forearm across the throat, but the barrel-chested man was bigger and heavier than her. He snapped his jaws and lunged at the same time.

She kneed him in the crotch as hard as she could and the zombie lunged again. *Damn. They don't feel that?*

A hand grasped the zombie's shoulder and spun it around. Wrist throbbing, Jen fished her tomahawk from its sheath.

Wayne had the zombie by the shirt and reared back with the bat, but the zombie was too fast and tackled him onto the seat across the aisle. Wayne shoved the bat handle into the zombie's mouth, but it didn't let up.

Jen glanced to make sure the girl was all right, then brought the pointed end of the tomahawk down toward the back of the zombie's head. It moved at the last second, and the point ended up buried in its shoulder.

"Shit."

Jen yanked the weapon from its shoulder and swung again, planting the point firmly in the creature's skull. It collapsed on top of Wayne.

Zeke still wrestled with his attacker. Its teeth were inches from sinking into his throat and his arms trembled with the strain of holding it back. *He's not going to last.*

The platinum blonde had turned and tore a chunk of meat from a teenage boys arm before turning and leering at the little girl.

Shit. Zeke's about to bite it, but I can't let that monster bite the girl, either.

Jen grabbed the barrel-chested zombie and yanked it off Wayne. "Help Zeke."

Without waiting for an answer, she spun, bringing the tomahawk overhead, and sliced the platinum blonde's arm. Less than a foot from the girl, the blonde turned and hissed at Jen.

Pandemonium broke out in the front of the car as the teenage boy turned and attacked several other passengers.

This shit's getting out of hand. Jen lowered her shoulder and rammed the platinum blonde to the side. It stumbled, then leapt. Jen ducked and straightened as the zombie landed on her. She catapulted the blonde into the wall, where it fell to the floor, stunned.

The little girl shrank against the wall between the seats. A quick glance toward Zeke showed Wayne knocking the snot out of the zombie's skull with the bat.

Jen fell upon the blonde and chopped at its head with the blade. Once, twice, three times. Her lungs burned with the effort. Blood splattered in her eyes, and she stepped back and wiped them with her sleeves.

The blonde lay in an unmoving heap.

Rodriguez ran to the other end of the car and picked up a phone cradled on the wall. "Engineer? This is Agent Rodriguez of Homeland Security. You are ordered to get us the hell out of here."

A man slammed into the outside of the door, his eyes wide in panic. He clawed the edge, straining to pull on it. It took a second for Jen to recognize the state trooper.

A large woman in a torn and bloody floral print dress grabbed him from behind. She twisted his head and sank her teeth into his cheek. Blood sprayed the glass on the car door as she ripped flesh and muscle from the trooper.

"Start this fucking thing now," Rodriguez screamed into the phone.

The train jerked, almost knocking Rodriguez off his feet, and it slowly made its way down the track.

The platform was blood-splattered carnage. No one was left alive. Dozens of zombies rushed the train but fell away as it pulled out of the station.

Jen lifted the girl onto the seat and let her wrap her arms around her neck again. Zeke and Wayne sat on the floor in the corner and leaned against the wall, catching their breath. The bloody remnants of their zombie lay in front of them.

Daniels stood over the third zombie, a bullet wound in its temple.

Of the six passengers that were already in the train car when Jen arrived, only two still breathed. One, a boy barely in his teens, stood in the corner with glassy eyes and a trembling lip.

Across from him a burly guy in biker colors and a porn star mustache stood over two dead zombies. Blood dripped from a machete he held. He cracked his neck. "Don't usually get my workout so early in the morning."

Zeke stood and stepped over bodies to get to the biker. He held out a fist for the biker to bump. "I'm feeling ya. My name's Zeke, and I'm a ninja."

Biker Guy glared at Zeke from beneath bushy brows, his grip tightening on the machete handle.

Zeke lowered his arm and backed away. "We're cool."

Rodriguez sat on a bloodied seat and talked on the phone.

"Who's he talking to?" Jen asked.

Daniels wiped his hands on his suit coat. "Cartwright."

Wayne pushed past Daniels and approached the boy. "You OK, buddy?" The boy remained quiet.

Wayne took a knee in front of the boy. "I'm Wayne. What's your name?"

The boy's gaze rose to meet Wayne's. "Jamarcus."

He pointed to a thirty-something man sprawled at Biker Guy's feet. "That's Uncle Floyd."

Biker Guy licked his lips and moved away from the body.

"I'm sorry about your uncle," Wayne said.

Not only hot, but Wayne's a saint, too? I feel like I'm stuck in the Hallmark movie from hell.

Jen's heart ached for the boy.

Rodriguez snapped his phone shut and stood. "Listen up. Cartwright's getting resources in New York to meet us when we stop.

They'll quarantine the train and go through it car by car, but we'll be the first car."

"Who's Cartwright?" Biker Guy asked. "For that matter, who are you suits?"

"Homeland Security agents," Jen said. "All of us. And Cartwright's someone who can get shit done."

Biker Guy eyed her up and down as if he'd just noticed her.

"I'll vouch for you," Jen said. "You'll get out of here with us."

Daniels' eyebrows rose and he exchanged a glance with Rodriguez, who shrugged.

Biker Guy nodded. "You're a helluva fighter. What's your name?"

"Jen. Jen Reed. And yours?"

"Call me D-Day."

Zeke smiled. "That's so cool. I want a name like that."

"D-Day?" Jen asked.

D-Day wiped a smear of blood off his forehead. "Did I stutter?"

He grunted and sat on a dry section of seat, facing away from the others.

Guess he's done talking.

Jen checked the serum. *Still there. Still intact.*

She sat next to the girl the rest of the way to New York City. She never said a word, even though Jen tried to get her name.

The train rolled into the station. Armed law enforcement lined the platform, while a set of armed men in civilian clothes, each wearing a red arm band, stood in a group to the side. *Militia. There has to be a hundred of them.*

When the train stopped, the militia members disappeared toward the rear cars. A squad of armed men dressed in black with helmets and vests approached their car, their rifles up and ready.

Rodriguez stood at the door and pressed his badge to it. "Agent Rodriguez," he yelled through the glass.

The SWAT leader spoke into a mic clipped to his shoulder, and a few seconds later, the door whooshed open.

Rodriguez stumbled back as the squad rushed the car. Calls of "all clear" came from the SWAT members as they fanned out in the car.

A man in a blue jacket with the letters FBI on it stepped in. "Agent Rodriguez?"

Rodriguez raised his hand, then pointed at Daniels. "Agent Daniels."

The FBI agent nodded. "I'm Hess. All the rest are with you?"

"All except the kids and the biker," Rodriguez said.

Hess stepped out the door and waved another agent over. "Get these kids to DCS."

The little girl clutched Jen's neck so tight, she coughed. Prying the girl's arms away, Jen said, "Come on, honey. These people will take care of you."

Tears rolled down the girl's face as the agent took her. She screamed, "I want to stay with you. I want to be safe."

Jen swallowed and dropped her gaze to the floor. *I'm the last person to be around if you want to be safe.*

11

———

Hess led them to another platform, where a line of people waited to board a train.

"This looks a lot more organized than Atlanta," Jen said.

Hess nodded. "We have a ton of people wanting to get on, but we preprocess them a couple of blocks away. Only those who are boarding are allowed in the station."

He walked right up the line to the front, where a couple of militia men with red armbands stood cradling AK-47 style guns.

"National security," he said. "These folks go on first."

One of the militia men eyed D-Day. "The big guy doesn't look government to me."

D-Day stared the guy down and cracked his knuckles.

"He's with us," Rodriguez said.

There's a surprise.

Rodriguez gave Jen a slight nod.

"We can't fit him in this car," Hess said, "but we'll get him a seat a few cars back." He called a militia man over and pointed at D-Day. "Get the big guy in the closest car to number one that you can."

"Yes, sir." The militia man led D-Day farther down the line of cars.

An older couple stood at the front of the line. The lady was shooting daggers at the group with her eyes. "We paid to be here," she said. "It's a shame some people don't know their place."

This bitch would make a good zombie.

One of the militiamen guarding the train pointed to the first car. "Go on in," he said to Rodriguez.

Rodriguez waved them on. Zeke pushed past the old couple and gave the lady one of his patented silly grins. She scowled.

They entered the car and Jen plopped onto the back seat and adjusted the serum bag on her belt. Zeke went to sit next to her, but Wayne slipped in first. Zeke frowned and took the seat in front of them.

He turned around, his arm on the back of the seat. "Do you think we'll see some action up north?"

Jen sighed. "I hope not. Shit's stressful enough as it is. I wish I knew how it's going on the front."

Zeke shrugged. "Call Howell."

"Howell?" Wayne asked.

"He's our contact at the Pentagon," Jen said. "He'll give us the straight poop."

Rodriguez and Daniels took seats on either side of the aisle in the middle of the car. They leaned across the aisle and spoke in low tones.

"Are you going to call him?" Wayne asked.

Jen broke from her thoughts. "Who?"

"Howell," Zeke said. "We were just talking about him."

"Oh, yeah." Jen pulled her cell phone from her pants pocket and flipped it open. She scrolled down the list of pre-programmed contacts. All the members of the team were listed as well as Cartwright, Mark, and Howell.

She highlighted Howell's name and pressed the Call button. It rang on the other end.

A click, then "Howell here."

"Sergeant Howell, it's Jen."

"Jen. I heard you had a hard time getting out of Atlanta."

Jen laughed. "Nothing compared to making our exit from Spokane."

"I heard that," Howell said. His voice became serious. "I've got a ton of shit going on here, what can I do for you?"

Jen swallowed. "What are we headed into?"

"In Boston? Big city with some small outbreaks here and there, but they've been keeping the lid on it."

"That wasn't a small outbreak in Atlanta," Jen said. "I saw how it started, and it spread faster than Big Bertha's ass at an all-you-can-eat buffet. I don't want to imagine it happening like that elsewhere."

Howell didn't answer.

"Howell, you still there?"

His voice lowered. "I'm seeing that same pattern. I know the brass are worried about it, but they can't break any forces off to go back east and deal with it. Did you know Boise and Las Vegas fell?"

Shit. "But what if we have an outbreak here that can't be put down?"

"Then we're lost," Howell said.

Jen frowned. *If I didn't know Howell, I'd think he's losing hope.* "I'll get this serum where it's supposed to go and we'll shut this shit down before it gets too bad."

"We're all counting on you, Jen," Howell said. "Let me know if there's anything I can do for you. I have access to local law enforcement reports, satellite images, and intel reports."

"Will do."

"And Jen, keep me updated. Don't bother Dr. Cartwright. Call me instead."

Really?

"OK. Talk to you later." The call ended.

Zeke peered at her over the back of the seat. "So what did he say?"

"Hordes are still making gains out west and there've have been flare-ups in the east like what we saw in Atlanta."

Zeke smiled. "More zombies to kill."

Wayne raised an eyebrow. "You actually looking forward to that, little brother?"

Zeke turned back around.

Heat rose in Jen's face. She elbowed Wayne in the side. He flinched. "What the hell?"

"Your little brother saved me more times than I can count," she said. "He's trying to keep his head in the game, so don't fuck him up."

Wayne gazed into her eyes, then said, "I can protect you."

"Oh, great. The big testosterone-fueled man is going to protect little old me." She poked a finger in his chest. "I've killed far more zombies than you've ever seen. Maybe I should protect you."

Wayne's lips pressed together and he looked away.

"I said Zeke saved me," Jen said. "I didn't say he protected me. We protected each other, and so did a lot of other people. Most of them are dead."

She sat back in her seat and crossed her arms. *Welcome to the real world, dude.*

Passengers boarded. The first were the old couple. They took the first seat on the right. The lady placed a coat-draped case between them. She glanced back and her eyes met Jen's. The old bag scowled and turned away.

What's she got in that box? Gold bricks? Or maybe something more valuable like a personality?

Zeke was twisted around in his seat, facing her. "Can't wait to get going, but there are still empty seats."

"I wonder how many seats are in this car," Jen said.

"Sixty-two," Zeke replied.

"Now how the hell did you know that?"

"I counted when we came in."

A thirty-something balding man with an enormous beer gut and a scowl led a mousy woman to the seat across from the old couple. "In here, honey," he said as he guided her to the seat.

The woman's eyes darted back and forth. It looked like a loud cough would be enough to send her into a panic.

Perfect person to be with in a zombie apocalypse.

The old lady up front surveyed her fellow passengers, most dressed in casual clothes. She whispered something to her husband.

Poor rich bitch has to put up with the rabble.

The doors whooshed closed and the murmur of conversation picked up in the car. Rodriguez and Daniels broke off their conversation and sat back in their seats.

A voice crackled from the speakers. "Ladies and Gentlemen, this is your conductor. We are about to begin our journey to Boston, Massachusetts, with stops in between. All cars are full to capacity and all seats taken, so please remain in yours. Nonessential cars have been replaced with passenger cars for maximum capacity, so there are no food and beverage services on this route."

"No beer?" Beer Belly wailed.

The train jerked and rumbled from the station. Breaking into daylight, it picked up speed. Jen looked out the window, squinting her eyes in the light. She jostled shoulder to shoulder with Wayne, but neither of them spoke.

The train rolled through the city and picked up speed. Several passengers leaned back and closed their eyes.

This'll be a piece of cake at this rate.

The conductor burst in from the next car and spoke in hushed tones to Agent Rodriguez. Rodriguez picked up the direct line to the engineer and listened. He pulled the phone from his ear and looked at the conductor, shaking his head.

So much for the piece of cake.

The conductor disappeared into the next car and Jen caught Rodriguez's gaze and shrugged.

Rodriguez beckoned Daniels over and whispered something to him. Daniels frowned.

Jen jumped up and made a beeline to the two agents. "What's going on?"

Daniels motioned for her to lower her voice. "Don't want to panic anyone."

"The engineer's not answering his intercom," Rodriguez said.

"Is that unusual?" Jen asked.

"According to the conductor, the only time that's ever happened was when the intercom wasn't working or the engineer had a medical emergency. Since they did a successful sound check before they left, he's concerned for the engineer."

"What have you got in there?" Beer Belly's booming voice filled the cab.

He stood in the aisle glaring down at the old lady, who cringed away from him. Beer Belly pointed at the covered case between the old lady and the old man. "There's something alive in there."

Rodriguez and Daniels exchanged a glance, and Daniels strode toward the front.

Passengers craned their necks to get a view of the disruption at the front of the car.

"Mind your own business," the old lady snapped. "You don't know what you're talking about."

"Oh, I don't, do I?" Beer Belly lunged and grabbed the case. The older couple latched onto it like their lives depended on it.

"Help," the old lady screamed.

Daniels reached Beer Belly and put a hand on his shoulder. "Let it go and sit down."

Beer Belly let go of the case. "Who the hell do you think you are?"

The old lady and the old man fell backward with the suddenly freed case. It slammed into the wall and fell to the floor.

Jen stood to see. The coat had fallen off and exposed a plastic animal carrier with a wire frame door. The door had popped open and something inside stirred.

With a deep growl a bloodied cat with piercing yellow eyes sprung from the carrier and landed on Beer Belly's thigh. He screamed when the cat bit through his pants and shredded his leg.

12

Daniels stumbled backward and the old lady let out a wail. "My Buttons. Don't hurt my fur baby."

Beer Belly swatted the cat off his leg, tripped, and fell onto his seat. His wife shrank against the wall.

The cat leapt onto Daniels' chest and clawed his suit. Daniels pulled his pistol and bashed the cat with the butt, knocking it to the floor, where it skittered underneath a seat.

Passengers pulled their legs from the floor and stood on their seats while the old lady went to her knees and crawled down the aisle. "Here, Buttons. Mommy's here."

The old man stumbled, clutching his chest, then collapsed out of sight.

Jen pushed past Wayne. "See if you can bash the cat."

She pulled her tomahawk while Wayne picked up his bat and Zeke unsheathed his katana.

"Not a lot of room in here to swing," Zeke said.

Beer Belly's wife screeched as her husband pounced on her, pinning her to the wall. He clamped his teeth on her throat and her cries died in a gurgle as he shook his head and ripped her throat out.

A gunshot went off and the back of Beer Belly's head disintegrated. He fell off the seat and sprawled on the floor.

The cat sprang onto a woman's chest and bit her shoulder. Jen charged and swung at the zombie cat. It leapt onto another passenger, and Jen's blade ended up in the wounded lady's neck. "Shit!"

The lady's cloudy eyes turned to Jen. *Already turning.*

Jen freed the blade, twisted the handle, and slammed the pointed end into the lady's temple. She dropped to the floor.

Zeke stood at the back, his katana at the ready, but he didn't attack. *He's afraid of hitting someone uninfected.*

Beer Belly's wife jumped on a twenty-something man's back and bit into the back of his neck while the old man had turned and proceeded to peel the flesh from his wife's cheek.

"Daniels," Rodriguez yelled.

Daniels stood in the middle of it all, his back to Jen. He spun when his name was called, and drool spilled from his mouth as he eyed a meal.

Rodriguez fired, the bullet entering Daniels' eye and spraying blood, flesh, and bone as it exited from the back of his skull.

The cat jumped onto the seat in front of Jen, its gaze locked on her. A flash from the corner of her eye, and an aluminum bat slammed into the spot the cat had been a second earlier.

"This shit's out of hand," Jen said. She raced to the door to the next car and grabbed the handle. Through the window, nervous passengers stood and stared at her.

She jerked the door open. "In here. Now."

Wayne slammed the bat into a charging zombie, hitting it in the ribs and knocking it to the side. Jen grabbed his shirt collar and yanked him off balance. "Leave it."

He stumbled into the next car and Jen followed. Zeke rushed in and Rodriguez stood at the doorway, firing wildly.

The passengers in the second car screamed and mobbed the back door.

Several zombies rushed Rodriguez, one up the aisle, two more leaping from neighboring seats.

Halfway through the door, he pulled the trigger and his gun clicked empty. He stumbled backward and slammed the door, but two bloodied arms prevented it from closing all the way.

The passengers bottlenecked at the back door. Jen grasped Wayne's arm and pointed at the fleeing passengers. "Help them out. We need the way clear in case we have to retreat farther. Make sure you keep the door propped open."

Wayne nodded and dashed to the back of the car.

Jen rushed to help Rodriguez. She chopped at one of the intruding arms, but it didn't withdraw and the door pushed wider a couple of inches.

Zeke struck the best he could with the limited room, but it did little good.

His teeth gritted and face red, Rodriguez strained to keep the door from flying open. "You go," he said. "We need you to make it to Boston."

"You can't let this door go and get to the next car in time," Jen yelled.

"I know."

"We're clear." Wayne stood at the back door. The last of the passengers were already halfway through the third car.

Jen pointed to Wayne. "Let's go, Zeke."

Jen dashed down the aisle and through the door. She turned just as Zeke made it into the car. The door Rodriguez held had opened more than two feet. Two zombies had pushed their upper bodies partially in, and more arms had snaked their way through, putting pressure on the door.

Rodriguez gave a groan and collapsed. A zombie wave poured over him and into the car.

Jen shut the door and it latched. Seconds later several zombies slammed into it, smearing the window in blood.

Jen turned to the others. "That's one solid-ass door—"

Zeke and Wayne stood halfway down the aisle battling five zombies. *What the hell?*

Jen unholstered her pistol and shot at a zombie in a beanie cap missing half its face. Rushing Wayne, it fell back as the bullet slammed into its chest, but quickly recovered.

Jen grasped the pistol in both hands and took a deep breath, then held it. She squeezed the trigger, absorbing the satisfying recoil and the sight of what remained of the zombie's face collapsing around its nose.

Wayne pounded the temple of another zombie with the bat and Zeke made an abbreviated slash with the katana and left a teen goth zombie with its neck halfway severed.

"Where they hell did they come from?" Jen yelled.

A blur zipped from her right, and she ducked just as the zombie cat sailed over her. *Son of a bitch!*

She holstered the pistol and yanked the tomahawk from its sheath as she scanned for the devil cat. "Where the hell did you go?"

Her eyes fell on the open door to the next car. "Tell me it isn't chasing the rest of the passengers."

She rushed the aisle, slashing and knocking zombies to the side. Wayne cracked the skull of a woman who collapsed back into two other zombies.

"Keep moving," Jen yelled. "Almost there."

Something grabbed her arm and she jerked back as a heavy man with a bloodied eye socket dipped his head to take a chunk out of her. Kicking out, she connected with one of his knees. He lost his balance and Jen threw him backward. He fell onto the floor in the doorway, blocking access to the fourth car. Jen brought the tomahawk overhead and jammed the point through the zombie's good eye and into his brain. He went limp.

Lungs heaving, Jen leaned on the doorway and looked into the fourth car. The outbreak had spread there and she faced more than twenty fresh zombies.

Wayne and Zeke had reached her. Eight more zombies pursued them, all the rest having been destroyed or moved into the next car.

"Change of plans," Jen yelled. "We stay in this car. Take the rest of them out."

Zeke stepped next to Jen. "Stay back." He pressed into the remaining zombies, his katana a blur around him. No longer worried about hitting a human, he spun, swung, and danced down the aisle, thinning out the remaining zombies until only one remained.

A shot took that one down, and Wayne stood behind Zeke with his pistol pointed at the zombie and a smile on his face.

More zombies entered the fourth car from the back and rushed up the aisle as Jen tried to close the door, but the heavy zombie she'd killed blocked the door from closing.

"Look," Zeke yelled.

Jen turned back to the third car. The old man was fumbling with the door latch.

"The old man's a fucking leader," Jen yelled.

The door between the second and third cars slid open and the horde burst through.

13

The old man lurched into the second car, his intense yellow gaze on Jen. She grabbed the dead zombie blocking their escape. "Help me."

Zeke and Wayne pitched in and they rolled the zombie out of the way.

Zeke ran into the fourth car and took a stance halfway down the aisle. Jen pushed Wayne through. "Back him up."

Wayne raced down the aisle and Jen stepped into the car, closing the door behind her. The horde up front held back, and the old man stumbled toward the door.

"Oh, hell no." Jen pulled her pistol and let the old man get closer. When he was only fifteen feet away, she slid the door open a foot and propped her gun against it for stability. A quick aim and a squeeze and she hit the old man in the neck. The horde roared and pushed forward.

Sweat pouring down her back, Jen aimed again. The horde had just about reached the old man and would be on her in a few seconds. Time slowed. Jen lined up the sights and held her breath. Fighting the urge to hurry, she squeezed slow enough to make sure she didn't pull the sights off target.

The pistol boomed and recoiled. A hole appeared in the old man's forehead and Jen leaned back, slamming the door shut. Three fingers made it through the doorway and were sliced off when the door closed.

The horde roared and banged on the door. Jen gave them the finger and spun to help out Zeke and Wayne.

Her breath hitched as she took in the scene. Zeke and Wayne stood side by side in the middle of the car. Waves of zombies pushed forward, the seats the only thing keeping them from sweeping over the brothers.

Jen aimed at a middle-aged woman in a bloodied pantsuit and put a bullet in her temple.

Wayne knocked back a zombie climbing over a seat.

Zeke beheaded a young man charging down the aisle, then spun and sliced at a teen goth girl who'd climbed on the back of a seat and squatted there like a gargoyle on a medieval church.

Jen shot another zombie about to reach Wayne. *We are so screwed.*

She holstered the pistol and drew the tomahawk. Darting forward, she planted her blade into a one-armed zombie's forehead. Stunned, but still undead, it struggled to its feet and Jen finished it off with a second blow to the same spot.

Another zombie pushed up the aisle between Jen and Zeke. Zeke was locked in a struggle with a wiry, athletic zombie coming over the seat. It had avoided the swings of his katana, but was kept off balance and unable to attack.

Jen took on the aisle zombie and swung sideways with the tomahawk, planting the pointed end in the zombie's temple. It dropped like its strings had been cut, but took the tomahawk with it.

No time to get it.

She yanked the pistol from its holster and shot the two closest zombies point-blank in the head. She shoved one on top of the other, which slowed a third that was creeping up on her.

Too many. Getting tired.

A booming voice came from the other end of the car. "Work your way to me."

Jen looked up. D-Day's head and shoulders towered over the zombies, his machete rhythmically mowing down the undead.

She retrieved her tomahawk and attacked with new energy. *Maybe we can get through.*

The bodies had stacked up in the aisle, which kept the zombies from rushing them full force, but also blocked Jen's way forward.

"We can't get them all," D-Day said. "Make your move now. Straight down the middle."

Zeke hopped onto the pile of bodies blocking the way and took out two zombies climbing over. His eyes were wide and maniacal and his face was splattered in blood.

Jen ran to Wayne. "Follow Zeke. I'll be right behind."

Wayne shook his head. "I'll take the rear and cover you."

Here comes the freaking testosterone. "I need you to help clear the way with Zeke. The rear is easy. Is that what you want to do?"

Wayne pursed his lips, then dashed to join Zeke. He leapt onto the body pile and jumped off with the bat over his head. He landed next to Zeke, the bat crushing a redheaded zombie's skull.

D-Day reached the brothers. Both of his bare arms were wrapped in clothing and taped. He used them to push back snapping zombies. Even when one latched onto his arm, its teeth didn't penetrate to the skin.

Smart idea.

D-Day glared at her. "Now."

Jen raced toward the others. She jumped onto the pile of bodies and used it as a springboard to leap down the aisle, avoiding several zombies spilling in from the seats.

D-Day turned and rumbled toward the back door like a human plow, his forearms pushing back the remaining undead.

Jen split one zombie's skull and avoided another's grasp as she hurried to catch up.

D-Day reached the back door and yanked it open. Zeke and Wayne sprinted through the door.

Six feet away, D-Day yelled, "Duck."

He swung the machete at Jen's head and she dove for the floor, tumbling through the doorway. She slammed into Wayne's shins, taking him down.

A zombie woman's head rolled in behind her and came to a stop between her outstretched legs.

D-Day slashed another zombie across the face, then backed into the car and slammed the door shut.

The zombies piled up at the door. Jen stood and brushed off her pants. "Thanks. Good thing for us you were on board."

He shrugged. "First thing I saw was people running down the aisle. It was like a cattle stampede. I looked to see what scared them and this car had a bunch of zombies tearing into people."

He patted his sheathed machete. "Figure I'd take a few of 'em out then join the cattle, but that's when I saw you guys."

Zeke sheathed his katana. "Maybe we should just stay in here. Both doors are secure."

A low rumbling came from beneath the seats. It grew into a maniacal growl, then a figure streaked across the aisle and disappeared under the seats on the left.

Jen hefted her tomahawk. "That fucking cat. That's what caused this shit storm."

"Then we've got to kill it." D-Day raised his machete.

"I'll get it." Wayne crept down the aisle, his bat cocked over his shoulder.

"Wait," Jen said. "We need to do this together."

The cat sprang at Wayne and he swung wildly, clipping the cat and knocking it back between the seats.

Wayne scrambled back to the others, his eyes wide. "Damn, that thing is fast."

Zeke kept his eyes on the seats. "How do you want to do this?"

Jen took a deep breath. "Zeke, you and I will each take a side of the aisle. We climb over one seat at a time together."

She pulled her pistol and handed it to D-Day. "Get down on the floor with the pistol. If the cat tries going underneath, take it out."

Wayne looked at her. "What do you want me to do?"

Now there's an attitude change.

"Stand back with D-Day and watch the aisle. In case D-Day misses, you're his backup if it charges him."

"I don't miss," D-Day said.

Jen climbed onto the first seat on the left. The next seat was clear, but she couldn't see all of the third seat.

Zeke crouched on the seat on the right, his eyes surveying the tops of the seats in front of him.

"Anything, D-Day?" Jen asked.

D-Day lay on his side with his back to the door and the pistol in his outstretched hands. "It ain't on the floor."

Jen caught Wayne's eyes. He nodded. "Ready."

"Next seat." Jen stepped onto the next seat as Zeke did the same across the aisle.

"I'm clear," she said.

"Same," Zeke said.

"Next seat," Jen said.

Jen froze as her lead foot touched the seat. She held up her free hand and listened.

A soft purring came from somewhere ahead. "Is that on my side?"

Zeke squinted and tilted his head. "Can't tell, but it's not far off."

"Still nothing on the floor," D-Day said.

Jen's heart pounded and her mouth went dry. *Is this it? Am I going to be taken out by a cat?*

She brought her other foot over and stood on the seat. Nothing in the next seat. She looked at Zeke and he shook his head.

"Next seat," she said.

With a high-pitched growl, the cat launched itself at Zeke's face. He ducked and brought his sword up. The cat sailed over him and missed the blade by a half inch. It landed on the floor in the aisle, then sprung at Jen without hesitating.

A shot went off and Jen flinched. The yellow-eyed beast sailed through the air, its claws out stretched.

Jen brought the tomahawk around with all her strength, but it would be seconds too late.

The silver barrel of an aluminum bat flashed by Jen's face, barely missing her, and slammed into the cat, sending it flying into the wall, where it hit with a crack and fell to the floor.

Another gunshot. "Got it," D-Day yelled.

Jen plopped to the seat and put a hand to her face. *That was too fucking close.*

Wayne stood over her, concern in his eyes. "Are you OK?"

Jen nodded. "Yeah. I'm good."

He nodded and turned.

"Thanks," Jen said.

He looked back at her and smiled. "We all watch out for each other, right?"

She found herself smiling back. "Right."

He held out a hand and she took it and pulled herself up. They stood face-to-face a few inches apart. His eyes were a deeper hazel up close.

He leaned toward her and her heart picked up again, but not from fear, not from exertion. His lips were inches away from hers. She closed her eyes in anticipation.

"Jen," D-Day said.

She blinked and stepped back from Wayne. *What the hell was I thinking? About to make out with a guy in the middle of a zombie apocalypse? It's like a bad movie.*

She turned to D-Day. "What's up?"

He pointed to her waist. "Didn't you have a pouch belted around you?"

Jen followed his gaze. The pouch with the serum was gone.

14

"The serum," she shouted. She checked the seats she'd climbed over and examined every inch of the floor.

"Fuck," she screamed.

"So it was important?" D-Day asked.

Zeke put his head in his hands. "Only the cure for the zombie virus."

"A cure?" D-Day said. "Then why the hell did Jen have it?"

"It's not the cure," Jen said, "but the closest thing to it. I was bringing it to a research lab in Boston to finish it."

Wayne put an arm around her shoulders. "Do you know where you lost it?"

She pushed away from him. "If I did, I would've known that I'd lost it. It could be anywhere in the cars ahead of us."

"Anywhere there are zombies," D-Day said.

Jen's phone rang. "Great. What's next?"

She flipped the phone open and put it to her ear. "Yeah?"

"Jen?" Cartwright's voice hit her like a ton of bricks. *Does this woman have a sixth sense about bad news?*

"Dr. Cartwright," Jen said.

Zeke's eyebrows shot up. Jen put the phone on speaker.

"What's the situation?" Cartwright asked. "Agent Rodriguez was supposed to check with me every hour."

"Rodriguez and Daniels are dead."

"What?"

Jen took a deep breath and let it out. "There was an outbreak on the train. Both Rodriguez and Daniels gave up their lives to keep me safe."

"And you're safe now?" Cartwright asked.

The best thing to do with Cartwright is tell her the truth up front. "We are right now, but we're going to have to go back into the infected cars. The strap on the pouch must've broken during the fighting. The pouch with the serum is in one of those cars."

The phone went silent except for Cartwright's soft breathing.

At least she didn't have a heart attack.

"You must retrieve it," Cartwright said.

No shit. Why didn't I think of that? "We're trying to figure out the best way to do that."

"Hold on," Cartwright said.

The phone clicked, then a tired voice said, "Howell here."

"Sergeant Howell," Cartwright said, "we need your help with the serum."

"Not sure what I can do," Howell said.

"We had an outbreak on our train," Jen said. "The first three cars are full of zombies and the serum is in there."

Howell's voice picked up. "Let me get a railroad contact on."

Another click. Jen looked at Wayne and he shrugged. Zeke was cleaning the blade of his katana on a discarded sweatshirt, while D-Day sat on the edge of a seat staring out the window.

"Jen?"

"Here."

"There are direct-line phones on the wall of each car. Pick it up and the engineer will answer."

"They've already tried that," Cartwright said. "The engineer isn't answering."

"Hold," Howell said.

He came back a minute later. "Railroad communications can't raise him, either. This is a bigger problem than just the serum."

"What do you mean?" Wayne asked.

"Boston is the end of the track. If that train comes in at its current speed, it'll crash and release the zombies in the middle of Boston."

"That's irrelevant," Cartwright said. "If it crashes, it could destroy the serum."

"Are there any surviving passengers?" Howell asked.

"We're not sure," D-Day said. "A bunch of them fled to the back, but we had a zombie cat going around biting people. This whole train could be full of undead."

Cartwright cleared her throat. "Who is that who just spoke?"

"D-Day," Jen said. "Without him, we wouldn't have survived."

"I've got you identified by satellite," Howell said. "You have some low bridges on your route that are over bodies of water. You can jump off into the water."

"But not without the serum," Cartwright said.

"I'm open to suggestions," Jen said.

D-Day stood. "Stop the train and open the doors. The zombies will wander off and we can go through the cars and find the pouch."

"Then we start the train back up and head to Boston," Wayne said. "But how do we run the train?"

Zeke smiled. "From the engine. We climb on the roof of the cars and walk right over the zombies to the engine."

Jen exchanged a glance with D-Day. The crazy-ass biker grinned. *He's eating this shit up.*

"Can you do it?" Howell asked.

Jen shrugged. "As good an idea as any."

"There's a station in Kingston, Rhode Island," Howell said. "It's pretty rural and I can alert the state troopers to set up there if you think you can stop it in time."

Wayne shuffled his feet. His head was down, but he'd been listening. "Even if we get to the engine, we don't know how to stop it."

"I'll get an engineer on the line to walk you through it," Howell said.

Jen looked at the others. Zeke grinned and gave her a thumbs-up. Wayne looked her in the eye and nodded. D-Day stood. "I'm up for it."

"Looks like it's a go," Jen said. "We'll let you know when we're in the engine."

"Roger," Howell said. "I'll be ready."

The phone clicked.

"Jen," Cartwright said.

"Yes?"

"Mankind is counting on you." The phone clicked dead.

Jen blew a raspberry. "What a stirring motivational speech."

D-Day pulled the handle for the outside door and slid it open with a whoosh.

Jen held her hands over her ears. "I hadn't realized how much of the noise the cars kept out."

"I'll go first." Zeke approached the door and stuck his head out, the wind making the spikes in his hair bend. The door was at the back end of the car. Zeke held onto the inside of the doorway as he swung the other half of his body out.

Jen's heart skipped a beat as he pulled himself outside. She ran to the door. Zeke was around the back corner of the car. "There are a couple of places to grab," he yelled as the wind battered him and his clothes flapped. "Make sure you have a good grip before you come around."

He looked up. "There are handholds all the way to the roof. Just take it slow and keep your grip." He disappeared around the corner.

Wayne moved to the doorway. "I'll go next." Without another word, he grabbed the inside handhold and swung himself around the outside of the cab. Even faster than Zeke, he disappeared.

D-Day moved next to Jen and grabbed the back of her shirt. "I'll hold you just in case. When you're ready to go around the corner, nod at me and I'll let go."

"Got it."

Jen grasped an inlaid metal handle just inside the doorway and positioned her right foot beneath it. D-Day grabbed her shirt. "Any time you're ready," he said.

Jen took a deep breath and flung her left arm and leg out and around the outside of the car. Her hand slid down the side and ran into a handhold but she couldn't hold on. Her heart banged like a bongo drum as her left side fell from the car. Lifted by the back of her shirt and pulled in, she was able to keep her balance and ended up back in the car.

"Don't know if I can do this," she said.

D-Day's eyebrows lowered. "Bullshit. Don't even think that. Did you feel anything to grab on to?"

She nodded. "About a foot lower than where my hand landed."

"Then now you know what to expect. Go again."

Jen licked her chapped lips. She bent her knees slightly, then leapt. Her hand slapped the smooth metal side of the car and slipped down. She curled her fingers and a split second later they slid into the handhold. She scrambled with her left foot and found a narrow outcropping to prop it on.

Looking up, she saw the handholds Zeke had talked about. Zeke stood on top of the roof and cupped his hands around his mouth. "Don't come up yet. Move to your left so that your right foot and hand are on something stable outside of the car."

Jen nodded. A couple of feet to her left were similar handholds. Jen nodded at D-Day and he released her shirt. She gulped. *No safety net.*

She gingerly brought her right foot to her left, then her right hand to her left. Arms trembling, she concentrated on the handholds on her left and moved her left hand to one and gripped it. Then her left foot to the one below it.

"I've got it," she yelled.

Zeke's beaming face looked down and he clapped, then motioned for her to climb.

Jen grabbed a handhold above with her right hand, pulled herself up, then found another with her left.

She stabilized her feet.

The train hit a sharp corner and Jen slipped, her feet flying out with the centrifugal force of the turn. Hanging only by her fingers, they began to slip.

15

Caught by the wind, Jen's leg's swung out from the train. She gritted her teeth and concentrated on keeping her tenuous grasp. Her legs slammed into the side of the car again and she winced. *Don't think I can take another one.*

Zeke and Wayne knelt at the edge of the roof, stretching their arms out, but she needed to be a couple feet closer.

Someone grabbed Jen's legs and she looked into D-Day's eyes. He hung out the door with one arm and had the other encircling her legs, preventing them from flopping in the wind.

"I'm going to give you a push," he yelled over the train's racket. "Only one chance for this."

Zeke hollered to her, "When he pushes, reach for our hands."

Jen nodded and looked back at D-Day. Fear froze her.

"You can do this," D-Day said. "You've got more balls than most men I've known. Don't overthink it, just reach for their hands."

Jen took a deep breath and swallowed.

"On the count of three," D-Day bellowed. "One...two...three."

He swung his body around still holding on to the doorway and threw her upwards. She reached out with both arms, and Zeke and Wayne grabbed them as D-Day let go of her legs. Her weight pulled on them and Zeke seemed to slip, but he regained his balance.

They pulled her close and she found footing and pushed as they yanked her to the top of the car.

She lay on her stomach, panting, the wind taking her breath away.

Zeke bent down to her. "You okay?"

She nodded. Wayne put a hand on her back. "Take your time."

She'd regained her breath by the time D-Day pulled himself onto the roof. He helped her stand, but said nothing.

"Thank you," she said. "Thank you all."

"Enough of this bullshit," D-Day said. "Let's get this train stopped."

Zeke led the way, hopping to the next car with ease. Jen recalled him practically flying over the empty space between two buildings in Spokane. *Mine didn't go too well. Good thing these cars are a lot closer together.*

With no more slips, they made it to the first car in minutes. Jen peered over the side.

The door to the engine stood open. A rail above it caught her eye. She pointed. "We can grab that and swing right in."

Zeke squinted his eyes against the wind. "We don't know what's in there. I should go first."

Wayne put a hand on his shoulder. "I should go first this time. If there are zombies in there, they'll go for me and you can swoop in behind them."

Zeke frowned.

"I don't trust anyone to cover my back more than you," Wayne said.

"OK." Zeke gave one of his grins.

Wayne climbed down to the bar. He squatted, facing the engine, and pushed off. He swung into the door and disappeared.

Zeke scrambled down and mimicked his brother's actions, vanishing inside in one fluid motion.

Wayne stuck his head out. "All clear."

Jen eased her way to the bar and took a minute to compose herself before she swung in. She tumbled onto the floor and stopped just before rolling into the wall. Wayne helped her up, then turned to examine a panel with switches and buttons.

He's stopped asking if I'm OK every few minutes. Maybe he'll work out after all.

D-Day landed on his feet like a cat. A big, hairy cat with lots of muscles.

Zeke pointed at the floor. A wide streak of blood painted it to the doorway. "Guess we know what happened to the engineer."

Jen pulled out her phone and called Howell. She put him on speaker phone.

"You all make it?" Howell asked.

"Of course," Jen said. "What have you got for us?"

"I've got an engineer standing by," Howell said. "You're about ten minutes out from Kingston, so I'll conference him in. Just a sec."

Jen peered out the window. Trees zipped by. Few buildings.

"Howell here. Do I still have you, Jen?"

"Yup."

"Reynolds?"

"I'm here."

"Who's going to play engineer?" Howell asked.

Zeke jumped up and down with his hand up. "Me. Me."

Jen and Wayne exchanged amused glances. "Zeke will stop the train."

"Give Zeke the phone," Howell said. "Take it off speaker so it'll be easier to hear. We don't want any mistakes on this."

Jen handed Zeke the phone and he glided to the controls, nodding his head and speaking into the phone.

"What's the Kingston area like?" Jen asked.

Wayne rubbed his nose. "A few roads and lots of trees, but the University of Rhode Island is nearby, so there could be a lot of people in the crosshairs."

"Sounds like a shitty tactical plan," D-Day said.

Jen put an arm around the gruff biker. "Thanks for the helping hand back there."

He didn't push her hand away or make a fuss, but his cheeks reddened.

"What branch of the military did you serve in?" Wayne asked.

D-Day's expression froze. "Army."

"My friend Mark was in the Army, too," Jen said. "Flew helicopters, then got screwed over by an officer and ended up doing convoys. Said he spent a lot of time waiting for an IED to explode underneath him."

One of D-Days eyebrows rose. "Convoys are the second craziest things to do."

"What's the craziest?" Jen asked.

"What I did. EOD."

"Defusing bombs?" Wayne asked.

"Yup. Convoys spent their time trying to avoid the explosives. We spent our time getting to know them. You can't do that job if you're sporting a full deck."

Zeke joined them, the phone still to his ear. "Brace yourselves. We're about to stop."

Jen found a corner and slid to the floor. She braced her feet against a console.

Wayne sat next to her and D-Day stayed on his feet, watching out the window.

The train slowed. Not much, but it definitely slowed. Zeke had the phone glued to his ear and he worked the console. The train's speed dropped until it was barely chugging along.

Zeke looked back. "Hang on."

The brakes were applied and Jen resisted the pull forward. Loud squealing and hydraulic sounds came from outside and the train slowed to a stop.

"I did it," Zeke yelled.

Jen took the phone from him and switched it back to speaker. "Howell, you there?"

"Haven't left. Everyone OK?"

"Of course, but I'm beginning to wonder if there's anything Zeke can't do."

Zeke grinned. "I've done it before. I had the best train simulator on my computer back home."

"What about the state troopers?" Jen asked. "Are they in position?"

"Checked with them minutes ago," Howell said. "They're ready. They've taken up position in the terminal."

D-Day grunted. "Guess it's time to get the show on the road. How about opening the car doors, Zeke?"

Zeke hurried to the console and pushed a button. "Done deal."

"Which one did you open?" Howell asked.

"Which one?" Zeke repeated. "All of them."

"Shit," Howell said. "There are ten cars and each carries sixty-two people. That's a ton to set loose all at once. I expected you to open them one at a time and let the troopers mop them up before you opened another."

Growling came from outside. Jen stuck her head out and looked back at the cars. She pulled her head back in. "They're pouring out of the cars."

"Close the damn door," D-Day said.

Jen pulled to slide it closed, but it didn't budge. D-Day and Wayne joined her, the three of them grunting and straining, but the door was frozen open.

"Find something to hide behind," Jen said. "And stay quiet."

The console that sat in the middle of the floor provided the best coverage, and Jen joined D-Day and Wayne there. Zeke squeezed between two consoles on the other side. *He's the only one skinny enough to fit.*

The zombies approached and the gunshots started. Jen peered around the console. Hundreds of zombies passed by. Several of them were dropped by bullets, but the rest went into a run.

Something tells me they don't have enough state troopers to take care of that.

A few minutes passed and no more zombies passed by. Jen crept to the door and peeked outside. The horde was attacking the terminal. *Looks like the troopers have their hands full.*

She stood on her tiptoes and peered out the front window. The zombies had massed and were pushing toward the terminal. *But that doesn't look like six hundred and twenty people to me.*

She turned to Zeke. "I think a bunch of them are heading into the trees."

Something ran into her back, whiplashing her neck and slamming her into a console. She fell to the floor with a heavy weight on her chest.

16

Jen's lungs emptied from the impact. She gasped for breath and choked on the graveyard fumes from the zombie.

D-Day grabbed the zombie's hair and yanked its head back before its snapping jaws could clamp onto her throat. The biker's machete cleaved the zombie's skull and it slumped.

Wayne knelt by Jen's side. "Come on. We have to go."

D-Day threw the twice-dead corpse out of the door and Zeke took up a position next to him while Wayne pulled Jen to her feet. She leaned on him and almost fell, but he wrapped an arm around her waist and kept her up.

Gunshots from the terminal increased.

"Now," D-Day yelled. "Head for the troopers."

Zeke let out a whoop and jumped out of the engine room, his katana over his head. D-Day hopped down a second later.

Wayne led Jen to the doorway. "I'll help you down."

Jen pushed him. "I can do it myself."

He grinned and climbed to the ground.

She jumped, almost losing her balance as her feet hit the gravel, but Wayne stayed back.

In full ninja mode, Zeke sliced an arm off one zombie, then spun and beheaded another. In contrast with his grace, D-Day bulled his way through the horde. He slammed the machete blade through one zombie's skull, then kicked another away before he bashed a third in the temple with the machete's handle.

More zombies fell as bullets flew from the terminal.

The terminal.

Jen pulled her tomahawk and stumbled toward the yellow building. Zeke and D-Day were keeping the front edge of the horde back and she was going to take advantage of the head start.

Coming around the front of the engine, a large woman with long steel-gray hair lurched toward her. Jen timed the zombie's movements with her own and swung sidearm, punching the pointed end of the tomahawk into the zombie's skull just behind an eye. The zombie fell against the engine and slid to the ground. *I'm getting the hang of this weapon.*

Wayne rushed to her and she let him lead her to the terminal's far side, where the troopers were positioned. They ceased firing as Jen and Wayne got closer then rushed out to help them to safety.

Jen leaned against the building, finally catching her breath. She looked up as Zeke and D-Day dashed around the corner.

"Is that everyone?" a sergeant asked.

Jen nodded. Five troopers shot into the horde. "Are there more of you?"

"On their way," the sergeant said.

"You've got to be kidding," D-Day growled.

Slipping the tomahawk back in its holster, Jen walked out from the side of the building. The horde of about fifty zombies stampeded toward them. She pulled her pistol and emptied a magazine of fourteen rounds, only killing five. *Shit. Still shaky.*

D-Day, Wayne, and Zeke joined her, and the charging horde was destroyed in minutes.

The sergeant walked over. "Thanks for the assist."

"That's not all of them," Jen said.

"What do you mean?"

D-Day nodded. "She's right. That was about one car's worth. And there are ten cars."

"They had to have gone into the woods," Zeke said.

The sergeant walked away and spoke into a radio, his face grim. He came back a minute later. "You folks need to get somewhere safe while we clear the area."

Jen scowled. "I need to get something out of the train first. Then we'll start it back up and finish the trip to Boston."

"I'm afraid that's not going to happen," the sergeant said.

Jen removed her badge from her back pocket and held it up. "I'm afraid it is."

The sergeant's jaw tightened, but he gave her a curt nod.

Jen strode toward the train. *Feeling like my old self again.*

D-Day took position on her right and Wayne lined up on her left. Zeke took the rear.

Jen stopped outside the doorway to the first car. "Zeke comes in with me and you two stand watch out here."

D-Day nodded. Wayne frowned and nodded.

Jen entered the car with her tomahawk cocked back. No sign of anyone.

Zeke crept up the aisle, and Jen followed. She checked the seats in each row, and the floor beneath them.

They reached the front of the car. "Nothing," she said. "I was sure it was here."

She strode to the door and stuck her head out. "Not here. Going to the second car."

Wayne and D-Day positioned themselves by the outside door to the second car.

Jen stepped through the doorway between the cars and walked down the aisle checking each seat. She stopped about halfway through and squinted at something on the floor at the other end of the car. *Is that what I think it is?*

"Found it." She ran to the pouch. It lay next to the doorway to the third car.

She knelt and picked it up. The strap was missing the buckle. "Sure as shit, it must've been stripped from my waist during all the action."

Pulling the zipper open, she looked back at Zeke walking toward her with one of his big goofy smiles. His jaw dropped and his eyes threatened to pop out of his head. "Jen." He sprinted toward her.

Hot coals burned into her forearm. She jerked her head around. A chunk of flesh and muscle had been ripped away, the grotesque wound wet and bloody. The edges of the wound turned black and spread up her arm as she watched.

A legless zombie lay on the floor chewing its prize.

Jen scrambled backward, then lost her balance and slammed to the floor. Zeke dashed past her. "No," he screamed.

His katana flashed and removed the zombie's head in one stroke. He knelt next to Jen, holding her wounded arm. "I'm sorry. I'm so sorry. I was supposed to protect you."

D-Day and Wayne rushed in and came to a stop, their eyes telling Jen what they were thinking.

"You have to kill me," she said.

Wayne looked away. D-Day's eyes grew cold and steely. *He's working himself up to it.*

A burning shock of pain exploded throughout her body and she screamed, her back arching. "The poison's moving fast. Do it now. I don't want to hurt any of you."

Zeke turned away for a moment, then back. He held a hypodermic needle.

Another flood of fire traced down Jen's spine. She gasped. Unable to speak, she shook her head at Zeke. *Don't waste it.*

Tears streaming from his red-rimmed eyes, Zeke plunged the needle into Jen's undamaged arm and depressed the plunger.

The serum entered her veins as cold as glacier water. The fire in the other arm had reached her shoulder. The icy serum shot up her vein and into her heart just as the poison reached the beating organ.

Jen screamed as they collided. Her heart seized and her body convulsed. Searing pain covered every inch of her body and the smell of dead flesh invaded her mind.

I'm turning.

17

J en floated in pitch black nothingness. No sense of sight, sound, or touch. *Am I dead?*

A voice in her head answered. "No. You are with us."

So I'm alive? Who are you? Where am I?

"You are neither dead or alive."

Fuck you. I'm not a zombie. My friends would've kept me from that.

"True. You're also not undead. You are a fascinating bridge between us and living humans."

Where am I?

"In our group consciousness."

What is that? And who the hell are you?

"Time for you to awaken and discover your fate."

WHO ARE YOU?

"You know the answer to that. I was so sad to see you fly away from Fairchild just as I and my troops arrived."

JEN'S EYES SLITTED OPEN. Blurry figures leaned over her. They were saying something, but it sounded like gibberish.

Her brain was on fire and her heart beat impossibly fast. A picture formed in her mind. She stood before the pit and the sailors rose, their arms outstretched toward her. She tried to flee, but her legs froze to the spot.

The overwhelming grave stench washed over her as the zombies gathered around her, then dropped to their knees and bent their heads as if they were knights kneeling before their queen.

She raised a hand to rub her eyes, hoping she'd wake up. She stopped, her hand in front of her face. The flesh had rotted, and hung in shreds. Glistening white bones shone through.

The voice came back. "You are one of us now."

Jen screamed.

VISIONS CAME AND WENT, from a fiery pit of molten rock she tried to escape from to iceberg-laden water she was drowning in. *No more pain. Please!*

"JEN."

She kept her eyes closed. Was this just another dream?

Closer, the voice said, "Jen, can you hear me?"

I know that voice.

She murmured, "Wayne?"

Wayne laughed. "Yeah, it's me. Can you open your eyes?"

Her eyelids were stuck together, but she strained and they popped open. A face hovered above her, blurry. "Wayne."

The blurry face shot away and someone nearby took in a lungful of air. "Wayne?" she asked.

Wayne's voice came, but this time it was shaky. "How do you feel?"

Jen blinked several times and his face came into focus. She smiled. "For once, I'm glad you asked. It was pretty shitty for a while, but I think I'm over the fever."

She rose on her elbows and Wayne scooted back. "What the hell's wrong with you?" she asked.

He swallowed, his Adam's apple bobbing on his neck. "You were bitten."

Jen raised the arm that had been bitten. It was wrapped in bandages and blood had seeped through and dried. She flexed it. "Doesn't hurt."

Zeke had given her the serum. "So the serum worked?" She looked around the room. A small office with two desks and two chairs, it smelled of grease and oil. She lay on a couch with a cheap plastic cover.

"Where am I?"

"My shop," Wayne said. "In Coventry, Rhode Island. D-Day found a couple of motorcycles. One had a sidecar, and we put you in it and rode here as fast as we could."

"Where are the others? Where's Zeke? I need to thank him."

Wayne glanced at a closed door. "They're in the shop."

Jen pushed herself into a sitting position and shook her head. "Still some cobwebs. How long was I out?"

"A day."

Damn.

She pointed to a door on the opposite wall. "Bathroom?"

Wayne nodded.

Jen pushed herself to her feet and used a desk as support as she stumbled toward the bathroom. Wayne backed up to the shop door. His hand gripped the knob as if he were about to make a run for it.

Jen ignored him and made it to the bathroom. Hanging onto the doorframe with one hand, she fumbled along the wall for a switch. She found it after a moment and flipped it on.

Sharp fluorescent light blinded her. She rubbed her eyes with the heels of her hands, then opened them.

The small bathroom had a standard toilet with a seat that had seen better times. The floor tiles were worn, but clean, and a sink with a rust stain down the back of the basin stood directly in front of her. A mirror hung on the wall above it.

She glanced in the mirror, then did a double-take. A worn version of herself, with torn dirty clothes and disheveled black hair, stared back at her.

A chill hit her body and she trembled. One brown eye peered back at her. Only one, because the other was deep yellow.

18

J en froze. "Holy shit."

She spun. "You need to kill me now. Before I finish turning and hurt you."

Wayne put his hands out, shaking his head. "No. You were bitten yesterday."

A bang came at the door. "I hear you talking," Zeke said. "Is she awake?"

Jen looked at herself in the mirror again. "I can't let anyone see me like this. Especially not Zeke."

The door burst open and D-Day strode in, shoving it to the side. "How is she?"

Jen shut her eyes.

Someone hugged her from behind. "You don't know how glad I am to see you alive," Zeke said.

Keeping her eyes shut, Jen turned and hugged him back. "Not sure I am."

Zeke let go of her.

"What do you mean?" D-Day rumbled.

Jen took a deep breath and exhaled. She opened her eyes.

D-Day's jaw went slack and he yanked his machete from its sheath.

Zeke's mouth formed a perfect "O," then broke into a smile that threatened to cut his face in half. "Gnarly."

He took a step toward her and she put her hands out. "No. We don't know if I'm dangerous."

D-Day remained silent, his eyes boring into hers as if trying to read her mind.

"I think she's OK," Wayne said. "She would've turned completely a long time ago."

"Come on," Zeke said. "You're the same Jen we all know and love. You just have the coolest eyes I've ever seen."

Jen lumbered to the couch and dropped onto it. "But we don't know if it's over. Remember that experiment with the old lady that gave O'Connor the heart attack? The serum delayed her turning."

"But not by a day," Zeke said.

"And now we don't have the serum," Jen said. "Our mission was to deliver it so it could be used to make a cure for everyone, not just me."

Zeke stood back, arms crossed. "I had to save you. I had no choice."

D-Day still had the machete in his hand.

Jen's eyes met his. "You can do it. We haven't known each other long."

"Oh, I'll do it," D-Day said. "But only if the time comes. I'm not a murderer."

Jen squeezed her eyes shut and leaned back on the couch. "My mission's changed. Since we no longer have the serum, we need to go back to Atlanta."

"That's the first sensible thing you've said since you woke up," D-Day said. "I'll take you in the sidecar, but we need to find a place to fill up."

"I've got an underground tank here," Wayne said. "You're welcome to it."

"Where Jen goes, I go," Zeke said.

Wayne exhaled loudly. "I knew you'd say that. Looks like Zeke and I are coming along."

D-Day rubbed his hands together. "Now that's settled, where can we get some grub?"

Wayne pointed toward the front glass door. "Burger place on the opposite corner of the intersection and a greasy spoon across the street to the left."

"Burgers it is." D-Day opened the door.

"Wait," Jen said. "I can't go out there like this."

Wayne frowned, then yanked a desk drawer open and rustled through it, finally producing a black pair of sunglasses.

He handed them to Jen. "This should do."

She put them on and looked in the mirror. "Close up, I can tell my eyes are different colors, but not that one is yellow."

"They'll do for now," D-Day said. "We'll pick up some mirror sunglasses after we eat."

Jen nodded. "I'm hungry, too."

She followed D-Day out the door and to the burger place. Zeke kept pace by her side. Wayne stopped and locked the shop's door before joining them.

Feeling better. Bet some food will take me to a hundred percent.

The restaurant had a few people in it. D-Day led them to a table in the back. Seventies' classic rock music played over speakers that looked like they'd seen better days.

A large sign hung on the wall that said, "Clam Cakes and Chowda Our Specialty."

A grimy-looking guy with a unibrow took their order. Jen chose a double cheeseburger.

"How would you like that cooked?" Grimy Guy asked.

"Raw."

D-Day and Wayne did a double take, and Zeke's mouth hung open. Grimy Guy looked at her, the furry caterpillar over his brow crinkled. "You mean rare?"

She glanced at the others, then grinned. "Let's make it well done."

Wayne visibly relaxed, while Zeke's mouth shut. D-Day went back to his complacent-looking expression. "Looks like you haven't changed that much," he grumbled.

Jen wolfed down her food, then sat back and finished her soda. A light belch escaped. "Feel like my old self again."

"You look like a celebrity with sunglasses on indoors," Zeke said.

Wayne laughed.

"I make these look cool," Jen replied.

Jen's fingertips tingled.

What was that?

Jen glanced toward the back wall. Nothing but booths and wall.

The tingling traveled up her arm and snaked down her spine. She turned her chair toward the wall. *Something's wrong.*

D-Day finished off a large shake, then put a hand up.

The music on the radio had stopped and it emitted a series of beeps. "This is the emergency broadcast system. Stand by for an important message from the Rhode Island Department of Emergency Management."

Someone at another table gave a loud *shhh* and the burger joint went quiet.

"There has been a zombie outbreak in Kingston," the radio said. "While that outbreak was resolved, Rhode Island state troopers report that break-outs have occurred in North Kingstown, Exeter, East Greenwich, Warwick, and West Warwick. Citizens in those areas are cautioned to arm themselves and stay in their homes or places of employment. Call 911 to report any zombie activity."

A couple of cop cars zoomed by with their sirens screaming. They were followed by SUVs full of men in camouflage uniforms, heading in the same direction Jen had just been sensing something.

"What's out in that direction?" D-Day asked.

"West Warwick," Wayne said. "Just down the road."

Chairs scraped the floor as the other table of diners hurriedly left.

"I want to go see," Jen said. *I have to go see.*

"Are you nuts?" Wayne said. "Why do you want to do that?"

Jen looked at D-Day. A small grin appeared on his face. *Damn, he always looks like he knows more of what's going on than everyone else.*

Zeke stood. "Because that's what we do, Wayne. We're Homeland Security agents, and we kill zombies."

"And there's no serum left to guard," Jen said. "Why not help out the locals before we return to Atlanta?"

"Damn straight." D-Day stood and headed for the door.

Jen shoved the last French fry into her mouth and rushed after him.

The two bikes roared down Tiogue Ave until it became Main Street. Several cars passed them going the other way. *Guess it's worth your rations to get the hell out of Dodge when the undead show up.*

The sidecar hit a pothole and Jen was thrown against the back. "Dammit. Rhode Island roads suck."

Lined with older-looking two-story houses, the area looked like it probably hadn't changed in fifty years.

Several pickups rode up on their ass and laid on their horns. D-Day and Wayne moved to the side to let them pass. Filled with men and women in a mishmash of camouflage and denim clothing, each wielding a variety of weapons, they sped by and disappeared up ahead.

The cracked sidewalks filled with pedestrians heading away from the action. Some carried possessions, but most had nothing more than the clothes on their back. A number of bicycles sped by on the road.

Two minutes later, they came to a number of vehicles blocking the road between a pharmacy and a two-story brick building. Police vehicles with their lights still going were parked next to civilian vehicles, including the trucks that had whizzed past them.

D-Day brought the bike to a stop several yards away on the grass outside the pharmacy. Wayne pulled up beside him.

The tingling had intensified and covered one whole side of Jen's body. The side she'd been bitten on. She rubbed her unaffected hand over the tingling arm and paused at the scar from the zombie bite. *What the hell is going on?*

Two armed men approached. "We've got an outbreak up ahead. Zombies everywhere. You folks need to turn around and leave."

Jen laughed. "Zombie is my middle name."

19

J en held her badge up. "Homeland Security. Agent Reed."
　　One of the men stepped forward and took the badge from her. He returned to his partner and they examined the badge and whispered between themselves. The man who took the badge looked up. "And these others?"

Jen pointed to Zeke. "Agent Tripp. These other men are with us."

The man with the badge tossed it to her. "You need to check in with the chief." He led her to a West Warwick cop giving orders to a group of men.

"You guys get on the right flank and hold them," he said. "We've got to keep them from spreading out of Arctic."

He turned to Jen as she approached him. One of the men who'd challenged her team whispered in the cop's ear.

The cop smiled and thrust out a hand. "Agent Reed? I'm Captain Leander. I'm in charge here."

Jen shook his hand, then pointed at Zeke and the others in turn. "Agent Tripp, his brother, Wayne, and D-Day."

Leander shook each of their hands, but gave D-Day an extra once-over. "What can I do for you?"

"What's your sitrep?" D-Day asked.

Leander looked from D-Day to Jen. She shrugged. "Good question."

He pointed to their left. "Outbreak started at the senior center and—"

Jen's tingling went into overdrive just as a twenty-something zombie with stringy, blood-matted hair stumbled from around the corner of the pharmacy.

Jen put up a hand. "Don't shoot."

With a puzzled expression, Leander waved his hand. "Hold fire."

The zombie was missing a chunk of meat from its left thigh, but it continued to limp toward Jen. She pulled her tomahawk and strode toward the zombie.

Someone behind her murmured, "What the hell's she doing?"

A sharp *shh* quieted him.

Jen's tingling became stronger, painful, as if a thousand needles were being jammed into the bitten side of her body.

The zombie's head tilted back and the hair covering the face fell away.

Jen winced and gritted her teeth. *Got to ignore the pain.*

She charged the zombie with the tomahawk cocked over her head. Swinging it down, she slammed the blade into the zombie's forehead, holding back enough to just wound it.

Facing the cops and militia, she held up a hand to stop a militia woman who was raising her shotgun. Leander shot the woman a glare and she lowered her weapon.

The zombie stopped and shuffled, turning to face Jen. She pressed her bitten arm to her side and gasped as a bolt of electricity shot up her side. *Got to take this thing out now. Enough experimenting.*

She stepped into her strike, bringing the pointed end of the tomahawk around and punching it into the zombie's right eye. It dropped to the ground, the goo from the punctured eye dripping from the tomahawk.

The pain, the electricity down Jen's side vanished. Jen panted. *That's some interesting shit.*

She walked back to the others. "Chief," she said, "we're going in."

"Do what you want," Leander said. "We're still waiting for more men before we push in, so we won't be able to help you if you run into trouble."

Jen grinned. *Who the hell in this world has been in more zombie trouble than me?* "Understood."

She moved several yards back from Leander and his people. Wayne, D-Day, and Zeke gathered around her.

"I want you guys to know what's going on. No secrets." She paused and looked at each in turn. Wayne had a look of concern, while D-Day's perma-frown didn't waver. Zeke couldn't keep still, moving his weight back and forth between his legs. *He's like an ADD sixth grader.*

"You wondered what the bite and serum might have done to me, besides the trendy two-toned eyes." She took a deep breath. "I can feel when a zombie is close by."

"What does that mean?" D-Day asked. "Feel?"

"I can't explain it very well, at least not yet. But I felt it all the way back at the diner. It got stronger as we got closer to this spot." None of their expressions changed.

"Look," she said, "when that zombie showed itself, the feeling shot through me like an electric shock. It hurt like hell, and it didn't stop until I killed it."

"Do you feel any other zombies around now?" Wayne asked.

She shrugged. "I have the low-level uneasiness I first felt at the diner. But the pain and high intensity sensations turned off like someone had flipped a switch."

"You get the most awesome stuff," Zeke said.

Jen rolled her eyes at him. "We'll see how awesome it is."

"And that's why you want to go in," D-Day said. "See if it happens again. Experiment."

"Bingo."

He slipped the machete from its sheath. "Let's do it."

"We've got our own zombie detector," Zeke said.

Leander walked over. "When are you going in? I've got my men positioned and we can cover you."

"Right now," Jen said. "Where are the cleared areas?"

He pointed to the left of the intersection. "Anything that way. All cleared."

Jen positioned herself out in front of the vehicles and the troops taking cover behind them. Sensations came from a one-hundred-degree radius up the street. *They're all over in that direction.*

She pointed to a bank. "We'll head there and start clearing out buildings."

D-Day took a step forward, but Jen put an arm out and he stopped. He glanced at her arm and then at her as if to say her puny arm could do nothing to stop him.

"Better let me go first," she said. "With this new sense, I might be able to detect a horde or an ambush quicker."

"Makes sense." He stepped aside.

Jen peered down the road to her right. It looked abandoned, the only thing moving was a sheet of newspaper blowing down the sidewalk.

Zeke stood next to her. "Where are they?"

Tingling ran up Jen's side. "They're out there."

She approached the bank's glass door, trying to peer inside for any movement. D-Day took up position on one side of the door, while Wayne took the other. "Zeke and I will go in first," she said.

Wayne pulled the door open and held it. Walking on the balls of her feet, Jen choked up on the tomahawk and crept in. Zeke had his katana held ready, and he entered by her side.

It was a small bank, and Jen could see most of it from the door. Nothing stirred, so she gestured for Zeke to approach the teller windows on the right while she took the left. She got up on her tiptoes to look over the counter. There was nothing but empty stools and papers scattered across the floor.

Wayne entered the building and crept toward the single restroom door. D-Day hustled to catch up with him. "Don't go wandering off alone."

D-Day pushed the door open, revealing a lightless room of shadows. Wayne reached in and flipped the switch. D-Day let the door close. "Nothing."

The tingling had dropped to almost nothing. It was like playing the kid's game Hot and Cold. The tingling increased when she was near a zombie, and died when they were far enough away. *I wonder if having buildings and walls between me and the zombies makes a difference?*

She walked toward the back door, which had an exit sign above it. The tingling slowly built back up. "This way."

The door opened into a back parking lot with an ATM drive. Older homes sat across the road.

Jen took several steps into the parking lot and looked down the street. *Still nothing.*

Zeke hitched his thumb to the right. "Do you want us to do this building next? If I don't get to kick some zombie ass soon, I'm going to burst."

The next building over was the back entrance to a store. A two-story white building with fresh colorful paint, it stood in sharp contrast to the bank with its barred windows and plain exterior.

Jen approached the store and stopped, clenching her teeth. The tingling down her side went into overdrive. "They're close. Be ready."

Wayne put a hand to his ear. "Listen."

The sound of hundreds of pounding feet came from down the road.

"Get in the building," Jen yelled.

20

J en dashed through the doors, nearly running over Zeke, who stood looking at the oncoming horde with a faint smile on his face. She grabbed him by the sleeve and pulled him inside.

D-Day and Wayne pulled the doors closed and followed Jen and Zeke into the small shop. She led them to the far side of the store where a staircase went to the second floor. No sooner had they reached the stairs than banging began at the back doors.

D-Day pointed at the store's front windows, which looked out over Main Street. Scores of zombies raced past, heading for the militia lines. Guns barked and men yelled as they engaged the horde.

"We're surrounded," Wayne said. "Can't go out the front or back."

"Then we go up." Jen climbed the stairs, which opened onto a landing with three closed doors. Jen opened the one straight ahead and turned on the light. A small office, it had an industrial metal desk, a reclining chair patched with electrical tape, and a cabinet overflowing with papers.

"Nothing in here." She closed the door and turned to the others. D-Day had opened one door and Zeke the other. He immediately closed his, holding his nose. "Just the bathroom."

D-Day stepped through the third door and disappeared for a moment. He stuck his head back out. "Looks like this is our best bet."

Jen followed Wayne inside. "An apartment?"

"A lot of these buildings that have businesses on the first floor have apartments on the second," Wayne said.

The banging downstairs increased. Jen crept to the top of the stairway. The left side of her body had gone practically numb from her built-in zombie detection alarm. *There has to be more of them.*

"I don't think we have more than five minutes before they're inside." She peered down the stairway trying to see the shadow-covered stairs. She flipped a switch on the wall and an overhead light buzzed, flickered, and went dark. "Shit."

She took her sunglasses off and put them in her shirt pocket. *Better.*

Wayne stood in the apartment doorway. "Come on."

She turned to him and he flinched. She almost felt like apologizing. *I wonder if any of them will ever look at me the same again.*

"I'm staying here," Jen said. "Top of the stairs is a good choke point."

Zeke pushed past Wayne. "Then I'm standing there with you."

Jen shook her head. "Narrow stairs. Only room for one. You should take that doorway to the apartment as a choke point. Keep the door closed. The three of you can defend it once it's breached."

D-Day tromped toward her. "Bullshit. We don't need heroes."

Jen smiled. "Looks like you're getting all emotional on me, big guy. Who said I was going to let myself get overrun? I'll hold this choke point until I can't hold it anymore, then I'm falling back into the apartment with you. I'll catch my breath while the three of you defend the door. That is, if you can handle it for a few minutes without me."

D-Day clenched his fists and lumbered back into the apartment. "Damn Homeland Security agents," he murmured.

Wayne followed him in, but Zeke didn't move. "You got bit because of me and I don't feel right leaving you out here to get bit again."

Jen's left leg spasmed. "The freaking zombies will be in here in another minute. I need you back in the apartment, and I won't take your shit. I've already been bitten and haven't turned, so I'm probably immune. That's more than I can say for you."

Zeke stared at her for a moment, then said, "I'll leave. But if I think you aren't coming back, I'm coming out to get you."

Jen grinned. "I expect nothing less. Now get the hell out of here."

Zeke disappeared and the door closed. The gunfire and the banging had reached a crescendo. *Sounds like they're hammering in the front door, too.*

Jen positioned herself two steps down the stairway and took a couple practice swings with the tomahawk. *I should be able to hold this thing for a while.*

A crash and the tinkle of shattering glass came from downstairs. Banging, as if furniture was being tossed aside followed, and underneath it all, the shuffling of dozens of feet.

A wave of zombies flooded the bottom of the stairwell, creating a pile of intertwined limbs and snarling, yellow-eyed faces. Blood poured from their wounds and predator eyes searched for prey.

Jen widened her stance and bent her knees slightly, swinging the tomahawk back and forth. Two zombies broke from the pileup and raced up the stairs toward her. Twenty steps, fifteen, ten.

The lead zombie's eyes burned into hers, but it stopped two steps away. Its head tilted as its gaze bore into hers. "One more step and I'm dropping your ass," she said.

The second zombie clambered to get over the first, but stopped as his eyes locked with Jen's.

What the hell? They look confused.

"You can't tell if I'm friend or foe, can you?"

She closed her human eye. Both zombies straightened and stumbled down the stairs. The pile of zombies at the bottom unraveled and headed into the store.

"Well I'll be dipped in dogshit."

Jen crept down the stairs and peeked out. The zombies poured out the front door and joined the street zombies attacking the militia.

Jen opened her human eye.

Boots stomped down the stairs behind her and Jen spun, bringing her tomahawk above her head.

Wayne and Zeke stood at the bottom of the stairwell, their weapons raised with puzzled looks on their faces. D-Day clomped down and leaned on the railing. "I guess you didn't need our help," he said.

Jen shrugged. "When you've got it, you've got it."

The horde on Main Street surged past, their attention on the militia.

Wayne stood next to Jen, watching them flow past. His hand brushed hers. Jen's heartbeat picked up. *We're going to have to do something about this when the time is right.*

She swallowed and turned to him. "Sorry I didn't leave you any."

He gave her his crooked grin. "That's okay. Looks like there's plenty more." His eyebrows lowered. "But what happened? We didn't hear any fighting and there are no bodies."

D-Day lumbered forward. "That's a question I'd like answered, too. What the hell's going on?"

Jen licked her lips. "They didn't attack me at first, I think because of my yellow eye. But they were thinking about it. So I closed my human eye, leaving only the yellow open, and they turned around and walked away."

"Holy shit," Wayne said. "They thought you were one of them."

D-Day didn't say anything, just stood there with his arms crossed and his eyes staring beneath bushy brows.

"Damn, Jen," Zeke said. "Someone's going to have to write a comic book about you." He laughed. "Zombie fighter Jen and her sidekick, Zeke the ninja." He took a couple of swipes with his katana.

D-Day went to the back door. "Totally busted back here. The front doors will keep out any strays but it's open season from the rear. We should move."

"What about the militia?" Jen said.

D-Day shook his head. "I ain't afraid of a fight, but attacking that mob out there would be suicide."

"He's right," Wayne said. "The militia was expecting reinforcements, and they'll do them a lot more good than we will. Besides, I think we need to find out more about your new...condition, and what you can do with it."

Jen sighed. "Agreed. We should probably move to the next—"

A sharp pain in her gut folded her in half. Wayne grabbed her and kept her from falling. "What's wrong?"

D-Day and Zeke rushed over.

"Don't know," Jen grunted. The pain subsided enough for her to straighten, but it was still strong and getting stronger.

She looked out the front window. The horde had passed, but one figure walked unsteadily toward the front door. An older lady, her skin hanging loose on her bony frame, shuffled to the door and peered in, her yellow gaze sweeping the room and resting on Jen. She reached out and pulled the door open. *A leader.*

Zeke stepped forward, his katana ready to attack. "What are you doing?"

Jen put her arms out, her gut still twisting. "Step back. Don't attack unless she does first."

Jen waited as the old lady shuffled to her. The zombie stopped and examined her from head to foot then stared into her eyes. A buzzing grew in Jen's head and the pain disappeared. Not unpleasant, the buzzing grew louder.

"You guys hear anything?" she asked.

"Not me," Zeke said.

"Nope," D-Day said.

"You're the only one," Wayne added. "What are you hearing?"

The buzzing reached a crescendo, then stopped. The feeling of being under a microscope rushed over her. "Do you understand me?" Jen asked.

The zombie continued to stare, motionless.

Jen took a deep breath and exhaled. "If you understand me, raise your right hand."

The zombie's right arm jerked up. Jen gasped. "Lower your arm." The arm dropped.

"Do you know who I am?" The zombie's right arm shot up. Jen's heart hammered her chest.

"Am I talking to the old lady who stands before me?" The zombie didn't move.

"If the answer is no, please raise your left hand." The zombie's left hand lifted.

Jen's breathing became shallow and rapid. She stumbled and Wayne rushed forward, putting his arm around her waist. She leaned against him.

"Jen?" he said.

She ignored him and locked eyes with the zombie. *Let's get to the nitty-gritty.*

Forcing the words from her mouth, Jen asked, "Am I talking to Butler?"

The zombie's right arm shot up.

21

Zeke jumped in front of Jen and knocked the old lady to the floor. She sprung at him as soon as she landed.

Zeke spun, the katana a blur.

"No," Jen cried.

The zombie collapsed at Zeke's feet and its head flew, striking Wayne's chest and bouncing onto the floor. Wayne scrambled backward, brushing his shirt. "Shit!"

Jen grabbed Zeke by the collar. "What'd you do that for?"

Zeke's eyes were downcast. "It was Butler. You said he needs to die."

"I wanted to find out more from him. I need to know why he keeps trying to contact me." Zeke wouldn't meet her gaze. *He did what he's always doing—protecting me.*

She released her grip and straightened his collar. "Sorry about the reaction."

A goofy grin spread across his face. "No worries."

"What do you mean when you say he keeps trying to contact you?" D-Day asked.

Jen licked her lips. Zeke and Wayne moved closer.

"The drones in the CDC basement," she said. "I think Butler could see through them, but he didn't have as much control."

Wayne rubbed his chin. "But he has clearer communication with leaders?"

Jen nodded. "I think so. First it was O'Connor and now this old lady. You saw what happened."

Wayne pointed out the front window. "Look."

The disciplined army of zombies had turned into an unorganized mob, but still pushed up the street in the direction of the gunshots.

"That leader must've been directing the drones," Zeke said. "Now they're just a normal, everyday horde."

D-Day lumbered to the back door. "Then now's the time to leave."

"Agreed." Jen followed him and stuck her head out of the door. "It's clear."

She crept into the parking lot and scanned the area. *Butler knows where I am. He'll find himself another leader sooner or later and have the whole horde rain down on our heads.*

Jen sprinted to the side of the next building and peered around it. The street was deserted. D-Day pushed up against her. "What do you see?"

"Nothing." She slinked out from cover. The small one-story building housed a jewelry store. "Nice bars on the window, but can't see shit from there."

Approaching the building, she craned her neck to get a good look at what lay ahead. Her zombie side went numb. *Looks like my spidey senses are tingling again.* The barred glass door of the jewelry store slammed open and an older man with balding gray hair, a huge beer belly, and organs hanging from a gash in his side lumbered forward.

D-Day swung his barrel toward the zombie, Zeke took an attack stance, and Wayne choked up on his bat.

The zombie stumbled past Jen. She put a hand up and gestured for the others to get back. The zombie seemed locked in on Wayne.

Jen ran in front of the zombie, blocking it. It stopped and glared, then shuffled around her.

She jumped in front of it again. "Stop."

Again, it went around her. *Even with my human eye showing?*

"Can I kill it now?" Zeke asked.

Jen grabbed the zombie and her body convulsed, slamming her to the ground. Her ears buzzed and everything grew darker. The last thing she saw before slipping into unconsciousness was Zeke's worried face hovering over her.

22

The buzzing grew louder until it reached a crescendo and became the whispering of a thousand voices. Blackness enveloped Jen—blackness so thick that not even a glint of light appeared.

What the hell? Am I dead?

She tried to stretch out her arms and realized she couldn't feel them. *Shit. I am dead.*

The whispering faded and a pinpoint of light appeared far away, but it grew as it came toward her. *Or am I going toward it?*

The circle of light sped toward her, filling her view then enveloping her in a blinding flash.

White. Searing white. Then it cooled and shadows appeared, becoming more distinct, until Jen found herself in a conference room, with six of the twelve chairs surrounding the table occupied.

Jen tried to move her head, look at the people around the table, but nothing she did worked. *Like watching a movie.*

A chubby thirty-something man with a shock of red hair adjusted his round wire-framed glasses and leaned forward. "I believe the risks of Project Svengali are unacceptable." He sniffed. "And all the rewards appear to be military." He looked at Jen. "No offense, of course."

The door opened and two more people took their seats. One of them sat to her right. Her view panned to him. *O'Connor.*

Her gaze switched to the other newcomer. *Dr. Preston. And where the hell's her wheelchair?*

The redheaded man sighed. "And where's our fearless leader? Isn't our time important, too?"

The door opened and in strode Dr. Cartwright. "Forgive my tardiness. My call with the president went over its allotted time."

She sat at the head of the table and scanned the room. "Dr. Morgan. Where is he?"

Her eyes zeroed in on Jen. A voice rumbled, surrounding her like a theater sound system. "He's in the middle of a necessary procedure and will join us as soon as he can."

Cartwright stared at Jen, a tic on her eyelid the only thing giving away her thoughts. "Very well," she said. "We shall proceed."

She nodded at a stick-figure-thin woman to Jen's right. "Williams, I've read your report. Please summarize for those present."

Williams bit her lip and shuffled a stack of papers in front of her before picking up a few. "We believe we may have found viable hosts."

She looked nervously at the others and continued. "We scoured our electronic systems for any possible matches. When we found nothing substantial, we were given access to all other government agencies and expanded the search." She pushed her black plastic glasses up her nose. "Still nothing."

"Get to the point," Cartwright said.

Williams licked her lips. "We sent teams to government archive sites to go through physical documents that were never digitized. Last week, one of our teams found a promising lead in an old Navy file."

She looked down at the paper in her hands. "They assigned a naval officer, Dr. Winston Burrell, to a whaling ship in 1871 to observe and gather data on the health of the crew during the voyage. His journal is quite boring until a stopover in Haiti where he writes about a meeting with a Vodou priest, what they called a houngan."

"A witch doctor," the redheaded man interjected. "Are we here for a ghost story?"

"Quiet, Dr. Stanley," Cartwright snapped. The redheaded man sat back in his chair and said nothing.

Cartwright nodded at Williams.

"Dr. Burrell obtained a powder from the priest that he claimed had restorative properties. The doctor makes note that he tried to buy the powder but the priest refused, saying it was dangerous in the hands of anyone but a priest." She looked up. "The doctor stole the powder.

"He also notes that the priest had revealed that the person treated with the powder could be controlled by another person, but the doctor discounted that as legend.

"They sailed off the coast of Alaska, almost reaching Wainwright by August. A stationary high over Siberia reversed the normal wind pattern and pushed the pack ice toward the Alaskan coast. As we know from other historical accounts, seven of the forty ships escaped. The others were trapped in the crushing ice."

The door opened and Dr. Morgan rushed in. Taking his seat, he looked around at the others. "My apologies. Don't let me interrupt."

Williams continued, "The men became sick, and lacking the proper medication, Dr. Burrell made a tincture with the powder, dissolving it in some rum he'd obtained in the Caribbean. He gave it to the men."

Dr. Morgan leaned forward with his elbows on the table. "Here's the good part."

Williams waited. When nothing more was said, she continued. "The men got better for a time, then grew suddenly worse. The first death happened within forty-eight hours. With no place to bury him, they put the man in the hold. When the second man died hours later, they opened the hold to store him there and the first man was alive and crazed. He attacked his crewmates, ripping the flesh from their bodies and consuming it."

"Zombies?" Stanley said. "Are you serious? Maybe if you'd gone to a higher-level institution for your studies, you wouldn't be talking about ridiculous things."

Williams shrank into her seat.

Morgan clasped his hands and laid them on the table. "She's merely giving you what was written in the reports of the time."

"Fortunately," Stanley said, "we're far more sophisticated today."

What an ass.

"Let her finish." Cartwright nodded at Williams. "Let's wrap it up quickly, shall we?"

Williams took a deep breath and exhaled. She put the paper down and looked at the others as she spoke. "Dr. Burrell reported them as zombies.

His last journal entry revealed that he was the only crew member who hadn't been infected. Other written Navy records reveal that those crew members walked the ice to other ships, infecting their crews. They eventually made their way to the mainland, near a small village called Point Wallace, where they froze in the subzero temperatures."

"What happened to them?" the rumbling voice asked.

"The Navy and Army sent men to collect them and bury them nearby beneath the permafrost. And so they remain today."

Stanley let out a heavy sigh. "I assume the so-called zombies are the hosts."

"So the plan would be to exhume these zombies?" the rumbling voice asked. "Then what? Bring them here? Isn't that dangerous?"

"No." Cartwright leaned forward. "Once Dr. Williams discovered this information, we scoured every piece of paper we had and found one more bit of information. It seems the government brought back samples of the zombies and studied them. It wasn't until almost twenty-five years later when science had advanced enough to detect viruses that they used that technology."

"So it is a virus?" Morgan asked.

Cartwright nodded. "The samples were destroyed, but the notes indicated it was a mycovirus."

"It attaches to spores?" Stanley said. "But that only happens with viruses that attack vegetation."

"Not anymore," Cartwright said.

"And zombies help us how?" Stanley leaned back in his chair and crossed his arms.

"Our mission," the rumbling voice said, "is to create the ability to control the troops of our enemies. This will end conflicts quicker without unnecessary risk of our own troops."

"I'm well aware of that," Stanley snapped. "What the hell do zombies have to do with it?"

Dr. Morgan removed his glasses and wiped his eyes. "Delivery mechanism." He put his glasses back on. "If we come up with a biological method of controlling the enemy, how do we deliver it?"

"Through zombies?" Stanley sneered.

"The perfect delivery method," Cartwright said. "They bite and infect others. The outbreak grows exponentially."

Stanley pursed his lips but said nothing.

Cartwright stood. "Further discussion is moot. The president has already approved."

She opened the door and turned, her gaze burning into Jen's. "Colonel Butler, draw up a plan for delivering spores to the mass grave in Alaska. They should be buried with the bodies for eighteen months, then collected. I expect the plan on my desk by the end of the day."

"Yes, ma'am," the rumbling voice said.

23

J en opened her eyes as far as she could and was barely able to make out D-Day on his bike. The vibrations on her back told her she was in the sidecar. "D-Day," she moaned.

He didn't react.

Can't hear me?

She tried to move, but only managed to raise a pinky finger. *What the hell's happening to me? And what about that dream? Or nightmare. I was in Butler's head, for crying out loud.*

Her body spasmed and she sank back into the shadows.

ARCTIC WIND WHIPPED past Jen's face as she stood in front of a squad of uniformed men digging. She tried to scan her surroundings, but she was back in the theater chair. *Shit. Butler again?*

One of the men shoveled up a chunk of earth, then staggered back covering his mouth and nose. The wind drove the scent up Butler's nose and his breath hitched. *And I get to smell what he smells. Freaking great.*

Butler wrapped a scarf to cover his mouth and nose and edged to the opening in the ground. "Get some light on this."

A soldier aimed his flashlight and lit the scene. *Yup. That's the sailors' pit.*

Two bearded sailor faces were exposed. One of the soldiers tapped them with a shovel. "Mostly frozen, but they're thawing."

"Let's get the damn fungus planted and cover them back up," Butler said. "Morgan? Hurry up."

Morgan, bundled up so Jen could barely make out his face, trudged into view. He removed a clear tube from inside his coat. It was filled with a brownish powder.

Butler turned around. *That's the direction of the village. Can't see a damn thing in this storm. That's how they did this without the villagers knowing.*

Butler turned back to the bodies as Morgan stood. "Get them covered up before this wind blows all the spores away," Morgan said.

Three soldiers filled in the opening to the pit.

Butler brought a radio to his lips. "Svengali One to Svengali Two. Ready for pickup."

The radio squelched. "Roger. Twenty minutes out."

Butler yelled at the soldiers. "Move your asses. You've got twenty minutes to make it look like no one's been here."

"IS SHE GOING TO LIVE?"

Zeke's voice.

Jen cracked her eyes open. Zeke sat next to her, looking behind him. "It's my fault," he said. "Never should have let that thing get so close to her."

"Screw the blame game," D-Day said. "Shit happens. Get over it."

Zeke pursed his lips.

"He's right." Wayne's voice came from in front of Zeke. "We just need to concentrate on getting her back to CDC. They'll know what to do."

"Zeke," Jen breathed.

Zeke's gaze dropped to her and his face lit up. "Jen! She's awake."

D-Day's face hovered over her. "Well, Spitfire. Looks like you cheat death again."

Jen gave him a weak smile.

"How are you feeling?" Wayne came into view.

"Weak. Confused. Can't do shit."

Zeke patted her arm. "You just relax. We've got this."

D-Day smiled. "We'll be back in Atlanta in no time."

Jen struggled to keep her eyes open, but lost the battle.

. . .

BUTLER ENTERED THE LAB.

Same one O'Connor used.

Morgan looked up from his desk. "What is it, Colonel?"

Butler's head turned from side to side. "Don't know. This whole Svengali Program just doesn't make sense to me."

"How's that?"

"It's just so off the books," Butler said. "I've been involved in hush-hush projects before, but why the hell does Cartwright report directly to the president? Even the Secretary of Defense is out of the loop."

Morgan frowned. "Does it matter as long as it works for national defense?"

A feeling of regret washed over Jen. *I'm getting his feelings, too?*

"I used to think that way," Butler said. "Sacrificed a lot of good men for the mission. Was it worth it?"

Morgan glanced at Butler over his glasses then went back to his work. "Just think if it works."

"We release the spores over enemy territory," Butler said, "then within twenty-four hours we control them. Sounds too good to be true."

Morgan didn't look up. "That's the idea."

Butler scoffed. "Nothing can go wrong with that plan, can it?"

THE TRAIN SWAYED UNDER JEN. She opened her eyes all the way. *Must be getting better.*

She lay across a seat with her head on Wayne's lap. He was fast asleep leaning against the window.

I could stay like this for awhile.

She peered across the aisle to where D-Day and Zeke sat, both out cold. Zeke leaned against D-Day and had his mouth open. A strand of drool hung off the corner of his lip, then dropped onto D-Day's arm.

Jen sighed. Were Butler's memories true, or did he just project what he wanted her to experience?

She eased herself into a sitting position. Wayne snorted and curled against the window.

Their car was empty. *How the hell did they manage that?*

She yawned. "I feel pretty good." She clamped her hand over her mouth. No need to wake the others.

Watching the countryside roll by the windows, she wondered if anything would ever get back to normal.

She leaned against the window and fell asleep.

THE DOOR to Butler's office burst open and Stanley strutted in, his fiery hair carefully coiffed and an intense look on his face.

He shoved a large envelope at Butler. "Hide this."

"What the hell are you talking about?"

Stanley pushed it at Butler again. "You don't want to know. Just hide it where no one will find it. Someone searched my office while I was out and I know they were looking for what's in the envelope. You're the only one I can trust. Take it and I'll come back for it later. I'll explain everything then."

Stanley opened the door and stuck his head out, looking up and down the hallway. Without another word he slipped into the corridor and disappeared.

Butler opened the envelope and removed several sheets of paper. Jen couldn't read them, her vision having been blurred. *Is he keeping me from finding out what's in the envelope?*

Butler returned the papers. "Son of a bitch. Even the president's in on it."

He rose and approached a six-foot cabinet in the back of the lab. Grunting, he slid it from the wall and slipped behind it.

His hand came into view and it held a penknife. Butler used it as a makeshift screwdriver to unscrew a vent cover several inches from the floor.

When he had removed the cover, he rushed to the desk and pulled a roll of duct tape from a drawer. He placed the envelope against the top of the air duct and taped it in place. Within a couple of minutes, he had replaced the vent cover and the cabinet.

He strode toward the door. "Got to let Morgan know what's going on. I'll need him if I'm going to have a chance to stop this."

· · ·

J‍EN J‍ERKED awake as the train slowed. She peered out the window. "Atlanta."

"Jen." Zeke stood up in the front of the car, his eyes wide and face red.

Jen raised her hand. "Hey, Zeke."

Zeke and Wayne hovered over her.

Better not talk about the memories yet. Not until I figure out what's true or not. She stretched. "Had a good nap. A little tired, but I'll live."

D-Day stood at the front of the car with his arms crossed and his eyebrows lowered. His eyes pierced hers. *The son of a bitch always looks like he can read my mind.*

The train came to a stop at a nearly empty platform. Militia and law enforcement were stationed every fifty feet.

Zeke handed Jen her sunglasses. "Better cover up."

She slid them on.

D-Day strode to the door. "Looks a lot different than the last time we were here."

Jen rose, grasping the seatback for stability. Wayne put an arm around her. "You can lean on me."

Jen let go of the seat and allowed him to keep her on her feet. She closed her eyes and his scent filled her nostrils. *If this were another time...*

The doors slid open and two militia men jumped on board, sweeping the car. As they worked their way down the aisle, an Atlanta policeman waved at Jen and the others from the platform. "Come on out, please."

Once on the platform, Jen watched a similar scene play out at each car.

The policeman, whose name tag had "Silverio" etched on it, looked each of them over. "Where'd you come from and what's your business here?"

Zeke displayed his badge. "Homeland Security. We're reporting to the CDC."

Silverio studied the badge for a moment, then nodded at Jen. "What's wrong with her?"

"Exhausted," she said. "Not bitten. Not infected."

Silverio motioned for three militia men to join him. He motioned to Jen. "Step forward."

Zeke opened his mouth, but the militiamen brought up their weapons. Zeke stood down.

Wayne released her and Jen shuffled to Silverio. She stopped inches away and glared at him. "Hurry the hell up. We've got a shit ton to do. In case you haven't heard, there's a war going on."

Silverio scowled. "Roll up your sleeves."

Jen peeled her sleeves back and showed her arms so that the bite scar wasn't visible.

"Turn them over," Silverio said.

Jen did, and Silverio's eyebrows rose. Two of the militiamen aimed their rifles at her.

"What's that?" Silverio asked.

Jen sighed. "I'm from Alaska. Had a bear encounter a couple of years ago."

Silverio bent over, examining her arm closely. "Looks like a human bite," he said.

"It was a black bear," Jen said. "Their bites are close to a human's. If it had been a grizzly, then my arm would be gone."

I hope he knows nothing about bears and believes the shit I'm shoveling.

"Guess you're OK."

A militiaman whispered in his ear. Silverio nodded at Jen. "Just remove your glasses so I can see your eyes and you'll be on your way."

"I have a condition where bright light triggers migraines," Jen lied.

Silverio drew his revolver. "It's not very light inside. Show me your eyes now."

The militiamen raised their weapons.

Zeke and Wayne moved to either side of her, and the presence of the burly biker towered over all of them. Mouth dry, Jen reached for her glasses. *This isn't going to end well.*

24

J en paused.

Screw it.

She dropped her arms and pushed past Silverio. "I don't have time for this bullshit."

Silverio grabbed her arm and she spun. "Let go or lose it," she said.

The policeman loosened his grip, but kept hold of her. "I have a job to do."

"I'm a Homeland Security agent," Jen said. "I have a bigger job than some local cop, and you're getting in the way of national security."

She pulled his hand off her. "We're leaving. If you've got a problem with that then shoot us. And when you're done you might as well put a bullet in your own head before someone else does."

She knocked a militiaman back with her shoulder as she strode from the terminal. Reaching the humid air outside, she took a deep breath.

"That was freaking awesome," Zeke said.

Wayne caught up with them. "We shouldn't hang around in case those guys grow some balls."

Unlike their departure from Atlanta, the grounds and streets around the train station were orderly. Passengers waited in cordoned-off lines that snaked through the surrounding streets.

M.A. ROBBINS

A black limo pulled up to the curb and Mark stepped out. "Anyone looking for a ride?"

Jen smiled and gave the big man a hug. "Been keeping busy?"

Mark's grin threatened to crack his face as he returned her embrace. "Not as busy as you, I hear."

Zeke and Wayne climbed into the limo. Jen put one foot in, but stopped when her gaze fell on D-Day, who stood several yards away with his arms crossed.

Jen ducked her head inside the limo. "Give me a second."

She ran to D-Day. "You're welcome to come with us. I'm sure I can talk Cartwright into giving you a job."

"No, thanks," D-Day said. "Last time I worked for the government, it didn't work out so great."

"What are you going to do?"

He shrugged. "I've got some brothers in Atlanta I can stay with for a while. It'll give me time to figure out my next steps. Maybe I'll head north again."

Jen nodded. "Thanks for everything." She threw her arms around him and he didn't resist.

"I'll be around if you need me," D-Day said. "For a couple of weeks, anyway."

"How will I find you?"

"I'll be staying in a house just south of Emory University. Get to Clifton Road and take it to Ridgeway Drive. Fourth house on the right."

Jen nodded. "I'll remember."

The limo's horn sounded. Jen faced it and put her forefinger in the air. She turned back to D-Day. "Stay out of trouble."

The big man's face broke into a fierce grin. "Shit. Me and trouble have had a lifelong friendship."

Jen jogged to the limo and climbed in.

The limo dropped Jen, Zeke, and Wayne off in front of the CDC Headquarters building. Within a few minutes, they stood before Cartwright.

She sat behind her desk with her fingers arched, her carefully neutral face composed. "Quite a journey. And the bottom line is we have no serum to work with."

Jen opened her mouth, but Cartwright put a hand up. "But we've got Dr. Preston working on a new serum." One eyebrow rose. "And we've got you."

Damn, she's practically drooling over me. Creepy much? "Do you think there's a cure for me?"

Cartwright's head cocked to the side. "What type of symptoms are you experiencing?"

Jen removed her sunglasses. "Yellow eye disease."

Cartwright's gaze locked onto hers. She rose and walked around the desk, never taking her eyes off Jen. "Amazing. Do you see any differently from it?"

"No."

"And what other symptoms do you have?"

Jen shrugged. *I'll be damned if I tell her anything until I find out what was on those documents Butler hid.* "Nothing else."

"Hmm." Cartwright returned to her seat. "We'll do some tests while Zeke and Wayne are gone."

"Gone?" Zeke said. "Where? When?"

"I'm sending you two, along with two other agents, back on the train to Boston. This time you'll return with Dr. Preston."

Jen bit her lower lip. *Once Zeke and Wayne leave I'll be alone, isolated.*

Zeke frowned. "Why us?"

"We're short handed," Cartwright said. "And I'm down another two agents."

Wayne shook his head. "Rodriguez and Daniels."

Cartwright nodded.

Something heavy and cold formed in Jen's gut. *I'm stuck. I can't refuse or Cartwright might suspect something.* "You guys better get going so you can get back."

Wayne gazed into her eyes.

Another place, another time, bucko. Jen swallowed.

Zeke gave her a hug. "We'll be back before you know it." He patted the katana's hilt. "There are more chances out there to kill zombies than there is in here."

Jen let go of Zeke, put her arms around Wayne's neck, and laid her head against his chest. "Get back here fast," she whispered. "I don't feel good about this."

Wayne wrapped his arms around her. "Then I shouldn't go," he whispered back.

"Something's going on and I'm getting close to what it is. If you stay, we'll be watched, and I need the space to dig around a bit."

He released her and stepped back. His gaze dropped from her eyes to her lips. Her heartbeat kicked up a notch. *Not a good time, but I don't give a shit.*

She raised her face and he eased closer. Jen closed her eyes in anticipation.

Zeke slapped Wayne on the back. "Come on. There are zombies to kill out there."

Wayne winced and let Jen go.

Damn, Zeke. It's no wonder your parents didn't have any more kids after you were born.

"Let me know if you need us and we'll be back as soon as we can," Wayne said. Jen nodded. Wayne and Zeke left the office.

Cartwright straightened her blouse. "Let's get you down to the lab." She stopped at the door. "Better put your sunglasses back on."

ONLY THREE OF the eight rooms with test subjects were occupied. *Are they running out of volunteers or does Cartwright no longer need them now that she has me?*

Cartwright opened the door into the large cavernous room and the zombies went into a frenzy. Jen hesitated, then stepped out of the hallway.

The zombies quieted.

Cartwright glanced at Jen. "Interesting."

Yeah. Interesting. Dumb-ass zombies making it worse for me.

She glared at the one closest to her, a husky guy with shoulder-length black hair matted with chunks of decayed flesh. He stared blankly at her. She met his gaze as she passed. *Why don't you at least growl?*

The zombie bared his teeth and let out a low, menacing rumble from somewhere deep inside.

What the hell? He heard me?

"He doesn't seem to like you," Cartwright said. "But you're having some kind of effect on them. No doubt about it."

The lab door opened and O'Connor's assistant, Randy, stood in the doorway. "I'm all ready for you." He blinked and looked at the zombies. "What got into them?"

"Something with Jen, and I need you to find out what it is," Cartwright said. "I'll check in later." She headed for the exit.

Randy nodded and stepped to the side. Jen walked into the room and he followed. "Why don't you sit?" he asked as he squeezed past her and plopped into the chair in front of the desk.

Jen took the seat next to him and rolled up her sleeves. "I'm right-handed." She stuck her left arm out.

Randy wiped her arm down. "This won't hurt."

He inserted the needle and Jen gasped. "Won't hurt?" she said.

He smirked. "I was talking about me, not you."

"For a guy who owes me big-time, you've got a funny way of showing your appreciation."

"Sorry," he said. "I get awkward when I'm uncomfortable."

He finished collecting her blood and bandaged her arm. Shaking the blood-filled tubes, he headed for the door. "Our fridge down here is on the fritz. I'll have to get these to the medical ward for refrigeration. Just hang tight."

As soon as the door closed, Jen rustled through the desk. "Aha." She took a small screwdriver from the middle drawer. Although she'd never noticed the large cabinet in her previous visits, it stuck out like a sore thumb as her eyes scanned the room.

She pulled on one side, her teeth gritted and muscles straining. It moved. Not much at first, but in several seconds she'd made a gap between the cabinet and the wall that she could squeeze into.

Sweat pasting her shirt to her skin, she wriggled into the space. Although there wasn't much light, the white vent cover was visible, just as she'd seen in Butler's memory. She soon had the cover off. She peered in, but it was too dark to make anything out, so she stuck her hand in and fumbled along the top of the vent. She touched paper.

Coughing from the dust, she ripped the envelope from its mooring and slid out from behind the cabinet and into the light.

The brown manila envelope had been opened, just as Butler had shown her. *But now I get to read it.*

She brought it to the desk and pulled the papers from it. The first page had the words *Top Secret* stamped in red, then it had a bunch of numbers to the left and a date of two years before.

Jen's eyes went to the text beneath it.

Dr. Linda Cartwright is assigned as the project lead for Project Svengali effective immediately. She will report directly to the Office of the President of the United States. All possible assistance and courtesy will be provided to her by all federal agencies.

Jen's gaze went to the big, bold signature at the bottom. *The president.*

She slid the paper to the side. The next sheet had the same stamp at the top and more numbers, but with a later date. She read the text.

Once the spores have been populated with the virus, they will be released in a small rural center by military aircraft. Twenty-four hours after the release, a research team will be inserted to test the virus's effectiveness. If the test subjects are sufficiently compliant, further tests will be conducted in a larger area.

If the second test is successful, further plans will be made to introduce the spores in all areas of the United States.

Jen swallowed. *"Sufficiently compliant"?*

She glanced at the signature at the bottom of the document. *Linda L. Cartwright.*

The lab door opened and Jen spun, hiding the documents with her body. Cartwright walked in. "All done with your blood?"

Jen nodded.

"Let's get you set up with accommodations," Cartwright said. "You'll be staying here in the building. Don't want your yellow eye accidentally exposed."

Cartwright put out her arm and Jen walked to the door, her pulse quickening. *How the hell am I going to get back and hide those papers? And put the cabinet back?*

As she reached Cartwright, the doctor peered past her to the desktop. "What is that?"

Cartwright walked to the desk.

25

J en froze as Cartwright picked up the papers and studied them. Jen thought of running.

That's not an option. Just play the cards you're dealt. "Is it true?"

Cartwright dropped the papers on the desktop and turned toward Jen. Her stern expression had softened. "I didn't want you dragged into this."

Jen crossed her arms. "Did Doc know?"

A horrified look crossed Cartwright's face. "Never. Like you, he was better off not knowing."

"So the plan was to create a mycovirus that would attach to spores and infect everyone?" Jen asked. "How were you going to keep from infecting yourself?"

Cartwright leaned on the desk, her hands at her sides grasping the edge of the desktop. "We planned on harvesting the spores from Alaska and modifying them to be short lived. Unfortunately, Mother Nature beat us to it."

"What about Butler and Morgan? Butler wasn't planning on taking down the government just so he could run it, was he?"

"No," Cartwright said. "When he found out Project Svengali would be used to control the civilian population and not just enemy forces, he played it straight, but watched and waited for the right opportunity.

Morgan fled, and we spent plenty of resources trying to find him. We had no chance, though."

"Why not?"

"Colonel Butler was in charge of the search," Cartwright said. "I have no idea if he knew of Morgan's escape ahead of time, or if he found him and they decided to work together."

Jen approached Cartwright. "But, why? Why control people? Does the president just want to be a dictator?"

Cartwright took a deep breath and exhaled. "You need to believe me. It's nothing like that. We just see that the human race is an unhappy, warring people. Imagine if all decision-making was taken from you. How you'd be happy with fewer of the unnecessary gadgets and toys this world offers."

The zombies outside the door went into a frenzy. "Someone's coming," Jen said.

"I called them," Cartwright said. "Panic button underneath the desktop."

Two burly security guards strode in. Cartwright pointed at Jen. "Detain her."

Jen reached for her axe and her hand slapped an empty sheath. *Shit.*

One guard grabbed her upper arm and she twisted away.

"Don't hurt her," Cartwright said.

The two guards came at her at the same time. Jen kicked one, missing his nuts and hitting his inner thigh.

The other guard tackled her to the floor.

She squirmed. "No."

He held her down while the other guard handcuffed her. "No," she screamed.

"Pick her up."

Both guards grabbed one of Jen's arms and lifted her to her feet. She stomped on the first foot she saw. Nothing happened. *Freaking steel toe boots.*

"Shh," Cartwright said. "You're all we have."

"To defeat the zombies or to turn everyone into slaves?" Jen spat.

Cartwright shrugged. "Why not both?"

Cartwright left the lab and the guards dragged Jen kicking and screaming after her. The doctor went to an empty cell and held the door open. "In here."

"Are you fucking kidding me?" Jen grasped the bars as the straight-faced guards tried to force her in. One of them peeled her fingers off one by one. She roared as each finger was pulled back. Her teeth gritted, she lost her grip and they shoved her inside. She fell to her knees and scrambled to her feet. The door clanked shut and she rammed it, but they already had it padlocked.

"Don't do this," she yelled, grabbing bars on the door and rattling it. "Zeke and Wayne will free me."

Cartwright stood back, her arms crossed. "Your friends won't be coming back from their mission. There will be an incident on board the train on the return."

A guard handed Cartwright the key to the lock. Jen glared at her. "Doc would be so ashamed of you."

Cartwright pursed her lips then turned and left, followed by the guards.

Jen bowed her head, pressing it against the bars. *I won't cry.*

She took a deep breath and exhaled. "I've never felt so alone," she murmured.

26

Jen looked at the zombie in the next cage. A middle-aged woman with bright red hair, she had no physical damage except a bloody stump where her left pinky finger should have been. The zombie stared at Jen with her mouth hanging open. "I'll bet those yellow eyes were once a deep blue," Jen said.

She plopped herself on the bed in the corner of her cell. "Fucking great. No Zeke, no Wayne, and no D-Day."

The zombies stayed as still as statues, each gaping at her.

"So is Butler looking at me through you? Butler, you in there? Raise your right hand for yes."

The zombies didn't move.

Jen got up and paced. "You've only communicated through leaders, so maybe you can't with drones." The zombies' eyes followed her movements.

She stopped and turned toward them. "Or maybe you can hear me, like a radio transmission instead of a phone." She approached the bars separating her from the redhead and peered into the zombie's eyes. "If you can hear me, Butler, I now know what went down. How you tried to save the country." She shrugged. "Maybe that's what you're still doing."

The zombie's gaze didn't change.

Jen sighed. "I don't know what I am now, and neither does Cartwright, but she won't have any qualms about cutting me open to find out." Jen threw herself at her cell door and yanked on it furiously. "I need to get the fuck out of here."

Panting, she leaned against the door. The zombies hadn't moved. "Now you're annoying me. Why don't you all just sit down?"

As one, they dropped to the floor in a sitting position.

Jen's pulse picked up. She pointed to the redhead. "Stand up."

The redhead rose and stared at her stupidly. The other zombies remained seated.

Jen smiled. "Eight zombies. That's like having a squad at my command."

She licked her lips. "I have my way out of the building. Now I just need a way out of this cell. And I think I know how."

27

R andy carried a tray of food to her cell two hours later. The guard took off the padlock and stood to the side with a wooden baton in his beefy hand.

Jen rose from the bed as Randy stepped in and the guard shut the door. "Hungry?" he asked.

Jen glared at him. "Really? That's what you ask? Hungry?"

Randy swallowed and turned to the guard. "Lock it up and give me five minutes."

The guard frowned.

"It's OK," Randy said. "It's part of an observation Dr. Cartwright has approved."

The guard slapped the padlock on the door and clicked it shut. "I'll be in the lab if you need me. Five minutes."

The door to the lab clicked shut behind him.

"Observation?" Jen asked.

Randy shrugged. "I had to come up with something. Can't believe it worked."

"You must think I'm not a danger," Jen said.

"I know you're not a danger," Randy said. "Cartwright probably sent me because she didn't think you'd attack me."

"She doesn't know me very well."

"Even if you do," Randy said, "I'm expendable."

He gestured to the bed. "Why don't you sit down and eat?"

Jen's stomach rumbled as he took the cover off the plate and the aroma of fried chicken enveloped her. She sat on the bed and took the tray from Randy, balancing it on her lap.

She picked up a leg and bit into it, the hot juices spilling down the sides of her mouth. In seconds, she finished the leg and dug into the mashed potatoes with a spoon.

Randy watched her. "The guard won't be gone long."

Jen squinted. "So what?"

"I want to help you."

"Because you owe me?"

"Something like that."

Jen put down the spoon. "Then have your head of physical security, Mark Colton, come see me."

Randy shook his head. "He won't come. Cartwright told him you were bitten and turned. She convinced him that he wouldn't want to see you this way."

"Then call Zeke and Wayne and let them know that Cartwright threatened to kill them. Have the decency to do at least that."

"She said she'll kill them?"

"Right to my face. They have two agents with them. My guess is those agents are the ones who'll do it. Tell them to get away as fast as possible."

Randy pushed a button on his phone. "They're in my directory. I'll call them as soon as I'm alone."

"And you'll let them know I'm here."

Randy nodded.

Jen downed a glass of water. "Why are you helping? I know you think you owe me, but aren't you on team Svengali?"

Randy shook his head. "I'd heard the name before, but had no idea what it was about until this morning." He crossed his arms and his eyes teared up. "All this bullshit. All those people dead. My mom and dad. My little brother. All because these assholes wanted to be in control." His hands clenched into fists. "No, I'm not on the fucking team." He glanced at the lab door. "But I'm letting them believe I am."

Jen put the glass down. "So why not just leave?"

"I may not know everything about Svengali and what's happened, but I do know one thing: you're the key to stopping this before we're all wiped out."

The lab door opened and the guard lumbered out. "Time's up."

Randy wiped his eyes with his shirtsleeve and gave Jen a slight nod. "I'll be back for the dishes. Take your time."

He stepped to the door. The guard looked at him.

"What?" he said.

"Strip."

"What?"

"We need to make sure she didn't bite you."

Jen nearly choked on the corn on the cob. She took a gulp of water. "You guys know I'm not a zombie, right?"

"Doctor said there's no proof your bite won't infect someone," the guard said.

I never thought of that. Could I bite someone and turn them into something like me? She turned away from Randy. "Go ahead. I won't peek."

She concentrated on her food while considering the possibilities. *What if my bite turned people into zombies? If they found that out, then I'd never get out of here. And if it turns them into a hybrid, Cartwright will want to milk that. Crazy bitch would create an army of them.*

The cell door shut. Jen turned.

"I'll bring you breakfast in the morning," Randy said. He walked off with the guard trailing him.

Jen looked at the zombie in the next cell staring at her. "What do you think, Red? Can I trust Randy?"

Red stared.

Jen sighed. "Never thought I'd say this, but I miss Zeke's rambling stories."

JEN SAT up and rubbed her eyes. "What the hell time is it?"

Rising, she scanned the room. The zombies were still prone in their beds where she'd told them to go. *Should've told them to close their eyes, too. They'd look less creepy.*

"Red," she said, "stand up and keep me company."

Red rose, slack-jawed, and faced Jen.

Jen laughed. "My bestie is a flesh-eating corpse."

The hallway door opened and Randy entered, followed by a different guard.

"About time," Jen said. "I ordered room service an hour ago."

Randy carried a tray into the cell and the guard locked him in. Jen sat on the bed and lifted the plate cover. "Bacon and eggs." She licked her lips. Just the smell made her less hungry.

Randy stood, his hands going into his pockets, then back out and clasped in front of him.

"What are you so nervous about?" Jen said with a mouthful of eggs. "Told you I don't bite."

"Once you've eaten, I need to get a sample," he said.

Jen laughed. "Don't give me one of those little cups. I've been sitting here overnight with no bathroom."

Randy removed blood collection supplies from his pocket. "Blood sample." He looked at Red, and then at the other zombies still in bed.

"What are they doing?"

Jen downed a glass of orange juice and let out an *ahh*. "Don't know. Maybe they're tired."

She stood and walked to the cell door. "How about a bathroom break? I'm about to burst."

The guard grunted and removed the padlock. With a baton ready to strike, he pulled the door open. "In the lab. Nice and slow."

Jen took her time walking to the lab. *What would Randy do if I could take this guy out?*

She entered the lab with the guard a few steps behind. The door closed behind him. "Bathroom's in the back."

Jen's eyes scanned the room. *Need something. A weapon. A diversion. Something.*

She shuffled into the bathroom and closed the door. The guard's foot stopped it. "It'll stay open."

"Bullshit, you creep. You get off on seeing the zombie girl pee?"

The guard's face reddened. "It'll stay open two feet wide. I won't see you, but you also won't be able to pull any funny stuff."

Jen sighed. *No help in here.*

Minutes later, she approached the cell door. Randy stood inside, his arms crossed. "Ready for the sample?"

The guard pressed closer behind Jen.

Oh, shit. I've got it.

She glanced at the zombies. *Blink your eyes.*

The zombies blinked their eyes.

Yes!

She stepped around the cell door, leaving the guard on the other side.

As loud and as fast as you can, attack the guard.

The eight zombies sprang to the bars with a roar, pulling and reaching for the guard. His eyes went wide and he took a step back, ready to defend himself.

Jen grabbed the cell door and slammed it into the guard, striking him on the chest and jaw. He stumbled backward, dropping the baton and covering his broken jaw with his hands.

Scooping up his baton, Jen charged him. He reached out for her, but she ducked and raked the baton across his kneecaps. The guard howled and collapsed. Jed swung the baton and clipped his forehead, knocking the back of his head into the concrete floor. He lay still.

Jen scrambled to her feet, ready for an attack from Randy, but he hadn't moved.

The growling and clambering continued. "Stop," Jen said. "Everyone quiet."

The zombies went still, their empty yellow eyes gazing at her.

Randy's jaw dropped. "Holy shit. They listen to you?"

Jen knelt next to the guard and checked his pulse. Still alive. *Good.* She rustled through his pocket and pulled out a ring of keys. "Did you make the call to Wayne and Zeke?"

Randy shook his head. "They took my phone." He gestured to the unconscious guard. "And one of these guys was always shadowing me."

"I'll have to find a phone and warn them," Jen said. "I hope they're not being watched as closely as you."

She went to Red's door and tried three keys before she found the one that opened her padlock. Before opening the doors, she made eye contact with each of the zombies. She pointed at Randy. "He's off-limits. Do not harm him."

Randy pulled his cell door closed. "Not that I don't trust you."

Jen let Red out and she shambled to a position behind Jen. Within minutes, Jen had all eight zombies freed. *I could just escape, but then Cartwright would come after me. Need to keep that from happening.*

"Hand me your security badge," Jen said.

Randy unclipped it from his belt and stuck it through the bars. "What are you going to do?"

Jen squinted her eyes. "Time to pay Cartwright a little visit."

28

The elevator doors opened on the second floor. Jen pointed at two zombies, an older woman with a shredded chest and a twenty-something man with the skin peeled from one side of his skull.

"Chase anyone you see," she said. "You harm no one. Just keep running and causing chaos."

The zombies dashed out of the elevator and down the hallway. A chorus of shrieks reached Jen as the doors closed.

When they opened on the third floor, Jen picked out two more zombies. She pointed to the left. "The Security Office is just down there. Take it over. Break every piece of equipment in the place. Go."

The zombies raced from the elevator and the doors closed.

After having sent zombies out on the fourth floor, Jen was left with two: Red and a muscular bearded man with a chunk of meat missing from his shoulder.

She pressed the button for Cartwright's floor. "You two will follow me."

The doors slid open and Jen stepped out. Soft music played from the speakers and she strode down the carpeted hallway to Cartwright's reception area. Cindy sat behind her desk and looked up as Jen walked in. "What are you—" The zombies appeared behind Jen. Cindy wrenched a drawer open and pulled a pistol.

Jen ducked. "Get out of here."

Cindy's shot took the top of the muscle man's head off and he dropped to the floor. She took aim at Red, but the zombie disappeared into the hallway.

Clenching the baton, Jen rushed Cindy and drove her to the floor, knocking the pistol from her hand. Jen wrenched Cindy's arm behind her and pulled her to her feet. Pushing Cindy toward Cartwright's office door, Jen said, "Open it."

The door opened into an empty office. "Damn," Jen said.

She pushed Cindy into a chair. "Move and I'll kill you."

She strode into the reception area and picked up Cindy's gun from underneath her desk before returning to Cartwright's office. "Where is she?"

"I don't know," Cindy said.

Jen aimed the gun at Cindy. "You're her assistant. You know, all right. Where is that bitch?"

Cindy returned Jen's glare, but said nothing.

"The bitch is right behind you," Cartwright said.

Jen spun and Cartwright stood in the doorway with a revolver pointed at her.

Jen lowered her gun. "Still looking for your ruby slippers?"

Cartwright gestured to Cindy. "Come with me. This facility is compromised. The outbreak is spreading rapidly."

Cindy walked over to Cartwright. "Where are we going?"

"To the roof. I have a helicopter coming."

"I thought they were all in the west," Jen said.

Cartwright shrugged. "Executive privilege. The president kept one for emergencies and he's sending it here."

"Are we taking her?" Cindy asked.

"Definitely," Cartwright said.

Jen jutted out her jaw. "I'm not going with a whacko like you."

"Whacko?" Cartwright said. "Is it insane to want peace and order in the world?"

Jen spat on the floor in front of Cartwright. "By taking away everyone's free will? You bet your ass it's insane."

"No matter," Cartwright said. "It's inevitable, and you're going to help make it happen quicker."

"Like hell."

Cartwright cocked the revolver's hammer back. "I'd rather you're alive for my studies, but undead should work as well."

Red sprinted into the room, colliding with Cindy and slamming her into the wall. Jen raised her gun and shot at Cartwright in one motion. A piece of doorway trim splintered and Cartwright ducked into the hallway.

A high-pitched screech pierced Jen's eardrums. Red clamped onto Cindy's neck and tore her throat out. The scream broke into a gurgle as Cindy slumped to the floor.

"No time for a snack," Jen said. "If we don't stop Cartwright now, we may not have another chance."

She raced out the door.

29

J en raced into the corridor. Gunshots and shouting echoed from both ends. A flash of movement caught her eye. The stairway door slammed shut. Jen ran to it with Red on her heels. Several fresh zombies rushed past them, one of them leaping onto a fleeing technician. He hit the floor, his blood soaking into the carpet as the zombie tore at his back.

Innocent people are dying. What the hell have I done?

Jen flung the stairway door open and caught a glimpse of movement above. Cartwright had a head start.

Taking the steps two at a time, they reached the next floor just as the door opened and a flood of humans rushed in, knocking her and Red down. Zombies poured in after the humans, chasing them down the stairs.

Jen rubbed the back of her head where it had banged into the wall. *Got to get Cartwright.*

A zombie streaked up the stairs and stopped in front of her.

Cindy.

All undead but Red and Cindy, stand down. Do not attack anyone.

Jen struggled to her feet and stared into Cindy's yellow eyes. "I don't know if that worked or not, but it's the best I can do."

Cindy stared back.

"Take us to the roof to find Cartwright, but don't get too far ahead of us."

Cindy ran up the stairs.

Jen gestured to Red. "Let's go."

Breathing heavy, she ran up the stairs, keeping Cindy in sight. More refugees passed them going down the stairs, but Cindy and Red ignored them as they followed Jen's directions.

Cindy waited at the top of the stairway. Jen caught up with her and bent over with her hands on her knees. Her chest heaved and her heart slammed her chest. "Top floor," she gasped.

Jen pushed the door open and stepped into a quiet tiled hallway. A corridor stretched ahead and another to the right.

Jen held the door open. "Get in."

The two zombies lumbered in and stopped.

Jen listened. "It's like the outbreak hasn't hit here yet."

A gunshot echoed down the corridor and a piece of the doorframe behind Jen exploded. Jen ducked.

An armed guard knelt in a room at the end of the hallway with a pistol propped against the door frame. He shot again, and the bullet buried into Cindy's shoulder.

Jen took cover around the corner. "With me."

The zombies followed.

Sticking her gun out, Jen fired off three blind rounds. The guard answered in kind.

"Who's betting Cartwright went that way?" she said. She peered farther down the corridor they hid in. "I wonder if there's a back way."

Footsteps came from the direction of the guard. Jen popped her head out and back in. A barrage of gunshots replied. Three more guards had made their way halfway down the corridor and another stayed back providing supporting fire. *Where the hell did those other guys come from?*

She fired two more blind rounds then peeked around the corner. The guards returned fire and Jen barely pulled her head back in time. *They're holding position. Too far away for us to rush them. But if I can get one of them on our side...*

"Girls, when I tell you, I want you to run out into view, pause, then run back here."

Jen ejected the pistol's magazine and checked the load. *Five rounds.*

With one in the chamber, that's not much. She slapped the magazine back in. "Got to make them count."

She moved as close to the corner as she could without being seen and turned to face the wall so when she stepped out into the hall she would face them. Squatting, she held the pistol in two hands and took a deep breath. *Don't rush.*

"Now, girls. Go."

The zombies ran past her and Jen leaned to the left and stretched out, landing on her side.

Bullets flew by and some hit solid wood and some smacked into undead flesh.

Take your time.

Lining up the sights on one of the three guards, she took a deep breath, then let half of it out. She squeezed the trigger.

The bullet hit the guard in the throat. He clutched his neck and fell over.

Jen was already aiming at the guard at the end of the corridor.

A bullet chipped the tile next to her, shrapnel cutting her cheek. She ignored the sting. *Girls, do the same thing again.*

The guns that were aimed at her swung toward the zombies as they exposed themselves to gunfire again. Jen concentrated on her target. With only half his body in the open, her aim had to be true.

Just as she squeezed the trigger, the first guard she shot rose, snarling, his yellow eyes gleaming. He attacked his two companions from the rear.

The pistol recoiled and Jen's target at the end of the corridor dropped his gun and grabbed his shoulder. She sent a follow-up shot, but missed as he rolled out of sight.

"Attack, girls."

The two guards had turned to face the threat from behind and realized too late they were surrounded. One of them wrestled with the zombie guard while the other shot wildly at Red and Cindy. Red pounced on him and tore open his shoulder with her teeth. Cindy tackled the other guard and chewed on his arm while the zombie guard went for his throat.

"Everyone to me."

The three zombies shuffled to Jen's side. *I wonder how many I can control at once? Butler can do millions, but he goes through his leaders.*

As she crept down the corridor to the open doorway, the other two guards rose. "Fall in with the others," Jen said.

She paused at the doorway and peeked inside. It was a large stock room with cabinets, a sink, and cleaning equipment. A trail of blood ran from the doorway to thick metal stairs that led to an upper level.

Can't see the whole thing. Someone could be up there.

Keeping her pistol pointed upward, she dashed to the stairs and pointed at one of the guards. "You first. Go quickly."

The zombie raced up the stairs and Jen followed.

The upper level was bare except for another stairway with a sign next to it that read "Roof Access."

"Could be a nice place for an ambush." Jen chewed her lip. "Got to be careful. I don't know how many guns she has up there."

A distant muffled sound caught her ear. *Sounds familiar.*

The sound came closer. *Thup thup thup.*

Time's up.

30

J en sprinted up the stairs. "Let's go."

A guard stood in front of the roof door, his pistol aimed at her. Jen swung her barrel toward him and stopped.

"Mark?"

"Stop there, Jen," Mark said.

Red stepped next to Jen as the other zombies crowded her from behind on the stairs. Mark's eyebrows rose.

"Cartwright was right," he said.

"Right about what?" Jen said. "What'd she tell you?"

"That you're not the Jen I know and love. That you're...different."

Jen sighed. "Some things are different, but I'm still the same person who fought all those battles at your side."

Mark shook his head. "That Jen never had her own zombie army."

"OK, smart-ass. That part's different, but it's still me."

Mark looked from Jen to the zombies and back. "Why would she tell me that if it isn't true?"

Jen tilted her head and listened. The helicopter had to be just overhead. "Because she's been lying to us since the beginning. She's the cause of this shit. She and her co-conspirators have been working on a way to control people."

"Put the gun down," Mark said. "I don't want to shoot you."

Jen jerked a thumb over her shoulder. "You do and I won't be able to save you from them."

Mark remained silent. *He's processing what tactical advantages and disadvantages he has.*

Jen took a step toward him he pointed the gun from her chest to her head. "Stop."

"Shoot me in the head?"

"Least I can do for who you were."

Jen gritted her teeth. "Look, asshole, I'm still me, and you're wasting time. Cartwright's going to get away."

Mark's eyes narrowed.

"Just step aside and get out of here," Jen said. "Get your family out and far away."

Another sound outside. Something hitting the roof? *The helicopter has landed. Out of time.*

"How can I prove to you I'm still me?"

Mark shrugged.

"How about that I haven't sicced these guys on you?" she asked.

Mark paused, then said, "You know I'll shoot you first, so you won't take the chance."

Dammit, you stubborn ass.

Precious seconds ticked away. Faces and events with Mark flashed through her mind. When they first met in her room. Talking on the roof and finding out his pain. Her saving his ass. Him saving hers. Zeke. Doc. *Doc.*

That's it.

Jen straightened. "Mark, if I'm not telling you the truth, I'll eat a bug."

Mark's expression remained unchanged, then his shoulders relaxed a little. He gazed into her eyes. "Jen?"

"It's me. A little fucked up, but you know me well enough to know that's a normal state for me."

Mark licked his lips, then straightened and lowered his gun.

Jen pointed at him. "Not only are you not to harm him or his family, but you will protect him from others. Human and zombie."

"Will that really work?" Mark asked.

"Who the hell knows? Move aside."

Mark stepped to the side.

Jen gave him a quick hug. "Promise me you'll get your family and get out of here."

"I promise. But I should help you get Cartwright first."

"I've got all the troops I need, and your mother and sister need you right now."

She turned to the zombies. "Follow me and attack anyone on the roof. Except Red and Cindy. You two stay with me."

Bulling the door open, she rushed onto the roof. Gunfire came from the Blackhawk that had landed on the far end of the roof. Cartwright was just boarding. Three guards next to the helicopter opened fire on the charging zombies.

No time for tactics. Jen broke into a full run toward the helicopter. *If I can get close enough to at least take a good shot at Cartwright...*

The helicopter lifted a couple of inches. One of the guards looked back at it and yelled. He and the others made a run for it, but were brought down by their fellow guards from behind.

The helicopter moved a few feet up and away from the roof. Jen's gaze locked on Cartwright's. For the first time, the bitch smiled.

Heat flared in Jen's face. "Cindy. Jump on the helicopter."

Cindy sprinted past Jen, making a beeline for the helicopter. Cartwright pointed at her and said something. The helicopter started ascending just as Cindy leapt. She missed the door and wrapped her arms on a landing skid.

Guards, follow Cindy. Get your weight on that helicopter.

The guards left their meal and streaked toward the helicopter. Cartwright gestured frantically and looked like she was screaming into her headset. The pilot gritted his teeth and the helicopter began to rise again.

The guards leapt. The first one missed and dropped out of sight, but the next three hit with two of them managing to hang on.

The helicopter descended. The pilot screamed into his mic and flipped several switches.

Jen slowed. "Red, I need you to take out the tail rotor."

Red shot past Jen and leapt at the rotor. She hit it and turned into a pink mist.

"Shit. That did nothing?"

The helicopter pulled away, the zombies still clinging to the skids. It barely made it over nearby buildings and it moved slow, but it was moving.

"Son of a bitch. She's going to get away."

The *thup thup thup* of the rotors changed rhythm and Jen shaded her eyes to get a better look. The tail rotor seemed to be slowing. As she watched, it stopped altogether.

"You did it, Red."

The helicopter started spinning, black smoke trailing from the rear. One by one, the zombies clinging to the skids were thrown off.

Losing altitude, the helicopter dropped out of sight somewhere near Emory University. Seconds later a thick plume of black smoke rose into the air.

31

Jen adjusted her sunglasses as she walked toward the helicopter wreckage. Two students stood next to the blackened skeleton and looked up as she approached.

"Hell of a thing," one student, a beefy jock-looking kid said. "Everyone thought all the aircraft went west, but they say the CDC kept one for emergencies." He kicked a burned piece of metal. "Shame they wrecked the damn thing."

The skinny long-haired girl next to him pushed one brown lock behind her ear. "I heard the military is pissed about it."

"Anyone survive?" Jen asked.

The boy shrugged, but the girl nodded. "I heard four died and one survived. At least long enough to go to the hospital. Good thing it's close by, the bodies were supposedly pretty burned up."

I heard. I think. Can't get a straight answer anymore. "Could you point me to Clifton Road?"

The boy pointed at a large building looming over the trees. "Just the other side of the hospital."

Jen hiked up her backpack. "Thanks."

WALKING up to the brick-faced house on Ridgeway Drive, Jen had an uneasy feeling in her gut. *Looks more like a typical suburban family lives here, not some bikers.*

She took the walk to the front door and rang the doorbell, fully prepared to tell the homeowner she had the wrong house. When no one answered, she shaded her eyes and peered through the window.

Inside looked just as nice as the outside. It had the kind of furniture she wouldn't dare sit on in case it broke.

An engine roared to life from somewhere behind the house. She crossed the perfectly manicured grass to the driveway that wound around to the back. A standalone garage came into view with its two overhead doors open. Three men and a woman worked on three motorcycles. Even among his own people, D-Day stood out, bent over and working on the sidecar.

Jen approached, and as soon as the woman shut off the engine she was gunning, Jen waved and said, "D-Day."

D-Day straightened as the others reached for weapons.

He put a hand out to the others. "She's cool."

Wiping his hands on a greasy rag, he loped to Jen. "Needing some help?"

She nodded. "A lot has happened. I'll tell you all about it on the road."

White teeth appeared under D-Day's mustache. "On the road. I like that. Where are we going?"

"West."

32

J en wiped up egg yolk with her last piece of toast and placed it in her mouth.

"What did Wayne and Zeke say?" D-Day asked.

Washing down the food with some orange juice, Jen put up a finger. "They're in Pennsylvania. Told them we're heading for Colorado so they have a general direction."

"Did you say Colorado, young lady?" An older man in faded jeans, a cotton shirt, boots, and a cowboy hat stood next to their table.

D-Day nodded. "What's it to you?"

"I didn't mean to eavesdrop," the cowboy said, "but you're heading right into the front lines. News this morning said the undead have overrun Salt Lake City and are heading east. They expect Colorado to be the next major battleground."

Jen downed the rest of her orange juice and looked from the cowboy to D-Day. "Then Colorado it is."

AUTHOR'S NOTES

In many ways The Hybrid is a lynchpin in the series. It answers some questions going all the way back to Book One, The Awakening, and sets the table for the rest of the series.

This was the first book of the series that was written after the The Awakening was released to the public, and reader reactions to the series gave me plenty of motivation and inspiration to keep the series moving along.

We're now heading into the fall and winter where my writing pace usually picks up. Other than a trip to Pittsburgh for Night of the Living Dead 50th anniversary events, and a follow-on to New England to see family, I'll be holed up in front of the computer, pounding away at the keyboard. Like you, I can't wait to see what happens next.

If you'd like to keep up with what I've got coming out, sign up for my email list at uprising.marobbins.com. You'll get a **free** eBook, new release announcements, updates, and even some drawings to win prizes like signed paperbacks and other unique items.

Thank you so much for reading the Hybrid. Know that I take no reader for granted and I'm truly humbled that you spent your time reading my book.

Till next time.

M.A. Robbins

ACKNOWLEDGMENTS

Thanks go to my wife, Debbie, for her steadfast support. Tamara Blain, editor extraordinaire at A Closer Look Editing, was a godsend for this book as events gave her a shorter turnaround time and she aced it with a smile. Domi at Inspired Cover Designs just keeps adding to her legend. To the beta readers, I really appreciate your input and honesty. You made the book better.

To all the readers, I've received such positive feedback since the series launched in May 2018. Rest assured that I'm putting my heart and soul into the books to provide you with top-notch zombie action. Thank you for reading!

THE RECKONING

BOOK FIVE IN THE ZOMBIE UPRISING
SERIES

CONTENTS

This book is dedicated to you, the reader of the Zombie Uprising. Thanks for joining me for the journey.

1

J en grimaced as she swallowed a cold forkful of scrambled eggs. *How do you screw up something so simple?*

The attendant at the motel dining room stuck his head in the door and flashed a smile. "How's everything?" he asked in a chirpy voice. He looked at her as if he could see through her mirror sunglasses. *If that were true, it'd wipe that smile off his face.*

She nodded to his question. "Fine. Got any hot sauce?"

Smile still pasted on his late-teen face, the attendant hustled to her table and pulled a small bottle of Tabasco sauce from his apron. Without another word, he disappeared through the door.

Jen sighed and splashed the sauce over her eggs. A commercial ended on the TV and the news came back on. Jen shifted her attention to the large screen on the wall.

"The war against the undead suffered a severe setback overnight," the grim-faced, perfectly coiffed news anchor said into the camera. A map of the United States was displayed behind him, a red line bisecting the country through Montana, Wyoming, Colorado, and New Mexico.

"This was the front line yesterday," the talking head said. The image changed with the red line moved out to eastern Colorado. "With Denver's fall in a massive zombie assault last night, our troops are in retreat to Kansas."

"Shit," Jen said.

A chair next to her squealed and she jumped. D-Day plopped onto the seat and placed a tray on the table. He gazed over the empty room. "Not their busy season, is it?" He nodded at the TV. "Does that say what I think it does?"

Jen watched as D-Day shoveled a whole sausage into his mouth. His eyes closed as he chewed and he made a satisfied rumble in his throat.

Jen rolled her eyes. *Guy can eat anything.*

"We need to get a damn disposable phone," she said. "I left Zeke and Wayne hanging. They don't know what's going on."

D-Day wiped his mouth with a napkin. "We'll do that first thing. There was too much military activity on the road last night to stop anywhere. We need to be careful."

"All they know is we're heading toward Colorado," Jen said. "Couldn't talk once Zeke told me about some new Homeland Security agents that were sitting near them. Couldn't take the chance on the wrong person finding out where we were."

"And their destination was changed from Atlanta to Pittsburgh and no one told them why," D-Day said. "There's something going on."

Jen took a swig of her orange juice and placed the glass on the table. "They're in danger. I just know it. Just like I know the government would be on us like flies on shit the minute I used my government phone."

"They can take care of themselves." D-Day gestured to the TV screen. "Looks like Butler's going to come to us if we wait for him."

The screen switched to a commercial from Homeland Security. A woman in hair rollers and with a shotgun explained how to detect and report zombie activity.

"We're in what, eastern Missouri?" Jen asked.

D-Day nodded. "Sikeston."

She dropped her fork on her plate and sat back. "We have to go to Butler, not wait for him. There are too many people between the horde and us. Too many that'll die."

"Can't we just find a leader so you can touch it and talk to Butler?"

"I don't know," she said. "Every communication through a leader has been Butler contacting me. Don't you remember that one we ran into just before we left Georgia? Couldn't get shit out of it."

"Maybe you weren't close enough to Butler. We're hundreds of miles closer to him now and he's heading this way."

Jen shrugged. "Worth a try. I had a few numbness episodes overnight, but none lasted long. They must be getting killed as soon as they turn."

D-Day pushed his plate forward. "We'll need to top off the gas tank before we go anywhere." He hitched a thumb over his shoulder. "Saw a convenience store with fuel pumps nearby when we pulled in last night. We can pick up a phone there, too."

Jen emptied her orange juice and stood. "Let's do it."

D-DAY STARTED THE HARLEY. Black smoke chugged from the exhaust as it rumbled to life. He motioned for Jen to get on, and she wedged herself between him and the sissy bar. "Wish we'd kept the sidecar," she said into his ear. "This seat hurts my ass after a half hour."

"A sidecar limits our maneuverability and uses more gas," D-Day said. "Besides, you'll get your own bike as soon as we find a decent one we can steal."

Jen put her arms around him and propped her feet on the passenger foot pegs. "I've never ridden a bike on my own."

D-Day tilted his head back and laughed. "You ride four-wheelers and snowmobiles, you can ride a bike." He accelerated and rode around the motel, then pulled onto an empty Highway 62. Almost immediately, a convenience store came up on the right. He pulled in, stopped at the pumps out front, and turned off the engine.

Jen squeezed herself out from behind the burly biker and walked up to the closest pump. She jiggled a padlock on the nozzle. "Locked."

A ding came from the convenience store and a twenty-something man in dirty jeans and a blue T-shirt that had seen better days sauntered toward them. Jen automatically adjusted her sunglasses to make sure they were secure on her face.

"Sorry," the man said. "Gas is only for those with ration vouchers, law enforcement, or government officials." He took a wide stance next to the pump and folded his arms. A pistol was strapped to his side.

"Then we're just the folks you can help." Jen reached into her back pocket and the man's hand went to his pistol grip.

Jen froze. "Just getting my ID."

The man glanced from Jen to D-Day, and back again. "Go ahead." His hand didn't leave the pistol.

Jen drew her ID and held it up. "Homeland Security."

The man squinted, then nodded. He pointed at D-Day. "Him, too?"

She nodded.

The man's shoulders lost all their tension and he gave her a smile. "Sorry for the caution. Had a station in the next town last week where an attendant was murdered. Sumbitches wanted the gas."

D-Day unscrewed the Harley's gas cap. "How about that lock?"

"Oh, yeah," the man said. He fished in his pocket and pulled out a ring of keys.

Jen nodded at the convenience store. "I'm going to pick up a few things. Need anything?"

"Could use a cold one," D-Day said.

"Any particular brand?" she asked.

The gas attendant pulled the padlock off of a pump. "Here ya go."

D-Day grabbed the gas nozzle. "Get me anything that's not light."

Jen smiled. "You've got it."

She crossed from the fuel pump island to the convenience store and pushed the glass door open, causing another high-pitched ding.

Standing in the doorway, she surveyed the store. Small and packed with goods, it looked like any of the thousands of stores across America. The glow from overhead lights bleached everything out, making it harder for Jen to see any detail through her sunglasses.

She picked up a small bag of chips from a display in front of her and noticed an older man behind the counter with his eyes locked on her.

Creepy.

She walked up to him and stared back. "Where can I find the beer?"

His gaze never wavered as he pointed behind her. "Fridge on the back wall."

"And a disposable phone?"

"Got 'em right under here." He patted the counter. "Remind me when you cash out and I'll fish one out for you."

The door dinged and the attendant walked in. Jen made her way down an aisle between displays of pastries and cookies on one side and magazines on the other.

She pulled the fridge door open and studied the beer singles.

Mumbling came from the register, and she glanced over at the attendant and old man speaking in hushed tones. The attendant pointed toward the pumps and the old man shook his head and jerked a thumb at a corkboard on the wall. He then shooed the attendant out of the store.

As she turned back to the fridge, a sharp pain stabbed Jen's gut, and bile rose in her throat. She put a hand on the door handle and steadied herself. "Zombie. Somewhere close."

She grabbed a sixteen ounce can of beer and turned. *Need to get to it before it's killed.*

Catching a flash out of the corner of her eye, she stood on her tiptoes and watched the old man disappear behind a door marked *Employees Only*.

"Are you shitting me?" She trudged to the counter and placed the beer and chips down. "Held up by an old man's bladder."

A muffled voice vibrated through the wall. Jen cocked her head. It was the old man, but wasn't clear enough for her to make out any words. *He does seem excited, though. What the hell is he up to in the bathroom?*

She gazed out the window. The young guy had engaged D-Day in conversation. The biker stood with his arms crossed, and nodded.

Come on, old man. Got to go.

Her gaze drifted to the counter. The old guy had left a half cup of black coffee and an open hunting magazine by his seat. Cigars and cigarettes spanned the display case on the wall, well out of reach of any light-fingered customer. Jen leaned over the counter to see where the phones were. "A freaking padlocked drawer?"

Fishing in her pocket for some bills, she plopped a ten on the counter. "Dammit. I'm just going to leave the money. We'll get the phone somewhere else."

She picked up the beer and chips and turned to leave, glancing at the corkboard the old man had been pointing at earlier. She stopped. "The fuck?"

A poster was pinned on the upper middle of the board. A Wanted Poster. Jen's black-and-white eyes stared back at her from it.

"Son of a bitch."

She tore the poster from the board and examined it. The picture was the one on her Homeland Security ID. "Ten thousand dollars for information leading to the arrest of Jennifer Reed," she read. "Do not approach. Consider her armed and dangerous."

"Time to go." She folded the poster, stuck it in her pocket, and picked up the beer and chips. The Employees Only door slammed open and the old man stood there, a shotgun pointed at her gut.

His face chiseled in stone, he aimed down the barrel. "Don't move."

2

Z eke yawned and his gaze fell on Wayne snoozing next to him at the back of the nearly empty train car.

Oh, yeah.

Two Homeland Security agents sat up front across the aisle from a sleeping Dr. Preston. The larger agent, Dickson, turned around and stared at Zeke. He had a phone to his ear and nodded before facing forward. The other agent, a slim older man with a bald head and a permanent scowl, leaned in to Dickson and said something Zeke couldn't hear.

Wayne stirred next to him. "How far out are we?" he muttered.

Zeke looked out the window. "I asked Preston a few minutes ago. He said Pittsburgh's not far."

Wayne straightened and scratched his head. He pulled his phone from his pocket and flipped it open. "Hear anything from Jen or Dr. Cartwright yet?"

Zeke shook his head. "Haven't tried in the past twenty minutes. Not being able to talk to Jen is freaking me out."

Wayne punched a button on the phone and put it to his ear. "Got me worried. We get diverted from Atlanta to Pittsburgh and Jen calls and says she's heading to Colorado, then clams up. And now her phone goes straight to voice mail. Something shady's going on."

"I'll never forgive myself if something happens to her." Zeke rubbed his thumb over the wooden hilt of the katana on his lap.

"Shit." Wayne made a face and closed the phone. "I've already left six messages." He leaned in to Zeke and lowered his voice. "I don't care what assignment Homeland Security has for us. When we get to Pittsburgh, I'm off to look for Jen."

Thurmond, the older agent, made his way back to them. His flat, black eyes fell on Zeke. "How're you guys?"

Eyes like a shark. "We're OK. Just eager to get back."

He nodded like he sympathized with them. "Part of the job."

"Anything wrong?" Wayne asked.

"Nope." Thurmond leaned over and peered out the window. "But you guys hang tight when we arrive at Pittsburgh. We're going to get the doc off first and get her to the CDC building then come back and pick you up."

Zeke glanced at Wayne and raised his eyebrows. *This is new.* "Why's that?"

"They're picking us up in a smaller SUV." He brushed the front of his jacket. "Can't all fit at once. The train won't be going anywhere, and you'll be safer in it than on the streets."

A heavy feeling crept into the pit of Zeke's stomach, but he smiled. "Sounds great."

Wayne maintained a poker face. "Yup. We're in no hurry."

Thurmond smiled, a slow creeping stretching of the lips that revealed a set of teeth so white they practically glowed. "Good."

He straightened and loped back to the front, plopping down next to Dickson. They huddled together and spoke in hushed tones.

Zeke tightened his grip on the katana's hilt. "What the hell was that?" he whispered.

Wayne opened his phone again and pushed a button. "Dr. Cartwright must know. Damn shame that Agent Rodriguez and Agent Daniels got themselves killed. They were all right."

Watching buildings pass by, Zeke frowned. "Not being able to talk to Jen has got me jumpy."

"I'm with you," Wayne said.

Zeke's pocket vibrated and two seconds later a voice from it yelled, "Get to the choppa! Get to the choppa!" Zeke fumbled to pull out the phone while it continued to scream. The ringtone grew louder as the phone cleared his pocket. He flipped it open and pressed it to his ear. "Hello?"

Dickson and Thurmond stared at him.

The phone clicked. "Zeke, say that you're sorry and you think I have the wrong number."

Sergeant Howell?

"I'm sorry," Zeke said, "but I think you have the wrong number."

"Who's that?" Wayne asked. Zeke put a hand up.

"Do not take the train into the Pittsburgh station," Howell said. "Get off beforehand. You and your brother's lives depend on it."

Zeke raised his voice. "I don't know anyone named Curtis."

"When you hang up, take a look at this caller ID and memorize the number. Call me back when you get away."

"I can't be any more clear, buddy," Zeke said. "You have the wrong number."

"Good luck," Howell said. The call clicked dead.

"Don't call back again," Zeke said. He slammed the phone closed and slid it into his back pocket.

Thurmond had risen and was halfway to him. Zeke swallowed.

"Problem?" Thurmond asked when he arrived.

Wayne looked back and forth between Zeke and Thurmond. Zeke willed him to be quiet.

"Just a wrong number," Zeke said.

Thurmond's scowl grew deeper. "Let us know if you need anything."

Zeke nodded and Thurmond rejoined Dickson.

"What the hell was that ringtone?" Wayne asked. "Didn't sound like Arnold Schwarzenegger."

Zeke licked his lips and glanced at the agents muttering between themselves. "It was from *Left 4 Dead*."

"What the hell's *Left 4 Dead*?"

"A video game." Zeke leaned toward Wayne and lowered his voice. "That was Sergeant Howell on the phone. He said we need to get off the train before we reach Pittsburgh."

"What?" Wayne said. "Why?"

"He didn't say and I didn't ask, but I think it has something to do with our new friends up front."

Wayne's hand rested on his pistol grip. "Why would they want to do anything to us?"

Zeke shrugged. "Who knows? They've been on the phone a lot. Someone's pulling their strings. And I don't think it's a coincidence that Cartwright and Jen are offline."

How they hell are we going to get off? It'll have to be on the approach to Pittsburgh when the train slows. Zeke pulled his phone out and flipped it open. He studied Howell's number, whispering it to himself several times as he read it. Closing the phone, he slid it back into his pocket.

"You want to show me?" Wayne asked.

Zeke glanced at the agents. "I've got it. I got good at remembering stuff when I did theater in high school, remember? Never forgot a line."

"Wait a couple of minutes and follow me." Wayne stood.

Zeke's heart leapt. "What the hell are you doing?"

Wayne strode up the aisle. Dickson and Thurmond turned.

"What's the problem?" Dickson growled.

Wayne pointed to the bathroom door at the front of the car. "Gotta go."

He pulled the door open and stepped in. The clunk of the lock was loud enough for Zeke to hear it.

Zeke's heart raced, but he stayed seated and drew his pistol from its holster. A minute passed and the lock clicked. Wayne stepped out of the bathroom with a disgusted look on his face.

"What's wrong with you?" Dickson asked.

"Someone made a mess in there and the toilet doesn't work." Wayne loped toward the back of the car. "I'll have to use the one in the next car."

Thurmond's mouth opened and closed, but nothing came out. He looked at Dickson, who shrugged.

Wayne winked at Zeke just before he crossed to the next car. The door closed behind him with a thud.

Thurmond and Dickson glared at Zeke. "He better be back before we get to Pittsburgh," Dickson said.

Zeke smiled. "How long till we get there?"

"Not long," Thurmond said.

As if on cue, the train slowed with a rattle. Zeke took a deep breath, stood, and strapped his sheathed katana to his back. "I'll get him."

Thurmond stood. "I'll go get him."

Zeke put a hand out in a calming gesture. "You two need to guard Dr. Preston, don't you? I'll bring him back. Take just a minute."

He opened the door and stepped through, letting it slam closed. *Don't look back.*

Passengers in the second car looked up as he entered. The bathroom's lock said it was unoccupied, but Zeke opened it anyway. Empty. *Where the hell is he?*

He smiled at an older lady in the front seat. "Did you happen to see where my brother went, ma'am? He came through this door a minute ago."

A man with a salt-and-pepper beard and eyebrows that looked like they needed trimming with hedge clippers jerked a thumb over his shoulder. "He went right through to the next car."

Zeke hurried through the back door and into the next car, glancing back as the door closed. His heart jumped into his throat as Thurmond stepped through from the first car with his pistol in his hand. He spotted Zeke and yelled, "Get back here."

The agent raised the pistol. "Stop."

Zeke took cover behind the door. *Too many people for a shootout.*

Thurmond shot, and the glass in the door's window shattered.

Passengers in both cars screamed and ducked behind their seats. Zeke dropped to one knee and fired a shot at the ceiling over Thurmond. The agent dropped to the floor.

Passengers had crowded the back doorway of Zeke's car, trying to get out. *Dammit.*

He peered through the broken glass. Thurmond was creeping down the aisle, his gun pointed ahead of him. His eyes locked on Zeke's and he fired at him. Zeke ducked, and the last remaining glass in the window was destroyed.

A scream from behind drew Zeke's attention. A middle-aged woman trying to flee had been struck and had fallen to the floor. Blood pooled around her motionless body. The crowd surged to the rear door, plugging it up. *No one's getting through there now.*

The passengers in Thurmond's car had escaped out the front, so Zeke shot at Thurmond. He missed. The door behind Thurmond opened, and Dickson joined his fellow agent, opening fire at Zeke. More passengers in Zeke's car fell, the yelling and screaming reaching a crescendo before it stopped for a second, then went up another octave.

The middle-aged woman crouched in the aisle, her yellow eyes locked on the frightened passengers. She leapt onto the pile and tore a young man's neck open. His blood sprayed over the crowd and they went into a full-blown panic, shoving and pushing to get away.

Two other dead passengers turned and joined in the bloody feast.

Another volley of rounds penetrated the door and only missed Zeke by inches. The agents were nearly on him.

Zeke pressed himself against the bathroom door.

Trapped.

3

Jen flung the beer at the old man and leapt for the cover of an aisle. She slammed onto the cold tile floor as the shotgun blast blew past.

Chunk-Chunk.

Rolling onto her side, Jen drew her pistol. Another shot from the old man, and several boxes of cereal exploded above her. *Dammit.*

She popped up and fired, missing the old bastard, but taking a chunk of wood off the doorway and forcing him to duck.

"I don't want to hurt you," she yelled. "Just put the gun down and I'll leave."

"Not a chance. I've got you trapped and the cops are coming. That reward money is as good as mine."

Jen jumped from the aisle and shot at the old man. He gasped and fired off-balance, the pellets shattering the front window.

Jen aimed at his chest and squeezed the trigger. The pistol recoiled in her hand and a hole appeared in the man's chest just below his right shoulder.

He howled, dropped the shotgun, and stumbled backward into the room.

Jen darted outside. D-Day had taken cover behind an old pickup that was peppered with bullets. He held his gun at the ready, but wasn't firing. *What the hell?*

Aiming her pistol at the attendant, she saw why. *That asshole's hiding behind a pump.*

She took off her sunglasses and holstered her handgun. *Let's see what he thinks of my pretty yellow eyes.*

The attendant shot at D-Day again and Jen bull-rushed him. He turned and his face slackened as his eyes locked onto hers.

"Zombie eyes!" she screamed.

Jen slammed into the attendant and drove him into a pump. They both bounced off, and the attendant collapsed onto his back. Jen kicked out and cracked his jaw with her heel. He lay still.

D-Day ran over and checked the attendant. "He'll be out for a while. What happened inside?"

Jen put her sunglasses back on and climbed onto the motorcycle. "Had to shoot the old man. Gave me no choice."

D-Day frowned, then looked around. "What about my beer?"

"Are you serious?" She slapped the seat. "Get your ass on this bike and get us out of here. The old man called the cops."

D-Day hopped on and started the bike, then kicked up gravel as he steered onto Route 62. Jen's stomach ached. *The zombie's still somewhere nearby.*

She tapped D-Day on the shoulder. "Go left."

D-Day hit the gas and followed her instruction. She closed her eyes. The tingling picked up and centered on her right side.

Sirens howled from behind. A cop car swung into the convenience store parking lot. D-Day accelerated.

Her right side had damn near gone numb. She yelled in D-Day's ear. "Take that next right."

He shook his head. "Cops."

"I don't give a shit. There's a leader over there somewhere."

Shaking his head, D-Day took the right, and the gas station, now almost a mile away, disappeared behind several buildings.

The numbness was so intense, Jen could barely lift her right arm.

A one-story building came up, a sign in front. In a flowery font, it said *Sikeston Nursing Home.*

"There," Jen said.

D-Day sped up and passed it.

"What the hell?"

"We can find a leader somewhere else," D-Day said. "No need to get caught here."

Jen gritted her teeth, but had no choice. *Every minute I'm not in contact with Butler, more people die.*

D-Day cut over to Route 55 North. The highway had little traffic and he goosed the accelerator. Jen stewed as she watched green fields zip by.

FORTY MINUTES LATER, they rolled off the highway at Exit 95.

Cape Girardeau. Never heard of it.

Another gas station with a convenience store came up on their left, and D-Day pulled in and stopped. Jen squeezed out from behind him and rubbed her sore butt. "Still wish we'd kept the sidecar."

D-Day scowled and turned off the bike. "You can be a pain in the ass when someone's trying to keep you out of trouble."

"Speaking of a pain in the ass," Jen said, "you should've stopped at the nursing home. Nothing's more important right now than contacting Butler."

D-Day crossed his arms. "What's your deal? Do you think just because you have your special super zombie powers that you don't have to listen to anyone else?"

Jen's face grew hot. "Why not? I'm the only person in the world who can stop this shit."

"No," D-Day spat. "You're not. Everything we've done has been as a team. It wasn't just you when we fought off the horde on the train. Seems to me it wasn't just you in Rhode Island. And from what I've heard from Zeke, it hasn't been only you since this whole shit started."

Jen balled her fists and got in his face. "I didn't ask for this, but I got it, and nobody but me bears the burden of it."

D-Day took a deep breath and exhaled loudly. "Look. You don't take advice well and you run head-on into shit. It's part of your charm, and it's worked out so far. I get that. But the day's gonna come when it costs you." He looked down at his feet. "And I don't wanna see you hurt."

D-Day being sentimental? Who would've guessed?

Jen stepped back. "I'm sorry. I know what you're saying, but it's the way I roll."

"Maybe it'll roll you right into a grave," D-Day said.

"I'll try to remember that."

D-Day nodded.

Jen spread her arms. "Still friends?"

D-Day grinned and pulled her into a bear hug. "Always."

A middle-aged man in faded jeans and a cowboy hat left the convenience store and jumped in a beat-up pickup. A cloud of black smoke blew out the tailpipe when it started. The truck rumbled down the road and disappeared in the distance.

Quiet enveloped them.

"This place looks dead," Jen said.

She took a step toward the store and D-Day took her arm. "What happened at that last stop? Why did those guys start shooting at us?"

Jen pulled the wanted poster from her pocket and handed it to him. He unfolded it and whistled. "So you're public enemy number one."

"I just thank God they didn't use the picture from my driver's license. I look like a total dork in it."

D-Day crumpled the poster and threw it in a trash can. "We can't have a repeat of that here. Maybe you should stay outside."

"Hell, no."

D-Day folded his arms. "I can get whatever you want."

Jen sighed. *He has a point.* "What I want is that cell phone so I can call Zeke and Wayne." She frowned.

D-Day nodded. "You got it." He took a step toward the store's front door.

"And get me another bag of chips," Jen said. "I didn't get to finish the last one."

Jen leaned against the faux brick wall of the store and surveyed the area. She turned away and pretended to look at something on the ground when a green sedan cruised by.

"Shit's got me paranoid now."

D-Day sauntered out of the store a few minutes later with a plastic bag in hand and a smile on his lips.

"You got what I asked for?" Jen asked.

He lifted the bag. "Got your phone right here."

"Great. What about the other thing I asked for?"

D-Day reached in, pulled out a bag of chips, and tossed it to her.

"That's what I'm talking about." She tore it open, spilling a few chips on the ground, and stuffed a crisp overcooked one in her mouth.

"How come these bags never open right?" she said. Crumbs fell from her mouth. "Oops. Sorry."

D-Day took out the disposable phone and read the directions to activate it. A few minutes later, he smiled. "Good to go."

Jen crumpled her chip bag and tossed it into a garbage can. "Let me have it."

Sitting on a picnic table next to D-Day, she took the phone, turned it on, and punched in Zeke's number.

I'd feel a lot better if he and Wayne were here. She pressed the Call button and then the Speaker button.

The ringback tone played loud and clear.

4

Zeke pressed against the bathroom door wishing he could melt through it. He jiggled the handle. *Locked.* He had the murderous agents in one direction and an evolving zombie horde in the other. *And here I am, the monkey in the middle.*

With a guttural moan, a beefy man in a torn and bloody business suit crept forward. Half of his face had been ripped away and his muscles and teeth lay exposed.

Zeke shot wildly and missed. The zombie approached as if it had all the time in the world. Zeke lined up his sight on the zombie's forehead and squeezed the trigger, but it didn't fire. He glanced at the pistol. The slide was open.

Empty.

The zombie leapt at Zeke. Without the time or room to unsheathe his katana, he brought his knees up and kicked the zombie in the chest as it landed. It flew into the aisle and scrambled back to its feet.

A fusillade of rounds came from the other car with a few of them hitting the zombie. *Damn thing didn't even flinch.*

Zeke drew a six-inch blade from his boot. The zombie sprung and landed inches away. Zeke brought the knife up and shoved it into the zombie's throat. Blood sprayed everywhere as the zombie pressed in, his teeth snapping inches from Zeke's face.

Holding the creature back with his free hand, Zeke pulled the knife out and ran it into the bottom of the zombie's jaw, through the roof of its mouth, and into its brain.

Its yellow eyes rolled up and it slumped on top of him.

The gunfire from the agents continued. Zeke wrestled the dead zombie and positioned it between him and the agents. He stuck his gun through the window and fired blindly into the agents' car. The gunfire paused for several seconds, then picked up again. Several bullets hit the dead body hiding Zeke.

The feeding frenzy in Zeke's car was coming to an end. Everyone else was either a zombie or food. Some of the undead broke through to other cars. Victims' screams filled the air.

Zeke leaned against the bathroom door. *Guess this is my last stand.* "I hope you get away, Wayne. Find Jen and protect her for me."

The bathroom door opened and Zeke fell backward, landing on his ass.

"Get up." Wayne grabbed his arm and tugged.

Zeke stumbled to his feet and Wayne slammed the door shut. Something large hit the other side.

"You were in here the whole time?" Zeke asked.

"Wasn't sure it was you until I heard you say my name. What the hell's going on out there?"

The gunshots paused, then picked up again. Shadows under the door had coalesced into a single large one.

"Those agents were trying to kill me," Zeke said. "Now it's Zombie City out there."

The train jerked and slowed again. Wayne peered out a small outer window. "Almost there," he said. "But we aren't getting out of this shitter anytime soon."

A yell came from outside the door.

"That sounded like Thurmond," Zeke said.

Bodies banged against their door and footsteps ran past. "They're moving," Wayne said. "One of the leaders must've opened the door. Those agents are screwed."

"What about Dr. Preston?" Zeke asked. "What happens if she's killed or turned? Isn't she the last best hope for a cure?"

The train came to a sudden stop, tossing Zeke into Wayne. Zeke steadied himself and looked out the window at a platform filled with armed cops and militiamen. Someone yelled, "Prepare to fire."

Zeke grabbed Wayne and pushed him to the floor.

"What the hell?" Wayne said. "Do you know how nasty this place is?"

Zeke jumped on top of him. "Stay low."

"Fire," came the bellow from outside.

The sounds deafening, bullets slammed into the car, broke out their window, and penetrated the wall. The zombie growls couldn't be heard, but the bodies running into the door and dropping to the floor could.

What took a few minutes felt like an hour. Someone yelled, "Cease fire." After several seconds of scattered gunfire, it went silent.

Zeke's heart slammed his chest. He studied the bullet holes in the wall. "How'd we not get shot?"

Some growling and movement came from the car, but it was mostly quiet. Zeke stood and held out a hand to Wayne. His brother took the offered hand and pulled himself to his feet while wiping his pants.

"Squad A, enter the cars from the rear. Squad B, from the front."

Boot steps came from the front of the train, followed by scattered shots. Within minutes, only the purposeful pace of human footsteps paced through the train car.

A slow, heavy set of footsteps came from the back of the car and stopped a few feet away. "Any sign of the targets?" a raspy voice asked.

"No, Captain," answered another. "Agents Dickson and Thurmond reported them on board as late as five minutes before arriving. They can't be far."

Targets? Us?

"What about Dickson and Thurmond?"

"Dead."

"And the doctor?" the captain asked.

"Same."

"Son of a bitch."

"Orders, Captain?"

A sigh came from the other side of the door. "Send another team through to mop up. I've got to call command and let them know their people are dead and the traitors have escaped."

The men left and Wayne opened the door. "We've got to get the hell out of here."

Zeke choked as the smell of slaughter assaulted his nostrils. He coughed. He put an arm across Wayne's chest. "Are you nuts? They're calling us traitors. We'll never get past all those militiamen. We need to wait until they've gone."

Wayne frowned. "Didn't you hear that guy? They're sending more in to mop up. What if they look in the bathroom?"

More boots nearby. *Shit.*

Zeke eased the door closed and pushed down on Wayne's shoulder. "We need to get on the floor and play dead."

"Why the hell do I have to be the one to get on the floor again?"

"You're already dirty. Why should both of us stink?" Zeke pressed harder. The militiamen were almost in their car. "Hurry," he whispered.

Wayne sank to his knees and splayed out on the floor. Zeke placed his sheathed katana on the floor next to Wayne and draped himself over his brother and sword, while facing away from the door.

Two voices came from the car.

"Would ya look at all these freaks," the first voice said with a slight lisp.

A deeper voice replied, "I hope they ain't gonna make us clean this shit up."

The bathroom door opened and slammed into Zeke's side. He clenched his teeth. *I think they broke a freaking rib.*

"Two in here," Lisp Voice said. "Dead."

Deep Voice sighed loudly. "Why do we get all the shit jobs? We didn't even get to shoot any of these fuckers."

A boot planted firmly onto Zeke's back and pressed down. Zeke stifled a gasp.

"Come on, Dan," Lisp Voice said. "You're wasting our time."

The boot's pressure released and a pistol was cocked a few feet away. Wayne stirred beneath Zeke. *Don't move, bro.*

"I'm gonna shoot some of these things anyway," Dan said. "Like they do in war movies. Make sure they're dead."

"They woulda attacked by now if they weren't dead," Lisp Voice said.

The boots tromped away from the bathroom and stopped nearby. A gunshot boomed.

"See," Lisp Voice said. "Waste of time. And don't let the chief find out you wasted bullets."

"Yeah, yeah." The boots clomped to the back of the car. The external door slid open. "Let's go get some chow," Deep Voice said.

Zeke let out a breath. "Let's get the hell out of here while we can," he whispered to Wayne.

The phone in Zeke's back pocket vibrated.

Shit, no!

The damn thing screamed, "Get to the choppa! Get to the choppa!"

5

J en bit her lip as Zeke's phone rang once...twice...three times from the phone's speaker. "He's not answering."

"Give him time," D-Day said.

The phone clicked. A lispy voice answered. "Hello."

Jen looked at D-Day, who shrugged. "Who is this?" she asked. "Where's Zeke?"

"This is Max."

Max who? "What number are you at, Max? I think I may have dialed wrong."

"Hell if I know," Max said. "You wouldn't happen to be calling some guy with a punk-style haircut and a long dangling earring with a skull at the end, would you?"

Jen swallowed. "Yes."

D-Day scowled. "His name is Zeke and his brother Wayne was with him. What the hell are you doing with his phone?"

Jen put a hand on D-Day's arm and pressed the phone to her chest. "Let's use honey on this one," she whispered.

D-Day folded his arms, but said nothing further.

"I'm with the Pittsburgh Militia," Max said. "A train of infected arrived at our station. We were just mopping up when we heard this phone. I took it from the pocket of the punk rocker. He's dead."

Jen's hand opened and the phone bounced off the ground. The world swam before her eyes. She leaned against a wall to keep from falling over.

"What was that?" Max asked.

D-Day picked up the phone. "She dropped the phone."

"What about Wayne?" Jen said. "His brother. He was with him. About an inch taller and five years older."

Voices muttered over the phone.

"Him, too," Max said.

Tears stung Jen's eyes. D-Day's scowl had morphed into a full-blown grimace.

"Hey, I'm sorry about your friends," Max said. "You can pick up the bodies if you can come by within the next few hours."

Jen's eyes stung. *Wayne. We never had the chance...*

And—

"Zeke," she breathed. He'd saved her so many times, and now he was gone.

D-Day held the phone up to her.

"We won't be able to pick them up," she said. "What will happen to them?"

"Placed in a pile and torched," Max said. His tone told her he didn't give much of a shit.

Jen looked at D-Day and shook her head. He hung the phone up. The floodgates opened and tears flowed down her cheeks.

D-Day pulled her into a hug. "I'm sorry."

She laid her head on his chest. "I've got to stop this zombie bullshit. Too many people I care about have died, and I can't take any more."

"So we need to find a leader?" D-Day said.

"Yeah. No more screwing around. I need to talk to Butler and shut this fucking war down."

"I asked in the store," D-Day said. "About hospitals. There's one less than a mile away. St. Francis."

Jen wiped her eyes and straightened. *Got to put my game face back on.* "How big?"

"Big enough."

Jen stumbled to the bike and climbed on. "Let's go."

D-Day sat in front of her and started the bike. He guided it out of the parking lot and north on South Mt Auburn Road. Minutes later the hospital complex came into view.

"It's a good-sized one," Jen said.

D-Day parked the bike near the main entrance. "Need a plan," he said. "They'll have armed guards ready to take out the recently dead. If they're like other hospitals, some of those guards will be off-duty cops."

"We need to get to the hospice ward," Jen said. "People are there to die and usually have private rooms. It'll give us cover from prying eyes."

D-Day watched an ambulance scream by. "Can't just go wandering around in there. We need to look like we belong."

"What do you suggest?"

He shrugged. "Maybe find a locker room and change into scrubs."

Jen rolled her eyes. "Just like the movies, huh? I have a better idea. Follow me."

Jen strode into the main entrance and up to the Information Desk. An elderly woman with thick-lensed glasses looked up at her and smiled. "May I help you?"

"Yes, ma'am. Our relative was admitted to the hospice ward of a hospital in town. We're from the East Coast and don't know which hospital it is."

The woman pushed her glasses up her nose and positioned her fingers over a computer keyboard. "Name?"

"Jones," Jen said.

The keys clicked as the woman quickly typed. She frowned at the screen. "No Jones, I'm afraid." She removed her glasses. "Maybe your relative is at Landmark Hospital. Or Southeast."

"Could be," Jen said. "We'll check there. Thank you."

She led D-Day away from the counter.

"Nice try," he said. "We can still find some scrubs."

Jen went to a map of the hospital. "No one wears scrubs in the hospice ward. They want it as homey as possible."

She traced the map until she found what she wanted. "Here. Let's go."

Walking at a clipped pace, she entered a corridor that bisected the hospital. D-Day hurried to keep up. When they reached the other side, Jen surveyed the lobby until she found what she was looking for. "Stay with me."

The young man wearing a headset sitting behind the Information Desk looked at her as she approached and put up a finger. "The pharmacy is open until five p.m.," he said into his mic.

One of D-Day's eyebrows rose. *Bet he didn't think they'd have more than one info desk.*

"Thank you," the young man said. "Have a good day."

He took off the headset. "I'm sorry, but I have an appointment and my relief hasn't shown up yet. I suggest you try the Information Desk by the main entrance."

Are you shitting me?

Jen leaned on the counter. "We've driven for hours from the East Coast to get here. We have a dying relative who's in hospice, but we don't know if it's this hospital or another."

"You can just go to the ward and ask. It's on the sixth floor."

"Please," Jen said. "It'll only take a second."

"I'm sorry." The man stood and put on a jacket. "I'm late for my appointment."

D-Day stepped to the counter, placed his ham-sized fists on it, and leaned forward. "You'll be visiting your own emergency room if you don't help us right now."

The man froze. D-Day lowered his bushy eyebrows, staring menacingly.

The young man plopped back into his chair and pulled the keyboard toward him. "Last name."

"Smith," Jen said.

Fingers flying over the keyboard, the man swore and hit the backspace key a few times before continuing. His right hand grabbed the mouse. "Betty Smith?"

D-Day straightened. "That's her. Betty." He took Jen's hand. "Let's go see Aunt Betty one last time."

Without another word, he led her to the elevators. When she glanced back at the Information Desk, it was empty.

THE HOSPICE WARD had soft carpets, muted colors, and a hushed atmosphere. They checked in with a receptionist and were directed to a room halfway down a U-shaped corridor. In it, a nurse sat next to a hospital bed with a shriveled ancient woman in it. A monitor by the bed displayed her vitals.

"How is Aunt Betty?" Jen asked.

The nurse stood. "It shouldn't be long. We don't expect her to last another twelve hours."

"So sometime tonight?" D-Day asked.

"Could be twelve hours or twelve minutes," the nurse said. "I'll give you some privacy." She left and closed the door behind her.

Jen paced. "I feel ghoulish, just waiting for this lady to die."

"Don't let it bother you." D-Day plopped in a cushy chair and sunk in. "What you're doing will save a lot of lives."

"I suppose," Jen muttered. She opened the curtains and looked out at a section of roof ten feet below the window. It extended out fifty yards ahead and another seventy-five to the sides. *Damn hospital's big.*

She pulled the drapes wider until the sun sprayed across the old woman's bed. "If I was dying," Jen said, "I wouldn't want it to be so gloomy."

The door opened. A cop sporting an M4 locked eyes with her. "There you are," he said.

6

A gunshot boomed just behind Zeke, and an invisible cloud of sulfur burned his nostrils. He clenched his teeth and steeled his muscles. Another shot went off. Then two more.

"You're just wasting ammo," Max said.

"So what?" Dan's deep voice cut in. "Makes me feel good."

"Captain finds out and your ass is grass."

The boot pressed on Zeke's shoulder. "Need my pistol practice. I'll just plug a couple rounds into this punk rocker and call it a day," Dan said.

Zeke tensed. *Please don't let the bullets go through me and hit Wayne.*

"What are you assholes doing down there?" yelled someone from outside the train.

"Shit," Dan said. "Chief's fucking coming."

The two militiamen hurried from the car. "Just finished, Chief. Nothing in there."

"Then what the hell were those gunshots?"

"Not us," Dan said. "Maybe another car."

Their voices trailed off.

"You can get off me now," Wayne said.

"Shh. Not yet." Zeke waited for several minutes.

Satisfied, he pushed himself up.

"Shit." He stretched his back and stepped out of the bathroom. "I'd like to kick that guy in the balls."

Wayne stood and wiped his pants with his hands. "I need a hot bath."

Zeke crept to a window and peeked out. The bulk of the militiamen were gone. "Still a few of them out there."

"Then we should wait till dark."

"No," Zeke said. "You heard them tell Jen she had a few hours to get our bodies. Sounds like they'll clean the cars out before nightfall."

A PAIR of militiamen walked by the open door. One of them said something Zeke couldn't make out and the other laughed.

When they'd passed, Zeke crept to the bathroom and retrieved his katana, still in its scabbard. "We might be able to see more if we go to the last car."

Wayne pulled out his club. "I'll lead."

"Just a second." Zeke strapped the scabbard to his back. "OK."

Wayne inched to the doorway leading to the next car. He stepped across a body mangled with bullets and slipped, landing on his chest with an *oof.*

Zeke grasped his katana's hilt and listened. "I think we're good. Keep going."

Wayne pushed himself up and padded into the car.

Zeke watched his feet as he crossed between cars. Bloody half-eaten organs, slimy and still fresh, littered the passageway. Bodies lay strewn across the aisle.

They skulked through the cars, each one a canvas of gore painted in crimson splashes and body parts. *Not one damn car escaped the infected.*

Wayne stepped into the last car and froze.

"What's up?" Zeke asked.

His brother didn't respond.

"Wayne?" Zeke pushed past him. He gasped.

The back half of the car was piled to the ceiling with the dead. With nowhere else to flee, the passengers had sealed their own fates.

The bodies seemed to be quivering. Zeke approached the pile and choked. Flies. The corpses were infested with them. Shimmering wings pulsated to create the illusion of movement.

Zeke took a deep breath and almost fell over. The air, thick with blood and slaughter, gagged him. He stumbled out of the rear car, dropped onto a seat, and put his head between his legs until the nausea passed.

Wayne, white-faced, plopped down across from him. "That's more death in such a small place than I imagined could ever exist."

"I've seen a lot," Zeke said. "Thought I'd seen everything, but this one caught me by surprise."

Footsteps sobered Zeke up. Someone was on board. He pulled his feet onto the seat and peered down the aisle.

Someone moved several cars away. *Is he walking to us or away from us?*

Wayne stared at his brother, wide-eyed.

"Out the door, now," Zeke whispered.

He slipped into the aisle, still crouched, and duck-walked to the door at the front of the car. Sliding down the stairs, he stuck his head out and looked both ways.

Two militiamen exited a car halfway up the train. They carried a dead body between them and swung it several times until they released it. It flew in an arc and landed on top of a small pile of corpses.

Wayne pressed against Zeke. "What's going on?"

"When I take off, you follow close behind," Zeke said. "Don't stop for anything, even if we're spotted."

"Right."

The two militiamen climbed back into the car. Zeke hopped to the ground and dashed across the open area to the end of a tall apartment building. He ducked around the corner as shouting erupted from behind. Wayne slid in behind him.

"They've seen us," he said.

Zeke peered around the corner and a bullet zinged off the building mere inches above his head. He pulled back and drew his pistol, then stuck it out and fired blindly. "Too many of them."

Wayne leaned out and fired. A flurry of rounds answered him. He barely pulled back in time.

Zeke glanced behind them. "Give them a half dozen rounds to think about then follow me."

Wayne nodded and moved to the corner. Zeke sprinted down the sidewalk. He came out at a four-way intersection surrounded on three sides by skyscrapers. Wayne was still twenty yards behind, so Zeke aimed past his brother and waved him on. A militiaman broke cover and Zeke shot. The man ducked behind a tree.

"Across the street," Zeke said as Wayne approached. "Don't stop."

Wayne zipped by him, and Zeke shot at the tree then followed his brother.

With no traffic in sight, they crossed the road and ran down Grant Street. They'd just passed a hotel when five militiamen fired from behind.

Zeke passed Wayne and cut through an alley then burst onto William Penn Place. He took a left and then a right onto Seventh Avenue. A single car streaked past.

Wayne pulled up beside him and bent over, his chest heaving. "Can't run much more."

Too much open street when there's no traffic. Zeke scanned the block. *That's it.* He dashed to a clothing store across the street and pulled on the handle. It opened and he waved his brother in. "Quick."

Wayne stumbled in and Zeke pulled the door closed. He ducked behind a display just as three militiamen rounded the corner and raced up Seventh Avenue.

Zeke sat on the floor and held a hand to the stitch in his side. "Think we lost them, at least for now. We need transportation."

"I need a damn shower and a change of clothes."

"Right," Zeke said. "We'll take care of that first, then we'll get out of here."

"How?"

"Howell. Got to get back to Jen. If Dickson and Thurmond were going to kill us, what are they going to do to her?"

"Dr. Cartwright wouldn't let that happen," Wayne said. "I think Jen's safer than we are."

Zeke peered down Seventh Avenue again. No one. "All I know is Jen is safest when she's with us."

Wayne straightened. "True." He scratched his head. "I could jack a car, but we'd still have the gas problem."

"Even then, we still have to find Jen." Zeke rubbed his chin. "We need to call Howell back. If anyone can get us to her, he can."

Wayne stood and brushed himself off. "They've got a men's section here. Let me wash up and change first."

"Make it fast," Zeke said. "Never know when these guys are going to come back."

7

J en fought the urge to pull her pistol on the armed cop. *Time to play it cool.*

"You were looking for us?" she said, "Sorry, but we're all out of doughnuts. You might want to try the cafeteria."

The cop, a twenty-something with close-cropped blond hair, displayed an easy grin. "Doughnut jokes? Going for the low-hanging fruit, aren't you?"

Jen's heart hammered her chest. *This guy isn't here to arrest us.*

"Name's Grimes." He put his hand out to Jen. She shook it, and he approached D-Day and shook his hand. "I'm infection control this shift."

He stopped at the bed and looked down at the old lady, then at Jen. "I'm sorry about Mrs. Smith."

"Thanks." Jen crossed her arms. "Aunt Betty lived a good life."

Grimes nodded and took on a serious tone. "I'm required by law to give you a briefing on the infection control procedure."

D-Day stood next to Jen.

"First," Grimes said, "Mrs. Smith is hooked up to monitors that will alert the nursing desk when her vitals have deteriorated enough to indicate an imminent death. Sometimes it happens like that—"he clicked his fingers—"but often, it's a process."

I can see this guy's going to be a pain in the ass and screw up my chances to get on the Zombie Psychic Hotline with Butler.

"When the alarm goes off, I come in," Grimes said. "If she's flatlined, you will clear the room immediately. Failure to do so is a felony."

He took in a breath and let it out, giving Jen a sympathetic gaze. "She's gone when that happens, so there's no use in you staying. Trust me, you don't want to be here when I do my job."

"What if she isn't flatlined?" D-Day asked.

"Then you can stay until she does," Grimes said. "But I will be here with you until it's time for me to do my job."

"Understood," Jen said.

Grimes looked from Jen to D-Day and back again. "Good. Please let me know if you need anything in the meantime. I'm at the nurse's station unless there's another patient in their last moments."

"Thank you," Jen said as Grimes left the room and eased the door shut behind him.

She turned to D-Day. "Well, that's a big-ass problem. What are we going to do with Barney Fife just outside the damn door?"

D-Day examined the doorknob. "Door locks from the inside. Not industrial strength, but could be enough to keep him out until we've done what we've come for. How much time will you need to make contact?"

"Assuming it works at all, who the hell knows?" Jen said. "In Rhode Island, it only took seconds. It's not like talking, but more like seeing a movie of what's in his mind."

D-Day grunted and plopped onto a cushy chair next to the bed. The old lady's chest rose as she struggled to take a breath. Jen rushed to the bedside. The lines on the monitor scribbled wildly like a toddler with a crayon.

D-Day launched from the chair and reached the door just as a red light on the monitor blinked and an alarm buzz sounded from in the hallway. He flipped the deadbolt and pointed to a huge solid oak dresser in the corner. "Help me with this."

The door handle jiggled. "Open up!" Grimes yelled.

D-Day tilted the dresser and it fell to its side with a boom. Jen positioned herself next to the biker, and they pushed it in front of the door.

"Open up before it's too late." Pounding rattled the door, but it remained closed.

The old lady's chest heaved and her eyes opened with only the whites showing. Jen rushed to her side and took her hand. "I hope this doesn't drag out."

Struggling for breath, the woman arched her back. Jen's pulse picked up. *I hope she's not suffering.*

Multiple fists pounded the door. "They got a battering ram or something?" Jen asked.

D-Day braced himself against the dresser. "Don't worry about this. Just take care of business over there as fast as you can."

The old lady's body convulsed and settled on the bed, the air leaving her body like a leaky tire. The monitor's red light flashed quicker, then went solid as the EKG displayed a straight line.

"She's dead," Jen said. She grasped the old lady's wrinkled hand tighter. And waited.

The frenzied banging at the door slowed and then something big hit. It rattled, but held. "They're getting serious," D-Day said. He pulled his pistol and checked the load. "You just concentrate on what you're doing."

Jen placed her free hand on top of the old lady's. "Come on. What's taking so long?"

The old lady's eyes sprung open, her yellow irises glistening in the sunlight. Jen tore her sunglasses off and the zombie's gaze turned to her.

"Butler," Jen said. "Do you hear me?"

The old lady's mouth opened and closed like a fish pulled from the water. A low moan came from its lips.

A shock shot down Jen's spine. Things went dark. Silent. *Butler?*

She stood on a city street, throngs of undead flowing past her as if she were a rock in the middle of a raging river.

You've got to stop. Too many innocent lives are being taken.

The scene switched to a rural area with sweeping fields. A black cloud spread over it, pushing farther across the land like a locust plague in the Old Testament.

I understand what's happened and that the shadow government needs to be stopped. But you have to stop taking innocent lives.

Everything went dark. A pinpoint of light appeared in the distance and grew closer. A figure stepped into the light.

Butler.

Butler as he was as a human.

In a flash, Jen stood next to him. He had his arms behind his back and a scowl on his face.

"I can't stop it," he said.

"But I thought you were controlling them."

"I am." He closed his eyes. "I was. There are too many now. I control the millions that are with me, but there are many more I don't."

"Then we're screwed because I don't think the military can stop them."

Butler opened his eyes. They glowed yellow. "We can. You and me."

"Me? I can barely control a half dozen of them."

"Come to me," Butler said. "I'll show you how. You're stronger than me. You're special."

A chill came over Jen. "Where are you?"

"Marching down Interstate 70 with my troops. Heading to Kansas City." Butler and the light floated away. "Meet me there. Kansas City."

Jen's eyes popped open. Chest heaving, she released the old woman's hand. "D-Day, we've got to go."

D-Day strained against the dresser. The doorframe had cracked and the door pushed in a quarter inch. "Where?" he asked. "We're fucking trapped."

The old woman sprang from the bed and landed on all fours. She eyed D-Day.

Get in the corner and stay there.

The woman skittered to the corner.

Jen rushed to the window. "They don't open. Maybe we can shoot them out and jump onto the roof."

"You think you're in a movie?" D-Day gasped. "It'll leave big pieces of jagged glass. Look for a red dot."

"A what?"

"A red dot at the bottom of one of the windows."

Jen scanned the bottom of the window in front of her. *Nothing.* She pulled up the drapes from the one on the left. *Same.*

Ripping the drapes away from the right window, she yelled, "Here."

"Shoot that one. It's safety glass."

The door slid another quarter inch. An eye appeared in the opening. "Open the damn door!"

Jen pulled her pistol and fired a round into the wall a foot away from the eye. The eye vanished and D-Day shoved the door back into place. She then stepped back from the window and swung the gun around. Three rapid shots and the window spidered into tiny pieces. She kicked at it, knocking the glass from the bottom part of the window. "We've got our exit."

"You go first," D-Day said. "I'll be right behind."

Jen hesitated.

"Now!" D-Day screamed.

Jen holstered her pistol and grasped the bottom of the window, lowering herself her full arms' length. Letting go, she dropped to the roof and rolled.

Reaching out with her mind to the old lady, she watched D-Day struggle with the door. The cops were pushing again, and D-Day would have little time to get through the window once he let up on the dresser.

You will attack the men who come through that door. Do not bite or harm them, but knock them over and go through the door. Do not bite anyone, but make them think you will.

She broke contact and ran across the roof before taking cover behind a ventilator cap. "Come on, D-Day."

A bang came from the window and D-Day swung his body out, letting go as soon as he was stretched out. Shouting and gun fire came from the inside the room. D-Day raced across the roof.

"Over here." Jen waved and drew her pistol. A cop appeared at the window, aiming his rifle out of it. Jen fired, and the cop jumped out of sight.

D-Day passed her, heading for a set of stairs. Jen sprinted down the stairs behind him to the back parking lot. Still running, an ambulance was parked at the emergency room entrance.

"Get in," D-Day said.

Jen jumped in the back and closed the door. "Let's go."

D-Day spun the ambulance around and it careened onto Silver Springs Road. D-Day accelerated and took a right on Williams Street. "Where are we going?"

"Kansas City."

D-Day laughed. "Kansas City, here I come."

Straight into hell, here I come.

8

Wayne stepped out of the men's room and let out a huge sigh. "Much better."

"Now you're all pretty again," Zeke said. "Give me your phone. Time to call Sergeant Howell."

Wayne reached into his back pocket and pulled the cell phone out. "It'd be nice to get some answers." He handed it to Zeke. "Still remember his number?"

Zeke tapped a finger to his temple. "High-capacity memory." He flipped the phone open, punched the number keys, and set it to speaker.

The ringback tone played once then the phone clicked. "Yes," Howell said.

"It's Zeke and Wayne," Zeke said.

"I'd nearly written you off."

"So did we," Wayne said. "What the hell's going on? Why'd those Homeland Security agents try to kill us?"

"Are you alone?"

"Yup."

Howell's voice lowered. "Shit's hit the fan. There was an outbreak at CDC."

"Is Jen OK?" Zeke asked.

"She's alive, but Dr. Cartwright didn't make it."

"Where's Jen?" Wayne asked.

"I'll brief you on that when I see you. Can you get back to CDC?"

Zeke put the phone on mute. "I don't like this. We've got Homeland Security agents trying to kill us, Cartwright's dead, and on top of that we don't know where Jen is."

"You think we should go after her on our own?"

Zeke frowned. *Got to get to Jen. We can worry about everything else later.*

He pushed the mute button.

"We're in Pittsburgh," he said. "And their militia's hunting for us."

"Hang on," Howell said. There was murmuring on the other end, then Howell came back on. "Are you near the train station?"

"We are," Zeke said.

"Find Liberty Avenue and take it west," Howell said. "Just before you get to the river, Point State Park will be on your right. A Blackhawk will pick you up there in an hour and bring you here."

"What about all the people trying to kill us?" Zeke asked.

"Can't discuss it on the phone," Howell said. "I've got CDC Headquarters vetted and we're safe here. So until the helicopter picks you up, be careful and don't trust anyone."

"Got it. See you then." Zeke hung up.

He handed the phone to Wayne and drew his pistol.

"What're you doing?" Wayne asked.

Zeke ejected the magazine and pulled the action back to reveal a round in the chamber. "Better be ready. We've got another hour of survival in Pittsburgh."

9

A highway interchange a half-mile ahead was jammed with motionless vehicles. Jen stopped her motorcycle on the side of the road and D-Day pulled up next to her.

"Looks like they're evacuating St. Louis," he yelled over the engine.

Jen shaded her eyes. People with backpacks and rolling luggage walked alongside the cars and trucks.

"It looks like something from a World War II film," she said. "Like a bunch of refugees."

A massive line of cars ahead led to the on-ramp. People stood outside their vehicles, talking.

"Let's get some info." Jen let out the clutch and eased the accelerator. D-Day had been right. While it wasn't quite the same as a four-wheeler, especially when it came to balance, the bike wasn't that hard for her to pick up.

She parked the bike behind an SUV and walked up to a group of four men gesturing and talking. One of them turned her way, his eyes admiring her, then darting to her side, where D-Day gave him a scowl.

She raised a hand. "How's it going?"

The other men stopped talking and turned. The first man to notice them, a beefy guy with curly hair around his head, but none on top, spoke.

"Just waiting," he said. "You taking the Poplar Street Bridge out of the city?"

Jen shook her head. "Trying to get through the city."

Another man laughed. "Good luck. All roads have been changed to one way, and if they're not packed with cars, they are with people."

D-Day folded his arms. "What's the best way to get to Kansas City?"

Curly Bald Guy chuckled. "Not the way you're heading. Ain't nobody going to KC. They're all jumping ship and getting the hell out of there."

"Yeah," said a beady-eyed young guy. "Why the hell do you want to go there? Not even the military guys are keen on heading that way. It'll be zombie central within a couple of days."

D-Day took a step toward the beady-eyed guy. "That's our business."

The young guy shrank back.

"Whoa, there," said Curly Hair. "We're all friends here. We're just trying to get out."

Jen peered down the road they way they'd come. "Why not head south, then head east? Doesn't seem like many people are going that way."

"Need to get over the river," Beady-Eyes said. "The military announcements said that the zombies don't cross wide bodies of water." He jerked a thumb over his shoulder. "Not many wider than the Mississippi."

Jen exchanged a glance with D-Day. *That's interesting.*

"I guess we can go around," she said.

D-Day shook his head. "We've got bikes. We can ride on the sidewalks if we need to."

Beady-Eyes pointed to the ramp. "Look. Line's moving."

The men scattered and jumped into their vehicles. The line moved up two car lengths and stopped again.

Jen strode to her bike. "Come on. Wasting our time here."

She started it and followed D-Day as he wove between cars and followed the road north.

An hour later they cruised down Tucker Boulevard into downtown. The number of refugees had slowly diminished the farther downtown they went. D-Day stopped at a red light. "Looks like we don't have to worry about traffic for a while."

A Humvee screamed down Olive Street. It slowed two blocks away and took a right, disappearing behind a tall brick-faced building.

"Just the Army," Jen said. "We should avoid them."

The light turned green and they continued down the road, passing the occasional pedestrian for the next few blocks. D-Day slowed and pulled off to the side.

"We should stop and eat," he said. "Who knows what's available on the way to Kansas City?"

"I'd rather get to Butler as soon as possible." Jen's stomach rumbled.

D-Day chuckled. "Looks like your gut doesn't agree."

"Guess you're right. Is there anything still open here?"

D-Day pointed to a small diner across Washington Avenue. The *Open* light was blinking and the door propped open.

They rode to the diner and walked in. A half dozen empty booths that had seen better days lined the front windows, while a couple of rickety tables sat beneath the harsh overhead lights. Salsa music came from the kitchen, but the dining area was empty.

"Anyone here?" Jen yelled.

No answer.

"I don't sense any zombies nearby," she said, "but the virus in me could still be mutating, so no use taking a chance."

She pulled her pistol and moved away from D-Day. The big biker whipped the shotgun from over his shoulder.

He pointed to himself and then to the left. She nodded and crept to the right.

The kitchen door opened. Jen swung her pistol around and pointed it at a short older woman carrying a stack of dishes. She let out an *eep* and froze.

Jen lowered the gun. "Sorry. Didn't mean to startle you. We're just looking for something to eat."

D-Day lowered his shotgun. "We're pretty starving."

The woman put the plates on the counter and pressed a hand to her chest, next to a name tag that said Donna. "You scared the life out of me."

D-Day stepped forward. "I'm sorry. We're just very hungry and would be grateful for anything we can get."

"I guess we're all jumpy right now." Donna wiped her hands on her apron then fixed her gaze on D-Day. "Eggs and toast. All I got left."

Jen's stomach rumbled again. "We'll take anything you can rustle up."

"Good." Donna handed her a remote control from her apron pocket. "In the meantime, you two can rest a bit. Scrambled eggs OK?"

D-Day sat on a stool at the counter. "Good by me.'"

Jen nodded.

Donna pointed to the coffee pots. "Help yourself." She disappeared into the kitchen.

Jen stepped behind the counter, filled a couple of cups from a steaming coffee pot, and placed them on the counter. "We should ask her what she thinks the best route out of town would be."

D-Day poured a mountain of sugar into his coffee and took a sip. "Maybe the TV could help."

"Right." Jen pointed the remote at the TV on the wall and hit the power button. It jumped to life. A reporter stood in front of a line of cars. Baby-faced and with long dark hair, she stared into the camera.

"Motorists have become frustrated outside of Kansas City," she said, "and fistfights have broken out along the massive lines of vehicles heading east. There have been reports of at least two shootings, and what remains of local law enforcement is stretched thin."

"Freaking people," Jen said.

D-Day refilled his cup and grabbed the sugar dispenser. "Assholes."

The TV switched to a male anchor in the studio. "Thank you, Mercy. That's Mercy Davis on location."

The picture zoomed in on him. "We will sign off in thirty minutes and close down the station. Most of our team will relocate east to our affiliate in Louisville, Kentucky. But one team will remain behind to continue reporting on the war. Mercy Davis, who you just saw, and Josh Newman, her cameraman, will stay in Kansas City to keep you up to date with the latest developments in the military's fight against the invading horde."

He stared into the camera. "From all of us in the newsroom, good luck and God bless."

The screen went dark.

Donna pushed backwards through the door and slipped two plates in front of Jen and D-Day. "Order up."

The aroma of the eggs had Jen's mouth watering. Donna dropped a set of utensils rolled in a paper napkin in front of each of them. "Enjoy."

Jen inhaled the eggs. "Didn't realize I was so hungry."

D-Day's plate was cleaned in minutes, too.

Donna beamed. "Nice to see such good appetites. Want more? Got to use up my eggs."

"You bet." Jen slid her plate over.

D-Day followed suit. "We need to get on the road after this."

Donna stopped halfway through the kitchen door. "You folks heading west?"

"Yup," D-Day said.

Don't want to bring attention to ourselves. "Not far west. I have an elderly aunt who's not too mobile."

D-Day glanced at her, then back at the TV screen. "Yeah. Aunt Betty."

A vehicle stopped outside the door and four soldiers entered the restaurant, laughing and joking.

Donna smiled at them. "Hi, boys. I suppose you'll take your normal spot?"

The lone corporal stood next to the last booth and gestured for the other soldiers to take a seat. "Thanks, Donna."

"I'll be back to take your orders in a second." Donna disappeared into the kitchen.

Jen kept her head down. "Maybe we should go," she whispered.

"It'll look suspicious if we just get up and leave," D-Day said.

"You folks heading out of town?"

Jen glanced at the soldiers. The corporal sat at the end of the booth, his attention on Jen and D-Day.

"Just grabbing a bite before we go," Jen said.

"Smart idea," the corporal said. "It's taking a lot of time to get over the river."

Jen nodded, but kept her eyes ahead.

The corporal shushed his companions then whispered something to them. They all went quiet. There was a rustle of paper.

Jen swallowed. *Please, please, please.*

Donna pushed through the door. "Ready to take your order."

"Just a second," the corporal said. "Maybe you should see if Jen wants something else first."

Fuck.

10

Z eke paced at one end of the CDC Headquarters conference room. "Where the hell is Howell? We've been here over an hour."

Wayne sat back in a chair with his hands behind his head. "I'd like to get going, too, but the fastest way is through Howell. It does no good to be impatient."

A sharp rap came from the open door and Sergeant Howell strolled in, his uniform crisp and clean. "Sorry to keep you waiting, but I'm still clearing some things up."

He sat at the end of the conference table and stared at Zeke. "Have a seat."

Zeke pulled out a chair and plopped into it. "Where's Jen?"

Howell leaned forward on the table. "I've got a lot to tell you, and Jen's only part of it."

Zeke crossed his arms. "Where's Jen?"

Howell sighed and leaned back in the chair. "Last we know, she and D-Day were heading toward St. Louis. That was a number of hours ago."

"Then we'll be going there," Zeke said. "Any chance of getting a car?"

"If you listen to what I fucking have to say, I'll get you out there quicker than that," Howell said.

"All right, all right." Zeke put his hands up. "I'm listening."

"There's a conspiracy that goes to the highest levels of government," Howell said. "And the members of this conspiracy caused the virus."

Wayne sat up straight. "You've got to be shitting me."

Howell shook his head. "Dr. Cartwright was a major player in the conspiracy. From what I've been able to gather, she had imprisoned Jen in this building's basement, but Jen was able to escape."

"That's my girl," Wayne said.

"You said Cartwright 'was' in the conspiracy," Zeke said. "She's dead?"

Howell nodded. "But the conspiracy is still alive and well. That's why you were targeted."

Zeke stood. "And if they're targeting us, they have to be targeting Jen, too."

"All civilian and federal law enforcement agencies have been alerted to apprehend her," Howell said. "And I recently discovered that the military is hunting her, too."

"How about your promise to get us to St. Louis quickly?" Zeke said.

Howell picked up a phone and punched a few numbers.

"This is Howell. I want our Blackhawk ready to go in five."

He hung up. "We'll need to stop and refuel once on the way, but we should be there in a few hours."

"We?" Zeke asked. "You're coming?"

Howell strode toward the door. "It'll be like old times. Let's get armed up. We're wheels up in five."

He led them to the armory, where they checked out new pistols and M4s, then went directly to the roof. A Blackhawk fired up its engine as they approached.

"Where'd you get this?" Zeke yelled. "Cartwright couldn't even tear one of these things away from the military."

"Cartwright wasn't in the Army. I know a lot of soldiers who owe me favors."

Zeke strapped himself in and helped Wayne get settled. The helicopter lifted from the CDC's roof and flew northeast.

11

J en whipped her pistol out and aimed it at the soldiers. The corporal who had recognized her froze halfway out of his seat.

She gestured with her gun. "Why don't you sit back down?"

The soldier eased into the seat.

"Hands where we can see them," D-Day said. He positioned himself next to Jen, his shotgun pointed toward the soldiers.

Donna stood with her mouth hanging open.

"Donna," Jen said. "Come around the counter, please."

Donna looked at her, but didn't move.

"Everything will be alright," Jen said. "Promise."

Donna shuffled to the front of the counter.

"The booth next to theirs." D-Day gestured to the soldiers. "Take a seat."

Donna slid in and slumped in the corner of the booth.

A burst of static came from the soldiers, and a muffled voice said something.

"Who's got the radio?" Jen asked.

A pimply private waved a hand. "Me."

"Where is it?" D-Day asked.

"On the seat next to me."

"I want you to slowly pick it up and put it on the table," Jen said.

The private nodded, then eased his hand to his left and lifted a radio into view.

"Put it on the table," D-Day said.

The private laid it down in front of him, then raised his hand back over his head.

Another burst of static. "Command to Charlie Twenty-Three. Command to Charlie Two Three. What's your status?"

The private's eyes got big and he looked away from Jen's piercing gaze.

"Answer that," she said.

D-Day looked at her and arched a brow, but aimed down his sight at the private. "You heard her."

The private reached for the radio, but the corporal grabbed his forearm. He glared at Jen. "What makes you think that's us?"

Jen snapped her pistol's action back, chambering a round. "Get your hand off him."

The corporal released his grip and the private picked up the radio just as the voice said, "Charlie Twenty-three, this is command. Over."

The private keyed the mic. "Command, this is Charlie Twenty-Three."

"What's your status?"

"Inactive. Getting something to—"

"Under duress," the corporal shouted. "Hostiles."

Jen rushed forward and knocked the radio from the private's hand. The corporal rocketed from his seat and drove her to the floor, knocking the wind from her lungs.

The radio crackled. "All units converge on the Washington Avenue Diner. Charlie Twenty-Three is down. I repeat, Charlie Twenty-Three is down."

Jen wriggled to get the corporal off, but he pressed down on her, his hands around her throat.

She caught a flash of D-Day's gun butt driving into one soldier's temple while another swung at his head and missed.

Jen struggled to breathe, but the corporal pressed harder. *Losing consciousness.*

She clawed at his face, but her strength had ebbed and he swatted her hands away. Motes swam before her eyes. A body flew past her line of sight followed by a dull thud.

Is this how it feels to die?

Lungs burning, she flailed at the corporal. His face loomed over her, his lips were pulled back in a snarl, and his eyes grew wide and crazed.

Eyes. My eyes.

Jen reached up and knocked her sunglasses off. The sergeant's face went slack and his grip loosened. Jen took a heaving breath and coughed.

"What the hell are you?" he said.

A gun butt slammed into the back of his head and he collapsed on top of her.

D-Day pulled him off and put out a hand. "Gotta get out of here."

Deep coughs wracked Jen's body. D-Day lifted her and set her on her feet. She swayed, but stayed upright. Unable to answer him, she nodded.

Donna still sat in the booth, her back against the wall and her knees to her chin. She shivered.

"Are...are you OK?" Jen stammered.

Donna stared at her and shivered harder.

What the hell?

Jen put a hand to her face. *The sunglasses. My eyes.* "There's nothing to be afraid of."

D-Day stood in the doorway. "Let's go."

Tires squealed outside and D-Day stuck his head out the door. He jumped back, slammed the door shut, and turned the deadbolt. "A Humvee and two crew cabs full of pissed-off soldiers just pulled up."

Jen stumbled to the kitchen. "There has to be a back door."

D-Day raced past her and through another doorway past the refrigerator. Jen glanced back to the dining area. Donna was unlocking the front door.

Shit.

Jen hurried through the kitchen and into the hallway D-Day had entered. He stood at a door six yards away, holding it open. "You're going to have to move quicker."

Jen jogged to the doorway and grabbed it to keep herself steady. Fresh air slapped her face and she inhaled as deep as she could. The motes disappeared from her vision and she pushed out into an alleyway.

Shouting voices came from the diner as D-Day slammed the door and dragged a couple of trash cans in front of it. He took her hand and pulled her along the alleyway. "That won't keep them," he said.

Banging came from the door. *We'll never make it.*

Jen and D-Day burst onto the street and raced to the other side then turned left. A bang came from the alleyway they'd just left.

"They've broken through the door," D-Day said.

A Humvee, maybe the same one D-Day had described, careened around the corner and headed straight for them. Jen's adrenaline kicked in and she sprinted between buildings with D-Day leading the way.

The Humvee screeched to a halt behind them and doors slammed shut. She dared one glance backward. Three soldiers, their M4s at the ready, dashed into the alleyway.

These guys are just doing their jobs. I don't want to shoot them.

D-Day reached the next street, and Jen follow him onto the sidewalk. He stopped and she slammed into him and fell on her ass.

A dozen soldiers stood in a semicircle around them, their M4s aimed at their chests.

12

The Blackhawk settled to the tarmac as a military jet blasted off the end of the runway. Even with headphones on, Zeke cringed at the roar of jet engines.

A crew cab truck pulled up twenty yards from the helicopter and a soldier climbed out. Zeke and Wayne followed Howell as he ducked out of the helicopter and jogged to the truck.

"Get in," Howell said.

The driver took them to a low-slung building at the other end of the flight line. A sign out front said *Operations*. Zeke hopped out and he and Wayne stayed on Howell's heels as he entered the building.

Several soldiers and a civilian sat at desks along a bland tan wall. The civilian looked up as they entered.

"Sergeant Howell," he said.

"Any word on Jen Reed?" Howell asked.

"As a matter of fact, she and her companion were picked up not long ago."

"In St. Louis?"

"That's correct."

Zeke's heart leapt. "When will she get here?"

The civilian tipped his head forward and peered over his glasses at Zeke.

"That's a good question," Howell said.

"They're not bringing her here," the civilian said. "They're detaining her elsewhere."

"You mean she's a prisoner again?" Wayne said.

Howell put a hand on each of the brother's shoulders and turned them away. "Let me handle this, guys," he whispered. "We'll get her."

Zeke frowned, but bit his lip. *Never letting her go off on her own again.*

Howell leaned on the civilian's desk and spoke to him in low tones.

The civilian answered, then Howell leaned down until his face almost touched the civilian's. The civilian stared into Howell's eyes as the sergeant spoke.

Howell straightened. "Where is she?"

The civilian's face had gone white. He scribbled on a piece of paper and handed it to Howell.

"Come on." Howell hurried out of the building.

Zeke looked at Wayne, who raised an eyebrow and said, "Glad he's on our side."

Howell opened the driver's door and jerked a thumb over his shoulder. "I've got this. Report back to your station."

The driver nodded and left.

Zeke hopped in next to Howell, and Wayne took the back. "She's not far away," Howell said.

They left the heavy military traffic of the airport and navigated to a near-deserted three-lane road heading southeast. "She's about fifteen minutes out," Howell said.

Howell had the truck doing better than fifty miles an hour. He passed two civilian vehicles heading the same direction and a Humvee driving the opposite way. The number of lanes dropped to two, and a few minutes later a sign told them they were on Dr. Martin Luther King Drive.

The buildings turned from residential to industrial as skyscrapers appeared in the near distance.

A one-story white building came up on the right as Howell slowed the vehicle. Surrounded by a ten-foot-high chain link fence, the building had no windows. An armed soldier stood at the gate and put up a hand as the truck approached.

Howell pulled up and rolled down his window. He flashed his ID. "Howell. You should have been told I was coming."

The soldier looked at Howell, then leaned down and peered at Zeke and Wayne. He backed away and spoke into a radio.

"What'd he say?" Zeke asked.

Wayne frowned. "Can't hear him."

The soldier stepped forward. "You'll have to back up and leave. You're not authorized to enter."

"Son of a bitch." Howell jammed the transmission into park and flung the door open, just missing the guard by an inch.

The guard put a hand on his sidearm. "Get back in your vehicle."

Howell paused. "Let me speak to whoever's in charge."

"Get back in your vehicle and leave," the soldier said. "Deadly force is authorized at this facility."

Zeke nudged Wayne and eased his pistol out. "We need to back Howell up," he whispered.

Wayne slid his handgun from its holster.

Howell's voice dropped. Zeke strained to hear him. *What's he saying?*

The soldier scowled, but spoke into his radio. Howell leaned into the open driver's side window. "You guys hang tight. I've got this. Red tape." He winked then walked with the guard a dozen yards toward the building.

Zeke and Wayne exchanged glances. "I don't like this," Zeke said.

A door opened in the center of the building and an older balding soldier stormed toward Howell.

"This guy looks like someone up the chain," Wayne said.

"An officer," Zeke agreed.

Gesturing emphatically, the officer snapped at Howell. Howell pulled a piece of paper from his pocket and shoved it at the officer, who snatched it from his hands and opened it.

As the officer read, his shoulders lowered and he no longer looked like he was ready to jump Howell.

Looking up from the paper, he handed it back to Howell, then nodded.

Howell jogged back to the truck and slipped behind the wheel. "Let's go get our girl."

13

Jen stared at the guard in the corner of the room. The soldier's gaze was on the wall above her head, but it drifted down until his eyes met hers and jerked away.

"Don't like these baby yellows, do you?" she said.

The guard remained tight-lipped.

She sighed and sat back in the worn metal chair. The chains between her handcuffs rustled. *Is D-Day close by? Are they boring him to death, too?*

The door opened and a balding, middle-aged soldier with an eagle on his shoulder strode in. He looked at the guard and jerked his head toward the door. The guard closed the door behind him.

"I'm Colonel Vesich." He pulled out the chair opposite Jen and sat, his eyes never leaving hers. "I have some questions."

Jen fought the urge to lick her lips. *Just stare. Make him uncomfortable.* "So do I. For one thing, what right do you have to imprison a federal agent?"

Vesich's eyes narrowed. *He's not used to back talk. This ought to be fun.*

"I don't answer questions," he said. "I ask them."

"Why's that?"

The corners of Vesich's mouth twitched.

This asshole's going to be easy to rattle.

"I'm Intel Commander in this sector," he said.

Jen leaned forward. "I don't care if you're Colonel of the Urinal. I'm not telling you shit until you give me some answers."

Vesich's face tightened and his hands clenched into fists. Jen glanced at them. "Gonna beat it out of me, asshole?"

The colonel pushed himself to his feet, his chair sliding back and bouncing off the wall. "You piece of shit." He pointed a trembling finger at her. "You're going to answer my questions one way or another."

That was easy.

A knock came from the door. Vesich ignored it.

"Where are the others?" he asked.

Others? Does he mean Zeke and Wayne?

"If they were up your ass you'd know it."

The door cracked open. "Colonel?"

Vesich spun around. "What the hell do you want?" Spittle flew from his mouth. "Can't you see I'm interrogating the detainee?"

"It's urgent, sir."

Vesich jerked the door open and stepped into the hall. A senior-looking soldier with an impassive face spoke to Vesich in a hushed tone.

The colonel closed his eyes and rubbed his forehead. "Fine. I'll take care of it."

The soldier left. Vesich turned toward Jen and grasped the doorknob. "I won't be long," he said. "If you still want to be a smart-ass when I get back, then we'll have a little wall-to-wall conversation."

He slammed the door.

Jen took a deep breath. *Don't push him too far. He looks like the kind that would enjoy beating a helpless prisoner.*

She strained to hear any movement behind the door, then wriggled her hands and tried to pull them through the cuffs for the hundredth time. *Shit.*

Her gaze strayed to the ceiling. A small mic hung six inches from a rafter.

"Anyone there? Yoo hoo. Why don't one of you frag that asshole colonel of yours? I'll bet he treats you like shit, too."

She sighed. "I fought with the military at Fairchild. Any of you guys hear about that one? Zombie city." She lowered her head. "A lot of brave soldiers died there."

She pulled on her cuffs. "Brave soldiers that didn't hide behind walls and microphones."

"D-Day," she yelled. "Do you hear me?"

Nothing. She leaned back and closed her eyes. *If that bald asshole comes back and tries something, I'm going to bite him. Then we'll see if I can infect humans.*

Footsteps came from the other side of the door. Not just one set. "Of course," she said. "Chicken shit colonel isn't going to work me over himself."

She slid her chair back and prepared herself to launch at anyone who came near.

The door swung in and Sergeant Howell stood in the threshold. *They sent him to beat me?*

A half-shaved head with a skull earring dangling from one ear appeared at Howell's shoulder. "Jen," Zeke said.

Zeke?

Wayne rushed past Howell and knelt next to Jen. He wrapped his arms around her and she leaned into him. "They said you were dead," she said.

Zeke stepped next to Wayne and handed him a set of keys. "We had to play possum."

Wayne took the keys and went to work on her cuffs. Zeke leaned over and hugged Jen so tight her back cracked.

"Take it easy, Hulk."

He released her. "Sorry."

She stood and wrapped her arms around Zeke's neck. "Missed having my protector with me," she mumbled into his shoulder.

Releasing him, she reached out for Wayne. He slipped in between her and Zeke. "What about me?" he asked.

Jen pressed her lips to his and he held her around the waist. She broke the kiss. "Does that answer your question?"

He smiled and moved in for another.

Howell cleared his throat. "Need to get on the move."

Jen gave Wayne a quick squeeze. "Duty calls."

She entered the hallway and stopped. "Wait. Where's D-Day?"

Howell nodded at the guard, who pointed at the next door.

Jen went back in the room, grabbed the keys from the cuffs, and hurried to the next room. She flung the door open and stepped in. A movement to her left and she turned. D-Day stood in the corner with a chair over his head.

"Really?" she said. "Watch too many movies?"

He lowered the chair and reached toward her, exposing his cuffs. "I was getting sick of that colonel. Figured I'd go down fighting."

She unlocked his cuffs and they dropped to the floor. "My hero."

He rubbed his wrists and followed her out the door. Zeke slapped him on the back. "Good to see you."

"I thought you two were dead," D-Day said.

Zeke laughed. "Can't kill us that easy."

Howell stepped forward and offered his hand to D-Day. "Sergeant Howell. Heard a lot about you."

D-Day shook his hand. "Likewise." He cast a questioning glance to Jen.

"Let's get back to base," Howell said. "We'll figure out our next steps from there."

Jen broke into the sunlight and took a deep breath, reveling in the fresh air. She jumped into the front seat and pushed Wayne to the middle, then took his hand and leaned her head on his shoulder.

Jen caught Vesich watching them drive away. She opened the window, extended her arms, and gave him both middle fingers.

Everyone laughed. "I'd like to beat him to a pulp," D-Day growled.

They arrived at the airfield Operations building. "Hang tight," Howell said. "I'll get an update and see what resources we have available."

When he disappeared into the building, Zeke turned to Jen. "What happened with Cartwright? Howell said she was in on the conspiracy."

"She was," Jen said. "She locked me up. Wanted to make me a guinea pig."

"Had us all fooled," Wayne said.

Jen nodded. "There are other conspirators still out there. Some at a high level. We're lucky to have Howell. Here's hoping he can get me to Butler."

"What's that going to do?" Zeke asked.

"I'm going to convince him to stop," Jen said. "Too many innocent people dying and undying. I have to show him that killing everyone isn't the only way to take out the conspirators."

Zeke crossed his arms. "You think a zombie leader's going to listen to that?"

Jen shrugged. "Depends on how much of Butler is left in his undead body, but it's my best play."

Howell stepped out of the building. "Just got word. The horde is closing in on Topeka, Kansas."

"Where's Topeka?" D-Day asked.

"Sixty miles west of Kansas City. After KC, there's little in their way until they get here." Howell pointed two buildings down. "Follow me to the armory and let's load up."

Wayne caught up with Jen halfway there. "Back into the shit again, I guess."

Jen took his hand and grinned. "I'm tired of screwing around with the army and ready to kick some zombie ass."

14

The Blackhawk followed Interstate 70 as it approached the outskirts of Kansas City. The occasional vehicle below zipped east toward St. Louis.

Zeke nudged Jen and pointed at a group of people walking along the road. Jen shook her head. *If we can't stop or slow down the horde, it'll catch up with these people.*

Tanks and Humvees drove the city streets, and troops were on the move. The Blackhawk crossed the Missouri River then descended toward a small airport on the city's north side and touched down on the tarmac.

The engine shut off and the rotors slowed. While Jen unstrapped herself and pulled off her helmet and headset, Howell jumped down and approached two soldiers who were walking their way.

Climbing down to the tarmac, Jen scanned the area. Helicopters and small aircraft came and went in an almost orderly manner. *Like there's not much going on.*

Howell joined her. "The attack on Topeka has started. Command is throwing some bombers at them to slow them down, but they're planning on making their stand here."

"I don't get it," Zeke said. "Why aren't they just bombing the hell out of them in Topeka like they did in Spokane?"

"Our inventory of ordnance is limited, and there's little production to refresh our stock." Howell's brow furrowed. "If they break through here, we're really screwed."

Jen frowned. "I need to get to Topeka. Getting Butler to stop may be our only hope."

"I'm up for that," D-Day said.

Wayne took Jen's hand. "You're not going without me."

Zeke patted the hilt of his katana. "You know me and Deathblade are ready for action."

"Deathblade?" Jen said.

Zeke's lower lip pushed out. "I've been working on a new name for a long time. You don't like that one?"

She clapped him on the shoulder. "It's perfect. You just caught me by surprise."

"Better name than that last one," Wayne said.

Howell rubbed his chin. "I'll arrange another helicopter. Should be some tall buildings in Topeka that we can land on. At worst, we can recon the horde and land at Lawrence's airport if needed."

"Lawrence?" Wayne said.

"Between here and Topeka," Howell said. "About forty miles away. That's the last decent-sized town before they get to KC."

Jen adjusted the M4 on her shoulder. "I'll take whatever I can get."

Howell walked back to the soldiers. One of them shook his head as soon as Howell spoke. Howell gestured with his hands and became animated.

Be nice to hear what they're saying.

After a few minutes of hand waving, the soldier gave a curt nod and stalked off.

Jen walked over to Howell. "We good?"

Howell nodded. "Took a bit, but he gave in when I reminded him who I work for."

"Who's that?"

Howell eyed Jen. "The Pentagon, of course."

BACK IN THE sky and leaving the city behind, the Blackhawk followed the Kansas River and flew past empty fields, roads, and subdivisions. Jen looked at the others and each seemed deep in their own thoughts.

When Lawrence appeared ahead, Howell's voice came through the head phones. "This is our fallback. The airport is just north of town and has a small contingent of Apache helicopters and support personnel."

Five minutes later they hit the Topeka. "Damn place looks like a ghost town," Wayne said.

The helicopter broke away from the Kansas River and followed a highway west out of town.

Jen's stomach grew heavy and a tingling raced up her arm as if she'd touched something electrical. With no zombies within sight, it couldn't be a run-of-the-mill leader.

Butler.

The tingling increased the farther west they went until her arm fell numb. Jen flexed her hand and tightened her bicep. *Still works.*

"Oh my God," Wayne said.

Jen strained to look out the windshield. They'd left the city and green fields. Copses of trees stretched westward paralleling the highway.

But a few miles ahead, the interstate and the surrounding landscape was covered in black, like a swarm of flies on rotting food. "Holy shit," she said.

The blackness spread as far to the left as she could see and stopped at the Kansas River to the right. Jen peered past the river. None over there. *Howell said they don't cross water.*

His voice came over the headphones. "Take us over the horde."

The Blackhawk climbed and followed the interstate. It flew over the horde seconds later as the zombie army swarmed toward Topeka.

Can't see shit from way up here. "Bring us lower," she said.

The pilot looked at Howell.

"They don't have weapons and can't fly up and grab us," Jen said. "And I can't see crap from here."

Howell nodded and the Blackhawk descended, hovering a couple hundred feet above the surging undead.

Jen closed her eyes and concentrated. *Do you hear me?*

A spasm wracked her body. She tried to open her eyes, but failed.

"Jen?" Zeke said.

Wayne took her hand. "You all right?"

A movie played in her mind. In it, she was one of the horde, running shoulder to shoulder with the other zombies. A helicopter hovered in the distance.

Butler?

"Come to me," a voice came from within her head.

I'm here. We need to stop this.

The Blackhawk was getting closer. "Come down to me. You and I must talk. Only way."

Can't land here.

"Land and I will find you."

"Jen!"

Jen's eyes popped open. D-Day had her by the shoulders, shaking her. "Wake the fuck up."

She pushed on his chest. "I'm back. I'm back."

Zeke's hands were squeezed into fists and Wayne had an arm around her, his brow furrowed.

D-Day sat down and strapped in.

"What the hell was that?" Howell said.

"We need to land," Jen said, her chest heaving as she struggled to catch her breath. "In Topeka."

Howell's gaze was laser-focused on Jen. She returned it and didn't waver. "I think I can stop all this, but I need to meet with Butler."

"You heard her," Howell said. "Topeka." The Blackhawk banked and headed east.

Jen sat back, crossed her arms, and closed her eyes. A nudge on her shoulder startled her. She kept her eyes closed. "I'm fine, Zeke. Just collecting myself."

"That was scary," he said. "It was like you were somewhere else."

I was. "I'm good."

She cleared her mind and willed herself to relax. *These episodes in Butler's head are draining the piss out of me.*

"Prepare for landing," Howell said.

Jen opened her eyes. *Here already?*

The helicopter slowed and descended. A rooftop appeared and the Blackhawk landed on it with a small bump.

The engine shut off and the rotors slowed. Howell gestured to the pilot to stay put and he hopped down to the roof. Jen and the others joined him as he walked to the roof's edge.

Jen removed her helmet. "How long do you think it'll take them to get here?"

Howell frowned. "We don't have a lot of time. What do you expect to happen here?"

"I have no freaking idea. Butler told me we need to meet in person."

"He told you?" Howell asked.

"We have this connection," Jen said. "It's always been through leaders that we've communicated, but we were far away from each other."

D-Day frowned. "I don't like this. Too many unknown variables."

"Doesn't matter," Jen said. "I have to do it."

"You can communicate with him without being in person," D-Day said. "Why take the risk?"

Jen put her hands on her hips. "Why are you fighting this?"

D-Day shrugged. "Instinct. This feels bad."

"It's my decision," Jen said, "and I'm going to meet Butler here."

"Thought you were going to take more advice," D-Day said. "Team effort and all that."

Is he really going to bring that up now? Screw it. I know what's best. "I am. I value your advice and have taken it into consideration, but my decision is the same."

D-Day nodded. "So be it."

Howell clapped his hands. "We need a game plan." He strode toward the roof entrance and opened the door. "We're on a hotel. Pilot's staying in the helicopter, ready to start it up and go. We have to secure the top floor and roof access."

D-Day lumbered through the door. "I'll set up at the top of the stairway. There may be more than one set of stairs, though."

"I'll check for more," Wayne said.

Zeke drew his katana, the blade catching the sunlight. "I'm not leaving Jen's side."

"Good," Howell said. "You two should set up in a top-floor room. We don't want them coming to the roof and cutting us off from escape."

Jen pushed past Howell and into the hotel. "Let's get going. We could be minutes from finally ending this thing."

A door at the end of the hallway stood propped open, and D-Day was on the landing with his M4 at the ready. The door at the other end was similarly open and Wayne was visible beyond it.

Jen tried several doorknobs. The handles moved freely without opening the door. "Shit. Bet they use those stupid cards."

Zeke pointed to a maid's cart in the hallway several doors down. "I'll check it out."

He ran to it and rustled through its contents. Jen joined him. "Find anything?"

He turned to her with a grin and held his hands out. "Got a bunch of those cool little shampoos."

"Are you shitting me?" Jen said. "What about a key card?"

"Oh, yeah." Zeke dropped the shampoos on a tray and searched the other cubby holes on the cart.

He stopped and held up a hand. A key card on a lanyard dangled over his head. "How's this?"

Jen swiped it from him and stuck it in the nearest door's slot. A light blinked red, then green. She turned the handle and pushed the door open. "Nice."

Waving at Howell, she called out, "Got a key."

"Good," he said. "But you should take a room closer to the roof exit."

"Great idea," she said. "Come on, Zeke."

She jogged down the corridor toward D-Day. He glanced at her and gave her a thumbs-up.

Jen unlocked the last door and entered. A typical hotel room with two double beds, a small bathroom with a shower, a TV, and a tiny refrigerator, it was clean, but unremarkable. She plopped on a bed and sighed.

His hands overflowing with shampoos and soaps, Zeke hurried into the bathroom.

Jen closed her eyes and laid an arm across them. "Seems like it's been days since I slept."

The door flew open and Howell burst into the room. "Look alive. Something's coming up the stairs."

15

J en rushed to the window and looked out onto the streets. "The horde shouldn't be here already."

Several cars sat abandoned and there were no signs of movement. She hurried back into the hallway. Howell and Zeke stood next to D-Day, who pointed down the stairs.

Howell cupped his hands around his mouth and yelled down the corridor, "See anything on your side, Wayne?"

Wayne peered down the stairs and shook his head.

"I don't feel anything." Jen strode toward Howell. "Even if there was just one leader nearby, I'd feel something."

"Maybe Butler doesn't control them all," D-Day said. "All of you get in the hallway. I've got this."

Zeke frowned, but D-Day gave him a gentle push. "Jen needs you."

Zeke nodded and stepped into the hall. D-Day closed the door behind him.

Howell checked his M4. "Where's that key card? I'll take cover in the doorway opposite of you. If you can't control the zombies and they look like they'll overwhelm us, lock yourselves in the room. I'll back into mine and draw them in."

Jen tossed the key card to Howell and glanced at Wayne. He had his rifle off his shoulder and ready to fire. She knelt in the doorway, propped her M4 up, and aimed at the stairway door. Zeke stood next to her and did the same.

Seconds passed. *Come on. Come on.*

A voice rumbled from behind the door. Another voice—a lighter one —answered.

Humans?

The door opened and D-Day stepped through, followed by a baby-faced woman and a husky bearded guy with a news camera on his shoulder.

Jen rose. "I know you. You're the reporter staying behind."

The woman smiled and approached Jen. "Mercy Davis, and this guy shadowing me is Josh Newman."

Jen reached out to shake her hand, but Mercy froze then took a stutter step backwards. Her mouth opened, but no sound came out.

My freaking eyes.

"It's OK," Jen said. "I don't bite."

"But you're infected," Mercy said.

Jen sighed. "It's a long story, but I'm no threat to you."

Mercy's right eyebrow rose. "Long story? Would you tell it to me, let me record it?"

This could be a good thing, if she can get it broadcast.

"I will." Jen put her hand back out. "You'll have the exclusive."

Mercy smiled then shook Jen's hand. "It's a deal."

"But we have a ton of zombies about to rain down on us," Howell said. "You two need go somewhere else."

"Somewhere else?" Mercy said. "We saw your helicopter land and hoped we could catch a ride with you. Our van's acting up and this isn't a good time to break down."

"No," Jen said. "They stay here."

Howell moved in next to Jen. "Why take the risk?" he whispered. "They're not armed and won't be of much help."

Jen looked at Mercy. "Excuse us a minute." She led Howell and Zeke into the room and closed the door.

"Even if I can get Butler to hold off any further attacks," she said, "we still have the conspiracy to deal with. What better way to bring it to light than through the media? If we can tell our story and have them document us stopping the attacks, we can get the people on our side."

Howell rubbed his chin. "Might work, but is it worth the risk of having to protect the newspeople as well?"

"I think so," Zeke said.

Good old Zeke.

Howell shrugged. "OK."

Jen returned to the hall. "We expect that horde to hit town soon. You'll be safe in this room."

Mercy squinted her eyes. "You're not leaving?"

"It's part of that long story," Jen said, "but I can't."

"Why would we need to get in that room to be safe?" Josh asked. "There aren't any zombies in the building, and the outside doors are closed. The zombies will just run by unless we bring attention to ourselves."

"Not quite," Jen said. "There's one zombie controlling them all, and he's coming to see me."

"One zombie's in charge?" Mercy asked.

"Maybe you should start that interview now," Zeke said. "Go in the room. I'll be out here and let you know when the horde arrives."

Jen nodded. "Guess there's no better time than the present." She entered the bedroom and turned on the light. "Let's get started."

Forty minutes later, Jen's stomach tingled. She put up a hand. "Have to cut off the interview."

"Why?" Mercy asked. "There's so much more to ask you."

Jen stood. "Remember how I told you I can sense leaders?"

Mercy nodded. "You sense one now?"

"Yeah." Jen opened the door and stepped into the corridor. Zeke stood at the window in the opposite room.

"See anything?" she asked.

"No." He pressed his face to the window and tried to see down the street.

The tingling sensation ran up Jen's spine to the base of her neck and radiated down her left side. She went to her room's window and peered at the street below. *Nothing's changed.*

Her gaze rose up the building across the street and stopped. A zombie, its deep yellow eyes staring at her, stood in a window two floors lower.

"Got one," she said. "Leader."

Howell rushed to her side. "Where?"

She pointed. "Two floors down and one to the right."

"Bet it's a scout. Won't be long for the others."

Movement in her peripheral vision caught Jen's attention. She peered down the street. A black wave washed toward them. *Holy shit.*

She stepped back from the window. "It's showtime. They're here."

Howell ran into the hallway. "Everyone at your position." He pointed at Mercy and Josh. "You two get in the room and shut the door."

Mercy scowled, then whispered something to Josh. She led him into the room.

Jen reached the hallway as the tingling intensified, numbing her whole side. She leaned against the wall and her body spasmed. Falling to the carpeted floor, she let out a gasp.

The movie projector in her mind flicked on and she found herself in the midst of the horde again, running down a street with buildings lining either side and then stopping in front of the hotel. The horde encircled it.

"I know where you are," Butler's voice echoed in her head.

I'm ready.

"I will send up two of mine."

Two of yours?

"Two of mine. Leaders, as you call them."

What about you?

"There are others with you. Mine will make sure it's safe for me."

Let me go so I can prepare.

Jen's eyes popped open. Zeke was on one knee by her side, rubbing her back. "What did he say?"

Jen put a hand out. Zeke stood and grasped it, then pulled her to her feet.

"He's sending two leaders ahead to make sure it's safe," she said. "Go tell Wayne to let them through if they come up that way."

"Got it." Zeke ran toward the far stairs.

Jen stumbled to D-Day's stairs. Howell stood next to the biker, talking, but rushed out to help Jen. "What's the news?"

Jen leaned against the stairway doorframe. "Butler's close. He's sending up two leaders first."

D-Day scratched his chin. "Smart move. Make sure we're not just waiting for them to show their faces and start blasting away."

A door opened somewhere below. D-Day leaned over the railing and peered down. "Someone's coming."

Howell pressed a hand against Jen's back. "You should get in the hallway by your room door, just in case."

Jen nodded. She took a deep breath. The tingling remained, but her balance had returned. She walked down the hall. Zeke rushed to her and together they waited.

Footsteps echoed up the stairwell. D-Day pointed his M4 downward and Howell moved next to him and did the same.

"What's taking them so long?" Zeke asked. "They could run up those stairs in a minute."

"Butler doesn't want to spook us," Jen said.

D-Day and Howell backed into the hallway, their guns pointing at two zombies taking easy steps through the door. One, a tall woman with an Afro, had no visible wounds. The other, a teen with a peach fuzz mustache, had a gaping hole in his chest.

"Let them come to me," Jen said. "You two stay there."

D-Day pressed against the wall as the zombies shambled by. Howell stayed his ground and the teen moved behind the tall woman to pass him.

The zombies stopped in front of Jen, their yellow eyes practically glowing.

"Tell him it's safe," she said.

Neither of the zombies moved nor made a sound.

"Butler's coming," Wayne yelled.

16

J en waved Wayne over. "Come here with me."

Wayne sprinted down the hallway and stood by her side opposite Zeke.

Jen's whole body was abuzz when Butler entered the hallway. He strode down the corridor like a king in a parade. His eyes never rested, moving from Jen to one of the other humans and back again. No one but Jen seemed to notice the air crackling with electricity as Butler stopped five feet in front of her. His two zombie scouts bookended him, their backs to the wall and arms at their sides like soldiers at attention.

A rustle from behind caught Jen's attention. Zeke had a two-handed grip on his katana, its blade perched over his shoulder. D-Day, Wayne, and Howell aimed down the barrel of their pistols at the undead colonel.

She caught movement from the corner of her eye. The door to her room opened and Josh stood in the doorframe with his unblinking camera taking in the scene. Mercy stood at his side, her mouth slightly open and her chin trembling.

"Lower your weapons," Jen said. Howell and D-Day lowered their firearms. Wayne hesitated for a moment, then did likewise. But Zeke didn't move. Jen put a hand on his arm. "Please, Zeke."

He broke his glare at Butler and looked at her, his expression shifting from one of hatred to concern. "Trust me," she said.

Zeke sheathed the katana, but didn't change his stance, his muscles taut and ready to spring into action.

"Come. To. Me." Butler spoke slowly, almost painfully, in a voice that sounded like wheels crunching on gravel.

The hair on the back of her neck stiffened. Jen took a step toward Butler, losing herself in the yellow depths of his gaze.

He reached out, and her hand went toward his as if it had a mind of its own. *This is going to hurt.*

Their hands clasped in a firm grip. A calmness flowed from Jen's hand and over her body. She closed her eyes and the movie began. *No. More than a movie. Like virtual reality.*

There she was, standing on the rooftop in Spokane, the *thup, thup* of the helicopter echoing behind her. A gunshot. The searing pain. Stumbling. Pitching off the roof's edge. The impact on the car. The darkness.

Then light. Awareness. The feeling of other infected souls. Of Butler doing what he'd done most of his adult life. Taking command. Directing his troops.

"You can do this, too," his voice echoed through her head. "Join me and we can root out those who caused the death of the earth."

Hundreds of thousands of zombies swarmed Fairchild AFB, pouring through the opening in the wall and flooding every building, every street.

I can control a few, but not an army.

"You are stronger than you know. I could feel your strength over the distances. You retain your humanity, and that makes you far more powerful than me. The ability is there. All you need to do is tap into it and we will be unstoppable."

I won't wipe out the human race to kill a few. I have a better way to stop them. A way for the people to see them for what they are.

"Then let us try your way. We shall—"

An explosion boomed through her mind and wrenched Jen back to reality. Her eyes popped open. Her arm was still outstretched, but Butler lay on the floor with half his skull missing. His zombie bodyguards screeched, their voices like nails across a chalkboard.

Disoriented, Jen stumbled backward from the scene before her. Someone grasped her arm, steadying her.

"Jen," Zeke said.

A hand went to her cheek and gently turned her head to the other side.

Wayne, his eyebrows raised and his eyes searching hers, said, "You'll be fine. I won't let anything happen to you."

Jen blinked as two more shots rang out and the screeching cut off. D-Day raised his M4 and aimed it behind Jen.

"Put it down," Howell said, "or I'll pull this trigger again."

Jen turned to face the barrel of Howell's gun ten feet away. She hyperventilated and her knees gave out. Zeke and Wayne held her up.

"Do you want Jen to die?" Howell asked.

D-Day laid his rifle on the floor.

"All your weapons. All of you."

D-Day dropped his pistol, then pulled the pistol from Wayne's holster and the one from Zeke's and tossed them to the floor.

Howell nodded and focused back on Jen.

"Why?" she said. "We were just about to get what we came for."

Howell pursed his lips, his gaze slipping from Jen to Zeke and back again. "This is part of what I came for."

Like slipping gears, Jen couldn't grasp what he'd said for a moment. She just repeated back to him, "What you came for?"

"He was the enemy." Howell adjusted his grip. "In war, you kill the enemy."

"It's not that simple." Enough strength returned to Jen's legs that she shook off Zeke and Wayne. "I was going to get him to pull the horde back. I was going to save lives. Who the hell knows what'll happen now."

"That's the second thing I came for," Howell said. "You. You'll come back with me. You'll control the horde."

Jen stared at him.

"Oh, come on," Howell said. "We know what you can do. I watched the security tapes from the CDC."

"We?" Jen said. "You're with them? The conspirators?"

"Patriots," he said. "We're in the most dangerous situation the world has ever known. It will take order and discipline to overcome it."

Heat flowed up Jen's neck and settled in her face. "You fucking asshole. You're the shitheads that caused the *situation*."

"Enough." He pulled a pair of handcuffs from his back pocket. "Come toward me. The helicopter's waiting."

"I'm not going with you."

He scowled. "I have to either bring you back to help control the horde for us, or eliminate you so you can't use it against us."

Goosebumps shot down Jen's spine. *Is this real? Is he going to kill me?*

D-Day sprung at Howell. The sergeant swung the barrel toward him, fired, and turned the gun back around to cover the others.

Jen gasped.

D-Day staggered, reaching out for Howell, and dropped to his knees. Jen took a step toward him.

"Stay back," Howell growled.

Jen pulled her pistol and shot at Howell without aiming. The round went wide. Howell returned fire and sprinted for the stairway.

Wayne dove for his gun. Jen lined up her sights on Howell's back, but he disappeared up the stairs.

"D-Day," she cried out. She knelt next to the biker's outstretched body and rolled him over. His glassy eyes stared at the ceiling.

Wayne rushed past Jen as she dropped her gun and cradled D-Day's head in her arms. Tears welled in her eyes.

Wayne hit the stairs, taking them two at a time, climbing out of sight in seconds. Gunfire echoed from the stairway and helicopter's engine roared over the shots.

Zeke grabbed his pistol and hauled ass to the stairs. Wayne met him at the entrance. "He's gone," he said.

"Shit," Zeke yelled.

"I should've listened to him instead of blowing him off," Jen sobbed.

"What?" Wayne put an arm around her. "Hey, it's not your fault."

Zeke stood next to her and drew his katana. "I'll take care of D-Day. Make sure he doesn't turn."

Jen shook her head and pressed the end of her barrel against D-Day's temple. "My fault. My responsibility."

D-Day's eyes snapped open.

Jen squeezed the trigger.

17

J en staggered backward, dropping her pistol. Wayne took her into his arms and she buried her face into his chest. Her shoulders shook as she cried.

Stonefaced, Zeke went into the room and peered out a window. "The horde's dispersing."

Mercy stepped into the hallway, her face pale and eyes wide. She gestured to Josh. "Turn it off."

He lowered the video camera.

D-Day was doing fine with his friends in Atlanta and I had to get him caught back up in all my shit. Dad and Doc, they had no choice, but D-Day did, and he chose to help me. And I basically told him to fuck off.

"What are we going to do?" Zeke asked. "How are we going to get that bastard?"

Wayne rubbed Jen's back. Mercy's attention was glued to D-Day's body as if she expected him to rise again. Josh's hand trembled as he fiddled with his camera settings.

What are we going to do? Good question. "We've got to get that video uploaded. Where's the best place to do that?"

"Local news station," Mercy said. "There's one not far from here."

"Define not far," Jen said.

"Three blocks west and a block south."

A bang echoed from the nearby stairway and dozens of feet pounded up the stairs. Jen's heart skipped a beat. "What the hell?"

Zeke raced to the stairs and peered down. "Zombies. Filling the stairs and coming this way."

Shit.

Another bang came from the opposite stairwell. "Sounds like they're coming in that way, too," Wayne said.

Jen pushed Mercy toward her room. "Everyone in here."

She closed the door and slid the deadbolt closed. Wayne and Zeke stood by the bed with their pistols out and ready. Josh and Mercy huddled in the far corner. *And still Josh has that damn camera going.*

Jen took position next to Zeke. She closed her eyes.

No tingling. No leaders. Can I control the drones?

She let her mind relax and reached out.

The stampede of feet reached their floor and rumbled past.

Something hit their door. It rattled.

Clear the floor.

Another hit on the door. Then another.

Jen's heart hammered her chest. She opened her eyes, took a deep breath, and exhaled. *Slow your breathing.*

Fists beat on the door and on the walls. They didn't have much time.

Jen approached the door and placed her palms against it.

"What are you doing?" Zeke asked.

She ignored him and concentrated. *Stop.*

The pounding picked up. *I did this in Atlanta. Why can't I do it now? Butler said I could.*

The door cracked. She imagined the zombies nearest the door and pictured them in her mind.

Stop!

The pounding on the door stopped. Other movement in the corridor continued.

Mercy's trembling voice came from behind her. "What's happening?"

"I've got control of some of them," Jen said. "Just the ones that were pounding on the door, but that's a start."

"That's good enough for now," Wayne said, "but you know we have to get out of this building and fast."

"Why?" Zeke asked. "We're safe here as long as the zombies can't get in."

"What do you think Howell is telling the army right now?" Wayne said. "With the horde in disarray, they're going to attack, and that means bombing. And where do you think Howell will tell them to hit first?"

"Shit," Zeke said. "Right here. To take Jen out."

Jen reached out with her mind. She could feel the zombies she controlled, almost as if she had a physical connection to each of them. Pushing out, she added another connection. Then another.

Clear the floor.

Feet shuffled in the hallway. Jen slid the peephole cover over and peered out of it. A space of a few feet had cleared in front of the door. The zombies she controlled pressed against the larger horde.

"I'm making progress," she said.

How many are outside the door? How many can I control?

Squeezing her eyes closed, she pushed with her mind and added another few zombies. Then something snapped in her mind as if a restraint had broken. She felt...full.

Leave the building.

The floor vibrated with the rumbling of footsteps fading away down the hall.

Faster.

The stampede started up again, but this time in reverse. Jen leaned against the door, keeping her concentration. The echo of pounding steps faded.

Putting her eye to the peephole, she squinted. "It's clear."

Zeke took her arm. "Let me go first."

She stepped back. He unlocked the dead bolt and eased the door open. Sticking his head into the corridor, he looked left, then right. "They're gone all right." He stepped into the corridor. Jen and Wayne followed. Mercy and Josh stayed in the room.

Scenes flashed in Jen's mind as if she were looking through multiple cameras in sequence. A view of the stairway as she moved down it behind a wave of zombies. Another in the street where she could see the hotel from a block away.

Am I communicating with that many?

She rushed back into the room and looked out the window. A hundred zombies crowded the street around the hotel, their heads angled up and all eyes staring at her. A chill shot up her spine.

Beyond the attentive zombie crowd, the other undead wandered aimlessly. She squeezed her eyes shut.

Everyone stop.

"Oh my God," Mercy's voice came from beside her.

Jen glanced at her. Mercy's eyes were wide and she held a hand over her mouth. Wayne leaned forward staring out the window, while Josh wedged in beside him, his unblinking camera aimed at the street.

Zeke stood at Jen's side, a smile on his lips. "Guess you can control more than a few." He gestured out the window.

Jen looked down into the group of upturned zombie faces.

"Oh my God is right," she said. "There's three or four hundred of them now."

"Give them another command," Wayne said. "Make sure this isn't a fluke."

Jen swallowed. "OK." *Everyone sit.*

As if they'd practiced it, every one of her damn zombies sat at the same time.

"Like soldiers moving in formation," Wayne said.

Wayne's pocket vibrated and a standard ringtone blared from it.

Jen raised an eyebrow. "Expecting a call?"

He shook his head, then opened it and held it out. Zeke looked at it and frowned. "Blocked number?"

Wayne pressed the speaker button. "Hello?"

"Put Jen on."

Howell? Heat rose in Jen's face. "I'm glad you called, asshole. I'm going to kill you, then make you my fucking zombie slave. You'll never rest."

"Are you done?" Howell asked. "You don't have much time."

"What the hell are you talking about?" she said.

"Surrender to me," he said. "Give me the video camera and all of the recordings. Do both of those things and your friends can all go free."

"Kiss my ass," she said.

Mumbling came from the speaker. *Who's he talking to?* Jen strained to hear the conversation, but couldn't make it out.

"We'd rather you work with us," Howell said, "but if you won't, you'll be eliminated. What do you—"

"Fuck you!" Jen snatched the phone from Wayne and flung it against the wall, where it split into three pieces.

"I guess he has your answer," Zeke said.

Jen stormed to the hallway. "Enough screwing around. Let's get to the news station and expose those assholes."

She stopped at the top of the stairs and checked her pistol's load, then holstered it. Adjusting the tomahawk sheath on her belt, she leaned over the railing and scanned the stairs below. "All clear down there."

"I'll go first," Zeke said.

Jen blocked him with her arm. "No. I'm the last one they'd attack. Until we know how much control I have with that big a group, I should be in front."

Zeke pursed his lips and stepped aside. Jen took the steps to the next floor and peered over the rail again. "Still good."

She took the following flight quickly and paused. Zeke was right behind her, Mercy and Josh a little behind him, and Wayne came down the stairs in the rear.

"No stopping till we hit the first floor." Jen kept a steady pace down the remaining stairs, reaching the first floor in minutes.

She opened the door to the empty lobby, which had floor-to-ceiling glass windows and double glass doors. The zombies still sat, their heads turned and eyes staring at her as she entered the lobby.

"This is freaking creepy," Zeke said.

Mercy hugged herself and hid behind Josh. Wayne's mouth hung slightly open.

Jen swallowed. *Stand.*

The zombies rose to their feet and watched her with impassive faces.

"Jen," Zeke said. "Can you do me a favor and tell us what you're telling them so we know if they do something different?"

"Good idea," Wayne said.

"Sure," Jen said. "I'm going to tell them to move away from the door."

The crowd of zombies shuffled back from the door.

Jen looked at the others. "I used verbal commands at CDC Headquarters, but not on so many. Looks like it works as long as they can hear me."

She grasped the door handle. "I'll wave you out once I feel it's safe."

Zeke pulled his katana and positioned himself next to the door. Wayne took the other side. "We'll be there if you need us."

She smiled. "I know."

Jen pulled the door open and walked into the sea of zombies.

18

Noone of the zombies moved. Other than Jen's own pulse pounding in her ears, there was no sound.

"Make more room for my friends."

The zombies pushed back, not taking their eyes off her.

She stepped back inside the building. Zeke let out his breath in a rush.

"Worried?" she asked.

"Always."

Wayne nodded at the zombies. "They seemed to obey you."

"They did." She gazed at the zombies. "I think we're safe, but be ready just in case. We'll go in the same order as we did on the stairs."

Mercy shivered.

"You going to be OK?" Jen asked. "We need you two. Not only to get the video uploaded, but to give us directions to the studio."

Mercy gave her a nervous nod. "Ready."

Josh lowered the camera. "Let's do it."

"Which way do we go?" Jen asked.

"Left," Mercy said, "to Southeast 6th Avenue. It's the first road we'll hit. Then take a right and we'll follow that road across the interstate and then two blocks farther."

Jen pushed the door open and stepped outside. Zeke took position at her side, his katana at the ready.

Not a zombie moved.

"Come on," Josh said. He put an arm around Mercy and half led, half pulled her out the door. Wayne followed, his eyes scanning the undead.

Jen turned to her left. "We will be walking this way. When we do, you will surround us and remove any undead from our path. You will ensure we're safe."

"Not exactly talkative, are they?" Zeke said.

"Nice and slow," Jen said, "let's walk to the street."

The zombies in front of her turned and shuffled forward. They moved away from the building's entrance, and members of her personal horde filled in on the building side. Jen got on her tiptoes and peered over them. As she'd commanded, the lead zombies pushed through the wandering undead.

"It's working," she said. "There seem to be enough of our zombies between us and the others that they don't know we're here."

They crossed the parking lot and stopped in the middle of Southeast 6th Avenue. Jen turned to Mercy.

"What street's next?" she asked.

Although no longer pressed into Josh, Mercy hadn't strayed far from his side. Josh, for his part, had his camera back out and recording.

"South Kansas Avenue," Mercy said. "Then a left. The station is the third door on the right."

"Walk three blocks to South Kansas Avenue then turn left and walk a hundred feet and stop," Jen said.

The horde shuffled forward.

"This is working well," she said. "We're the first people in history to have a zombie escort."

Zeke put a hand up. "Do you hear that?"

"What?" Jen asked.

Wayne looked to the sky. "Plane. We need to get away from the hotel."

"Run," Jen yelled.

The horde surged forward, and Jen picked up her pace.

The rumbling grew louder.

"Not just one plane," Wayne said.

A vision played in Jen's mind. She was running at the edge of the horde as it ran into a large group of undead. Her zombies began dropping away as they were blocked from moving forward.

Jen pulled her tomahawk. "Get ready to fight. We're losing some of our cover."

The top four floors of the hotel exploded behind them, the blast waves knocking Jen to the pavement. She pushed herself up on her elbows and watched as another strike hit the flaming building.

Howell.

She scrambled to her feet. The shock wave had knocked down every zombie and human in a two-block radius. She grabbed Zeke's hand and pulled. "We've got to find shelter."

Zombies stirred. She reached out with her mind. *Reassemble around us.*

A dozen zombies stumbled to her side.

"Shit. I lost control of most of them." Jen pointed past a gas station to a two-story building with a brick facade. "Run."

Other zombies staggered to their feet and turned toward Jen. The zombies she controlled knocked over those in front as Jen jumped over undead bodies. She glanced behind her. Zeke engaged two zombies attacking from the side, beheading them in two swift strokes. Wayne barreled shoulder-first through a group of three zombies, knocking them down like a raging bull.

A zombie swiped at Mercy, and Josh swung the camera, connecting with its jaw. It dropped, but three more rushed them.

"With me." Jen spun and rushed one of the zombies attacking the news crew. She planted the tomahawk's point into its temple and pushed it to the side. Zeke appeared and kicked one zombie back and slashed at another. His katana wedged in its skull, but it didn't die.

Jen slammed it in the back of the head and split the skull. The zombie fell, almost taking the katana with it.

Her escort of a dozen zombies fought off a growing number of the undead, but two of them had already fallen.

"We've got to get to that building," Jen yelled. "Zombies, lead the way."

The remaining escort dashed toward the building, knocking attackers to the side. Two more of the escort went down.

Another sound caught Jen's attention. A number of *thup thups* echoed off the buildings.

"Helicopters," she screamed. "We can't let them spot us."

Wayne put an arm around Mercy and led her away as he swung his club in a sweeping arc to clear one side. Zeke kept the zombies on the other side at bay.

They rushed to the building, the zombie escort reaching it first.

"Clear them away from the door," Jen yelled.

Her undead troops pushed back the few zombies in front of the entrance. None were within ten feet when Jen reached the tall glass door.

She pulled on the metal bar and the door swung open. She turned to wave the others in and froze.

Two Blackhawks and four Apaches flew into sight from behind a tall building. They hovered over the burning hotel.

"Get in now," Jen screamed.

Josh flew through the door with Wayne and Mercy right behind him. *Where the hell's Zeke?*

Twenty yards away, a score of zombies closed in on Zeke, blocking him from reaching safety.

19

Z eke's katana glistened in the sunlight as he whirled and sliced, parried and slashed. But as soon as he struck a zombie down, another took its place.

Jen pointed at Zeke. "Go help him."

Four of her zombie escort remained, and they dashed toward Zeke. Each of them engaged one of the undead. Jen drew her pistol and took out four more in rapid succession.

Their efforts created a hole in the zombie lines.

Jen waved Zeke over. "Come on."

Zeke sprinted for the door. Jen glanced at the helicopters. Two Apaches headed toward them as the others flew to the east. Zeke streaked through the door. Jen pulled it closed and engaged the dead bolt. A dozen zombies slammed into it.

"Away from the windows." She herded the others through a waiting area and into a hallway.

The Apaches flew closer until they sounded like they were directly over the building. Jen closed her eyes and reached out with her mind. *Nothing.* "I'm not connecting with any zombies."

A brief buzz came from outside. Jen peeked out a window. Dozens of zombies lay shredded in the road. Another buzz and another group of zombies dropped.

"Shit. They're taking out the horde," Jen said.

"What's wrong with that?" Mercy asked. "Sounds like a good thing to me."

Jen backed into the hallway, keeping her eyes on the carnage in the street. "Now that Butler's not here to control the horde and coordinate their attacks, they're sitting ducks for the army." She turned to Mercy. "And until we can broadcast your video, that's not good for us. They may just be able to sweep the zombies back."

"Which means they could march in here at any time," Zeke said. He darted down the hallway.

"Where are you going?" Wayne called out.

"We need a way out of here," Zeke said.

Jen ran after Zeke. "Good idea. If they're distracted out front, we might get out the back."

Open doors lined the hallway, all of them offices. Jen ducked into one at the end of the corridor. She rushed to the window and pulled the blinds up, exposing an alleyway. "Perfect."

She popped the latch, lifted the window, and stuck her head out. Clear at one end, the alleyway was blocked at the other by a middle-aged zombie leaning against the wall. It streaked toward her, but slowed a few yards away. Staring into her eyes, it stopped and tilted its head, then turned and stumbled back the way it had come.

Jen closed the window and joined the others in the hallway.

"What'd you find?" she asked.

"There's another door, but a ton of zombies right outside it," Zeke said. "How about you?"

"I've got a window that opens into an alley. Perfect cover to get us to South Kansas Avenue."

"Why don't we just wait here?" Mercy asked.

"Because the army will send more helicopters, and soon," Jen said. "Once they've cleared the streets, the troops will move in. We don't have much time to get to the studio and get your shit uploaded."

Jen moved in front of Mercy. "Look at me."

Mercy's gaze met hers.

"You're the key to this. We need you."

Mercy pursed her lips, then nodded. "Let's go."

"Now you're talking," Zeke said.

Jen led them to the alley window and opened it. She hopped through it just as another burst of gunfire spat from above, then helped Mercy through.

Zeke hopped out and crowded Jen from behind. Mercy pushed past him. "I'll show you the way."

Putting a hand across Mercy's chest, Jen said, "Hold up. I go first."

She strode down the alley until she stood face-to-face with the middle-aged zombie. "Out of my way."

The zombie moved to the side.

"Looks like I'm getting some control back. Hang on for a second." She closed her eyes and reached out. One connection, six, fourteen, twenty-three, thirty-eight.

Jen saw the alley entry from the street side. Fifty or so zombies gathered in the road and one of the Apaches floated into view.

She opened her eyes. "Get ready to run your asses off. Mercy, where's that door we're looking for?"

"Third on the right."

Jen peered around the corner. The third doorway was a pair of heavy-looking solid wood doors. *Look like they could withstand some force.*

"I've got almost two dozen zombies under command," she said. "I'm going to send them orders to clear the way to that door. When I tell you, get your asses to the third set of doors. Two big wooden ones. Get inside. Don't stop for shit." She eyed Zeke. "No stopping to fight."

Zeke bounced on the balls of his feet. "OK. OK. Let's get going."

Jen took another look into the street. *Clear the way from the alley to the big wooden doors down the street.*

The zombies under her control rammed the other zombies, knocking them clear of the route.

Jen took a deep breath. "Let's go."

She dashed onto the street, her eyes glued on the news station doors. She glanced at the others. All were right behind her.

Only twenty more yards.

A flash of red and yellow blinded Jen. A giant hand picked her up and flung her onto the asphalt. She lay in a stupor. Something warm and wet trickled down her cheek.

What the hell?

20

E ars ringing, Jen pushed herself up on her elbows. A blaze raged not far up the street.

She coughed, rolled over, and managed to get up on all fours.

What the hell happened?

"Jen," Wayne said. "Come on. Get up."

He staggered to his feet and shuffled to her. Grasping her shirt, he pulled. Jen stood and nearly fell over, but Wayne's grip prevented it.

"I feel like I just woke up on New Year's morning," she said.

Zeke stumbled to her side. "What was that?"

Wayne pointed to a building up the street fully engulfed in flames.

A block in the other direction, zombies rose to their feet. Jen shook her head to clear cobwebs and pointed at the rising zombies. "My head's screwed up right now. Can't control myself, much less any more zombies."

Zeke took her hand. "Come on, I'll get you in the building."

"What about Mercy and Josh?" Jen asked. "We need them."

Wayne turned around. "I see them. I'll get them in. You just go."

Jen let Zeke guide her. He caught her once as she tripped over a prone zombie, but they made it to the door and inside the building intact.

Zeke leaned her against a wall and pressed a button. An elevator door slid open seconds later.

"Electricity," she said. "Good sign."

She grabbed a rail in the elevator car and kept herself upright. The doors slid closed and the sound of upbeat soft music filled the car. "Are you shitting me?" Jen groaned. "The end of the world and I have to listen to this shit?"

The doors opened and Zeke helped her into a well-lit carpeted waiting room. He eased her onto a couch and plopped down beside her.

Lying back, Jen put a hand to her throbbing temple.

The stairway door flew open and Wayne and Josh stepped out, carrying Mercy between them. A trickle of blood ran from Josh's scalp, down his brow, and dripped off the end of his nose.

"Is she OK?" Jen asked.

They laid Mercy next to Jen. "I think so."

Eyes closed, Mercy didn't move. Jen pressed a finger against her carotid artery. "She's got a pulse. That's a start."

Josh pointed down the hall. "Equipment I need is down there. I want to get this footage up as quick as possible."

Jen tried to stand, but fell back to the couch. "Shit."

"Stay here," Wayne said. "I'll go with him."

"Mercy's the editing whiz," Josh said, "but we can't wait. I'll have to upload the raw footage."

"Do it," Jen said.

The two men hurried down the hallway.

Jen leaned forward, head in her hands, and rested her elbows on her knees. Closing her eyes, she relaxed the muscles in her face and neck. The cloud in her mind cleared.

Tingling ran down her spine. *What the hell?*

It became more intense and Jen straightened.

"What's wrong?" Zeke asked.

"There's a leader nearby." She rose to her feet and wobbled. Zeke jumped up next to her and held onto her arm.

"You should take it easy," he said.

Jen ignored him and walked to the window. She peeked through the blinds.

Hundreds of shredded zombie bodies filled the street. Hundreds more shambled over them. An Apache hovered over a building two blocks away, its guns silent.

Zeke crept up next to her. "The army took out a bunch of them."

"Why aren't they firing anymore?" Jen asked.

"Probably out of ammo," Zeke said. "I talked to one of their pilots at breakfast one time at Fairchild. He said their chain gun spits out 625 rounds a minute, but can only hold a total of 1,200. That's why they fire in bursts. Even then, they run out fast."

Movement down the street caught Jen's eyes. Several Humvees and two tanks came into view. Dozens of soldiers crowded behind them. The zombies in the street turned and sprinted for them. Machine guns chattered and the zombie threat was eliminated in seconds.

"Shit," Jen said. "With no leader, there's no horde. With no horde, the army just mops them up."

A sharp pain seared her gut. "There's more than one leader, and they're close."

"What's happening?" Mercy said.

Jen turned to Mercy. "How are you feeling?"

Mercy shook her head. "Like shit." She looked around. "Where's Josh?"

"He and Wayne went to load the video," Zeke said. "They're just down the—"

The lights went off. The hum of the air conditioning faded. A yell of frustration came from the hallway.

Jen pulled the blinds up. Indirect sunlight filled the room.

Another chatter of gunfire came from outside. The troops were passing their building. Jen stepped back out of sight and doubled over as another stab seared her stomach. Zeke put a hand on her shoulder. "Jen?"

Wayne and Josh rushed into the waiting area. "Fucking power's out," Wayne said.

Jen panted. The pain eased and she straightened. "What was your first clue, Einstein?"

"Did you upload the video?" Mercy asked.

Josh shook his head. "I was seconds from getting it out."

Wayne kicked a chair. "What the hell's going to screw us up next?"

"The army's invading," Zeke said. "They've cleared our area."

Mercy rose from the couch. "What if the power outage is local? There's one more news station at the university."

Jen dropped into a chair as more battle sounds crept in from a distance. "Sounds like the army's launched a full assault against the city. I don't think we'll have a chance to find another station."

"It shouldn't take them long to clear the zombies out," Wayne said. "Now that the undead are disorganized."

Another stab in the gut. Jen closed her eyes. *Only one way to stop the pain.*

She rubbed her temples and tried to relax. *I know you're here. Where are you?*

A video played in her mind. She stood in a street, surrounded by zombies. An explosion sounded and the camera swung left, pointing down the street. Four blocks away, a mass of tanks and Humvees rolled into view. Fire spat from their mounted machine guns and mowed down any zombie in their path. Several dozen soldiers paced the vehicles, their gunfire added to the mix.

I need you, Leader. And others like you.

The camera tilted.

Gather the zombies around you.

Zombies sprinted to the leader's side.

Show me.

The leader turned slowly, panning its gaze over a hundred zombies, all still.

Send them to attack.

The zombies stampeded toward the soldiers, who mowed them down before they could get within a block.

Help me reach the others.

A buzzing surrounded Jen and she couldn't tell if it was in her own head or the leader's.

Like an explosion, the one viewpoint she had became two. Then four. Then ten. Ten video screens in her mind's eye, each with a different viewpoint.

Ten leaders?

She slowed her breathing.

Gather as many zombies as you can and get to the corner of South Kansas Avenue and Southeast Sixth Avenue fast.

The scenes on the screens bounced as the leaders ran. Jen focused on the one that stayed still, and her viewpoint zoomed to that one screen.

The soldiers had stopped as the street before them filled end to end with zombies. They opened fire, mowing down rows of the undead. More arrived to fill their places.

Jen zoomed back to see all ten screens. She concentrated on four of them at the top.

Attack the soldiers from behind.

The scenes in those screens changed as the leaders followed their orders. She zoomed back to the leader facing the soldiers.

Attack.

The leader sprinted toward the soldiers. Zombies fell to its left and right as the horde closed in on the enemy. Twenty yards from the soldiers, the screen went blank.

Jen switched to the other four she'd ordered and picked out one. The horde raced up a street and turned. A Blackhawk swooped overhead, but didn't fire. Another horde merged with the one she watched, swelling its ranks.

One more turn and the backs of the soldiers appeared a block ahead. The soldiers yelled and turned their weapons toward the oncoming horde.

Too late.

Like ants on a dropped ice cream cone, the horde swarmed over the infantry and their vehicles, clawing, biting, and chewing their way to victory.

Jen swallowed the bile that hit the back of her throat. *Never wanted it to come to this.*

Someone shook her. "Jen."

She opened her eyes and looked into Zeke's worried face.

"We need to get out of here before the army starts clearing buildings," he said.

Jen rubbed her eyes. Even with them open, the communication lines with the leaders hummed in her head.

"We don't need to move," she said. "The army's about to get their asses kicked out of this city."

21

Jen watched the progress of the attack through her multiple leaders. The army did their damage and took out tens of thousands of her zombies through bullets and bombs, but the numbers were too overwhelming.

"Holy shit," Zeke said. "Will you look at that?"

Jen joined Zeke and the others crowded around the window.

Several Humvees sped by, followed by troops on foot running their asses off.

Jen opened the window and stuck her head out. A tsunami of zombies poured down the street toward her. *Looks like one of those battle scenes in movies set in the Middle Ages.*

The Humvees reached the intersection and screeched to a halt. One heartbeat and they were swarmed by two hordes, each hitting them from a different side. The gunner of one Humvee was yanked from the vehicle and tossed into the pulsating mass of undead flesh, where he disappeared.

Zombies tore another gunner apart, pulling his arms off as easy as a kid could pull off a fly's wings. The soldier wailed as a zombie ripped his throat out.

The foot soldiers grouped together in the middle of the street, firing into the two hordes coming for them from either side. The mass of zombies washed over them.

Jen staggered from the window and fell to her knees, puking on the two-toned carpet. Zeke put a hand on her shoulder.

The window slid shut and Wayne was at her side, grasping her under the arm. She stood with their help and they guided her to an overstuffed chair. She fell into it.

"What have I done?" she said. "Mark always said the soldiers were innocent and that we shouldn't harm them." She dropped her head into her hands. "I've killed hundreds of them in minutes."

Wayne knelt before her and embraced her. "You're doing what needs to be done. You didn't kill those men. People like Howell and Cartwright did."

She looked at him. Josh stood off to the side, his camera pointed at her. She found herself not caring.

"I know that here." She pointed to her temple. "But not here." She pointed to her chest.

"How many are you controlling?" Zeke asked.

Jen took a deep breath. "Hundreds of thousands. Maybe a million."

Mercy gasped.

"I close my eyes and I see through their eyes. I can choose just one to see, or I can see many, like how a fly sees."

"You're all kinds of awesome," Zeke said. "You've got superpowers no one's ever heard of before."

Jen gave Zeke a weak smile. *Don't ever lose that innocence.*

She closed her eyes and watched her zombie army overwhelm the enemy. They reached the edge of the city and the ragged remnants of the army fled east on Interstate 70.

Go no farther.

The zombies stopped.

Jen opened her eyes. "The army has been driven from the city. We need to see if we can find another news station."

"There's another one," Mercy said, "but it's halfway across the city."

Jen pushed herself to her feet. She wobbled and Zeke grabbed her arm, steadying her. "I'm good," she said. "Let's get going."

They took the stairs to the ground floor and exited into the entryway. She cracked the door and peeked through the opening. *Zombies. Everywhere.*

She eased the door shut. "Let me make a few adjustments."

Clear South Kansas Avenue.

Pounding feet rushed by the door.

"What did you tell them?" Zeke asked.

"Sorry," she said. "Forgot you can't read my mind. I told them to get off my damn street."

She opened the door and walked to the middle of the empty street. Turning around, she waved the others out. "It's safe."

Zeke pranced to her side. "This is so fucking awesome. Do you know how awesome this is?"

Jen smiled and spread her arms. "Not one zombie on South Kansas Avenue."

"You told them to get off South Kansas Avenue?" Wayne asked.

She nodded.

He pointed to an intersection. Zombies packed the crossroad on either side of South Kansas Avenue. "Looks like they took it pretty literally."

"What happens when we get close to them?" Mercy asked. "Will they attack us?"

Jen scratched her head. "Hadn't thought of that. I'll order them to lay off you guys."

These people that are with me right now are your allies. Not only will you not attack or bite them, but you will assist and protect them.

She smiled. "Order given."

"Let's test it out." Zeke sprinted toward the intersection.

"Zeke," Jen yelled. "Wait." She ran after him.

Zeke slowed as he approached the intersection and withdrew his katana. He crept toward one of the hordes, stopping twenty feet away. Not a zombie moved.

Jen caught up. "Don't you think we should test this on a smaller scale?"

Zeke shrugged. "Better to find out now if it doesn't work."

He strode toward the zombies. Hundreds of yellow eyes shifted toward him, but not one of them moved. He stepped nose to nose with a twenty-something zombie with a half-shaved head and spiked purple hair on its unshaven side.

Jen came up behind him. "Looks like a zombie version of you."

Zeke coughed and backed away. "Maybe you could order them to take a bath?"

"Looks like it works." Wayne approached Jen from behind. "Can we go find that news station now?"

Josh came closer, his ever-present camera taking in the scene. Mercy kept the big videographer between her and the horde. "It's a long walk."

Jen jerked a thumb at an SUV parked down the street. "Let's ride."

They tried three abandoned vehicles before they found a serviceable one. The late-model crew cab truck started right up after Wayne found the keys in the visor. "Which way?"

Mercy pointed. "Follow South Kansas Avenue until you get to Southwest 21st. Take a right and follow the road until you get to the university. The studio's in there."

Wayne hit the gas, squealing the tires and throwing everyone back in their seats. He laughed. "Sorry. Not used to this accelerator."

They reached Southwest 21st and he slowed. As it had been with every other intersection, zombies packed the crossroad.

"I'll take care of them," Jen said. *Clear Southwest 21st from South Kansas Avenue past the university. And clear the university grounds.*

As one, the zombies turned and ran into side streets as if a giant invisible broom swept them aside.

"Damn," Wayne said. "I'm not all geeky like Zeke, but that is impressive."

"Thanks," Zeke said.

"For what?"

"Calling me a geek. I let my geek flag fly proudly."

Wayne grinned and let up on the brake. "Anytime, brother." He turned onto Southwest 21st and gassed it.

"In a hurry?" Jen asked.

"No traffic," he said. "No lights to worry about."

Jen looked at the traffic lights. "Shit. I hadn't noticed the stoplights are all out. Doesn't give me a lot of hope that the power's on anywhere."

Minutes later, the university's sign appeared on a neatly manicured lawn to their right.

"Next right," Mercy said.

Wayne turned onto the road and followed it, winding through the campus.

Mercy pointed at a one story concrete building on the left. "There."

Wayne parked in front.

Jen jogged to the door. "Let me go first. I told the zombies to—"

"Your zombies," Zeke said.

She sighed. "I told my zombies to clear out of the university grounds, but I'll check just in case."

Pulling her tomahawk, she opened the door and stepped inside. The lights were out and she could barely see a few feet ahead. Fumbling her way to a window, she pulled the curtain aside. Light flooded the room.

She checked out a few offices, then went back to the entrance and pushed the door open. "All clear, but it looks like there's no power here, either."

Mercy and Josh pushed past her and made a beeline for a door in the back. They disappeared behind it.

"What's next if this doesn't pan out?" Zeke asked.

Hadn't thought that far out. "Guess we'll have to find another station."

Mercy appeared, her shoulders slumped. "No good."

"Where's the next station to check?" Wayne asked.

Jen chewed her lip. "We can spend the whole day looking for unicorns in this dead city. We should move on."

"You sure about that?" Wayne asked. "Seems safer to me to try every-thing here. Who knows how it is out there?"

Jen took a deep breath. "My mind's made up. We go to Lawrence."

"You mean that town we passed?" Zeke asked.

Jen nodded. "It's what? Twenty-five miles away? The horde can reach that in an hour. They don't get tired, remember?"

"I don't think it's got a news station," Mercy said. "It's pretty small, and I've never heard of one there."

"Then what?" Zeke asked.

"Then we keep going on to Kansas City," Jen said.

22

J en tapped Wayne on the shoulder. "Pull over here."

He maneuvered the Humvee through the packed horde and to the side of Interstate 70.

Jen sat back in her seat. They'd cleaned the inside of the vehicle as best they could, but the stench of death still hung in the air. "We need to keep as hidden as possible in case the Air Force strikes. I can control the horde from the rear."

She closed her eyes and organized her many views from the leaders. They ran across grassy, rural areas and down the empty highway. No sign of the army.

"Do you suppose the military's retreated and left Lawrence?" Zeke asked.

"They didn't have a lot there when we came through," Wayne said. "I'll bet they're setting up their line in the sand at KC."

Jen listened to their conversation even as she watched her zombie army's progress through the leaders' eyes. "Let's get moving again."

"It'd help if you told your friends to leave ten feet or so around the Humvee," Wayne said. "I've accidentally run over several of them already."

"No," Jen said. "We'd be too easy to pick out from the sky. Howell knows if he takes me out, the battle's over. Running over a few zombies here and there is a small price to pay."

"OK." Wayne pulled onto the highway and paced the zombie horde. He looked at the speedometer. "Keeping at just above twenty-four miles an hour."

Jen switched her focus to one leader, the leader she'd sent earlier with its thousand-member horde. It raced up a grassy embankment with an interchange on its right. Houses and a school lay in the distance.

"My recon has just hit Lawrence," she said.

"The one going in on the south side?" Zeke asked.

She nodded.

The leader's horde spread out and they raced down streets and through yards. No sign of any humans. Nothing in the sky.

Jen opened her eyes. "No resistance so far. They're going to the university. When they get there, I'll take a look and see if there's any signage for a studio."

"How far out are we?" Zeke asked.

"Our leading edge should be hitting north Lawrence any minute," Jen said. "We're ten minutes behind them."

She tilted her head and stared in the distance. "Recon's at the university and has spread out." She went quiet for a minute, then her eyes came back into focus.

"No station," she said. "Looks like we'll need to get to KC."

Recon, move through the city to the eastern edge, then work your way north to join up with the main forces.

"Wait," she said. "Helicopters on the leading edge."

"Are they firing on the horde?" Wayne asked.

Jen squeezed her eyes shut. "Four helicopters. Mix of Blackhawk and Apaches. Flying over the horde, but not firing."

Wayne jerked the Humvee to the left, running over several zombies and nearly flipping the vehicle as it jumped the curb.

"What the hell?" Mercy said.

Goosing the accelerator, Wayne broke through the zombies and swerved just in time to avoid a parked tractor.

Jen tracked the helicopters through her leaders. "They're not far off."

As if on cue, the *thup thup* of multiple rotors came from their right. The Humvee veered onto a dirt road, kicking up a cloud of dust. Two long red buildings loomed ahead.

A burst of machine gun fire kicked up dirt just ahead of the Humvee. A Blackhawk zoomed past.

"We need cover," Jen yelled.

Wayne steered onto an open field and zigzagged toward the buildings. Another burst from a chain gun barely missed. An Apache overshot them and turned around.

One of the buildings came up fast. The Humvee straightened and sped toward a half-open warehouse door. Several rounds hit the Humvee and Mercy screamed.

"Anyone hit?" Wayne called out.

Jen looked around at the crew. No blood. "We're good."

"Then hold on," Wayne yelled.

More bullets flew by as the Humvee rammed into the partially open door, knocking it to the side. The vehicle zipped into the building and Wayne slammed the brakes, narrowly avoiding pallets of wooden boxes and barrels. He brought the vehicle to a stop.

"Everyone out," Jen screamed. "Weapons ready."

She jumped from the Humvee and took position behind a metal barrel, her M4 pressed to her shoulder and aimed toward the door. Wayne took cover behind a crate, while Mercy hid behind a forklift and Josh knelt next to her, pointing his camera at the door.

Jen raced back to the Humvee and pulled out two M4s. She shoved them at Mercy and Josh. "Time to grow a pair."

Mercy looked at the M4 in her hands as if Jen had just given her a snake. "I don't know how to use this."

"Point and shoot." Jen rushed back to her position and checked out their situation. *Wayne ready. Mercy and Josh, who the hell knows? And Zeke.*

"Where the hell's Zeke?" she said.

Zeke popped up in the Humvee's gunner position. He took hold of the mounted M60 and fed a belt into it. "Haven't had a chance to shoot one of these babies for months."

A helicopter sounded as if it were landing just outside the open door, then its rotor sped up and it left. Another one did the same, and then a third. Jen caught a glimpse of the third as it rose past the open door.

"We've got company," Wayne said. "Be ready."

A figure clad in black streaked through the door and ducked behind some heavy machinery. "Damn, that was too fast to fire on," Jen said.

The figure popped up and fired at Wayne's position. Several more dark figures entered the warehouse and took cover.

Jen shot back at the lone gunman and ducked when two others returned fire from different positions. The chatter of the M60 cut off the soldier's fire.

Popping her head up for a second, Jen fired a burst and then ducked back down, but not before more soldiers infiltrated the building.

"How many are there?" she said.

Wayne moved a couple feet to the side, then popped up and fired. He took cover as return fire raked his position. He looked at Jen. "At least two dozen and they seem highly trained."

"What are you saying?" Jen asked.

"We're screwed."

A shot came from Jen's right and a spark pinged off the top of the Humvee, inches from Zeke. He dropped into the cab.

Shit. They're flanking us.

She crawled several feet to the end of a stack of boxes. Several more rounds fired, one of them from somewhere behind her. She looked back. Mercy hid behind the forklift, a curl of smoke drifting from the end of her barrel. *She does have some balls after all.*

A fusillade of shots came from the soldiers. Jen peeked out from the side of the boxes. At least a dozen soldiers moved forward in a crouch, their weapons blazing.

Jen aimed at one on the far end. She tracked him and slowly squeezed the trigger. The soldier dropped and the others hesitated.

That was enough for Zeke to pop out the side of the Humvee and fire several times with his M4 before jumping behind cover. Several rounds pinged off the floor where he'd stood seconds before.

"Jen."

Jen turned.

"Can't you get some of your zombie troops in here?" Wayne asked.

What the hell? Why didn't I think of that?

She closed her eyes and zoomed in on the leader with the strongest connection. *Go to where the helicopter sounds are coming from. Attack the soldiers in the big red building. Remember those you are ordered not to attack or bite as they're in the building, too. Kill everyone else.*

The leader turned and fought his way through the horde. He broke free, but the red building wasn't in view.

Listen for the helicopters.

A bullet whined over Jen's head.

Her arm tingled. Another leader was close. Very close. But this one was unfamiliar to her.

She closed her eyes and connected. The leader was somewhere dark. Flashes of light caught its eye. A man stood, shot a gun, and ducked back down.

That man was Zeke. This guy's in here with us.

Look down.

The zombie looked down. Its black uniform had a hole in the gut where blood leaked out.

It's the guy I shot.

Attack anyone in this building who's dressed in black.

She looked at Wayne. "We've got some help. One of them has turned."

He gave her a thumbs-up and fired another round. Jen peeked out and shot at one soldier only fifteen feet away.

A man screamed and the firing stopped.

Jen peered over a crate. Several soldiers retreated to a far corner, where several shots rang out. She aimed at the back of a retreating soldier and squeezed the trigger. He fell out of sight and she aimed at another.

The M60 came to life and three of the soldiers were peppered with rounds that tore through their bodies.

The screaming stopped and Jen heard nothing above the *thup thup* of the helicopters' rotors. One set grew louder and a shadow darkened the doorway.

Jen glanced at the doorway. An Apache floated mere feet from the ground, its cannons pointed into the warehouse. A burst of light exploded from one of them, and Jen's world turned upside down.

23

Jen bounced off the wall and slammed onto her back while debris rained on her. Choking, she struggled to regain her breath and tried to roll over, but her legs were pinned to the floor.

Another flash and another explosion farther off rattled the building and shook the floor. Jen's ears rang and her eyes filled with grit.

"Fuck!"

She lay helpless, trying to gain her senses. She couldn't see anything beyond the destroyed crates she'd taken cover behind. *Got to clear my head.*

A shadow crossed her chest and she stared into the flat eyes of a soldier. The muzzle of his M4 pressed against her head, he said something.

"I can't hear you."

He bent closer and yelled. "...now who...you think you can...asshole."

Jen felt along her hip for her knife. She kept her eyes locked on the soldier and shook her head. "All I heard was you telling me you're an asshole."

The soldier scowled, grabbed the front of her shirt, and lifted her a few inches off the ground. He said something, none of which she caught. She stared blankly back at him.

Teeth gritted, he knelt down to her and put his mouth next to her ear. "Sergeant Howell has requested your presence."

Jen's fingers played across the hilt of her knife. She pulled it from its scabbard and shoved it into the soldier's side.

He roared and stumbled to his feet. Another soldier appeared at his side and steadied him. He spoke rapidly to the stabbed soldier, who pointed at Jen and said something. The second soldier drew his 9mm pistol and aimed it at Jen.

It had to end somehow. I just hope the others get away.

The soldier with the gun was jerked off his feet and into the shadows. The soldier she knifed glanced over his shoulder then looked down at her, screaming something. His eyes wide and drool coming from his mouth, he seemed to be pleading with her.

A gnarly hand grasped his throat and pulled him from sight.

The ringing in Jen's ears increased and she dropped into a pool of black.

FLOATING IN THE AIR, Jen's body jerked back and forth. *Am I flying?*

Back into the black.

JEN'S EYES FLUTTERED OPEN. A light with an unmoving fan hung from the ceiling above her. She turned her head and the bones in her neck cracked. "Shit."

She lay on a bed in a plainly decorated bedroom. The shade on the one window was drawn.

Propping herself on her elbows, she coughed. *Where the hell am I?*

Footsteps paced outside the door and the low murmur of voices seeped into the room.

I can hear again.

She slid to her feet and almost fell over from a shot of pain jabbing her left shin. Sitting on the bed, she slid her pant leg up. Dried blood and an ugly sprawling bruise spread across her shin. She felt around the area and winced.

Seems stable. Not broken. Just hurts like hell.

Easing herself to her feet, she held onto the bed frame for support. She limped to the door and cracked it open, then peeked out into a kitchen. Zeke stood by a sink, his face smeared with soot and a cut across his cheek.

Wayne sat at a table taking a sip from a coffee cup. "Tastes good, but you made it a bit too hot."

"I'm a ninja, not a waitress."

Mercy sat across from Wayne, her gaze far off. Josh had his camera in front of him and seemed to be tightening something with a tiny screwdriver.

Jen pulled the door open and stepped into the kitchen.

"Jen!" Zeke rushed over to her and clamped his arms around her.

"Careful with the merchandise," she said.

Wayne reached out. "Want some coffee?"

She took his hand. "How long have I been out?"

"About twelve hours," Zeke said. "You were pretty out of it."

Jen eased into a chair. "What happened?"

"Your troops arrived." Wayne rose and pulled back the window curtains. A couple dozen zombies stood outside, wandering back and forth.

"Where are the rest?" Jen asked.

Zeke frowned. "That's all of them."

"But there had to be a couple hundred of them."

Wayne cleared his throat. "Those things not only took out all of those soldiers, but they even climbed on one of the helicopters and brought it down."

"Did they?" Jen felt a little burst of pride.

"You ought to see the wreck," Zeke said. "It's a miracle any of them made it. Those helicopters strafed them pretty good."

Jen closed her eyes and reached out. The rest of the horde was intact and in Lawrence.

Take cover in buildings near you and await further orders.

She opened her eyes to a quizzical look from Wayne.

"I ordered them to lay low," she said.

Wayne nodded. "Good idea." He stood and put his empty coffee cup in the sink. "The nearest news station is in KC, have I got that right, Mercy? Josh?"

Mercy broke from her trance. "Oh. Hi, Jen."

Jen shot a look at Wayne and he shrugged.

Josh closed a compartment on the camera. "You're right. KC is our best bet."

"But won't they be waiting for us there?" Zeke said.

Jen cracked her neck. "Doesn't matter. We'll kick their asses out of there, too."

"Have you still got enough troops?" Wayne asked.

Jen closed her eyes. "Let me check."

The screens appeared in her mind's eye. "Holy shit. There are more."

She chose one where the connection was the weakest. The leader stood on the side of a road surrounded by zombie drones. A sign was posted a dozen or so yards ahead, but Jen couldn't make it out.

Run up to the next sign.

The leader raced to the sign and stopped. Its drones converged around it.

Look up at the sign.

The leader's view rose. The sign said *Omaha 76 miles.*

Jen opened her eyes. "Farthest one is seventy-six miles outside of Omaha. Isn't that north of here?"

Wayne whistled. "That's damn near two hundred miles north. You've got a hell of a reach."

"I think the more I use it, the stronger it's getting."

Zeke pulled his pistol and checked the load. "Shouldn't we be going? We've got some ass to kick."

Wayne pushed his chair back and stood. "Sounds like a plan."

Ten minutes later they were back on Interstate 70 in a late model SUV.

"I guess the Humvee took some hits," Jen said.

"That beastie wasn't going far," Wayne said. "I'm good at fixing vehicles, but even with a fully equipped shop at my fingertips, that thing wouldn't be going anywhere for a while."

They took Interstate 70 across the north of Lawrence to the bridge over the Kansas River. "Stop on the other side," Jen said.

Wayne pulled off on the first exit after the bridge. He stopped in front of a set of gas pumps and jumped out.

Jen hopped out of the SUV and stretched. "I'll get the troops moving."

She closed her eyes. *All of you in Lawrence proceed east on I-70 to Kansas City. Full run.*

She watched the screens as leaders left buildings and raced for I-70. Within minutes, the highway was packed with zombies crossing the bridge over the Kansas River.

Zeke shaded his eyes and watched them run past. "Are they all going over the bridge?" he asked.

"I told them all to go to I-70, so I suppose so."

"But isn't that a bottleneck?"

Jen shut her eyes. "Let me try something."

Several leaders raced down I-70 toward KC, but others stood behind the bottleneck at the bridge.

She zoomed in on one leader.

Leave the bridge and go down to the river.

The leader pushed its way through the horde then sprinted to the river's edge. The dark water flowed by swiftly.

Turn around. Let me see your group.

The leader scanned the zombies gathered around it. There had to be two hundred or more.

Swim across the river and continue to Kansas City on I-70.

The leader didn't move. None of its group entered the river.

Swim across the river.

No movement.

Was the connection lost? *Turn around three hundred and sixty degrees.*

The leader turned. The zombies in its group still crowded behind it, but none seemed to have moved.

Swim across the river.

Still no movement.

Jen opened her eyes. "I think we have our answer."

"What's that?" Zeke asked.

"Howell was right. The zombies won't cross the river."

"You mean like swim?"

"Swim, walk, whatever."

Zeke scratched his chin. "That's going to slow us—"

The bridge erupted in flames, tossing chunks of concrete and body parts in the air.

"Take cover," Jen yelled.

24

J en ducked under the gas station's awning. A second explosion rumbled from the south.

She ran through the connections in her mind, but several were missing.

Debris rained down and a dust cloud settled on the bridge. When it cleared, Jen gasped. A hundred-foot span of the bridge was missing. The zombies still lined up on the other side.

"They may be running out of bombs," Wayne said, "but they're being smart in how they're using them."

Mercy huddled next to Jen. "There's another set of bridges at Vermont and Massachusetts Streets."

"Let me guess," Jen said. "They're south."

Mercy nodded.

Wayne jogged into the convenience store.

"Great time for a doughnut fix," Jen called after him.

He came out and spread a map on the SUV's hood. He pointed at the I-70 bridge. "This is us."

Moving his finger along the Kansas River, he said, "And the river goes all the way to KC."

Jen craned her neck to examine the map. "So the horde still has a clear path there. Looks like the army's just keeping them from coming in on I-70."

"Look at KC," Zeke said. "It's split into three sections by the Kansas and Missouri Rivers. By blowing the bridge, the horde will be isolated in the south."

"So what?" Mercy said. "Why does that matter?"

Jen pointed to the top third of KC. "That's why." Her finger rested on the downtown airport. She looked at Wayne. "Remember when we came through there? They had advanced aircraft set up."

Wayne whistled. "They'll be able to reload chain guns and bombs damn quick."

"We've got to knock that airport out," Zeke said. "But how? We have no aircraft, and Jen's zombie army will be sitting ducks in the south part of the city."

"Give me a second." Jen squeezed her eyes shut. *Everyone stop.*

All movement ceased.

Those of you in Lawrence, close your eyes.

Only nine screens still displayed anything.

Jen zoomed in on the first one. *Omaha. When I give the order, attack Omaha. That'll draw any assets from Offutt Air Force Base.*

She moved to the next screen and directed the leader to the nearest road sign. *Wathena.*

"Find a town named Wathena on the map," she said.

The map rustled. "Here it is," Wayne said. "It's seven miles east of St. Joseph."

"Where's that?" she asked.

"Fifty-five miles north of KC."

"Is there a river?"

"Yup. The Missouri. One bridge over it, just like Lawrence. You'd have to cross the bridge to come south into North KC."

Jen opened her eyes and blinked to get them back in focus. She leaned on the hood and examined the map. "We'd have the same problem. Even if the city is abandoned, it's big enough that the military is apt to have eyes on it. By the time the horde makes the bridge, they'd have it down."

Her gaze drifted down the map. "Here." She stabbed a finger at a town forty miles northwest of Kansas City named Atchison. "It's not a major city and has a bridge that spans the river. If we have a chance of getting the horde across, it's there."

"But what about us?" Zeke said. "We still need to upload the video."

Mercy cleared her throat.

"We should go into KC alone to do that," she said.

"Why's that?" Wayne asked.

"Once the zombies are in the city, the bombing and stuff starts, right?"

Jen nodded. "Probably."

"Then the power goes out."

Jen and Wayne looked at each other. "Why didn't we think of that?" he said.

Zeke clapped Mercy on the back. "Good thinking."

Mercy's face reddened. "Thanks," she murmured.

THIRTY MINUTES LATER, Wayne drove the SUV onto I-70 and sped east.

"I've got my troops broken into three groups and I'm communicating with one leader," Jen said. "This has to be how Butler was able to level up and command so many at one time."

"I'm still jealous," Zeke said. "Wish there was more of that serum."

Jen grasped his forearm and lowered her voice. "No, you don't."

Zeke broke from her gaze and looked out the window.

The Omaha horde had assembled on the outskirts of Omaha and awaited orders. The Kansas City horde still ran toward KC. Jen estimated they should be ten or fifteen minutes from the city's south side. The Atchison horde was due to arrive on the outskirts of Atchison in thirty minutes.

"All of them are still on track," she said. "They all have orders to attack their targets when I give the word. Atchison's got the farthest to go, so I'll have to time the diversionary attacks precisely."

"When do we get to KC?" Zeke asked.

Wayne turned and gave him a toothy grin. "At the speed I'm going? Twenty minutes."

"You look like you're having too much fun," Jen said.

"Driving a vehicle with some balls, and no cops to worry about? Nah."

Jen went back to monitoring the hordes.

Fifteen minutes later, the Kansas City horde arrived at the outskirts of South Kansas City. "KC's in position," Jen said.

"And we're here, too," Wayne said.

Jen peered out the windshield at the signs for Kansas City. "Mercy? Do you know where we're going?"

"Josh has this one," she said.

Josh leaned forward. "Take the exit for 670 East. It'll take us over the Kansas River and into downtown."

He pointed at a sign on an overpass. "There it is. Exit 421B."

Wayne maneuvered the SUV onto the ramp, followed the curve, and approached the bridge. "Looks like this bridge is still intact."

"I'm not seeing any working traffic lights," Jen said.

Wayne slammed a fist on the dashboard. "Dammit. No power again?"

"We don't know that," Mercy said. "Those lights could be out even if the power's on."

Josh pointed over Wayne's shoulder. "Big cloverleaf up there. You want I-35 south, then get off at West 20th Street and go east."

Wayne took the first off-ramp on I-35 after the cloverleaf and took a left at the stop sign. Houses, half-hidden by trees and bushes, gave way to brick buildings and warehouses.

"Go up to Main Street," Josh said. "Take another left there and it'll lead you into downtown."

Jen stuck her head out the window and searched the sky. Nothing. No sign of aircraft.

They hit downtown and Josh guided Wayne to a sixteen-story building. He stopped the truck in front of a set of double-glass doors.

Jen jumped out. Other than the SUV's doors closing, there still was no sound, no movement. A chill ran down her spine. "You'd think I'd get used to the silence."

Wayne looked around. "I know what you mean."

Josh pulled on the doors. "Shit. Locked."

"Stand back," Zeke said. He slid the M4 off his shoulder. Josh scrambled out of the way, and Zeke shot a burst of three rounds at the door.

Cracks spidered from the bullet holes.

"I guess that didn't work," Josh said.

Zeke handed Jen his rifle and approached the damaged door. He took a wide stance and concentrated. With a short bark, he lashed out with his foot, nailing the glass and knocking a chunk into the lobby. He reached inside the opening and opened the dead bolt.

Pulling the door open, he stood to the side. "After you."

Josh grinned and entered with Mercy at his side.

Wayne bumped fists with Zeke as he passed.

Jen put up a hand. "Wait." She cocked her head.

A Blackhawk zoomed over the building.

"Shit."

She hurried into the shadows of the lobby.

The Blackhawk hovered above the intersection next to the building. A loudspeaker squawked. "Time to give up."

A pair of Humvees squealed around a corner two blocks down.

"How the fuck did they do that?" Jen asked.

Wayne peered out next to her. "Don't know."

"I'll bet they still have working satellites," Zeke said. "I read about them on the internet."

"Shit," Wayne said. "They were probably tracking us the whole way."

"Mercy," Jen said, "you and Josh get your shit uploaded. They want me so I'll draw them away."

Wayne grabbed her arm. "I'm coming with you."

"Me, too," Zeke said. He had a crazy, excited look in his eyes.

They dashed down the sidewalk and into an alleyway. Dodging trash cans and debris, they raced to the other end. One of the Humvees stopped at the entrance and two soldiers jumped out and gave chase.

Wayne pulled his pistol and shot a few rounds in their direction. The soldiers took cover. Jen added a few rounds of her own.

You asshats can't fire back, can you? Need to take me alive.

They burst onto the next street right in front of the other Humvee. It screeched to a stop and Jen rolled over its hood. Zeke made a flying kick at the driver's door as it opened and slammed it closed. Wayne zipped past him and ducked into the alley across the street with Jen.

The Blackhawk flew past overhead in the direction they were heading.

Jen glanced back. Zeke was catching up. She looked past him. No one gave chase.

What the hell?

She slowed as she approached the alley's entrance. Wayne paced her. "What's wrong?"

Four soldiers stepped into view. They had rifles Jen didn't recognize pressed into their shoulders.

Jen raised her pistol, but the soldiers shot first. A sharp pain made her wince and drop her gun. A dart of some sort stuck from her shoulder. She pulled it out and stumbled. Her vision blurred.

"No."

Wayne dropped to the ground next to her.

"Jen," Zeke said.

Another shot and he stumbled.

The world spun.

Attack!

Jen fell to the concrete and into the darkness.

25

J en opened her eyes and the world spun. She rolled to her side and
puked.

"It's OK," Wayne said. "That'll pass."

Groaning, Jen squinted in an attempt to see through the blackness. "Where are we?"

Wayne's voice came from her left. Not close, but not too far away.
"Don't know. I've only been awake for ten minutes or so and haven't seen
anyone."

"Zeke?" Jen asked.

"There's someone breathing heavily," Wayne said. "Got to be him."

"My hands," she said. "Handcuffed."

"And chained to the wall," Wayne said. "I pulled on them. Solid."

Jen pushed herself into a sitting position and scooted her back into the
wall.

A cough came from in front of her.

"Take it easy," Wayne said.

Zeke's slurry voice pierced the darkness. "Is Jen OK?"

I'm the first thing he's worried about. What'd I do to deserve that guy? "I'm
good."

A tumbler turned and a door opened. Light spilled in and Jen clamped
her eyes shut.

"You're awake," Howell said. "Good. Let me see how you're doing."

A click and the light grew brighter.

Jen cracked her eyes. Howell stood in the doorway with his hands on his hips.

The rustle of chains to her left drew her attention. Wayne sat up, shading his eyes with his bound hands. On the other side of the room, Zeke lay on his side with his head buried in his arms.

"The drugs will wear off soon," Howell said. "Once it does, we'll bring you food and water." He spread his arms. "We don't want to hurt you. All we want is your cooperation."

"That'll be the day," Jen said. *Need to see where my troops are.*

She closed her eyes and concentrated, reaching out with her mind. *Who's the closest? Where are you?*

Nothing but darkness.

"I forgot to tell you," Howell said. "Jen's been given an extra drug. It screws with your focus, your concentration. After all, we don't want you rallying your undead hordes. At least, not until you're doing it for us."

Jen glared at Howell. "You think after all this I'm just going to be your puppet? How about I line the horde up and have them bend over so you can kiss their asses instead?"

"We need you," Howell said, "but don't think our patience is limitless."

He stepped out of the room and eased the door shut. Jen dropped her head forward. *How the hell are we going to get out of this one?*

"Don't lose hope," Wayne said.

She looked over at him.

He smiled. "Think of what we'll do after this shit is over."

"Haven't given that much thought," she said.

"Yeah," Zeke said. "I'm visualizing slicing that asshole's head off. Makes me feel all warm inside."

Wayne pulled his knees up and rested his arms on them. "Maybe you should think about after. Where are you going to live? Can't go back to Alaska."

He's trying to keep my spirits up. Even though I know what he's doing, it's still working.

"Where will I live?" she said. "Haven't the foggiest."

"What'd you think of Rhode Island?" Wayne asked.

Her eyes met his. "Rhode Island? With you?"

He smiled. "Why not?"

Warmth flooded her chest. *Why not?*

The door cracked open and Howell stuck his head in. "Someone wants to see you."

He pulled the door back and stepped to the side.

Cane in hand, Dr. Cartwright limped in.

26

"Hello, Miss Reed."

Cartwright?

"I can see by your expression that I'm the last person you expected to see." She pulled a metal folding chair inside and sat. Howell leaned on the doorframe. *If I could stand, I don't know which one I'd kill first.*

A snippet of memory bubbled to the top of her mind. "The college kids said that one person was pulled from the helicopter crash site."

"Bravo." Cartwright did a sarcastic clap. She looked at Howell. "If she's remembering things, then the drug is probably wearing off. See to it she gets a new dose."

Howell nodded.

Shit. That's the last time I'll let them know how I'm doing.

"I need you, Miss Reed. Our country needs you."

"You need your asses kicked is what you need."

Howell chuckled. "That's one of the things I liked about working with you. You've got attitude. But it's time to play ball. We've got you. All of you."

Jen's pulse kicked up a notch. "I don't believe you."

"You can believe it," Cartwright said. "We even have the video your friends were trying to upload. Seems our troops got to them just in time."

"Bullshit. You're a fucking liar. Every damn word from your mouth's been a lie. I'm just glad Doc's not here to see it."

Cartwright stiffened.

Howell sighed. "Maybe you'll believe this." He rapped his knuckles on the door. A soldier came in carrying a video camera.

"Look familiar?" Howell asked.

"You've seen one, you've seen them all," Jen said.

Howell turned it so the monitor faced Jen. He pressed a button on the side and the monitor came to life. There was Butler and Jen in the hallway of the hotel. Butler's head exploded and the camera swung to Howell, his gun still aimed down the hallway.

Jen's heart sank. "Where are Mercy and Josh?"

"They're no longer an issue." Howell gestured to the soldier and he left the room with the camera.

Zeke strained against his chains. "What does that mean? You killed them, didn't you?"

Cartwright looked calmly at him. "For national security purposes."

A sergeant appeared next to Howell and whispered into his ear. He nodded and stepped aside.

The sergeant waved a corporal in. They descended on Jen. She kicked out, hitting the corporal in the shin. He grimaced and grabbed her legs, pinning them to the floor.

"No," she screamed. "Get the fuck off me."

"Leave her alone," Wayne yelled.

The sergeant pulled Jen's bound hands up, immobilizing her arms. He slid her sleeve down and produced a hypodermic needle.

Jen struggled, but they held her fast. "You fucks! No!"

"I'm gonna kill you assholes," Zeke shrieked.

The sergeant plunged the needle into her arm. Jen wriggled and screamed.

Cold steeped into her veins and bile rose in the back of her throat. The sergeant removed the needle and stepped back. "Let her go."

The corporal released her and jumped back, but not before Jen lashed out with her foot and slammed her heel into his calf muscle. He hobbled from the room.

Jen pulled herself up. "That won't do shit, because in the end I'm going to kill you both."

Leaning on her cane, Cartwright stood. "I hope you understand we don't have time for games. We need your help soon."

She limped out the door.

"What does that mean?" Zeke asked. "No time for games?"

Howell sighed. "It means she and I wish Jen would cooperate on her own." He raised an eyebrow. "What do you say, Jen? Make it easy and get back on the team."

"Fuck you."

Howell pursed his lips and sighed. "We know how much Zeke means to you. Don't make us go there."

"I'm not afraid of you," Zeke said.

Can't let him hurt Zeke.

"Your answer?" Howell asked.

Jen stared at Howell, keeping a poker face.

Howell shook his head. "So that's it, is it?" He stepped out of the room, keeping his eyes on her. "Sergeant Doyle."

The sergeant pulled his pistol and aimed it at Zeke.

Jen's heart jumped into her throat. Zeke yelled something unintelligible and Wayne threw himself against his chains.

Falling to her knees, Jen begged, "Please, don't."

Sergeant Doyle swung the gun barrel around to Wayne and fired two rounds.

27

Wayne dropped to his knees, two holes in his chest leaking blood.

"Wayne!" Jen screamed.

Doyle calmly walked from the room. Howell stood in the doorway for a moment, then closed the door.

Wayne looked down at his wounds then over at Jen. Tears flowed down her face and her throat thickened. "Wayne," she whispered.

He fell on his side and his body convulsed. Once. Twice. Then he was still.

Head down and hands pressed to his forehead, Zeke cried, his whole body trembling.

Numbness enveloped Jen. *What have I done?*

A wave of emotions crashed over her and she clenched her fists, raised her face to the ceiling, and wailed. A long, low sound that hollowed out a part of her soul.

"It's done. We lost. AND IT'S MY FAULT! Why didn't I listen to D-Day? Why didn't I take everyone else's advice? Why did it always have to be my way?"

Sobs wracked her body.

A chain clanked. Jen's head popped up.

Wayne rose unsteadily to his feet. Facing the wall, he stumbled, then turned, his yellow eyes surveying the room.

28

"Wayne?" Jen pushed herself to her knees. Wayne turned his head at the sound of her voice and stared at her.

"Are you still there?" Jen asked.

Wayne's head tilted as if he was trying to understand what she'd said.

Zeke pulled himself to his feet, his face red and puffy. Wayne's gaze snapped to him and he launched himself at his brother. Reaching the chains' length, his feet went out from under him. He slammed to the floor on his back.

"It's me," Zeke said. "Your brother."

Wayne scrambled to his feet and strained at the chains, trying to get to Zeke. Spittle flew from his mouth as he struggled to break free.

"Stop," Jen said.

Wayne went still.

"You can control him?" Zeke said. "The drugs don't work."

"Wayne," Jen said. "Sit."

Wayne dropped onto his ass.

"Damn," Zeke said. "How'd that work?"

"I think it's because he can hear my voice," Jen said. "I can't connect through his mind, but I can through his ears."

Zeke wiped his eyes. "Howell and Cartwright don't realize that. They think all your control is through the mind."

"Right," Jen said. "So I can keep Wayne still until we find a way to give him peace."

"No."

"No? What the hell are you talking about?"

"Wayne can still help us," Zeke said.

Heat rose in Jen's face. "Are you fucking kidding me? He's your brother. I'm not gonna use him like a piece of meat. How can you even think of that?"

Zeke sighed. "He's my brother and he'd want us to do this. He wanted nothing more than to keep you safe. And that's all I've wanted since we met in Anchorage—to protect you."

Jen put a hand to her forehead. "I don't give a damn what you want. Listen—"

"No, you fucking listen!"

Jen's eyebrows shot up and her mouth hung open.

"That's right," Zeke said. "You fucking listen to me for once. You just went on about how you never listened to anyone else and now you're doing the same thing."

He stabbed a finger at her. "It's more than you. If you don't survive, then what's left of the United States will be under the boots of a few tyrants. Hell, maybe even what's left of the rest of the world won't be free anymore."

Jen's mouth moved, but she couldn't speak.

"It isn't all about you," Zeke said. "Time to put on your big girl pants and realize that."

Her heart pounding, Jen scowled at him. She opened her mouth to speak, but Zeke cut in.

"I love you," he said. "Wayne loved you. Let us both help you."

Jen's mouth clamped shut. *Wayne loved me?*

As if he were reading her mind, Zeke said, "That's right. He loved you. He was going to tell you once this was over."

"What happened to him," she stammered, "it's...it's my fault."

Zeke shook his head. "No. But if you don't do everything you can to defeat these assholes, then it will be your fault when they've destroyed the world."

Jen struggled to her feet, her knees shaking. *He's right. D-Day was right. I can't change what's happened, only what's going to happen.*

She wiped her face with her hands. "You're a little shit sometimes."

Zeke's lips trembled. "I am. But I'm also right sometimes."

Jen nodded. "Let's figure out our next steps."

Zeke opened his mouth and Jen's hand shot up. He didn't speak.

"Just one thing before we get busy," she said.

"What's that?"

"I love you, too."

29

J en sat against the wall. "I think we're ready."

Zeke nodded. "Not great odds, but better than we had."

"We're outnumbered now," Jen said, "but if this works that'll turn around."

Wayne sat still, his eyes following the conversation. Jen turned to him.

"Wayne, wipe your hands on your wounds, then wipe them all over your head."

Wayne looked down at the bullet holes in his chest and rubbed his hands over them.

"Now rub them on your head."

He placed his hands on top of his head and smeared the blood into his hair and onto his skin.

"Again," Jen said.

After she had him repeat the process several times, she said, "Put your hands at your side."

Wayne did as she asked. His entire head was slick and shiny with blood.

"What do you think?" Jen asked.

"Looks like someone beat him in the head," Zeke said.

"It does, doesn't it?" Jen gestured to Wayne. "Lie down."

Wayne went to the floor on his side.

"Close your eyes and don't move," Jen said. "You won't move for any reason until I say 'attack.' When I say 'attack,' you will attack anyone within your reach. Bite them."

Zeke cleared his throat.

Jen put a hand to her mouth. "Sorry. Wayne, you won't attack Zeke. Ever."

Zeke gave her a thumbs-up.

Jen rubbed her eyes. "Now we wait."

THE DOOR'S lock clunked and it swung open. A corporal stepped in with two trays of food and two bottles of water. He made a wide arc around Wayne, then placed the trays on the floor and slid them toward Jen and Zeke with his boot. "Sergeant Howell said you should eat up." He tossed them each a bottle of water. "And drink up."

Jen unscrewed the bottle and took a gulp.

The corporal watched her. "The team will be here in fifteen minutes to give you another injection." He turned toward the door.

"Can you do something before you leave?" Jen asked.

The corporal glanced back at her. "What's that?"

Jen gestured to Wayne. "Can you get him out of here, please? He's really beginning to stink."

The corporal examined Wayne from a distance. "What happened to him?"

"He went nuts and kept ramming his head into the wall," Zeke said. "Probably frustrated he couldn't get to us."

The corporal took a step toward Wayne. "He looks dead, but that's not my job."

"I'll tell Sergeant Howell you said that," Jen said.

Frowning, the corporal looked at her then back at Wayne. "Fuck it."

He pulled a set of keys from his pocket and bent over Wayne.

"Attack," Jen yelled.

The corporal looked toward her with a puzzled look then screamed as Wayne bit into his arm.

"Don't let go," Jen said.

Breathing heavily, the corporal pounded Wayne in the head with his free fist, but Wayne had his arm trapped. The corporal's attacks slowed and he fell onto his back and lay still.

"Let him go," Jen said. "And find his keys."

Wayne dropped the corporal's arm and picked the keys up from the floor.

"Toss them here."

Jen caught the keys and freed herself.

The corporal rose.

Jen pointed to herself and Zeke. "You will not attack either of us. You will protect both of us."

She scrambled over to Zeke and released him. He stood, rubbing his wrists. "I'd give you the biggest hug right about now but I know there's no time for that."

She pulled him in and squeezed. "Always enough time for you."

"Still friends?" he said.

"That'll never change." She released him. "Now let's grow our little army. My inoculators should be here any minute, and have I got a shot for them."

30

J en stuck her head out the door, then stepped out into a large room with a low ceiling. Fluorescent lights revealed tables with boxes and pieces of equipment that lined the walls. Two windowless metal doors, one to Jen's left and the other to her right, were closed.

Zeke joined her. "Any idea where we are?"

A big vehicle rumbled by, its vibrations hitting the bottom of Jen's feet.

"Sounds like a semi," she said.

Zeke looked around. "No windows. Maybe we're in a warehouse."

"Maybe." Jen popped back into the room.

The two new zombie soldiers stood in the corner with Wayne and the first soldier. "Stay with us," Jen said.

She pulled the pistol she'd taken from one of the soldiers and, with Zeke at her side, strode to the door on the right. She pressed her ear against it.

"More rumbling," she whispered.

She put a finger to her lips.

"Helicopters." She glanced at the zombies. "Zombies stay here. Zeke, with me."

She eased the door open and stepped into a corridor lined with stacked boxes. Glass windows in the double doors at the hallway's end showed the inside of a cavernous hangar.

"Hold here," she said.

Jen rushed up and peered through the windows.

An Apache and a Blackhawk, both parked in the hangar, had their cowlings removed. A soldier in a T-shirt jumped out of the Blackhawk. He picked up a toolbox and strode out of the hangar.

Something moved to Jen's left and she shrank away from the window. A soldier walked by, an M4 slung over his shoulder and a Beretta strapped to his hip. He stopped three feet from the door.

It's that asshole, Doyle.

Jen slunk back to Zeke.

"That murderer Doyle's on guard out there," she said. "But he's there to keep people out. Doesn't seem he's worried about keeping us in."

"We should grab him," Zeke said. "Find out where we are."

"Good idea. Come on."

Jen led Zeke to the double doors. The guard hadn't moved.

Easing the door open, Jen slipped into the hangar with Zeke right behind her. She pressed the barrel of her gun to Doyle's temple. "Don't move."

Doyle put his hands up.

"Put your hands down," Zeke said. "Call attention to yourself and this won't end well."

"OK." Doyle lowered his hands.

"Walk backwards with us," Jen said. "We're going inside."

Jen guided Doyle into the corridor while Zeke held the door open. Once inside, she pushed the sergeant against the wall. "Grab his shit."

Zeke took Doyle's pistol and rifle.

"Turn around," Jen said.

Doyle glared at her. "What do you want?"

"Where are we?" Jen asked.

He didn't answer. Jen popped him in the mouth.

That wiped the look off his face.

"Where are we?" she repeated.

"Downtown airport. North Kansas City."

"And where are Cartwright and Howell?" Zeke asked.

Doyle's lips pressed tightly together and a drop of blood ran from the corner of his mouth.

"Really?" Jen said. "I can do worse than a punch."

"How about something easier?" Zeke asked. "Where's your chow hall?"

Jen squinted at Zeke. *What the hell? Does he think we're going to stop for lunch?*

Doyle must've wondered the same thing based on the look he gave Zeke. "Two buildings down from here."

"Is it big?" Zeke asked.

Doyle shrugged. "I guess so."

"How many does it seat?"

"I'm done answering shit."

Zeke turned Doyle's wrist and looked at his watch. "11:45 a.m."

Jen looked at Zeke. *Brilliant.*

She placed the barrel of her gun to his forehead. "Last chance. Where are Cartwright and Howell?"

Keeping his eyes ahead, the guard remained silent.

Jen looked down the corridor. "Wayne, come here, please."

The door opened and Wayne lumbered to her. Doyle's eyes widened.

"What do you think of your work?" Jen asked.

Doyle licked his lips and closed his eyes.

"One more time," Jen said. "Don't give me the answer I want and Wayne will snack on your face."

A drop of sweat rolled down Doyle's cheek. "The command center. Small building. Two down from here."

"Which way?" Zeke asked.

"Left as you leave the hangar."

"And the chow hall? Which way is that?"

"Right."

Jen and Zeke exchanged glances.

"Guess we got what we need," Jen said.

Doyle glared at her. "Won't do you any good. You're fucked, and I hope I can be the one to put a couple of rounds in your little punk rocker friend there. Make him and his brother a matched set."

Jen spoke through clenched teeth. "You look like a guy with leadership qualities, and we're in need of another leader."

She dropped the gun to his chest and pulled the trigger.

Twice.

31

Doyle stood to the side with the rest of the soldiers.

"You'll lead the soldiers to the chow hall," Jen said. "It's noon and it should be full."

She turned to Wayne. The more time she spent with Zombie Wayne, the less he seemed like her Wayne. "Wayne will go with me and Zeke to the command center."

Zeke checked the load in his M4. "The soldiers should concentrate on biting as many as they can as quick as they can."

"Not stay around and snack?" Jen said. "Good point. You soldiers will bite anyone you can. As soon as you've bitten someone, go bite someone else."

She looked at Zeke. "I miss anything?"

"I don't think so."

Jen peered into the hangar. *All clear.* She pushed the door open. "Soldiers, you have your orders. Attack now."

Doyle raced out the door, followed by the three drones. They were out of sight in seconds.

Jen drew her pistol. "Let's go."

She darted across the hangar. *No use playing it too safe. The diversion at the chow hall should be enough.*

Zeke sprinted ahead of her and waited at the far side of the hangar entrance. Wayne stopped silently beside him.

Peering around the corner, Zeke called back. "Clear." Jen darted out of the hangar and past a parked tug and a pallet of equipment.

She made a beeline for a small one-story building with a single door at its end. Just as she neared it, an older soldier pushed through the door. Jen slammed into him, knocking his ass back into a room with a conference table and chairs in the middle and communications equipment lining the walls.

A burly soldier jumped up from the table and drew his pistol. Jen took a wild shot at him and he ducked. Zeke burst into the room and went into a roll. He came out of it and sprung to his feet, slamming the butt of his M4 on a burly soldier's forehead.

Howell launched from a chair and bull-rushed Jen, knocking her on her ass. "Dr. Cartwright," he barked.

Cartwright limped toward Howell.

Oh, no you don't.

"Wayne, attack."

Wayne pounced on a shrieking female radio operator while Zeke pulled his pistol and shot at Howell. Howell winced and grabbed his shoulder.

Jen leapt onto the conference table, rolled across it, and hit the floor, blocking Cartwright from reaching Howell. Howell ducked out the door.

"Everyone line up," Jen yelled.

The radio operator rose, her yellow eyes flashing.

"You keep still," Jen said.

Zeke lined up the remaining soldiers and relieved them of their weapons. "Got 'em all."

Jen nodded. "Everyone take a seat."

Cartwright glared at Jen as she took a chair at the head of the table. "What do you think this is going to accomplish?" she asked.

Gunfire erupted outside and Jen ducked. Zeke crept to the window and peeked out.

"Looks like there's some trouble at the chow hall."

Jen smiled. "Imagine that."

"What do you want?" Cartwright asked.

"What do I want?" Jen lined up her gun sights on the old bitch's nose. "I want Wayne back. D-Day. My father." She got her face down to Cartwright's and screamed, "I want Doc back. Remember him?"

Cartwright closed her eyes and swallowed. "Hysteria won't do any good. I can offer you safe passage from the base."

A radio speaker crackled. "This is Howell."

Jen exchanged a glance with Zeke. Zeke rushed over to the radio panel the voice came from. He picked up a mic and keyed it. "What the hell do you want?"

"I want to talk to Jen."

Jen strode to the panel and Zeke handed her the mic. She pressed the button. "I'm talking to a dead man."

"You're on an active military airfield with hundreds of armed men. Don't act like you've got us by the balls."

"Maybe you didn't notice your zombie problem," Jen said.

The radio speaker clicked. "Perhaps you should take a look yourself."

The gunfire ramped up. What the hell?

Jen lifted a window blind and peered toward the chow hall. Zombies poured out of the building and raced toward a half dozen Humvees lined up on the tarmac. Each Humvee rapidly launched grenades from their mounted Mark 19 launchers.

The horde was destroyed in minutes.

"It was a pretty good idea," Howell said. "But you're dealing with soldiers. We have tactics. What do you have?"

Jen ran back and grabbed the mic. "I have Cartwright, asshole."

"You have the queen," Howell said. "But that doesn't match up when I have all of my other pieces."

Shit. I was sure we had them on the ropes.

"You have five minutes," Howell said.

"And then what, shithead? Are your Humvees going to grenade me?"

"Of course not," Howell said. "We have an Apache five minutes out that has two missiles remaining in its load. I've ordered it to return and use those missiles to destroy the command center."

Jen swallowed. *Was that a checkmate?*

"You can still surrender," Howell said.

"Blow this building up and you kill Cartwright," Jen said.

"Definitely not what I want," Howell said. "But Dr. Cartwright would agree it's our best move."

Jen locked eyes with Cartwright. The steely old bitch didn't flinch.

Looks like we're not getting out of this one after all.

32

Jen strode to Zeke. "Come with me."

She pointed to the hostages. "Wayne. Zombie Radio Girl. Watch them. Bite anyone who moves."

Guiding Zeke to the corner of the room, she lowered her voice. "Any ideas?"

"Tell me what you think first," he said.

She took a deep breath, then slowly released it. "At best we can take Cartwright out. That's something, I guess."

"What about the other hordes? Have you tried them lately?"

Jen slapped her forehead. "What a fucking idiot I am." She put up a finger and closed her eyes.

A single view appeared. *Wayne.*

He stared down Cartwright. *Move six inches to your right.*

Wayne shuffled to his right. "Son of a bitch," Jen whispered.

Have Radio Girl scratch her nose.

Radio Girl's hand lifted and rubbed the side of her nose.

Jen opened her eyes. "It's coming back," she whispered. "I can command Wayne."

Zeke scratched the bald side of his head. "That's good news, but he's practically right on top of you. Can you get any of the others?"

"Maybe. I'll try." Jen shut her eyes. *Anyone else out there? How about the Kansas City horde?*

Something flickered in the darkness. *Kansas City horde?*

A new view appeared. Thousands of zombies flowing down city streets, gun and rocket fire hitting them from the tops of buildings and helicopters. Zombies fell in droves.

"I've got Kansas City," Jen whispered. "They're doing what I ordered. They're attacking and it's keeping the military busy."

"What about Atchison?" Zeke asked.

Jen furrowed her brow. "Nothing yet. No Omaha, either. I sent Omaha and Kansas City in to keep the military busy so the Atchison horde could slip through."

"Without Atchison, we're screwed," Zeke said.

Atchison horde, are you there?

"Nothing," she said. "How much time left?"

"Four minutes," Zeke said.

Atchison? Come in.

Another view shimmered then died.

Come on, Atchison.

The view blinked on then held steady.

Jen focused on it. Zombies streaked down railroad tracks with a river to their right. They approached a sign.

Look up.

The sign came into focus. *Downtown Kansas City Left Lane.*

"Got anything?" Zeke asked.

Jen opened her eyes and smiled. "Cavalry's coming."

33

"How long before they get here?" Zeke asked.

"Don't know exactly, but soon."

A familiar sound came from the flight line.

"Shit," Jen said. She lifted a window blind. An Apache descended to a hundred feet from the tarmac and off to the side of the Humvees. "We're out of time."

Howell's voice came over the radio. "Time to make a decision."

Jen gritted her teeth. *How do we buy time?*

She glanced at the hostages. Cartwright's gaze burned through her. *Let's make you useful, you bitch.* "I got it," she whispered to Zeke. "Follow my lead."

She strode to the radio, picked up the mic, and keyed it. "Howell."

"All I want to hear is your surrender," he said.

"How do I know you aren't planning on killing us if I give up and join you?"

"Why would we do that?" Howell said. "We want your abilities. Hell, we could've already killed you."

"We're going to let the hostages go first," she said. "That will make our surrender simpler."

"That's a start," Howell said.

Zeke's face dropped. Jen whispered, "Buying time."

He gave her a slight nod.

She checked in on the Atchison horde. The railroad tracks they ran on split into multiple tracks all going in the same direction. The horde spread out even more.

Show me.

Jen swallowed. Thousands. Hundreds of thousands.

Run your asses off. I need you here now.

Zeke poked her shoulder and Jen blinked.

"No more waiting," Howell said. "You've got one minute to release the hostages or the Apache fires the missiles."

Jen licked her lips. The soldiers around the table looked at her with hope. Cartwright gave her a flat stare.

"Wayne, Radio Girl," Jen said. "Come over here with us. Let everyone leave the building."

As soon as the zombies moved aside, the soldiers jumped up from their seats and scrambled out of the building. Cartwright didn't move until they all had gone.

"You haven't lost," she said. "You'll see. I think this will be the best outcome for you, and everyone else."

Cartwright rose, leaning on her cane, then hobbled to the door.

"Cartwright," Jen said.

Cartwright paused, but didn't turn.

"Who said we lost?" Jen said.

Cartwright limped through the door.

"What now?" Zeke asked.

Closing her eyes, Jen said, "The cards are on the table. Time to see how they play out."

34

The Atchison leader followed the train tracks around a curve and the airfield came into view only a hundred yards away.

There are soldiers in the middle of the runway. You will turn them all, then continue on to swarm the rest of the airfield. Remember my friend, Zeke, who's with me and is untouchable.

The zombies raced past a huge hangar next to the end of the runway and the whole airfield opened up to them. Like an avalanche, the horde rumbled down the tarmac.

Jen opened her eyes. The window blinds were raised and Zeke watched the battle unfold. Jen rushed to his side.

Shouts came from the line of Humvees. Several soldiers dropped their rifles and ran while the others opened fire. The Apache turned to bring its power to bear.

Zombies fell in droves to the Humvees' grenades and the soldiers' bullets. Still the horde came. When the leading edge went down, the next wave rolled over them and pressed on.

The Apache let a missile loose. It hit the horde dead center on the leading edge, the explosion rattling the control center. Body parts and bits of gore rained down on the airfield and a huge gap appeared in the zombie lines.

"Holy shit," Zeke said.

The zombies streamed forward, clamoring over the broken bodies of their comrades. The impact had been no better than pissing on a forest fire. The Apache banked and flew off.

Jen tuned into the leader.

The leader reached the Humvees and barreled through. He sprung and landed on the back of a fleeing soldier. The soldier rolled over, panic in his eyes, and attempted to fend off the leader.

Howell.

Bite his ass.

The leader latched on to Howell's throat and shook its head violently, ripping away flesh and tissue. Howell's screams ended in a gurgle.

Show me the rest of the soldiers at the Humvees.

Rising, the leader scanned the carnage.

Where's the old lady?

With no more resistance on the flight line, the zombie horde dispersed across the airfield, into the buildings, and as far out as the river's edge.

The leader went to each body inside the Humvees, but none were Cartwright.

Shit. Did that bitch get away?

A bloody figure stumbled across the carnage.

That one. I want to see that one.

The figure stopped as if it were under remote control. It turned and staggered toward the leader.

Cartwright.

With an arm hanging by a thread and yellow eyes unwavering, Cartwright stared straight ahead as she obeyed her leader.

Jen opened her eyes and clapped Zeke on the back. "Howell and Cartwright have been turned. Their asses belong to me now."

35

S ix Months Later

THE TAXI DRIVER pulled onto the I-70 bridge above the Mississippi. Jen peered out the windshield toward the checkpoint at the bridge's midpoint. No sign of Zeke.

After bringing the cab to a stop at the twenty-foot-tall gate, the driver jumped out and opened the trunk. Jen pulled her pack out and slung it over her shoulders. She handed the driver a bill. "Thanks."

He tipped his hat, climbed into the taxi, and drove back into Illinois, passing a Humvee approaching the bridge.

A guard strode out of the entry control point. "This is a restricted area."

Jen turned toward him and he took a step back. "Sorry. Didn't recognize you." He returned to the gate shack.

The Humvee pulled up. It had government plates and a placard on the side. A ninja stepped out of the passenger side, adjusted the katana strapped to his back, and jogged up to Jen.

The guard came back out. "Can I see your ID, please?"

Pulling a black tab down on his shirt, the ninja exposed a badge.

"Why don't you take your hood off?" Jen said.

"Forgot," Zeke said. He pulled the hood off and gave her one of his goofy smiles. He looked at the guard. "Captain Tripp, Zombie Quick Response Unit."

The guard squinted at Zeke's badge, then nodded and went back inside.

"Doing pretty good for yourself," Jen said.

Zeke shrugged. "They let me wear a ninja uniform and kill zombies. What more could a guy want?"

Jen laughed. "America can sleep safe with you on the job."

"It's working so far," Zeke said. "A few zombies cross the bridges and we take them out, but the Mississippi keeps the bulk of them away."

He snapped his fingers. "Almost forgot. We have a vaccine for the mycovirus."

"Damn," Jen said. "That didn't take long once we cleaned out the assholes in the government. Why haven't I heard about it?"

"It's not official yet," Zeke said. "But I hear things because of my position."

"Oh, yeah? Like what?"

"The network's doing a documentary on the whole thing: the conspirators, the outbreak, everything. You'll be a celebrity."

Jen sighed. "I already am and it sucks."

"I guess," Zeke said. "They've asked me to be a technical consultant. They're going to use Mercy and Josh's footage."

Jen licked her lips and gazed across the bridge into St. Louis.

Zeke shuffled his feet. "I guess it doesn't matter since you won't be around anymore..."

This is going to be harder than I thought. "I haven't seen you much since Wayne's funeral. I stopped in Rhode Island on my way here and visited with him. Left some flowers."

"That's good," Zeke said. "I stop by anytime I can." His eyes became moist. "You two made a great pair."

Jen nodded. *Still too soon to think about.*

"Anyway," she said, her voice thick. "Time for me to go."

He took her hand. "Why don't you stay? We can use you in the ZQR."

Jen looked down and scuffed a foot on the asphalt. "Zeke."

An awkward silence fell between them.

She swallowed. "You know I'd love to stay. You're like the little brother I never had." She hitched a thumb over her shoulder. "But I need to be out there. Out with the zombies. Keeping things controlled."

"But you're half-human, too," he pleaded.

Jen scooped him into a hug. *How many times have I had to say goodbye to someone I love?*

"It's because I'm human that I'm doing this," she said. "And I'm the only one in the world who can."

Zeke sighed and pulled back. He wiped his eyes. "I know."

Jen patted the tomahawk on her hip. "Guess I better get going."

Zeke stepped past her and gestured to the entry control point. "Open the gate," he yelled.

A hum came from the gate then it rolled slowly to the side.

Jen bent down and squeezed Zeke in her arms. "You take care." Her eyes burned. *Please don't let me cry.*

"You, too," he said.

She kissed him on the cheek and whispered, "Thank you for protecting me. I never would've made it without you."

Letting go of him, she strode through the gate.

"Will I ever see you again?" Zeke called out.

Jen stopped. *I don't know.*

She turned and waved. "Of course you will."

He waved back, a big smile on his face.

Jen adjusted her pack and strode into an uncertain future.

KEEP UP TO DATE

Keep up to date on new releases, book recommendations, free offers, and free drawings by subscribing to the M.A. Robbins mailing list at uprising.-marobbins.com

THANK YOU

Thank you for reading the Zombie Uprising. I hope you've enjoyed it.

Can I ask you a favor? Please leave a review on Amazon or Goodreads because all reviews help other readers decide on books to add to their reading list.

AUTHOR'S NOTES

It's been a wild ride from the tundra of Northwest Alaska to the mighty Mississippi. I've enjoyed the heck out of writing this series and appreciate all the feedback. This last book took a little longer to write because life doesn't stop even when my head's stuck in another world. There were some gloomy days that were brightened by a review, an email, or a Facebook post. They made a big difference. Thank you.

So we leave Jen and Zeke for now. I've got tons of ideas for stories; far more than I could ever manage to write in one lifetime (and I'm no spring chicken). I'll continue to write stories that I hope are interesting to you.

Guess I better get at it. Until next time.

M.A.

ACKNOWLEDGMENTS

My wife, Debbie, is my life. We met when we were from rival high schools and worked at a McDonald's together. That was several lifetimes ago. Our first conversation consisted of me saying something unflattering about her school and her dumping a milkshake over my head. How could I resist her after that?

Domi at Inspired Covered Designs knocked another one out of the park. It's so awesome that I don't have to sweat how the cover will look. It's always a guaranteed winner.

Same goes to Tamara Blain of A Closer Look Editing. I do my best to send her the cleanest manuscript possible, but I know I don't have to worry when it's published. Tamara will catch my silly typos, lack of commas, and too many commas (I suck at commas).

Beta readers get the manuscript before Tamara and make sure the story itself makes sense, is exciting, and flows well. Thanks to this book's group of beta readers: Ami Agner, C. Deanne Bourgeois, Lyn Eubanks, Marinda Grindstaff, Wayne Tripp, Rachel Wagner, and Helen Zawacki.

ALSO BY M.A. ROBBINS

The Tilt Series
   The Tilt, Book One

Printed by Amazon Italia Logistica S.r.l.
Torrazza Piemonte (TO), Italy

12276708R00469